CRAIG HALLORAN

THE SUPERNATURAL
BOUNTY
HUNTER
FILES

BOXED SET
BOOKS 1-5

The Supernatural Bounty Hunter Files Boxed Set
Books 1-5
By Craig Halloran

Copyright © 2015 by Craig Halloran
Print Edition

TWO-TEN BOOK PRESS
P.O. Box 4215, Charleston, WV 25364

ISBN eBook: 978-1-941208-83-0
ISBN Paperback: 978-1-941208-84-7

www.craighalloran.com

Edited by Cherise Kelley

Smoke Rising The Supernatural Bounty Hunter Series: Book 1 Copyright © 2014 by Craig Halloran
I Smell Smoke The Supernatural Bounty Hunter Series: Book 2 Copyright © 2014 by Craig Halloran
Where There's Smoke? The Supernatural Bounty Hunter Series: Book 3 Copyright © 2014 by Craig Halloran
Smoke on the Water The Supernatural Bounty Hunter Series: Book 4 Copyright © 2015 by Craig Halloran
Smoke and Mirrors The Supernatural Bounty Hunter Series: Book 5 Copyright © 2015 by Craig Halloran

Publisher's Note
This book is a work of fiction. Names, characters, places, and incidents either are the product of the author's imagination or are used fictitiously, and any resemblance to actual persons, living or dead, events, or locales is entirely coincidental.

TABLE OF CONTENTS

Smoke Rising 5
I Smell Smoke 141
Where There's Smoke 265
Smoke on the Water 387
Smoke and Mirrors 505

CRAIG HALLORAN

THE SUPERNATURAL
BOUNTY HUNTER
FILES

SMOKE RISING
BOOK 1

PROLOGUE

T HE MAN-LIKE THING LURCHED UP and smacked Smoke in the chin.

He staggered back.

It started walking down the hall, arms dangling at its sides and a hole clean through its back and chest.

Sidney took aim.

Blam! Blam! Blam!

It tumbled over with its kneecap blasted apart.

"Good shot." Smoke wiped his brow and headed after their fallen attacker where it writhed on the floor. "I think it's a zombie." He pointed his weapon at its head.

Blam!

"Zombies aren't real," she said, catching her breath and holstering her gun.

CHAPTER 1

HUNTSVILLE DETENTION FACILITY, ALABAMA

"ARE YOU NERVOUS?" THE WARDEN asked.

"No," Sidney said. "Why would I be?"

Warden Decker shrugged. Dabbing the sweat on his brow with his handkerchief and tucking it back in his pocket, he hustled forward and swiped his card. Nothing happened. He swiped it again and again. An unseen latch popped.

"Ah, there we go." He opened one of two heavy metal doors and stepped aside. "It's an old place. Not made for all this technology. I miss the sound of those keys jangling on my hip some days."

"Thank you," she said, crossing into the next room.

"You're welcome, Agent Shaw."

The pair entered a long hall made of cinderblock wall, lined with barred windows. Agent Shaw's short heels echoed on the marble floor. The prison was old, but it had the smell of fresh paint that still lingered on the pale grey walls.

The thickset black man cleared his throat. "I've been the warden these ten years, and I have to admit, I've never had a situation like this."

"Like what?" She adjusted the strap of her black leather satchel on her shoulder.

"We just don't get a lot of visitors from the FBI, that's all. And you have to admit, the situation is very unique." He was smiling as he glanced over at her. "Isn't it?"

"For you, I suppose, but I've been doing this for quite some time."

"Visiting prisoners in sweat-rank prisons?" He huffed. "You didn't sign up for that, did you?" He let out a little laugh. "Sounds more like something a foolish young man would do, like me."

She showed the slightest smile on her face. Dark hair was pinned up behind her head. She wore a dark-blue pants suit with a white shirt. She reminded him of his daughter, in a white sort of way. Too confident for her own good.

"My job requires me to go to a lot of unique places, but I'll admit, Warden Decker, I don't think I've been to a place as humid as this."

"They've been working on the A/C for twenty years, and it still never works right. I'm from the South, and I still never get used to it." He dashed the sweat from his eyes. "Sorry. But this hallway has no ventilation at all."

"It's all right. The academy's prepared me for worse."

He stopped at the next set of doors, readied his swipe key, and paused.

She dipped her chin and eyed him. "Something on your mind, Warden?"

He leaned on the door, took out his blue handkerchief, and wiped his neck. "I just got to know. Why do you need to see him?"

"That's confidential."

"I know that, but ... it's so strange. Listen, Agent Shaw. I'm the warden. Certainly you can give me some nugget of information. After all, he's my prisoner. I'm pretty familiar with him. I'm pretty familiar with all of them. We have the worst of all sorts here: dangerous maniacal bloodthirsty killers. Of course, I've seen some of them cry like babies before." He gave her a quick finger shake. "But we don't have—and never have had—anyone like him."

"Sorry," she said, looking at the next set of doors.

They were painted white, with the word "LIBRARY" stenciled in black where the window glass had been replaced with steel.

"Is this really a library?"

"It is." He tapped on the metal. "This is how we make do. I don't think we get the same level of funding as the G-Men"—he looked her up and down—"or G-Women do. Are you sure I can't stay inside with you?"

"I'll be fine." She shifted her satchel from one side to the other.

He took a breath and swiped his card. "All right then."

CHAPTER 2

T HE LATCH POPPED, AND THE warden pushed the door open. It was a library as expected, with stacks and rows of books. The musty smell reminded Sidney of her days in high school. She'd done a lot of reading back then. Large wooden tables were lined up neatly, resting on old hardwood floors.

Two correction officers in grey shirts and black pants held synthetic stocked shotguns on either side of a table. A man in an orange jumper sat there between them. His head was down over a newspaper and his dark straight hair dangled over his face.

Her heart thumped behind her temples.

"I can stay inside, just out of earshot," the warden said, patting the semiautomatic pistol on his hip.

She lifted a brow. "I don't think he'll try to escape, or even to hurt me, for that matter. It's not in his profile."

The warden blocked her view of the prisoner and whispered, "I've read his profile too. Several times. He has a dark side to him."

"I know, but don't all men?"

Warden Decker nodded and stepped aside. "Come on, men." But at the last second, he turned to her and said, gradually getting loud enough for the prisoner to hear, "As long as you stay out of the stacks, I've got eyes on everything. Just signal when you're finished."

The guards came forward, eyeing her as they passed the threshold.

"Uh, Warden—"

Warden Decker held his hand up and led them out.

Sidney glanced over her shoulder as the doors began to close, just in time to see Warden Decker swallow. Her heart skipped a beat as the door sealed shut. She turned and faced the prisoner.

Pull it together. He's just another creep, Sidney.

She approached him, heart thumping. It was even hotter in the library, and she could feel the sweat beading above her lip. Her eyes slid toward the camera globes above. *Those things better be on.* She dropped her file on the table, dragged a chair back, and sat down. The man across from her, eyes still down, turned a page of the newspaper.

"John Smoke," she said, scooting her file in front of her and opening it. "I'm Agent Shaw with the FBI. How are you doing today?"

Without glancing up, he said, "You're different than what I expected. What are you, about five foot eleven? That's tall for a gal. And you're even wearing flat shoes. The last one I met was a sawed-off dumpling with Coke-bottle glasses. I didn't like her so well." He scanned the paper, turned the last page, folded it up, and pushed it aside. He clasped his fingers together and looked down into her eyes. "Volleyball. I bet you played collegiate volleyball."

Smoke was hawkish, but handsome. His chestnut hair was thick and cut just above the neck. His eyes were dark with a burning fire behind them. He was a strong-chinned, lean, well-knit man with hands the size of mitts.

"This is business, Mister Smoke, not a social call."

"You know"—he eased back in his chair—"you aren't exactly what I figured for an FBI woman. I was expecting someone a little less, well, a lot less—to keep it professional— appealing. I have to say, it's a nice surprise." He scratched the scruff on his cheeks. "Shaw. Is that your maiden name?"

Sidney didn't have a ring on. "I'll ask the questions. You just answer them."

"Well, you haven't asked anything yet." His voice was a little rough, with a hair of charm behind it. He clasped his fingers together and rested them on his head. "I'm all yours."

"All right, Mister Smoke—"

"Smoke," he interrupted.

"Excuse me?"

"Just call me Smoke." He winked. "That's what everyone calls me."

"Sure," she said. "First question then. Are you interested in getting your sentence commuted?"

He shrugged.

I'm starting to hate this guy. Sidney had interviewed dozens of prisoners over her career. She'd negotiated deals with many. Every time she mentioned someone getting their sentence commuted, their eyes lit up. Smoke's hadn't.

"You're less than a year into a three-year sentence," she continued. "And when I say commute, I'm not talking about months off. I'm talking about years."

Rubbing a bruise on his cheek just below the ear, he said, "I've become pretty fond of the old place." He glanced around. "It speaks to me."

"Warden Decker says you and the other prisoners don't get along so well."

"He's such a worrywart. Nice guy, though."

"I've been informed that there's a bounty on your head." She leaned forward. "In most cases, the superior numbers get you. One slip-up or payoff of the guards will get you killed in here."

"It keeps me sharp," he said.

"Getting killed?"

"People trying to kill you is always the best training."

"I see," she said. "And I guess I shouldn't be surprised after reading your file." She leafed through some pages. "You've had quite a career for a man under thirty. Navy SEAL. Ex-Washington PD. Bounty Hunter. Prisoner. Now that's a resume."

"Chicks dig it."

"There aren't any *chicks* around here, and there won't be for the next two years. The funny thing I came across is how you wound up here in the first place. You are a decorated veteran, though not without some marks. Tell me, why'd you leave the SEALs?"

"I didn't like the pay."

"Oh, the pay," she said, eyeing the file and nodding, "but that's not what it says here. The gist I got was that you are difficult to control. Insubordinate. You struck an officer."

"He had a big mouth."

"He was a general."

"He had a really big mouth." He shrugged. "And I got an honorable discharge. I hope you read that far."

"I see," she said. "So you didn't like the military?"

"Listen, Agent Shaw. I loved the military. But there is a lot of standing around, training, and waiting. I got bored."

"It doesn't say that here."

"Do you believe everything you read?"

Interesting. But at least he's talking. "Let's skip over the Washington PD and talk about why you became a bounty hunter."

"Better money."

"Really? So you're all about the money?"

"Yes."

"I don't believe you."

"I don't care."

Typical stubborn man.

"Fine. Let's talk money then. The last goon you brought in was worth ten thousand."

"It should have been fifty, and I still haven't received payment for that."

"No?" Sidney said, cocking her head. "Well, I wonder why *that* is?"

Smoke looked away and growled in his throat a little. He mumbled something. Sidney leaned forward and turned her ear toward him. "What was that?"

The room seemed to darken when Smoke's eyes narrowed. He slammed his fist on the table. *Wham!* "He had it coming!"

CHAPTER 3

HEART RACING, SIDNEY FLINCHED BACK. Smoke's eyes were smoldering fires. Behind her, the doors burst open, and two guards dashed in. The first one drove the butt of his shotgun into Smoke's chest, toppling him over. In a second, both barrels were lowered toward his chest.

"Don't you move, Smoke," the first guard said. "Not an inch."

"Are you all right, Miss?"

Face flushed red, Sidney jumped from her chair. "Get your sorry asses out of here!"

"What?"

"Did I signal for the cavalry?"

"Well…"

"Did I?" She pointed at the cameras.

"But—" the first guard started.

"Jeff," a voice shouted from just outside the library doors. "Moe! Let's go!" It was Warden Decker. His chest was heaving and his face beaded in sweat. He loosened his tie. "Now!"

With hesitation, the guards lifted their barrels and backed off, eyes never leaving Smoke.

"Sorry, Miss."

Sidney glared at him.

"Er … Sorry, Agent Shaw."

Sidney waved the warden off, and he showed her a squeamish grin. Seconds later, the doors closed again, leaving her all alone with Smoke. She turned and found him in the chair, with a slight smile on his face. She hid a gasp. She hadn't even heard him move. No rattle of metal nor scuff of chair. Nothing. She resumed her seat.

"How's your chest? I bet that hurt."

"I've been hurt worse." His eyes were dancing. "You're prior military too, aren't you?"

"Let's pick up where we left off before you had your little tantrum, shall we? I believe you were saying you're upset that you haven't been paid."

"I took a major thug off the streets. A top dealer." He rolled his shoulders and grimaced a little. "I should have been paid. I was tossed in here instead."

"The judge didn't see it that way." She glanced through the file. "It says you acted with extreme prejudice."

"The man's a killer. A murderer."

"That's for the courts to decide. And we can't just go around maiming people."

Smoke lifted his brows. "Even if it saves a life?"

"You cut off his index finger."

"No, I cut off his trigger finger."

She wanted to laugh but held it back. "Most people only have one trigger finger. You cut off two."

"I can shoot right- or left-handed. Can't you?"

"I've never had the need. As for you, well, I'd venture to guess your little act of mutilation didn't sit well with Mister Durn. That's probably why he put the prison hit on you."

"Huh, well, I've been a bounty hunter a long time."

"You've been one four years."

"That's a long time." He crinkled his brow. "Anyway, I've achieved a lot in that time. Helped a lot of people. But some of those judges aren't so helpful. Durn has deep pockets. It's no surprise he paid the judge off and got me sent inside here."

"Maybe the judge was coerced."

"He should be willing to die first."

Sidney nodded. Smoke had a point, but it was all speculation. She picked up the file and fanned herself with it.

"It's in the past now. Let's talk about the future. Are you interested in hearing what I have to offer or not?"

He shrugged.

"Yes or no, if you please."

"Does it involve working with the FBI or any other law enforcement agency?"

"Absolutely."

"Then no."

"Why?"

"You've read my file. I don't play well with others. Too many rules. Not enough action. That's why the bad guys get away. Besides, I don't trust them. If I did, I'd probably be doing what you're doing."

"Come on." She leaned back. "We aren't all bad."

"See, you just admitted it."

"Admitted what?"

"That most of you are bad." He tilted his head back and let out a laugh. "Hah."

"That's a common expression."

"Says the girl scout. And I bet you think those cookies you're selling are good for me, too." He shook his head. "No one is as blind as he who will not see."

"My eyes are wide open."

"I'm sure they are, but my answer is still no."

"So, you'd rather sit in here for two more years plus and let more criminals get away?"

"There are plenty of criminals inside here that are in need of my correction." *Difficult. Difficult. Difficult.* The man across from her seemed content, however. It was weird.

"So long as I'm here, will you just listen to my offer?"

He shrugged. "Sure."

"The FBI has a list." She clasped her hands together and rested them on the table. "The typical America's Most Wanted. You're familiar with it, I'm sure."

"Uh-huh. Say, what kind of perfume are you wearing?" He sniffed the air. "It's different. Good, but different."

"The Marshalls have their lists. The Washington PD has their lists too," she continued, "more on the local level. You've dealt with them all, and disregarding the last case, you've done an exemplary job."

"Yeah." He yawned and eased back until he lifted the front legs of his chair from the floor, then started gazing around. "I know all of the lists. It's what I do."

"But there's another list, one that isn't on the public record. It's called—"

Smoke's brows lifted, and his chair legs hit the floor. He leaned over the table and spoke.

"The Black Slate."

CHAPTER 4

I'VE GOT HIM.

"Let me see the list," Smoke said, unable to hide the excitement in his voice. "I knew it existed."

"Oh, did you now? You don't sound so sure."

"It was a theory."

"Based off what? The Black Slate has very little activity. It's very low profile."

"True, but I know all the lists pretty well. I've studied the cases, the files, at least whatever I could get ahold of. But there was always something missing. I don't look for what they show or say, I look for what they don't show or say." He drummed his fingers on the table and stared at the file. "All of those lists I figured were nothing but busywork that hid the real people. Good for the papers. Good for accolades and medals. But they never bring in the top-dog criminals." He stretched his fingers toward the file. "May I?"

Sidney slid the file away. She wanted to give it to him, he seemed so eager, child-like even.

"Not without clearance, and I don't see that happening if you aren't on board with this. Don't fret it. The list isn't in here, just the first assignment. Are you interested or not?"

Smoke pulled his fingers back. "Tell me more. I'm curious. Why does the FBI want to use me as a resource?"

"All right, I can answer that. Let's just say that our resources are stretched thin. Even though the Black Slate, as you call it, is important, other matters have higher priority: border security, domestic terrorism, cyber-attacks, white collar crime. There are only so many agents, and they can only keep tabs on so many things."

"Sure, sure, and I'm supposed to believe the NSA doesn't keep tabs on any of these things? Don't you share information with each other?"

"Like I said, the FBI has priorities, but the Black Slate is still a threat, it just isn't as high up on DC's agenda."

"Ah," Smoke said, "Washington DC, home of the greatest truths and the greatest lies."

"You have a skewed outlook on things," she said. "Where does all this come from?"

"I read a lot of books."

"What kind of books?"

"The kind that aren't on the bestseller lists."

"I see." She nodded. "Is there anything you care to recommend?"

"Nope." Smoke's chair groaned as he shifted. "So this character on the wanted list, tell me about him. Has the FBI tried to catch him?"

"Yes, for years and without success. I've studied the file. We've gotten close, only to see him slip from our grasp time and time again. And these are veteran agents. They speak as if he's a ghost or something."

Smoke tilted his head. "Maybe he is?"

"I don't think so."

"Maybe he's like Bruce Lee and they just can't handle him?" He made some quick chops with his hands. "Wah-tah!"

"I'm certain that's not the case, but several agents were wounded in hand-to-hand combat."

Smoke's eyes widened. "Maybe it's the ghost of Bruce Lee?"

"You are a strange man."

"So, do you have a picture? A name?"

"Are you in?"

Smoke beckoned with his fingers.

Sidney pulled a picture from the file and shoved it over. It was a surveillance shot of a small dark-haired man in a blue suit, stepping out of an SUV. "His name is Vaughn, Adam Vaughn. They call him AV."

Smoke's brows buckled as he studied the picture.

"Is this the only picture you have?"

"The only one on me, and it's the best one we have."

"This guy's about five foot five. Hmmm, and he almost has the unibrow thing going. Spanish descent. Sharp features. Hard-eyed." He rubbed his chin. "Where's the last place they cornered him?"

"DC."

"And what is he suspected of?"

"Trafficking."

"Trafficking what?"

"Everything."

"So you have testimonials?"

"Some living and some dead."

Smoke shoved the picture back across the table.

"All right."

"All right. Does that mean you're in?"

"No, all right as in I'm thinking about it."

CHAPTER 5

SIDNEY JOGGED THE MONUMENTS ROUTE in DC. She checked her watch and heart rate. She was thirty minutes into the run, and her thighs and legs were starting to burn.

Thirty more to go.

It was Saturday, mid-morning, and the sun almost warmed the fall air. She hated running when it was too cold. She didn't like getting up early either, not on Saturday. There were other tasks at home she liked to do. But today was different. This wasn't her usual route or scene. She had another meeting. Her former boss wanted to meet. Outside the office. Privately. First time for everything.

Wiping the sleeve of her grey hoodie across her brow and picking up the pace, she passed two joggers, older, wearing 80s Adidas leisure. She smiled as she ran by. They probably moved much faster thirty years ago. She jogged by several people, strollers, tourists. It wasn't the best time to run, but she liked the extra work that came with running through the slow masses. She picked up on things.

A man sitting on a bench wearing a leisure suit and winding his watch. A group of older women walking at a brisk pace and laughing. One had purple leggings on. Another straightened her red wig from time to time.

She weaved her way around the reflecting pool three more times. Her lungs labored, and her feet burned. She checked her time, pushed on, passed the World War II Memorial and sprinted across the street toward the Washington monument, where she slowed to a walk. Hands on her hips, she strolled toward the monument until she saw a man sitting on a bench, waving.

"Sid! Sid!"

Soaked in sweat, she trotted over. He stood up and opened his arms wide. He was as tall as her, broad and heavy, balding with a handsome smile on his face. She stopped short of him.

"I'm soaked in sweat."

"It's all right," he said in a comforting voice, "I have my raincoat on. Come here."

She sighed and made her way into his arms, which braced her in a bear hug, taking more wind from her. "Easy now, Ted." She patted his back.

"Sorry." He released her. He was still smiling. "I've missed my favorite trooper. It's been awhile." He clasped her hands and held them tight. "You look great."

"Sure I do," she said, brushing the damp hair from her eyes. "You look great yourself."

He patted his stomach. "Maybe twenty, thirty, forty pounds ago." He lumbered back to his seat and sat down with a groan. He patted the bench. "The desk and meetings are killing me."

"Are you sure it isn't the burgers and French fries?" She took a seat.

"It's those buffets at the lunch meetings, I swear it. Marge keeps me on a strict diet." He scratched the top of his head and squinted one eye. "But that diet's not very tasty. Salad, salad and more salad. I try, but I can't figure it out."

"Maybe you should start running again, like we used to."

"Ah," he nodded, "I miss that. Well, your company, not so much the running."

His full name was Ted C. Howard, and Sidney still didn't know what the C stood for. He was the first assistant director she'd worked for. Over fifty years old now, Ted still had the thick-set frame of his football days that he always loved to talk about. He was a good man. Energetic. A good mentor. He'd taught her a little about everything—and a lot about little, when he started to ramble. He was like family. An uncle of sorts.

"So, how was Alabama?" he asked.

"Hot."

"Good country down there," he said. "Nice fishing. Nice people."

"Not where I was," she said, smiling. She bent over and redid the laces on her shoes. "But I'm sure you'd find good company."

"True," he said. "Did I ever tell you about the last time I was down there? I was thirty-nine and ..."

Aw crap. Here we go. Cut him off before you end up in tomorrow.

"Yes, you told me," she interrupted. Maybe Ted had told the story, and maybe he hadn't, but she was pretty sure she'd heard them all. Some of them two or three times, as he'd told them to other people when she was around. "What's this about, Ted?"

"Oh." He seemed disappointed. "How'd your interview with Mister Smoke go?"

Cocking her head, she looked him in the eye. "You know about that?" All she had told him was that she'd come back from Alabama. She hadn't mentioned anything about anyone she'd met.

"I spoke with Warden Decker. We go way back."

"Of course you do." Ted had a catalog of contacts. He had access. If he wanted to know something, he'd find it. "And does your office have an interest in my case? I thought you were handling more of the border cases."

Ted reached into the pocket of his navy trench coat and pulled out a paper bag. It was full of nuts. He tossed one toward the nearest squirrel that was skirting by.

"I'm not keeping tabs on you, Sid, but I have checked up on you from time to time." He flicked another nut out. "But this was different. A little bird dropped me a wire of peculiar interest. I felt compelled to look into it."

"And?"

"The Black Slate. I know a little something about that." The creases deepened over his eyes. "I don't like the idea of you working on this. The way they're going about it is peculiar. It seems … dangerous."

Ted had never been like this before, and they'd navigated some dangerous waters. Why the concern now?

"Danger's part of the job. You told me that."

He laughed. "I think that's a quote from a movie. It's true, but probably much shorter and more eloquent than I would have put it." He flung out a few more nuts where many squirrels had now gathered. "Don't take me wrong. You're as fit to do this as any. If I was in the field, I'd want a piece of the action too." He groaned. "Don't ever get promoted, Sid. They anchor you with cinderblocks to that desk. I should have been a cop. Did I ever tell you—"

She grabbed his shoulder. "Back to the Black Slate, please. John Smoke? You wanted to talk about him."

"Yes, John Smoke. Now that's an odd one. A good candidate on the surface, but all the paperwork below the surface is blacked out or missing."

"You mean I didn't get the entire file?"

"You got enough. I got a little more. That's why I talked to Warden Decker." He pointed at the squirrels. "Look at them. I haven't done this in years. Crazy little rodents. I met a man once who had a squirrel living in the hood of his hoodie. It was after Hurricane Hugo hit Charleston. Construction guy. One of the strangest things I ever saw." He turned and smiled at her. "In a good way."

She glared at him.

"Sorry." He flung the rest of the nuts aside and dusted his hands off. "Truth. Warden Decker likes the guy. But, we aren't the only people taking an interest in him. Decker clammed up when I prodded him. Leaves me uneasy."

"Well, Smoke has neither accepted nor declined my offer, so maybe there's nothing to worry about."

"Interesting, but I assume he'll take it."

"Why's that?"

"I just have a feeling. That said, be careful. I did some deeper research on similar projects like this that failed. The Black Slate is marred with a dark history. They've tried mercs, bounty hunters, and others of their ilk before."

"And what happened? It didn't work out?"

"They're dead. Some, not to mention many of our agents—who aren't even in that file you were toting—are gone without a trace." He peered up at the Washington Monument. "I don't like this, Sid. Just use extraordinary caution." He got up and extended his hand. She took it, and he pulled her up with ease. "I'm serious." He patted her shoulder and started to walk away. He stopped and turned. "Say, how's the Hellcat doing?"

Unable to contain her smile, she said, "Doing great."

"Hah. You stole her from me. I'll never forget that." Moving on, he waved. "Call me if you need anything."

"Good seeing you, Ted. And thanks."

I think.

CHAPTER 6

S IDNEY'S EYES POPPED OPEN. SHE rolled over and grabbed her buzzing
phone. Sitting up in bed, blinking, she read the screen. There was an
address. A time. And the text came from her supervisor, Dydeck.

"Are you shitting me?" She checked the time. 4:30 a.m. She groaned and
fell back into her goose-down pillows. "What does he want now?" she mumbled.
"Ugh. Why does he get up so early? Why does he feel compelled to bother me?
So early!"

Her toes touched the cold hardwood floor, and she crept into the bathroom
and started the shower. The small bath steamed up quick, and into the hot water
she went and soaked it up. Five minutes later she was out, drying off, and on
the go. She tore the plastic off her dry-cleaned clothes. Seconds later, she had
everything on but her shoes and headed for the kitchen.

The studio apartment west of Reston, Virginia didn't offer much. Its eight
hundred square feet was furnished from secondhand shops and goodwill stores.
A mid-size bed, a small sofa, recliner and a kitchenette with two stools under the
bar.

She turned on the television and followed the blurbs on the news. It was
Monday. Forty-five degrees and a rainstorm was coming.

"Great."

She grabbed the blender out of the sink and loaded it with ice, protein mix,
two eggs, fresh veggies and ice and blended it all up. Eyes intent on the news,
she poured the mixture into a travel mug and rinsed the blender out before
abandoning it in the sink. She snatched her bag from the kitchen bar, clicked
the television off, and headed for the front door. She opened it and stopped.
Something didn't feel right. He fingers fell to her waist.

"Ah!"

She shuffled back to the bed and grabbed her weapon from under the pillow. A
Glock 22. .40 S&W. Inside her closet, she took her shoulder holster and strapped
it on. She paused, staring into the small closet. Another pistol and shoulder
holster hung ready. What Ted had said hung in her thoughts. *Use extraordinary
caution.* It was a strange phrase. The way he'd said it even more so. At 4:42 am,
she was inside an FBI-issued Crown Victoria and rolling down the road. Fifteen

minutes into the ride, the rain started in heavy splatters on the windshield. She turned on the wipers, which left streaks of rain, and the defroster wasn't working well either. She wiped the condensation with her hand and sighed. The rising sun was a blur in her eyes. She slipped on her sunglasses.

It's going to be a long week.

While she drove down the road, Sidney's thoughts were heavy. Typically, she headed into the office at 8 a.m. She'd push paperwork for a few hours then go to meetings and briefings. That was seventy percent of the job, maybe eighty. The rest of the time she was in the field. When Dydeck called her out in the field, it could mean anything. Homicide. Drug busts. Stake outs. Talking to clients and informants. Anything dealing with problems or potential problems at the federal level. From time to time they were a cleanup crew of sorts, when the local brass of Washington got their hands too dirty. It was a part of the job she didn't care for.

Two hours later and south of DC, she exited the highway and entered a residential neighborhood along the Potomac.

Homicide?

Dydeck liked to surprise her. He was good about that. He had a way of working them into a little bit of everything, which she liked. Most of the agents were assigned to a particular unit, but Sidney floated along the rim, where the full range of her talents could be put to use. She was classified as special field ops. Not to mention her paperwork. She was thorough, her wording in sync just the way the top brass liked it. The Bureau loved paperwork. Without it, they'd eliminate most of what they did. She hated it.

Her brakes squeaked to a halt as she parked in the driveway of a contemporary one-level home in a lower-middle-class neighborhood. A For Sale sign was in the yard, and there were also signs in the other two yards at the end of the cul-de-sac. Two other cars were there, black SUVs.

Why don't I have one of those?

Through the rain, she could make out one man on the porch in a dark trench coat, standing by the door. She didn't know him.

Aw, great.

No uniformed local law enforcement. That ruled out homicide, but she'd been to plenty of these scenes before. The estranged family members or children of Washington's finest often wound up in dark places: overdoses, suicide, domestic squabbles. The FBI often covered it up before the news outlets caught wind of it.

She grabbed her gear, popped open the door, and dashed through the sloppy wet grass and onto the covered porch.

"Agent Shaw?" the stocky man said, smiling. He had a warmth about him. She showed her ID.

He glanced at it. "Lousy morning, isn't it."

"You bet."

"I'm Tommy," he said, extending his hand. "Nice to meet you."

She shook it.

"You too."

He opened the door. "They're all waiting for you."

Inside, the house was dimly lit by a lone floor lamp in the living room. There, three men in dark suits waited. Sitting on the large raised hearth was a fourth man in an orange jumpsuit, shackled with his head down.

"Welcome, Sidney," said a man standing off in the corner and putting away his phone. He was in his forties, well-knit, with his head shaven. His eyes slid over to Smoke and back to her. "Well, what do you think?"

"I have to admit, I'm surprised, Jack. And I'm not even including the location. I was under the impression this would be handled downtown. Aren't we outside of protocol?"

"Yes and no. All the paperwork is covered on my end. On the prison end. At the assistant director's end. But hey, it's the list. We have to keep it low." He scratched his head. "And I have to admit, I didn't even know there was a list until a month ago. Huh. Gum?"

"No thanks." She folded her arms over her chest. "So, where do we stand? I'm not really familiar with running things without explicit directives."

"I know that." He nodded to one of the other agents. The man handed another file over. "The directives are in here. Everything we have on the mark as well, including his last known location." He approached and brushed his shoulder against hers. Tapped the file. "Never seen anything like this in twenty years, plucking a low-life out of the prisons to do our job." He sneered at Smoke. "You have two weeks, pal, and then it's back in the hole." He winked at Sidney. "If he gives you any crap, just call and we'll cut this silly mission short." He walked over to Smoke and kicked the man's foot with his boot. "Mind yourself."

The door opened, and another man in a trench coat entered, holding a newspaper over his head with one hand and a briefcase in the other. The man was slender and stoop shouldered, and he wore glasses that looked too heavy for his nose. His frosty eyes met hers.

"Agent Shaw, what a displeasure."

"Agree, Agent Tweel. I couldn't be less happy to see you."

Agent Cyrus Tweel didn't look like much, but he was proven. Sidney had graduated from the academy with him.

Agent Tweel dropped to a knee and popped his briefcase open. "Let's get on with this, shall we? I have more important things to do than waste time on experiments."

Smoke's head tilted up. His gaze fell on Cyrus.

"Jack," Sidney said, "What's going on here?"

"Tracking," Jack said. "We can't lose sight of him. Not for a second. Surely you know that."

Cyrus held up a two-inch needled syringe filled with clear liquid. He flicked it with his fingers.

Smoke rose to his feet. "No one is going to Snake Plissken me!"

"You'll do what you agreed to," Jack said. He nodded to the other agents, who seized Smoke by the arms. "Now be still." Jack pulled out a stun gun. "Or it'll be my pleasure to use this on you."

"No!" Smoke said, struggling against the agents. "No!"

CHAPTER 7

"That needle better not get within a foot of me!" Smoke said.

"What's going on here, Jack?" Sidney said. "What the hell is in there?"

"Something new," Jack said. He pointed to Smoke. "You agreed to this. You better settle yourself."

"I didn't agree to any injections! Screw this! Put me back in prison."

"Jack!" Sidney said, stepping in front of him. "What is it?"

"A vaccination."

"No one is giving me any shots!" Standing taller than the rest, hands cuffed behind his back, Smoke squatted down and drove his shoulder into the agent on his left. The man teetered over but held on, dragging the three of them down in a heap.

"You're going to regret that," Jack said. He stepped around Sidney and pointed the stun gun at Smoke. "I don't have time for this."

Sidney shoved his hand aside.

Jack misfired. The taser prods buried themselves in one of the agents. He jerked, spasmed, and writhed on the floor.

"Dammit, Sid! What did you do that for?"

"This isn't protocol!"

"It is. Read the file. I tell you it is." He shoved by Sidney and drove his toe into Smoke's gut.

"Oof!"

"Settle down, hot dog! Take your medicine!" Jack said. He put his knee on Smoke's neck. "Cyrus!"

Smoke bucked and squirmed.

Zap!

Smoke jerked and writhed.

Behind Sidney, Cyrus had tased him.

"Give him more juice," Jack said. "He's still squirming."

"Gladly," Cyrus said, squeezing the trigger.

Pop. Pop. Pop.

Smoke screamed out, "Aaargh!" A second later he collapsed on the floor, disheveled and coated in sweat.

"Whew!" Jack said, getting up. He ran his forearm across his brow. "What is that man made of?" He helped up the agent who'd caught some juice from his taser. "Sorry about that." He let out a heavy sigh. "Agent Shaw, I'm letting this incident go. But if you ever act insubordinate again, I'll black mark your file."

"But Jack—"

He stepped up to her.

"But Sir!"

He reached into his pocket and grabbed a handkerchief. "Get in line, or I'll withdraw my consideration."

Sidney started to say, *Yes, Sir*, but held her tongue.

"You go right ahead, *Sir*. This entire incident is way out of bounds."

"No, you're out of bounds, Sid."

"I'm not the one who lost control of this situation. That's on you, not me. That's no way to treat a person. He's a decorated veteran."

"He *was* a decorated veteran. Now he is some ex-con vigilante hot dog idiot."

She glanced at Smoke. Cyrus was driving the needle into him. "Hey!"

"Back off, Sid," Jack said. "Tohms! Yo, Tommy!"

The man she'd met outside came in.

"What the hell are you doing out there? Didn't you hear the racket?"

"Er …"

"Never mind," Jack said. "Just help Muldoon to the car. He's shaken up."

"Right," Tommie said. He glanced at Sid. There was a bit of sympathy in his eyes. He mumbled as he passed. "Cyrus is an a-hole."

"I heard that," Cyrus said.

"Good," Tommy replied. He helped Muldoon back outside, closing the door behind him.

Jack raised his palms up. "Let's start over. The vaccination. I had to do it. Orders. And that's all I know. It's a vaccination."

"Is there something wrong with him?" Sid said.

"Well, I'm just assuming it's for your protection … and his."

Smoke groaned on the floor.

Cyrus locked an ankle tracker on him.

"Who's keeping tabs on him," Sid said, "me or you?"

"Check your phone?" Cyrus said. "There's an app you need to download. Twenty four seven location. Just don't let your phone go dead. Don't lose it like the last time, either."

"Shut up, Cyrus."

"Listen, Sid," Jack intervened. "This is a strange case. I have my orders. You have yours. Execute them, and I'm sure it will all make sense after everything hashes out. Got it?"

"Sure, I got it."

"Good."

"So," Sid said, "is this headquarters?"

He pointed to a peg on the wall.

"Those are the keys. You can work out of here, or you can work out of his place."

"I'm sure she'd like to take him back to her place." Cyrus snapped his briefcase shut. "Probably why she took the assignment. She always had a thing for damaged guys."

"Cyrus, get going," Jack said.

Agent Tweel departed with a frown, slamming the door behind him. That left only Jack, Smoke, the other agent, and herself in the room.

"Get the car warmed up, Danny," Jack said.

That left only three.

"Sid, I'm sorry for how this went down. You're my best. You know that. But I can't have you questioning me in front of others. Not like that. Respect the chain."

"I know, but—"

"No, the only butt I'm going to have is yours if you cross that line again. Capisce?"

She nodded.

"Good." His eyes slid over to Smoke and back. "I don't know what to make of this. He's all yours though. Read the file. Stay away from the office. Don't hesitate to call. In two weeks this will all be over. Things will be back to normal."

"You say that as if you don't think we can bring this guy in."

"Well, the odds are against you. I'm told no one has ever brought one in. And by the look of things, I don't see that changing." He squeezed her shoulder. "Good luck, Sid."

She could feel his heavy gaze on her back as he headed for the door. It sent a chill through her. She didn't turn.

"Goodbye, Sir."

CHAPTER 8

SID PEEKED OUT THE CURTAIN in the bay window and watched the black SUV back out of the driveway and roll out. The chill between her shoulders didn't ease. It seemed everyone knew something they weren't telling. First her old boss, Ted, and now her current boss, Jack.

Behind her, metal clanked on the floor.

In a single motion, she spun around and ripped her pistol out. Smoke sat on the hearth, undoing the cuffs on his ankles.

"Freeze!"

He didn't move a muscle.

"Key. Toss it over to me."

He flicked it at her feet. "You don't think I can work shackled and with this prison garb on, do you?"

"No." She holstered her weapon. "But I won't have you playing pickpocket either. Just be still." She gave him a once-over. A moment ago, he'd been completely disheveled, and now he seemed perfectly fine. He should have been laid out still. "Are you all right?"

Smoke nodded. "Maybe a little achy, but that's more from the vaccination than the taser."

"I don't know what that's about."

"Don't worry about it."

She cocked her head. "You seemed pretty upset about it, and now you're not worried."

"Nope."

"So that was a show?"

"Yep." He held his arms out. "Can you please unlock these?"

"So, you know what the shot was?"

"Yep."

"And they don't?"

"That's right."

"Are you going to tell me?"

"Are you going to take these cuffs off?"

"Answer my question first."

"No, I'm not going to tell you what the shot was for. But I will tell you I have a condition. Nothing contagious, but I've had that shot before."

"Who makes those shots?"

"Don't worry about it." He extended his wrists. "It's just a thing. A private thing. I have my right to privacy, you know."

She tossed him the key.

What in the world is going on?

Smoke had been injected with something, and he was the only one who knew what. He had a fit and had taken a walloping for it. Someone beyond pay grades was overseeing this. Watching Smoke. And so far, everything that was going on made absolutely no sense to her.

Smoked unlocked the last set of cuffs and tossed them on the floor. He unzipped his jumpsuit and slipped out of it.

"What are you doing?" she said, averting her eyes. Her glance revealed his lean body was packed with hard muscle.

"Changing," he said, walking over and grabbing a duffle bag in the corner. He emptied the contents of his bag and slipped on a pair of jeans, a black t-shirt, and work boots. "So, you and Cyrus have a past." He repacked the bag and threw in the jumpsuit. "He doesn't seem like your type."

"I beg your pardon?"

Smoke tossed his duffle bag on the counter. "Aw, come on. It's obvious you two dated. But I can't imagine why you broke it off. He seemed so ... charming. Beady eyes and all."

"You have wonderful powers of perception." She opened the file and set it on the kitchen table. "But if it's not related to this case, keep it to yourself."

"Sure." He walked over and stood by her side. "But tell me, why did you go out with him? Let me guess: you thought his drive and intelligence outweighed his meager frame and uber-bland personality."

"No." She kept her eyes on the papers in the file.

"You have a thing for short guys?"

"Mister Smoke—"

"Smoke." He smiled. "Just call me Smoke."

"Grab a chair."

Smoke took a seat and hitched one booted foot on the table. It had the ankle tracker on it. "They might as well have left the handcuffs on. Ridiculous."

Sid downloaded the application Cyrus had sent her. A minute later, Smoke's location was on the screen. She showed it to him. "Works great. Things are looking up. Now, let's discuss our current situation... First, whatever you have in mind, you run by me first. Second, you don't go anywhere without me."

"I need to hit the head."

"Third." She looked at his boot on the table. "Keep it professional."

He dropped his foot on the floor.

"All right, but I really do."

"Make it quick."

He got up. "I missed prison chow this morning too." He patted his stomach. "I'd really like to have some pancakes."

She looked at him. "I don't care."

He picked up his duffle bag.

"Where are you going with that?"

"If you don't mind, I'm going to shave." He rubbed his chin. "This scruff makes me feel dirty. Now that I'm out of prison, I want to feel clean again."

"That really doesn't matter to me."

Smoke walked away and flipped a hallway switch.

"No bulbs."

Sid heard him checking switches until he finally stopped and a door near the back of the house closed. She checked the monitor on her phone. *Good.* Inside the file were more pictures of Adam Vaughn. He wore plain clothes and kept a personal network of goons close by. Most of the footage wasn't the best, as it came from security cameras and the locations were erratic. Different banks. Restaurants—some expensive, others dives. AV seemed to have friends in high and low places. She became engrossed. There were pictures of weapons caches. Unidentified men slaughtered. There were pages of documentation with the letters blacked out.

What good is this?

There was an envelope inside she'd overlooked. She opened it. A brief letter was typed out on bureau letterhead.

Agent Shaw,

Due to the unorthodox arrangement of this assignment, you will need to keep the following items under consideration.

John Smoke is a convicted criminal with special skills. Don't underestimate him.

You have eyes on him and we have eyes on him. Allow him free range. We'll let you know if he needs to be reeled in.

If any alien objects or circumstances or individuals are encountered, notify your superiors immediately.

Trust your instincts and good hunting,

The Bureau

"Who on earth wrote this?" She glanced at her phone. Smoke's beacon hadn't moved. "It can't be from the bureau."

It was a first: a cryptic, unprofessional, unsigned letter. It made her wonder if Cyrus or Jack were playing a joke on her. But the bureau stamp. The make of the paper. She'd seen it before. It was nothing short of top brass bonding. She shook her head.

I guess there's a first time for everything.

She put the letter back inside the envelope and slipped it into her bag. *'Allow him free range', it says.* She smirked. *He doesn't need to know that.*

There was a squeak from down the hall. The turn of a faucet. The faint sound of water echoing.

Are you kidding me? A shower? Really? I thought he was hungry.

She glanced at the tracker on her phone. Nothing had changed.

One by one, she entered the location coordinates into her phone. Ten minutes later she was done.

Sidney brushed her hair aside. "I need a map." Her belly groaned. "Someone needs another shake." She gathered all the items up and stuck them back in the file folder. Calling out, "Let's get this show on the road," she made her way down the hall and listened at the door. The shower was still running. She rapped her knuckles on it. "Hey."

No reply.

She checked her tracker, and it showed no changes. She knocked again.

Her fingertips started to tingle. She drew her gun and tested the door handle. Locked.

"John? John Smoke?"

No reply.

She stepped back and delivered a heavy kick. The hollow door burst open. The mirror was steamed up, and the ankle tracker lay resting on the back of the toilet. She picked it up.

Damn. How'd he do that?

CHAPTER 9

ANGRY, SIDNEY RIPPED THE SHOWER curtain back.

Smoke was in there.

"Hey! Do you mind?"

"What! Do I mind?" She looked away and slung the ankle tracker at him. "Put that back on!"

"I didn't want to get it wet," he said, chuckling.

"It's waterproof, imbecile!" Sidney left the room. Her face was flushed red. *How in the world did he do that?* "Get dressed and get out here!"

"I'm coming," he said from inside the bathroom. "What's the matter, Agent Shaw? Did you think all of your plans had gone up in Smoke?"

How did he do that? She stormed down the hall. Paced back and forth. Smoke rattled her. Nothing ever rattled her—until this assignment. *Get it together, Sid. Get it together.*

A few minutes later, Smoke came out. He was drying his dark hair off with his towel.

"Sorry about that," he said. "I didn't mean to startle you."

"I kicked the door in. You didn't hear that?"

"I was singing," he said, screwing up his face, "I think. Sometimes I get really into it."

"I didn't hear any singing." She glanced down at his ankle. The ankle tracker was back. "Care to explain?"

"I have my secrets."

"Do you want pancakes, little boy?"

"Okay, I made some calls."

Her head tilted over. "How did you do that?"

"I borrowed one of those agents' phones. The one who got a piece of taser." He held it out. "He can have it back now."

She snatched it from his hand and slipped it in her bag. "Who did you call?"

"My crew."

"And they remotely disarmed the ankle tracker?"

"Sure. Not a problem. And this model isn't one of the best ones. As soon as I gave them a model number, they laughed. So, they looped the signal and I unsnapped it. Easy peasy."

"Are you testing me, Mister Smoke?"

"I'm just knocking some dust off, Agent Shaw. We're going up against something big, and I need to be sharp." He tossed the towel aside and came closer. "I could have just vanished, you know."

"True, but then I wouldn't buy you any pancakes."

"Mmm," Smoke said. "That's good." He stuffed in another forkful of buttermilk pancakes slathered in syrup. He was half through his second stack. "You really should try some."

"No thanks," Sidney said again. She took a sip of coffee. She hadn't been inside an IHOP since she was a teenager. "I'm fine."

Smoke shrugged and stuffed in another mouthful. Over the past hour he'd proven himself to be the most elusive garbage disposal she'd ever known. He was a bit of a chatterbox too, asking her bizarre question after question that she ignored and dodged until they arrived at their high-carb destination.

She checked messages on her phone. Text. Email. Her niece, Megan, had dropped her a quick text that said 'Hi' with a smile and a unicorn. It had been a while since she heard from her. Her sister, Allison, had issues.

"What's the matter?" Smoke said, gulping down his second Coke and motioning for the waitress.

"Nothing." She set down her phone. "Tell me about this crew of yours."

A waitress took away his glass. "I'll be right back, Hun."

"Thanks," he said. "Sure, my crew. Right. Well, not much to tell. Just two friends that help me track things down. They work the inside, and I work the outside."

"Do they have names?"

"Fat Sam and Guppy."

"And this Fat Sam and Guppy are the ones that helped you hack into FBI property."

He nodded and shoved more pancake in his mouth. "Mmm! I swear, this makes me feel like I haven't eaten in months. Prison food has no flavor to it. And we never get pancakes or waffles, either. Which do you prefer?"

"Neither." She straightened herself in her seat. "Are you about finished?"

"Huh? Well, no. This is a carb load. The protein load comes next." He eyed her and her plate of half-eaten bacon. "You look like someone who knows something about that."

"Are your friends criminals?"

Smoke sat up and leered down. "No. Why would you say that?"

"I need to know what I'm dealing with. 'Fat Sam and Guppy' doesn't tell me much of anything." She took another sip of coffee. "You have to admit, it sounds shady."

"'Fat Sam and Guppy' sounds shady to you?"

"Yeah."

He shook his head. "Well, they say perception is everything."

The waitress returned with his third Coke. "Anything else, hun?"

Smoke looked at Sidney.

She glanced at the windows. The rain was pouring down, and the chill in her bones had finally faded. She gave him a nod.

Smoke held up the menu and pointed.

"I want this and this."

"Anything else?"

"I'll let you know when I'm through."

The waitress brushed by him. "You do that."

"Sure," Sidney said. "You do that. So, you were talking about Sam and Guppy?"

"No, you were talking about them." He took a drink. "Listen, they are legit. No record."

"Which implies they haven't been caught."

"Sort of, Agent Shaw … or Sidney … or Sid—can I call you that?"

"Let's keep it professional."

"Ugh … Agent Shaw, how suspicious are you of this hunt? I mean, think about it. They don't want you in the office. That limits resources. Instead, they want you to tail me as I go on a hunt. And you said yourself they weren't following protocol. Doesn't that worry you?"

"A little, maybe."

"Good. You're honest. Frankly I'm a bit worried too. Not in a scared way, but in a 'I'm pretty sure I'm being manipulated' kind of way."

"Then why do it?"

"It's the Black Slate. Bad people are on that list, and I like the idea of putting them away. Say, mind if I take a look at that file now?"

"Can you handle it while you're eating?"

"I'm a multitasker," he said, taking another big bite of pancakes.

She opened her bag and handed over the file. Smoke rummaged through it, his dark eyes scanning the contents. He was an attractive man. Boyish, yet dark. She noted white scar lines on his hands. A broken finger that hadn't healed well.

"He's a swarthy-looking Spaniard."

"Why do you say he's a Spaniard?"

Smoke shrugged. "He has some interesting haunts, too. Ew, look at all these dead guys. That's not good. Why did you show me this while I was eating?" He stuffed the papers inside the envelope. "I'm going to need a copy of this."

"It's confidential."

"Really?" He laughed. "I don't think there *is* such a thing these days."

The waitress returned and set down two steaming omelets surrounded by hash browns, all on one plate.

"Aw, you put them on one plate. That was really sweet of you. Thanks, sugar." The waitress pinched his cheek. "If you weren't my son's age, I'd take you home with me." She looked at Sidney. "You found yourself a good one here. Big eater. I like a man that lets you feed him."

"Uh, we're not ..." Sidney started, but the waitress moved on.

"Are you a good cook?" Smoke said, sharpening his knife with his fork.

"I can make an omelet."

"Well that's better than the last girl I dated."

"This isn't a date."

"Easy, I'm just making conversation."

"Let's stay on point, Mister Smoke."

"You see, there you go again. Just call me Smoke."

She held her tongue. She wanted to call him something else, but didn't.

"Agent Shaw, let me tell you how I expect things to go. I need information and a couple of days. I want to go to my place. Sort through some things. When I'm ready to move, I'll let you know and ... we go."

"That's not going to happen. We're going to go back to the house and plan things out. We only have two weeks to resolve this."

He tilted his head back and closed his eyes. "Ugh. This is why I work alone."

"And you'd still be working alone if you hadn't gotten carried away with your last job."

"Just two days, that's all I ask. You take some time and I take some time. After that, I'll fill you in and be more willing to cooperate. Please."

The letter did say to turn him loose, but she wanted to hang on. That was her nature. Her training. This scenario was the complete opposite of everything she'd been taught. It irked her.

"You can take the ankle tracker off. That's the biggest problem. Why did you show your cards on that one?"

"Perhaps I was showing off a little."

"Here's the deal. You stay in the house. I drop you off. I pick you up. If I show up and the ankle tracker is there but you aren't, it's over."

"I'll keep it on if you insist, but take a moment. Don't you see the problem this ankle tracker presents? It's a distraction for us, nothing more. It doesn't benefit either of us. It only benefits *them*."

"Them?"

"You know," he said, eyeballing around. "Them."

I actually understand his point. "I tell you what, Mister Smoke. You finish your meal, we go back to the house, lay out a plan, and we'll see how it goes. Easy peasy?"

He dug into his omelet. "Good enough for me."

Her phone buzzed. It was another text from her niece, Megan. Her heart stopped. The text read:

Sorry to bother you, but I haven't seen Mommy in three days. I'm scared. A frowning icon followed.

CHAPTER 10

"What's going on?" Smoke said.

Sidney pulled the sedan into the driveway of the house, put it in park, and looked at him.

"Here's the deal. You go inside. You don't leave."

"Come on," he said. "You've been frosty the entire ride. What's going on? I can help."

"Get your bag. Get out of the car. Get inside the house."

Nodding and raising his hands in surrender, Smoke reached into the back seat and grabbed his duffle bag. He popped the door open to the sound of pouring rain outside. "Let me come."

"I'll be back tonight. Just go."

Smoke stepped into the rain, shut the door, and dashed onto the covered porch.

Sidney didn't wait to see if he went inside. She hit the gas, squealed out of the driveway, and blasted the car through the rain.

"Dammit!"

She was torn. On the one hand, she hated to let Smoke out of her sight. On the other, she didn't want him in her personal business.

It took her an hour and a half to get to her sister's apartment, talking to Megan the entire ride. The nine-year-old was tough, but scared. Sidney wheeled into the apartment complex, which consisted of twenty three-story brick buildings, a pool, tennis courts, and a gym—all of which were long past their glory days.

She parked, headed up the grass to the screened patio of her sister's porch, and knocked on the metal frame of the screen door.

"Megan? It's me, Aunt Sid."

A cute little face peeked through the blinds, and its watery eyes brightened. Megan unlocked the door, flung it open, ran outside, and hugged Sidney.

Sidney picked her up and carried her inside.

"It's all right. It's going to be all right."

Using her foot, she closed the door behind her and sat down on the couch with Megan latched onto her. Sidney's heart burst in her chest.

Allison had better not be using again.

"All right, Megan, all right. You're safe. I'm here." She pushed Megan back and wiped the tears from her eyes. The little girl's long brown hair was braided back in a ponytail. Her face was sweet and innocent with freckles on her nose. "I'm going to take care of you."

"I-I was doing fine. I even made it to school the last two days, but the storm scared me. I thought Mommy would be home by now, but she isn't. Do you think she's mad at me?"

"No, no, no, of course not." Sidney took a breath. Megan was a capable little girl. She'd learned how to take care of herself when she was little. An independent little thing. "She probably got lost again."

"Will you find her, Aunt Sid?"

"I will." She hugged her niece again. "I will."

Her sister, Allison, was younger. She was a runaway. An addict. A mess. Sidney could never make heads or tails of her problems, but she always tried to protect her. No matter what, Allison stayed in trouble. It was heartbreaking and infuriating.

"Are you hungry?"

"No," Megan said, "I had some cereal."

"Do you want to go stay with Nanny and Grandpa?"

"Can't you just stay here with me?" Megan looked at her with sad eyes. "Until Mommy comes back?"

"I'll see what I can do, but I have to call Nanny and Grandpa first."

Megan shrugged. She looked adorable. Little blue jeans. A flowery pink-and-purple shirt. "They'll do."

Sidney didn't stick around after her mother arrived. Keeping the reunion short, she hit the road and headed to Allison's ex-boyfriend's ... Dave was his name. According to Megan, he'd been coming around and staying over from time to time. The last time she'd seen Dave and Megan together, it hadn't ended well.

If she's with him, I might kill both of them.

She drove the car into another neighborhood a little better than the one where she'd left Smoke. The sidewalks and driveways made up the edges of well-kept lawns. Leaves were in piles and bagged at the end of the drives. She pulled along the sidewalk across the street from Dave's house, 104 Dickers Street. The windows were barred. The screen door was a wrought-iron security door. The garage door was closed.

Somebody's made some changes since the last time I was here.

She checked her phone. Smoke's beacon remained in place.

He'd better be there.

The blinds were shut, but light peeked out at the corners. She waited. Dave was a dealer. A clever one. He moved small quantities to subsidize his government assistance. He hadn't worked in years—or ever, for all she knew. She waited another hour. Cars splashed by. Water poured into the grates. It was 2:15 p.m. when she looked again. She needed to get back to Smoke. She needed to find her sister.

I need to put an ankle tracker on her!

She drummed her fingernails on the steering wheel. Chewed on her lip.

Aw, screw it.

She popped the trunk, opened her door, and stepped out into the rain. From the trunk she grabbed an umbrella and opened it up. A car rolled by, splashed her legs, and pulled into Dave's driveway. She noted the plate.

A couple of young men in hoodies jumped out of the car and rushed onto the stoop. One started pounding on the door. The other was yelling.

"Hurry up! It's cold as hell out here!"

The door opened. Sidney hid behind the umbrella until she heard the door close, then made her way across the street and waited beside the front door on the stoop, craning her neck toward the window. The voices were muffled, and the driving rain splattering all around drowned out the details. She closed the umbrella, shook it off, and waited. Ten minutes later, the door opened. She stepped back and whipped out her badge.

The dilated eyes of the young men lifted toward her.

Sidney held her badge up and said quietly, "Disappear."

The two scurried through the rain without a glance backward.

Sidney caught the door with her umbrella and slipped inside.

"Shut the door, you idiots!" a voice said. Dave appeared in the foyer. His eyes widened. He dropped his can of beer. "Aw shit! How'd you get in here?"

Sidney closed the door behind her and locked it.

"Hey, hey," Dave said, holding his hands up and backing away into the living room. "I didn't do anything."

"Sure you didn't, Dave. Sure."

Dave wasn't a bad-looking guy. He had a mop of brown hair and strong features. A scruffy beard. The plaid pajama pants and Bob Marley T-shirt did little to enhance his demeanor. His eyes were weak and yellow, and he smelled like reefer.

"You can't be in here," he said. "It's illegal."

"Where is Allison, Dave?"

His eyes flitted around the room. A bong sat on the coffee table in front of a new plush sectional sofa. A video game was playing on a seventy-inch flat-screen TV.

"I haven't seen her."

"Do you remember what happened the last time you lied to me about her?"

Grimacing, he rubbed the white scar on his forehead.

"Yes."

Sidney got closer and bounced the handle of the umbrella on his shoulder.

"Don't make me use this."

"What are you going to do with an umbrella?" He laughed. "Let me guess. Stick it where the sun don't shine and open it?"

"Aw, that's my darling Dave. Smart-ass dope head and everything." She stepped on his toe. "You know what, Dave? I really like your idea."

"You would, seeing how you don't have any of your own." He tugged his foot out. "And as I recall, you got into quite a bit of trouble the last time you barged in here, didn't you?"

"Oh, you gonna call your uncle again, the congressman?"

"Yep."

"Hmmm," she said, tapping the umbrella on his shoulder. "I think he's in danger of losing this next election. Yes, I'm pretty sure he's done for."

"No he isn't. He's up in the polls."

She smiled.

"I'll take my chances."

She brought the umbrella handle down between his eyes.

Crack!

"Ow! You bitch!"

Crack!

"Ugh! Stop it!"

"Stop it what?"

"Sid!"

Crack!

"Agent Shaw! Okay? Agent Shaw!"

"Dave, this is the last time that I ask. Where is she?"

He swallowed hard and looked away.

Sidney made it over to the coffee table, picked up the bong, and started to pour the water out on his new couch.

"Be nice, now. I didn't do this. I swear it's not my fault."

"Where IS she?"

"I-I..."

Sidney dropped some more water on the sofa.

"Aw ..." Dave moaned.

"If you like, Dave, I'll be more than happy to confiscate your inventory."

"Not without a warrant."

She poured out the bong and dropped it on the couch.

"Dammit, that's new!"

She took out her phone.

"I'm out of patience. One call, and a swarm of local law enforcement will be here."

"You wouldn't dare. Not after the last time."

She started to dial.

Dave turned tail and ran up the steps.

"Allison! Allison! Run!"

Sidney surged up the stairs and stormed down the hallway just as Dave jetted into a bedroom and slammed the door behind him.

Sidney pounded on the door.

"Open up! I'm not playing any games! Get out of there, Allison!"

"Screw you, *Agent* Shaw!" Dave yelled.

She kicked the door in.

Dave stood inside an unkempt bedroom with the window wide open. One leg hung outside the sill.

She grabbed him by the arm, jerked him inside, and wrestled him to the floor.

"No more games, Dave."

"You're too late," he said, laughing. "She's already gone."

She checked outside the window. There was a deck and stairs that led down into the backyard. There was no sign of Allison.

"She left you a message, Sid," Dave said, sitting up and rubbing his head.

"Really, what was that?"

He giggled. "You are so stupid."

"Am I? Why is that?"

She heard the rumble of a garage door opening.

"Because," Dave said, "she was never up here to begin with. It was all a distraction, you stupid b—"

She socked him in the jaw, rocking his head back to the carpet. *Whap!* She dashed downstairs and opened the front door. A jungle-green Jeep Wrangler sped out of the garage down the street and disappeared around the corner.

"Damn!"

CHAPTER 11

SIDNEY RUSHED TO HER CAR and slung open the door. Taking a seat, she glanced back at Dave's house. A blind in one of the top bedrooms peeked open. She saw the faint outline of two fingers.

Wait a minute.

She took a second and closed her eyes, envisioned the Jeep Wrangler speeding away. There was a lone driver hunched over the wheel. Big. Husky. Allison could have been hidden in the back seat. Or maybe not. She had a feeling. An instinct.

That little dope-headed witch is still in there.

The garage door started to close.

Crap! Move it, Sid!

She couldn't let Dave lock her out again. And she dared not force herself in, not after the last time. She was probably in enough trouble already. She sprinted across the street, right in front of an oncoming car. It squealed to a stop, and the driver laid on the horn. She kept moving, eyes intent on the lowering garage door. She wasn't going to make it. She made a decision and did a stupid thing.

Sidney drew her gun and slung it under the garage door. It skidded over the driveway, clearing the opening by inches and disappearing inside. The door stopped, rattled ... and began to lift. She heard a voice inside scream. Up the door went. One foot. Two feet. It stopped and renewed its descent. Sidney rolled underneath it and inside. She spied her gun, scrambled to it, and found Dave's wide eyes.

"No!" he said, making his way back inside through the door. "No! Get out of here!"

Sidney snatched up her weapon and charged the closing door that was slamming shut. She lowered her shoulder and plowed into it. The impact jarred the door open. It jarred Dave.

"You get out of here! This is illegal!"

She drove her knee into his crotch. She shoved him inside the garage and watched him spill onto the floor, cry out, and writhe. She slammed the door shut and locked it.

Upstairs, she heard footfalls scampering over the floor. There was something about them—lithe, child-like, familiar. She made it upstairs in seconds. A woman with long dark hair, blue jeans, and a black T-shirt ambled across the hall into another room and stumbled inside the door.

"Allison!"

Two bare feet slipped into the frame, and the bedroom door started to close. Sidney stopped it with her foot and shoved it open. She looked down at her sister. Allison was a smaller version of herself, but soft and supple. She was shaking. Her face was sad. Tears streamed out of her eyes. There were needle tracks on one arm.

"I'm sorry, Sid. I'm sorry."

"Shut up," Sidney said. "Do you know how long it's been since you left Megan?"

"A day?" Allison sniffed.

"Three days!"

"No," Allison said, shaking her head. "It, it can't have been."

"Well, it has."

Allison started to bawl. Tears streamed out of her sunken eyes and over her pouting lips. "I'm a lousy mother."

"You're a lousy sister too. Get up!"

"What? Why? I'm not leaving. I don't deserve to go back."

Sidney reached down and grabbed her arm.

"Get up!"

Allison jerked away. "No!"

Here we go. Her little claws are coming out.

"I'll take you out of here in handcuffs."

Allison pounced on her legs and drove her to the floor. Sidney cracked her head on the door frame, drawing spots in her eyes.

"No you won't!" Allison screamed. She sprang out of the door.

Angry, Sidney snatched her sister's ankle and climbed onto her back.

"Get off me! Get off me! Dave!"

Sidney wrenched Allison's arms behind her back. Her sister squealed. She bound up her wrists and slipped the flexi-cuffs on her. Allison resumed her bawling.

"Get up. I'm not carrying you."

"No," Allison said with a defiant sob. "No."

She grabbed Allison by the ankles and started dragging her toward the stairs. Her sister kicked at her and yelled.

"I hate you! I hate you, Sid! I hate you! Why can't you mind your own business? Why can't you leave me alone!"

This wasn't the first time the sisters had gone round and round. It all started in their teens. Allison liked to party. She liked the attention. She liked boys. Drugs. Excitement. Sidney bailed her little sister out time and again. It got old. It had made her mom and dad old.

"Why don't you grow up, you little brat! You have a daughter. Go to church and find Jesus or something." She hauled Allison down the carpeted stairs.

"Hey!"

"Get up, then!"

At the landing, Allison started to rise. She eyeballed Sidney. She spat in her face.

Sidney slapped her across the jaw, and Allison stumbled back to the floor. Her little sister wailed. "I hate you, Sid. I hate you."

Sidney dragged her to her feet and said, "You don't hate me. You hate yourself."

Family. It mattered, even though her sister was a wild one who often ruined the best-planned Thanksgiving. Sidney loved her sister, even though for the last decade she'd wanted to choke her. And there was Megan. How could Allison neglect Megan? The little beauty was about one step from a foster home if she and their parents didn't intervene.

Please God. Please don't let that happen.

Sidney pulled into a gas station alongside the pumps. It was evening now, and she'd just spent the last three hours helping her parents get Allison settled down. They were all distraught, and none more so than Allison had been when she was finally reunited with Megan. She had shaken all over and sobbed, begging forgiveness. All Megan had said was, "It's going to be okay, Mommy."

Megan was a strong little lady.

Sidney whipped out her credit card, pumped gas, ran inside the station, and grabbed some coffee. Black. No cream. No sugar. No straws. She dropped two bucks on the counter and left, ignoring the greasy-haired clerk's toothy smile at her.

Creep.

She racked the nozzle, grabbed her receipt, and hopped back inside the car to lean back against the headrest and take a long sigh.

Lousy weather. Lousy day. I should have transferred south when I had the chance. What was I thinking?

Family. She rubbed the knot on the side of her head.

Love hurts.

She took a sip of coffee and checked her phone. Smoke's location hadn't changed.

He'd better be there—probably wants more pancakes.

She put the car in drive, sped out onto the main drag, and gunned it onto the highway. Her thoughts were riddled with her family. The burden on Mom and Dad. Dealing with Allison's problems. And Megan. This was one of the things she hated about her job. She loved her duty. She loved her family. But duty presided over family, and it hurt in times like this when they needed her.

"It's all right," her mother, Sally, had assured her. "We understand. It's our job to handle this. We'll get her on the mend."

Her father, Keith, had agreed and nodded his head. Both of her parents were strong, but they were heartbroken, and they weren't getting any younger. She could see it in their eyes. She heard the worry in their voices, not just for Allison, but for her. They didn't like the job she did. It was dangerous. And oftentimes Sidney felt selfish. It tore at her.

Block it out. Block it out, Sid. You can't take care of everybody.

Sidney had to live her life and be available when she could.

"Just do the best you can, Sid," her father had said, giving her one last hug. His hugs were always warm and comforting. "Do the best you can."

I try, but it never feels like enough.

CHAPTER 12

I T WAS 8:14 P.M. WHEN she pulled into the driveway of the FBI house. Smoke's beacon was still strong, but the porch lights were out, and so was the lamppost at the end of the drive.

He's not here. I know it.

The front door was locked, and none of the inside lights shone. She took out the house key that Jack had given her and fumbled around with the lock until she got it. Inside she went, testing the switches until she made it to the lamp between the living room and kitchen and switched it on.

With caution she made her way down the hallway. A dim light showed beneath one of the doors. She put her ear to it and heard voices on the other side. She drew her weapon, turned the knob, and opened the door. A set of wooden stairs led into a basement she hadn't accounted for. Weapon first, she crept down them.

The basement was partially finished. There were hook-ups for laundry and an unfinished shower. The framework of two-by-four walls was laid out. There was an empty fireplace and a rec room or den of some sort. A flat-screen TV was on. In front of it was a plaid sofa, and there was an old recliner that didn't match beside it. A news show was on the screen. A lady doing the weather.

What is going on here?

She noticed a wooden kitchen table with some papers fanned out on it. A pizza box and a two-liter of soda. Some power tools and drywall were lying nearby on the floor. There was a map hanging on a plywood wall.

A commode flushed.

Sidney whirled around.

Smoke stepped out from behind a narrow bathroom door. He lifted his hands up.

"Easy, Shooter. I'm just taking a ten-fourteen, is all." He eyed the gun and cocked a feeble smile. "Glad you're back. Is everything okay? You look like you've had a long day."

She holstered her weapon.

"What is going on here?" She glided back to the table and took a closer look at the contents. The file folder was on the table. Her blood pressure spiked. "You stole my file."

Hands still up, Smoke said, "I can explain."

"Can you now?"

"Sure, I, er ... okay, I stole it, but only so that I could work on things while you were gone." He walked over to his map and pointed at the red circles. "See, now we can take another angle on things."

"You made a mistake."

"I'm sorry," he said, "but I stayed put. I bet you thought I wouldn't, didn't you?"

Her stomach gurgled.

Smoke opened the pizza box. "Half ham and onions and half Hawaiian. Please, have some."

"How did you get this?"

"Uh ... Delivery."

"And how did you pay for it? Did you spend my money too?"

"No," he said, "I'd never do that." He tapped his head. "I have many numbers in my head. Hey, my accounts are still good."

"Well, you did one thing right today."

"I did? What's that?"

Sidney picked up a slice of pizza and took a seat on the sofa.

"I like Hawaiian."

The old sofa was comfortable. It reminded her of the times she and Allison would stay in their grandparents' basement for long weekends. She bit into the pizza.

"I could warm it up," Smoke said. "I came down here and saw that some of the breakers were off, but I let them be. I didn't want any nosy neighbors dropping by for a greeting. I like my privacy."

Sidney yawned. An image of Megan came to mind, and she forced it out again. She studied the television. "So, you're getting reception down here."

"I spliced into the box."

"Cable theft is a crime," she said with a laugh.

Smoke eased into the recliner.

"So, I'm here. You're here. What's the next move?"

I have no idea.

"You look beat," he continued.

"I look beat? Really?"

"Sorry, I guess *tired* is a better word."

She finished off the pizza and dusted off her hands. She wanted to lie down, but she forced herself off the sofa instead and headed toward the map.

"Where did you get the map? Did the pizza guy deliver that too?"

"Er ... well, you shouldn't be surprised at what you can get delivered these days. As a matter of fact, Amazon—"

CHAPTER 14

"**O**PEN THE DOOR! OPEN THE door!" Smoke yelled.

Sidney popped the locks.

Smoke swung open the back door and stuffed the hefty body inside. The back sagged and bounced with the impact. Smoke shoved the man over, hopped in the back seat with him, and shut the door.

"What are you doing? Have you gone mad?"

"Did I make it?" Smoke asked, scanning the dash.

"Make what?"

"Make it back in ten minutes?"

"Are you kidding me?"

"No, you said ten minutes. I made it, didn't I?" He pumped his fist. "Yes, one of my best extractions ever!"

Sidney stared at the man in the back seat. It was Rod Brown. A white cotton tank-top barely contained his belly. His plaid boxer shorts were half turned around. He was out. Out cold.

"Go," Smoke said. "Go! I think someone might have seen me."

"No."

"Yes!" Smoke said. "I see someone coming."

A flashlight coming from the condos cut through the dank night.

Sidney dropped the transmission into drive and sped away. "Do you know how many laws you've broken?"

"Let's see …" He counted on his fingers. "Breaking and entering, and kidnapping. Two."

"Two to start with."

Rod Brown groaned.

Smoke socked him in the jaw. *Whap!* "And battery."

"You're an idiot!"

"Look," Smoke said, "the way I see it, he's a criminal."

"So are you."

"No—aw, let's not get into that. That said, guys like him don't operate within the rules you hold so dear. They break them. And we aren't going to get anywhere following the FBI playbook." Smoke huffed. "Guys like this laugh at those tactics. If you want to get this done, then we need to fight fire with fire."

"We need to not break the law."

"Then you shouldn't have come along, Agent Shaw. I'm pretty sure that's the reason they hired me to do this: I can get my hands dirty. You can't." He shoved Rod's sagging body over toward the window. "Let me out, and you walk away from this."

"No." In the rearview mirror, she saw Smoke banging his head against his headrest.

I'm in charge, not you.

"So what's the next step in your brilliant plan? Are we going to beat the whereabouts of AV out of him?" she asked.

"Something like that, but my methods of intimidation are a bit more subtle."

"Waterboarding?"

Smoke laughed. "Sure. Why not? Let's swing by Walmart and pick up some bottled water and towels."

Sidney drove the car down into a marina along the Potomac and parked in the shadows where a stretch of highway passed over. She turned and faced Smoke. "Next time, let's put him in the trunk."

"Next time, huh?"

"You know what I mean."

"Sure. Say, where are your flex cuffs?"

She popped open the glove box and handed him two pairs.

Smoke fastened Rod's arms behind his back and bound his ankles. He rummaged through Sidney's gym bag.

"Hey!" She snatched a pair of her panties from his hand. "Do you mind?"

"No," Smoke said. He found a sweatshirt and covered Rod's head. "There. I think we're ready to go now." He handed over her gym bag. "All set. Time to wake him up." He put his finger to his lips. "Let me do the talking."

"Fine. Just don't get carried away." Interrogations. She'd conducted plenty. *Let's see how you handle this.*

"Great, now turn the heater up."

She did.

Smoke nodded. "And cover your ears."

"Why?"

Smoke pinched Rod's inner thigh.

The big man bucked in his seat and let out an ear-splitting howl.

Sidney covered her ears.

Smoke grabbed Rod by his neck and squeezed. "Quiet, Rod, and we'll make this quick."

"Who-who are you?" Rod stammered. "What's going on?"

"I just have a few questions." Smoke changed his voice to something, rougher, darker. "Tell me what I need to know, and I'll let you go."

"Screw you! Do you know who I am?"

"You're Rod Brown. Another one of AV's disposable buttholes."

"Huh? What did you call me? A disposable—"

Smoke punched his face through the sweatshirt. "Shut up!"

"But—"

Punch!

"I don't like your accent. Where are you from, Rod? Pennsylvania? Jersey?"

"Baltimore."

Punch!

"I thought I told you to keep quiet. And I hate Baltimore." Smoke winked at Sidney. "Now, simple question. Where can I find AV?"

Rod remained still and silent. The rising heat was fogging up the windows. Sidney fanned her neck.

"I asked you a question, Rod."

Rod said nothing.

"Oh, I see. Now you're going to be quiet."

Punch.

"Listen, moron," Rod said. "You can punch me all you want, but I don't know any AV."

"Sure, sure you don't. And I'm Mary Poppins."

"You sound like her to me, you frigging putz!" Rod thrashed at his bonds. "Now let me out of these things, you idiot, and I won't have to frigging kill you!"

Smoke reached under the sweatshirt, hooked his fingers into Rod's nose, and lifted him up out of his seat. It was one of Sidney's favorite pressure points. A simple restraining technique. *Impressive.*

"Ow! Ow! Ow!"

"Do you know who AV is, or don't you?"

"Yes! Yes!"

"Are you going to sit still?"

"Yes! Ow! Yes!"

Smoke released him.

"Good, Baltimore Rod. Now we're getting somewhere. So tell me—you're one of his crew—where is he?"

"Look," Rod said, huffing for breath, "Let me do both of us a favor. Whatever you have with AV, drop it. If you pursue it, then you're dead already."

"So you know where he is?"

"All I know is when and where I'm supposed to be. He may or may not be there. Listen, whoever you are, I don't care." Rod's voice started to break. He balled up a little. "Don't cross AV. Don't make me cross AV. It's worse than death, what he does to people who cross him. Worse than death."

An uncanny chill raced down Sidney's spine. She glanced at Smoke. One of his brows was cocked over his eye. He mouthed some words to her. "What do you make of that?"

She shrugged.

He held a finger up, reached into his pocket and handed her a smartphone. He nodded to Rod.

Sidney turned it on. It needed a passcode. *Great.* She thought about it as Smoke went back to work.

"When's your next meeting with AV?"

"Two days."

"Oh, that was pretty quick. I think you're lying, Baltimore Rod." Smoke lightly touched his fingers on Rod's leg.

"Eek! What was that?"

"A spider. Well, a tarantula to be exact." He tickled Rod's leg again.

Rod screamed. "Get it off me! Please! Get it off me!"

"What's the matter, Rod? Are you scared of a little, er, well, a big bug with eight hairy legs?" He barely touched the hair on Rod's leg again.

"Ah!" The big man bucked and twitched. "Stop it! I meet him tomorrow. Late afternoon! Stop it!"

"Where?"

Rod fell silent.

"My spider is a biter, Rod."

"Please, man, please. You don't want to do this. If I tell you, AV will figure it out. AV knows everything. No one can get close to him, no matter how hard they try. Trust me, man. Trust me!" He sobbed. "It's a death wish."

Sidney had seen plenty of men under duress before, but she hadn't expected this. Given enough pressure, loyal foot soldiers rolled on their bosses all the time. This was different. Rod had fear. Real, earnest fear.

Hmmm… She decided to try a passcode on Rod's phone. *Let's see how dumb you are.* She typed in his building and room number. 1211. She got access. *Yes!* She showed Smoke. His brows lifted. She began sifting through Rod's emails, contacts, texts, and interesting applications. It was sparse. *Great. A burner.*

"Where are you meeting tomorrow?" Smoke said.

"Aw geez, don't make me, please."

"I'm going to leave you in here with Mister Tarantula. Leave him on your face. How does that sound, Rod?" Smoke tickled his leg.

"Ah! No! No!"

"Ah, yes, yes," Smoke said.

"It's Drake. A club called Drake. He meets us there. Oh man. Oh man, I can't believe I told you." He balled up and started to rock. "I'm a dead man. You're a dead man. All loose ends must go."

CHAPTER 15

S MOKE PUT ROD IN A sleeper hold and silenced the man's hysteria. "Sorry," he said, "that was getting old."

"Agreed." Sidney tossed the phone back to Smoke. "So what's the plan now? Are you going to tuck him back in bed?"

"We could drug him."

"I don't have any drugs. Do you?"

"I was thinking we could buy some."

"Dumb idea. I guess you didn't think things through." Sidney fastened her belt and put the car in drive. In two minutes they were back on the highway.

This is a mess. A total mess.

"You did good," Smoke said.

"I beg your pardon?"

"You did good. You have good instincts. Going after Baltimore Rod was a good call. He *is* stupid, and he was easy to break."

"I think some luck should be factored in there, seeing as he was home. What if he hadn't been?"

"Well, he was though, wasn't he?"

Sidney fought off a yawn.

"Tired?"

She ignored him. Exhausted was more like it. It had been an unexpectedly emotional day, and she hadn't handled it well. *I need to get better at this.*

"I think we should follow your suggestion and tuck Baltimore Rod back in bed."

Sidney caught Smoke's eyes in the rearview mirror. "Why is that?"

"Why do you think? You suggested it."

"You first."

"Aw, can you just be forthcoming for once and let me be the devil's advocate for a change?"

"All right, Mister Smoke, let me share my thoughts. You're an idiot! All you had to do was verify that Rod was in there. We could have tailed him. Bugged him. Done something vastly more subtle."

"That might have taken days. Maybe weeks."

CHAPTER 16

BUZZ. *BUZZ. BUZZ.*

Sidney pushed her face out of her pillow and checked the clock on the nightstand. 5:34 a.m. Not even four hours' sleep. With a groan, she sat up. Her eyelids were heavy. She rubbed her neck, stretched out her arms, and yawned.

If that's you, Jack, I'm going to kill you.

Rubbing her eyes, she checked her text messages. There weren't any.

"Great. Phantom buzzing in my sleep now."

She toggled through her features. There was a red update on the tracking app. "What's this?"

She opened it up. Smoke's beacon had moved. It was no longer sitting safely at Benson Park Estates. It was on the move. Miles away. Sidney jumped to her feet.

"Sonuvabitch!"

She stubbed her toe on her bed post.

"Dammit!"

She limped to her closet, grabbed a pair of jeans and a pullover shirt, and slipped them on. She holstered up and tied on her shoes. Inside of two minutes she was squealing out of her parking spot and then back on the road.

She tied her hair back in a ponytail, then rubbed her puffy eyes. It wasn't raining, but the window was frosted up. She rubbed it with her hand and turned up the heater.

"Piece of crap car."

She shivered and checked the beacon. Smoke was moving. West. Toward Annapolis. She laid on the gas.

I'll intercept him in the Interceptor. She laughed. It was a long-standing joke that cops and agents made about the old cars. *Then I'll kill him.*

Hankering for coffee and listening to the moan in her stomach, she plowed down the road. She was angry. Jack. Cyrus. Smoke. They all made her mad. Each was unreliable. Unpredictable. She didn't like it. But she didn't mind the excitement that came with it.

I'll show 'em.

She eased back in her seat and turned on some talk radio. The aggravating conversations were certain to keep her alert. Awake. Promises and failures. A chronic rinse-and-repeat cycle of wasted taxpayer dollars.

Clear your mind, Sid. Focus.

There were a lot of things to take in. Change was one of them. She didn't like change. She liked routine. She liked a plan.

"Some things you just can't plan for," her father often said. "Always assume everything is out of your control, aside from yourself."

She hated it when he said that, right along with the smile that came with it. It made her feel like she was doing something wrong. She did things right. She saw to it others did things right as well.

Cruising down the road, she regained her focus. She'd been off her game.

Too much time behind the desk.

She had yelled and cussed. It showed a lack of self-control.

No more of that. You're a pro, Sid. Be a pro. No surprises. No letdowns.

She unholstered her Glock, ran her fingers over the barrel, and stuffed it back in the holster.

I need to get to the range.

She felt jumpy. Edgy.

I don't like feeling this way.

The frost on the windows cleared, revealing the moon's bright glow. An eerie haze hung in the sky, concealing parts of it. Up ahead, a pack of animals darted across the highway. She squinted.

"What the heck?"

The dogs were big dark silhouettes padding across the concrete and vanishing over the guard rail and into the woods. A chill went through her.

Those were wolves.

She shook her head. *Maybe coyotes. No, coyotes aren't that big.* She slowed the car down and eased onto the berm. *No. Get after Smoke, Sid. No time to fool around.* She laid the gas back on and zoomed up the road. *Those were wolves, though. I know it.* Ted's words came to mind. *Extraordinary caution.*

Cruising at ninety, she closed in on Smoke's beacon, which had come to a stop off somewhere south of the John Hanson Highway. She took the machine up to ninety-five before slowing for the next exit, then followed the beacon down the greenway beyond the condos and plaza to a lonely stretch of road miles from the nearest highway.

What on earth is he doing out here?

That's when another thought crossed her mind. What if it wasn't him at all? What if one of his crew was leading her on a wild goose chase? It had been at least twenty minutes since his beacon stopped moving.

Erase your doubt. Follow your leads.

The beacon led her down a grave stretch of road that ended in a grove of tall trees. A gravel parking lot greeted her, accompanied by a lone warehouse lit up with neon signs. One sign read Chester's in bright orange and green flames. There were a few motorcycles and muscle cars on the scene. Beer cans and broken glass littered the parking lot.

What is he doing here?

Sidney checked the beacon. She was on target. She brought the Interceptor to a halt a hundred feet from the front doors. Fog was lifting into the early sunrise. A man in jeans and a leather vest lay face down in the parking lot. Fresh blood from a broken nose dripped on the ground. There was a gentle rise in his chest. She took out her weapon and crept to the doorway.

What have you gotten into, Smoke?

Inside the bar she could hear loud hillbilly rock playing.

Just when I thought it couldn't get any worse.

She pushed the door open and peeked inside. A gunshot cracked out.

Blam!

CHAPTER 17

S IDNEY CROUCHED DOWN OUTSIDE THE door.

Blam! Blam!

The shots were coming from inside the warehouse, somewhere above her head. Adrenaline pumped through her veins.

Crash!

Glass rained down into the parking lot from above her head. A man fell onto the hood of an old white Camaro. Groaning, he rolled off the hood and onto the ground.

Sidney peeked up and around the corner. A figure stood looking out of the oversized window pane. It was Smoke.

"Freeze!" she said. He vanished. She turned her attention to the other man, who was stumbling away. He hopped onto a motorcycle and started it up. "FBI! Freeze!"

He revved the engine.

"Don't make my day," she said, pointing her weapon at him. "The first hole goes in your gas tank. The next hole goes in your head."

He raised his hands over his head. His sagging face was skinned up, and his chin was bleeding.

"Sure thing, lady. Sure thing."

"Aiiyee!" a man screamed.

Sidney turned just in time to see another man flying through the window. He crushed the roof of the Camaro.

Vrooom!

The biker revved up his engine and started to speed out of the parking lot.

Blam! Blam!

Sidney put a bullet in his tank and another in his back tire.

"Get on the ground now!" she said.

The man obeyed.

She bound his legs and wrists with flex-cuffs.

"You didn't have to shoot my bike," he said. "Stupid bi—"

She shoved his face in the ground and rubbed it in the gravel.

"What was that?"

"Nothin'."

Smoke landed on the Camaro's hood, a tall figure in a dark shirt and jeans. He dragged the man who had crunched in the roof to the ground.

Sidney trotted over. "What are you doing?"

Smoke had a dangerous look his eye. He punched the man in the face. *Whap!*

"Taking care of unfinished business."

"Stop!" Sidney said, holding her weapon on him. "Stop now!"

Smoke let go, and the man sagged to the ground.

"Who is he?" Sidney watched the man gather himself into a sitting position.

The man was in his forties, shaven head and black bearded. Dusky skinned. Tattoos covered his naked arms. He was thickset. Formidable. Valuable rings dressed his fingers below all of the knuckles except for two of them. His trigger fingers were missing.

"Ray Cline?"

"Sting Ray," Ray interrupted, spitting blood. "You're going to die, Smoke. Die in a horrible way! Oof!"

Smoke kicked him in the gut.

"What was that, Ray? Say, how did that hit that you put on me go down, in prison? Not so well, did it?"

"Back off," Sidney stepped between them, keeping her eyes on Ray. She had become familiar with his file when she studied up on Smoke. He was a killer. A drug lord. A career criminal. For some insane reason, the system had let him out. "I'll handle this."

Ray started laughing.

"You want to handle me, Pretty?" He winked at her. Blood dripped off his chin. "Help yourself then."

She handed Smoke another pair of flex cuffs and covered Ray with her weapon.

"Secure him."

Smoke slipped the flex cuffs around Ray's neck.

"No, no, no!" Ray said.

"Yes, yes, yes," Smoke replied.

"No," Sidney said. "Just the wrists."

"I can make it look like an accident," Smoke said.

"The wrists," Sidney said. "Take care of it while I call this in."

"Wait," Smoke said, cuffing Ray's wrists behind his back. "Before you do that, let me show you something."

"Yeah," Ray said, "let me show you something too, Pretty."

Smoke rabbit-punched Ray's ribs and hauled him up to his feet.

"Not another word, fiend," he said in his ear. "Not another syllable." He shoved Ray back toward the warehouse bar.

"Are you coming or not? You need to see this."

Sidney followed. The intensity in Smoke's voice compelled her. He was angry. It stirred her.

Inside, there was a long bar, a band stage with instruments, high tables scattered about, and a checkered dance floor. Smoke pushed Ray toward a metal stairwell that led up. Two goons were knocked out cold by the threshold.

"Watch your step." Smoke banged Ray's head into the doorframe. "I'd hate to see you get hurt more than you already are." He banged his head into the door frame again. "No, I wouldn't."

At the top of the stairs they entered an office with a large one-way mirror overlooking the dance floor. The furnishings were fine leather and well-crafted oak. A kitchenette. A bar. An apartment of sorts. Bags of cocaine and cash were on a black velvet pool table, along with dozens of small bottles full of pills.

At least a million worth of dope and cash.

Sidney stepped over another prone body, one of three more men whose blood had been spilt on the floor.

"He has a nice little empire here, doesn't he?" Smoke said to her.

"I've seen bigger," she said, "But without probable cause there isn't a case here."

"That's right, Smoke," Ray said with a sneer. "You don't have a case with me, you frigging renegade. You're toast, Smoke."

Smoke shoved Ray onto the sofa and tied his legs to the sofa's foot with the man's belt. One by one, he tore open the cocaine bags and slung them out the window.

"I'm going to kill you, Smoke! Stop doing that!"

"That's evidence," Sidney added.

"Whose side are you on?"

"The law's."

"Yeah, the law's, you stupid bastard," Ray added.

Smoke chucked bundles of cash out the window.

"That's enough," Sidney said, "I'm calling this in."

"Just one more minute," Smoke said, "You haven't seen anything yet." He tilted his head toward another door. "Check there."

She eyed him.

"It's clear. Go ahead."

"Something you want to tell me, Ray?"

The drug lord looked away.

Butterflies started inside her stomach. Smoke's tone. Ray's feverish look. What was on the other side of that office door? She grabbed the brass door knob and shoved it open. A short hallway, maybe twenty feet long, greeted her. A heavy door stood at the end. On the left, or the front side of the warehouse, was an open office with computers. A black man in a biker vest was laid out on the floor. She walked up to the door and glanced back. Smoke stood just outside the doorway.

And behind door number 1 we have ...

She pulled open the door and gasped.

CHAPTER 18

CHILDREN WERE INSIDE. SIX IN all. They wore aprons and masks. Wide-eyed, frail and skinny, their hollowed eyes froze on her.

Sidney's heart sank. Blood drained from her face.

The children kept working. Scales. Baggies. Small piles of pills and cocaine. Latex gloves stretched over their little hands. Not a one of them could have been more than ten. Girls and boys. Eyes weak and glassy.

Her knees gave a little. She swallowed. "It's okay. I'm here to help. I'm the police."

A little Latino boy dropped his utensils, ran over, and hugged her. Within seconds, they had all closed in and embraced her. Tears streamed down their faces. Her own eyes watered. Her heart ached. Their lithe bony bodies pressed against hers.

"It's okay. It's okay. Let's find you something to eat." She picked two of them up in her arms. The others hung on her legs and waist. She gently yelled down the hallway, "A little help please."

Smoke picked up a few of the children and took them into the office. He peeled their tiny fingers off Sidney and set the children down at a table. There was a refrigerator that had some sodas inside. Some Doritos were in the cabinet over the bar. He filled their hands and said, "Eat."

Their fear-filled glances fell on Ray's hard eyes.

Sidney's temperature rose. Her cheeks turned red.

"You're going away for a long, long time, Ray."

"Am I, Pretty? I don't think so. You see, those kids … heh, heh, well, they're all *my* kids."

"I'm sure that isn't so," she said, stepping between Ray and the kids. "I'll see to it this all sticks."

"Good luck with that, Pretty. The only thing that's going to get stuck, though, is you."

Her fingers danced on her gun. She wanted to wound him. Shoot him. Make him pay for all that he'd done.

"You won't shoot me." Ray chuckled. "You have a career. A pension. Hah. You wouldn't want to lose all that, would you."

"True," she said. "But that's not why."

"Really, why is it then?"

"It's because I don't want to set a bad example for the children." She looked at Smoke. "Do you mind removing him from our sight so they can eat in peace?"

"As you wish." Smoke undid the belt, picked Ray up by the scruff of the neck, shoved him toward the outside window, and leaned him over the edge. "Time to fly Smoke Airlines again."

"No! Wait! What are you doing?"

Smoke, much bigger than Ray, hoisted him up over his shoulders.

The whine of police sirens cut through the air.

Sidney rushed to the window.

Three police cruisers pulled into the parking lot. It was the county sheriff.

"Ah ha ha!" Ray laughed. "My cavalry has arrived."

A nagging feeling crept between Sidney's shoulders.

Smoke started to heave Ray out anyway.

Sidney grabbed his shoulder. "No, don't. Put him down." She messed with her phone. "We have to let the law sort this out."

"Amen to that," Ray said. "Amen to—ow!"

Sidney elbowed him in the nose.

The scene was ugly. Sidney had called in her colleagues at the bureau. Ray had called in his the moment Smoke arrived. The two parties fought over jurisdiction. Possession. The children. Smoke was handcuffed in the back of a bureau SUV. The only thing going for them was that nobody had died.

"Stupid, Sid. Really stupid." That was all Jack said when he showed up an hour later. "He needs to go back in the hole."

"I'll handle the paperwork," she said. "It's not that bad. Nobody died. The media hasn't arrived."

"Oh, really. It's not that bad? You have an ex-con going vigilante. You've pissed off the county sheriff's department. I can imagine a dozen lawsuits being filed from all this." He rubbed his forehead. "None of the charges will stick!"

"I can handle it."

"You're what, going to make something up? Lie?"

"No," she sighed, "embellish."

Jack's face turned red. "Embellish!"

"Don't you raise your voice to me, Jack. You saw the drugs. The lab. The children. Don't you act like this can't stick." She poked him in the chest. "We've handled worse. I seem to remember doing a few favors for you."

"Get ... get over here." He pulled her away from prying eyes and ears. "Listen to me. You are out of your lane. This is not part of the Black Slate. No, you blew it. Your little soldier over there is going back to the jail cell where he belongs. Experiment over. And you will be spending a lot more time behind the desk."

"Wait a minute. It's only been one day. I'm supposed to have two weeks."

"Tough. Now get in your car, go home, and report back to me in the office tomorrow so you can get started on all the paperwork you wanted."

"No," she argued. "We have a lead on AV."

Jack looked up into the sky and shook his head. "I could almost let this slide." He locked eyes with her. "Except there's another detail you missed. Congressman Wilhelm gave me a call late yesterday, and let's just say it wasn't so pleasant."

Crap!

Congressman Wilhelm was her brain-dead sister's boyfriend Dave's uncle.

"I gave you the benefit of the doubt, Sid. I sympathize with you regarding your sister. But now this?"

"Sir—"

"No sirs, Sid! Go home. It's over." His phone buzzed inside his suit pocket. "Excuse me." Jack walked away.

Sid headed for her car.

I can't believe this!

Smoke sat in the back of a black FBI SUV. She shot eye daggers at him through the tinted windows. She could have sworn he waved.

Good riddance.

Things were beginning to clear up. Ray and his men were gone. The children had been taken by protective services, leaving only a few men from the sheriff's department. One of them passed her by and in a low voice said, "Now you're in the crosshairs. Beware, Agent. Beware."

"What?"

He tipped his cap and kept on moving. Seconds later, the deputy sheriffs and their cruisers were gone, leaving only her, Jack, and Agent Tommy Tohms—and Smoke, but he was locked up. She popped open her car door and started inside.

Well, at least the kids are safe.

"But sir?" she heard Jack exclaim. His face reddened. "But—" He looked at his phone. "Dammit!" He started to throw it on the ground, but stopped short. He marched over to his SUV and opened Smoke's door.

"Get out!"

Smoke eased his big frame out of the car.

"Uncuff him, Tommy."

Smoke handed Tommy the cuffs.

Jack snatched them out of Tommy's hands and slung them away. He pointed his finger in Smoke's face. "Don't get my agent killed, you stupid sonuvabitch. Let's go, Tommy."

"But my cuffs!"

"Let's go!" Jack glared at Sid. "You got your wish, Sid. He's all yours."

Ten seconds later, Smoke and Sidney stood in the parking lot all alone.

She got into her car, feeling a little bit elated.

Smoke joined her.

"I have one question," she said.

"Shoot."

"How in the hell did you get here?"

CHAPTER 19

"H UNGRY?" SMOKE ASKED.

Sidney rolled her eyes. She was torn between mad and happy.

Smoke patted his belly. "I always get hungry after an adventure like that."

"I don't care." She accelerated up the highway.

"It's early. I know a diner around here that makes great pancakes."

"No."

"Excellent coffee too."

Yes.

"No."

"Come on, Agent Shaw. You can't be that sore at me. We did a good thing back there."

"'Sore at you?' Really? Is this the nineteen fifties? Who says that anymore?"

"I picked it up from some old timer in prison. He said that a lot. 'Don't be sore at me, boss.' It kind of stuck." He popped open the glove box. "Got any snacks in here?"

She leaned over and slammed the glove box shut.

"No."

Smoke shrugged. He adjusted his seat backward, locked his fingers behind his head, and closed his eyes. Seconds later he was snoring.

You have got to be kidding me!

She glanced over at him. His athletic frame filled out his black T-shirt and jeans. His knuckles were scuffed and swollen, and there were white scars on his bare arms.

He wouldn't be so bad if I didn't hate him.

She backhanded him in the chest.

He lurched up. "What—what?"

"You're on duty. No sleeping."

"So now we're a team, are we?"

"Where's the diner you were talking about?"

Smoke's dark eyes scanned the signs on the highway. He rubbed his jaw. "Two more exits. You'll love it."

"We'll see."

The diner wasn't much, but the silverware was clean. It was an old dining car in the front with much more built on in the back. Blue stools hugged the chrome-trimmed counter. The floor was hardwood, and the booth they sat in was a soft blue vinyl. A gas fireplace burned at one end. It was warm. Cozy.

"Nice, isn't it?" Smoke stuffed in a mouthful of pancakes that looked like they were stacked to his chin. "Ever seen a fireplace in a dining car?"

Sidney picked through her eggs and bacon. "No." She took a sip of coffee. *Mmmm ... good coffee.*

"How's the coffee?"

"It's all right."

"Would you like to try my pancakes?"

Yes.

"No." She scraped up the rest of her eggs and washed them down. "Are you about finished?"

Smoke looked at his stack. "No. Are we in a hurry?"

"Yes."

"For what? AV isn't supposed to show until five. We have plenty of time." He flagged down the waitress. "Could I get another Coke, please?"

"Sure thing."

"I'm still catching up from prison time," Smoke said to her. "I hope you don't mind, but I'm hungry."

"Fine, take your time." She checked the messages on her phone. "You clearly know what you're doing. And your friend, Ray, when he's released—say, tomorrow—will be thankful for your intervention."

"It wasn't supposed to go down that way."

"Really?" She leaned forward and looked him in the eye. "And how was it supposed to go down?"

"You weren't supposed to show up." He cut up his sausage and pointed at her with it on his fork. "I had it all under control. I told you, just leave me be."

No.

"All right, so I don't show up, what happens?"

"I have my ways. I nullify Ray and his gang and secure the kids." The waitress returned and put his Coke on the table. "Thanks. The kids are the main thing. Once they're safe, I burn the place down."

"Arson? That was your brilliant plan. Committing a felony."

"I'm just kidding."

She shook her head. "No, no you aren't."

"Come on." He tried to catch her eye. "You know you feel good that we put some bad guys down and saved some kids. Everyone is better off now."

She balled up her fist and said through her teeth, "That wasn't our mission."

"He put a hit out on me. He's slime. Do you have any idea how many people have disappeared under his watch?"

"That's not the point."

"How many women and children?"

"You don't know that."

"Yes, yes I do. I studied him for months. I have files inches thick I can show you." He reached over and grabbed her arm. "Justice was served today, and it didn't take a pile of paperwork to dispense it."

His grip was warm and strong. She pulled away.

"Let's go."

"But I'm not finished."

She tossed two twenties on the table. "You are now."

CHAPTER 20

THE DRAKE. THAT WAS WHERE Rod had said AV would be. It wasn't at all what Sidney expected.

"That's different," Smoke said.

A series of barges formed a small city along the Potomac on the Virginia side of the river, south of the Torpedo Art Museum. A lighthouse could be seen in the distance. Standing on the wharf that jutted over the river and led to the barrages was a lone sign that pointed to the Drake.

"Let's go," Sidney said.

The Drake was a hotel-like building that sat on top of the backs of four barges. Pleasant music drifted down the pier that ran alongside it. The salivating scent of food drifted into her nostrils. She led with Smoke in tow, drifting in with the crowd that traversed the docks. Along with the hotel/restaurant getaway there were small stores and local artists. Beatniks, preppies, hippies, all sorts walked, talked and made polite conversation.

"Great," she said. A long line of people had formed outside the restaurant at the Drake.

"Shall I put our name on the list?" Smoke said.

"No, let's go around. Come on."

The Drake plaza sat on a huge boardwalk and deck. People gathered around the railing watching the boats and ferries. A few hard faces fished. A staircase led down to a boat dock and slips on the back of the floating city. Men in dark suits stood on the docks, helping men and women from their boats. Sidney could see the bulges of body holsters concealed under their jackets.

"Pretty seedy," Smoke said.

Sidney took a closer look at the men fishing. They were holstered up too. And so were some of the common folk milling about. She counted at least ten well-armed men and women. Guns for hire. Bodyguards. Goons.

"I'll be. We're on private property," she said under her breath.

"Yep," Smoke said. "It seems like AV has thought of everything. A criminal's safe house. An excellent escape route with immediate access to three states. I like it."

"It seems you convicts all think alike." She smiled up at him and hooked her arm in his. "Oh, don't frown. Buy a girl a drink, why don't you." She tugged him along. "Come on. We can't make our intentions obvious."

"I don't have any cash."

"And that's why there won't be a second date." They made their way up to the hostess stand.

"Name and how many?" the hostess said.

Sidney looked up at Smoke.

"Er, two, and the last name is Ferrigno."

The young waitress wrote it down and handed him a pager. "Okay, it will be at least an hour, Mister Ferrigno. You can get some drinks on the plaza while you wait." She smiled. "Next."

They grabbed two long-necks from a beer stand and took a seat on a bench overlooking the river.

"A toast," Smoke said.

"No."

"I'm just trying to act natural," he said. "Forgive me; I haven't been on a date in a while."

"This isn't a date." She took a sip of beer. "And don't get wasted on that beer. I might need you."

"Really?"

"It's a figure of speech."

"If you say so." He tilted the bottle to his lips and guzzled it down. "Ah!"

"What did I just say?"

"What? I've been in prison. Can you blame me?"

"No more." She eased back on the bench and crossed her legs. The chill from the river was worse than she expected. It was a starry night. "This place is full of all kinds of everything."

"It sure is." Smoke cleared his throat. "I wonder who Drake is?"

"I only care who AV is. You should too."

A group of men in tuxedos with women in fine jewels crested the steps that led down to the dock. Eyes forward and faces drawn tight, they marched straight for the restaurant.

"I'll be."

"What?"

One of the men was Congressman Wilhelm, with his troupe of lackeys. His beady eyes turned her way. There was no avoiding his gaze.

She nudged Smoke.

"Kiss me."

"Wh—"

She pulled his face down to hers and locked her lips with his. He pulled her body into his. A charge went through her.

Good kisser. Three. Two. One. Through the corner of her eye, she saw Congressman Wilhelm move on. She held the kiss a moment longer and broke it off. "That'll do."

"Do you mind telling what that was all about?"

"Yes, I do mind." *What is Wilhelm doing here?*

"Ex-boyfriend?"

"No."

"Animal attraction?"

"Don't get any ideas. I might explain later."

Locking his fingers behind his head, he gazed upward into the stars. "Oh, at least you've given me plenty to think about."

Me too.

Smoke pulled the flashing pager out of his pocket. "That was quick."

"Sure was." Sidney felt eyes on her and noticed a few cameras on the lamp posts. A pair of eyes along the railing drifted away from her. A woman at the beer stand spoke into her wrist and looked away. "I have a feeling Rod Brown gave us up."

"Maybe." Smoke cracked his knuckles. "Say, are you going to finish that beer?"

She took a long drink and handed it over. "Knock yourself out."

Smoke chugged it down. "Ah!"

Please don't burp.

"Buuuurp! Whoa!" Smoke tapped his chest. "Sorry."

Sidney got up and started toward the restaurant. A mix of six men and women wearing dark pea coats hemmed them in with hands on their holsters.

CHAPTER 21

A DUSKY-SKINNED WOMAN WITH DARK CORNROWS stepped forward, rolling a toothpick from one side of her mouth to the other. She had a hard edge in her voice.

"My name is Gina. I speak on behalf of the Drake. You need to leave."

"I beg your pardon, Gina?"

"Listen, Miss." The woman rolled the toothpick to the other side of her mouth. "This is private property. The Drake Management doesn't want you here."

"I don't follow." Sidney glanced at the tattoos crawling up the rough-cut woman's neck.

"I don't need to explain myself. I know you saw the private property lines. You're trespassing."

No, I'm getting close to something. AV must be here.

The woman stuck her fist inside her palm and cracked her knuckles. "Now, I'm asking nicely. Don't make me mess up that pretty little face of yours." She cracked her neck from side to side. "I'd love to do it."

"I'm certain that's not going to happen."

Gina took a step closer and leaned forward. "Listen, tramp, I've busted up men and women in the octagon. These hands are lethal weapons. And here, heh, well, I'm free to use them. I've left the bloodstains of my victims on the deck before. Just ask them." She tipped her chin. "What do you think about that, Pretty?"

"I don't think a woman acting like a man makes for much of a woman."

Gina's eyes enlarged. "What!" She shoved Sidney in the chest.

Sidney absorbed the push, lowered her hip, and launched a roundhouse kick. She caught Gina flush on the chin. Gina smacked the deck face first, spilling her blood.

The men closed in with fingers itching on their weapons.

Sidney whipped out her badge. "FBI, back off!"

The wary-eyed men eased back.

"Her assault on a federal officer just gave me probable cause to search this place. Come on." She led Smoke through the gathering crowd. "He's in there. I can feel it." She rushed past the hostess stand.

Smoke tossed the hostess the pager. "The Ferrignos will be seating themselves tonight."

Sidney carefully picked her way through the tables while scanning the crowd. The Drake had two levels: the main floor of booths and tables decorated in a high-décor riverboat look, and the upstairs level, which was roped off for private parties.

"Up there." Sidney eyed a man who was quickly moving along the balcony. He spoke to another group of men who were seated. It was Congressman Wilhelm and his party. Sidney stepped under the balcony, evading their concerned glances.

"The only way out of here is back the way we came. I didn't notice a fire escape. Did you?"

Smoke was at her side. He peeked up at the next level. "Apparently the Drake doesn't like OSHA, either. I saw him."

Sidney pulled him back. "Saw who?"

"AV. He's up there at your ex-boyfriend's table."

Some of the goons in pea coats eased their way into the restaurant without creating a commotion.

"Are you sure you saw him?"

"Yep."

"Let's go up then." Heading for the stairs, she was cut off by a bald thickset bodyguard in a dark grey suit. She flashed her badge. "I need to get a message to Congressman Wilhelm. It's urgent federal business."

He took a hard look and glanced up at the balcony. Someone gave him a nod. He removed the velvet rope and stepped aside. "Go on up. But just you, lady."

Smoke's fist crashed into the man's rugged jaw.

Whop!

The henchman sagged onto the stairs.

Up they went, side by side. At the top, two other henchmen awaited them. Sidney's fingertips danced on her weapon. "Move."

The pair of men parted, and at the top a table awaited with eight guests. One of them was Congressman Wilhelm. The other face she recognized was Adam Vaughn's.

"Agent Shaw," Congressman Wilhelm said, lighting up a cigar, "may I ask what you are doing here?"

"I could ask you the same," she said.

"I don't answer to anyone less than a senator."

"I'm sure your voters would love to hear that."

The congressman chuckled. "They only hear what I want them to hear." He squeezed his date's knee with the hand bearing his wedding ring. "And they only believe what I want them to believe."

A few more henchmen crowded near the table. Congressman Wilhelm had a secret service agent on one side and his baby-doll date on the other. One seat over from AV, Rod Brown sat in a blue suit, eyeing a spot on the table.

"As always," Sidney said, "you seem to be on top of things, so I assume you know you're dining with a wanted man?"

"Beg pardon?" Wilhelm's eyes slid toward AV, but shifted back to her. "What are you talking about? You're not here to pester me?"

"No," she said, taking out her flex cuffs, "I'm here for Adam Vaughn."

"Adam? What on earth would you want with Adam?"

Adam Vaughn's fine features darkened. His eyes scoured his men.

"That isn't any of your business, Congressman. But I'm sure your spineless sources will fill you in soon enough. Mister Vaughn, I need you to come with me."

"Stay put, Adam," Wilhelm said, tossing his napkin on the table and getting up from his seat. "You listen to me, Shaw. You need to get out of here. Get out of here now. You're in deeper than you know." He plucked out his phone and started to dial. "Relax, Adam. I'll handle this."

Adam Vaughn was an attractive man, small in stature, with a head of coarse black hair and heavy eyebrows. He wore a white shirt with an open collar underneath a blue pin-striped suit. His eyes narrowed and his jaws were clenching. The atmosphere was ripe with tension. Sidney felt Smoke slide in behind her. She glanced back. His eyes were laser locked on AV.

"Let's go, Mister Vaughn," she said, using more authority this time.

AV had turned his attention to Rod. The big man's head was beaded with sweat.

"Rod," AV said in a European accent that was more deadly than charming, "look at me."

Rod lifted his chin, started to turn, and began shaking uncontrollably.

"I'm sorry, AV. I'm sorry!"

"Nobody's sorry, Adam," Wilhelm said, covering his phone. "I'll take care of this in a moment." He rolled his eyes at Sidney. "You really don't know what's good for you."

"Betrayer!" Adam jumped up from his seat and lunged at Rod.

Sidney drew her weapon. "Back off, Mister Vaughn!"

AV lifted his palms and backed off. "You're dead to me, Rod." He spat on the table. "Dead!" He came out from behind the table and faced Sidney. "You'll soon be dead to me too."

"Turn around — *oof!*"

AV kicked her in the gut, dropping her to her knees. He ducked under Smoke's lunging arms and leaped over the rail and crashed onto a table below. A cry of alarm went up all over the restaurant.

Smoke catapulted off the rail and charged after AV, who was dashing toward the exit.

Sidney scrambled to her feet and headed for the stairs, tripping over Wilhelm's feet.

"Watch your step, Agent Shaw," he said with a sinister grin. "Watch your step."

CHAPTER 22

S IDNEY HIT THE LANDING AT the bottom of the steps just as Smoke vanished through the front doors. Panicked people spilled into her way.

"Move it!"

A path slowly parted between feeble bodies and bewildered faces. She powered through them, shoving a man and two women down. "Does anyone know what move means?"

While she was rushing by the hostess stand, two peacock goons blocked her path. She blasted two warning shots into the floor.

Blam! Blam!

One goon dove left and the other dove right. Everybody screamed. Through the door Sidney went. Sprinting on long, fast legs, she surged out onto the deck and saw Smoke racing through the crowd thirty yards away. AV vanished down the steps leading to the docks. Smoke disappeared right after him.

Get down there, Sid!

At the top of the stairs, two more gunshots cracked off. The bodyguard on the dock was blasting away at the slithery Smoke.

Sidney took aim.

Blam!

Her bullet ripped through the back of the man's shoulder, spinning him to the ground. Down the stairs she went, sidestepping the big man and kicking his pistol into the water. After Smoke and AV she went, weapon ready. A pitch-black 30-foot cabin cruiser at the end of the dock started pulling out of its slip.

No you don't! She sprinted toward the end of the dock. *Faster, Sid! Faster!* Adrenaline surging through her limbs, she put everything into her jump. She sailed through the air. *I'm going to make it!*

Her foot clipped the edge of the boat, making for an ugly landing. She tumbled and bumped her head on the table. Bright starry spots drew in her eyes. She rubbed her head and forced herself up to her feet. A man in a captain's hat was up the stairs behind the wheel. She took aim and said, "FBI! Shut it down!"

The man remained unmoving. Sidney went up the steps and put the gun to his neck.

"I said, shut it down."

The man turned to face her. His face was pasty, hair ratty and stringy, eyes hollow and lifeless.

She gasped. Something evil, unnatural lurked behind his sunken eyes.

In a burst, the creepy man shoved her aside and lumbered stiffly down the stairs.

"Freeze!"

He kept going.

She fired a round at his leg.

Blam!

Unfazed, he stepped up on the edge of the boat and fell into the black water.

Sidney rushed down the steps and looked over the rail. The man was gone. Only the captain's hat remained afloat.

I know I hit him ... it.

"Sid!" a voice cried out. "Sid!"

She twisted around. Smoke's voice was coming from inside the lower cabin. She burst through the doors. Smoke's big frame had AV pinned down on the floor. The smaller man twisted away and sprinted toward Sidney. Smoke tackled his legs and launched a quick punch in AV's ribs. The man sagged.

"Cuffs!" Smoke said, chest heaving.

"What?"

"Flex cuffs!" he added, sucking for air. He wrenched AV's arms behind his back.

AV jerked them away.

"You are one strong little man!" Smoke punched both sides of his ribs again. *Whap! Whap!* "I'll have no more of that, you swarthy Spaniard."

"I'm not Spanish, you fool!" AV spat on the floor. "I'm something else."

You're something else, all right.

Sidney kneeled down and put her gun barrel to AV's temple. "If you don't remain still, something else of yours is going to be splattered all over the floor."

AV's struggles eased. He gazed up at her. His eyes were black pools. Insidious. Primal. Evil. Hair rose on her neck. Without averting her eyes, she handed Smoke the cuffs. He crisscrossed AV's wrists and bound them.

"Do you have another pair?"

"I always have another pair," she said, handing them over.

Smoke tied down AV's legs, leaned back against the bed, and caught his breath.

Winded herself, Sidney sat back on the steps and wiped her sleeve across her forehead. She then asked AV, "Is there anyone else on this boat we should know about?"

"Do you see anyone else?" he said with a sneer. "It's just me and a couple of soon-to-be dead people."

Smoke kicked him. "Where's the captain?"

"He jumped overboard."

"Really?" Smoke said, cocking his ear, "then who's driving the boat?"

The blaring sound of a boat horn ripped through the chill night air.

Sidney's eyes widened. She jumped to her feet, darted up the stairs, and raced up to the captain's chair. A river barge was almost on top of them. She spun the wheel right and pumped down the throttle. The fore of the boat rose high, and the propellers sank the aft of the boat into the water. Sidney hung onto the wheel. The massive bulk of the barge cruised by with little more than a foot to spare.

That was close.

She throttled down the cruiser and watched the barge pass by.

Too close.

She scanned the black water. The barge's wake beat against the hull. There was no sign of the captain—and she was certain the captain wasn't any man at all. Cruising down the shoreline, she caught movement along the bank. A drenched figure lumbered out of the water, up the shore, and disappeared into the woods. A chill went through her.

That's wasn't a man. I swear it!

CHAPTER 23

"EXCELLENT JOB, SID," SAID JACK Dydeck. "Just excellent." He paced the floor with his fingers locked behind his back. They were back at the house: Jack, Tommy Tohms, Sidney, Smoke, and a couple of other agents. AV sat cross-legged, head down, by the fireplace. "You erased a name on the Black Slate in one day?" He put his hand on her shoulder and squeezed it. "I'm proud of you, Sid."

"There's really no need. It's my job, and I can't take all the credit." She nodded at Smoke. "He helped."

Smoke sat quietly on the sofa, eyes intent on AV. He hadn't said much of anything since they journeyed back from the Potomac and Jack and his men picked them up.

"I'm sure he did," Jack said. "We'll be sure to send him some new books to read back in prison."

"Wait," Sidney said, "I thought we had two weeks?"

"Sure, to get Mister Vaughn here. That's all over now."

"Hold on." Sidney was not hiding the irritation in her voice. "There are reports. Interrogations. Investigations of his operations. The list goes on. I want to be thorough."

"We'll handle that, Sid. You go get some rest and we'll talk tomorrow."

"No, I'll handle it."

Jack offered a smile. "Tomorrow. Back in the office. Around noon. We'll await Mister Vaughn's caretakers." His tone became stern. "You look exhausted, Sid. We can stitch up this mess tomorrow. Go."

"What about him?" She looked at Smoke.

Jack sighed.

"Tell you what: seeing how the two of you caught headquarters with their pants down, well," he scratched his head, "they aren't sure what the next step is. I'm waiting on their call to advise me on what to do with Mister Smoke, so the two of you head up the road and grab a bite to eat. I'll call you back after Mister Vaughn is picked up. We'll take it from there. Fair enough?"

"I'd rather stay," Smoke said. His eyes were still glued on AV.

"I don't care." Jack glowered at him. "You can go eat or sit here handcuffed."

"Come on," Sidney said to Smoke. "Let's go."

Slowly, Smoke rose from the sofa and headed out the door. Sidney was one half-step behind.

"Give us a couple of hours, Sid," Jack said. "I should have it all wrapped up by then."

"All right," she said, glancing down at AV.

His eyes fastened on hers. "Soon, Pretty. Soon."

Goosebumps rose on her arms. She tore her gaze away and went back outside. She was short of breath.

"You okay?" Smoke said.

She swallowed and took a breath. "Yeah. Let's go."

"You've been awfully quiet," Sidney said to Smoke. They were sitting in a truck stop restaurant almost ten miles up the road from the house. Smoke's burger and fries were getting cold. "Did you lose your appetite?"

"Tell me about that captain again."

"I don't know." She covered her yawn. "It was dark. I've been tired." She took a sip of coffee. "His face was clammy. Veiny. Like a, well, I don't know."

"Like a zombie?"

"I wouldn't take it that far." She wrinkled her forehead. "Zombies don't drive boats. It might have been sick from something."

"You said *it* again."

"Him. It. It was ugly. Ugh. He was ugly. Just let it go."

"But you said you shot him. Hit his leg. But didn't slow him."

"Adrenaline."

"You said he walked up the shore and disappeared."

"It might have been someone else. It was too far to see."

"I don't think anyone else would have been swimming in the Potomac." Smoke pushed his plate aside, scooted back into the booth, and stretched his legs out.

"Make yourself comfortable, why don't you."

Smoke closed his eyes and rubbed his temples.

He's getting weird on me.

"Are you all right?"

"I have a confession." His eyes were still closed.

Oh great. Please don't give me some sappy story about the last time you ate Pop-tarts with your sister.

"Great. There's a Catholic steeple down the street."

"I'm worried." He opened his eyes and looked worried.

"So?"

"I don't get worried."

"Well, I guess you're just one of us now."

"AV. He's not normal."

"No, most criminals aren't. What's the matter? Are you afraid he won't be a good cell mate?"

Smoke raised his eyebrows at her.

"Sorry. That was uncalled for." She leaned forward. "It's been a really long day."

"Agent Shaw, did you get a good look when AV jumped off the balcony?"

"I was there."

"Well, so was I. There aren't many people aside from Olympic athletes who can jump that far in a single bound." He sat up. "He made a mistake and ran for the boat, thinking the bodyguards would stop us. If he had run into the city, we never would have caught him."

"So he's fast."

"And strong." Smoke narrowed his eyes at her. "I have a hundred pounds on him. It took all I had to wrestle him down."

"He's in shape. Adrenaline. Maybe he's on something. That wouldn't be a first. My father told me he saw a man on PCP burst out of his handcuffs once."

"No," Smoke said in a hushed voice, "I'm telling you, he's not normal. Just like that captain isn't normal."

"Don't overthink it." She finished off her coffee and checked her phone. No messages from Jack yet, and it had been two hours. She yawned. "I wonder why this is taking so long."

Smoke started to ease himself out of the booth. "I say we head back." His eyes were restless. "I have a bad feeling."

Can't disagree there. But I'm not going to let him spook me either.

"Sure, why not." Sid fetched some bills out of her bag. "Do you want a doggie bag?"

"What?"

She dropped the money on the table. "Lighten up a little, will you?"

Driving down the road, Sid couldn't shake the butterflies from her stomach. Smoke was uncomfortable. It made her uncomfortable.

What is his deal?

She'd texted Dydeck before they left and hadn't heard back. Jack was always quick to reply. Ahead, the half-moon shone brightly behind the rising mist of the late evening. She barreled down the exit ramp, merged onto the highway, cruised a few more miles down the road, and turned into Benson Estates.

A pack of dogs darted across the road. Sidney slammed on the brakes. Her heart was jumping.

"Whoa." Smoke leaned forward in his seat. "Were those coyotes?"

"Coyotes aren't that big," Sidney said, peering into the night. The pack had vanished behind the houses. "Those were wolves."

"Like timber wolves? I don't know about that. But they were big. Shepherds, maybe."

"Wolves, trust me. I'm pretty familiar with the breeds of dogs." She let off the brake pedal and eased on up the road. It was the second time she'd seen them in a day.

"Care to fill me in?"

"No."

"So, you used to be a veterinarian?"

She didn't reply.

"Really? Is it that hard to share the smallest detail of any of your history?"

"No. I'm just staying focused right now." Driving slowly, she surveyed between the houses they passed. "Just keeping it professional."

"I agree, but I think you should work on tuning up your social skills."

After a long pause, Sidney said, "I was a K-9 cop in the Air Force."

"Oh." Smoke nodded. He sniffed the air. "Funny, you don't smell like a canine cop. They usually have a scent about them."

"I'm not one now, obviously."

"Just a little humor, Agent Shaw. Take it easy."

She almost cracked a smile as she pulled the car alongside the curb of the house. The two black SUVs were still in the driveway.

Unbuckling his belt and getting out of the car, Smoke said, "It doesn't look like anyone else has shown up." He headed for the front door. Sidney followed in step behind him. The lights were on inside. The front door was wide open. No sounds came from within. "That's weird."

"Sure is," she said, drawing her weapon.

Smoke stopped at the threshold. His arms fanned out, shielding her.

"Wait."

Sidney's body tingled with tiny fires. She slipped underneath Smoke's arm and stepped inside. Blood dripped from the fireplace mantle. The stench of death was thick. She gasped.

CHAPTER 24

S IDNEY STUMBLED BACK INTO SMOKE, mumbling, "No ... no."

Blood pooled on the floor. Splattered on the walls. Two agents lay in mangled heaps of flesh. A man was disemboweled, his frozen gaze fixed on the hearth. It was Tommy Tohms. A woman lay with her elbow and neck snapped. The third agent sat on the sofa, coated in blood. His head was missing. Twisted clean off.

Sidney swallowed hard and choked out a cry when she saw the head lying on the fireplace grate. It was Dydeck.

She started shaking. This was inhuman. Uncanny. She dropped her weapon. Her knees sagged.

Smoke caught her. "Let's get you to the car."

"No." She gasped, wiped the tears from her eyes, reached down to pick up her weapon, and took a deep breath. "I can handle this."

"This is madness. Not a lot of people can handle madness."

Sidney took another deep breath and straightened herself. "Not a lot of people can handle me mad either. Let's get to the bottom of this."

AV was gone. Sidney noticed the busted flex cuffs on the floor.

Smoke was squatted down, eyeballing them. "These weren't cut, they were torn," he said, covering his nose. "Whew ... Death stinks."

Sidney held her stomach.

Don't puke. Don't puke.

Blood coated the walls in the living room. It dripped from the ceiling. It looked like a Cuisinart had ripped through the agents in the room.

"What could have done this?" she asked herself.

"These are claw marks. A wild pack of canines perhaps."

"Dogs wouldn't do this."

She studied Dydeck's headless corpse. She'd lost a few friends in the field, but none that she knew well. Her heart ached. Dydeck had a wife and three children.

Lord, no. Lord, no. This can't happen. Not like this. Not to Dydeck.

He was hard-nosed. Not always right. But she liked him. She liked him a lot.

Dydeck still had his weapon in hand. It had been discharged. She turned. The same with Tommy Tohms.

"Do you see any bullet holes?" She pulled some latex gloves from her inside pocket and checked the cartridge on Dydeck's weapon. It was empty.

He couldn't have missed. Not at this close a range.

"Two in the wall over here," Smoke said, fingering the holes, "and one nick in the mantle."

"There should be more," Sidney said, brushing the hair from her eyes. "This magazine is empty."

"I don't see anything else," Smoke said. "They must have filled something with lead."

Sidney noticed a pair of holes on the blood-stained floor.

"Here's another. Geez." She took out her phone and dialed headquarters. It wasn't her first instinct, but it was protocol. She wanted to call Ted, her old boss. A woman's voice answered.

"This is Agent Sidney Shaw—"

She heard the squeal of brakes and pushed the blinds up.

"Hold on."

An unmarked black van had pulled into the driveway. Four men in FBI jackets came out and slammed the doors shut.

One of them was Cyrus. "Agents down. More agents arriving on scene at 241 Benson Estates. Send forensic team and homicide." Cyrus spilled in the doorway and stopped in his tracks. His eyes widened and his face turned ashen. "What the hell?" He jerked out his weapon and pointed it at Smoke. "Freeze!"

Smoke raised his arms over his head.

"Cyrus." Sidney cut in between the two men. "They were dead when we got here. Lower your weapon."

Three other agents poured into the room with their weapons drawn.

"Did you clear the house?" Cyrus said.

"Not yet, I just got—"

"Secure the house," Cyrus ordered his men. "Now! You," he said to Smoke. "Don't move." He grabbed one of the agents by the sleeve and said, "Cuff him."

"That's not necessary," Sidney objected. "He's done nothing wrong."

Smoke's arms were jerked behind his back and he was shackled. "Don't forget to double-lock them," he said.

"Stay with him," Cyrus said to the other agents. He looked at Sidney. "You, come with me." His eyes drifted toward the fireplace. He blinked and leaned in. "Is that ... Dydeck?"

"Yes," she said. "Cyrus, I just arrived a few minutes before you. How come the transport was late? It should have been here over an hour ago to take Adam Vaughn away."

"Sir," one of the agents said, coming from downstairs. "We have another agent down, but she's breathing. The rest of the home is secure."

"Call an ambulance," Cyrus said, rushing down the hall and down the steps.

Sidney was right on his heels. At the bottom of the stairs a woman in an FBI vest lay still. Sidney swallowed. The agent—a short-haired black lady—was crumpled up in a heap.

"Back broken," said one of the agents, a short wiry man with a mustache. He shook his head. "Probably from the fall. A bad spill." He patted her leg. "Hang on, honey. Hang on."

"Don't touch her," Cyrus said, kneeling by the woman's side. "Wait for the ambulance to arrive."

"She didn't fall," Sidney said, gazing at the stairwell. There was a large indentation in the drywall. "She was thrown."

Cyrus stood up, glanced up the stairwell, and said, "That's not possible." He eyed the spot. "Maybe it was already there."

"I don't think so," Sidney said.

"Well, I don't care what you think, Agent Shaw." Cyrus's forehead started to bead with sweat. "Forensics will decide that. You need to decide how to explain all this."

"Me?"

He got in her face. "Yes, you!"

"Hey, Cyrus," the short agent said, "look at this."

Cyrus took out a pair of glasses and put them on. "What is it?"

"She has something in her hand," the agent said. "It looks like hair."

Sidney leaned in. The hair was long, dark brown, and very coarse. Cyrus scooted over and blocked her view. She said, "Do you mind?"

"As a matter of fact, I do." He rose up, stood in front of her, and pointed up the stairs. "Go."

"I beg your pardon?"

"I'm the senior agent on the scene," he said. "And you are going."

"Going where?"

"Going home."

CHAPTER 25

HAP! WHAP! WHAP!
Sidney laid into the heavy bag that hung in the gym.
Whap! Whap!

Sweat dripped from her brow.

Whap!

Chest heaving inside her Under-Armor hoodie, she walked over to a nearby bench and twisted the cap off her bottled water. It was Saturday, two days after the massacre at Benson Estates. She'd spent all day Friday doing paperwork, and she hadn't heard a word about the case since. Cyrus didn't return her texts. He'd iced her. She finished off her water, crushed the bottle, and tossed it in a can. *Damn him.*

The gym had a little bit of everything going on and was fairly busy for a Saturday. Men and women pushed weighted sleds. Cross trainers pushed their clients to the limits. Sweating bodies churned on treadmills and elliptical machines lined up row-by-row in front of the wall-mounted television. The entire gym smelled like sweat, and the music playing gave it energy.

She ripped a sidekick into the bag. Launched another and another.

A man walking by stopped and watched. He was a little shorter than her, red-faced, and all muscle in a little T-shirt. Tattoos of daggers and snakes decorated his shoulders. He nodded and smiled. "You really know how to work that bag. Impressive."

Great. "Thanks." She paused. "Are you waiting?"

"No," he said, shaking his chin. "I'm enjoying watching." He looked her up and down. "You really are something. How long have you been working out?"

"Listen—"

"Tommy. Tommy's my name." He extended his hand. "Weightlifting is my game."

She laughed. "Tommy, you really need to go."

"I can't leave without your name."

She walked over the padded floor to her gym bag, grabbed her badge, and held it in front of Tommy's widened eyes. "Here are my initials. Now beat it."

He eased back but kept smiling. "Well, FBI, you are one fine agent. You can cuff me any time."

"Can I shoot you too?"

He swallowed. "Er ... No." He blinked a couple of times, turned, and walked away.

Loser.

Sidney worked the bag again. Combos of kicks and punches. She loved kick boxing. It had been a passion of hers since she was nine. Her arms became heavy. Her black stretch pants were soaked in sweat. She unleashed some more roundhouse kicks.

Whap! Whap! WHAP!

She took the sparring gloves off, tossed them into her gym bag, and headed toward the treadmills. The ghastly images from the crime scene still burned in her mind. Dydeck was dead. Good agents were dead. One paralyzed. And somewhere, a killer was out there running free. Could it have been Adam Vaughn? It wasn't possible. But that wasn't what bothered her most.

Smoke was gone.

She climbed up on a step mill, punched in the time and intensity, and started walking.

Things had gotten ugly between her and Cyrus when he'd told her to leave. She had objected. The mousy man with frosty eyes had responded by having Smoke carted off behind her back, with no goodbyes between them.

"Your boyfriend is headed back to prison. You'll have to get your kiss goodbye some other place, some other time."

It gnawed at her gut. After a forty-five-minute workout, it still stuck in her craw.

Maybe I should go for a run. Or go shooting.

She gathered her things and exited the gym into the biting wind, headed for her car. The Interceptor wasn't alone. A man wearing a brown leather Donegal and a tweed trench stood there.

"Ted?" She looked around the parking lot. "What are you doing here?"

"I just came to see how you were doing."

"Really." She unlocked the car and tossed her gym bag inside. "Why?"

"Come on, Sid. Agents died. You were there. I saw the pictures." He grimaced. "In all my years, I've never seen ... well, never. Let's just leave it at that. How about we go and get something to eat?"

She crossed her arms. "How about you tell me what's going on? I should be in on this, you know."

"Headquarters is in turmoil at the moment. It almost takes an act of God to keep these incidents out of the papers." Hands stuffed in his pockets, he leaned his shoulder on the car. "When I heard the news, I thought it was you in that bloodbath. I'm glad you're still alive."

"Still?"

"Ah, don't start that." He rolled his eyes. "Quit picking sentences and expressions apart."

"Didn't you teach me that?"

"I don't know." Looking at her with his soft eyes, Ted reminded her of the old actor named Brian Keith from movies she watched with her father. Tough, yet soft in a very manly way. "Probably. Let's get out of this cold and go eat. There's a nice little greasy spoon around the corner."

She pushed her back off the car. "Nice little greasy spoon? I don't think so."

He chuckled and offered his elbow. "Aw, come on. I've never seen anything in there that could bite you."

They made their way out of the parking lot and down the sidewalk, brushing by many passersby.

"Sir, I have to have a part in this. I was there, I brought in AV, and now I'm cut out? It doesn't make any sense."

"The Black Slate doesn't make any sense either. Those files are off the books. I'm trying to make sense of it myself."

"And what have you learned?"

"Huh, well, from what I've gathered, the Slate precedes the FBI." He cleared his throat. "It's a mystery where it came from."

"Wouldn't that make the people on the list really old ... like you?"

He laughed.

"And," she continued, "Adam Vaughn didn't seem very old. He seemed little older than me."

"Over time, the list ... it changes, I guess. I don't know."

"Well, who keeps the list updated?"

"I don't know that either."

"What do you know?"

He pointed at the sign on the door of a restaurant. The stenciled lettering on the glass door read: The Wayfarer. He opened the door and nodded. "We're here."

The smell of fried food and cooking oil wafted into her nostrils. Soft rock music and the clinking of dishes caught her ear. She stepped inside. "Great." She shivered. "At least it's warm."

"Come on." Ted led her toward the back of the quaint but deteriorating establishment that hadn't changed since the fifties. He stopped at a booth and began speaking to someone.

She couldn't see the person until Ted stepped aside. Her eyes grew. Her heart skipped. It was Smoke.

CHAPTER 26

"H ELLO, AGENT SHAW." SMOKE HOISTED a Coke. He wore jeans and a dark sweater under a black leather jacket. His face was clean shaven. "Did you miss me?"

Yes.

"No."

Ted removed his coat, hung it on a hook on the booth, and took a seat opposite Smoke. Just he and Smoke practically filled the booth. "Uh ... let me scooch over."

"That's all right." Sid grabbed a chair and dragged it over to the table, closer to Ted's side. She sat down, rested her clasped fingers on the table, and looked at Ted.

"Er, well, I guess we don't need any introductions." Ted took off his cap and placed it on the table. Scratched his head. "A little stuffy in here. Waitress!"

A young man came over in a dirty apron with quaffed brown hair dominating one side of his head. The pen in his hand looked heavy. "Yeah, man."

"Er, double cheeseburger with everything, fries—no, onion rings, and a sweet tea." He eyed Sidney. "And you'll be having?"

"Nothing."

"Mister Smoke?"

"I already ordered."

It better not be pancakes.

The waiter nodded. "Coming up, man."

"All right, man." Ted glared at the waiter's back. "Man. Man. Man. Man. Doesn't anyone say sir anymore?" He looked at Sid. "All right, I'll quit. But if he screws my order up, no tip."

"Sir, can we get down to business?"

"That's my girl. Okay, they still want you on this case. You got AV before, they think you can get him again."

"*It* again," Smoke said.

"Wait a second," Sidney interrupted. "Who wants us on this?"

"One at a time." Ted held up his palm. "First, Sid, I can't tell you that. I'm not really sure myself, but for the interim, I'm your new supervisor."

Unusual, but good.

"Second," Ted said to Smoke, "Adam Vaughn is not an *it*. Some person or persons took him out of there. The evidence confirmed that."

I don't think so.

Smoke sat up. "Did the evidence lead to the discovery of Bigfoot, too? An animal or something like an animal tore through those people like the Tasmanian devil. It wasn't a person."

"Just settle down a moment. Your mission"—he pointed at Sidney and Smoke—"is to find Adam Vaughn. Bring him in. Alive. Find him, and we'll find the fiend that did this to our agents."

"Just us?" she said.

"Yes."

"What about resources? Cars? Weapons? Tactical support? Is Mister Smoke going to be armed or not? And what about his ankle tracker?"

Smoke stuck out his boot. No tracker. With a smile, he said, "All gone."

"Ted, how am I supposed to keep track of him then?"

"You'll just have to work together." He leaned forward. "Ah, food is coming."

The waiter had a tray full of food. Three hamburgers and two chili dogs and plenty of fries. He set a burger and fries down in front of Ted.

Ted's face reddened. His voice darkened as he said, "I said onion rings."

"No man, no, you didn't," the waiter said, setting the other baskets in front of Smoke. "I can get some, man, but it will be extra."

The veins in Ted's neck started to bulge. He glared at the young man.

"No, it won't."

"Take it easy, man. I'll get your rings. Stat." He sauntered off.

Smoke squirted ketchup on his fries and Sidney fought against her giggles.

"What?" Ted said, checking the contents of his burger.

"Nothing," she replied. A giggle erupted.

"All right, now what's so funny?"

"You sounded like Batman," Smoke interjected. Then he imitated. "*I said onion rings.*"

Sidney's face flushed and her giggles continued. She stopped herself. "But it was way better than 'Do you feel lucky, punk?' I thought that was coming."

Ted snatched up his burger and stuffed it into his mouth. "Screw both of you." Ketchup dripped onto his shirt. "Aw, dammit."

Sidney caught a playful look in Smoke's eyes. She felt a spark inside.

Sense of humor a plus. Stuff your face with unknown parts of a swine, minus.

"So, Ted, it's just us then? Again, who is my backup?"

"It's you and him." He swallowed his food. "And me. He reports to you. You report to me. The clock is still ticking on your two weeks. Remember, this is off the books. The less everyone else knows, the better."

Smoke dipped one of his fries in the ketchup. "So there's a mole in the FBI then?"

That's what I was thinking.

"No, there isn't any mole. Just loose lips and big-eared busybodies." Ted tucked a napkin under his chin. "I have enough on my plate without any more probing questions. And so far as I'm concerned, until it's over, the less I know, the better." He bit into his burger.

"Wherever you go, we're going together," she said to Smoke.

"Fine, but that might be a bit awkward when we're sleeping." He leaned closer. "Does that mean I'm staying at your place?"

Sidney's eyes got big. "No, you know what I meant!"

"Ha," Ted laughed. "He turned the tables on you, Sid. I like that."

"I've got everything I need: my own ways," Smoke said, tapping his head, "and my own gear. Just step aside and let me make this happen." He looked straight into her eyes. "I want this murderer as much as you do, and at some point you're going to have to put some trust in me."

Sidney shook her head. "We'll see."

Ted grumbled at the fries in his basket. "Where the heck are my onion rings?"

She glanced back at Smoke. "So, do you have any leads?"

He drained his Coke and clopped the plastic tumbler on the table. "Nope."

CHAPTER 27

"Y OU KNOW," SMOKE SAID, RIDING shotgun in the Interceptor, "there's one thing I can't figure."

"About what?" Sidney said.

"AV. If he turned into a werewolf—"

"A werewolf?" *Oh lord, please don't be some Twilight geek.*

"In theory."

"Uh, stupid theory." She pulled the car to a stop at the light. "I think I like the Bigfoot idea better."

"Well, you saw a pack of wolves for yourself. So did I."

"And you thought they were coyotes. Perhaps they were were-coyotes?" The light changed, and she eased on the gas. "That said, I'm not liking your theory. It's ludicrous."

"My point is, AV's clothes were gone. Not a stitch. If he turned into a werewolf or something else, there would have been evidence of something." He pointed up the highway. "Take the next exit."

"So, you're ruling out the supernatural then?" She nodded her head. "Good for you."

"Well—"

"Well, I won't have any of it." She accelerated. "Monsters don't roam Washington."

"Hah, Washington's full of them. They just prefer human form." His head turned right. "Uh, you missed my exit."

Sidney jammed on the brakes and shifted into reverse. She eyed the rearview mirror and gunned the gas.

"Hey," Smoke said, "there's a lot of traffic coming our way. Not a good decision."

"What's the matter, are you afraid I might run over a groovy ghoulie?"

"A what?"

"Nothing." A few car horns blared as they whizzed by. Sidney gunned the Interceptor down the exit ramp. "How much farther?"

"About three miles." He shifted in his seat. "Are you telling me your skin didn't crawl when you stood in the middle of that bloodbath?"

"No, my skin didn't crawl."

"Your friend's head was twisted clean off."

Her throat tightened a little. She thought about Dydeck's family. The funeral. A closed coffin was never a good thing. "I'll let forensics figure that out."

"And I guess you'll read it in the reports you'll never see. Ha." He pointed right. "Turn there."

She hit the blinker and turned right down a blacktopped road marred with low spots and potholes. The car plunged into a pothole and lurched upward.

Smoke stared out the window. "You just lost a cap."

She kept driving.

"Aren't you going back for it?"

"No."

"But that's littering."

"No it isn't."

"Yes—"

She hit the brakes, lunging Smoke forward. Putting the car in reverse, she hit pothole after pothole. Coming to a stop, Sidney put the car in park and got out. Outside, she located the hubcap, picked it up, walked over to Smoke's door, opened it, and dropped it in his lap. She got back in the car again.

"What do you want me to do with this?"

"Shove it."

Smoke flipped it around between his hands. "Usually these old cars are nothing but black rims. It'll probably look better without it anyway." He tossed the cap in the back seat. "Take the next left. Another mile up or so."

Sidney's knuckles were white on the steering wheel. She couldn't shake the image of Dydeck's headless body from her mind. She knew his wife, Jean, and his children, Larry and Zoey. Her heart ached for them.

"Are you all right?" Smoke said.

"Fine."

"This is strange." He cleared his throat. "And I know plenty about strange. I've seen bodies after fifty-caliber bullets ripped through them. At least, I've seen what was left of them. I saw plenty of people decapitated in the desert. It's gruesomely horrible. That said, I've never sensed anything like this before. Eerie."

Goosebumps rose on her arms as she wound the wheel to the left. Sidney couldn't deny the eeriness she felt either, or the sickness the scene stirred inside her.

They passed by some small homes and trailers.

"Next right," Smoke said.

Ahead, an old gas station sign was mounted on a light pole twenty feet in the air. Below it was an old service station, neatly kept. It had two closed garage bays on the left and the store front on the right. The gas pumps were gone, but the overhead canopy remained. It all had been converted into an apartment or house of some sort.

"This is where you live?" she said. The place was almost forty minutes from D.C., east of the Potomac. "Strange place for a gas station."

Smoke popped open his door, but before he got out he said, "It's an old place. Mostly for the locals and family. I picked it up at an estate auction several years ago." He closed the door and headed toward the apartment. "Are you coming?"

Her palms started sweating.

Strange place to be with a strange man.

CHAPTER 28

S HE PICKED UP THE FILE on AV and made her way after him, eyeing the garage bays.

"What's in there?"

"That's where I keep my friends," he said, reaching inside his pocket and producing a set of keys.

"Ah, Fat Sam and Guppy then?"

He tilted his head back and laughed. "You remember! No, but I can't wait to tell them you said that." He stood at the door beside the large block glass window. The heavy grey steel door had both a keypad and a key hole. He stepped in front of her and punched in the code. "I hate carrying keys."

Me too.

Smoke shoved the door open and stepped aside, gesturing. "After you."

Sidney crossed over the threshold. Her heart raced a little.

What is wrong with me?

She took a long draw through her nose. The glass wall offered little light to an otherwise dim room. It was quiet.

"Hold on." Smoke brushed by her. He stopped at a circuit box and pushed up the black handle. The overhead incandescent lights came on, and the room hummed with life. "That should be better."

A sofa, kitchenette, refrigerator, cupboards, and an island with two stools made for a quaint apartment remarkably similar to her own. An office desk and computer monitors filled one back corner. Two tall dark-green gun safes filled another. It was a lot more modern and cozy than she expected from seeing the outside.

No back door.

"Make yourself comfortable." He sat down and turned on the computer. "As best you can, anyway. It's not much for entertaining. And ignore the cobwebs; I haven't dusted in over a year."

"Ha ha." She took a seat on the sofa, tossed the folder on the coffee table, and opened it up. "So, bounty hunter, you don't have any leads?"

"Nuh-uh." He pecked the keyboard of his computer. "But give it some time and I'll have something."

Adjacent to him, she squinted her eyes toward the monitors. There were four in all. The biggest displayed security camera feeds from outside. Smoke's broad back blocked the front screen from her view. *This is awkward.* She pulled out a picture of Rod Brown, AV's goon.

"Maybe we should check up on Rod Brown."

Smoke stopped typing and swiveled around in his chair to face her.

"I already did."

"What? When?"

"Yesterday, right after they took the leash off." He cocked his head. "You look angry. Are you angry?"

Sidney's nails dug into her palms. She'd been put on ice, but Smoke had been given free range? *Ted's going to get it.* "What did you find?"

"Rod's dead."

She leaned forward. "Dead how? I didn't see anything in the news about it."

"FBI covered it up after I called them. Just like the other one."

Sidney's pulse quickened. Her jaw muscles clenched.

Smoke rose out of his chair and gestured at it. "Have a seat. I'll show you what I discovered."

"Oh, I can't wait to see your big discovery, but I'm fine where I am. Just tell me what you did."

"I went to Rod's apartment, picked the lock, and went inside. His blood was everywhere, just like we saw at Benson. The only difference was Rod's head was … missing." He turned and plucked away at the keyboard. "I took a few pictures of the scene before I called. Can you stomach it?"

She eased her way over and gazed at the monitor. Blood soaked the carpet and was splattered on the walls. Rod's corpse lay headless on the floor. A queasy feeling sank into her stomach and weakened her knees.

"It takes time to get used to it," Smoke said, easing back. "But it's best you don't."

"Did anyone report a disturbance? Screams? Someone must have heard something."

"Growls," he said, taking hold of the mouse.

"I don't think werewolves lock doors."

"Maybe someone else did. Besides"—he clicked on another file—"the residents did report seeing something tall and hairy sprinting through the streets."

"There are such things as bearded runners, you know."

He opened up a video file. "True. But here's a little local footage I hacked into, from the condos."

"You hacked into?"

"Sort of." He pointed at the screen. "Just watch."

The video clip showed a view of the condominium complex's parking lot. It was nighttime, and most of the spaces were filled. The lamp posts illuminated much but not all. A tall figure— distant from the camera angle—glided along the perimeter wall.

Sidney's spine tingled.

The image was unclear, but its shoulders were hulking, and a snout looked to be protruding from its face. It jumped, grasping the high wall's ledge and pulling itself over with ease. Then it vanished. It all happened in a few seconds.

"Go back," she said, "frame by frame."

Smoke toggled the keyboard. The video wound back frame by frame.

"There's something in its hand."

"Yeah, I know," Smoke said, zooming in. It looked like a dripping skull was clutched in a big paw. "I'm pretty sure that's Rod's head."

CHAPTER 29

T HE HUMAN BRAIN IS A powerful organ. It can detect the difference between reality and the finest computer-generated images. What Sidney saw wasn't a hoax, but that wasn't the problem. What she saw wasn't human. The limbs were too long. The movements impossibly fluid.

"Maybe a seven-foot-tall ape escaped from the zoo," Smoke said, powering down the monitors. "Or maybe there is a Sasquatch, even though I always figured him to be bigger."

Sidney rubbed her head.

"It's a lot to take in," Smoke said. "I have some aspirin."

"No." She made her way back over to the sofa. "Just give me a moment."

Smoke turned on a TV that hung on the wall. The local news was on.

"You know, it always amazes me how deft the FBI are at covering things up. The sad thing is, I don't think there's enough news time to air all the stories they cover up. And if there were, people would be overwhelmed by the reality of the horrible world we really live in." He sat down on the other end of the sofa and kicked his boots off onto the table. "And in the last few days, I've learned the world is even worse than I thought it was."

"We need to learn what we can about the Drake." She stared at the big screen. "I spent my time poking around the last two days, and I picked up a few things. It's owned by a real estate investor. Aside from the hotel and restaurants, I found almost nothing. There isn't even a website about the barge island on the river."

"Sure, follow the money. I'm sure the IRS has something."

"I made some calls to some friends, and they're pretty tight-lipped right now." She spread some of the file pictures out on the table. "But I did learn the Drake Corporation operates a lot of subsidiary companies. They own most of these locations that Adam Vaughn frequents."

"I think he'll show up."

"Where? Here?" She shook her head. "He's hiding somewhere."

"He's cocky. He'll be out and about."

"We can't stake all of those places out, and they'll be looking for us."

"True, but that's why I have Fat Sam and Guppy on it."

She rolled her eyes and got up. *Damn, I'm still in my gym clothes.* "I'm going.

If you can control yourself, stay put and I'll swing by and get you tomorrow." She looked around. "Say, do you have a phone?"

"I have a burner."

"Let me have it." She pulled her phone from her bag. "Here's mine."

They each put themselves in the other's phone as a contact.

"Wow, you just gave me your number and I didn't even ask for it. I'm flattered."

"I'm not."

Her phone buzzed. She grabbed it from him. There was a text from her mother.

It read: Allison's gone.

Racing down the road, Sidney pounded on the steering wheel. "I don't need this right now." Her phone rang. "What's going on, Mom?"

"It's been seven hours, Sidney, and we can't find her anywhere." Her mother sobbed. "I'm worried."

"This isn't the first time it's happened," Sid said, accelerating up the highway ramp. "Aren't you used to it?"

"Never, but Megan," Sally's voiced cracked, "it's not fair to Megan. It breaks my heart and makes me so angry. And sad!"

"Did she steal a car? How did she get out of there? You're five miles from anywhere."

There was a silence.

"Mom, you *are* five miles from anywhere, aren't you? The camp, not the house?"

"We thought the house would be a nice change."

Sidney squeezed her phone. Her parents used to be tough as nails, but over the past few years they'd gotten softer. Almost feeble in many ways.

God, don't let that happen to me.

"Your father and Joe are out looking for her now. I'm sure they'll find her."

No, they won't.

"Mom," Sidney softened her voice, "Allison's going to have to figure this out on her own. You've given her all the love you can. There's nothing more you can do."

Sobbing, her mother said, "You're a good girl, Sid. You know how to say the right things."

"I'm just repeating what you told me."

"Oh!" her mother said, perking up. "I hear the garage door opening." There was a pause. Suddenly, she screamed in the phone. "It's Allison! He's got Allison! She looks okay!" *Click!*

Sidney looked at her phone and said to it, "Are you frickin' kidding me?"

Buzz ... Buzz ... Buzz ...

Sidney stretched her arms through her bedsheets, fingers searching for her phone. Bright morning light peeked in through the apartment's blinds. She found her phone. 8:00 a.m. "Ugh. Already." She'd been in bed by 2:00 am, but it felt like five minutes ago. *Screw it.* She set the snooze and sank back into her bed.

Buzz ... Buzz ... Buzz ...

She forced her heavy eyelids open. Her phone was still clutched in her hand. 8:08 a.m. A crack of sunlight gleamed in her eye. Sidney's bare feet crossed the cold floor to the window, where she pulled the curtains closed. *That's better.* She set the snooze again and crawled back under the sheets. A few things raced through her mind. Smoke. Allison. Megan. Smoke. She drifted off to sleep. She dreamed. Smoke. Fire. Satin sheets.

Knock. Knock. Knock.

She lurched up in bed. A thin film of sweat coated her body. Her phone read 8:13 a.m. *That's odd*, she thought, panting a little. *It shouldn't have gone off yet. Sounded like a knock.* Yawning, she stretched her arms out wide. Normally she was on the move by six, except on the weekends. *I'm not even sure what day it is.*

Knock. Knock. Knock.

Her eyes widened. She grabbed her Glock and headed toward the front door in nothing but a black T-shirt and panties.

She'd been in this apartment a year, but only one time had this door been knocked on—by a couple of college guys who lived a few doors over. It had been an invitation to one of their parties. They never looked her way again after she shoved her badge and an earful of her legal authority in their faces.

Sidney checked the peephole. Smoke stood on the other side, holding a tray of coffee and wearing a pair of sunglasses.

How does he know where I live!

CHAPTER 30

"**W**HAT ARE YOU DOING HERE?**" she said through the door.

"I was in the neighborhood and thought I'd bring some coffee over."

A playful thought entered Sidney's mind. She swung the door open.

Smoke's jaw hung in the air.

She plucked a cup of coffee out of the carrier, said "Thank you," and shut the door in his face. From the other side of the door she heard him say, "I thought I'd come over and we could get a jump on things."

"Really, and what kind of things did you want to jump on?" She set down the coffee, headed to her room, grabbed a pair of jeans and a maroon sweater, and slipped them on. She could hear his reply through the door.

"It's not like that."

"You're a man, aren't you?"

There was a pause. "Well, it's kinda like that, but not the way you think. I have a lead."

She buttoned her jeans. "Hold on." Inside the bathroom she brushed her teeth and clipped her hair up. *No.* Back in the bedroom, she found an FBI-issued ball cap, put it on, and laced up some rubber-soled boots.

"Aren't you going to invite me in?" Smoke said.

And break my last seven months of chastity?

She checked herself in the mirror again and strapped her weapon on. She saw her bed reflecting in the mirror.

Just let him in. Long enough is long enough.

"Hello?" she heard him say. "The biscuits are getting cold."

The biscuits are getting cold? The fires inside her dimmed. *Cheap thrill killed.* She pulled her hat down, grabbed her coffee and bag, and opened the door.

"Don't ever do this again," she said, locking the door behind her, "and you can explain how you found me later." Her stomach growled. "Where's my biscuit?"

"Oh," he said, rubbing his neck. "I was joking about that. I ate on the way over."

She glared at him.

"Nice hat," he said, eyeing the three big letters. "Not exactly discreet considering where we're headed."

"And where might that be?" She scanned the parking lot. "And how did you get here?"

"Automobile." He pointed at the parking lot as they made their way down the stairs. "I can drive too, you know."

"Well, we won't be finding out about that anytime soon." There was an old VW bus, red with a white top, she hadn't seen before. "Please tell me you aren't driving that."

He looked at the bus. "That? No." He pointed to the space on the other side, where there was a primer-gray Camaro. A mid-eighties IROC version. "Those are my wheels."

"We'll take the Interceptor."

"It's too slow."

"I didn't think we were in a hurry." She headed for her car. The windows were frosted over. The trunk groaned when she opened it up and grabbed the ice scraper. She handed it to Smoke. "Get to work."

"My car's warm and ready. The bucket seats are cozy."

"Please stop." She grabbed her jacket from the back seat and then started up her car. "Hurry up, and then get in."

Scraping, Smoke said, "I have all my gear in my car."

"And I have all my gear in mine." She closed the door and took a sip of coffee. Flipped on the defroster. The fan rattled. Her neck tightened. Smoke's suggestion seemed more promising.

Nah, let him scrape.

Finishing up, Smoke rapped on the window with his knuckle and said with icy breath, "Why don't we take both cars?"

Her nostrils flared. *Screw it.* She shut off the engine, got out of the car, and locked it.

Smoke tossed the scraper in the trunk and started to close it.

"Hold on." She took out a black duffle bag that clattered with metal and swung it over her shoulder. "All right."

Smoke clamped the lid down, headed for his car, and opened up the passenger side door.

"This isn't a date." She placed her bag in the back seat.

"No, it's common courtesy."

Sidney took her seat and Smoke closed the door. Seconds later, they were roaring down the road. The Camaro's acceleration pinned her to her seat. It had a roll cage inside, and the dash rattled and squeaked. Smoke filled up his racing seat. His head almost touched the ceiling.

"I appreciate you letting me drive," Smoke said over the hum of the engine. "That's one thing I hate about prison. I don't get to drive anywhere."

"Don't get used to it. We have a stop to make."

"Stop, why?"

"Take the next left, a right and then another left."

"Sure, where are we going?"

"Just do it." *Turn about is fair play.*

She took the lid off her coffee and took another drink. Smoke was being extremely cooperative for a man who had problems with authority. He was up to something. His behavior was way outside of his profile. Smoke made the second left.

"Turn here."

They entered a facility full of orange-doored storage garages. He pulled his car to a stop at the key pad. "Uh ..."

"Seven six seven five."

He punched it in, and the gate glided open.

"Straight back and to the right."

Smoke cruised toward the back, where cars, boats, and RVs were parked in rows. He pulled into an open slot.

She picked up her belongings, got out, and said, "Wait here."

"Can I at least get out?"

"Sure."

A few minutes later she pulled out in a Dodge Challenger Hellcat: phantom black, with flame-orange stripes on the hood and pinstripes on the side. She pushed on the gas, unleashing a throaty exhaust note.

Smoke took off his glasses. Brows up and eyes wide, he strolled over.

"I think I'm in love."

"With me, or the car?"

"Heh ... I'll get my stuff."

CHAPTER 31

CRUISING DOWN THE HIGHWAY, SMOKE ran his fingers over the dash. "Seven hundred and seven horsepower, the most powerful production engine." He bobbed his chin. "Now that's something. I read about these in prison. Pretty new. How'd you come by it?"

"Police auction," she said, fingers hugging the heated steering wheel. *I've missed my baby.* "I outbid a lot of interested people. Pissed off many men."

"I bet."

"It came down to me and Ted." She plucked her shades from the console and put them on. "At the end of the day it was my Hellcat, not his."

Glasses off, Smoke inspected everything. "He missed out. So why the attraction?"

"Love cars. Love the name. My dad actually had some comics with a superhero named Hellcat I kind of liked." *Too much information, Sid.*

Smoke smiled. "Ah, very interesting."

"Not to mention the rear-wheel drive and all the awesome power. It's sort of a given."

"So, was this a drug runner's car?"

"Snagged north of the Arizona border. The auction was in Texas. I drove him all the way home."

"I thought cars were *hers?*"

"Does he look like a *her?*"

He shook his head no.

"I'm heading south, you know," she said. "Unless there's another direction I should be going."

"Right, right. No, south is good." He poked at the GPS. "Do you mind?"

"It would help to know where I'm going." She checked the speedometer. It read ninety. The feel of the road, the sound of the engine, she lost herself in it. She eased off the gas and set the cruise control at seventy. "So tell me about this lead. How did you get it?"

"Fat Sam—"

"And Guppy. Sheesh, I should have known." She switched lanes. "I'm wondering if they're even real."

"Oh, they're real, but it's important that I keep my resources secret." He finished tapping on the GPS. "There we go."

"What is that?"

"Mitchell-Bates Hospital. Closed as of 2004. One hundred and seventy-five beds. Three floors and a basement." He took a drink of coffee. "Two miles from the highway. Once public and now private property."

"And who owns it now?"

"A real estate developer, which is a subsidiary of ..."

"The Drake Corporation."

"Actually, Drake Incorporated. We checked at the Secretary of State's office, which wasn't easy seeing how three states are in the immediate area."

"So there are lots of companies, different names and doing business as?"

"Yep." He nodded. "And no real names."

"And I guess they all pay their taxes."

"Do you want me to find out?"

"No." Sidney had done her share of white-collar investigations. Digging through layer after layer of false names and companies was interesting. The top lawyers and accountants dotted every 'i' and crossed every 't' on the good ones. In the most thorough cases it took an act of God to bring them down, and that was only after years were exhausted in the court systems that the enemy knew too well. *This is a lot deeper than just one man.*

"Shadow companies like the Drake probably benefit from a few congressmen and senators in their pockets."

She thought of Congressman Wilhelm and the last words he had said: "Watch your step."

Things were quiet the next ninety minutes of driving, and then she took the Grandview Road exit. A pair of steel-crafted yellow swing gates barred the road that led into the parking lot.

"Looks like we walk from here."

"I'm not leaving my car out here," Sidney said. She got out and made her way to the gates. A heavy padlock down inside a steel mesh cage held the gates together. She scanned the area. The Mitchell-Bates Hospital sign was in disrepair. No cameras were mounted on the light poles leading to the entrance. Only the sound of highway traffic caught her ears. She drew her weapon, shot the lock off, swung the gate open, and got back in the car.

"Subtle," Smoke said.

She put the car in drive. "Let's get this over with."

CHAPTER 32

"MAYBE HE IS, MAYBE HE isn't in here," she said, driving forward. "Perhaps Fat Sam and Guppy are wrong."

"They aren't wrong."

"Maybe there's another way out."

Smoke shrugged.

As they rolled up the road between the tall trees, the rising sun dimmed behind misty clouds. The brisk wind stirred the leaves on the parking lot as they approached. The small brick hospital stood in a woodland of falling leaves and pines. Not a car was in the lot. Patches of tall grass popped up through the blacktop.

"He's in here, huh?" she said to Smoke. "It looks pretty abandoned to me."

"It's a lead," he said. "Besides, looks can be deceiving. There's another side to the building, you know." He shook his head. "Man, this is the worst recon ever."

"What's that supposed to mean?" she said, reaching into the back seat for her gym bag. She took out another shoulder holster. A Kevlar vest. Another Glock was ready, along with two fifteen-round magazines. She slipped off her jacket, put on the Kevlar vest, and put the jacket over it. "I don't think there's that much to recon."

"Then why are you gearing up like that?"

"Because I don't normally get to." She pulled the car under the canopy that led to the emergency room entrance, opened her door, and dropped a foot outside. "Are you coming or not?"

"Pop the trunk."

She followed him to the back of the car, where he opened his oversized gym bag. He put on his own Kevlar vest and strapped a pair of 9mm Beretta pistols to his hips. He finished by stuffing a single-action army sheriff's pistol in the back of his pants.

"A revolver?" she said.

"It's sentimental."

"All right, cowboy." As she turned toward the hospital entrance, something caught her eyes. She froze.

A white-grey wolf stood twenty feet away, teeth bared. Its muscular back was more than waist tall. It was one of the biggest canines she'd ever seen.

"Uh, Smoke?"

"Yeah?" he said, turning. "Oh ... that's one big dog."

Sidney's back tightened. Her fingertips tingled. She knew dogs but not wolves. They were wild. Ferocious. She reached for her weapon.

Before she could even touch it, the wolf had snarled and sprinted away.

Sidney jumped when Smoke closed the trunk.

He had a tire iron in his hand. "Let's go catch that werewolf."

"I think it will be a few more hours before any of them come out." She took the tire iron from his hand and made her way onto the landing. A set of sliding glass doors were closed, and the side entrance steel door was locked. She wedged the tire iron in between the doors and started to pry. The doors cracked open an inch. "A little help," she grunted.

Smoke gripped the door's edge and gave a powerful tug. The doors split apart another foot. Straining, he said, "Think you can fit?"

"Ha," she said, squeezing through. Smoke forced himself inside, and the doors sealed shut with the tire iron outside. "Ew," she said, covering her nose. "It smells like the dead in here."

Inside, the lighting was dim other than the natural light from the windows.

"Do you hear that?" Smoke said, tilting his head. The sound of electricity hummed inside the walls. "Something is going on in here." He started forward, shuffling by the old waiting room chairs and into the ER. There were several gurneys with rotting curtains hanging around them. "What do you think? Follow the smell?"

Sidney remained behind Smoke's shoulder and followed him into the central hall, plugging her nose. *This is disgusting.* The long hallway was darker because the patient room doors were closed, blocking the sunlight. Smoke stopped at one of them and pushed it open. It groaned on the hinges and swung inward. *Is he visiting somebody?*

It was a two-patient room with soiled linens rotting on the beds. The air was musty, rotten, and stale.

Sidney coughed. "Do you have a thing for bad smells?"

Smoke glided to the window and stood where the daylight crept in through the blinds. He pulled them aside with two fingers. "We aren't alone."

Sidney took a look. Smoke was right. More cars were parked behind the building: two navy-blue cargo vans and several dark sedans. A box truck was backed into the service drive. All of it was shadowed by the tall trees that snuffed out the bright rising light.

She glanced up at Smoke. "I can't say I'm glad that you're right. Come on."

"I'd be disappointed if I was wrong."

Heading out of the room, she came to a stop. Footsteps and the shuffle of feet came from the room above. The steps creaked and were moving down the hall. Sidney followed the sound down toward the emergency exits. Smoke was a large shadow behind her. The doors were closed at the stairwell, but she heard the latch of the doors above pop open. She slid to one side of the doors, and Smoke took the other. Her heart thumped in her chest.

After about thirty seconds, Smoke shrugged. "They either went up or went back." He popped the door open and peered inside the dark stairwell. "Huh, there's a basement too. I have a coin. Heads we go up, tails we go—*ulp*!"

A hand shot out and pulled Smoke into the stairwell. The door slammed shut behind him.

CHAPTER 33

"**S**MOKE!"

Sidney shoved on the door, but there was no give. Something blocked the other side. She thrust her shoulder into it. It cracked open and slammed shut. She could hear the scuffle of a fight on the other side. A man screamed.

"Smoke!"

Wham!

A heavy body rocked the door. She heard the heavy blows of bone on bone and flesh on flesh. Hard smacks. Kicking. Punching. Wrestling. She found her flashlight and shone it through the rectangular portal. A bloodshot eye blinked in the light. The face was scarred. Subhuman. She tapped the nose of her gun on the glass.

"Back off!"

The face ducked away.

She lowered her shoulder, rammed into the door, and winced. No give. She wanted to shoot. Blast away, but Smoke was over there, fighting for his life.

Come on! Come on! Think, Sid! Think!

"Back away, Sid," Smoke roared from the other side. "Back away!"

Sidney stepped aside. The door flung inward. Smoke appeared, dragging another man in a headlock.

"Stay away from the door," Smoke warned. The door clasped shut. Footsteps scurried up the stairwell. "Stay here." Smoke wrestled the struggling man to the floor and wrenched the man's arm behind his back. *Pop!* The shoulder was dislocated, but the man didn't cry out.

"What are you doing?" Sidney said.

Chest heaving, Smoke replied, "I'm immobilizing him." He wrenched the man's other arm. *Pop.* The other shoulder gave.

Sidney's stomach turned.

The man-like thing thrashed with purpose, arms hanging limp as noodles from the sockets. Its face was ghoulish and veiny. It gathered itself on its feet.

Smoke swept the legs out from under it.

It crashed back-first to the floor.

Smoke pinned it and jammed his gun barrel in its chest.

"Don't kill him," Sidney ordered.

"I hit him with everything I had. He didn't even grunt."

"That's not a license to kill."

"You're just going to have to trust me on this, Agent Shaw." He squeezed the trigger.

Ka-blam!

The man-like thing lurched up and smacked Smoke in the chin.

He staggered back.

It started walking down the hall, arms dangling at its sides with a hole clean through its back and chest.

Sidney took aim.

Blam! Blam! Blam!

It tumbled over with its kneecap blasted apart.

"Good shot." Smoke wiped his brow and headed after their fallen attacker where it writhed on the floor. "I think it's a zombie." He pointed his weapon at its head.

Blam!

"Zombies aren't real," she said, catching her breath and holstering her gun.

"I don't know," Smoke replied.

She kneeled down. Whoever or whatever the man was, it didn't bleed: it oozed. It still moved. Her skin turned clammy. "This is sick."

"Good thing we're in a hospital."

Sidney eyed him. "How many were in there?"

"Just two. One I think was a man. I kicked him solid in the balls." He cracked his neck. "That's when I dragged this fiend out of there. Do you think it's that captain?" he said, referring to the man driving AV's boat she'd mentioned earlier.

"No, but his skin is just like what I saw." She took out her phone. "No signal."

"No surprise." He tipped his head toward the stairwell. "How about I scout it out?"

"How about we scout it out? But another approach would be better, seeing how they know we're here." She made her way into another patient room and peered out through the window. None of the cars had moved. "Doesn't look like we scared anyone off, either."

"Not yet," Smoke said, leaning on the door frame. "But I say we take it to them."

If AV was here, then he certainly knew they were here. It might take hours to clear the building, not to mention the unnatural elements that surrounded them. What kind of man had they just taken down? It had attacked, but it hadn't tried to eat them.

It's not a zombie. There's no such thing as zombies. She headed back into the hall. The man-like thing on the floor was still moving.

"Strange," Smoke said, looking down at it. "I thought the head wound would kill it."

"This isn't a movie. This is reality."

Smoke switched weapons. "And this is a forty-five automatic loaded with hollow points." He pointed at the writhing thing's heart.

Blam.

It stopped moving.

He blew the smoke rolling from the barrel. "Critical hit."

Irritated, she said, "Will you stop shooting?"

"We needed to know how to take these things out, and now we do."

"A bullet in the heart does that to anything." She made her way back down the hallway, stopping and listening at patient doors from time to time. On the other side of the hall, Smoke did the same. She traversed the hall, passing the elevators. She heard a ding and turned back.

Smoke stood in front of the elevators. The up button glowed with light. The doors split open and he half-stepped inside. He looked at her and said, "Going up?"

"I'm not taking the elevator." She crept in halfway and pressed buttons two and three, grabbed Smoke's arm, and pushed him out. She ran down the hall with Smoke on her heels. Flashlight ready, she entered the stairwell, jogged up the steps, and stopped on the second floor landing. She peered through the door's portal. Figures crowded in front of the elevator down the hall. One of them was limping.

"That's the guy," Smoke said, cocking his pistol. "It has to be."

Sidney counted four men, but she didn't see any weapons. It was odd. One of them disappeared into the elevator. Necks craned forward until the man stepped out into view again. Voices mumbled among themselves, and the group spread out, vanishing into patient rooms and behind the nurse's station.

"Ambush," she whispered to Smoke.

"I say we start at the top and work our way down. Give them something to think about."

"Agreed." She turned her flashlight up the stairwell and took it two steps at a time. She stopped halfway to the first landing. A man stood there in ragged clothes, hollow-eyed and ugly. He held a grenade-sized object in his hands.

"FBI! Hands up!"

The man's thoughtless expression didn't change as he dropped the grenade down the stairwell. It bounced off the first step.

Smoke scooped it up. "Stun grenade." He flung it back at the man.

Sidney squeezed her eyes shut and covered her ears.

Flash! Boom!

The sound inside the stairwell rocked her senses. She saw dizzying spots and sagged down the steps. There was ringing, ringing and ringing, and everything faded to black.

CHAPTER 34

A SPLASH OF COLD WATER SNAPPED Sidney out of her sleep. Wide-eyed and head aching, she tried to spit the gag from her mouth. Something bit into her wrists, which were tied behind her back. Her feet were bound as well.

"Huh, huh," a man said, lumbering by with a plastic bucket in his hands. He was thickset and bald. He wore a heavy blue sweater, grey sweatpants, and white tennis shoes. He poured the bucket of water on Smoke, who sat on the floor by her side, bound the same way.

Smoke coughed and sputtered.

The man walked away and disappeared through a double doorway.

Spitting the gag from his mouth, Smoke said, "You all right?"

Sidney nodded. Other than a piercing headache and stiff limbs, she was fine. They looked to be in the basement cafeteria, judging by the checkered tiles on the floor. They weren't alone, either. Below the incandescent lights were more people, working at tables. They wore masks, gloves, and dark-grey scrubs. Some sat at the tables and others stood. She didn't have a clear view of what they were doing. Not a one glanced their way.

"See that?" Smoke said in a low tone. Two goons in pea coats lorded over a lone table. It had their guns and gear on it. "Be patient."

It was easier said than done. Sidney had never been captured before. Never been a captive of any sort. The revolting smells didn't help, either. She strained against her bonds. Her eyes watered.

"Save your energy," Smoke advised.

Balled up, she let her body go slack. Smoke was right. She focused on what the others were doing. A small figure that looked to be a boy taped up a box the others had loaded and moved it to a stack in the corner. *Hmmm.* Five people in all were making packages of some sort. It reminded her of the scene at Sting Ray's bar. Children being exploited. She clenched her teeth.

A small bell rang. The workers stopped what they were doing, and without a glance among them they departed from the room.

With great effort, she spat the gag from her mouth and gasped.

"Feel better?" Smoke said.

"No. Hey!" she yelled over at the guards. "I'm a federal agent. I demand to know who is in charge."

The men remained frozen in place without a glance her way. Each one had a shotgun strapped over his shoulder.

She heard Smoke's belly grumble. "I don't think they're serving pancakes."

"No," Smoke said just as the set of doors that led into the hallway opened. Two ghoulish men with clammy skin, wearing denim overalls, walked in. "And I don't think they're here to take our order."

The men came toward them with strong stiff movements. The first one grabbed Smoke by the collar and heaved him up on his shoulder. The second one did the same to Sidney. Draped over the ghastly men's shoulders, they exited the room into a dark hallway and entered another. Sidney's goon set her down in a padded office chair. An antique walnut desk in a well-furnished office was in front of her.

Behind it sat AV in a high-backed leather chair.

His eerie henchmen moved to either side of him.

"I have to admit," AV said, filing his nails, "This is a surprise. I normally fetch my enemies myself. But in this case, you came straight to me." He wore a dark-purple dress shirt with rolled-up sleeves, revealing his hairy arms. The glow of two floor lamps against the back wall brought out the sheen in his waves of jet-black hair. He seemed small between his goons. "Agent Shaw, didn't I mention that I would kill you?"

"Yes, I recall you threatening a federal agent."

AV laughed. "And yet, here you are." He waggled his finger at her. "Did you not see the bodies of your friends? Were they not torn to shreds?"

A coldness overcame her.

"Ah," He continued, "you look confused. He eased back in the chair and rocked a little. "Let me fill you in." He licked his teeth. "I'm a werewolf."

Sidney laughed despite the truth behind his words and the tingling that shot up her limbs. "Congratulations," she said. "That must explain the fleas."

"Good one," Smoke said with a nod. "And I told you so."

AV picked up a pistol that lay on the desk. It was Smoke's Colt .45, black matte and pearl-handled, sheriff's model. He popped open the chamber and emptied the bullets out of the cylinder. They were silver. "Either you're a fan of the Lone Ranger, or you are as stupid as most men are."

"Really?" Sidney said, looking over at Smoke. "He's not a werewolf."

"Ah, a skeptic. I love a skeptic." AV opened a drawer and pulled a knife out. The wavy blade looked ancient. He turned in his chair and grabbed the hand of one of his goons and placed it on the desk. He skinned the hair off its arm. "Sharp, isn't it?" The knife bit deeper, and he peeled off the skin, exposing the muscle beneath it.

Sidney's skin crawled.

"See, he doesn't even scream." The listless goon leaned back into attention. AV stuck the knife in its thigh. "And he makes for an excellent knife holder." His dangerous eyes narrowed on Sidney. "Can you explain that, Agent Shaw?"

No.

"We call them deaders."

We?

"Cursed flesh brought to life. Flesh automatons made for our bidding. Capable of executing simple commands. Fetch. Fight. Kill."

"That's quite an accomplishment," she said, twisting her wrists behind her. *I need to get out of here.* "Do you have a patent on it?"

"Humph," he said, plucking a pen from its holder and writing on something. "How did you find me? I need to tie up that loose end."

"It wasn't that hard," Smoke said. "Those wild wolf dogs led us here."

"I don't think so," AV said. "But no matter. I'll figure it out soon enough."

"So, who is 'we'?" she said, turning her ear to him. *Keep him talking.* "I can use all the leads I can get, because you're only the first guy, I mean werewolf, on my list."

"Your tongue is sharp, Agent." He leered at her. "I'm reconsidering."

"Reconsidering what?"

"Twisting your head off first." He picked up a phone that looked to be hers. "You have family, don't you?" He turned her phone toward her. A picture of Megan, her niece, appeared.

How'd he get in there?

"You've seen what I can do," he continued. "Imagine what I could do to her." The blood rushed through her temples. Her heart sank. *No!*

"Of course, that would be merciful," AV said, flipping through the pictures. "Maybe I'll have her turned into a deader."

"I'm going to kill you," Sidney replied.

"No, Agent Shaw, I am going to kill you." He rose from his chair, pushing it back, and stretched out his arms. "Both of you. I've been waiting to wake you for hours." He cracked his neck from side to side. "Nighttime is my time." He crushed her phone in his fist and dropped the remains on the desk.

"Told you he was strong," Smoke said, straining at his bonds.

Sidney's heart quickened. *What is happening?!*

AV started to change. His body stretched and convulsed. Coarse hairs sprouted from his face and arms. Muscle bulged and bone groaned. His purple shirt split at the seams. A short snout protruded from his jaws, and his head stretched toward the ceiling. In seconds, AV went from a man to a full-blown werewolf. Evil and lust lurked behind the yellow eyes that rested on Sidney.

Horrified, she sagged in her seat and turned her head away.

This isn't real! This isn't real! This isn't real!

CHAPTER 35

"What's the matter?" AV said, his voice now something monstrous—throaty and raw. "Has your sharp tongue dulled?"

Sidney had seen horrible things, both in real life and in the movies, but nothing compared to the supernatural transformation she'd just witnessed. It was unnatural. Evil. Yet somehow ... alluring? Utterly afraid, she pulled her knees up into her chest.

"That's what I like to see," AV said, coming from around the desk. "The brave woman turned into a little girl again." He leaned over her. "Your fear feeds my craving."

She felt his hot breath on her neck. Now she couldn't deny there was something seductive and powerful about it. Her iron will started to cave.

"Yes, yes, Agent Shaw. Give yourself away." He brushed her hair aside with his clawed finger and turned her chin toward him. "Experience every pleasure I can offer that needs awakening in the dark corners of your soul."

He ran his claw down her face, over her chest, and rested his powerful hand on her thigh and squeezed.

She moaned. Dark fires ignited within. She was powerless in the clutch of the uber-man before her.

"Maybe I'll keep you around after all." He ran his finger down her thigh. With his claw, he sliced the cord that bound her ankles. He twisted her around and cut the bonds from her wrists.

Her shoulders sagged. Her body was loose. Languid.

He eased her legs apart. "It's been quite some time, hasn't it, woman?"

Lost in his power, her head fell over on her shoulder. She wanted him. She loathed him. Her eyes found Smoke's. He had a fierce look about him. Seeing the sweat bead on his forehead, a glimmer of her senses returned. AV took her chin and turned it away.

"Don't worry about him—he's a dead man, but you might have a promising future ahead."

"Sidney! Close your eyes! Think of pancakes and butterflies."

What kind of man says that?

"Deaders, kill that fool!" AV ordered. "Feed his corpse to the wolves. I'll be needing Agent Shaw all to myself."

Pancakes and butterflies? The flames of passion turned to angry fires. *Pancakes and butterflies!* She kicked AV's groin with all her force.

He slammed back into the desk.

"Fool woman!" He lurched forward and backhanded her in the face, spinning her like a top from the chair so that she tumbled over.

Her head rang, and all she saw was bright spots and stars.

AV put his big paw on her head and tugged her up to her toes by the hair. "I'm not big on second chances, Pretty."

A clamor rose. Smoke, somehow free of his bonds, wrestled against the clutches of the deaders.

"Excuse me," AV said a moment before he slung Sidney into the wall.

She smacked into it hard and sagged to the floor. Groaning, she forced herself up to her knees and spat blood.

"Run, Sidney!" Smoke urged. "Run!" He slipped away from the deaders only to find himself cornered by AV. The werewolf sneered down on him. Smoke punched him in the throat and poked him in the eye.

AV roared. His claws slashed out.

Smoke twisted away, ducked, and popped up with a knife in his hand. It was the ancient blade that AV had planted in the deader. He cut into the monster's slashing arms, spun under a powerful blow, and drove the blade home into AV's abdomen.

The werewolf staggered back against the wall.

"No! No!" AV cried. "You stabbed me with the Blade of Hoknar. Darkness falls. Darkness falls." He slumped back against the wall, and his eyes began to close.

Sidney got up and wiped the blood from her mouth.

"That was close."

Smoke skipped away from the deaders, who wandered the room but didn't attack.

Laughter rumbled in AV's throat, and his mighty form rose again. He plucked the blade from his stomach and showed a mouthful of sharp teeth.

"Fools." He hurled the blade at Smoke.

The big man plucked it out of the air, spun, and buried it hilt-deep in the heart of a deader. He ripped it out and said, "Sid, get out of here!"

"Oh please," AV said, "no one has ever escaped alive." He wiped the saliva dripping from his fangs off of his chin. "I just need to decide which one of you to kill first." He chomped his teeth. "Deader, kill her. I shall kill him." AV sprang from one side of the room to the other. His heavy frame drove the evading Smoke to the ground. His fists came down with speed and power.

Sidney ran for the door.

The dead man cut into her path. Fingers clutched at her waist and tore a belt loop off her pants.

She slugged it in the face.

It leered back into her eyes. Soulless. Empty. Its grabby hand locked around her wrist and slung her to the floor.

She hit hard. "Ugh!"

The deader held her in a fierce grip and pummeled her with its free fist. The hammering blows rocked her body.

She kept her shoulder up to absorb what she could and kicked her hardest with her legs. Her heel connected with its jaw.

"Nuh!" it said, sounding almost human.

With an angry shout, Sidney twisted her wrist free and was on her feet again.

The werewolf had Smoke pinned to the wall by the neck. Smoke's shaky hand was pointing at the desk. The gun. The bullets. Silver nodules caught her eye. She snatched the old wheel gun up. Strong hands grabbed her feet and jerked her to the floor.

"Ulp!"

Crack!

Her head bounced off the edge of the hardwood desk. She saw red.

"No!"

She kicked it in the face.

"No!"

Her heel crushed its nose in.

"NO!"

She ripped her foot out of its grip and scrambled away on all fours. The other deader lay still, with a knife stuck in its chest. She ripped it out and turned just as the deader dove on top of her. She drove the blade into its chest and pushed it off her.

Smoke!

She pushed off the floor. Smoke held on for his life against the werewolf. Sidney plucked a bullet from the desk and loaded it into the chamber. She cocked back the hammer. "Let him go, AV!"

The wolfman froze with the battered Smoke held tightly in his grip and said, "You don't really think that will work, do you?"

"Only one way to find out."

"Aren't you here to arrest me? After all, I'm no good to your handlers if I'm dead. They need the knowledge within this body."

"Shoot him," Smoke spat out from busted lips. "Shoot him now."

"Let him down," she warned. The adrenaline cleared her mind. She felt in control again.

"Certainly," AV replied, lowering Smoke's busted frame to the ground. "But I don't think you have strong enough cuffs to hold me. Remember what happened the last time. And another thing, silver bullets don't really kill werewolves."

"Then why are you doing what I say?"

"Because I enjoy the game." In a flash, he rocketed by the desk toward the office door.

Sidney fired. *Blam!*

The wolfman burst through the door with a wounded howl and vanished into the hall.

Sidney peeked down both ways. AV the werewolf was gone.

CHAPTER 36

"That was fast," Sidney said, rushing over to Smoke. She helped him to his feet. His hair was matted in blood, and his face was swelling. His Kevlar vest was all torn up. "Are you going to make it?"

He straightened up. "I had my doubts." With a bloody hand, he picked up the other bullets from the table. "Why didn't you shoot him?"

"They want him alive."

"They? Don't let your overzealous sense of duty get me or you killed, Agent Shaw. " He stepped past her and plucked the knife out of the deader's chest. He flipped it around and faced her. "He's a murderer. And murderers must die." He pointed his finger in her face. "I told you he was a werewolf. Now hand over the gun."

"No." She held out her hand. "Hand over the bullets."

"It's my gun."

"I'm not arguing with a twelve-year-old."

Smoke's face drew tight as he handed over the bullets. "Fine. Just, the next time you hesitate, remember—he twists people's heads off!" He made his way into the hall and knelt down by some blood drops on the floor. "Seems you clipped him, and my guess is he didn't like it."

"Follow the blood," she said, loading the bullets into their cylinders. As she made her way down the hall toward the cafeteria, one of the double doors squeaked open. Smoke darted in front of her. A shotgun blast rang out. She flattened on the floor. Aimed her weapon.

In a burst of motion, Smoke jerked one of the pea-coat men through the door and ripped the shotgun from his grasp. He lowered the barrel to between the man's eyes.

"No, no man! Please, don't shoot me."

Smoke kneeled down, pressing the barrel deeper into the man's face. "Where's Mister Vaughn?"

"Who?"

Smoke punched him in the gut. "The werewolf."

"Aw man, aw man, I don't know!"

"How many others?" Sidney piped in.

"Just me. Just me."

"Liar," Sidney said, backing into the cafeteria. There were no signs of anybody anywhere.

Pop! Pop! Pop! Pop! Pop!

Bullets ripped through the air from the other end of the hall.

Smoke dragged the man into the cafeteria.

"Who was that?"

"The other man, Allen. Like me, he stayed to finish you off." He chuckled. "And if he doesn't, the others will."

Smoke looked up at Sid. "We've got to go. Time's wasting."

Pop! Pop! Pop! Pop! Pop!

"Yer gonna get wasted, all right," the goon said.

Smoke took the shotgun stock and clocked the goon in the jaw. "I hate big talkers." He nodded at the table. "Get the gear. I'll cover the hall."

Sidney moved, picking up pistols and holsters.

Ka-Blam! Ka-Blam!

She whipped around. Smoke was gone. "Dammit."

He reappeared back inside the door with another shotgun strapped on his shoulder. "Got him."

She took a moment and caught her breath. *Is this really going on? Werewolves and zombie-like men called deaders?* She swooned a little.

Smoke wrapped his arms around her waist and steadied her. "We aren't finished yet. And I think you're going to have quite a shiner, but I can live with it."

"Look who's talking," she said.

Smoke's clothes were blood-soaked in some parts.

The cafeteria suddenly became quiet. She remembered what AV had said: no one ever left alive. She took a shotgun from Smoke's shoulder and pumped the handle.

"Until today."

"Until what today?"

"Nothing," she said, looking at the floor. She found AV's blood. "Let's go."

The blood trail led into the darkness of the stairwell. She turned on her flashlight.

Smoke cut in front of her. "You shine. I'll lead." He took off up the steps, clearing the first floor and heading up the second flight. He cracked the door open.

Pop! Pop! Pop! Pop!

Bullets blasted into the stairwell doors.

"Turn off the light and cover me," Smoke said.

"Wait."

He surged through the door.

Sidney laid down shotgun cover fire into the middle of the hall. Shots cracked out from everywhere. Muzzle flashes flared. Shielded behind the door, she cracked off a few more rounds and everything fell silent. Now that it was night, the hallway was almost pitch black. The seconds seemed like minutes as she peered into the shadows.

Pop!

A man cried out. A group of shadows tussled in the hall. Something cracked. Another man screamed.

Blam! Blam!

"It's clear," Smoke said, his voice hollow in the blackness of the hall. "Come on. There's still a trail of blood."

Just as Sidney eased into the hallway, the fine hairs on her neck rose. She started to turn. A hairy paw clamped down on her shoulder and dug its sharp nails into her skin.

"I'll take this," the soft savage voice of the wolfman said, sliding Smoke's pistol with the silver bullets out of the back of her pants. "Set down your weapons and stop resisting. You don't know what you're missing."

Hot saliva dripped onto her neck, arousing her carnal senses. Compelled to obey, she set the shotgun and pistol down.

"I'm not so bad, Pretty," AV said, wrapping his powerful arm around her waist. He picked her up off her feet like a child. "Come quietly now and everything will be fine."

She wanted to believe him. Her rigid body slackened. "No," she managed to say.

"Yes," he replied, moving down into the stairwell's blackness.

In a twisted moment of fate, her terror turned to attraction as she felt herself being carried over the threshold of wickedness. Everything she knew to be right suddenly turned wrong. Reaching deep inside, she found a spark and tried to cry out against her captivating bonds.

AV clamped his hand over her mouth. "Sssh…"

CHAPTER 37

THE SECOND-FLOOR DOORS TO THE stairwell flung open, and Smoke emerged. He hurled himself down the stairwell, crashing into Sidney and AV. The jolt knocked her loose from the werewolf's clutches.

"Fool!" AV roared, lashing out and striking Smoke in the chest.

The hardened soldier crashed into the wall. The stairwell lit up with bright barrel flashes.

Ka-Blam! Ka-Blam! Ka-Blam!

Smoke unloaded his shotgun into AV's chest, rocking the werewolf backward.

Click.

"You're a dead man!" AV roared.

Sidney crawled through the darkness as she heard heavy blows smacking into flesh. Man and monster cursed and snarled. *I have to help!* A clatter of metal skidded over the landing. She dove toward it and felt the cool pistol clutched in her fingers.

Whap! Whap! Whap!

Punches and angry howls filled the stairwell. The heavy scuffles and grunts were inseparable. Weapon ready, she rushed into the fray, grabbed a handful of coarse hair, and fired.

Blam!

A shrieking howl split her ears, and a swipe of claws knocked her from her feet. She fired again at the sound of feet fleeing up the stairs.

Blam!

Smoke grabbed her hand and moaned, "Stop! Only three more bullets left."

They helped each other to their feet. Smoke leaned on her, limping down the stairwell. He looked like he had crawled out of a mine field.

"We need to get you help."

He spat blood. "I'm fine."

"You don't look fine."

"Well, I look better than most guys who've slugged it out with a werewolf." He groaned. "We need to kill this guy."

"We need more help."

"Follow the blood. I think we've almost got him." He pointed at bloody footprints on the floor. "Staggered. You got him good."

The blood trail led to the emergency room and then to the door of a locked office. She peered through the portal. AV sat in a chair, digging medical pliers into an abdominal wound. He plucked out a bloody silver bullet and tossed it to the floor.

Sidney tapped on the glass and pointed the barrel at him.

The werewolf's eyes widened.

She fired.

Blam!

Cat-quick, he sprang away, crashing through the window and into the parking lot.

"Missed. Dammit!"

Smoke busted the door handle off with a fire extinguisher and kicked it open.

"True, but I think you scared him off," Smoke said, stepping inside and looking out the broken window. "And the hunt starts all over."

"Did you hear that?" she said.

An engine flared up with a gentle roar. A second later, a maroon Cadillac Escalade sped through the parking lot. AV the werewolf filled the seat.

"You've got to be kidding me." She took aim. Smoke pushed the barrel down.

"I think the Hellcat has a better chance of not missing."

She took off, racing into the ER waiting room. The sliding glass doors were sealed and the main entrance door wouldn't open.

Smoke picked up a row of seats and hurled them through the glass. "After you," he said.

Sidney jumped down the steps and flung open the car door.

Smoke slid over the hood.

"Don't you ever do that again!" she said, firing up the engine. She shifted into reverse, hit the gas, and swung the car around. Dropping the car into drive, she stomped on the gas, smoking the wheels.

"Nothing like the smell of burning rubber in the evening," Smoke said, crawling into the back seat. "Sorry about the upholstery."

"What are you doing?" she yelled at the rearview mirror.

Smoke popped down the rear seat, pulled his duffle bag from the trunk, and crawled back into the front seat. "Getting this," he said, holding an M-16 assault rifle with an M203 grenade launcher mounted under the barrel. "A real beauty, isn't it?"

"Illegal as hell!"

"I won't tell if you won't. Jealous?"

Yes. "No."

"Well, get after him. It's time to blow Fang Face away."

The engine roared as they raced up onto the highway. AV's bright red taillights weaved in and out of traffic about ten car lengths ahead.

"Looks like he knows we're coming." She changed lanes, pushing on the gas. "And don't you dare discharge your weapon. There are civilians everywhere."

Smoke rolled down the window. "Don't you have a siren or something?"

"No, Starsky, I don't."

A grin crept onto Smoke's busted lips. "Just pull alongside."

"What are you going to do?"

"Blow his doors off."

Barreling down the highway one lane over, Sidney caught up with AV.

"Perfect!" Smoke yelled.

AV slammed on his brakes.

The grenade blasted out of the barrel and tore out a section of the guard rail.

"You missed?" Sidney said.

"It happens." Smoke started firing short bursts of bullets. *Takka takka ... takka takka ...*

AV turned the Escalade off at the next exit.

"Great, he figured that plan out," she said, cruising after the SUV. She was three car lengths from the bumper.

"Get closer," Smoke said, shooting out the back windows. "I need to get the wheels."

"No," she said, "he might slam on the brakes."

"You're joking."

"No, wouldn't you do th—"

The SUV's brake lights blared. The huge car started to screech.

Sidney hit the brakes and slung the wheel over to the right. She hit the berm and skidded by until they came to a stop.

"Perfect," Smoke said, crawling out the window. He fired the launcher over the hood.

Toomph!

Inside the cab of the Cadillac, AV's fierce yellow eyes shone like moons. The entire front end of the SUV exploded.

Ka-Boom!

The front of the car was engulfed in flames.

"That ought to do it." She got out of her car.

Smoke approached the burning car and unloaded a few more rounds into it.

Takka takka ... takka takka ....

There was nothing left but a ball of flame and black smoke. Smoke circled with wary eyes, barrel lowered toward the flames. The driver's side door opened with an eerie groan and fell onto the pavement.

AV the werewolf stepped out. All of his fur was smoking.

Smoke let him have it.

Takka takka ... takka takka ...

AV barked a wolfish laugh. "Fools, you can't kill me!" The werewolf's eyes narrowed on Sidney.

She went for the pistol as the monster closed in. She brought the weapon up and fired a blast into the ground where AV once stood.

Hurtling through the air, he landed on top of her. The breath was knocked out of her, and the pistol clattered over the road. AV wrapped his claws around her neck and squeezed. "Goodbye, Pretty!"

Crack!

AV's wolfish head jerked forward.

Smoke locked his rifle under AV's neck and pulled back with both arms. AV released his grip on Sidney.

Gasping for breath, she crawled away.

"Get the gun!" Smoke yelled.

The werewolf bucked and slung like a bull.

Smoke held on to the rifle and rode the werewolf like a cowboy.

Sidney searched for the pistol. A glimmer of metal rested underneath her tire. Snatching it up, she rolled to a knee and took aim. AV now had Smoke in a headlock.

"One shove," AV said, concealed behind Smoke's body, "and I break him. Walk away, and I'll let him live. I'll let both of you live."

She didn't have a clear shot. Little more than half of his head was exposed.

"Take the shot," Smoke sputtered. "You've got to take the shot and forget about me."

"Touching," AV said, applying more pressure to Smoke's head.

The large man's face turned purple. She heard bones popping and cracking.

Her eyes found Smoke's.

His lips spit out two words. "Center mass."

"Time's up, Pretty," AV said. He howled at the moon. "And I don't think you can hit me anyway."

In a burst of motion, Smoke shifted his leg behind the werewolf and flipped him over.

Sidney fired.

Blam!

Both men lay on the road, and only one of them started moving.

Smoke peeled the werewolf's arms off him. Hair, claws, and wolf face retracted. In seconds, Adam Vaughn was back, wearing only shorts made from spandex. He had a bullet hole in his heart. While examining the body, Sidney noted a strange brand on his back shoulder: a rising black sun that seemed to be bleeding.

"Good shot," Smoke said, groaning. "Can I have my gun back now?"

She started to hand it to him and stopped. "I have a question first."

"All right."

"How did you get your hands free, inside AV's office?"

"Diamond dust on my fingernails." He flashed his hands. Where there wasn't blood, they twinkled a little.

"Did you learn that in the SEALs?"

"No, it's from a Punisher comic book."

"Is that from the prison archives, Smoke?"

He smiled. "Finally."

EPILOGUE

THE NIGHT BECAME EVEN LONGER. Fire trucks arrived. Local law enforcement and the FBI followed. No one listened, and Smoke was back in handcuffs. Sidney spent an hour arguing her case, only to have Ted arrive in his brown trench coat and clear things up in five minutes.

"A werewolf?"

"Don't judge me, Ted." She yawned. She didn't really care if he believed it or not. At the moment she was happy to be alive.

"I know, but that corpse looks like a man." He watched the emergency crew bag AV up. "Next time take a picture. Maybe a video. And we wanted him alive."

"I tried. We both tried, sort of." She touched her lip and winced. "At least I don't have prom tomorrow."

"What?" Ted shook his head.

"Nothing. So what happens to him?" she said, looking at Smoke. He was sitting in the back of a police cruiser, all stitched up.

"Back to prison, I guess." Ted patted the hood of her car. "Man, I can't believe you outbid me by a dollar. A dollar! The Hellcat sure is pretty."

Sidney wasn't paying much attention. Her thoughts were on Smoke, AV, deaders, the Black Slate... Many things. But mostly Smoke.

"Go home," Ted said, rubbing her shoulder. "Come in when you feel like it tomorrow."

A wrecker hauled the SUV off and the ambulance pulled out with AV's body.

"I'd rather head back to that hospital."

"Sid, there's a dozen agents over there already. Damned if we didn't find more missing children." He scratched his head. "What you did was a good thing. Another good thing. Take comfort in that. As for your friend, I'll do what I can."

An FBI agent shut the cruiser door on Smoke, got inside the car, and sped away. Her friend had vanished. Her chin dipped and she sighed. Then the rain came down.

The next day, stiff as a board, Sidney headed into the office. Five hours later, she turned in her statement of events to Ted. It was fifteen pages long.

"Geez, Sid." He put on his glasses. "It's just a report, not a bestseller."

She scanned the trophies, pictures, and colorful memorabilia on his wall. "What's the matter? Are you worried it might cut into football?"

"No. Well, yes." He huffed a breath and looked up at her. "Sid, I'm sorry, and I want you to know that I'm glad you're all right. But deaders? What is a deader?" His desk phone rang. He picked it up. "Ted." His face darkened and he hung up. "Dammit." He picked up her report and grabbed his dress coat. "Got to go."

He was gone, leaving her all alone. She slipped out of his office, grabbed her bag, took the elevator, and went to her car. The old Interceptor. *At least it's not raining*. The rattle in the dash was even worse than before. She turned up the radio and headed for Mildred Bates hospital. Driving up the entrance, the first thing she saw was a great yellow crane with a wrecking ball. She pulled into the parking lot, parked, and got out, gaping.

The entire hospital was rubble. A dump truck loaded with debris rode by. The company name and logo, she instantly recognized.

Drake.

Her phone buzzed. A picture of her sister, Allison, and niece, Megan, popped up. The text below it read: Watch your step.

CRAIG HALLORAN

THE SUPERNATURAL
BOUNTY
HUNTER
FILES

I SMELL SMOKE
BOOK 2

CHAPTER 1

B *uzz. Buzz. Buzz.*
Sidney rolled over in her bed and grabbed her phone. The clock read 4:32 am, Tuesday morning. She sat up, rubbed her eyes, punched in her security code, and read the text.

It was from Cyrus Tweel, her new supervisor.

The text read:

Come immediately.

"Aw, crap."

She shuffled toward the bathroom. Inside, she turned on the shower then brushed her teeth until the mirror steamed up. She flung her garments into a hamper, and then, stooped under the showerhead, she let the hot water run down her neck.

Enjoy the little things in life.

The last two months had been lousy. Cyrus Tweel, her ex-boyfriend, had replaced Jack Dydeck as her supervisor. Every time she thought about Jack, she envisioned him sitting there with his head torn off. The funeral for him had been horrible. His wife, Jean, was a waterfall of tears. She could still see one of Jack's boys pounding on the closed coffin saying, "I want to see my daddy. I want to see my daddy." The moment shook her. It shook everybody, it seemed, but no one talked about it.

She lathered up her hair with shampoo and groaned. "Ugh." She rinsed the soap from her eyes. "Great job."

Her old supervisor, Ted Howard, had been elusive since their clash with Adam Vaughn. It was shortly thereafter that Cyrus was named as Jack's replacement, which infuriated her. Cyrus was a solid agent, but he was a suck-up. That was one of the many reasons she had stopped dating him.

She stepped out and began drying off, her thoughts still on the Black Slate. No one spoke about it. She tried to pry at Ted for information, but he gave nothing away. She worked out her frustrations at the gym, hammering away at heavy bags late in the evening. When that didn't work, she always ended up doing midnight searches about the Drake, werewolves, and deaders, trying to fit these things together. Ted had called her out for using FBI resources and tried to put an end to the searches. The trail had gone cold, but she had to keep digging.

She blow-dried her hair, which she'd had cut to a shorter length. She could still feel one of the deader's clammy hands pulling at her locks. It was a nightmare that had awoken her more than once, coated in sweat. Toweling dry, she headed into the cold air of the bedroom that rose goosebumps on her arms, grabbed some clothes, and put them on. Seconds later, she was geared up and inside the kitchen. She flipped on the switch to her coffee brewer and got a warning light.

"Great."

Sidney routinely loaded up the pot the night before and had it set on a timer. Last night wasn't her night however. She'd slogged in the door extra late before pecking at the computer a few hours and crashing on the bed. She refilled the coffee pot, loaded the grounds, and set it to brew. The aroma brought a thin smile to her lips.

Cyrus can wait.

Normally, she'd get a move on, but Cyrus was never satisfied, late or on time. He was much worse than Dydeck: emails, texts—his micro-management methods were overkill.

Maybe I should try another agency.

Five minutes later, she had the coffee in her travel cup and was headed out the door. Nearby, the Interceptor sat covered in a thin layer of frost. She shivered inside the cab, grinding the ignition until the engine fired up. Waiting for it to defrost, she sipped on her coffee. *Waiting's good.*

She texted Cyrus back.

On my way.

He replied:

You should have been here 10 minutes ago!

I can't believe I dated that guy! She put the car in reverse, backed up, slammed it into drive, and sped out of the quiet parking lot onto the highway. She turned on the radio and started singing along with a corny tune. "*I think it's gonna be a great day.*"

CHAPTER 2

"I T'S ABOUT TIME, AGENT SHAW," Cyrus said with a sneer as he checked his watch. The sly man in round spectacles wore a dark blue suit and FBI logo'd tie. His beady eyes were calculating and penetrating. "What did you do, take the bus?"

"Traffic was really bad," she said. They were inside an apartment building that the FBI had been conducting surveillance from, overlooking a small abandoned strip mall. A chain link fence surrounded the facility, including the parking lot. Cameras and other equipment were set up in front of the window. The computers monitored the activities on the streets.

"At five in the morning? Don't feed me that load of crap."

"Just tell me why I'm here," Sidney said, rolling her eyes, "and try to tone down being such a dick."

An agent sitting at a desk snickered.

Cyrus glowered at him, and the guy's neck reddened. Then he turned back to Sidney. "Watch yourself, troop."

"Don't call me that," she said, walking away. "Ever again." She thought about Dydeck. He was a good man, and even though they had avenged him, everything still felt unfinished. "So, a move is about to be made."

"We got a transaction alert from our insider," an agent said. He was a well-knit black man in a blue FBI jacket. His name was Harvey. "The deal should go down this morning." He pointed toward the kitchenette. "Coffee?"

"Sure," she said, taking a Styrofoam cup from the stack.

The case they were on had been going for months, but she'd only been assigned to it a few weeks ago. More drugs. More problems. The cartel's smuggling operations became more sophisticated and refined with each passing day. They were impossible to keep up with. For every player the FBI took down, three more stepped up in his place. No guilt. No shame.

"So," Cyrus said, keeping his voice low and cornering her near the coffee, "you look kind of tired. Were you up all night chasing zombies? Or were they chasing you?"

"Back off, Cyrus."

"I need to make sure you aren't distracted from the mission. Are you?"

She glowered down at him. "The only thing distracting me is you."

He touched her arm, leering at her. "That's my job, Sid."

She pushed past him and stood in front of the monitors, clenching her jaw.

Harv glanced up at her and shrugged. There had been some leaks about what happened with the Adam Vaughn case, and word had spread that Sidney had reported an encounter with a zombie. She had no doubt that Cyrus has seen her report and had something to do with that. He'd been hounding her ever since. She'd hounded Ted about the leak, but he said he had nothing to do with it, so she did her best to ignore it.

"We have some movement," Harv said, adjusting his headset. "White box truck. Two in the cab."

Sydney watched the monitors. The driver hopped out of the truck and unlocked the gate. Back into the truck he went. The truck wheeled around the building and backed into the loading dock of a small abandoned department store. Cameras had been set up at adjacent buildings overlooking a long-gone strip mall.

"I don't want to miss anything," Cyrus said. "Call in a drone."

"Yes, sir," Harv said, typing into his computer. "I'm on it."

Cyrus put a headset on and tossed another set to Sidney. "Gear up," he said.

While she slipped the device on her head, another vehicle pulled inside the fence, a black Corvette.

"That's our man, McCall," Cyrus said. "Must be nice going undercover and flashing all that money. Poor bastard."

"I told you I'd do it," Harv said.

"Maybe next time."

"Count me in too," said another voice in the headset.

"And me," said another. It was a woman. They were all part of the team on the streets.

"All right, let's maintain radio discipline," Cyrus added, crossing his arms over his chest and looming over Harv's shoulder. "This is McCall's third time inside. Something has to go down at some point."

Agent McCall pulled the Corvette around back and alongside the truck. He stepped out with his briefcase in hand and gave a quick nod.

Cyrus clapped his hands. "This is it!"

Sidney's spine tingled. They'd been waiting for the signal for over a month and now it came. *I wish I was down there.* Agent McCall was good, but everyone needed back-up. High caliber traffickers were trigger happy. Agent McCall slipped out of sight, either into the building or into the truck.

The room fell quiet for a moment, then Cyrus broke the silence.

"Everyone breathe easy. This might take a while. Lacy and Carl, do either of you have an angle on McCall?"

"No."

"Ditto."

"Just remember," Cyrus continued, "once they start rolling out, McCall will send another signal, so no one get jumpy until I say go. They're probably checking for a wire now."

The operation wasn't the biggest, but it was important. The traffickers dealt in arms, munitions, and drugs. The men McCall dealt with weren't high up the chain either, but their bosses were, and that was who the FBI wanted. Get names. Get voices, and have it all recorded by a small device built into the handle of a briefcase.

"How's our signal?"

"Solid," Harv said, leaning forward, "let's hope it's recording."

"Hope's for sissies," Cyrus said, smiling over at Sidney.

Such a tool.

Five minutes turned into ten and then fifteen. Cyrus started to pace, saying from time to time, "Be patient everybody. The last few months are down to the final minutes."

Sidney's palms were sweating. *This is taking too long.* She checked her watch. 5:38 am.

"We've got movement," said one of the outside agents.

The box truck was pulling out of the dock.

"Any eyes on McCall?"

"Negative."

The box truck sped up the ramp. A spark of light on the monitors was mirrored by sharp pops of gunfire. McCall was holding his side, staggering up the ramp and blasting away in the dark.

Cyrus cried out, "Stop that truck! Execute!"

CHAPTER 3

S IDNEY BOLTED FOR THE DOOR.

"Hold it, Agent Shaw," Cyrus said, grabbing her by the arm.

She twisted out of his grasp. "Are you insane?"

"No, I'm in charge. Now stay in here!"

With an inner growl, Sidney returned to her spot behind the monitors.

Three FBI SUVs sped through the gates, and two more blocked the entrance. The box truck weaved through the parking lot in chase until one of the SUVs slammed into the driver's side. In seconds, agents in body armor and holding M-16 rifles had the truck surrounded. The drivers exited the box truck with their hands up. Instantly, the agents took them to the ground.

"Now that's a clean takedown," Cyrus said with a nod. "And I'm not even breathing heavy. Well done everyone. Someone get to McCall, pronto."

Sidney's nails dug into her palms. It was hard to watch something like this from afar and not get involved. On the screen, she watched FBI agents rushing to McCall's side. Inside her headset she heard one say, "It's bad, but he's breathing."

"All right, get him stabilized. An ambulance is on its way." Cyrus slapped Harv on the shoulder. He had a worried look in his eye. "Good work. We'll go check it out. Come on, Agent Shaw."

Finally. She followed him out the door and down the stairs. By the look of things, Cyrus had taken control and bottled up what could have otherwise been a very ugly situation. Of course, that all depended on whether McCall survived or not. Clearly something had gone wrong. *Let's see how he handles it.*

Rushing out of the stairwell and across the street, they cut between the cars blocking the gate.

"Ambulance coming," Cyrus said, slapping one of the hoods. "Move these things!"

Jogging across the parking lot, they came on the scene. Two men lay on the ground, hands cuffed behind their backs. Each wore nice street clothes. One was tattooed and bald. The other was taller, long-haired, and lanky. Each had an edge about him.

Cyrus kneeled down, grabbed the taller one by his locks, and said, "My agent better not die."

Somehow, the man shrugged. "The only good agent is a dead agent."

Cyrus stuffed the man's face in the cement and ground it in a little.

"Sir," one of the other agents said, "Come take a look at this?"

The thugs stirred on the ground, watching Cyrus walk over. Sidney made her way behind him, stopping at the back of the box truck that was wide open. Inside were munition crates and round blue barrels. Seated along the wall and wide-eyed were children.

"Aw," Cyrus said, rubbing the back of his head, "are you shitting me?" He shook his head and activated his Blue-tooth. "Call Child Services too." An ambulance with flashing lights roared into the parking lot and sped by, stirring the wind. "How's McCall?" No reply. "Carl. Lacy. What is the status on McCall?"

Carl's voice was flat. "He didn't make it, sir."

"Dammit," Cyrus whispered. Everyone's chin dipped a little.

Sidney felt her heart sink. McCall was one of their best agents. Flashy. Confident. Well-liked. His loss was a wound. Like Dydeck's.

"Heh heh heh," said the bald thug lying in the parking lot. "What's the matter, agent? Pretty Boy didn't make it? Heh heh heh … that's what you get for trying to fool us. But it looks like we fooled you."

"Somebody shut him up," Cyrus said, turning his back and rubbing his temples.

"I hear you agents have been dying like flies around here lately," said the other dealer.

Sidney's heart skipped. Something about the way the man said it jolted her. She fastened her eyes on the men and said to one of the agents, "Did you get them patted down?"

"Yes, ma'am."

"I don't think they did a very thorough job," the bald one said. He winked. "How about you come on over and pat me down, sugar. I'm pretty sure they missed my crotch, and besides, my balls are itching. Heh heh."

Sidney walked over, squatted down, and put her knee in his back. She grabbed his thumb and twisted it.

"Yeow!" the dealer cried out.

"Are they still itching?"

"Yes!" he spit out.

She cranked up the pressure.

"Argh!"

"How about now?"

"No," he puffed. "No, dammit!"

Just as she released him, she noticed a mark inside the palm of his hand, a black sun dripping blood. A sliver of ice raced down her spine, making her toes tingle. It was the same mark she had seen at the hospital where she encountered the deaders and Adam Vaughn. *This can't be a coincidence.*

"Sid," Cyrus barked at her. "Get over here."

She hated the sneering tone Cyrus used on her. It riled her up. She walked up to him and said, "Don't 'get' me again."

"Fine. Will you just take custody of the children and sort them out before Child Services arrives?"

"Sure, you're the boss."

Inside the box truck, some of the agents had cracked open the crates: assault rifles, ammo, grenades, and bags of pills and powders. It was enough to start or incapacitate a small army. Sidney climbed into the truck and crawled among the children. Each was ragged, dirty—and hungry, by the looks of them. "I'm Agent Shaw, and I'm here to help you. Can you tell me your names?"

A small black boy with lighter skin, maybe eight years old, spoke up first. "My name is James." He cocked his head and touched her cheek with a gentle hand. "Your hair is different."

She pulled back and put her hand inside his. It was fragile and cold. "I'm not sure that I follow, James. What do you mean, different?"

"I think it was longer last time."

Sidney's memory flashed. James's face was suddenly familiar. He was one of the children she and Smoke had rescued from Ray Cline's joint back in October. *Sonuvabitch, this can't be happening!* She scooped the boy up in her arms. "Cyrus, we have another problem."

CHAPTER 4

INSIDE HER CUBICLE, SIDNEY HAMMERED at the keyboard. *This doesn't make any sense.* She'd sent emails. Made inquiries. But the children she'd rescued months earlier had disappeared into the system. She snapped the pencil in her hand and tossed it in the trash. "Dammit."

"You okay?" a woman said, walking up behind her. It was Sadie, a black co-worker, a little heavy, in a plum pantsuit. She had a warmth about her. "Because I don't think your keyboard can take much more."

Sidney spun around in her chair. "It's that noticeable?"

Sadie set down her coffee mug that had a picture of two children on it. She rested her rear end on Sidney's desk. "So what's going on? It's Cyrus, isn't it? You and him are a thing again, aren't you?"

"No," Sidney said shaking her head. "Lord no."

"Good. Because I don't like him."

"Does anybody?"

"True," Sadie said, hoisting up her coffee cup. "So, fill me in."

"Aw, just a dead end on those kids is all. Makes me wonder who's protecting the children from Protective Services."

"You don't actually think they're going to be very forthcoming about losing children, do you? After all, it is just another government agency."

"One that loses children?"

"Well, maybe they didn't. Maybe it was the foster home."

"They can't ever tell me anything about that." Sidney shook her head and clenched her fists. "I could just punch somebody."

"You know, Sid, you've been pretty frustrated lately. Are you seeing anybody?"

"What do you mean?"

"What do you mean, what do I mean? Are you getting any?"

No!

"Come on," Sadie continued with a smile. "It's just us girls talking."

"I don't have the time."

"Hah, you're single. You've got the time. Me and Reggie have two children: baseball, football, soccer, basketball," Sadie huffed, "not to mention coaching, shopping, cleaning, and cooking. And we find the time. Heck, we make the time, else we'd kill each other."

"That's different. You're married."

"And you're single." Sadie leaned closer. "A long time single, and the longer you stay single, the longer you're going to be single. Don't get set in those ways, else you're going to be an old maid forever."

"No, I won't."

"That's what my sister says, and guess what—still single. And every time she finds a good man, she picks him apart. She's set in her ways."

Great warm-up. I'm going to have to listen to this same crap from Mom over Christmas.

"You know," Sadie said, peeking around, "there's some new faces around here that I'd love to introduce you to."

"I'll never date another agent."

"They aren't *all* agents. Most of them are just nerds, college boys wanting to change the world. Look down this way." Sadie motioned her over, peering around the cubicle. "That's Greg. Blond hair. Blue eyes. Nice butt in those trousers."

Sidney wheeled her chair and looked down the aisle. "I don't see anybody."

Sadie started laughing. "You looked. Ha ha. Sid, you need a man even worse than I thought you did."

Sidney slapped Sadie's leg. "You witch!"

"Don't be disappointed. There is a Greg, as described. I'll introduce you to him."

Sid pushed back toward her desk. "No thanks. I need a matchmaker I can trust."

"Aw, that's cold. You know you can trust me."

"And why's that?"

"Cause I ain't a man."

"No, but you're just as ornery. See you around, Sadie," she said, turning around.

"Say, I didn't come over here to rile you. I want to help." Sadie looked over her shoulder. "I have a close cousin in Child Protective Services. Why don't you give me something so I can snoop around?"

Sadie was an executive secretary who had as much authorization and access as most field agents. She'd proven to be very helpful on more than one occasion, not to mention that she did most of the supervisors' and assistant directors' work for them.

Sidney jotted down some names and contacts on a legal pad, tore it off, and handed it to her. "Thanks."

Sadie snatched it out of her grip and said, "You're welcome."

Glad that's out of my hair. The last thing I need is to be reminded that I don't have a boyfriend or husband. There'll be plenty of that talk tomorrow. Ugh. She enjoyed the holidays, but things would be a little tense dealing with her sister, Allison, who was still holed up at her parents', along with Sidney's niece, Megan. Sid had made one visit for Thanksgiving, and it had turned ugly. Allison didn't hide her resentment of Sid.

Her desk phone rang. Ted Howard's name popped up. She hadn't met with him in weeks. She picked up the receiver. "Agent Shaw."

"Sid, can you swing by?" Ted sounded a little tense.

"Sure, when?"

"Now would be ideal."

"Okay, I'll be right—" The line went dead, "There? Great." Normally, Ted gave her a heads up on what he wanted to talk about. But not today. The tension in his voice left her uneasy. She picked up her bag and got up out of her seat. A nice-looking younger man was standing behind her in a white oxford shirt, burgundy checked tie, and khaki pants.

Morning glory. He's fresh out of the frat house.

"Hi," he said, rubbing the back of his blond head. "I'm Greg. Uh, Sadie says you need to see me. She says your computer needs a tune-up."

Sidney laughed out loud.

"I'm missing something," he said, swallowing. His eyes glanced down at her chest.

"Apparently not," she said, disappointed. "And my computer's just fine. Nice meeting you, Greg." She walked by Sadie's desk on the way to Ted's office, one floor up from hers. "Nice try, Sadie. It only took him five seconds to glue his eyes on my boobs." She kept going.

Sadie hollered after her, "You can't fault a young man for looking when you have a body like that, you prude."

Sid made her way to the elevator, laughing inside. Normally, her suit jacket concealed her ample curves. And it was a rare day when she wore a skirt. Waiting at the elevator, she noticed a few agents approaching. *No time for chit chat.* She took the steps and made her way to Ted's floor, stopping at his secretary's desk.

"Go on in, Sidney. He told me he was expecting you."

"Should I knock?"

"No, go on in," the secretary said, eyeing her up and down. "I like that outfit. Why don't you dress like that more often?"

Sidney grabbed the door handle and started her way inside. "Because I work here."

Inside, Ted was sitting at his desk with a stern expression on his face. Filling one of the two chairs in front of him was a man with short dark hair in a grey suit. Both men stood up as she entered and closed the door behind her. The man in the grey suit turned and fastened his engaging eyes on hers. Her heart skipped under his heavy gaze.

Glorious morning!

CHAPTER 5

"HELLO, AGENT SHAW," SAID SMOKE. His presence seemed to fill up the office. "How have you been?" The tall man's suit coat bulged in the arms.

"Never better," Sidney said, taking the open seat in front of Ted's desk. "Looks like prison life has been treating you well. Did you make that suit in there yourself?"

"It was either this or vanity license plates."

"I see," she said, turning her focus to Ted. "So you surprised me. Care to fill me in?"

"The Black Slate is back on the table," Ted said, taking a black file folder from his drawer. "They appreciated the thoroughness of your report."

Sidney reached for the folder, but Ted pulled it back. She said, "Who appreciated the thoroughness of my report?"

"You'll know when they want you to know."

"Come on, Ted. It's been two months already, and now it's suddenly back on the table."

"Things take time. It could have been longer. But you two are back on it. At least, Mister Smoke has agreed to it."

"So you two have visited?" She narrowed her eyes on Ted. She'd been left in the dark again.

"We talked," Ted said, loosening his tie.

"In person or over the phone?"

"Sid, don't start this."

"First," she said, poking her finger into his desk, "you send me in to recruit him. Then, I'm sent out to hunt werewolves with him only to have him slammed back in prison again, and not a single word about it until now. I don't work like this, not with you. Not with anyone."

Ted leaned forward, resting his big elbows on the table. "Don't think you are the only one being put in an unusual predicament, Sid. You get your orders. You follow them. Or did you forget that?"

"This is why I'm a civilian," Smoke interjected.

Sidney shook her head. She hated being left in the dark about anything. Even worse, just when she'd managed to bury her memories of Smoke and everything that happened at Mildred Bateman hospital, it all cropped up again, like a volcano blasting out memories and emotion. "I'm sorry," she said to Smoke, "but didn't you volunteer for this?"

"The food's still better outside of prison."

"You don't look like you've missed any meals."

"Thanks for noticing."

She turned back to Ted. "Why the secrecy, Ted? Why?"

"They," Ted said, "who it seems I can't not mention, wanted to wait until the end of this last assignment of yours was resolved."

"And this revolves around me how?"

"As I am told, you and Mister Smoke are the first to bring in a member of the Black Slate in ten years."

"So there are other werewolves."

Ted rolled his eyes. "Man, I really hate that word. But, no, not a werewolf, just another wanted criminal. I don't know much more than you do, but I do know that."

"So I guess we aren't getting any government-issued silver bullets?" she asked.

"Aw," Ted grunted, "let's forget that last bounty and talk about the new one." He pushed the file over. "Shall we?"

Sidney snatched it up. "Hold on a second, Ted. What about the case I'm on? I can't just walk away from it. We found one of the same kids that we picked up from Ray Cline."

"We did?" Smoke said, sitting up.

"I did," Sidney added.

"Cyrus will handle that, Sid," Ted warned. "Drop it."

"I'm not going to drop it. Children are in danger. Something is wrong with the system."

"It's being taken care of."

"No it isn't."

"Sid, you have to have faith in the system."

She sat back and groaned. She'd heard that plenty of times. For the most part, the system did hold together, but in this case something was wrong. Really wrong. "I'd rather stick to the case I'm on." She looked at Smoke. "No offense."

"She doesn't play, then I don't play," Smoke said.

Ted rose out of his chair, and with a raised voice, he said, "Let me remind you that neither one of you have a choice in the matter. Mister Smoke—"

"Call me Smoke."

"*Mister* Smoke, it's the Black Slate or you go back to staring at the grey slate, not to forget the time in solitary you have coming... "

Solitary? Why would he have solitary? Sidney noticed a nasty scrape on the right side of his face that was a little swollen.

"... and you, Agent Shaw, will follow orders or be faced with insubordination. Now don't buck me on this. If I could give you another assignment, I would, but I can't. It's this or nothing. Nothing being, you might be out of a job," he said to her, "and you might go back to prison even longer," he said to Smoke. "Do I have your cooperation or not?"

Smoke shrugged.

"Sir, yes, Sir!" Sidney mocked.

"Don't push me, Sid. Don't push me."

She could see Ted's harsh expression drain a little. He didn't like this any more than she did. He had orders, and he'd follow them. It was just the way the chain of command worked, and in the grand scheme of things they were all way down on the pecking order. She opened the black file folder. Inside was the portrait of a beautiful lustrous-haired woman with a wicked look. "Interesting."

"Her name is Angi Harlow," Ted said with a sigh, "also known as Night Bird."

Smoke leaned over and glanced at the picture. "Why do they call her Night Bird?"

"I don't know," Ted mumbled, uneasy. "Maybe she can fly or something."

Sidney shuffled through the pictures. There were more crime scenes. Drug labs. Munitions. Blood. She swallowed hard. There were dead bodies too. Some disemboweled. Others in bits and pieces. The last photo was of a man, dead in a cemetery. His eyes were missing from a body half covered in ravens. Sidney's chest tightened. *This is not normal.* She glanced up at Smoke.

"Let's go find her nest," he said, "and burn it."

CHAPTER 6

"**Y**OU AREN'T BURNING ANYTHING," TED said. "Bring her in alive."

"And we have how much time to do this?" Sidney asked.

"Mister Smoke's out for two more weeks, and the clock has already started."

"Now?" Sid said. "My leave starts at the end of the day, and it's Christmas Eve tomorrow."

"Figure it out," Ted said, taking his seat and fumbling through his desk. "And thanks for reminding me." He punched keys on his desk phone. "Jane, where's my gift?"

"Bottom drawer on the left," said his secretary.

Ted reached down and produced a small flat box wrapped in bright colors. "Ah, very nice." He got up, walked across the office, and put on his coat and hat. He opened the door, turned to Sid, and said, "Everything you need to know is in the file."

"Sir, what am I supposed to do with him?" she said, throwing her thumb back at Smoke.

"You'll figure it out." Ted gestured for them to leave. "Let's go. The bad guys don't stop just because it's the holidays."

Sidney headed out of the office with Smoke right behind. *Man, this is so weird.*

"Jane," Ted said, "I'll be back in Monday. Merry Christmas everybody."

Sid saw Jane watching Ted's lumbering form dash for the steps and disappear through the doorway. Jane sighed and shook her head then glanced over at Smoke. Her smiling eyes were filled with him. Sidney tapped his arm. "We have to go."

"Sure," he said. "Nice meeting you, Jane."

"You too, Mister Smoke." She batted her eyelashes. "I hope I see you again soon."

"Come on," Sidney said, taking him by the elbow and steering him down the hall. She began nosing through the file as they headed down the stairs. The black file folder was almost a half inch thick. It had a white tab on it marked Harlow. There were names, dates, pictures, and locations. The main thing that caught her eye was the Drake logo. That and another. A black sun.

"Can I see that?"

"No," she said, pushing her way through the elevator door and heading for her desk. As soon as she got there, she put on her jacket. Smoke was watching her. His handsome face stared right into her eyes. "What?"

"You seem rattled."

Pull it together, Sid. Man, he looks nice in a suit.

She plopped down in her chair. "I'm not really big on one-eighties. Pull over a seat, why don't you."

Smoke reached across the aisle and dragged a four-legged chair into her cubicle and sat down.

"Okay," she said, scooting away, "not exactly built for two." She took half the papers out of the file and handed them over to Smoke. A sealed envelope fell out, marked Shaw. Smoke beat her to it. She snagged it away. "For my eyes only."

Inside, she found another letter like the last one, on old Bureau letterhead. It said almost the exact same thing.

Agent Shaw,

Due to the unorthodox arrangement of this assignment, you will need to keep the following items under consideration.

John Smoke is a convicted criminal with special skills. Don't underestimate him. He's dangerous. Unpredictable. Possible escape risk.

You have eyes on him and we have eyes on him. Allow him free range. We'll let you know if he needs reeling in.

If any alien objects or circumstances or individuals are encountered, you should notify your superiors immediately.

Seek Mal Carlson for assistance when needed.

Shadow cover authorized.

Trust your instincts and good hunting,

The Bureau

Whoa! Shadow cover? Who is Mal Carlson?

"What does it say?" Smoke said without glancing up from his papers. "Let me guess. I'm a dangerous criminal who can't be trusted, and if any strange circumstances arise, then notify your superiors immediately."

Sidney stuffed it back in the envelope. "It says if you don't do whatever I say, I get to shoot you."

"I like the sound of that."

"What, me shooting you?"

"No, me doing whatever you say."

Sidney flushed around the collar. "Let's get something to eat." She took his papers and put them in the folder and stuck it inside her satchel. "I imagine you're up for some pancakes."

"I was thinking milkshakes."

"Come on." As soon as she started up, a voice interrupted.

"Who do we have here?" Sadie said, warming up to Smoke with her hand extended.

He rose from his chair, took her hand, and said, "I'm Smoke."

"No, you're smoking."

"Sadie!"

"What? He is."

Sidney pushed Smoke toward the elevator. "We're going."

"Where you going? I want to come too," Sadie said, "My lunchtime just started."

"We aren't coming back."

"Now that's my girl," Sadie said with a smile. "Glad to know you're listening to your sister Sadie."

Leading Smoke away, Sidney whirled back and whispered harshly at her friend, "You're filthy."

Sadie walked away laughing.

It left Sidney smiling, but she caught herself as she turned around and entered the elevator with Smoke. They had made it down one floor when the door opened. A man with frosty eyes entered. *Morning glory!* It was her supervisor, Cyrus Tweel.

CHAPTER 7

"**W**HAT DO WE HAVE HERE?**" Cyrus sneered as the elevator doors closed. "And what's the convict doing here?"

Smoke wedged himself between Sidney and Cyrus.

Cyrus leaned right; Smoke leaned right. He went left; Smoke went left. It almost made Sidney giggle. "I have new orders," she said, fanning the file out in front of Cyrus's face.

"My ass you do. You're still on a case."

I love pissing him off. "Take it up with Ted."

"Black Slate file, huh. Will you get out of my way, you goon!"

Smoke poked him in the chest, knocking Cyrus back a little. "I haven't forgotten about that injection you gave me."

"You lay another finger on me—"

Smoke crowded him against the buttons. "I'll break you."

Cyrus pushed back. "Back off, troglodyte."

"That's enough, Smoke," Sidney said. "Cyrus!"

"I'm guessing you two are going on another zombie hunt. Hah." Cyrus tightened his tie. "What a joke."

"What's the matter, Cyrus? You can't handle being in the dark on this one?"

"I know more than you know about, Sid." The elevator opened, and he stepped out. "And just so you know, I took a pass on it. It's a joke, and so are you and your ex-con—" The doors closed.

Smoke was shaking his head.

"What?" she said.

"I can't believe you dated that guy."

"Why do you care?" she said, grinding her teeth.

"It's such a mismatch, is all."

"I'd think you'd have figured out by now that it didn't work out."

"I've figured it out, but I'm pretty sure he hasn't. He eyes you like chattel."

"Chattel?"

"You know—"

"I know what chattel is." The elevator doors split apart, and out she went, with Smoke close on her heels. "A little space, if you don't mind."

"Sure," he said, eyeing the lobby of the FBI building. It wasn't the J. Edgar but one of the larger post-modern satellite offices a few miles outside DC.

"Just to be sure," she said, "you didn't drive, did you?"

"No. Are you still in the Interceptor?" He scooted ahead and opened the exit door for her.

That was nice. "Yep," she said, stepping outside into the biting cold. "Tell you what, I'll let you scrape the frost off the windows."

"It would be my pleasure."

I do not understand this man. Smoke's actions had been very contrary to everything she'd read about him in his file—and in those strange letters, too. His military record made him out to be an insubordinate hot head. A loose cannon. For the most part, he'd been nothing but amiable and reliable. To her at least. *He's playing me. He must be.* "It's pretty cold," she said, "you still in the mood for a milkshake?"

"I thought I said *milkshakes?*"

Geez, he's corny. She popped the trunk open and tossed him a scraper. "Work up that appetite, big boy." *Did I just call him big boy? Why did I say that?* Inside the car, she fired up the engine and turned on the heat. Her phone buzzed. It was her mom, Sally. *To answer, or not to answer.* With a sigh she picked up. "Hi, Mom."

"We're eating at four tomorrow." Her mother's voice was as sweet as it was lovely, but it had a pressing tone about it.

"I know, you told me."

"What's the matter, Sidney? You don't sound so well. You're still coming."

"I just got a new assignment, and I have to tidy things up."

"Don't you dare show up late, Sidney. I need you here." Sally started to whisper. "Allison is such lousy help, but Megan shows promise."

"I'll get there as soon as I can."

"You have to be here to help me cook. It's tradition."

In truth, Sally did all of the cooking while Sidney stood around listening to her talking. She was pretty sure most everything was ready already.

"I'll do my best." She covered the phone and moaned. It wasn't that she didn't want to be home with her family. She did, but Allison made for such a distraction. *I've got to be there for Mom and Dad. They'd be there for me.*

"We had some excitement around here the other day," Sally said. "A very nice man stopped by and said he was in the area looking at properties."

"Uh-huh."

"Of course we told him that we weren't interested in selling, but he was very, oh, how would you call it—suave. He seemed European. Very persistent."

"Mom, I've told you about people that run these scams. Business people like that don't just show up at your front door." *Sheesh.* "Did he try to sell you a security system too?"

"Why no, but he said his company would pay good money, and you know how much your father talks about moving to Florida this time of year."

"I wish I was in Florida this time of year," she mumbled.

"What was that?"

"Nothing. You didn't invite him in, did you?"

"It would have been rude not to, and besides your father was here." Sally sighed. "They spent an hour talking about the Redskins. The only Redskins I like are the kind that have potatoes in them. That's what I told him. The man almost spit up his tea from laughing so hard."

"Listen, Mom, quit letting strangers in. These are dangerous times we live in." Her palms became clammy as she thought about the text she had received with a picture of Megan that read

Watch your step.

Smoke opened the car door and slumped into the passenger's seat, jostling the car. He started blowing into his icy red hands.

Sidney clicked the heater up a notch.

"All right, I'll see you tomorrow, Mom."

"Wait, wait a second," Sallie said, still hanging on the line. "This man is legit. He even left a business card."

"Those aren't exactly hard to come by, Mom."

"It says Edwin Lee. And the nice logo reads ..."

Sidney lurched up in her seat as soon as her mom finished the sentence.

"... Drake Properties."

CHAPTER 8

"**I** HEARD THAT," SMOKE SAID WITH a concerned tone.

"Heard what?"

"Your Mom talks pretty loud. So, let's get up there and find out what's going on."

"Excuse me, but I'll be dropping you off, or you can get out of the car now."

"Sidney, who are you talking to?" Sally said on the other end of the line.

"Nothing, Mother. I'll see you soon." She hung up her phone, backed the car out of her spot, and sped away.

"I think I should come with you," Smoke insisted. "Anything that involves Drake is tied to our cases."

Sidney wasn't going to admit it, but she didn't really hate the idea.

"I'm dropping you off."

Smoke tossed his duffle bag into the back seat. "I'd rather you didn't. I can help."

"Maybe you should take some time to visit with family."

"I can't. Just like you, I have my orders." He buckled his seatbelt. "Just tell me what Sally said."

Sidney scowled at him. "How'd you know my mother's name?"

"You know I have my ways."

"It's kind of rude, don't you think?"

"You know everything about me, don't you? My parents. Place of birth. Every military mission?"

"I'm authorized to know that."

"That doesn't exactly seem fair now, does it?"

Sort of yes. Sort of no. "You'll get over it." She switched lanes and merged onto the interstate, then glanced over at him. "What happened to your face?"

"Oh, this." He brushed his fingers over the ragged scar. "It seems Drake has many accomplices in prison. They came after me when I asked too many questions."

Sidney's chest tightened. "What kind of questions?"

"There were a few dudes with those black-sun tattoos." He shrugged. "They weren't very forthcoming. It's okay now."

"What did Ted mean about you going into solitary confinement?"

"Well, after the fight—"

"Fight? What fight?"

"You know, the four of them cornering the one of me fight." He rubbed his scabbed knuckles. "It landed me two weeks in solitary and four of them in the hospital, but"—he smiled—"they still have solidary coming."

It made her uneasy. Were they coming after her, too? Why?

"I'm sorry to hear that."

"I'm fine. It wasn't anything I couldn't handle, considering the last scrap I was in."

"You're talking about AV."

"Yep."

Damn. I hate being reminded of him. She squeezed the wheel until her knuckles turned white. *Damn evil people. Don't swear about it. They aren't worth it. Morning Glory! I hate evil people! That doesn't exactly work, either.* "You'll be fine on your own, I assume?"

He shrugged. "I think Fat Sam and Guppy have a Christmas tree."

"What does that have to do with anything?"

"I just haven't been out for Christmas in a while. And I know a few places that make a decent home-cooked-like meal. There's this one place called Humphreys. It's all pine walls, stone fireplaces, and baskets of buttered hot rolls."

"It sounds wonderful."

"It would be if I was with my family." He tapped on the dash. "But it's better alone there than in the hole in prison. You know, I never thought about it, but it's always possible this could be my last Christmas. After all, you never know what this new mark, uh, what's her name, Black Bird? No telling what might be in store for us, considering what we ran into the last time."

What he said made her mad. Not because of him but because her heart ached a little. It made her think of the first time she had missed Christmas with her family. It had been her first military mission, and she had thought she would never make it home ever again. "Fine," Sidney said in almost a growl, "you can come with me."

"I appreciate it," he said, nodding. "So, I take it Sally's a good cook?"

"Yes, very good." Sidney floated the car down the next exit and re-entered the interstate, heading north. Her mom would have a hundred questions for Smoke. And even more for her. "My mom's pretty nosy, so keep it professional."

"I will," he said. "So, can you tell me a little more about what she said on the phone about Drake?"

"Edwin Lee. That was the man's name."

Smoke produced a phone from his pocket and started to text.

"What are you doing?" Sidney said.

"Checking in with Fat Sam and Guppy. They worry about me."

"That's a load of crap," she said. "You don't share confidential information."

"That's not confidential. It wasn't in the file, was it?"

"No, but I have another file, my trust file, and you just broke it. I'll check into this with my own sources. "

"Aw ... I'm sorry. But you can't trust your sources. That's how they track what we do."

"Tough. No more sharing our information." She held her hand out. "Now give me the phone."

"What?" he pulled it away. "No, it was hard to get this burned."

"Hand it over."

"No."

"You just lost my trust," she said. "Do you want to earn it back?"

"Maybe."

She made his window go down. The icy air battered the cabin.

"What are you doing?" Smoke said. He tried to roll up the window, but she had it locked.

"Chuck it."

"Why?"

"I told you why. Now chuck it."

"You're being a bit extreme, aren't you?"

"I have trust issues." She glowered at him.

Smoke sighed and tossed it out the window.

Good boy! "Excellent," she said, rolling up his window. "If I want you to have a phone, I'll get you one. Do you understand?"

"No, no I don't understand, but I'll live with it, your worshipfulness." He glanced at the semi-truck passing by. Its wheels were kicking up slush and salt from the road, coating the windshield. "Say, that truck ... can you see the logo on it?"

Sidney turned up the wipers. "No. Why?" The semi-truck, passing on the left, swerved into her lane. She pumped the brakes and rode onto the berm.

The truck kept coming, sideswiping the Interceptor. *Wham!* Metal groaned and popped.

Sidney slammed on the brakes. The car's front end caught up underneath the trailer, and the semi-truck wheels ran over the hood, crushing it. The car did a three-sixty, spun across the road, and careened into a ditch. The air bags deployed with loud pops, busting her in the nose. Stunned and bleeding, she heard Smoke saying, "Are you okay? Are you okay?"

CHAPTER 9

THE ENGINE CAUGHT FIRE, AND the interior started to fill with grey smoke. Sidney's fingers fumbled over her seatbelt as the heat rose. It wouldn't unbuckle.

"Hang on," Smoke said.

She started coughing. Smoke sawed at her belt with a knife. "Get the folder. The folder's in my bag!" she said. The belt came loose, and Smoke dragged her out through the passenger door.

Whoosh!

The entire car went up in flames.

"The folder," she said, coughing. "Put me down. We need that file folder. It's in my bag." She rushed back toward the car.

Smoke caught her by the arm. "Let it go," he said. "It's over. We're lucky to be alive after that hit."

Sidney watched the Interceptor go up in flames. Bright orange flames and black smoke rolled out from under the hood and through the windows. She had thought about torching it herself on more than one occasion. It was a good way for a bad car to go. Still, it shouldn't have caught fire and burned like that.

"Here," Smoke said, handing her cell phone to her. "I saved this."

"Thanks," she said, taking it and sliding it into her pocket. "Say, what were you saying before that truck ran into us?"

"I was saying that the truck, the black semi, was marked Drake Transportation Industries."

After the first fire engine arrived, it took four more hours to clear the scene. Covered in a blanket, Sidney was cold, stiff, and sore. She rubbed her head. Speaking to the officer on scene, she finished off the last of her statement. "Mind if I take a look at what's left of my car?" The tow driver was loading it up on the trailer. "Sentimental, you know."

"I don't think there's much left to see," he said, taking the report. "And you probably should go to a hospital."

"I'm okay." She limped toward the tow truck, grimacing. A fireman in a yellow coat and hard hat was standing there. "You see many cars after a wreck go up in flames like that?"

"It happens all the time in the movies but not so much in DC—or on a Crown Vic. Those are pretty safe cars. That's why cops used them. A decade ago." He tipped his hat at her. "But I've seen stranger things happen."

"Thanks," she said. She turned to the tow truck driver. He was a burly roughneck in dirty overalls. "What about you? Have you seen many cars go up in flames?"

He spat juice on the sludgy ground. "It happens. But it's odd how some of the metal just melted. Like there was an accelerant or something. I've seen paints and coating that burn like hot welds." He spat again. "That was back in my military days." He winked at her. "Hush hush. You didn't hear it from me." He hopped into his cab, hung his waving arm out the window, and said, "So long."

The tow truck pulled away, revealing Smoke standing on the other side. He had his duffle bag strapped over his shoulder. Patting it and saying, "Fireproof," he walked up and handed her what was left of her satchel. "Not fireproof. I peeled what I could off the carpet."

The satchel was charred leather, but a few pages from the file folder remained intact. She rubbed her head. "Are they trying to kill us or scare us?"

"I don't think it makes much of a difference to them."

Angry, she set her jaw. "Well, it makes a difference to me."

The police officer from a moment earlier was waving them over to his sedan. He said, "Do you two want a lift or not? I've got things to do."

Sidney sulked in the back seat. At her side, Smoke was oddly quiet and staring out the window. She'd given the policeman directions to the storage yard that housed her Dodge Hellcat. On Smoke's advice, she'd sent a text to Ted stating that the accident was only a fender bender and she had other means of transportation. *Screw 'em*, she thought. *They aren't completely honest with me, so I won't be completely honest with them.*

It was 7:32 pm when the officer dropped them off. "Are you sure you don't need anything else?"

"We're fine," she said. "Thanks, Officer Parrish."

"No problem, ma'am."

Within the next five minutes she had the Hellcat pulled out and was speeding down the highway. She passed the spot where they crashed. *Better their car than mine. RIP Interceptor.*

Sidney fumed inwardly in silence the entire ride home. Someone was coming after her, her family, and her friends. It was personal now, and all she could think of was Congressman Wilhelm's last words. "Watch your step." *Perhaps I need to pay him a visit.*

"We'll take it to them, Agent Shaw," Smoke said, resting his head against the glass and closing his eyes. "You can count on it."

She eased the car off the highway and onto a gravel road dusted in snow. It winded two miles deep through the woods until they passed by two stone pylons. The gravel road jostled Smoke from his snoring.

He sat up. "Are you a farm girl or something?"

"I think you probably already know the answer to that is no."

Ahead, some red and white lights were flashing. She wheeled around the curve and came to a stop on the edge of the gravel driveway to her parents' home. An ambulance was parked in front of the garage.

"Good Lord," Sidney said, rushing out of the car. "What now?"

CHAPTER 10

S IDNEY RUSHED INTO THE HOUSE. Her first fear was that her sister had overdosed. Instead, she found her father sprawled out on his recliner, surrounded by two paramedics.

"Will you get away from me!" Keith wore a brick-colored flannel shirt under a pair of jean overalls. The sleeves were rolled up. His grey hair was a frizzled mess. "Sally, why did you do this? I'm fine, I tell you. I'm fine."

Sally stood nearby wringing her hands. Her frosty blonde hair was up in a bun, and she wore a plum-colored apron. "You hush, Keith. I'm not having you die on me."

"I'm not dying," he growled back, rolling his eyes. "It's heartburn, I tell you."

"You're all clammy," Sally argued.

"You need to clam up. I told you I was fine." Keith rolled his thick neck around and saw Sidney. "Sid!" His face brightened. "Will you arrest these men?"

"Sidney!" Sally exclaimed, rushing over and grasping her arm. "Talk some sense into him."

"What happened?" she asked.

"He collapsed on the sofa."

"I did not," Keith said. "I just tripped because I felt a little dizzy, and your mother went into a panic." He glared at one of the blue-clad paramedics. "Let me go."

"His blood pressure is high," one of the paramedics said. She was a no-nonsense burly woman. "But the heartbeat is strong. We need to take him in and run some tests on him. Be on the safe side."

"Of course my blood pressure is high. It's the holidays, isn't it. And you, ball breaker, aren't making life any easier. Now get in your death wagon and get out of here."

"Keith!" Sally said. "You settle down right now! And apologize to that young lady. They're trying to help you."

"No, they're trying to take my money." He pulled his arm away from the man who was taking his pulse. "Well, guess what? I don't have any money. No insurance, either."

Sidney walked over to the paramedics. "Give me a minute."

"And you are?" the woman paramedic said, eyeing her.

"A lot more difficult than him if you care to find out."

"We're just doing our job," the woman said, stepping aside.

Sidney kneeled alongside her father and clasped his calloused hand. It was warm but not clammy. "What's going on, Dad?"

"Nothing," he said.

Keith was a retired deputy sheriff with over thirty years on the force. Hard as nails. He once cut the tip of his finger off and tried to stitch it back on himself. Now he had a missing finger to show for it, down to the second knuckle.

"How do you feel?" she said, rubbing his palm. "Really?"

Keith looked away. "Crowded."

He looked tired, too. His grey eyes sagged a little, and deeper creases were in his face. Decades on the force had caught up with him and perhaps something else too. Allison. Sidney's stomach sank. Allison was wearing them down.

"Dad, do you really think you're all right?"

He nodded her over and whispered in her ear. "Don't tell your mother, but I think I forgot my medicine." He choked. "Don't let them take me to that hospital, Sid. I won't go. Mortimer died the last time he went. I won't go, I tell ya. I won't."

Mortimer was his younger brother, her uncle, who had died the year before from the flu. They'd taken him in for fluids, and he'd never come back out again. It had sapped a good bit of her father's hardened resolve. Her iron-clad father had become mortal.

"All right. Just sit tight."

She led the paramedics outside. "Did you pick up anything serious?"

"No," the woman said, "but you never know."

"He says he didn't take his medicine."

"That'll do, but I still advise caution," the lady said. "But I see your mind's made up, and I'm pretty sure his is too. We'll get on out of here."

Sidney handed her a business card. "Thanks. And if you can, send this bill to me."

"Sure, no problem."

Back inside, Sidney's mother was sitting on the couch talking with Smoke. *So much for introductions.*

"Sidney, you didn't tell me you had a handsome new partner?" She patted Smoke's leg. "And he's a nice one. Tall, dark—"

"Mom, I think I smell something burning in the kitchen."

Sally jumped up. "What?" Her bright eyes widened. "My pies!" She shot a look at her husband and rushed into the kitchen. "You burned my pies."

"I didn't burn them." Keith let out a breath and watched the ambulance back out of the driveway. "Ah, I feel better already. Say chief," he said to Smoke, "toss me that remote. And Sid, think you can grab my pill case from the medicine cabinet?"

She started down the hall. Megan, dressed in pink and purple pajamas, wrapped her arms around Sid's legs.

"Aunt Sidney! I didn't think you were coming until tomorrow." She sniffed and looked up at her. "Why do you smell smoky? Is that blood on your nose?"

Sidney hoisted the little girl up on her hip. "You know, you're going to make a great detective some day."

"I want to be an FBI agent like you so I can waste the bad guys."

"Oh, and where did you hear I did that?"

"Grandpa," she said cheerfully.

"Well," said Sid, carrying Megan into her parents' bathroom with her. "I'm certain that you're going to grow up to be whatever you want to be." Inside the medicine cabinet she found a plastic pillbox with each day of the week. Half of the cabinet was filled with prescriptions. *Do I have this to look forward to? Insane.* She handed the pill case to Megan. "Take this to Grandpa, and don't let Grandma see. Okay?"

Megan nodded yes. "You can count on me." She saluted and disappeared into the bedroom.

Wish I could say the same about your mother. She rummaged through the cabinet. There were pain pills, muscle relaxers, high blood pressure pills, cholesterol regulators, and anti-depressants. *Geez!* She checked some of the dates. They were recent. *Allison!* She snapped the mirrored cabinet shut and began washing her face off. She scrubbed her hands with vigor.

Allison! Allison! Allison!

Her younger sister had begun the art of parental manipulation at an early age. Her being the youngest, her parents let her get away with it. Allison was every bit as charming as she was conniving. She used her beauty shamelessly to get whatever she wanted. Most mortal men found it impossible to tell her no. *Hussy. Where is she anyway?* Sid had just finished drying her face off when she heard her sister's concocted laughter coming from the living room. Sidney threw the hand towel down on the sink and headed out there.

Smoke sat in the middle of the couch smiling. Megan was on one side. Allison was on the other. Long legs crossed and brushing against his, wearing only a flimsy pink top and white cotton yoga pants, she left little to the imagination. She tossed her hair and laughed some more. "You are so funny," she said, twirling her finger in her hair. "Much more than the last one. What was his name?"

Shut up, you hussy!

CHAPTER 11

"Cyrus," Sidney's father answered.

"Frosty," Smoke said, perking up.

Sidney cut between them. "Time to change the subject."

"Cyrus Tweel?" Smoke said to Sidney.

"So you've met him," Allison said. "Too bad for you, I'd say." She checked her nails. "But he was a good match for my sister."

"Drop it, Allison," Sidney warned through her teeth.

"Oh, get over it. That was years ago, but it seems like it was yesterday." Allison giggled as she eyed Smoke. She leaned forward, offering a generous view of her ample boobs. "I was sitting right here, nursing Megan—"

Sidney closed in on her sister. "Stop it, Allison."

Allison put her hand on Smoke's thigh and let out a haughty little laugh. "You know what he looks like, right?"

Smoke nodded.

"Well, the little worm got down on one knee and proposed to my sister in front of everybody. Ha. You should have seen the look on Sidney's little face. She looked like she swallowed a rodent."

"It made for a frosty summer day," Keith said, shaking his head. "I'll never forget it."

It took all of Sidney's willpower to keep from strangling Allison. Her eyes were daggers. *I hate you.*

"So—" Smoke started.

"I said no." Sidney slunk over to the love seat adjacent to the fireplace and took a seat. It was a day she'd do anything to forget. She liked Cyrus, but the relationship had topped off after several months of dating. She'd been ready to move on but had dragged it on too long, and he had made his move.

"She really did say no," Allison said, pressing into Smoke's shoulder and eyeing her sister. "Right then and right in front of everybody. You should have seen his face: like a wounded dog that quickly became dark and angry. And my sister says I'm a tease."

"No," Sidney interjected. "I say you're a hussy."

"Sidney!" Sally exclaimed, re-entering the room with a tray of cookies. "We will not have that kind of talk in this house, especially over the holidays. Now leave your little sister alone." She set the tray down on the coffee table and faced Smoke. "What would you like to drink?"

"Milk is always best with cookies, if it's not a problem."

"Milk goes great with a lot of things," Allison said.

"Allison," Sally said, "go and put something decent on."

"This is decent, don't you think—John, is it?"

Smoke turned his head toward Sally. "I always respected my mother's wisdom, and I think your mother's is very much the same."

Sally's face lit up like a Christmas tree, and with an approving nod, she shuffled back to the kitchen.

Allison stood up with a huff, ran her fingers along the waistband of her yoga pants, and slunk out of the room, saying, "I'm sure I can find something much more traditional and boring in Sidney's room."

The tightness in Sidney's chest started to ease, and the room's atmosphere lightened. She found Smoke's eyes searching hers with a curious look in them. *What must he think of me? And Cyrus? Damn!*

"Aunt Sidney," Megan said, crawling up on the love seat and laying her head on Sid's shoulder. "What's a hussy?"

Damn.

About an hour later, Sidney sat on the hearth with Megan sleeping on a pillow in her lap. She flipped the business card her mother had let her see through her fingers. Edwin Lee with Drake Real Estate Appraisers. A voicemail picked up when she called the number.

"I can't say, Sid," Keith said, yawning. "He seemed all right. Not a twitch about him."

"So a man shows up out of the blue and you just let him inside?"

"Your mother did that."

"He was nice, and he looked cold," Sally said, knitting a bundle of bright green yarn. She glanced at Smoke. "Would you like some more cookies, John?"

"No thank you." He patted his belly. "Those were fine though. I love chocolate chips and pecans. And what were those white chocolate things with the peanut butter in them?"

"Oh, those are Ritz crackers, Jiffy dipped in melted chocolate …."

Sidney let her mom ramble on. Holidays were her thing: cooking, talking, and making merry. She hadn't always been so jovial. Her parents had been stalwart, once upon a time. They had two girls and two older boys, and her mother had taken a switch to every one of them on more than one occasion. But now her mother wouldn't swat a fly.

"Sid, I'm sorry. I don't hear so well. I can't see, either," Keith started, clearing his throat. He picked something up off of his end table by the recliner. "And I have to use this magnifying glass to read my comic books. I never believed my father when he told me, 'Getting old's not for sissies.' Well hell, he was right."

She brushed Megan's hair aside. Megan was sweet, smart, and adorable. Sid wished she had more time with her. The little girl didn't deserve the hard life Allison put her through. No one did. She sighed. "Dad, where did he sit?"

"Right there, where John is. Why?"

"Did he go anywhere else?" she asked. "Use the phone or anything?"

"No. Sally," he said, interrupting her mother's story. "Sally!"

Her mother jerked up. "What did I tell you about using that tone with me?"

"If you'd answer me the first time I wouldn't have to."

"What do you want? I'm talking."

"I know that. Everybody knows that. You're always talking." He rolled his eyes at Sidney. "Always. And it ain't to me. It's to the wall, the cat, the dog, the plants."

"What is your question?" Sally demanded.

"Did that man go anywhere else in the house besides the couch?"

"No," she said, looking up and tilting her head. "Um... Oh, yes, he asked to go to the bathroom."

"Speaking of which," Smoke said, "may I make use of your facility?"

"Certainly, John, second door on the right down the hall."

As soon as Smoke got up, the house phone started ringing. It was an olive green handset from the eighties. No caller ID to be found. Sally picked it up and in a welcoming voice said, "Hello, Shaw residence." She made a sour face. "Smoke?" Her brows buckled in concentration. "Oh, John Smoke. Yes, he's here." She made an excited face at Smoke, who'd stopped in the hall. "And may I ask who's calling?"

Sidney's eyes fastened on Smoke. He shrugged.

"Okay," Sally said. She covered the phone receiver with her hand. "Uh, John, it's a Mister Guppy for you. That's a funny name, but he sounds friendly."

Smoke walked over and took the receiver from Sally. "Thank you." He held the phone to his head. "Smoke." His eyes scanned the room. "Uh-huh ... uh-huh ... thanks." He hung the phone up and said to Sally. "Thank you."

"Is everything all right?" she asked.

"Just fine," he said, "but I don't think my bladder will hold out much longer." He headed for the bathroom.

"I have the same problem," Keith said.

"I really like him," Sally said to Sidney. "I hope he's your partner for a long, long time."

Sidney shook her head, gaping. *What was that all about?*

CHAPTER 12

A T 10:42 PM, EVERYONE WAS in bed asleep except Sidney and Smoke. The coals in the fireplace had gone dim. Her eyes were heavy, but inside some fires still burned. Smoke sat on the couch, still in the grey suit, but the jacket and tie were undone. He looked relaxed. Casual.

"So you grew up here," he said, glancing over at her. "It's a nice place. I like the knotty pine on the walls."

"My grandparents built it and left it to my mom. They died kinda young."

Smoke stretched back his elbows over the back of the couch. "Well, I guess I should catch some sleep. I guess the loft over the garage is that direction?" He pointed toward the kitchen.

"Just a second," she said, getting up from the hearth and taking a seat in her father's chair across from him. "Care to share what your friend Mister Guppy had to say? That was a nice trick, by the way."

"Oh, that. Sure, I thought you'd never ask."

"Sure you did." She crossed her arms over her chest. "Now out with it."

Smoke pulled a small device out from under the coffee table to show her. It was digital wire. A bug. "I'm pretty sleepy. Some fresh air would be nice."

Sidney headed for the sliding glass door and pulled it open. She shut it just as Smoke stepped outside. The frigid air felt as if it had teeth on it.

"Think there are any others?"

"No," he said, following the steps off the front porch and walking toward the triple-bay garage. "I looked, but I'd say that was it."

"Well, let's destroy it."

"Nah. Just leave it be. There's nothing for them to hear once we leave, and I doubt they'll be monitoring once we're gone. This kind only works a few weeks anyway. They're messing with you. They're messing with us."

"Who is?"

"Whoever doesn't want us to pursue the Black Slate."

Her boots crunched over the gravel path that led around the house. It was a nice moonlit evening, just freezing cold. She remembered running around this house with her brothers and sister and cousins, all playing spotlight late into the night. She accidentally brushed her hand against his as they rounded the corner. He held hers gently for a moment and let it go. *He's still warm.*

She blew her icy breath into her hands and rubbed them together. "I'm guessing someone on the Black Slate doesn't want us pursuing the Black Slate."

"The best criminals own a piece of everybody. Just look at your buddy Congressman Wilhelm. He may be the one behind it all. I can only imagine there's a bundle of money on the table. And money and blackmail win elections."

"I'd hate to think this is all about politics."

"It's always about politics. That's all DC cares about. People around here lose their minds during an election cycle."

"And their jobs." She plucked a rock off the ground and dropped it back onto the gravel pathway. "So, what did Mister Guppy say about Edwin Lee?"

Smoke made his way into the yard and leaned back on the split-rail fence. "What makes you think it was about Mister Lee?"

"Come on, I don't have time for games, Mister Smoke."

"Are we back to that again?"

"Back to what?"

"Mister Smoke? After all we've been through? At least your parents call me John."

"So I should call you John?"

"No, I like Smoke, but your parents can call me John because I'm a guest in their home."

She shivered. "What did Guppy say?"

"He wanted to wish me a Merry Christ—"

She punched him in the shoulder. "Out with it, please."

"All right, I'm just teasing. You really should loosen up over the holidays some." He cocked an eyebrow at her.

She glowered back.

"So, Guppy found Edwin Lee."

"And?" she said, shivering.

"There's several hundred in the United States, and fifteen in DC. Fourteen don't match the description." He cracked his thumbs. "The fifteenth did." He looked up at the distant tree line. "I bet you have a bundle of deer out there."

"And?" she said again, not hiding her agitation.

"And he died in 1943. Buried in a place called Red Vine Cemetery, southwest of DC."

Sidney stretched her visit as long as she could stand it and departed her parents' home late Christmas afternoon. Smoke, to her surprise, blended in quite well and was very smooth, brushing off all of Allison's advances. It pleased her, watching him handle himself so well where most men tended to stumble. Rolling onto the highway headed south, she set the Hellcat on cruise control.

"Where are we headed, Agent Shaw?" Smoke said, staring out the window.

He sat dressed in blue jeans and a black shirt under a dark leather jacket. A holster holding a gun was strapped to his side.

"Red Vine Cemetery. I want to see that grave."

"Not a bad call."

"Did you have something else in mind?"

"We have to start somewhere, but I might have picked a place out of the file folder. Out of what's left of it, anyway."

They'd gone through the remains of the file back at her parents'. There was little left to start on, but Sidney remembered plenty of what she'd seen and jotted down her notes. It was one of her things: studying something once and not forgetting. Names, places, and events easily stuck in her mind. "I'm sure there's another file."

"Well, I have a feeling those files aren't digital. Looks like it was dug out of a metal file cabinet from the old days."

"Perhaps."

Smoke patted his stomach. "I appreciate the hospitality. I haven't been a part of something like that in a long time. I like your family."

"I bet you liked Allison."

"She's something, all right. But your Mom was the one who kind of got me."

"What do you mean? What did she say?"

"She said she thought I was a *goodly* child and asked me if I had any baby pictures."

Sidney laughed. "Yes, that was strange. Try not to take it the wrong way. She's pretty old-fashioned with her words. She always says something odd about everyone. It used to be pretty embarrassing growing up."

"What did she say about Cyrus?" he said without looking at her. "Did he come over much?"

Ugh! Why did you have to ruin a perfectly normal conversation? She didn't reply.

"Did you ever envision yourself married to him?" he pressed.

"I don't want to talk about it. And why do you have such an interest in it?"

"He's a jerk. I've never understood why so many women go for such big jerks. That's all."

"There's more to him than meets the eye."

He turned his head. "Is there now?"

"Not like that."

"What do you mean, not like that? What were you talking about?"

"I thought you were—ugh, never mind. Drop it."

The next few hours were driven in silence. No radio. No chatter. Just her driving and Smoke, eyes closed and maybe sleeping. She liked him. Every time Allison neared him, a fire had lit inside her. But she couldn't blame her sister for trying, and he wasn't the first man they'd fought over. Allison hadn't flirted with

Cyrus, though, and that had ended up being a confirming sign. *Quit thinking about it and get back to the business at hand.* But she didn't stop thinking about it. She couldn't. The way he'd handled himself with her parents was genuine and impressive. *And they like him.* But it was ludicrous for her to fall for a man whose home was in prison. She pulled off the highway, entered the nearest gas station, and pulled alongside the pumps.

"Why are we stopping?" Smoke asked, rubbing his eyes.

"Getting a little gas and coffee." She popped open the door. "Want some?"

"Gas, or coffee?" he said with a smile.

"Or neither."

"Large black coffee, and if you don't mind, some nacho Doritos would be nice."

At least they don't serve milkshakes.

"Just pump the gas," she said, scanning the card on the pump and walking away.

Inside the store, Sidney prepared two large coffees and paid the clerk.

He was an older black man with a lazy eye, wearing a Santa cap on his head. "I hope you've had an extraordinary day," he said with a smile. "Now you be careful out there, or the holiday spooks will get you."

That's an odd thing to say.

Back inside the car, she waited for Smoke to stop pumping and get inside. Finally he hopped in. She handed him his coffee, saying, "You used high octane, didn't you?"

"Of course," he said, taking the cup. "Hey, no Doritos."

"No," she said, putting the car in drive and motoring out of the lot. "No Doritos." *What am I, your mom? Geez, I don't get this guy.*

Another twenty minutes of driving and things remained quiet. Smoke sat huddled over his coffee, sipping and looking away.

Is he pouting?

She checked the GPS on her phone. Red Vine Cemetery was ten miles from the nearest highway in Springfield. The road leading up to it was dirt and gravel with a heavy night fog rolling over it. She pulled off to the side in the tall grasses beside a tall iron gate that was chained shut. Black gargoyles loomed on the top posts with wings spread and screeching faces. There was something alive about them. She popped the trunk and got out.

Smoke slid out of the car, eying the metal fence. "This looks like the ancient ones in Savanna."

She picked up a flashlight and checked her weapon, eying the moon in the sky. She grabbed another gun, a Glock 22, and clipped it on. She kept the .40 caliber ready in her free hand. She closed the trunk and Smoke was nowhere to be found.

No he didn't.

CHAPTER 13

THE FENCE AND GATE WERE eight feet high, and the top rails were spiked. It was odd. Most cemeteries didn't have fences around them. And there was something else peculiar, too. She ran her fingers over the wrought iron. The metal was in excellent condition, almost new. After pushing her gun and flashlight between the rails and setting them down on the other side, she grabbed the ice-cold rails and squeezed them. *Here we go.* She shimmied up the rails, got her boot on the topside, and swung herself over.

Rip!

One of the barbs at the top ripped through her coat and into her shoulder. Grimacing, she hopped down to the ground and grabbed the gun and flashlight. She touched the throbbing wound. Warm blood wet her fingers.

Not good. She peered through the murk. *Dammit, Smoke, where are you?* Treading through the tall lawn, she took note of the graves and markers. Many were tall limestone works with crosses and other ornate types of pylons and pillars. There were stone sarcophaguses too, with a few cracked and damaged. There were hundreds of marble headstones as far as her eyes could see, glinting faintly in the moonlight. Sidney waded through the mist that hung just above her ankles. A sound caught her ear. She stopped.

Shnnnk … Ffffp … Shnnnk … Ffffp … Shnnnk … Ffffp …

It was the steady rhythmic sound of a shovel digging into the earth. Sidney crept toward the sound.

Shnnnk … Ffffp … Shnnnk … Ffffp … Shnnnk … Ffffp …

A figure in shabby clothes stood waist-deep in a grave. A man with a broad back and hunched shoulders scooped out large shovelfuls of dirt and tossed them aside. There was something extraordinary about the man as he slung the dirt aside. The shovel was huge, almost the size of a snow shovel. The ominous silhouette kept shoveling without any source of light. Spidery legs of warning crawled up her arms.

Shnnnk … Ffffp … Shnnnk … Ffffp … Shnnnk … Ffffp …

She turned on the flashlight and readied her Glock and slid in behind him. There was a body in a burlap sack, bound up in thick cords of twine beside the grave.

"FBI," Sidney said, shining the light on the man's back. He was big-framed. Arms bulged. A nasty scar was carved deep in his bare skull. *He should be freezing.* "Drop the shovel and let me see your hands."

Shnnnk ... Ffffp ... Shnnnk ... Ffffp ... Shnnnk ... Ffffp ...

Dirt landed on Sidney's boots. "Drop the shovel and get out of the grave, sir."

Shnnnk ... Ffffp ... Shnnnk ... Ffffp ... Shnnnk ... Ffffp ...

Sidney growled in her throat. *Men never listen.* She stepped around the side of the grave to get a better look at him. He kept his head down. *He might be deaf, but he can certainly see the light.* She shined the light in his face.

The foreboding man stopped and looked up. His marred face had dead eyes. He snarled. The shovel swung.

Shit! A deader!

Sidney jumped. The shovel clipped her heel, and she pitched backward hard onto the ground. Her gun fell from her grasp. The man grabbed the hem of her pants and hauled her into the grave. She drove her heel into his mouth. Clocked him in the head with the flashlight. The deader's grip was iron, his power unnatural.

"Screw you, Frankenstein!"

She let loose a flurry of kicks in his face, rocking his thick neck back. Using a jujitsu move, she twisted her leg free of his grasp and scrambled out of the hole. In the darkness, she clutched through the tall grasses for her gun.

"Murrr!" the deader moaned, climbing out of the hole wielding the shovel. He raised it over his head and brought it down hard.

Sidney rolled left.

The shovel bit into the ground beside her head. The deader ripped it from the ground and swung another decimating blow.

She ducked under the swipe. Spying her gun, she snatched it up and blasted away.

"Eat Glock, you ugly undead sonofabitch!"

Blam! Blam! Blam! Blam! Blam! Blam!

The deader staggered backward, shovel slipping through its grasp, teetering on the lip of the grave.

Blam! Blam! Blam! Blam! Blam! Blam!

Goo oozed from the hole in its chest as it toppled into the grave.

Thud!

Chest heaving, Sidney leaned over the grave.

The deader's arms shot up.

Blam! Blam! Blam!

The deader's arms fell down.

Morning Glory. She took out another fifteen-round magazine and reloaded. *What was that goon made of?*

A man rushed toward her. She aimed for his head. He raised his arms. It was Smoke. "Where in the hell have you been?"

"Sorry," he said, peering into the grave. "Another deader?"

"I guess," she said, glaring at him. "Now, if you don't mind, where were you?"

"While you were fumbling through the trunk, I saw somebody running and went after them."

"And you didn't think to tell me."

"When a wolf chases a rabbit, he doesn't think about it."

"So you think like a dog?"

"I said I was sorry. You're a big girl, Agent Shaw. Get over it." Then he said with a little guilt in his voice. "I really didn't anticipate any danger. I should have known better. Sorry."

She could see the heavy look in his eye. He meant it. And he was right. She didn't need to get into the habit of relying on someone else. "Just give me a heads-up next time."

Smoke sauntered over to the grave marker and ran his fingers over the engraving. "You need to see this," he said.

She took out her phone, turned its light on, and shined in on the marker. Sidney read it out loud: "Edwin Lee. 1865-1945. A humble servant of the Drake Foundation." There was a black sun rising at the top. She looked at the body on the ground, covered only with the burlap sack. "You thinking what I'm thinking?"

Smoke cut away at the cords with a knife and peeled the burlap away from the face.

Just as her mother had described lay the cold dead face of Edwin Lee.

CHAPTER 14

"WEIRD," SMOKE SAID, LOOKING AT the dead body. "Really weird. He doesn't look like a deader. Practically a fresh corpse." He glanced at Sidney. "You're bleeding."

"I don't have time to bleed," she said.

Smoke started laughing. "I can't believe you just said that. Is there something you're not telling me? Did you used to be part of the secret SEALS or something?"

The willies that had been creeping through her bones started to subside. She needed some humor, something real and tangible in what was become a bizarre world. "My father and brothers were big fans of the movie."

"And you weren't?"

"Well, I liked it too—the first twenty times."

"It was a pretty popular phrase among the seals," he said, "I've just never heard a woman use it. I like it."

"So, assuming we haven't woken the dead, did you find what you were chasing?"

"Disappeared into a mausoleum." He pointed over a ridge of tombstones. "That's when I heard your shots." He nudged the body of Edwin Lee with his boot. "What do you want to do with him?"

Good question. According to her letter from the Bureau, she needed to call it in. Then again, this was a shadow operation, which gave her liberties with her decisions. She took some pictures of Edwin Lee, the tombstone, and the deader. "Let's go check out this mausoleum."

After traversing through fifty yards of grave markers and willow trees, she came to a stop in front of an ancient rectangular structure. Standing almost twenty feet tall and just as wide, it towered over the other structures. Gargoyles adorned the corners. Vines crept over the stained glass windows and twisted along the columns to the entrance. A pair of brass doors at the top of the steps were split open.

"In there?" she said.

Smoke nodded.

"Maybe he or she slipped back out."

"Only one way to find out," Smoke said, starting up the steps and pulling open the door. The hinges creaked from the effort. "I'll go first."

"But you don't have a light."

Smoke disappeared inside. Sidney ran up the steps after him and shined her phone light inside. It was wholly inadequate, and she regretted busting her Maglite on the deader's head. She could see Smoke well enough, however, and rows of marble burial markers. There were dates carved in them and initials but not full names. She snapped a few pictures.

"Do you mind?" Smoke said, running his fingers over the burial vaults. "You're screwing up my night vision."

"Do you have super powers I should know about?"

"Maybe," he said, tapping his knuckles on the stones. "Huh. Doesn't make sense someone would run in here without anywhere to go."

"Only those windows." She shined the light toward the top. The stained glass windows at the top were all intact. "Or down through the ground."

Smoke pressed his ear to one of the burial chambers.

"Listening for a ghoul's heartbeat?" she said, eyeing the floor and walls. There wasn't anything out of the ordinary. "I think whoever it was already left."

"I don't," Smoke said. "I can smell them."

Oh boy. Sidney sniffed the air. There was nothing extraordinary. "Really, and what do they smell like?"

"Fear." He ran his hands over the markers and started pushing. "Help me out. There has to be a catch or something."

Sidney gave it a half-hearted effort, running her fingers over cold stone after cold stone. She pushed in a little here and there. "It's just a mausoleum, not the Temple of Doom, Indiana."

"I take it you don't like my plan."

"I think we stumbled on plenty to start with already." Her shoulder throbbed, and she was getting colder. "I think it's time to go."

"You aren't all right, are you?"

"This isn't how I normally spend the holidays."

Wuppa—Wuppa—Wuppa—Wuppa—Wuppa ...

"That's a chopper landing," he said, heading for the door.

Sidney followed him outside. Sure enough, a large helicopter landed in a nearby clearing. Its whirling blades pressed down the tall grass and stirred the leaves on the willow trees. Men in dark garb spilled out the chopper's doors and rushed at them with bright lights and assault rifles.

"This is bad," Smoke said as the men surrounded them from all angles. "Really bad."

Shielding her eyes, Sidney took out her badge and held it up over her head.

"Don't move another inch, lady," said a voice filled with authority.

"I'm Agent Shaw with—"

Budda-budda! Budda-budda!

One of the armed men squeezed off a few rounds at her feet.

"When I say don't move, that means not anything!" His voice was muffled by a mask of some sort. "Especially your mouth. Try me again, and I'll saw your legs off."

CHAPTER 15

"LOCK YOUR HANDS ONTO YOUR head," the soldier demanded. "Now!"
Slowly, Sidney put her arms over her head. Smoke's hung ready
at his sides. *Just do it!* she wanted to say but didn't. She had no doubt
the half dozen men she could make out meant business.

"Looks like we have a wise guy on our hands," the soldier said. "Teach the
trespassers a lesson."

"No!" Sidney cried out.

The muzzle flashed.

Budda-budda! Budda-budda!

Bullets tore up the landscape in front of Smoke's toes. He didn't flinch.

"I'll be," the leader said. "Plenty of guts to splatter in this one. Take him
down."

Two figures darted from behind the lights. One of them launched the butt of
his weapon into Smoke's belly. He doubled over.

Zap!

The second soldier prodded Smoke in the back with a stick that was some
sort of taser. Smoke twitched, growled, and started to rise.

The soldiers laid into him.

Zap! Zap! Zap!

Smoke sagged to the ground, clutching at the air.

"That'll take the starch out of him," one said, twirling his stick in the air. He
slapped it in his hand. "How about we take a little starch out of her, Boss? I bet
Barbie pees herself."

"Just fetch me her ID," the leader said.

"Aw," the man said, strutting over. He snatched Sidney's badge. The men
were soldiers of a sort, clad in dark body suits padded in body armor and wearing
rectangular goggles and some sort of masks over their mouths. "Sidney Shaw, FBI
agent." He glanced down her backside. "Not bad. Boss, can I keep this one? She's
got a nice — *oof!*"

Sidney slammed her knee into his nuts. The other forces closed in with stun
sticks ready.

Zap!

She twitched from head to toe and toppled to the ground. Everything tingled. Her bones hurt. She watched the sky above blinking as more men in strange masks crowded around her. One of them called her a bitch. She was pretty sure she knew who it was.

Just doing my job, she thought.

"What's the plan, Boss?" said one of the mercenaries. "This is a great place to bury them. Alive would be nice."

"I'm not very fond of suggestions. Perhaps I should bury you. Nothing like a shovelful of dirt to silence you," said the leader, kneeling down alongside Sid.

"Sorry, Boss."

The leader brushed Sidney's hair from her eyes. "It's so hard to find good help these days, Agent Shaw. The younger ones are so, eh, exuberant. And stupid, for that matter." There was some polish in his voice behind the mask. "I hate stupid people." He pulled out a stainless steel pistol. The muzzle flashed.

Blam!

Sidney saw the body fall.

"Leave him," the leader ordered. "The servants shall dispose of him." He ran the muzzle of the gun along Sidney's chin. The hot barrel seared her flesh.

"Uh…" The man's tone and demeanor were those of many cold-blooded killers she'd studied. Nerveless men who didn't flinch executing torture. Mutilation.

"Agent Shaw, I assume you don't have a warrant. Blink once for yes."

She did.

"Good," he said. "But I find it very strange that you are here. Why would that be?"

Can't exactly help with that right now.

"I see, you still can't speak. How rude of me. What's this?" He took off his goggles. He was fair-haired and pale, with pitch-black eyes. He fingered the wound in her shoulder. Blood was on his finger. A hunger filled his eyes. "Mmmm … delicious, I bet." He removed the mask over his mouth. His face was long and slender with a strong dimpled chin. He licked the blood and closed his eyes. "Delicious indeed."

You better not be a vampire. You can't be a vampire.

The leader gazed into her eyes, lending her a full view of his becoming face. He cradled her in his arms. Her head flopped back, exposing her neck to him. The leader bent down and brought his lips to her neck.

This can't be happening! No! She moaned. *No!*

His teeth sunk into her skin. She squirmed. "No."

"Ah-hahaha!" the leader laughed. "I'm screwing with you, Agent Shaw. I'm not a vampire, but I always wanted to be one." He cocked his head and stared hard into her eyes. "But there are worse things out there than vampires, love. Take my word for it."

I know. They're called lawyers, jerk. The numbness and pain started to wear off. *Save your energy, Sid. Save it.*

"But I do have a bit of a dilemma here. Normally, I just kill people that trespass and have them buried. You however, are a Fed." He scratched his neck. His nails were unusually long. "And the Feds cause problems. Questions. Investigations. Hmmm. My boss likes to keep things quiet. And I don't like my boss showing up, so I like to keep things quiet too." He gazed into the sky. "Damn. I really hate loose ends."

Sidney watched him stand up and hang the barrel of the gun over her face. *He's going to shoot me. God, please don't let him shoot me!*

CHAPTER 16

"H MMM …" THE BOSS SAID, tilting his head with the moon hanging over his shoulder. "I like you, Agent Shaw. You and your friend can live, for now. But I suggest you stop your snooping around. The game you're playing is far too dangerous for the common man—or woman." He motioned to his men. "Drag them outside of the gate and leave them. Maybe the cold will take them." He walked off, heading toward the chopper.

A hand clutched Sidney by the hair and dragged her limp body over the grass. Smoke was being dragged by two men behind her. His head was slumped downward. Her teeth started to chatter. It was a miserable existence, being dragged.

"Hurry up," one of them said. "The boss might leave us." The soldiers picked up the pace. "It'd go quicker if this big bastard wasn't so damn heavy. I say we kill 'em both. He'll never know."

"You saw what happened to dumbass Franklin back there, didn't you? You want a hole in your head too?"

"Good point," said the man dragging her. "But a bullet in the head's an act of mercy compared to what I've seen other upstarts get. The Cage. Ew. That's nasty."

"Clam up, will you. I don't need reminded."

They came to a stop just outside of the gate. Sidney could see the Hellcat's taillights and mufflers. The soldiers dragged Smoke by her side and kicked him in the ribs a few times.

"All right, that's enough," one said. He started closing the gate. "Let's go. I'm pretty sure they'll be dead soon enough anyway. He'll make it look like an accident is all. Enjoy the cold, agents."

They all piled in the chopper, and it took off.

Wuppa—Wuppa—Wuppa—Wuppa—Wuppa …

It was below twenty outside, and if she didn't get moving she'd be a Popsicle in an hour. *Come on, Sid. Move.* Her fingertips scraped at the dirt. Her teeth still chattered. *This sucks!*

Smoke rolled over with a heavy groan and crawled toward her.

Thank God!

"Hang in there," he said, rummaging through her pockets.

What! What in the hell are you doing?

He produced her key fob and pressed the button. The taillights flicked on.

You'd better be starting the engine.

Smoke rose to his feet, staggered toward the car, and pulled the door open. He pulled out his duffle bag and unzipped it.

Now you're pissing me off.

He produced an army green tube and stretched it out to full length.

That's a LAW rocket! He's insane! She had fired the light anti-tank weapons before during Air Base Ground Defense training in the Air Force. But those had been blasting caps. This was the real thing.

Smoke hefted it onto his shoulder and took aim at the rising helicopter.

"No," she managed to croak out. "No."

Watching the chopper rise, Smoke took his hand off the trigger and collapsed the weapon back into its compact size. Jaw jutted against the moonlit sky, he shook his head as the chopper flew out of sight.

Thank God. The men deserved it, but she didn't want their blood on her hands. She didn't want it on Smoke's either.

He walked over, picked her up, and cradled her in his arms. "I hate loose ends. It'll come back to bite us." Smoke set her down in the passenger seat and buckled her inside. "Looks like I finally get to drive."

"Don't you dare," she mumbled.

Smoke fired up the engine and pressed on the accelerator, which let out a vicious exhaust note. "What? Did you say something?"

Pinning her to her seat, the Dodge Hellcat's back wheels tore the gravel off the road. After a couple of minutes, the seat began warming her rear, and the heater thawed her icy cheeks. She glanced over at Smoke. In the dim light he reminded her of a modern-day road warrior. She kinda liked that about him. "Don't get too comfortable, Mad Max."

"Hah. Now he was an interceptor. But that wasn't a Hellcat."

She shifted in her seat and made herself a little more comfortable. Held her hands in front of the heater. The nerve-jangling effects were beginning to wear off. But Smoke had been tasered at least three times. *He shouldn't be moving.* "So, was that LAW rocket a parting gift from the SEALS?"

"Nope."

"You were about to kill all of those guys, weren't you?"

"Maybe. Don't you think they had it coming?"

"I'm not a judge. I'm an agent." She rubbed her temples. "Man, this is one rotten Christmas."

"I've had worse," Smoke said, adjusting the rearview mirror. He glanced at her shoulder. "That might need stitches. I can handle it, if you like. But you need to put some pressure on it."

Sidney had a few things to consider. A trip to the hospital would generate paperwork. She was a shadow agent now, and maintaining a low profile would take some getting used to. There were other bizarre matters too. The deader and the body of Edwin Lee. She still needed to confirm that. Grimacing, she searched her pockets. Panic seized her.

"What's wrong?" Smoke said.

"That man, the Boss, he must have taken my phone!"

On Smoke's insistence, she let him take her back to his place. It wasn't like her to not put up a fight, but his words persuaded her. Now, she sat on his kitchen counter inside his service garage apartment. The gas heater made a soft roar overhead, which gave the place a cozy feeling. Her shoulder throbbed, however. Sitting too long and staying awake on depleted adrenaline had stiffened her body.

"I'll be back," Smoke said, heading for his bathroom. "You might want to remove your jacket, and you'll probably need a clean shirt. I can help out with that one."

With a few grunts, she slid her jacket off and dropped it to the floor. The shoulder of this shirt was ripped and soaked in blood. She debated taking it off or not. *Screw it. Life's too short to be modest.* Off the shirt went, leaving her in only her bra and slacks.

Smoke returned with a towel, a damp washcloth, and a medic kit. "Did you learn that move from your sister?" he said, eyes fixed on hers.

"Ha ha. If it were my sister, there'd be no top at all and your sofa-bed would be unfolded."

"Ouch," Smoke said, inspecting the wound. "Sounds like you're feeling better, but it's pretty nasty."

"Just get on with it."

He went to work. Wiping off the blood. Cleaning the wound. Threading the needle. "Four or five should do it. It might sting a little."

She didn't look away. She looked right at him. His warm presence and rock-steady hands drew her in. Her blood began to sizzle. They'd only spent a few days together, but it felt like a lifetime. The needle dug into her arm. Her eyes watered.

"You okay?" he said, fixated like a surgeon on the wound.

"Never better," she said in his ear, eyeing the wound.

He ran another stitch through. "Good. That's two … that's three … and four." He knotted it off and clipped it with scissors. "All done."

"That was fast," she said with bated breath, looking into his eyes and resting her good hand on his neck. She rubbed his cheek and earlobe with her thumb. Her body was throbbing. "Good job."

"You're a wonderful patient," he said.

Her lips drew closer to his. "And you're a wonderful—"

Smoke withdrew just as the sound of an approaching car caught her ear. *Morning glory!*

CHAPTER 17

H EADLIGHTS ILLUMINATED THE WINDOW BLINDS. Smoke went for his gun. She went for hers. The sound of tires crunched over the driveway. He peeked through the blinds, pulled back, and headed to the other side of the room.

"Who is it?" she said, standing in her bra and slacks, holding her gun.

Smoke opened up a dresser drawer and withdrew a T-shirt. He tossed it to her. "Put this on. We have company."

"Good company or bad company?" she said, slipping the shirt on. It was a little tight and had a battle helmet and axe logo on it. "Whose was this, your girlfriend's?"

"I used to be smaller." He put away his weapon. "It's a sentimental treasure."

Knock! Knock! Knock!

Smoke made his way over to the door and swung it open. A short stocky man, bald-headed and bearded, bustled inside. A woman, taller, followed in behind him. Her honey blonde hair was pulled back in a long silky pony tail. Her winter jacket did little to hide her generous curves. Smoke closed the door behind them. She was older than Sid, over forty, but without a wrinkle and nary an eyelash out of place. *I hope I age that well.*

"Nice shirt," the woman said with a voice that was a little Lauren Bacall-like. She looked Sid up and down with very pretty eyes then took off her coat and handed it to the other man. She wore a sleeveless black top adorned in silver sequins and a pair of Buckle jeans. "I used to have one just like it."

"Hey," the man said to Sid, "The Darkslayer. I like that." He hung the woman's coat on the wall and did the same with his. He wasn't tall for a man but stocky as a bull, with thick forearms bulging beneath his flannel sleeves. His voice was warm and friendly. He had a rugged charm about him. He walked over and extended his hand. "They call me—"

"Guppy," Sidney said, taking his hand in hers.

Guppy's eyes lit up. "You can call me Gil if you don't like Guppy. I don't mind."

"Well, you don't look like a Guppy."

"I'd say not. I've been telling everyone that for years." He scratched his brown-red beard and glowered back at Smoke.

"So why the name then?"

"Well, it is my last name, after all."

"Ah," she said. "So it's Gilmore Guppy."

"Er, no," Guppy said, scratching the back of his bald head. He mumbled. "It's Gilligan actually. Gilligan Guppy."

"We tried Double G, but it didn't stick," Smoke said. He slapped his hand down on Guppy's brawny shoulder. "So, Guppy it is. And over there is Fat Sam."

Fat Sam had moved away and taken a seat behind the computer.

"It'll take some time, but she'll warm up to you," Guppy said with a wink.

"I have to admit," Sid said, "neither of you are what I expected, especially in her case. She's so—"

"Stacked," Smoke interjected.

Sid narrowed her eyes on him. "I was going to say gorgeous and female."

"Thank you," Fat Sam boomed, pecking away on Smoke's computer.

"Yes, she's the fat with a PH kind. Pretty hot and tempting, wouldn't you say?" Guppy said, raising his brows.

"I get it," Sidney said, glancing at the woman.

"And Sam's short for Samantha," Guppy added.

"I think she figured that out already," Sam said.

"And she's grumpy," Guppy whispered.

"I heard that."

"Well, I have to admit, your arrival is a bit peculiar." Sid made her way over to the computer desk and looked over Fat Sam's shoulder. The monitor had pictures from the Drake graveyard on it. The ones she had taken. *How in the world did she get those?* On the desk, she noticed a phone similar to the one she thought she lost. A jolt of fury went right through her. "Smoke!"

"Oh, I meant to tell you, I found your phone," he said.

She jerked her phone off the cable. "Garage! Now!" *Jerk!* Smoke made his way into the garage, and she shut the door behind them. She wanted to hit him. She poked him in the chest. "Why didn't you tell me that?"

"Easy," he said, putting his hands up, "you don't want to tear those stitches."

"I'm going to tear your tongue out if you don't give me some straight answers!"

"Is this an interrogation?"

"It's betrayal," she said, walking away. In one of the garage's double bays, his IROC Camaro was on a lift with a new fiery red paint job on it. *When did he do that?* On the other side, two motorcycles were covered in tarps. Last time there had only been one. Boxes of Snap-On Tools hugged the block walls, and long shelves were filled with neatly organized parts.

"I shouldn't have taken it," he said, "or at least I should have given it back. But I wasn't sure how forthcoming you'd be with the information. We need it."

"I'm here. We're well past that point."

Dejected, he said, "I'm sorry."

Her fires simmered down, but it still hurt a little. She wanted to trust him. Even worse, she had trusted him, letting things hang out with only a bra on. She wanted to take the T-shirt off and throw it at him. She wanted him to take her in his arms and kiss her. *Damn men!* "So, this shirt, was it Sam's?"

"Still is, I think." He stretched his arms up on the bottom of his car that hung on the lift. "We aren't a thing. Her and Guppy stay over sometimes."

"I don't want to know anything else." *Keep it professional.* She headed for the door. "But it's nice knowing you kids have sleepovers." She opened the door and stepped inside, then shut it behind her. Guppy and Fat Sam were seated at the desk, staring at her.

"Is the squabble over?" Sam said.

No! "Yes." She made her way over to them. "Care to fill me in on what you're doing?"

"Trying not to freak out," Guppy said, staring at one of the four monitors. He got up from his chair. "Please, Agent Shaw, have a seat."

"I'm all right."

"I insist."

Sidney obliged. *Nice guy but probably lying to someone.* "What are you freaking out about?"

Sam twisted her head around. "Are you shitting me?"

"Language," Guppy warned.

"Oh, I'm sorry for my French. I meant to say, are you joking?" Sam clicked on the mouse and pulled up four images, one on each monitor. The tombstone marker of Edwin Lee. Edwin Lee's corpse. The 1943 obituary and photo of Edwin Lee, and finally the deader. "That's what we're talking about. Craziest shit I ever saw."

"Ahem."

"Sorry again. Craziest slat … oh never mind. This is Nucking Futz! Yet at the same time, it's awesome."

"Sorry about her," Guppy said, shaking his head. "She's still got a lot of alley cat in her."

Sam spun around her in her seat to face Sid. "Tell me more about the werewolf." Her green eyes gleamed. "Smoke wouldn't talk about it, but you'll tell me. Tell me everything."

"I'll think about it," Sidney said, leaning toward the screen with the deader on it. "I'm curious. Do you think you can identify that guy?"

"Maybe, why?" Sam said, zooming in on the image.

"It might give us some more insight. Man, he's huge. You don't notice so much when they're trying to kill you."

Sam and Guppy gave each other odd looks. "Boy, Smoke is right," Guppy said, "you really are a Hellcat."

Sidney showed a wry smile. She squinted her eyes at another image on the screen with the tombstone. She pointed at it. "Zoom in on that."

"Okay." Sam zoomed in.

There was a figure with gleaming eyes peering at them from up in the tree. Its shape was fuzzy.

"Cat maybe," Guppy said.

The shape was odd but familiar. "Pretty big cat. Are those wings on its back?"

"Probably an owl," Sam offered.

Smoke crept back in the room and offered his insight. "Not a cat. Not an owl. It's a gargoyle."

CHAPTER 18

"OH, PLEASE," SIDNEY SAID. "IT's not a gargoyle."

"Oh, please be a gargoyle," Sam said, toying with her onyx and diamond necklace with her eyes glued to the screen. "Smoke, this is so much more exciting than the wife-beating drug dealers we're used to."

"And stopping those people isn't a good thing?" Smoke said.

"Sure, but taking down wife-beating werewolves is so much cooler."

"Am I missing something?" Sidney asked, staring at Smoke.

"She prattles. Don't worry about it."

"Hmmm, I think it is a gargoyle," Guppy said. "Yep, I'm with Smoke. Gargoyle."

Sidney recalled a bad movie she'd seen years ago with friends, called *Gargoyles*. It had really creeped her out then, and the talk of them creeped her out now. *Strange bunch. Just a little too into this.* "I think we need a little more proof. I'm sure forensics can find a scientific explanation for what that is."

"Don't be such a Scully," Sam said, tilting back in her chair. "You've seen deaders and a werewolf. I don't see any reason you can't add a gargoyle to the supernatural kingdom."

"I know what I saw, but we don't really have proof of any of that, so don't go calling the papers."

"Not even the *Enquirer*?" Sam said with a huff.

"Or the *Sun*?" Smoke said with a laugh.

"Don't forget the *Weekly World News*," Guppy added.

"Sure, call the *Lone Gunman*, why don't you?" Sidney said, laughing at herself. They all fell silent and stared at her. "Oh, it's funny when you say stupid things, but not when I do, is it?"

Guppy shrugged his heavy shoulders. "We just weren't of the impression that you were funny is all."

Smoke nudged him.

Sidney folded her arms over her chest and cocked her head. "And why would you be under that impression?"

"Er, well ..." Guppy scratched his head. "I think I hear something in the garage. I better go check it out. Probably them raccoons again."

Smoke put his finger up. "I'm going to get a shower." He tugged at the neck of his shirt. "Phew, I can almost feel what I'm smelling."

Almost instantly, Sidney found herself all alone in the studio with Sam, whose decorated fingernails were a blur on the keyboard. Sid resumed her seat beside her. Everything about Sam was impeccable, from the type of shoe she wore to the onyx wrap that held her blonde ponytail in place.

"What?" Sam said, keeping her eyes on the monitor.

"Nothing," Sidney said. "Well, not exactly nothing. I really like your fingernails."

"Thanks. Too bad I can't say the same about yours."

"Excuse —" Sidney fanned out her hands. The maroon polish was dull and chipped off. Polishing her nails wasn't one of her better habits. She was a little more practical about such things. "They do look pretty crappy, don't they?"

"Yep," Sam said, smiling out of the corner of her mouth. "But I imagine FBI girls need to be a little more practical, especially when you're fighting deaders and such. You might want to sprinkle a little diamond dust on them though."

"I suppose." She nodded. "I have a question."

"About me and Smoke I bet."

"Yes."

Sam turned in her chair and looked into Sid's eyes. "We don't have the right chemistry."

Sidney locked her fingers in her lap and leaned back with an inner sigh. But another question pecked in her mind. She opened her mouth to speak.

"No, we haven't done it," Sam said, "and let's just leave it at that. Smoke's a special guy, but even he gets a little misaligned sometimes." She resumed her pecking on the keyboard. "That's all I can say, because it's starting to get a little weird."

"Fair enough," Sidney said. "So, Sam's short for Samantha?"

"My mom was a fan of the *Bewitched* show. Well, I was too, a decade later. Huh. There I go, dating myself."

"I used to watch that with my mom and *I Dream of Jeannie* too."

"Well, at least your mom had sense enough not to name you Samantha Jean."

Sidney burst out in laughter.

"Yeah, laugh it up. Everyone else does." She started to laugh herself. "I hated it growing up, but it's kinda cool now. Goes well together. Don't you think?"

"Sure, if you live in Alabama."

"Ha ha." Sam shook her head. "I went to one of those snobby private schools. I was a little heavy, really had a thing for Little Debbies and hot donuts as a kid. My parents never told me no to anything until after they were dead."

"Oh." Sidney stopped laughing. "Sorry."

"I'm just screwing with you. Made you stop laughing, though."

"That's messed up."

"But it's effective."

It wasn't half bad having a friend to warm up with for a change. For the most part, all she had was Sadie. *Sam and Sadie. Now that would make one heckuva girls' night out together.*

"So, as I understand it, you have a file on this weird shit—I mean slat?" Sam asked.

"Yea, how'd you already know about that?"

Sam just looked at her.

"He's really sneaky, isn't he?" Sidney said.

"An oversized fox. Don't underestimate him."

Sidney made her way over to the kitchen table to pick up the charred remains of their case file. She noticed a coffee pot in the corner.

"I like the way you're thinking," she heard Sam say.

Does everyone have ESP around here? She found a pack of grounds, readied the pot, and returned to the computer station. She dumped the file on the desk. The envelope from the Bureau slipped out on the floor.

Sam snatched it up. "What's this?"

CHAPTER 19

S IDNEY SNATCHED THE CHARRED LETTER from Sam's dazzling fingertips. "It's mine."

"Secret orders, huh?" Sam's eyes narrowed on her. "Now's not the best time to keep secrets. You need to trust someone."

The door to the garage opened, and Guppy bustled in, sniffing the air. "Is that coffee brewing?"

"Hey, Guppy," Sam said. "You'll never believe this."

"Believe what?"

"Sid has secret orders."

Smoke appeared out of the bathroom, drying his hair and wearing only a beige terrycloth towel. The strapping man's muscles flexed as he breathed in the aroma. "Ah, coffee."

Sidney unglued her eyes from his hard belly and turned back to the file on the desk. "We need to get going on this Night Bird case, before the jailbird back there has to go back to his nest." She plucked out a picture of Angi Harlow and set it on the table. The edges were crisp. "I recall seeing some notes about her being a philanthropist of sorts. There were several similar locations that she had in common with Adam Vaughn too. That might be a starting point."

Sam slid the picture over and stared at it. "She's a true beauty. Look at those cheekbones. I'll do a search and see if I can find anything on her. But I'm sure there's a thousand Angi Harlows in the system."

"Think it will get flagged?" Sid said, fanning herself with the Bureau letter. "We need to be careful."

"I'm careful," Sam said, typing.

"What's this?" Smoke said, snatching the letter from Sidney's hand.

"Hey!"

He took the letter out, held it high over his head, and started reading it out loud. "'Agent Shaw, due to the unorthodox arrangement of this assignment, you will need to keep the following items under consideration.' Interesting. 'John Smoke,' that's me, 'is a convicted criminal with special skills.'" He made a quirky face. "'Don't underestimate him.' Which you already have. Several times." He changed his voice to something dark and hoarse. "'He's dangerous,' like Batman.

'Unpredictable,' like Miley Cyrus. 'Possible flight risk,' like DB Cooper." His voice changed back. "'You have eyes on him and we have eyes on him.'" He glanced around with widened eyes and shrugged. "'Allow him free range.'" He stopped and looked at Sid. "*Allow him free range.*" He wagged his finger at her. "It seems you're not being completely honest about things either. Shame. Shame." He continued. "'We'll let you know if he needs reeling in.' Blah, blah, 'alien objects,' blah blah, 'notify your superiors. Seek Mal Carlson ... for assistance when needed.' That's new. 'Shadow cover authorized.' That's cool." He switched back to his Dark Knight voice. "Trust your instincts and good hunting. The Bureau." He handed her back the letter. "Sooner or later, you're going to have to figure out who you're going to trust: us or the Bureau. I'll be back. I have to brush my teeth. I have a foul taste in my mouth for some reason."

Sidney shrank in her chair as he walked away. She swore his cheeks had reddened. "I bet I seem like a real ass, don't I?"

Sam kept up at the keyboard while Guppy poured a mug of coffee. He walked it over to her. It was a white mug with a dragon and sword logo on it.

"Thanks," she said.

"Don't mention it," he said. "And don't worry. He's only a little mad. He'll get over it."

"I've got nothing on Mal Carlson, but I've found a few good Angi's," Sam said. "I'll see if I can tie any of it in to Drake." She shook her head as she talked. "Drake has a plethora of subsidiaries. They're as bad as government pork barrel companies."

Glimpsing through the remains of the file, Sidney noticed a tattoo on a dead man's arm. "Look for anything with a black sun incorporated into it. That might help."

"Sure," Sam replied.

The bathroom door popped open. Smoke appeared in a black T-shirt and jeans. His dark brown hair was still damp but combed back. He made his way over to the kitchen counter, where Guppy had him a mug of coffee ready. "Did you bring the kit?"

"It's in the car," said Guppy. "I'll fetch it." He headed outside and returned shortly with a red medical kit in his hands. He opened it up and took out a packet with a syringe. Then he cleaned off the inside of Smoke's elbow with alcohol and a cotton swab.

"What's going on here?" Sidney said, getting up out of her chair.

"We're checking to make sure that I'm not a werewolf," Smoke said. "We have to send the bloodwork to Transylvania Labcorp."

"Ha ha," she laughed. "No really, what's going on?"

"Okay, since you seem genuinely concerned, we're testing my blood to see what your boyfriend Cyrus injected into me months ago."

Sidney had forgotten about that until Smoke brought it up again in the elevator. It was pretty clear that it agitated him. "He's not my boyfriend."

"Sorry, I meant ex-fiancé."

Sam wheeled around in her chair. "You were engaged? When did this happen?"

She shot a look at Smoke. His playful smile was showing. "I wasn't engaged." She shook her chin at him. "I said no."

"Oh," Sam said, turning back around. Her fingers became a blur on the keyboard, "Cyrus Tweel. Let's get a better look at you."

"What? Wait, what are you doing?" Sidney said. Pictures of Cyrus suddenly picked up on the monitors. *Morning glory!*

"Ew, you were engaged to this creepy little guy?" Sam said with her head cocked.

Guppy walked over for a closer look. "Him? You and him?" He pointed at the screen. "Look at those cold beady eyes. I bet his great granddaddy was a horse thief."

"Again," Sidney interjected, "we didn't get engaged. I said no."

"But you slept with him, right?"

Sidney pushed her hair back over her head. *She's worse than Sadie!* "Let's get back on the track that doesn't have anything to do with my sex life, okay?"

Sam spun back around in her chair, facing Sid. "My door's always open when you want to talk about it." She turned back around.

Behind her, Smoke was chuckling. Sidney turned and punched him in the shoulder.

"Ow," he said, flatly.

"Now what's this bloodwork all about?" she asked.

"Just a second and I'll tell you," he said.

Guppy drew blood from Smoke's arm then proceeded to inject the blood into a large glass vial of solution. He was stirring the blood in with a clear liquid when the most bizarre thing happened. It started to shine in the light.

Smoke's face turned grim.

"Yep, you were right," Guppy said to him with a frown. "They've got the Glow in you."

Smoke smacked his fist on the kitchen counter.

Wham!

CHAPTER 20

"THE GLOW?" SID ASKED. "WHAT is that?"

"It's a tracking serum," Guppy said, disposing of the syringe in a biohazard bag. "Experimental stuff."

"I've never heard of it."

"Well, don't be surprised. It's relatively new and not used very much. Mostly tested by the Department of Agriculture on animals."

Sidney thought about the letter from the Bureau. *We've got eyes on him.* She had wondered how that could be, and now it made perfect sense.

"It'll wear off, Smoke," Guppy said, trying to sound reassuring. "And it's never been proven effective."

"Are there any side effects?" she asked.

"Don't know." Guppy rubbed his chin. "Are there, Smoke?"

"Aside from headaches, blurred vision, and nosebleeds, I'm perfectly fine." He shrugged. "Of course, fighting for your life causes some of that."

Sid wanted to reach out and touch him. She couldn't imagine how hard it would be to be used as someone's lab experiment. She noticed a sad look in Sam's eyes. Behind her was a clip of Cyrus's face. *Has he known all along where Smoke was? Where I was? The bastard!*

"I'll get more tests done and see how diluted it is. Maybe it's down to the final days."

"Apparently, it's lasted for months. I feel like a collared dog."

"How does this *Glow* work?"

"It's a bit like the dye they put in you for bloodwork. It spreads through the body and can be picked up like a radio signal. It has a frequency. *They* tune into it." He snapped up the lab kit. "But, just because it's in you doesn't mean that it works. Remember that, Smoke."

He nodded. "I've made it this far. I'll be fine."

Sidney yawned. She had another dozen questions that she'd like to ask, but she'd had enough. Their knowledge of the Glow impressed her. How did they know about it? What kind of access did they have? She had a last name now, and it was time she learned a little bit about them. "It's been a pleasure," she said, picking up her things. "But I'm going home to get some shut eye." She opened up the door. "I'll swing by tomorrow, assuming you'll still be here."

"Uh, bye," Sam said, waving her fingers with a funny look on her face.

Smoke and Guppy weren't even looking as Sid closed the door behind her. She felt a load fall from her shoulders when she fired up the Hellcat's engine. She needed space. Time to settle herself. She wanted to look into a few things on her own. Who they were and what the Glow was. She dropped the car into gear and sped off down the road. *Need to make sure they aren't all full of bullshit.*

Sidney tossed all night in her sleep and woke up with a slight headache. Fully dressed, she sat on the sofa watching the TV and sipping coffee. The local news was on. She laughed a little. The lead anchor wore a burgundy tie and had a caterpillar moustache. *What a clown. I bet everyone's seen the movie but him.*

She soaked it in for almost thirty minutes, getting updates on traffic and weather before she turned the TV off. It was a habit, watching the news, but Guppy's words gave her another perspective that she hadn't given much thought to before. *Plenty of conspiracies, so little proof. Or is there?* She took a seat behind her laptop at the counter and punched in her password. Her FBI mailbox had a few canned messages and something else.

Yes!

Her shadow authorization access had come through. She began clicking through various websites, setting up passwords and entering authorization codes. After about thirty minutes of answering security questions to various sites, she sat back in her seat.

Who shall I look up first?

Being an agent of the FBI, there wasn't much you couldn't look up about an ordinary citizen. It came with the job. But any inquiries fed into the system, and those checks were reviewed by someone else in the agency. She didn't want anyone else knowing what they were doing. *I wonder what database Sam is hacking? Crap, I didn't get her last name. Way to go, Agent Shaw.* She typed Gilligan Guppy into the database.

Guppy's face, social security number, and birthday popped up. His work history was nothing out of the ordinary. If anything, it was too ordinary.

"Service Manager at Walmart?" She shook her head. "He's not working at Walmart. Auto Zone maybe." She felt a little guilty doing research on him. Clicking from link to link and place to place, she found everything she could. It was clean, all the way down to the bank records and credit cards. Guppy was just an ordinary citizen living his life day by day. Not married. Next of kin all deceased. "That's odd."

She gently rubbed her aching shoulder that itched a little and took a sip of coffee. She thought about some of the things that Guppy had said. "They only show you what they want to show you." *Huh, they could be FBI for all I know. Great.* She plugged in Angi Harlow. Nothing popped up remotely close to the pictures she'd seen.

Knock. Knock. Knock.

The knocking sounded familiar. *Smoke?* She made her way over and looked through the key hole. A courier in a blue uniform stood on the other side, holding a package. She opened the door.

"Are you Sidney Shaw?" he said with frosty breath. He had freckles, and dark red hair spilled out from underneath his cap that was almost pulled over his eyes.

"Yes."

"Special delivery. Sign here, please."

She eyed the box. The cardboard was solid black. "Does it say who it's from?"

He looked at his digital pad. "Mmmmm, an M. Carlson." He shrugged. "I guess you weren't expecting it. Do you want me to return it?"

"No." She signed the pad and took the package. "I know him. Thanks."

"Have a nice day."

She closed the door in his face, staring at the package. There weren't any postage markings on it at all, but a letter was slipped inside a sealed plastic bag stuck to the box. She shook the box. It had some heft to it. She put her ear to it. *Is that ticking?* Her fingers went numb. She closed her eyes and put her ear to it again. *Phew, nothing.* She peeked back through the keyhole. The courier's van motored out of the parking lot. It was black with white stripes along the side. The lettering on the van read Jebco Deliveries, in red.

She set the box down on the coffee table and took a seat on her couch. She tore the letter off and opened it up. The typed letter read.

Agent Shaw:

Looking forward to meeting you soon. I'll let you know when I'm available. In the meantime, take advantage of the contents of this package. You'll need it ... soon.

Regards,

Mal Carlson

CHAPTER 21

"**W**HAT COULD THIS BE? AND who is Mal Carlson?" she said, opening the briefcase-sized package. Inside was a black case with a latch on it. There was a note attached. It read:

Hold onto this case. I'll need it back.

"Sure thing, buddy."

She clicked open the clasp and lifted the lid. The inside was filled with black foam, like many gun cases she had seen. There was a knife in a case about eight inches long. The grooves in the hilt perfectly fit her hand. The curved edge was as keen as anything she'd seen. In another slot were two loaded fifteen-round magazines, fit for her FBI-issued weapon.

"Interesting."

She pushed out a bullet. It had a unique full-metal casing that had a blue sheen to it. The tip was pointed and tipped with a tiny red dot. Sidney had seen plenty of ammo in her days. It reminded her of a tracer round, but it was still unlike any ballistic she'd ever seen.

"Guess I won't know until I shoot it."

In the middle of the case was a folded shirt that felt like a thin sweater of some kind. It was dark gray, tightly woven, and flexible, if a little heavy. Its waffle texture reminded her of long underwear. Dark copper stripes ran up and down the middle and around the arms.

"What the heck is this for?"

The longer she stared at the shirt, the more compelled she felt to put it on. *Why not?* She took off Smoke's T-shirt and slipped this on like a second skin. The flexible top hugged the curves of her body. It felt warm, almost like a part of her. It breathed well too. *I like it.* Her body became more alive. The throbbing inside her stitched shoulder eased. She felt energized. There was something inside the fabric. *Copper or magnets maybe.* She picked the knife up. *Hmmm?* She ran it across the sleeve of her arm. It didn't cut the odd fabric.

"Wow."

Inside the box she noticed a pair of pants, the same make-up as the shirt. She shrugged, switched out of her jeans, and slipped them on. Her blood tingled. She wanted to run a hundred miles.

What is this stuff made of?

The heightened sense of her body was exhilarating but natural. She slipped her clothes on over the outfit and laced on her boots.

Time to go … somewhere.

She snapped up the briefcase, grabbed a new bag out of the closet and transferred her gear, got her travel mug, and headed out the door. The bite of the icy air was muted by the suit, nipping at only her fingers and nose. She was firing up the engine of her car from the outside when she noticed a man walking down the sidewalk with his hands inside his jacket pockets. Her eyes met his. It was Smoke.

"Ah, I see you got one too," he said, looking at the briefcase. He jogged in place with high knees. "Tell me you got a suit too. It's amazing. I've heard about them but never believed they existed." He stretched his arms. "Man, I feel great in this."

An image of Smoke in only the suit flashed through her mind. *I bet you look great too.* "Did you drive?" she said, opening her door.

"No."

"And Sam and Guppy are?"

"Doing their thing." He rubbed his hands together. "Do you have any more coffee inside?"

Don't tempt me in close quarters. "No. Get in, let's go." She got in.

Smoke eased in beside her. He had a piece of paper in his hand. "Some places we might want to check out first. Philanthropies tied into Drake." He set it on the dash. "Fat Sam and Guppy are on it too."

She put the car in reverse, started to ease out, stopped, and shoved the car back into park. She turned and looked at him. "What are you doing here?"

"What do you mean?"

"You? Here? Now? Tell me why."

"I just happened to be in the —"

"Don't bullshit me!" She wasn't sure why she let it out, but it felt good. "The man I read about in your file is a lone wolf. Independent. Bucks authority. But here you are, completely out of the ordinary. What are you up to?"

"I'm changing my ways."

"I don't buy that."

"Why does it matter?" He slid a knife out of his jacket. It was like the one she'd received. "Did you get one of these, too? It's made of a unique steel alloy I haven't figured out yet."

"Listen, dude. I can't count on you one minute and not the next. I need you to be accountable."

"Well, I'm here," he put the knife away, "so I'm accountable. And being unpredictable is kind of my thing."

The muscles in her jaw tightened. The military and the Bureau were all about teamwork and reliability.

"I know what you're thinking, Agent Shaw. 'The machine breaks down, we break down.' Man, we used to love to watch that movie. Good stuff." He cleared his throat. "But too much blind loyalty also creates vulnerabilities. The element of surprise can escape us, and sometimes that's the edge you need when taking on an unknown enemy."

It made sense, but it wasn't satisfying. "Fair enough." She put the car back into reverse.

Smoke put his hand on top of hers and looked her in the eye. "You can count on me."

His words seemed to have a deeper meaning to them that penetrated her to the heart. She swallowed. "We'll see."

CHAPTER 22

THEY SPENT THE BETTER PART of the morning and afternoon chasing down dead ends. Restaurants. Hotels. A couple of local stores. Angi Harlow was a gorgeous woman. Her stunning looks would make an impression on anyone. Not one person was forthcoming with anything. No surprise. Not a flinch.

Sitting in traffic waiting on a stoplight, Sidney sighed.

"It's only the first day," Smoke said. He drummed on his knees. "In time something will reveal itself."

"What leads did Sam and Guppy take?"

"Probably the good ones."

"Great."

"I'm joking."

"No," she said, "you're probably right. I'd do the same thing." Her stomach groaned.

"I know a great place nearby called Pancakes and Butterflies."

"What?" She looked at him. "Really?"

"Yes." He shook his head. "No."

"Why'd you say that anyway?" The moment in the clutches of AV the werewolf popped in her mind.

"It was a joke. Sorry. I shouldn't have brought it up."

She could still feel the wolfman's hot breath on her neck, her will caving in. "No, it's fine. Your annoying words saved that day. It wouldn't be so bad to talk about it, maybe."

Smoke straightened up in his chair. "Really?"

Why not. After all, I don't know a lot of other people who have met a werewolf. "Let's check off the last place on the list, and then we'll go grab some chow."

"Sounds good to me. Chowabunga."

Sidney shook her head. *Please stop saying things like that.*

The last stop was the Hilton Renaissance Hotel. She pulled the car into the front. Smoke rolled down his window and flagged the valet. "I'll handle this."

"Sweet ride." The valet was Indian, pleasant faced with a broad smile. "Lots of horsepower. It would be my pleasure to park it."

"We aren't checking in." Smoke held up a picture. "Have you seen this woman?"

The valet's eyes lit up. He said, "Have I seen her. I'm pretty sure I have. You can't forget a face like that. Wowza!"

Sidney looked at Smoke, shaking her head. *I can't believe it. I've been asking questions all day to nothing, and he only asked one.*

Smoke shrugged.

"This is serious," Sidney said.

"I'm being serious," said the valet.

"When's the last time you saw her?" Smoke said.

"Can't say for sure," the valet replied, rubbing his white-gloved thumb and fingers together.

"Do you mind?" Smoke said to Sidney, "I left all my cash back at home."

"I don't have any cash either. It's the digital age, you know."

"Aw, that's too bad," the valet said. He tipped his cap. "See you later."

Smoke's hand shot out of the window, grabbed the man by his coat collar, and jerked his head inside the car window.

"Hey, man! Hey, Man! Hey!" the guy squirmed. "We can Square up on my phone?"

"Shut it," Smoke growled in his ear. "Now tell me what I want to know, unless you want me to bite your ear off."

Smoke's dark tone put a shiver through Sid. *Morning glory.*

The man went stiff, his eyes boggled in his head. He said, "Like Mike Tyson?"

"Exactly."

Sidney stuck the picture in his face.

"Yes. Yes! That's the bird lady. Very hot. Very hot. Good tipper."

"How long since you last saw her?" Smoke said.

"She like to party. She like to party," the valet sang in a jingle. "And wiggle that thang." He bobbed his head. "Can you let go of me please?"

"No."

The man made a pleading look at Sidney.

"When?" she said.

"Aw, these people are heavy hitters. She's got a serious crew. I'm talking spooky."

Smoke shook him.

"All right. They checked in last night. Went out a couple of hours ago and haven't been back since." He grimaced. "Please don't screw up my uniform. It's all I got, mean guy."

"Where'd they go?" Smoke said.

"Clubbing down the road. Took a black Jaguar. Black wheels rolling behind her. Park City Nights. You know, right? Park City. Park City."

"Never heard of it. Why don't you fill us in?"

"The underground. You know, the old place. I've been there once. They go there. Bad crews. Bad crews."

Smoke glanced at Sidney then said to the valet, "There better be a place, or I'm coming back for your ear."

"You'd really bite it off?"

Smoke held his knife up to the man's eye. "Nope." He pushed the man away.

Sidney accelerated back into the street. "A little dark, don't you think?"

"Didn't have much of a choice without any cash." He eyed his knife. "Besides, a little fear in the belly never hurt anyone. It's better than a knife anyway."

"I just never figured you for the tormenting type."

"Good. Let's keep it that way." He tucked the knife away and pulled something else out. A smart phone. He started texting. "Let's get something to eat."

"Now? We just got a lead."

"I've passed it on," he said, putting the phone away. He patted his belly. "Let's eat."

"No, we're going to pursue this lead first."

"Come on, I don't do so well on an empty stomach. I'm starving. I almost chewed that guy's ear off." He made a sour face. "And that just ain't right."

"No."

"Let Sam and Guppy do their thing. The Drake and their people know we're out here looking for someone. They might know the entire thing. Besides, I have the Glow in me. Let's lay low. When the time is right, we'll do the right thing." He pointed. "Take the next left at the light and head three miles downward. Great steaks and pancakes."

Sidney pushed her blinker down. *Fine.* "I'm only doing this because I was about ready to eat that man's ear too."

Smoke laughed. "You get cranky when you're really hungry, don't you."

"No." *Yes. Mother always said that. Allison too.* "I think it's the suit. It's like I'm burning more energy."

"If you say so. How's the shoulder?"

"Good."

Not much was said after that until they parked and went inside the restaurant. It was located beneath an apartment complex and displayed the modern décor of a restaurant chain. The food smelled good, and being just past dinner time, it was busy. The hostess sat them down in a booth in the corner.

Sidney studied the menu. "I don't see any pancakes."

"That's the dinner menu. They'll have them."

The waiter came over. "Drinks?"

"Water," Sidney said.

"Coke and two orders of pancakes." He glanced at Sidney.

"Uh ... just bring me the grilled chicken salad and a cup of tomato Florentine soup."

"Certainly," the waiter said, dropping his pad back in his apron. "I'll be back with your drinks."

Sidney checked her phone. 6:33 pm. *Where does the time go?*

"So," Smoke said, easing back in his chair. "Are you ready to talk about werewolves?"

CHAPTER 23

"**I** HAVEN'T SLEPT THE SAME SINCE," Sidney said, finishing off her salad. "Not bad but not my best. It was getting better, but now after this last incident, I'm not so certain."

"I've never been much of a sleeper," Smoke said. He'd almost finished off his second stack of pancakes and downed his third Coke. "I think you're right."

"About what?"

"These suits. They burn more calories or something. I'm still hungry." He jabbed his fork into the flapjacks and stuffed them in his mouth. "Not that I mind eating."

He had a drop of syrup on his grizzled chin. It didn't bother her. Nothing about the way he ate or drank bothered her at all. It was odd. There were plenty of things she'd find to pick a person apart. But not Smoke. Not yet. Something about his raw nature was enjoyable to watch. "Maybe you aren't getting it all in your mouth." She pointed at his chin.

"Oh." He wiped off his chin with the cloth napkin. "Sorry. How barbaric of me."

"Barbarians don't use utensils."

"You're right." Smoke dropped his fork, picked up the rest of the pancakes with his hand, and stuffed them in his mouth, grunting. "Mmmm."

Why did you have to do that? Everything had gone pretty well up to that point. They'd discussed the werewolf, the deaders, and the Drake. It was all a common bond only the two of them shared, and it was comforting. Almost like a good date, and she hadn't been on one in a long time. *And now this?* Her expression didn't hide her disappointment.

"What?" Smoke said, trying to clean off his sticky hands. "It's a joke. Just lightening up the mood a little. You're looking at me like this is a bad date or something." He set down the napkin. "I don't think this is going to do it. I'll be back."

She watched him go, gently shaking her head. *Lighten up, Sid.* She'd been around plenty of frivolous men in the past. Silly gestures hadn't bothered her before, at least not during her time in the military. But in the Bureau, things were always serious. *Screw it. I'm under shadow cover now. No one else is around.* She took her fork and stabbed his last bit of pancake and stuffed it in her mouth. *Oh, that's good.* She swallowed down part of his Coke. *And that's good too. Man I wish I could put it down like he does.*

The waiter showed and said, "Can I take this out of your way?"

"Yes. Take all of it, and I'm ready for the check."

Smoke returned just as the waiter was taking everything away. "I wasn't finished," he said, taking a seat. "Or was I?"

"You were," she said.

"Fine. Well, I return bearing good news."

"Really, from a trip to the restroom?"

"It's a text from Sam." He held up his phone.

It read:

She's here and this is freaky. Laterz.

"There's a picture." He pulled it up. The image was dark, but the distinct features of Night Bird's face were defined well enough. She was dancing in a mish mash of people.

"Who parties like that at this time of day?" Sidney said.

"Freaky people."

The waiter came back and set down the check. "I'll pick it up when you're ready."

"I got it," Smoke said, reaching into his back pocket and producing a thin wallet. He removed some bills and handed them to the man. "Keep the change."

You butthole! "I thought you said you didn't have any cash."

"It slipped my mind."

"Right."

"Besides, I was saving it for our dinner."

"You tormented that poor guy."

"I gave the otherwise boring man something to talk about." He put his wallet away and got up. "We can go back and tip him if you feel so bad about it. You're driving."

She narrowed her eyes on him and sighed through her nostrils. "Let's just go."

That sat in their car across the street, eyeing the entrance to the club. Every five to ten minutes or so, an expensive car or limo would pull in front of an older office building. They'd been staking it out for over an hour.

"Here comes another one," Smoke said, using a small pair of binoculars. A dark green limousine pulled alongside the curb across the busy street.

A burly bouncer with almost as much neck as head opened the limo door and escorted three well-dressed people, a short man and two women in furs, into the alleyway that was shared with the next-door building.

"Is that all rich people do, party day and night?"

"I wouldn't know," Smoke said.

"Me neither. Though I have been at a few federally funded banquets, helping out the Secret Service."

"Ah, the Secret Servants," Smoke said with a nod.

"No, Secret Service."

"That's what I said, Secret Servants."

Here we go. Conspiracy time. "I have plenty of good friends in the service."

"Hah, that's a lie."

"No it isn't."

"It is, because I don't think you have *plenty* of friends of any kind."

True. "Fine. Acquaintances."

Smoke continued. "Unless you've spent time at home with them, you don't really know them."

"All right, all right. I don't want to get into this right now. But those guys and gals are willing to take a bullet for someone, so I'm willing to give them the benefit of the doubt."

"Touché."

Thank you, Lord. "So, mister bounty hunter, what's your next move: wait for them to leave, or go in there?"

"What do you think?"

"I'm giving you *free range* on this one, but if you'd rather I didn't—"

"Sam sent me the password," he said.

"We've been sitting here an hour when all along you had the password." *And why do you text with Sam all the time and not Guppy?*

"I didn't figure you'd let the valet park your car."

True. "Or you could give me the password and I'll go inside alone," she said.

"I was thinking it should be the other way around."

"No. I trust the valet more at this point."

Smoke gave her a look.

She gave him one back. "So what's the plan to bring her in once we're inside, bounty hunter?"

"We isolate her from the pack."

"Pack? I don't like the sound of that."

"I'm not worried." Smoke lowered his binoculars from his eyes. "Somehow I don't think someone that calls themselves Night Bird is a werewolf."

"She's on the Black Slate. I have a feeling she must be something. I'm not exactly eager to find out what that is."

"Don't worry. You can count on me. We'll take her the other way out. Easy peasy."

"Why don't we take this other way in?" she said. "I'm assuming Sam and Guppy told you where it is?"

"Now you're catching on." He showed a little teeth. "But there's a catch."

"I'm listening."

"We can't go in with any weapons."

CHAPTER 24

Park City Nights. The club was expensive, yet seedy all the same. Sidney and Smoke hung back at the bar. The mirrored cabinet stocked with top shelf liquors gleamed. The wine glasses and goblets were fine crystal. The music that thumped in the room was loud but manageable for conversation.

"Would you like something to drink?" said the bartender. He was a lean black man, white shirt and black bowtie. A very clean look about him.

"Edmund Fitzgerald," Sidney said to him.

"Make it two," Smoke added.

The bartender gave them a funny look. "Coming right up." He made his way down to the end of the bar, opened up the cooler, and returned with two beer bottles with sinking ships on them. He removed the caps. "Enjoy."

Sidney took a taste.

"Interesting choice," Smoke said. His Adam's apple rolled as he gulped. "Ah. Much better than the beer they make in prison."

"Don't get carried away."

"Who, me?"

She eased up onto the stool, eyeing the dance floor. Lithe hard-bodied women danced in gleaming jewels and fine linens, their movements seductive and erotic. Sidney's throat tightened. There was something ancient and fascinating in how they moved. Almost like a ritual. *Geez.*

"I don't see her yet," Smoke said in her ear.

It brought her back to reality. She scanned the rest of the room. Half-naked women in bronze bird cages cavorted and grinded amid men huddled in conversation. The sinister atmosphere crept into Sid's bones. Stirred her soul. These were not the people of the streets she'd sworn her protection to. They were something else.

Smoke bobbed his chin to the beat. "Man, this place is filled with evil boogers. It's like I can smell it. Want to dance?"

"No," she said, taking a sip. *I want to drink.*

"I think it would be better than sitting here like a couple of toads. Come on. Show me your moves. I'm sure you have at least one."

"Oh, I've got more than one. You'll just have to take my word on that." She spied the dance floor. The women frolicked and shimmied all over the men and one another. Shameless. Inviting. "I've never seen people dance like that so early in the day before."

"It's after midnight somewhere, so I guess that's why they're letting it all hang out. Before long I bet they scream and shout."

"I bet you'd like that."

Smoke shrugged his brows and finished his beer.

A deeply tanned muscle man in a sliver of a gothic T-shirt walked by. There was a tattoo on his neck with a rising black sun on it.

"We've definitely got the right place," Smoke said, watching the man walk away. "The stink of Drake is all over it."

On the dance floor, the sultry dark and dusky women and their partners parted on the floor. A magnificent woman walked into the center. *Angi Harlow.* She wore a long silver dress trimmed in feathers and sequins with a plunging neck line. The curves of her body were without flaw. Her eyebrows sparkled with glitter. The music changed into something dark, passionate, and ceremonial. *What is going on here?*

"Night Bird is one fine lady. It's a shame she's a soul-sucking criminal," Smoke said, taking his last sip of beer. "Makes me thirsty."

Sidney had been to a Persian wedding years back and enjoyed the incredible dances. This was like that but with ten times the passion and filled with erotic steam. *Morning Glory. They're gonna rip their clothes off at any moment.* She took a long drink. Smoke nudged her out of her trance.

"Four o'clock," he said, eyeing the edges of the dance floor. "And eight o'clock. Huh, rock around the clock it seems."

Goons. Bullish men in dark suits and glasses stood around the edge of the dance floor with their arms crossed over their chests. *She really does have a lot of henchmen.* There was the bulge of a concealed gun underneath each man's jacket. Sidney knew the type. A lot of former athletes and vets who liked the spicy benefits of the macho life turned mercenary. It reminded her of a movie scene with Columbia drug lords. *The Night Bird Cartel. How nice.*

"Hey," said the man sitting beside her. "Hey, gorgeous. You want some?"

He's wasn't handsome, but his clothing and watch were exquisite. He had five lines of cocaine lined up on the bar. He seemed familiar.

"No, thanks."

He grabbed her arm. "Come on. I insist."

"No, thanks," she said, plucking his fingers away.

"Nobody tells me no, lady." He grabbed at her. She backed into Smoke. Two large bouncers appeared and locked their arms around her accoster. They picked him up off the floor. "No, no, I'm sorry guys," the man pleaded. "I was just flirting with the lady!" They escorted him out of sight.

"Interesting," Sid said, watching the bartender wipe the cocaine off the counter. She turned her attention back to the dance floor. Hips and shoulders swaying, Night Bird had her hungry eyes fastened on Smoke. One of her goons on the edge of the dance floor approached.

The bulldog of a man was bald and wore heavy rings on his fingers. "Night Bird wants to dance with you, fella," he said in a thick accent.

"I'm with someone," Smoke said, "and I'm not the best dancer."

The man, broader than Smoke but not quite as tall, cracked his neck from side to side and said, "Get out there now, before I put all those pretty teeth out."

"I—"

"Bub," the goon said, "she ain't a patient lady, and I'm not a patient man."

"Sure," Smoke said, setting his bottle on the bar. "I'm going." He eased his way around the thug, headed to the dance floor, and took Night Bird's extended hand in his.

Sidney felt flames shoot through her as the woman's hand caressed his back and went over his butt and down the backs of his legs. *Damn Dirty Bird!*

CHAPTER 25

FTER ABOUT TWO MINUTES OF bumping and grinding, the music changed to something slower and more seductive. Ears red underneath her dark locks, Sidney was impressed with how Smoke handled himself. *He's a decent dancer. I'll give him that.* The strapping man towered over the men and women on the starlit dancefloor, except for Night Bird. In her heels, she was almost as tall as he. As the music slowed, the exotic woman wrapped her arms around his waist and drew him in close.

Can't wait to see you in your bird cage, whore.

As Sid finished her thoughts, she found Night Bird's eyes on hers. The woman's mysterious gaze was inviting as she nestled her head against Smoke's muscular chest. Like a flash of the camera, she winked. Sidney's head spun a little, and she bumped back into the bar. She felt those icy spiders crawling over the goosebumps on her arms.

What was that?

It was that same seductive power that AV had over her, paralyzing her reason and opening the gates to her lusts. She took a long draw from her beer and looked away.

Get it together, Sid. Butterflies and Pancakes!

It didn't help that Smoke seemed to be enjoying himself. He smiled as his lips moved in conversation. Sidney wanted to know what he was saying to her and what she was saying to him. She realized she needed to distract herself. She started counting. The guests. The entertainers. The staff, bouncers, and most importantly, Night Bird's bodyguards.

Eight thugs. Great.

Extracting their mark wouldn't be easy. All of the men were armed with pistols or possibly small Uzis. A single elevator, the one they had taken, led up and out. By it was posted a guard who was almost as wide as the elevator itself. She turned and motioned to the bartender.

"Another beer from the lakes, my lady friend?"

"No thanks. Um," she smiled and wiggled up to him. "I was kinda curious. What happened to that guy snorting all of those lines? I feel bad for him."

"Don't feel bad for that guy. He's a real jerk, a good tipper, but a jerk. He should have known better."

"I just don't want to see anyone get hurt. I'm a peacemaker. He'll be all right, won't he?"

The bartender's eyes drifted toward the kitchen doors. "Lady, don't ask questions that you don't want the answers to, especially in a place like this." He leaned closer. His tone became grim. "You're new, so I'm going to cut you a break and pretend you didn't ask me anything. Do you understand?'

Sidney swallowed and widened her eyes. "Sure." *You've given me all I need.* "Uh, where's the powder room?"

He pointed. "That way."

"Thanks."

Passing the kitchen on her way to the bathroom, she slowed and cracked open the windowless door. About ten people were busy at work in white outfits and red aprons. A waitress in a feathered cocktail dress bustled by. Making a quick scan of the area, Sidney noticed a service elevator in the rear. Perfect. A man was seated by it in a metal folding chair. His suit jacket was draped over the back, and he had two pistols strapped under his heavy shoulders. A shotgun rested in his lap. *Not perfect.*

She headed for the restroom and glanced at Smoke, who still danced comfortably in Angi's clutches. *Horndog.* The restroom was long, with many stalls crafted in white marble stone that rose from the floor to the ceiling. Sidney walked by a half dozen sinks in front of a huge vanity mirror trimmed in cherry wood. Beside them sat a small lithely built woman in a feathered mask. A basket of toiletries, same as those on the sinks, sat on her lap.

Weird. Too weird.

Sidney took the faucet farthest from the woman in the bird mask and turned the water on.

"Ow!"

The water was steaming hot. She glanced at the woman, who had her head cocked to the side. The black bird eyes faced her.

Get used to it. Ignore it.

She checked her face. Her make-up was a far cry from what she'd observed on the other women. Her clothes were far from up to snuff either.

How out of place must we be?

She washed her hands and had begun to rinse them off when the moaning started.

"Uh, uh, uh ..."

A man and woman were cavorting in one of the stalls. Their moans got louder, the rollicking more pronounced. Sidney took a deep breath and adjusted her hair. The little attendant appeared with a steaming cloth on a plate. Sidney plucked it up with her fingers.

"Thanks."

She wiped her neck down. *I think it's going to take more than this to get the filth off of me.* She dropped it on the plate, and the little attendant walked away and put the washcloth in a bin then returned with a basket of toiletries. Sidney took a closer look at them. *Geez! Some of this stuff is a hundred dollars an ounce.* She picked out two tiny perfumes and a small shampoo bottle and crammed them in her pocket. The attendant's bird eyes were glued on her.

"Aw, you won't tell."

Sidney felt a strange compulsion overcome her, staring at the tiny woman in the mask. Something was not right. It creeped down her spine. Looking deep into the eyes, she stretched out her fingers toward the mask. The figure didn't move away. She glanced at the tiny fingers holding the basket. They reminded her of her niece, Megan. *No. Not another child.* She started to pull the mask up.

Wham!

The attendant jerked away at the sound of a stall door banging open. A giggling woman and a man with devilish good looks staggered by. Tucking his shirt in and buckling his belt, he winked at Sid and said, "Good evening."

The stall woman adjusted her skintight dress, slung her bra over her shoulder, and added as they strutted out, "Maybe next time you can join us?"

Sidney stood alongside the sinks shaking her head, thinking, *Ew, they didn't even wash up after that. Now I know why they're called the filthy rich.* Giving the little attendant no more thought, she headed back out into the club. Making her way back to the bar and spying the dance floor, she noticed something out of place. Smoke and Night Bird were gone.

CHAPTER 26

SMOKE AND NIGHT BIRD WEREN'T the only ones gone from the dance floor. The bodyguards had vanished too. *Those oxen shouldn't be too easy to hide.* She cut through the tables and patrons until she found herself on the other side of the room. Several well-concealed alcoves dotted the back. The heavy curtains were drawn on most of them. Sidney got a peek inside the closest one. Girls. Men. Sex. Drugs. She moved down the row.

Ah, follow the goons.

A pair of body guards stood on either side of the alcove at the end. The other guards were spread out nearby.

Play along, Sid. Play along.

She weaved her way toward them showing a dreamy look in her eye. She said to the nearest bodyguard, "Have you seen my friend? Tall guy. Kind of handsome?" She added a hiccup. "He was just dancing with that gorgeous lady. I want to party with them."

"Just move along," the man said. "If Night Bird wants you, she'll let you know, and I ain't heard nothing about her wanting you. Consider it a good thing. So move along now, prissy."

I am so gonna take you out first, you nose-pierced jerk.

"But," she said, batting her eyelashes, "can I at least go in and say hi?"

"No." he looked her up and down. "But, maybe on my break, if you do me a favor, I can work something out." He patted her ass.

I hate this guy. I hate this place.

"What did you have in mind?" she said.

"Well," his eyes widened. He touched his finger to his ear and cocked his head. He looked back at Sidney. "Huh, seems you have the okay to go in." He leaned in closer and whispered in her ear. His breath was heavy with cigarettes, but his soft words were perfectly clear. "That's too bad. I was doing you a favor." He pulled the heavy maroon curtain back and stepped aside. "Nice meeting you, lady."

Doing me a favor? I don't see how.

Sidney gave the man a funny look and drifted inside. Smoke sat back in a comfortable booth looking as innocent as a Boy Scout. A small round table offered drugs and drinks. Night Bird was beside him, glued to his hip. One long leg was draped over his, while her free hand toyed with the hair around his ears.

"Is this your little friend, John?" Angi said, offering a playful smile. "She's tall for a woman. Finely crafted. I like that. What is your name, dearie?"

"Sidney."

"Hmph," Night Bird said, "fitting. So, why don't you come and join us." She fanned her free arm out toward the other three people in the room. Two women's hard bodies were only clad in feathery lingerie. A chiseled man with long brown locks and the looks of a Chippendale dancer sat drinking a bottled beer in only cutoff sequined trousers.

I think I've seen enough.

"I think it's time to go, *John*," Sidney said, lifting her brows.

"Oh, dearie," Night Bird said, squeezing Smoke's thigh, "he's not going anywhere. But maybe you can have him back tomorrow. He's such a fine drink of water. I can't wait to bathe with him."

Sidney's chest tightened. "John, it's time to go."

Smoke didn't reply. Instead, he sat in a daze.

Aw, crap! She's done something to him.

"You're starting to bother me, dearie," Night Bird said. "I think it's time you moved along." She glanced at the scantily clad man. "Be a dear, Bulldog, and escort our lady friend out."

The well-defined man's bulging muscles flexed as he stood up.

Sidney laughed. He was maybe five and a half feet tall, and she towered over him. "He's cute, but really," she said, staying him with her hand. "Please, I'll show myself out. I don't want you to hurt yourself"—she glanced at his pants— "Bulldog." She backed up toward the door. "John, it's time to go. Pancakes and Butterflies."

"Pancakes and Butterflies?" the woman said. "My dear, what on earth are you talking abou—"

Night Bird slumped forward and crashed through the table.

Bulldog growled at Sidney and closed in with clutching fingers.

In a flash, Sidney put everything she had into a roundhouse kick that broke Bulldog's jaw. He collapsed on the floor and didn't move. The two women in the room started giggling, and one lit up a joint for the other.

"I take it you have a plan to get out of here," Smoke said. He had Night Bird draped over his shoulder.

"You drugged her?"

"It's an unethical method, but effective," Smoke said, staring at the curtains. "Every situation is different. So, did you disable all the bodyguards?"

"What? Disable them? Exactly how would I do that? I don't even have a gun."

"You take one of theirs."

Sidney stood by the curtain, felt the material, and listened. It was amazing how quiet the room was on account of the heavy fabric. She could barely make out the music. "I have an exit plan at least. That's more than you have, *John*."

One of the girls started clapping. She said, "I like this game. What is it?"

"Hey," the other girl said, taking a toke. "What happened to Bulldog? And why do you have Night Bird over your shoulder, new guy?"

"Where's the other exit?" Smoke said. His eyes flashed, and his tone was urgent.

"Why? What are you going to do?"

Suddenly, one of the girls let out an ear-splitting shriek.

Smoke shrugged his shoulders at Sid. "Run for it!"

CHAPTER 27

ONE OF THE BODYGUARDS STEPPED inside the curtains. Smoke plowed over the man and kept going. Sidney didn't stick around. She burst through the curtains just as the second bodyguard lowered his gun on Smoke's back. She chopped him in the neck and twisted the weapon free of his grip. She turned.

Aw, crap!

The other four bodyguards were up, weapons drawn and moving. Alert men. Formidable. They didn't see her coming. She squeezed the trigger.

Pop! Pop! Pop! Pop!

Two men collapsed, clutching at their legs and crying out in pain. Sidney jumped over them and sprinted after Smoke and his assailants, out into the larger room of the club. That was when the music stopped and the screaming started. A sea of bodies came to life and moved in a wave of panic. A heavyset woman in a sparkly tube top crashed into Sidney, knocking her to the floor.

Hell's bells!

She scrambled to her feet and shoved her way through the throng of sweaty bodies toward the kitchen door. Two bodyguards disappeared inside. She was almost there when another woman grabbed her, yelling, "Help me! Help me!"

Sidney slapped her in the face, widening the woman's eyes. "Help yourself, halfwit!" She stormed toward the kitchen door and heard gunshots crack out on the other side.

Blaat-at-at! Blaat-at-at! Blaat-at-at!

The kitchen help dashed out as machine-gun fire ripped through the metal pots and stainless cabinets. Sid went in low, spied a man blasting away with his back to her, and fired.

Pop! Pop!

He collapsed bleeding on the floor.

Blaat-at-at! Blaat-at-at! Blaat-at-at!

She dove behind a rolling counter and peeked underneath. *Feet, feet, where are you?* She saw a pair of filthy sneakered feet shuffling over the floor tiles and took aim.

Pop!

"Ow! Sonuvabitch! My foot!" His shooting became wild.

Blaat-at-at! Blaat-at-at! Blaat-at-at! Blaat-at-at! Blaat-at-at! Blaat-at-at! Blaat-at-at! Blaat-at-at! Blaat-at-at!

"I'm gonna kill you! I'm gonna kill you good!" said the bodyguard, spraying the room with bullets. "Where are you! Where the hell are you!"

Blaat-at-at! Blaat-at-at! Blaat-at-at! Blaat-at-at! Blaat-at-at! Blaat-at-at! Blaat-at-at! Click. "Aw, hell."

Whop! Thud!

From under the counter, Sidney saw the man fall flat on the floor. *Whew!*

"Sid? Come on!" Smoke yelled out.

She popped up and saw him. "What about the guy at the elevator?"

Ka-Blam! Ka-Blam!

"You talking about me?" said a hard voice. "Come on. Take my elevator."

Ka-Blam! Ka-Blam!

"Shoot him, Sid!"

"Yeah! Go ahead! Try and shoot me!" The man started clearing the kitchen aisles, one shotgun blast at a time.

Ka-Blam! Ka-Blam! Ka-Blam!

Sidney scurried from one side of the aisle to the other and got a bead on the man. She took a knee and fired center mass.

Pop! Pop! Pop! Pop! Click.

The big fella teetered backward into the counter, jostling the shot-up pots and pans. "Oof," he said. "That stung. Good thing I'm best friends with Kevlar." He snarled and pulled his two pistols out. Lowered the barrels on her. "Your elevator's going down, lady!"

Sidney dove down the aisle.

Blam! Blam! Blam! Blam!

"Where'd you go, little rabbit?"

BLam! Blam! Blam!

Pinned down with nowhere to go, she crouched behind the counter. *Think of something, Sid. Think!*

"Last call, you squirrely little bitch!" A hail of bullets ripped through the counter.

Blam! Blam! Blam! Blam! Blam!

Bong!

The gunshots stopped.

Bong?

"Sid, are you coming?"

She glanced over the counter. Smoke was standing in the elevator, Night Bird still in tow. A huge frying pan was in his hand. He tossed it out on the floor with a clatter. She got up and ambled over. A bullet grazed her ankle.

Inside the elevator, Smoke said, "You all right?"

She pressed the button going up and glared at him.

More bodyguards spilled into the room and rushed the door, which hadn't yet started to close. Smoke filled the doorway, cradling Night Bird in his arms. "I wouldn't shoot if I were you."

The men's itchy trigger fingers froze. A few eternal seconds went by, and finally the doors closed.

"You're an idiot," Sidney said.

"Me, what did I do?"

"You started a date in the middle of a mission."

"I just went with the flow. Sometimes the best plan is to let things happen and strike when there's an opening."

"Oh, you had an opening all right," she said, looking at the woman in his arms. "A pretty big one."

"Hey, I'm dedicated to the mission, whatever it takes," he finished with a wry smile.

"This isn't On Her Majesty's Secret Service, and you aren't James Bond."

"Don't be a Moneypenny." He glanced at her ankle. "Looks like you're going to need some of my services again."

"It's barely a flesh wound."

The elevator came to a stop.

"Here," Smoke said, handing Night Bird over to Sid, "hold her."

As soon as the elevator doors parted, his hands snaked out and jerked in a man carrying a pistol. He slammed the man into the back wall and snatched up his gun. "Switch me." He hefted Night Bird over his shoulder and gave Sid the gun.

Outside the elevator, they went down the service ramp that led outside. A cold rain was pouring down. After splashing down the street, they raced up the sidewalk, crossed over the intersection, and ran to the parking spot where the Hellcat waited.

"Hurry," Sid said, opening up the door, eyeing the valet station to the club across the street. The husky bodyguard was talking into his wrist as he scanned the streets.

Smoke stuffed Night Bird in the back seat. "Let's go," he said, hopping into the passenger seat.

"Stop! Stop!" The bodyguard had spotted them. He pulled out his gun. Others came to his aid. "Stop!" *Pop! Pop! Pop!*

Sidney stomped on the gas, and the car sped away. She watched a swarm of angry figures diminish in the rearview mirror and took the next turn down the street. "I better not have any bullet holes in my car!"

"Are you blaming me?" Smoke said.

"You're the one who said to park in the street."

"It was just a suggestion—and a good one, seeing how we're making a clean getaway. You should thank me."

"We'll see after I inspect the Hellcat later." She took out her phone and said, "Call Howard mobile."

A voice grumbled on the other line, "Yeah, Sid?"

"Ted, Night Bird's in custody. Where's the safe spot?"

"Already?" he said.

"Safe spot, Ted. Safe spot."

"Oh, oh, all right. Let me see. Are you on the road?"

"Yes," she said, irritated.

"Okay, keep moving and I'll text you directions. Give me a minute. Bye." He disconnected.

Sid looked over at Smoke, who asked, "What did he say?"

"He's texting directions. It'll be a minute."

A coldness slipped into her body. In the rearview mirror, an image appeared. It was Night Bird leaning over her seat. A strange, somewhat demonic expression was creased in her face. Her lacquered lips parted, and she said in a bewitching voice, "Pardon me, but where are we going?"

CHAPTER 28

T RYING HER BEST TO KEEP her eyes on the road, Sidney said to Smoke, "I thought you sedated her."

"I did," Smoke said, looking back at Night Bird.

The woman leaned forward from the back seat and placed her hands on either side of both headrests. "Sedate me? Ha. I'm immune to your toxins and poisons."

Sid noticed the long fingernails on the woman's hands. There was something unnatural about them. "I see you didn't restrain her either?"

"I didn't feel there was a need," Smoke said. Night Bird was toying with his hair. "She shouldn't have woken up until tomorrow."

"Don't worry," Angi said to both of them, "I won't run. I never run." She eased back into the back seat. "Interesting, a little tight, but cozy." The exotic woman cocked her head in quick shifts and whistled a bird song. Her dark spacey eyes were in another world.

"I think you better restrain her," Sidney said from the corner of her mouth.

Smoke opened the glove box and took out a set of flex cuffs. He twisted his shoulders around toward the back and said, "Do you mind?"

"Oh," Angi said, offering her wrists. "I don't mind at all. I enjoy being tied up. How about you?"

He secured her. "Not so much."

"And what about your uptight friend?" Angi touched Sidney's ear.

Sid jerked away. "Sit back, bird lady."

"Humph." Night Bird eased back and resumed her bird song.

For someone who'd been apprehended, the woman was very much at ease. Not the slightest worry creased her face. *This really isn't right.* Sid's phone buzzed. Directions from Ted appeared, to the safe location. It was twelve miles away. She glanced back at Night Bird. *I can't handle her tweeting another minute longer.* "Hey! Night Bird. Shut your beak."

Night Bird quieted. "No need to be rude. I am capable of mercy, you know."

"What is that supposed to mean?"

Angi let out a frivolous laugh. "You two don't know anything about me, do you?"

"Such as?" Smoke said.

"Blind mice," the woman said. "The innocent can be so delicious." She chirped out a flittering sound. "The Black Slate. I know I'm on that dubious list. You aren't the first to find me, and you won't be the last either." She checked her nails. "I'm not one for hiding."

She's way too confident. I should probably shoot her now.

"So," Night Bird continued, "are you the pair that took down the wolf man? He was such a cock. But I admit, we were impressed. Two mortals taking down the wolf. I would have lost a bundle on that bet, not that money matters." She clapped her hands together. "Good for you."

Not good. Again, someone knew more about what was going on than Sid did. But didn't most criminals? *Keep her talking.*

Smoke beat her to it. "He wasn't so tough. Just bad dog breath walking on hind legs. I look forward to taking out more of them."

"Oh ho!" Angi leaned forward. "I like a man who is cocky. Even a mortal one."

"Everyone is mortal," Sidney chimed in.

"Really?" the woman said. "I know a lot of dead people who are still living, including me. Don't be so sure of yourself ... Agent Shaw."

What is she talking about? Sid's fingernails drummed on the wheel. Night Bird had said too many odd things. *Mortals.* She talked as though she was a demi-god or something. But she was so confident when she spoke. Everything she said had the stamp of truth behind it.

And Night Bird, she sat back in her seat with a confident smile, staring out the window. The voluptuous debutante seemed invincible.

Sid stopped at a light and turned the wipers off.

"Huh," Smoke said, looking out the windshield. Large black birds flew across the night sky and landed on the nearby power lines. They squawked at the car. "Are those crows or ravens? I've never seen birds like that fly at night before."

"They do what they're told," Night Bird said. "And they are ravens."

"Aren't they the same?" Sid asked. "Black. Annoying. Ugly."

Angi sneered. Her voice became a hiss. "You had best watch your tongue, little woman. You know not of what you speak."

"No surprise that you know a lot about them," Sidney said, watching Angi in the mirror. "I've heard a lot of people call them rat birds." The light turned green, and they accelerated forward.

Smoke stared out of his window.

This is getting creepy. The birds were following them. Sidney gunned the gas a little more. "Do they like cheese?"

"I can tell you what they don't like," Night Bird said in a very dark tone. "They don't like people."

"Ah," Smoke said, looking inquisitive, "so that's why they crap on my car?"

"Oh, John, please don't you start," Night Bird said. "I've grown fond of you. Of course, I'm always fond of my pets, especially the lab rats. They're so entertaining."

"Lab rats?" Sidney said. They were approaching the safe zone drop.

"Well, it's a bit more of a modern terminology, but every decade or so, a group of fools such as yourselves shows up to take the likes of us down." Night Bird sighed then whistled a dreary tune that was impossible for a human. "We toy with them until we bore of their games. And then we wipe them out."

Sidney's hand slipped to her Glock, inside the door pocket. "So, care to fill us in a little more on who *we* is?" She glanced at the sky. It was cloudy, but no moon was out. "Would that *we* be the Drake criminal network?"

"Such children," Angi said, shaking her head. "I think it's too late for your education. Besides, some things, you are better off not knowing. Your minds aren't ready to comprehend them. But soon enough, the world will be ready. This is just the beginning."

This needs to be the end. As harmless as she seemed, Night Bird's calm cool collectedness was a tad on the frightening side. Sid looked up from the highway and noticed a black helicopter landing in the distance. It was FBI. They landed about a mile off the road at an abandoned truck stop. The tightness in her neck eased. *Good! They can have the bird-loving loon.*

"It seems my escort has arrived. I so hate those flying metal machines," Night Bird said. "So loud, and they smell nasty."

As soon as they pulled into the lot, they were surrounded by agents clad in body armor and armed with M-16 assault rifles.

What is up with all the hardware? Badge out and up, Sidney exited the car. Smoke helped Night Bird out of the back seat.

"This was fun. Too bad we'll never do it again," Night Bird said, leaning on his chest. She sucked her teeth. "I just love the dark and charming kind." Two agents pulled her away and marched her toward the chopper. "Ta ta!"

A sea of ravens landed on the truck stop's roof, on all the cars and trucks, and all over the pavement, pecking and squawking.

Sidney shooed them away from her car. "Get!" She looked around. "Who's the agent in charge?"

A Chinese man in full gear walked up with his rifle slung over his shoulder. He stood eye to eye with her and had a small mole under his left eye. He extended his hand. "Agent Ramsey."

"Do you have any paperwork or anything that needs to be signed off?"

"No. I was just told to get my ass down here ten minutes ago. We rolled off another job to come to this one." Agent Ramsey looked at the chopper. "I was expecting something a lot less fine and a lot more dangerous. Who is she?"

"Huh, well, I guess I can't really tell you that. But thanks for the back-up."

Agent Ramsey touched the microphone in his ear. "Once the bird's out of site, we're all clear." Watching the chopper lift off, he shrugged. "Nice meeting you, Agent Shaw. Nice car too. Be careful you don't get any bird poop on it." He kicked at a raven and walked off.

Sidney eased up alongside Smoke. His gaze hadn't left the chopper. "What do you think, easy peasy?"

He slowly shook his head. "Maybe too easy peasy."

Watching the helicopter drift up and away, Sid's eyes widened. An agent from inside the chopper was plummeting toward the ground. Her heart jumped. "Oh no!"

CHAPTER 29

A GENTS SPRINTED TOWARD THE BODY that had crashed to the ground, but Sidney's eyes remained transfixed on the scene above. The chopper wavered in the air, hung in place for a moment, then spun in a three sixty. Her keen eyes picked up a struggle in the cockpit. A wrestling of bodies.

What on earth is going on?

Another man was hurled out of the chopper doors. "Aaaiiyyeee!"

More agents scrambled in aid then slowed as they gazed up. Something alive emerged from the reeling chopper. A giant bird of some sort.

"My Lord," one agent said, gawping. "Are those wings?"

Among the distant commotion, a bird with the head of a woman dropped from the chopper and into the sky. Like an eagle, the bird-woman clutched a screaming agent in her talons. She soared overhead, making a cackling shriek just one hundred feet above.

"Night Bird's a harpy?" Smoke said, drawing out his pistol.

"A what?" Sid said, taking aim.

Night Bird circled above. Her great wings of black and grey feathers spanned fifteen feet. Everything from her chest down was covered in feathers, and her face was still human. It was radiant but in a dark and supernatural state. Suddenly, she dove and flung the agent from her talons. The screaming man soared head over heels and smashed into the FBI van.

"Run!" Agent Ramsey said, pointing toward the sky. "Take cover! Now!"

The helicopter descended in their direction. Legs churning, Sid sprinted away and took cover behind a parked bus. The chopper plunged into the blacktop.

Boom!

A fiery explosion erupted, spraying the parking lot with bits and pieces of metal. Black birds scattered everywhere, taking to the air in droves and diving down in a black swirl of terror on the other agents. Men and women were flayed, and they screamed.

"Come on," Smoke said, scraping Sidney off the ground and onto her feet. "Let's move!"

Wading through the sea of birds, they headed for the car. A shadow glided over them, cackling. It was Night Bird. She snatched another agent off the ground and pumped her wings, racing into the sky, up, up, up, a speck in the dim light. Suddenly, the woman dropped from high above and smashed through the truck-stop roof.

Sidney's stomach turned in the chaos. *This is mad! Hitchcock madness!*

FBI agents fired bullets into the sky. Night Bird weaved and darted with grace and speed, cackling the entire time. In a streak of feathers, she closed in on one man and sliced his throat open. Blood spilled from the gaping wound.

Sidney blasted away at the evil creature as it did aerial somersaults in the sky. Her bullets clipped off some feathers that sprinkled the air. Night Bird and her ravens continued their assault on the other agents, who scrambled for the cover of their cars, plucking the birds from their ankles and faces.

"Strange that they aren't after us," Smoke said, taking cover behind the fuel pumps beneath the canopy. "Keep an eye out for her."

Sidney dashed the sweat from her eyes. Underneath the truck depot's cover, the ravens darted in and out, squawking. She fired at three of them. *Pop! Pop! Pop!* They dropped from the sky.

"Good shooting," Smoke said, "but you might want to save your bullets. There's at least a thousand more to go."

Sidney's mind raced. Her heart pumped from terror. Nature had run wild, and she'd seen at least five agents fall in the chaos. "We have to end this!" She marched out from underneath the oversized canopy and eyed the sky. There was no sign of Night Bird. "Where are you?"

"Looking for me?" said a voice from above. It was Night Bird, standing on top of the roof in her full glory. Her feather-coated body still maintained her voluptuous figure, but her arms were turned into wings with hands, and razor-sharp talons had become her feet. The bird-woman's face was dark and twisted, yet beautiful. "Here I am!"

Sidney fired.

Pop. Pop. Pop.

The spray of bullets hit center mass, drawing a gusty laugh from Night Bird. "Your mortal weapons cannot hurt me." She took flight and disappeared into the sky.

Smoke eased along to her side and said, "Which bullets are you using?"

"Government-issued loads, why?"

Smoke popped the magazine of his weapon and showed her the blue-tipped bullets within. "I think I have a pretty good idea what these are for." He slapped the magazine back in. "If she comes back, let me take the next shot." He scanned the sky.

"Why don't you let me handle that? I think I'm a better shot."

"No," Smoke said, shaking his head, "I don't think so."

"Even if those pretty bullets work," she said, "we're supposed to take her in alive, you know."

"After she killed all those people?" Smoke set his jaw. "I don't think so."

Good point. Good men and women were down. Many dead. Ravens pecked and clawed at their flesh. Capture would be mercy to the murderous fiend.

"And to think I kinda liked birds up until now," he said. "But Night Bird is going down."

"I'm sure they aren't all bad. But I think we need to take her alive. Those are my orders."

In an instant, the ravens stopped squawking and took off in flight, disappearing into the night sky.

"That was weird," Smoke said, surveying the lot.

The surviving agents stumbled around assisting one another. In the distance, Sidney recognized the silhouette of Agent Ramsey. *Good.*

"Oh, I beg your pardon," a familiar sultry voice said. "Are you searching for me?" Night Bird stood near the pumps behind them, back in human form and completely naked. She held out her blood-caked hands and wrists. "I surrender."

Smoke aimed his gun at her chest.

"Please don't," Night Bird said, eyeing his gun. "I don't want any part of your little blue bullets." She touched her ear. "We birds have very keen hearing, you know. I'm glad I was paying attention."

"She's unarmed," Sid said, readying her own weapon.

"She only looks unarmed."

"What's the matter?" Night Bird said, approaching them, "Are my perfect breasts a threat to you?"

"Sorry, Agent Shaw," Smoke said, "but I don't play by your rules." His finger tensed over the trigger.

"Stay where you are, Night Bird," Sid said, stepping between the bounty hunter and the woman. "Smoke, ease up."

Night Bird stopped, lifted her hands above her head, and dropped to her knees. "I'm really sorry about your comrades, but my temper got the best of me when one of them groped me." She offered a coy smile. "I'm over it. I'll play nice from now on."

"Don't trust her, Sid," Smoke said in a growl.

Duty. Despite the carnage, Night Bird had to be taken in alive. Those were the orders. Sid was a good soldier, and she'd follow them as long as she could. She pulled out her flex cuffs and said, "Hands behind your back."

"You are a faithful soldier, Agent Shaw," Night Bird said, placing her hands behind her back, "but you should have listened to your friend." She opened her mouth wide, and an ear-splitting shriek came out.

Sidney's stomach turned and her knees buckled. She hit the pavement and the world started spinning. In front of her, Night Bird rose up, still unleashing the hellish sound. Sid felt bile rise up in her mouth when the horrendous sound stopped. She spat it out.

Ahead, Night Bird's body convulsed and transformed. Muscle, sinew, and bone popped and crackled. Feathers sprouted out. The bird woman shuffled over and grabbed ahold of Smoke. The big man's long limbs trembled. His gun lay inches from his fingers. Sid's ears were ringing. She tried to find her own gun but couldn't move. She couldn't feel her fingers. *Ugh!*

Night Bird was a much bigger bird than she was a woman. She scooped Smoke up in her talons, spread her great wings, took flight, and disappeared into the night sky.

Sidney's mind cried out, "Noooooooooooooooo!"

CHAPTER 30

H EAD DOWN, SIDNEY SAT INSIDE the Wayfarer's Way restaurant, stirring
her spoon in her chicken tortellini soup. It was midday, two days after
Night Bird flew off with Smoke. Since the chopper crashed. Since good
FBI agents died.

I can't believe he's gone. I can't believe they're all gone.

She glanced at the front page of the Washington Post on the table. The
headline read:

FBI AGENTS PERISH IN TRAGIC TRAINING INCIDENT.

Conspiracies and accusations followed. The community was shocked.
Television, Internet, and radio buzzed with theories about terrorist activities.
Everyone had a theory. Everyone was wrong.

How many other fabricated stories have I believed before?

There had been plenty of incidents with loose ends she had previously taken
at face value but had begun to reconsider. Pan Am's Malaysia Flights. Seal Team
Six. Was any of it true? Everything she read in the paper was a lie. What else was?

She rubbed her temple with one hand and took a sip of soup with the other.
It tasted funny. Not that she'd eaten much. Everything tasted funny since Night
Bird's screech. The jarring sound still echoed in her ears. She could still see
Smoke's body being hauled through the air like a carcass. It left her cold inside.
She should have trusted him. She should have let him take Night Bird down.
Now, he might be gone forever. *I failed him.*

She closed her eyes and sighed. She felt as if something was eating her
from the inside out. After the incident, it had taken her thirty minutes to get
back on her feet. By the time that happened, help had come, sort of. Men and
women covered from head to toe in hazmat-type attire administered aid and
whisked the dead away in minutes. It was bizarre. Not of one of them spoke or
identified themselves. Agent Ramsey did all of the talking while they patched up
his bleeding arm. Sid was in a haze eyeing the sky. By the time they shook her
out of it, everyone was gone. She was taken to a small hospital and released the
day before with orders to stay away from headquarters and meet her boss at the
Wayfarer. Finally he came.

Ted Howard entered the restaurant, hung up his coat and hat, and took a seat across from her.

"How are you doing, Sid?"

She held up the paper. "It's all a lie."

"Aw, come on. You know we can't print what you and the other agents saw, especially when none of it can be verified." A waitress approached with her honey brown hair up in a bun. "Coffee and the special," Ted said.

"Coming right up."

"I'm surprised you can eat," Sidney added, pushing her soup away.

"I'm not hungry, but I am a creature of habit. You know that." He leaned forward with an uneasy look on his face. "Sid, you're going to have to let this one go."

"What do you mean, *let it go?*"

He swallowed, and his eyes drifted before they found hers again. "The Black Slate is shut down for now. At least until the smoke clears. Ah!" He shook his head. "Sorry, bad choice of words. Let me rephrase. Until the dust settles."

"What do you mean, Ted? I have to go after him. We have to go after him."

"You know bloody well that the Pentagon is all over this one. At least until the media moves on to something else." He rolled his sleeves up, revealing his meaty forearms. "But there will be an investigation, and that will take weeks. Heck, months. This won't go away for a long time."

"I have to find him, Ted. You know that. We can't just forget about him."

"If he was an agent, sure, but he's not." He lifted his finger up. "And before you get mad at me, you know that my hands are tied on this one."

"Just because he isn't an agent doesn't mean he's worth any less."

"Yeah, well they don't see it that way. He's a convict. Expendable." He frowned. "That's probably why they signed him up for this gig."

"And what about me? Am I expendable?"

"You were his Bureau liaison, Sid. His handler, not his partner." He nodded at the waitress, who dropped off a steaming cup of coffee. "I told you to use extraordinary caution, didn't I? You jumped into the shark tank feet first. You have to back off of this."

"You know I can't do that. I'm a vet. He's a vet. You're a vet. We don't abandon one another, come hell or high water. He wouldn't do that to me."

"Sid, your report says that a giant bird flew away with him." He clenched his jaws. "I can't believe you wrote that."

"That's what happened, Ted!" She clenched her fists. She wanted to hit the table but restrained herself. "What if we can find him? When Dydeck was alive, he and Cyrus injected Smoke with a serum called the Glow."

"The Glow? I've never heard of it."

She wanted to reach across the table and slap him. All of his answers were too convenient. He had to know something. "Can you look into it?"

"Sure. All right. Fine."

"I'm being serious, Ted."

"So am I. I promise."

She picked at her lip. That might take forever, and Smoke would be long gone or dead by then. She needed something now, but she had nothing. She didn't even have a number for Fat Sam or Guppy. "What about Agent Ramsey? Why don't you talk to him? Plenty of agents saw what happened."

"And plenty of agents want to keep their jobs," he said matter-of-factly.

"Are you kidding me?"

He shook his head. "Sorry." His food arrived, a loaded cheeseburger and fries.

"So what am I supposed to do then, bury my head in the sand?"

He squirted ketchup on his plate. "Be patient and see how things turn out."

"And what about John Smoke?"

"I know you liked the guy. I liked him too. But given his background, you're just going to have to pray his own survival skills get him out okay." He took a bite of his burger. "Sometimes that's all you can do."

"Pray?"

He shrugged. "It works sometimes. I once had a friend—"

"Ted," she said, getting up from the booth. "Just check into the Glow. I'm going home ... for now."

"Aw Sid, don't go like this—"

She made it out of the restaurant before he finished and headed for her car. *I'm such a fool!* She opened the Hellcat's door, got behind the wheel, and fired the engine up. *Perhaps a long drive through pigeons will help.* Her phone buzzed. It read Unknown Caller on the screen. *Fat Sam and Guppy?*

"Hello?"

"Agent Shaw," an unfamiliar voice said. "It's time to go after Smoke."

CHAPTER 31

"WHO IS THIS?" SIDNEY ASKED.

"Mal. Mal Carlson," the man replied. His voice was cool but serious. "And your first question should probably be, 'Where is he?'"

"Or, maybe it should be, 'Where are you?' assuming you are Mal Carlson." She turned left on the next street. "Mister, I have no idea if you are who you say you are."

"Well, you got the case with the bullets I assume?"

True. He wouldn't know that otherwise. "Yes."

"Do you have on the *Zweite Haut* suit I made you?"

"Sweet heart?"

"*Zweite Haut* is German for second skin," he said with a testy tone. "I haven't thought up a good name for it. It's a trivial thing. Do you have it on?"

"No."

The man sighed. "Oy. Well, tell me you do have it with you."

"Why, don't you have another one?" Sid was a little irritated with all men right then.

"As a matter of fact I do, Agent Shaw, but your comrade, Mister Smoke, is wearing it, and I'd like to have them both returned intact, but I need your help."

Well, at least I'm not the only one who gives a damn. "Let's meet."

"There is no time for that, Agent Shaw. Within a day I'm certain they'll... well, we'll never see him again."

Half a dozen questions raced through her mind. How did he know where Smoke was? Why should she trust him? And who in the world *was* Mal Carlson? She pulled off to the side of the road. "I have the suit."

"And it's in the case, I assume."

"No. It's in the back seat of my car."

"You need to put it back on."

"I'm not putting it back on. It needs a wash," she said, reaching into the back and sniffing it. There was a pause on the other side of the line, followed by a groan. "Are you still there, Mister Carlson?"

"I'm here, but please don't stop by the cleaners. That's a quarter million dollar suit you've been wearing. And those bullets, a thousand dollars each. You still have those, don't you? And the case?"

"Let me guess, it's worth a million?"

"With the contents, yes, without them, well, look, it's sentimental. Don't lose it. Now, get dressed and ready to go."

"Go where? How do you even know where Smoke is? Nobody else does."

"The Glow," he replied.

She thought about Ted. Maybe he was moving faster than she thought. "How did you know about that?"

"Because I'm the one who had it put in him—and we need to get moving before the signal is lost." There was pecking on a keyboard. "I'm sending you directions."

Sid's phone buzzed inside her palm. She checked the screen. "Got them. What is this place?"

"A nineteenth-century bird sanctuary. It was an estate of an old English lord from the seventeen hundreds." He coughed. "But I don't have much history on it, just what was in the local papers that have been transferred to microfiche. It's now owned by an eccentric group of philanthropists."

"Anything tying the property to Drake?"

"Oh yes. The land is under a trust managed by Drake Property Enterprises."

Sidney pulled off the shoulder and headed down the road. The location was about 45 miles away, northwest of DC. "So Mal, now that I've seen deaders, werewolves, and now a harpy, do you care to fill me in on what is going on?"

"All in due time."

"Now is the time!" She squeezed the wheel. "Come on, Mal—Mister Carlson, you need to give me a heads-up on what's going on. I need something of substance. If I'm going to risk my neck, I'd like to know what in the heck for."

"In this case, you're doing it for your friend," he said matter-of-factly.

Sid could hear his rustlings and peckings on a computer in the background. *Morning glory! I don't need this crap!* "Just tell me more about the Black Slate and what I'm up against."

"I'd rather have you focus on the task at hand."

"Well, it's a bit of a drive, and I think I'm just as ready as I was the last time." Her car roared up the highway ramp and merged with traffic. "Just a nugget. Something meaningful."

"This enemy, the Drake—which is just a name—has been around a long, long time."

"Humor me. How long?"

"We're talking ancient times."

"Like, BC?" she said.

"I can't confirm it, but yes. There's evidence of it all over the globe, but it's never viewed in the proper light."

"Why don't you just shed some illumination on it then?"

He sighed. "All right. Just suppose that myths and legends aren't a shadow of the truth but real. At least some of them. There's a lot of silly stuff out there too, and you have to learn how to discern what should be ignored. Ahem. That said, these people, be it from fallen angels or demons, have always been among us, in one form or another, lending others their power. That's what you're dealing with here."

"Demons?"

"More like the spawn of demons. I like to think of it as manifestations of evil. It takes all sorts of forms and develops all sorts of powers. The evil seed planted in the body makes for supernatural mutations of sorts."

It was hard to hear and believe, even though she had seen it for herself. *This is too big a pill to swallow. I'd be choking on it if I hadn't seen it for myself.*

"I know what you're thinking, Agent Shaw. Even seeing is not believing. People see only what they want to see, and this enemy of which we speak, they thrive on our ignorance. Hence the world that crumbles all around you."

His words crept into her soul. "Can you tell me ... why me, and why now, if this has been going on so long?"

"For the most part, men and women have fought the good fight and kept it under control. But you don't hear about these heroes in the history books. Very little is known about them at all. They've battled and driven the fiends into their dark holes, but there's always meddling underneath the surface. Like snakes, they slither out and suck good people down."

Sounds like a bad fantasy series. "And what is your part in all of this?"

"Oh, I guess it's just my predestination to find these evil toads. Keep your phone handy, Agent Shaw. I'll call you back in a few minutes. Remember, fight the good fight."

The line went dead.

"Wait!"

CHAPTER 32

THIRTY MINUTES LATER THERE WAS still no word from Mal Carlson.
Great, great, great, great, great!

Sidney followed the GPS directions and found herself traveling down a lonely stretch of roadway accompanied only by tall pines. She took the left split at the fork in the road. Dusk was settling, and the landscape was changing, revealing an assortment of trees of all shapes and sizes. There were stone markers along the road too, some bigger than cars and others the size of tires. An old split-rail fence linked them.

Things became odd as the road winded. The trees changed. Thick roots seemed to burst through the ground like animated things. The heavy brush looked ominous and impenetrable. What had been a colorful forest by day was fast becoming a deadly and dreary one by night. The kind that campers disappear in. Colorful birds darted over the road from tree top to tree top. Some seemed unusually big. Their chirping was shrill and creepy.

Bird sanctuary my butt.

As she pulled on ahead, a pair of bright yellow eyes reflected her headlights. The four-legged creature bounded away along with the rest of the pack. Wolves. Big furry bodies disappeared like shades in the forest.

Not again.

She wanted to turn around. She didn't belong here, but Smoke didn't either. Finally she found herself passing underneath an old iron archway covered in vines and ivy. The lettering read Dummerville Bird Sanctuary. Half a mile ahead a lone manor stood against a backdrop of tall creepy oaks. Made from rough-hewn stone, the estate house, the size of a small resort, became bigger as she approached. Exotic cars and limos were parked all over the huge lawn, and a few people milled about at the front entrance. One man in a tuxedo was smoking with a woman in a fur coat. Each of them wore a bird mask that covered the eyes and nose.

This must be the place.

She parked the Hellcat on the lawn, leaving some room away from the rest, and waited. Another car pulled up to where a valet waited. He took the couple's keys, took the car, and parked beside her. The man lumbered out of the car in an old doorman's uniform. His skin was clammy and pale. He glanced over at Sidney's car. She let out a soft gasp and pressed against the seat.

Deader! She closed her eyes, clutching her gun to her chest. *Look away! Look away!*

The deader's heavy footsteps crunched over the grass and back toward the estate.

Sidney let out a soft sigh and grabbed the sweetheart suit. *No back-up, Sid. No problem.* Cramped inside her car, she slipped out of her clothes, slid the suit on, and redressed. Her body began to warm and energize. She picked up her gun and readied a second magazine. *Glock is my back-up.* She slid the knives Mal had sent to her and Smoke into her boots.

Just as she started to exit her car, another one wheeled in beside her—a razor-blue Jaguar XE. Two men exited from the front, and two giggling ladies exited from the rear. All of them swayed a little. One of the men handed each of them a mask and said, "We can't forget these ladies."

Sidney got out of her car and turned on the charm. She sauntered up to the man who had handed out the masks. She fingered his chest. "You wouldn't have another one of those would you? I forgot mine, and my boyfriend, well, ex-boyfriend maybe, got mad and went inside without me."

"He left a pretty thing like you out here all by yourself?" He hiccupped. "What a dick. Sure, I have another." He popped open his trunk and gave her one that was black with feathers and silver sequins. He pointed to his face. "Find me later though. You owe me a favor."

One of the girls hooked her arm in his and said, "Come on Reggie. The only one owing you any favors is me."

"Sure sure, babe. Whatever you say," he said, winking at Sidney from behind his mask. "Come on lady. Head on inside with us. It's as cold as a snowman's ass out here."

Feeling underdressed, Sid opened up her trunk and grabbed a coat her mother had gotten her for Christmas. Still in the box, the long winter coat was deep brown with fur trim around the neck. She put it on and said to the group, "Let's go party."

Approaching the manor, Sidney stayed close to the others. An imposing man in a hawk mask gave everyone a once over. Reggie held up his ring, and the man in the mask nodded. Behind the guard, on either side of the door, were deaders in doorman uniforms that looked to be a hundred years old.

"I love the looks of these men," one girl with a squeaky voice marveled. "So undead."

"They're undead all right," Reggie said, stuffing a fifty in the hawk-masked man's breast pocket. "Just don't get too close."

"Why?" the girl said, stepping closer and cocking her head.

The young man goosed her. "Boo!"

She squealed. "Stop that Reggie! You almost made me pee myself!"

"Sorry, babe." He slung his arm over her shoulder. "But you haven't seen anything yet."

Sidney caught a glimpse of a signet ring on his finger. It was a golden head with a rising black sun stamped in the middle of it. A dreadful feeling overcame her. Not for the men so much as the girls. They had no idea what they were in for. Sheep being led by wolves to the slaughter.

Inside, the atmosphere was heavy. Dreary music filled the massive foyer made from cut stone and marble. A banquet room with buffet tables and a bar was on the right, and a huge ballroom was on the left. People didn't dance. Instead, dressed in evening attire, they talked and touched, and some kissed. Every one of them had on a bird mask. There were eagles, hawks, pigeons, ravens, cardinals, robins and even parakeets and canaries.

I bet there's a pecking order to all of this.

There seemed to be. Men in dark suits wearing hawk masks were spread out along the walls. Their builds were similar to the men from the club. Women in scanty outfits of revealing silk wore bright pink and yellow canary masks. A few muscular bruisers in blue jay masks sauntered around carrying trays with drinks and small packages of pills.

I bet Allison would love this place.

Sidney broke off from the others and began milling about, careful not to jostle anyone. She picked up on a few conversations but nothing of note. Money. Politics. Sex. That was the gist of it. She grabbed a drink from one of the trays and leaned against a post. She noticed more oversized bird cages. Inside them were bird-masked shirtless men, covered in neon colors with war paint and wearing only buckskin pants. Some danced. Others stood with their arms crossed over their bare chests.

Allison would definitely love this depraved place. Her phone buzzed.

Unknown Caller

The message read:

Are you in?

Sidney responded with a *yes.*

Describe?

She texted back: *The filthy rich in bird masks. Men in loincloth and cages. Want a picture?*

How many?

Two-hundred +.

Odd for this time of day. Something must be going on. Much artillery?

Yes.

Find Smoke and leave. Make sure you have the suit.

I didn't come to make new friends—and screw your suit. What about Night Bird? She'll have to wait.

Sid put her phone away. These cryptic messages from Mal Carlson were of little benefit at all. Not to her anyway. But he did point out one odd thing: the unique time of day for the gathering. Unlike the late-night hours mingling at the club, this had more of the feeling of a buildup for an event. She headed for the buffet and decorated her crystal plate with extraordinary cuisine. The aroma of fine spices was arousing. She took a few bites. *This is wonderful.*

"Are you enjoying yourself?" said a man in a robin mask and a tuxedo. He sounded young and was well built. His cologne was enticing.

Sidney nodded. "Yes. You?"

He rubbed his hand up and down her arm. "Not yet. Say, aren't you hot? I bet you are." His voice was smooth and persuasive. "Why don't you let me help you take that coat off?"

"I just got here." She eased away. "Maybe later." *Never!*

"I'll be close," he said, walking away.

Find Smoke! Get out of here!

The music stopped and the chatter quickly subsided. Everyone gazed up at the balcony at the top of the stairs. There was Night Bird.

CHAPTER 33

NIGHT BIRD STOOD PROUDLY AT the top, hands on the rail, in a glorious white feathered gown. Her outstanding features almost made Sidney forget about the monster that lurked behind them. She spoke. "Guests, one and all, welcome to my abode. I'm sure you're enjoying yourselves."

Some laughter broke out, and a few cheers echoed and died.

Night Bird clapped her hands. "Are you ready for the main event?"

The crowd shouted back. "Yes!"

"Are you sure?" she said, playfully.

"Yes!"

"Then step aside, children, and let the Battle of the Bird Cages begin!"

Sid moved out of the banquet room and over to the ballroom, where the people gathered in a big circle eyeing the floor. The center of the floor slid back like a great eye, making a gaping hole in the middle.

Morning Glory!

The men and women started chanting and pumping their fists. "Bird Cage! Bird Cage! Bird Cage!"

A great raven made from blackened iron rose from the gaping floor, rising higher and higher. It was perched on a round metal bird cage maybe twenty feet wide and over ten feet tall. It filled almost a third of the room.

You have got to be kidding me.

She glanced up at the balcony. Night Bird stood looking downward with two deaders in pea coats on either side of her.

On the main floor, the serving men in hawk-masks opened up the door to the big cage. Other servants pushed the smaller bird cages with men inside over and let them out. Inside the cage they went, and the door was latched shut. The men inside—each coated in bright colorful war paint—were well built: stout and hard muscled. One shadow boxed, stretched and warmed up. The other stroked his wild beard. Somewhere a gong sounded, and the room fell silent.

Sidney controlled her gaping. *Really, they couldn't go see this anywhere else? Couldn't they just stay home and watch* Fight Club?

Night Bird spoke up. "No mercy. Winner take all!"

The crowd let out a cheer.

Sidney pushed her way through the throng. Now was the best time to find Smoke. Someone had to be holding him somewhere. *Wouldn't surprise me if there was a dungeon in here.*

Night Bird raised her arms and lowered them.

Bong!

Sid glanced back over her shoulder. Up inside the cage, the men circled. One, sleek and bald, jabbed at the brawny bearded one. His blows smacked into flesh. The bearded man snatched the man by the arms and drove his knees into his chest. In a blink, the bald man was hoisted over the bearded man's head.

The people roared.

A second later, the bearded man slammed the struggling man head first into the floor. *Crack!* The witnesses gasped, and the ballroom fell silent. The bald man moved no more.

The bearded fighter beat his chest and let out a triumphant howl. He flexed his muscles and yelled up at the balcony, "Who's next? Who's next?"

The crowd started chanting. "Wild Jack! Wild Jack! Wild Jack!"

Wild Jack? It was the name of a legendary MMA fighter. Sidney hadn't recognized him with the beard. He had been clean-shaven and worn a Mohawk, if she remembered it right. *This is insane, not to mention highly illegal.* She took out her phone and sent a text to Ted Howard. *Night Bird or no Night Bird, I'm breaking this party up. I'm a witness to a murder.* She pressed send, but the signal bar was dead. *No!*

Bong!

"Well done, Wild Jack," Night Bird said. "Are you ready for another?"

"I'm not even warmed up yet," he shouted up to her, "But yes, milady, I'm ready."

"Excellent, because we have a newcomer that I think you just might find worthy." She clapped her hands. "Bring him in!"

A pair of grand double doors opened underneath the balcony. Another bird cage was pulled in, containing a man with his back turned to them with his head down. The people murmured and pressed toward the cage.

"Make a hole! Out of the way!" said one of the hawk-masked men.

Oh no! Sidney's gut churned. She squeezed through the crowd and crept up on the cage. She got a good look at the face. It was Smoke. His shoulders were bruised, his complexion pale, and he had a sick and haggard look about him. His weak eyes met hers. "Smoke?"

His head lifted, and he coughed. "You need to go," he said in a raspy voice. "Just go."

Keeping up with the cage, she said, "What happened?"

"What didn't happen?" He winced. "Just go. They'll see you. Forget about the Slate." His eyes hardened. "Forget about all of this and go."

"But—" she stammered.

"Move it, woman," said one of the servants, shoving her aside. They started pushing the crowd back from the cage. "Clear out! All of ya!"

The throng eased back and Sidney drifted in with the masses. A hollowness filled her. Smoke's rock-solid demeanor was gone. A world champion MMA fighter waited inside the cage, grinding his fist into his paw. *I have to stop this. He'll die.*

The crowd hummed with new energy.

Smoke's disheveled form lumbered out of his cage and stepped over the bald man's dead body. Stooped over, his battered muscular body was riddled with cuts, scrapes, and bruises. He shuffled toward the center of the cage, facing his aggressor. The cage door closed with a clank.

"This is going to be a massacre," one man said.

"I hope there's blood this time," added a woman.

"There's blood. There's always blood," the man in the eagle mask replied. "Wild Jack will bring it all night long. He's never been defeated."

Sidney's chest tightened. Her fingers went to her gun. *What am I going to do? I can't watch him die.*

"Kill him, Wild Jack!" a strong voice cried out. "No mercy on that man! I want to see blood on those hands."

Sidney cocked her head and looked at the man. He had a husky bowling-pin build and meaty hands. He squeezed the hips of the women on either side of him.

"Wait till you see this, girls. Wait and see. That bastard in the cage has it coming."

Congressman Wilhelm!

CHAPTER 34

S IDNEY'S JAW MUSCLES TIGHTENED. IF Congressman Wilhelm was there, who else was? All around her, people in bird masks talked, some in different languages and others with bad American accents. They all wanted blood. Mayhem. Death.

Who are these people? Why don't they get in the cage!

She shuffled through the crowd toward the cage, bumping Congressman Wilhelm, jostling his drink.

"Idiot! Watch where you're going!"

She didn't turn.

Night Bird clapped her hands, and the crowd fell silent. "Life to the victor! Death to the fallen! Agreed?"

The people shouted back in agreement. Inside the cage, Smoke stood a few paces away from Wild Jack with his shoulder dropped. The bearded warrior, all lathered up, mopped the sweat from his brow. He spat. "This man doesn't seem fit for fighting!"

"I don't expect him to put up much of a fight," Night Bird replied. "He crossed me. That's how I want it."

"I see," Wild Jack said, stroking his beard. He pumped his fists in the air. "I'll make it a prolonged and painful death then!"

Smoke burst into motion, striking Wild Jack in the throat. The burly man's eyes popped wide. The seasoned fighter brought his fists down. Smoke slipped behind the man and locked Wild Jack's arms and neck up. The bearded warrior gagged, and his face quickly went from beet red to purple.

Get him, Smoke!

Wild Jack slapped at Smoke's arms, spat and struggled. The muscles in Smoke's corded arms bulged. His face filled with strain. Wild Jack's eyes rolled up inside his head, and Smoke took him to the floor.

The crowd unleashed a fury of angry boos and profanities. It didn't matter. It was over.

Smoke released Wild Jack, rose back to his feet wincing, looked up at Night Bird, and shrugged.

The gong sounded, and the crowd quieted.

"I didn't even give the signal to start the match, and that's cheating," Night Bird said. "Not to mention that I said it was to the death. I see Wild Jack is still breathing. Or should I say, sleeping?"

The attendees craned their necks toward the cage and murmured.

"Kill him yourself," Smoke said back to Night Bird.

Night Bird laughed. "Oh, that's noble. How quaint. But either you can kill him or I'll have to kill her." She pointed straight down at Sidney. "Take her!"

How did she know?

The array of guests turned on her. The brutes in the hawk masks shoved the masses aside and came straight for her. Sidney pulled out her gun and fired three shots into the ceiling.

Blam! Blam! Blam!

Screams and frightened cries were followed by dozens of people scrambling for the doors. Sidney lowered her head and melded in with the rampaging throng.

Try to find me now, you idiots!

As the crowd pushed toward the main entrance, she noticed two men in suits pushing Congressman Wilhelm out the door. The bodyguards in bird masks formed a blockade at the main entrance, patting everyone down with force. Above, on the balcony, Night Bird was screaming, but Sidney didn't look back. Instead, she snatched a parakeet mask from one woman's face and disappeared underneath the stairs that led up to the balcony. Gathering her thoughts and catching her breath, she waited.

I've got to get Smoke out of here.

Five minutes into the wait, she switched masks, slipped off her coat, and reentered the scene. The manor was half empty. The excitement from the gunfire had dulled. The servants were picking up the mess. Others searched. The remaining party guests had resumed their talks, making up half-baked stories. Eyeing the balcony, Sidney noticed Night Bird was gone.

Where could that bird brain be?

She huddled with a crowd of talking guests that had gathered near the cage. Smoke was still inside, sitting on the floor, head down and shivering.

What is wrong with him?

Checking her surroundings, she eased closer to the cage and cleared her throat.

Smoke didn't move.

Putting a stagger in her step, she teetered around the rim and hiccupped from time to time.

Smoke crawled over on his hands and knees, saying, "Water. I need water."

She whispered. "It's me, Sid."

"Water," he replied, then under his breath he said, "I know. I can handle this. Just go." He coughed.

"Are you all right or not?" she said, still whispering.

He cocked his head back toward Wild Jack and said, "Better than him." He coughed again. "What a tool. If you're going to stick around, get the keys. But I suggest you go. Night Bird has keen instincts."

"I'm not leaving without you."

"Then we might not be leaving at all." He looked deep into her eyes. "Are you sure you're all right with that?"

"I'm good. Let me go find you some water."

"A milkshake would be better."

Now that the crowd had settled down, the hawk-masked guards began making rounds and patting everyone down. Sidney still had her gun tucked down in her pants. *Great.* She made her way over to one of the banquet tables, kneeled down, and put her gun beneath the curtains. She then sauntered over toward one of the guards with her hands raised over her head.

"Yoo hoo, you haven't searched me yet," she said to the nearest one. She nuzzled up to him. "Pat me down, and be sure to be thorough. And if you do a good job I'll pat you down too!"

The guard grunted. "Be still."

She draped her arms over him and pulled him close. "How can I be still with a brute like you around? Hmmm?" *Lord, he smells like English Leather.*

He ran his hands over her chest and waist, taking full advantage of the moment.

"You have great hands."

"I'm a student at a massage therapy school." He patted her rear. "You're clear."

"No doubt you'll be a good one," she said, tickling his chin. "Anything else?"

"No," he said, starting to walk away.

"Oh, well, can I get that man in the cage some water? I feel sorry for the dear."

There was a grinding of gears and a clank of metal. The giant bird cage started to lower back into the floor.

"I think it's a little late for that now, but don't worry, he won't be thirsty much longer."

"Why do you say that?"

"Because dead men don't thirst."

CHAPTER 35

SIDNEY RETRIEVED HER GUN AND made her way up to a gathering crowd that stood watching the cage go down into the floor. Smoke sat inside the cage, head down.

"Bummer," someone said, "no more violence. Let's go."

The cage sunk into the darkness and rattled when it hit bottom. Gears grinded and the floor began to close.

"Wow, it looks like he's being swallowed whole. Too bad for that loser," a man said, guzzling a bottled beer. "Better him than me. I wonder where they find these goons anyway."

Sidney crept toward the rim. The hole was seconds from closing.

"Hey, lady, you better back off. That floor will cut your leg off." The man laughed. "It wouldn't be the first time that happened, either."

The light over the grand birdcage faded.

Sidney swallowed. *I'm not losing you again.* She jumped on the sliding door of the closing circle.

"Are you crazy?" the man said. "Get off of there!"

Crazy enough! She jumped through the narrowing doorway into the darkness. She hit the top of the cage with a bang and rolled down the side, hitting the floor hard. "Oof!" Slowly, she sat up, rubbing her hip and shaking her head.

"What have we here?" The man's voice was gruff. He approached, tall and lanky and wearing a pea coat. "Looks like a little bird fell out of her nest." He extended his hand. "Let me help you up, my dear."

She reached for his hand.

He took it, started to pull her up, and drove his booted toe into her gut.

She doubled over with a groan.

"Men, I got her! I got—*ulp!*"

Smoke stretched his arms through the bars and grabbed the man's neck and collar. He jerked the man's face into the metal. *Bang! Bang! Bang!*

The man sagged to the floor with his face bleeding.

"Find the key," Smoke urged. "Hurry!"

Sidney fumbled through the man's pockets and belt and found nothing. A scuffle of feet and agitated voices echoed down the corridor. "He doesn't have it."

Smoke reached into the front of her jeans and pulled her gun out.

"Hey!" she said.

He marched over to the cage door and shot the lock off. It sounded different underground.

Pop!

And then he stepped outside and tossed her back the gun. "Thanks," he said, coughing.

They stood in a cavernous room, almost the size of the ballroom above. Oaken barrels lined the walls. Shelves were stacked up to the ceiling, loaded with unknown materials. The walls were cut rock, and three stone corridors led out. Smoke took her by the wrist and pulled her toward the one farthest from the onrush of guards.

Blat—at! Blat—at! Blat—at!

Sidney's legs churned. Bullets whizzed by her head. Rock chips scattered from the wall. She returned fire.

Pop! Pop! Pop! Pop!

Smoke pushed through the exit door and bounded up the stairs. She kept pace, stumbled, bashed her knee on the metal step, and carried on, grimacing. They rushed through the door at the top and found themselves in a grand kitchen. They dashed to the other side of the room and found themselves inside one of the main halls.

Voices cried out from all over. Footsteps echoed off the hardwood floors.

"Stay close," Smoke said.

"No, you stay close," she replied. "I'm rescuing you. It's not the other way around."

Smoke coughed. "If you say so."

They took a curved stairway going up, away from the sound of voices. At the top was a long hallway with many bedroom doors. She jiggled the handles on one side. Smoke tried the other. The opposite end of the hall was a dead end.

"Any luck?" she said, glancing back over her shoulder. Smoke was gone. A door gaped open on the other side. "Smoke?" A heavy scuffle caught her ear. Inside, a deader had Smoke by the waist and picked up off the floor.

"Close the door," Smoke spit out. He drove an elbow into the deader's eye socket. The lifeless creature shrugged it off and slammed him to the floor.

Sidney closed the door and locked it, closed in, and took aim.

Smoke shook his head. "Don't shoot it!"

"Why?"

"Too loud." The deader got his tireless arms around Smoke's neck. "Knife," Smoke choked out, stretching his clutching hand and eyeing her ankle. His face reddened. "Knife, now."

She slid the blade from her boot.

"Don't just stand there, stab it!"

"Stabbing's not really my thing."

"Give it!" Smoke snatched the blade from her hand and drove it backward into the deader's eye. The creature's body stiffened, but it held on. Smoke twisted inside its grip, ripped himself free, plunged the blade into its heart, and gave it a twist.

Churk!

The deader went limp.

Gasping, Smoke wiped the blade on the bedspread. "Stabbing isn't really your thing?"

She shrugged. "It seemed weird."

He staggered toward the window. "Some rescue." Peering outside, he said, "I think you can make a break for it from here." He opened the window. "The ivy's pretty heavy on these walls."

"And just what do you think you'll be doing?"

"Bringing in Night Bird."

"You need to forget about her."

"Nah," he said, shaking his head. "Not after what she did to me. Did to those others. She's going down."

She grabbed his chin, looked straight into his eyes, and said, "There's too many, Smoke. Let's cut our losses and go. You're sick."

"I'll be fine." He tried to nudge her toward the window.

"You weren't fine five minutes ago."

"Of course I was," he said, coughing. "It was all going according to my plan until you showed up."

"Me?" She backed up into the room. "You'd be dead if not for me."

He shook his head. "No I wouldn't."

The closet door popped, and with a creak it slowly opened. It was dim inside. *Probably some partygoers.* Sidney peered inside, weapon ready. "Come out with your hands up."

A pale and ghastly figure rushed out of the closet.

Sidney's finger froze on the trigger.

A knife flashed and stabbed her in the gut.

CHAPTER 36

T HE GUT-BUSTING BLOW PICKED SIDNEY up off her feet. Agony raced
through her body. Instinct took over. She fired the Glock.

Blam! Blam! Blam! Blam! Blam!

The spray of bullets blasted the deader back into the closet.

Smoke rushed over. "Sid! Sid! Are you all right?"

Clutching her stomach, she shook her head quickly, saying, "I don't know." It
felt as if the monster had punched a hole through her. All of her innards ached.

Smoke pulled the belly of her sweater up. "Whoa."

"Is it that bad?"

"No. Your second skin held."

"It's called a *Zweite Haut* suit."

"Sweet heart?"

"Something like that. It's German. Where's yours?" She groaned as Smoke
helped her to her feet. Her knees buckled, but Smoke caught her. *Man, it hurts.*

"Not sure. Why, am I in trouble?"

"Probably. It's worth more than the both of us put together."

"Well, at least it kept you together."

A heavy pounding came at the door.

Wham! Wham! Wham!

"Open up! Open up!"

"Just a minute," Smoke said in a feminine voice. "I'm not decent." He dragged
Sidney to the window.

Gunshots cracked out from the other side of the door. Wood chips blasted
through the holes.

"Hang on," Smoke said, hefting her onto his shoulder.

"Let me down, I can climb."

"You can barely move."

He eased out of the window, gripped the vines, and scaled the wall to the
ground like an ape. He sprinted out into the back courtyard. Angry voices called
out after them. Gunfire followed.

Feeling as if her guts were falling out, Sidney aimed her weapon and cracked
off some cover fire.

Blam! Blam!

One man fell out of the window. "Ahhh!"

Nice shot, Sid! Wish my combat arms instructors could have seen that. They'd never believe it.

"Hang on!" Smoke said, running at full speed. "I'll get you to safety."

Whoooosh!

A great shadow dropped from the sky and knocked them sprawling to the ground. Sidney fought her way up to her hands and knees.

"You ruined my party!" Night Bird squawked. The bird woman's face was contorted with demonic fury. Her wings were spread, and her razor-sharp talons clawed up the dirt as she bird-walked forward. "I will make you pay!"

Sidney raised the barrel of her gun, aimed center mass, and said, "Glock you." She squeezed the trigger.

Click.

Night Bird snarled. "I'm going to rip you lab rats apart!" She lowered her head, pinned back her wings, let out a shriek, and charged with unnatural speed.

The shriek paralyzed Sidney. She hunkered down, fighting to regain her faculties.

Night Bird landed on top of her. The talons dug into her body, and Sidney cried out. She felt her body lift from the ground and rise toward the sky. Something slammed into Night Bird and dragged the monster to the grass by the neck. The talons released her.

"You dare!" Night Bird shrieked at Smoke. "I've had enough of you, mortal!" Her wings lashed out, cutting Smoke along the eyes. Bigger and stronger than the man, she pinned his legs down with her talons. Her talon-like fingernails tore into his skin. With superior strength and speed, she pummeled him.

Smoke struck back, stabbing with the knife.

Night Bird bit his wrist and wrenched it free. "Fool! For hundreds of years none of your kind have ever stopped me." She shrieked in his face.

Smoke covered his ears. He sagged to the ground, nose bleeding. His body was cut to ribbons, and he slumped over on the blood-slicked grass.

Night Bird spread her wings in triumph and squalled.

A fire lit inside Sidney. She snaked the other knife out of her boot and charged the harpy.

"Eh?" Night Bird turned her head a split second too late.

Sidney jumped and jabbed the knife deep between Night Bird's wings.

The monster let out a squawk so loud it bent the leaves on the trees. Somewhere, glass shattered. "Nooooooooooo!" Night Bird slung Sid from her back, spread her great wings, and took to the air, under the moonlight. The higher she went, the more she wavered. Finally, she spiraled in a downward cone and crashed into a storehouse nearby.

Oh, please be dead!

Sid crawled over to Smoke.

He lay prone on the ground, struggling to rise and wiggling his fingers in his ears. "Did you stab her?"

"Yes," she said, holding up the knife.

He poked the other magazine in her pocket. "Why didn't you just reload and shoot her?"

I forgot. She didn't see her gun anywhere on the ground either. "I just wanted to stab her, I guess." She shivered. "I think I've had enough of this cold. Let's make sure she's dead and get inside."

"I don't think that's our call," Smoke said. Looking over her shoulder, he raised his hands.

They were surrounded by at least a dozen gun-toting goons.

Sid's teeth chattered, and she thought, *Don't say it.*

But they did.

"Freeze!"

CHAPTER 37

"**D**ROP THE KNIFE, LADY!" ONE of the guards said.

Sidney let it slide from her fingers. "I think you can take the masks off now, bird boys. I think your boss is dead."

"She's not our boss," one man said, hauling Sidney up to her feet.

"Is that so? Then who is?"

"Button your lip," the man said, picking up her knife, "or it might get cut off." Behind her a man stuck a rifle muzzle in her back, shuffling her forward. "Let's go."

She glanced at Smoke. Blood was caked all over him. He tried to fight off the cough in his chest.

"This is a horrible rescue," he said to her. "You know that, don't you?"

"If you'd cooperate, it'd be just fine."

A rifle butt gently clocked both of them in the back of the head. "Shut it," a man said.

Whumpa! Whumpa! Whumpa! Whumpa! Whumpa! Whumpa! Whumpa!

A helicopter soared in overhead, shining its floodlight on them like a small moon in the sky.

"This is the FBI! Drop your weapons and surrender!" an amplified voice called out from it.

The guards, some in bird masks and others in pea coats, fled toward the house.

"FBI! Last warning!"

A second chopper soared over and landed closer to the house. A tactical team in gas masks spilled out of the helicopter's bay, cracked off some blasts of gunfire, and unleashed smoke grenades. Within minutes, the FBI took control of the situation. Night Bird's bodyguards were face down in the grass. FBI agents in vans and SUVs spilled into the driveway a few minutes later.

Sidney grabbed her phone. "I'll be." Her text had gone through.

"What?" Smoke said.

She showed him the phone with a reply from Section Chief Howard.

Almost there. Hang tight.

She shifted around and said to Smoke, "I told you I was rescuing you."

"No, I'm pretty sure they're rescuing you."

"So that's her, huh?" Ted said, watching Night Bird being loaded into an ambulance on a gurney. She was in human form and had an oxygen mask strapped to her nose.

"No, that's an *it*," Sidney said, pulling the blanket tighter over her shoulders. "And you better hope *it* doesn't survive."

"I look forward to you telling me all about … it," he said, patting her shoulder. "But most of all, I'm glad you're all right."

"Well, I have plenty to tell you, but I'm positive you're going to hate my report."

"At least it'll be entertaining."

The wind stirred the ground, and a bird mask made of raven feathers rolled up on Ted's shoe. He picked it up. "Strange masquerade party."

"They're strange people." Sidney looked over at the back of the other ambulance, where Smoke sat on a gurney. A paramedic was stitching him up. "Does he really have to go back … tonight? He's sick, you know."

"Afraid so. By the looks of things, he's lucky to be alive, like you." He eyed Smoke and then looked at her. "You like that guy, don't you?"

"He's a good soldier. I don't think he deserves what's being done to him."

"Probably not. I'll see what I can do about his living conditions. I figure he deserves that much." Ted surveyed the scene. "Sheesh, this is a mess. Half of these people aren't even citizens. We can't figure out where some of them are from. Some days I just don't recognize my country anymore. I swear I'm going to wake up one day and everything I knew will be gone."

"You could be right," she said.

"Ted! Ted!" Waving his hand over his head, Cyrus ran toward them. "You need to get inside and look at this place." He glanced at Sid. "Hey." Then he was back to eagerly addressing Ted. "Anyway—weapons, drugs, you-name-it's in there. All of these agents are going to be up for accomplishments after this bust!"

Just after he said it, agents came rushing out of the manor. Flames roared with fiery life in the windows. In moments, the entire manor was ablaze.

Cyrus gawped. "Oh no, oh no, oh no! Somebody call in the fire trucks!"

Boom! Boom! Boom!

The ground shook, and the manor collapsed into a pile of rubble.

"I can't believe it," Cyrus said, squeezing his head. "All of the evidence. It's gone."

Sidney walked away shaking her head and headed toward where Smoke now stood. "Are you going to make it?"

"Yea. You?"

"I think so." She extended her hand. "I guess you have to go back now."

He grabbed her hand and squeezed it in his. "Seems so."

Two agents put a coat over his shoulders and led him toward a Bureau car. Her heart sank. She said over to him, "Until next time then?"

"You can count on me."

CRAIG HALLORAN

THE SUPERNATURAL BOUNTY HUNTER FILES

WHERE THERE'S SMOKE
BOOK 3

CHAPTER 1

A LONE INSIDE SECTION CHIEF HOWARD's office, Sidney sat chewing on a pen cap. She stopped and scribbled a name on her notepad.

Mal Carlson.

He had sent her several texts over the past few weeks. They didn't say much. Greetings. Almost gibberish.

How are you?

Checking in.

Anything strange?

Be alert.

Sometimes she replied, sometimes she didn't.

The office door popped open, and Ted's secretary, Jane, stepped inside. Refined in her appealing and professional dress, she said, "He just pulled in. Can I get you anything, Agent Shaw?"

"You could tell me where John Smoke is."

Jane offered a smile. "I wouldn't mind knowing where he is myself. Are you sure I can't get you anything?"

"No, thank you," she said, turning away. She heard the door close behind her. A whiff of Jane's perfume lingered in the air. *I wish I felt as together as she looks.* She sketched an hourglass on her notepad. And waited. Jane knew plenty more than she'd ever let on. That's what good secretaries do, and they are often privy to what is said and never documented. Jane always eased out of Sid's inquiries. *I hate that about her.* But she respected it too.

Buzz. A new message appeared on her phone from her mother. It read:

Don't forget to check on her.

Allison and Megan had headed back to DC. Her sister had convinced their parents that her head was better and she was ready to go back home. Supposedly she had a job lined up. Allison was well educated and capable. She had a degree in nursing, but she never really applied herself to it. Instead, she enjoyed working in campaign offices with high-profile people, and it was election season.

Sidney texted back:

I will. Love U.

She turned the phone off and tucked it away. *As if I don't have enough on my plate already. Hah!*

Life had changed, but it hadn't. She went through the routine. Eat. Work. Sleep. Good sleep was hard to come by. Now she slept with restlessness, knowing that the monsters under her bed or in her closet were real. But no one wanted to talk about them. There wasn't anyone she could confide in. Instead, she came in once a month to meet with Ted. Otherwise, she was a shadow. Sometimes as she lay in bed she wondered if any of what happened had been real.

Werewolves. Deaders. Harpies. Gargoyles. Cage fights. Plenty of other agents had also witnessed what she had seen, but no one talked about it. In today's world of mass communication, that didn't seem possible. She'd been completely cut off from the investigations and interrogations at the Drummerville Bird Sanctuary. She scratched on her pad. *Maybe they want me to think I'm crazy.*

The door opened, and Ted entered. "Sorry, Sid." He hung his coat and cap on the rack. "Got a late start with the grandkids in. Honestly, I'd forgotten about this meeting until Jane reminded me. I must be slipping." He walked over and patted her on the shoulder. "I hope you'll forgive me." He glanced at her pad. "Is that a portrait of Mr. Smoke?"

She glanced down at the paper. *Lord, it is!* "No, just another person of interest." She watched Ted take a seat behind his desk. "Nice to know you've forgotten about me. I'd like to think the Black Slate carries more interest."

He held his hands up and waved them from side to side. "It does, it does. Please don't go on the attack again. I just got here."

She leaned toward his desk. "No, it doesn't. You don't even want to think about it, and you know it. I bet we wouldn't even be meeting if you didn't have an obligation to."

His eyes drifted a moment before they found her again. "That's not true. You know how fond I am of you, Sid." He unbuttoned his sleeves and rolled them up. "But I am not now, nor have I ever been comfortable with this Black Slate stuff, not since day one. The fact that you are on it is the worst part."

"You don't think I can handle it."

"No. Well that's not entirely true. Five agents died last time, right? You were there. Not that I don't feel for those agents. I do, but you're just different." He locked his eyes on hers. "I don't ever want to go to your funeral."

"I'm touched, but it comes with the job, you know."

"Sure, all agents are at risk. We all know that. But a greater rate of mortality comes to those who deal with this Black Slate." He wiggled his mouse while he put on a pair of rectangular glasses. His monitor came to life. He logged in. "And well," he sighed, "I've lost a friend before to the peculiar circumstances that come with it."

Interesting. Sidney settled back in her chair. Ted might be a little grizzly on the outside, but he was all heart on the inside. When agents died, he felt it. "So you were close to this person? How did they die?"

"Disappeared is more like it." He rubbed his neck. "I was two years out of the academy. She was my supervisor. Deanne, one of the few people in this world who ever intimidated me." He smiled and locked his fingers behind his neck. "She was magnificent. Merciless in interrogation. The tougher they were, the harder they fell. She'd have them crying for their mommies. Confessing everything. You'd watch through the one-way glass, hear that penetrating squall that turned your guts out, and watch a man's entirety collapse."

"Wow, she really made an impact on you."

"She made an impact on everybody. One time, we were on a presidential detail, and I swear he saluted her. Ha. She was the Rambo of the interrogations unit." He got up and opened the small fridge and grabbed a water. "Want one?"

"No, thanks. So, she really got you worked up, huh Chief."

"Aw," he shooed her with his hand. "Not like that. Well, maybe. I'd be lying if I said I hadn't thought about it, but hell Sid, she scared me."

"Do I scare you?"

"No no no, that's not what I'm getting at. But your toughness makes me think about her sometimes. Not many have that edge like you have. It's a gift in this profession."

"Thanks. What did happen?"

Ted leaned his head back like he was looking for the answer on the ceiling. "Huh, good question. She called me into her office one day, sat me down, and told me she was leaving and that I would be her replacement." He rubbed his chin. "All she had was a cardboard box. You know, the kind that hold reams of paper. Her possessions didn't fill half of it. Of course, back then you were lucky to have an office with a window air conditioner in it." He glanced around his office. "Look at all the shit I have. If she came back, well, I'd be embarrassed." His eyes grew sad. "We're just so damn soft nowadays."

Sidney chuckled.

"What?"

"Nothing." She shrugged. "Just funny to hear my hard-nosed boss say that. I don't think your baubles are too much to be ashamed about."

He stuck out his chest. "No, I guess not. Besides, Margie won't let me put them up at home, so it might as well be here." He eyed a fish on the wall. A bass every bit of two feet long. "Did I ever tell you—"

"Yes!" Sid widened her eyes. "So that's it. She left, and you never heard from her again. How did you know it was the Black Slate she was involved with?"

"She left with few words, but she said, 'You'll do well.' I asked about her assignment, and all she said was 'If they wanted you to know, they'd tell you.' And out the door she went. I never saw her again. She became a ghost."

"So how do you know she was on the Black Slate?"

"I got a postcard in my mailbox at home years later." His voice became low and quiet. "It was a picture of an eerie castle somewhere in Europe I guess. Like something one would see or imagine from a scene in Transylvania. It said, 'Ted, monsters are real. Avoid the Slate.' She didn't sign it, but I knew it was her writing. I always thought it was a joke. A gag. It was almost two decades later that I learned it wasn't."

"Do you still have the postcard?"

"Yeah." He opened up his drawer, reached down, and withdrew a small yellow envelope. He tossed it to the edge of the desk. "I've never shown it to anyone, aside from Margie."

Sidney bent back the clasp and took out the postcard. The edges were still clean and crisp. The picture of the castle nestled in the hills above the fog seemed almost as real as a view from a window. She read the message. All seven words. *Seven. Interesting choice.* A small sketch in the bottom left corner shot a chill through her bones. It was a black sunrise.

CHAPTER 2

"So," Sid stared at the card, "can I borrow this?"

"Uh, no." Ted said, rubbing his lip with his finger. "Why would you want to?"

"What if there's more to it than meets the eye, and you missed it?"

He reached across the desk with his hand out. "I don't think so."

"You're pretty attached to it, aren't you? I wonder what Deanne would think about that." She fanned herself with the card. "I bet she'd be touched."

Ted's forehead crinkled. "Give it back."

Boy, he really is attached to it. "Do you have a picture of her?"

"No."

"What was her last name?"

"Just forget about it, Sid." He patted his desk with his meaty fingers. "The card, please."

She took her phone out and brought up the camera.

"Don't you dare," he said. "I don't want every detail of my life to be a digital record. They have a file on me in the computers already."

She gave it one last look, dropped it back in the envelope, and handed it over. *I've seen all I need to see anyway.* "Thanks for sharing."

He stared at the envelope with a pained expression on his face. He sighed and handed it back to Sid. "Here. Just try not to lose it. So, how has the last month been?"

She tucked the postcard away. "Oh, let's see. I've been inside archives doing research as ordered. Pretty boring. Sorting. Filing."

"I thought you liked that kind of stuff."

"No, I'm just better at it than anybody else. What I like is being in the field and not shackled inside a library basement that everyone but the janitor has forgotten about. Do you have another name on the Black Slate for me or not?"

Ted looked away and wrote a note on a piece of paper. "No."

He's not telling me something. "So then I can assume that everything is suddenly right in the nefarious underworld I've discovered, the one no one else wants to talk about." She folded her arms over her chest. "I guess if no one talks about it, it's not real. Huh, Ted? Is that why I'm not in the office? Why I'm isolated? Because I might disrupt the status quo?"

"Don't get so heated. No one has forgotten about you. You just aren't a priority right now. We have borders, elections, terrorist threats, endless investigations, and budget cuts, not to mention an unruly media." He took a drink of water. "The Slate is low on the pecking order, and they haven't so much as sent me a peep about any of it. No files. No nothing."

"Do I just wait?"

"You're still under shadow cover. Why not enjoy it? And don't make it sound as if you aren't doing anything. I know you're snooping around over something."

True. She'd still been digging up all the dirt should could on Drake and its conglomerates. Black suns. They kept popping up in the shadows. "I've been practicing *extraordinary caution.*"

"And I couldn't be happier," he said, clicking through his emails. "Man, it's going to be another long day." Without taking his eyes off the screen, he said, "What you're doing is better than sitting in meetings all day. It's a wonder we get anything done around here." He clicked through a few more emails, shaking his head and muttering to himself.

Sidney sat back in her chair and watched his eyes toggle up and down the screen. A couple of minutes had gone by when she spoke up. "Excuse me, Chief? Are we finished here?"

"Oh, sorry Sid." He swung his shoulders around. "I believe we are."

"You're joking."

"I don't have anything else. I really don't."

"So you invited me to a meeting about nothing?"

"It's routine, you know that. Most meetings are about nothing. They're just a nugget on the schedule."

She got up quickly and glared at him. "Well I hope you get a medal for it." She headed for the door. "This is ridiculous!"

"You haven't been dismissed, Agent Shaw." He got up, crossed the room, and met her at the door. He put one hand on her shoulder and took her hand in the other.

She felt a piece of paper in it.

"Same time next month, Agent Shaw. Now, let me get that door for you."

"See you around next month, maybe." She nodded at Jane and made a bead straight for the elevators. Passing cubicle after cubicle, she felt eyes slide over her body and drift away when she faced them. A young woman with her head down rounded the corner and bumped into her, dropping her phone on the floor.

"Excuse me," the woman said. She was a blonde in her late twenties, dressed in an FBI polo and slacks.

"No problem," Sid said, picking up her phone and handing it to her. "Have a good day."

"Say," the woman said, "you wouldn't be Agent Shaw by any chance?"

"Yes, why?"

"Nothing. I just heard Sadie talking about you one day to some of the newer agents. And older agents. Pretty much everybody." The woman offered her hand. "I'm Rebecca Lang, data analyst." She rolled her eyes. "Pretty boring job, but I'm going to be a field agent, eventually." She pushed her glasses up. "I'm just not a very good shot, but I've also heard you're one of the best. Any chance you can teach me sometime?"

Sidney looked down at her. "There's nothing I can teach you that you haven't already been taught. Practice more, Agent Lang." *I'm going to kill Sadie.* Without another word or glance, she headed for the elevator but turned left and pushed through the fire door into the stairwell. *I suppose some time at the range wouldn't hurt me either.*

Heading down the stairs, she'd almost forgotten about the note. Given the peculiar nature of the delivery, she'd kept it tucked inside her palm. Head down, she averted her eyes from the cameras in the stairwell. That was one thing that didn't bother her about being in the remotely located archives. She didn't feel as if she was being watched all the time. But headquarters was different. Too different. If someone's eyes weren't on her, someone else's were. *They.* Ted always mentioned *them* but gave her no idea who *they* were. She wasn't even certain that *they* were agents. She still wasn't certain about a lot of things. Too many things.

She popped the fire door, crossed through the lobby, and exited through the front doors. Her breathing eased. Keeping pace with the crowd, she made her way to her car a few blocks down. That was one thing she didn't mind so much about shadow cover: blending in. Jeans. Sweater. She wasn't any different than anyone else on the street. *There's something to be said for anonymity.*

Checking traffic, she crossed the street and headed for her phantom-black Hellcat. The twenty-inch wheels on the boss machine made her smile. She unlocked the door, took her seat, and closed herself inside. With a push of a button the engine purred to life. She sank into the leather and closed her eyes. *Ah, that's better.* She rubbed the note inside her hand and tried to guess what it said. *Probably the name of a new pizza place or a microbrewery that's just opened.* Opening her eyes, she unfolded the paper and read a short list.

Alexandria Detention Center

Deanne Drukker

Extraordinary Caution

CHAPTER 3

SIDNEY DIALED UP THE ALEXANDRIA Detention Center. A man picked up. She asked, "Do you have a Deanne Drukker incarcerated?"

The man replied, coughing. "Sorry. Fighting a cold. Are you wanting to schedule a visit?"

"Maybe. Right now I'm just looking for her, actually."

"Well, the name doesn't sound familiar. Let me check." He started to hum an eighties rock melody that was broken up with coughing. "Nope. No Deanne or Drukker. Are you sure that's the right name?"

"I'm sure," she said, pulling out of her parking spot.

"You might want to call around some other places, Miss. Did you call the local police on this?"

"Not yet." She stopped the car at the red light. *Why would Ted give me her full name? Why the detention center?*

"Miss, are you there? I've got another call if we're finished here."

"Smoke," she said. "Is John Smoke housed there?"

"Oh yeah, Smoke's here. Are you family?"

Her blood pulsed through her chest. "Really. Uh, No."

"Ah, girlfriend. What's your name? I'll see if he has you scheduled."

"Does he get many visitors?"

"Not many people do, but he does better than most. I see he's expecting someone. What is your name?"

It better be Fat Sam or Guppy. "It's Sidney. I'm probably not on the list, but I'd like to see him."

"Well, Sidney, are you finally going to show up this time?"

"What do you mean?"

"Well, protocol calls for him to schedule someone before they come. He's had your name on here every Thursday for the last several weeks. Pfft. If you're coming, show up sometime between now and noon. Time's up after that. We can't wait to see you." The line went dead.

What game is he playing?

A correction officer escorted Sidney through the halls of the detention center. Their footsteps echoed off the hard white walls. He opened the door to the visitation room and stepped aside.

"He'll be with you soon, Miss."

Inside, there was a sofa, a small round table, and four chairs. The walls were painted a pale yellow, and a painting of an old man fishing in the sea hung on the wall. The checkered tile floors were scrubbed clean, and the smell of Clorox lingered in the air. It was one of the better detention centers she'd been inside. The chair scraped across the floor as she took a seat. She took off the jacket they'd given her to wear. The watch commander had said her sweater left little to the imagination. She'd told him she was FBI acting in official capacity. And he'd said he didn't care. She checked the time. 11:15 am.

Two minutes later, Smoke came through the door. He wore a beige jumpsuit, and his hair was shaved down to about a quarter inch. The imposing man took a seat across from her and looked deep into her eyes.

"So, you've been expecting me?" she said, pushing her sleeves up on her sweater.

"For about seven weeks," he said. "How have you been?"

"Bored."

"Huh-huh," Smoke laughed, tipping his head back a little. "You think you're bored. I think you miss me."

"You're the one writing me in for visitations," she said, remaining poised. "You've been here the entire time?"

"I have, and that's why I thought you'd have been here sooner." He eyed her. "You really didn't know I was here, did you."

"Not until today. A little bird told me."

"A bird, huh?"

"Not that kind of bird." She glanced at his hair. "So, are you going back in the military? You look like you're fresh off the bus and just left the base barber."

"We had a lice outbreak."

As if being almost obscene wasn't bad enough, you have to follow up with that.

He rubbed his hand over his head. "It takes some getting used to, but it will grow back."

Let's hope. "It doesn't really matter." She brushed her own hair aside. "Are you going to stay here for the duration?"

"Seventeen months to go, maybe six with good behavior, but I'm not for sure. I'm just marking the days until time is served."

Clearly Smoke didn't need to be imprisoned, and seeing him there hurt. She wanted him out. *At least I know where he is now.* "Any other visitors, Sam or Guppy?"

He shook his head. "No, they don't swing by. It's better that way." He patted the table with his fingers. "So, do you have your sweet heart suit on?"

"No, just my own skin."

He leaned forward. "Did you return it to Mal Carlson then?"

"I still don't have any idea who he is, but he sends me texts from time to time. They don't make a lot of sense."

"Can I see them?"

"No."

"Can you tell me what they say?"

"Not much of a point in it. Just weird stuff. Common courtesy and such." She crinkled her nose. "Kinda juvenile actually."

The chair groaned as Smoke eased back into his seat. "I see. So you don't have anything interesting to tell me? Black suns? Odd investigations? Semi-truck trailers running you off the road?"

"Nothing worth mentioning." An odd silence followed and the distance between them seemed to grow. On the one hand she wanted to talk to him about everything. Her family. Her work. Drake. Section Chief Howard and Deanne Drukker. But she held her tongue. "And you? I see you aren't battered up like the last time. I take it there's been no more attempts on your life?"

"Not as much hostility here." He leaned onto the back legs of his chair, stretched his long arm out, and pounded on the door. "Guard!"

"What are you doing?" Sidney said in alarm.

"Well, if you don't have anything else to say, then I guess this meeting's over."

CHAPTER 4

LATER THAT DAY AT THE FBI's indoor shooting range, Sidney blasted away at a silhouette. She emptied her magazine on the target and snapped in another, took aim, and squeezed the trigger.

Blam! Blam! Blam! Blam! Blam... click.

She popped out the magazine and set her weapon aside on the counter. When she hit the switch, the target floated to her. Her bullet groupings were tight. Quarter-sized holes appeared inside the head, the heart, and two inches below the target's lower abdomen. She plucked the chart off the clip and replaced it with another.

"Nice grouping," said a feminine voice behind her back.

Sidney turned and found herself facing Agent Rebecca Lang. The young woman wore yellow shooting goggles and hearing protection, standard issue, like Sid's. Slight of build and wearing loose-fitting clothes, she seemed undersized for all of her gear.

"So, what's his name? Or is it a her?" Rebecca continued, gazing at Sid's target.

"Its name," Sidney said, opening up another box of bullets, "is none of your business."

"All right," Rebecca said, making a slight wave. "I'll carry on then. I just thought since I happened to be taking your advice and just happened to be down here at the same time, I'd say hi. And now that is said, I'll say goodbye." She turned her back and began to step away.

Aw, geez. "Hold on a second, Agent Lang."

The younger woman turned and faced her.

"Sorry, but it's been one of those days. I apologize." She looked at her target with the holes in it and let loose a small laugh. "Pretty obvious, isn't it?"

Rachel nodded and smiled. She was nice looking, professional, and carried a determined look about her. "I think it would make for a pretty cool poster. Maybe keep it on your wall in your cubicle. Put a note on it saying, 'Ask me what happened to the last guy I dated.'"

"Kinda dark, don't you think?"

"I'm a data analyst, not a comedian. Just trying to make some honest conversation."

"I'm not in much of a talking mood right now." She fed bullets into her magazine.

"You've got some pretty fast fingers," Rachel said. "Is there a trick to that?"

Sidney loaded one bullet in after the other, saying, "Press and slide. Press and slide. I used to fill magazines for my father when I was a kid. He was a sheriff. I'd go to the range and help him and his deputies all the time. By the time I was sixteen, I could outshoot all of them." She slapped in the magazine, twirled the gun on her finger, and stuffed it in her holster. "We watched a lot of westerns, too."

"They don't teach that at the academy. Any chance you could show me that roll?"

"Show you that roll?" Sidney shook her head and flipped the switch. The target glided out toward the back wall. She flipped the switch off. The paper silhouette lingered about twenty-five feet away. "This is how I roll." Cat quick, she slid her Glock out of the holster, took aim, and blasted away. In seconds, the magazine was empty. Empty bullet casings rattled off the floor. She holstered her gun and flipped the switch.

Rachel stepped closer, eyeballing the target.

The target had holes that formed two eyes, a nose, and a mouth.

"Is that a belly button or a bad shot?"

"It's a belly button," Sid said, taking down the target. She had a wry smile. "A little something I learned watching *Lethal Weapon*. Ever see it?"

Rachel shook her head. "No."

Sidney reloaded, twirled the gun on her finger, and holstered it. She said to the woman, "I love shooting. That's why I'm good at it. And if you don't love it, chances are you won't ever be any good at it. We're best at the things that we love most. That's not always good in some cases, but it's often true." She patted Rachel's sidearm. "Do you love that weapon?"

Rachel shrugged her brows and shoulders.

"Well, I love mine. That's the difference. Find out what you love, and do it." She gave her the ole Ted Howard squeeze on the shoulder. "Good luck with that. I've got to go."

"Is there anything you love more than shooting?" Rachel asked.

Without turning back or slowing, Sidney said, "Of course, but loving your weapon is so much easier."

"I'm an attorney."

"Oh really," Sid said, rolling her eyes. She'd stopped at a restaurant to grab a bite to eat on her way home. The place was busy. Lots of suits and ties. A working crowd. Not wanting to wait for a table, she'd settled in at the bar. "Well, let me take my panties off and give them to you right now. So impressive. Please. Your place or mine?"

"Look, I was just making conversation," he said, pushing back his hair. "I wasn't trying to brag or anything."

"Of course you were." She fixed her eyes on his and took a swig of beer. "And you said 'I'm an attorney' as if that were something rare. Have you ever picked up a phone book? Have you?"

He eased back and said, "Yes."

"There are more attorneys in there than anyone else. Almost double. So pray tell, what makes attorneys so special?"

"I-I…" he loosened his tie and took a half-step back. "I swear I didn't mean it that way."

"Yes, you did. But let me tell you what is special: plumbers. You see, plumbers are useful. They fix things. Your kind, they just make a mess of things."

"I'm not a divorce attorney. I'm not even a trial lawyer. I'm a title attorney. That's all."

She narrowed her eyes on him. "Did I say anything about divorce lawyers or trial attorneys? Are they bad or something?"

"Look, I just think there are stereotypes, and plenty of them are accurate, but that doesn't mean we're all bad. We've done plenty of good things."

"Really? Well, please tell me one good thing your profession has done."

He rubbed the back of his neck. He had a little curl in his tawny hair, soft eyes, and a gentle smile. Lean but well built. "Look. I'm sorry. I don't have very much experience in the bar scene. I just thought you were pretty and maybe I could buy you a drink." He turned away and waved. "See ya."

Sidney shrank back on the bar stool. The man, right around her age, settled back down at his table, alone. *A title attorney. Probably lying.* She drained her beer and set it back on the bar.

"Another, Miss?" the bartender said, wiping down the bar.

"Uh, sure." She didn't drink much, and when she did, usually one was her limit, but tonight was different. Smoke had given her the cold shoulder, and she suddenly felt more alone now than ever. Something needed to fill her. *Cold beer. Why not?*

Sidney stirred in her bed. There was a rattle in her bedroom. She eased her gun out from underneath her pillow, heard a soft scuffle of shoes, turned, and pointed.

"Easy! Easy!" said a man, dropping his pants to the floor and raising his hands.

She lowered her weapon and rubbed her aching eyes. "Damn." The clock on the wall read 2:10 in the morning.

"Sorry," the man said. His name was Roy, the title lawyer she'd met earlier. After another beer, she'd cozied up to him at the restaurant, and things had steamrolled from there. "I didn't want to wake you." He glanced down at his trousers. "May I?"

"Go ahead."

He slid his pants up and tucked in his shirt. "Is this a one-night thing, or can I call you again?"

"It's a moment of weakness on my part."

"You don't have to be so glum about it. I'm pretty sure we both had an excellent time."

Not going to argue there. "Just consider it your lucky night."

He tightened his belt. "Maybe you should consider it your lucky night." He flashed a nice row of teeth. "You yelled out my name a few times, as I remember."

"I don't think so."

"Hmmm." He snapped on his watch. "Maybe that was me yelling out your name. Hope I didn't disturb your neighbors. It's a nice area you live in here." He sat down on the bed and put his shoes on. "Are you sure I can't call you sometime?"

"Look, you're a nice guy, but no thanks."

"Yeah, I know. The nice guy never gets the girl. I've heard it before. Bad girls don't like nice guys."

"I'm not a bad girl."

"Uh, I just finished sleeping with you, and well, by my standards—which are well coordinated with the likes of Maxim magazine and such—you're a bad girl." He got up, slipped on his suit jacket, and said, "Are you sure you won't reconsider?"

Maybe. "I'm sure."

"Sidney, you're a magnificent woman." He started across the bed and tried to kiss her.

She placed her hand on his face and pushed him back. He mumbled a word, awkward in her hand. "Just get going, Roy. And don't swing by or look me up." She patted her gun on the pillow. *He's not a bad guy. Fit. Effective. A second time is considerable.* "I mean it."

"Loud and clear," he said, saluting. A buzz erupted inside his pocket. He fished the phone out and answered. "Yeah. Yeah."

Sidney cocked her head. There was an irritated woman's voice on the line.

"I'm on my way. Long night, it'll be fifteen minutes. Thirty tops. I love you too. Kiss. Kiss."

Sidney's eyes widened. "You're married!"

Roy started backing toward the door. "Hey, you didn't ask. I thought it was cool."

"I didn't ask because I didn't see a ring on your finger!"

"Pfft! How dated is that? Sorry, but you should have asked." He turned the doorknob and began his exit. He eyed her up and down. "Besides, bad lawyers don't wear wedding rings. Especially ones that are actually divorce attorneys." He flashed his teeth. "Thanks, you hellcat, you."

As Roy closed the door, she just shook her head.

CHAPTER 5

SIDNEY SCRUBBED A RUSTY SPOT around the drain of her bathroom sink with a Brillo pad until her elbow ached.

"Why won't you go?" she said through clenched teeth. She rinsed the spot and the rust was still there. "So be it." She removed the rubber gloves, tossed them in a plastic pail, and headed to the kitchen. There she placed another coffee pod into the machine. The coffee maker vibrated on the counter a little, and thirty seconds later she had another fresh cup of brew in her hand. She looked at the five empty pods on the counter and swept them into the trash bin. *Get it together, Sid.*

It was 6:37 in the morning, and she hadn't been back to sleep since Roy left. She'd showered. Cleaned. Washed and dried. Her apartment, normally well kept, was now spotless. Counters were wiped clean. Not a dirty dish in the washer, the sink, or on the counters. All of her clothes were folded or ironed and hung. No dust bunnies lurked under the bed. She took a drink out of her coffee mug. It was a keepsake from her Air Force days, with a logo of a skull wearing a beret and the letters ABGD. *Air Base Ground Defense. Those were the days.*

She mopped a thin film of sweat from her brow with a dishrag. *I think I may need to shower again.* Meandering into the bathroom, she thought of Smoke. She couldn't get his brush-off out of her mind. She couldn't think of anything she'd done wrong, either. *I didn't do anything wrong.* Deep inside, her feelings stirred. She'd done something. Inside the tub and shower, all of the porcelain had a nice sheen. No soap buildup surrounded the drain nor watermarks the basin. Everything smelled clean. *Not gonna be enough.*

She put on a set of gym clothes, packed a duffel bag, got in her car, and drove to the gym. The showers there were plenty hot after a good workout, and the sauna would do her good. Still, the more she tried not to think about Smoke, the more he cropped up, a stealthy intruder invading the privacy of her mind. *Why the sudden rejection? Was there a message in it? What was his reason?* They hadn't even talked about the Black Slate, AV, or Night Bird. She didn't have anyone to talk with about those things.

Inside the gym, she had a purpose-filled workout, hammering at the heavy bag. Large drops of sweat splatted on the rubber-coated floor, forming tiny puddles. She wiped it up with her towel and headed for the sauna. There, she spent twenty minutes listening to a pair of older women discussing the sexual inefficiency of their husbands and planning a girls' trip to Vegas. The shower she took was hot, pleasant, and without any busybody neighbors. Refreshed and dressed for work, she left the gym and headed for her car.

"Excuse me, Agent Shaw?"

She turned. There stood a husky man in a weather-beaten trench coat and a Redskins ski cap that hung over his ears. He had s shifty gait as he approached.

"That's close enough, Mr..."

"Davenport. Russ Davenport." He tipped his scruffy chin that went well with his scratchy voice. "I'm a reporter for *Nightfall DC*."

"Never heard of it," she said, easing back toward her car. "Care to explain how you know who I am?"

"Well, I'm an investigative reporter in the middle of an investigation. Surely you understand, being an investigator yourself."

"Oh, I understand. You're stalking a federal officer."

"It's still a free country. I'm just making conversation with a fellow citizen with whom I might have something in common. That's all."

"So, you've been waiting for me in a parking lot?"

He glanced back at the gym and patted his tummy. "I'm not one for working out much. It interferes with my fully processed diet." His eyes darted around before they fixed back on her. "Look, I'm not a troublemaker. I just have a question."

She popped open her car door. "Then you'll have to contact the FBI and go through the proper channels. They have a media center. I'm sure you're well acquainted with the Freedom of Information Act. Go there, or else you might find yourself in prison."

"You're working on the Black Slate," he interjected. "Have you seen any werewolves lately? Giant birds, maybe?"

She froze. *No way!* She held his gaze and shook her head. "DC is full of a lot of crazy things. A lot of people see one thing, and someone else sees another."

"I got proof," he said, raising his double chin. There was a satisfied look on his chubby face. He withdrew a plastic bag from his pocket. There was a large feather in it. "Look familiar?"

"No."

"I found this at the truck stop where that FBI chopper crashed. Normally I don't report on those bigger stories, but on social media there were some tall tales—of a giant bird, for instance." He coughed into his fist. "Well, how did I come across this?"

"DC is notorious for its really big pigeons."

"True, Agent Shaw, but this isn't that kind of feather. You see, I've got a friend who works in the Smithsonian. He's in the ornithology department—that means birds. He freaked out when he saw this. He said, 'I've never seen anything on this planet like it.' I almost didn't make it back out of there. Really creepy."

"Maybe you should have just left it with them. I'm sure they would have paid good money."

"As you can see," he opened his jacket, revealing a cheap shirt and cheaper blue trousers underneath, "I'm not into money. I'm into the truth. I know there are monsters out there, and I know that you have seen them. Just tell me more about what you saw."

"Oh, there are monsters all right, Mr. Davenport. You know as well as I do that this town is full of them. But the kind you're talking about, well, I don't have any proof on anything." She got inside her car and started to close her door. Russ grabbed the door. She tried to pull it shut, but his strength was firm. "You need to let go."

"You might not have any proof, but you have your word. Eyewitness testimony is the most convicting."

"And many eyewitnesses are also known to be convicts."

"You aren't a convict."

"How do you know for sure? How do you know anything for sure?" She closed the door, started the engine, and pulled out of her spot. She heard him yell out and say, "Nice car!"

Gunfire cracked out of nowhere. *Pop! Pop! Pop!* She flinched and checked her mirror. Russ was on the ground, clutching his chest and bleeding on the pavement.

CHAPTER 6

GLOCK READY, SIDNEY RUSHED OUT of her car toward Russ. He lay on the ground, moaning. Scanning the parking lot, she didn't notice any threat, just some gaping onlookers.

She pointed at one and said, "Call 9-1-1!" She kneeled at the man's side. He had two bullet holes in his side. Placing her hands on it, she applied pressure.

"Oh!" he said in alarm. His face was ashen. Eyes wide open.

"Easy, Russ. Easy. Help's coming."

His jittery gaze held her eyes, and he said, "Why would anyone shoot me?"

Because you know something you shouldn't know. She shushed him. "Save your strength, okay? Help is on the way." A small crowd gathered. "If you can't help, step away!" Most gawked, and a couple of others pulled out their phones. *Indecent idiots!*

"Dude, I might catch a shot of him dying," said a young man in a ski cap, tank top, and baggy sweatpants. He had more tattoos than teeth. "Wouldn't that be cool?"

"Yeah, man," said another one. "Pretty sick. Get closer. I want to show my girlfriend. She loves this stuff."

Someone get here now, please! "Has anyone called 9-1-1 yet?"

"I did."

"Me too."

"Agent Shaw," Russ said in a raspy voice. Blood bubbled from his mouth. "Getting shot hurts like hell."

"Don't talk. Try not to talk. Save your energy."

"I need to tell you something, in case I don't make it." He convulsed and twitched. "Aw geez, it hurts."

"Don't say anything," she said, cocking her head. Sirens. Loud and clear. *Hurry!* She bent closer. "Just hang on Russ. Can you do that for me? Hang on."

"I'm trying." He coughed blood.

"Dude, that's sick!" the young man said. "Get closer on that. It's awesome."

Sidney clenched her jaws and checked Russ's pulse. It slowed. He was losing lots of blood. *Please don't die.*

"Agent Shaw, you must listen," Russ croaked out. "They're watching. They're always watching."

Who's watching? She wanted to ask, but she couldn't. Not when his last moments were upon him. She needed to save him. *Why shoot him and not me?* "Save your strength. Help's here. They're going to take you to the hospital and save you."

"I'm already saved," he said. His eyes fluttered. "And I hate hospitals. Fight the good fight, Agent Shaw." He reached up and touched her cheek. His eyes were glassy. "I just wanted to help." His bloodstained fingers slipped down her cheek.

"Dude, did he die? Did he die?" one punk said. "Did you get it?"

The ambulance pulled in, and the paramedics pulled out. Police officers took control of the scene.

"Miss," said a paramedic in a blue EMS uniform. "You've done all you can. We got this."

She backed off as they loaded Russ onto the gurney. He wasn't moving. Into the ambulance he went. They shut the doors, and the vehicle sped away. *What just happened?*

"I got it all, dude. I got it all."

She whirled around and faced the pair of young men. "Excuse me." *Try reason, Sid.* "That man's a friend of mine who may or may not have just died. I'd appreciate it if you'd delete that video."

"Sorry, lady, but stuff like this is too hot." He eyed her up and down, nudged his friend, and thumped his nose. "But maybe we can work something out."

She closed in, looked him in the eye, and said, "Oh yeah? What did you have in mind?"

He rubbed his lower lip with his index finger, licked his teeth, and said, "I was thinking…" He grabbed her arm.

Perfect. She grabbed him by the wrist, twisted it behind his back, and slammed him into the pavement.

"Ow! What's the deal? Get off me!"

She took out her badge and stuck it in his face. "You just assaulted a federal officer. That's the deal, worm!"

The other young man took off running. She held her badge up and said, "Officers! That man's a suspect in the shooting." She drove her knee into the punk's back and said, "So are you, maggot."

"Hey, I didn't shoot anybody!"

"That's not for me to determine. That's up to the courts. You don't have any priors, do you?"

"A couple." He struggled. "Look, I'll delete it. Just let me go. I don't want any trouble. I'm sorry. Really, I'm sorry."

"Do it," she said, lifting her knee off his back.

Chin on the ground, hands holding the phone in front of his face, he pulled up the video. He hit the trash bin icon. "There, it's gone."

"Let's hope, but this isn't the end of the investigation, just the beginning. It's gonna be a long day, bub."

"But I have class."

"No, you don't. And that's not my problem." She pulled him up to his feet. "Did it even enter your mind to do something to help the man?"

"Why? He probably wouldn't do that for me." His eyes grazed over her body. "I'd help you out though."

Loser! "Officer!" She flagged a cop over. "This one's ready to make a statement, and so am I when you're ready."

It was late Friday morning, a day after the shooting at the gym. Sidney sat inside the Wayfarer's Way, sipping coffee and picking at her plateful of eggs and bacon that was pushed off to the side. She had a newspaper under her nose. There was a little blurb about the shooting. It said Russ Davenport was in critical condition. The police blotters had it down as an accidental shooting.

This is crazy.

Two bullets in the lungs in a full parking lot wasn't an accident. Witnesses said they'd seen a car drive by, chasing after another. Both of the vehicles were SUVs, dark paint, big rims. She hadn't noticed the vehicles at all. Everyone figured it was a gang, but she knew better.

She folded up her paper and pulled her plate of food over. The portions were huge. *No wonder Ted likes to meet here so much.* She figured he dreaded meeting her anyway, but he had to, given the nature of yesterday's incident. Her name, tied with the agency, was all over the blotters. But her name wasn't in the paper. Not that it should be, but it very easily could have been. The FBI didn't want that kind of local attention.

"Can I freshen you up, honey?" asked an older woman holding a steaming pot of coffee over the table.

"That would be great, thanks." Sid shoved her mug over and watched the woman fill it to the brim.

"No cream or sugar?"

"No."

"There you go. Anything else?"

"No, thank you."

She checked the clock on the wall. 10:32 am. Ted was late, and he wasn't normally late. She shifted in the booth and pulled up a website on her iPad. www.nightfalldc.com. It was more of a tabloid than anything else, but it had a strong following. There were stories about crimes that never got reported. Strange happenings at the nightclub scene. Sidney had spent a couple of hours scanning the past year's worth of articles and stories. Russ Davenport's name was on most of them, but that wasn't all she learned. Russ Davenport wasn't his real name, rather a pseudonym. And to make things more interesting, she still didn't know what his real name was.

A text popped up on her iPad from her sister, Allison. It read:

Can you watch Megan this weekend? Need serious help. Mom and Dad in Florida.

"She must be joking." Sid started to reply no but pulled back. A weekend with Megan might be just what she needed. She didn't want Allison to know that, but why punish the kid? Megan probably needed a break too. She texted back.

I'll think about it.

Great. It could be a career-defining moment. Thanks, Sis.

That's odd. The nature of the text almost seemed cheerful. Positive. *She's probably high.* Sidney sighed. *I guess I'll find out soon enough.* She checked the time. 10:36. *Where is he? He could at least text or something.* She took out her phone and pulled up Ted's number. *Screw this. I've got things to do.* A bell rang on the old restaurant's front door, and a man in an overcoat, suit, and tie entered. Sidney frowned. It wasn't Ted, it was Cyrus Tweel.

CHAPTER 7

C YRUS SAT DOWN IN THE booth and dropped a paper satchel on the table. "Hey, Sid." He raised his finger up and half-shouted at the waitress. "Coffee. Two creams. One sugar." He drummed the table and settled himself into the booth. "I hate this place. Smells old. Feels old. Never understood why Ted's so fond of it."

"Probably because people like you don't come here."

"Oh-oh," he said, drumming the table. He pushed back his round wire-rimmed glasses. "Why the frosty reception?"

"I was expecting Ted."

"Ted was called into something bigger—we can only assume—and hence, he dispatched me, your supervisor, to have this little meeting with you." He plucked a piece of bacon off of her plate and bit into it. "Man that's greasy." He dropped it back on her plate and wiped his hands off. "You should switch to turkey bacon or no bacon at all. That would be wise."

"And you should keep your hands to yourself." She straightened up in her chair and locked her fingers together and rested her hands on the table. "What's the meeting about? I assume it involves the incident from yesterday?"

"Never assume anything," he said, smiling. "No, I've been briefed on the incident and so has Ted, but this is entirely different." He shoved the paper satchel her way. "It's the next Black Slate assignment."

"Really?" she said, staring at the file. She fixed her gaze back on him. "You seem almost chipper about it."

"Oh, not really. Look Sid, I've gotten wind of some of the reports, and maybe I haven't been very clear about what I think, but I will be now." He pecked his index finger on the file. "This is a career killer. Get away from it."

"It's my assignment. I've been picked for some reason, and truth be told"—she pulled the file toward her—"I like it."

His face deflated a little and he said with a shrug, "It's your career." The waitress delivered his coffee and set it on the table. He took a long sip and made a sour face. "Good lord, this coffee tastes as old as the building."

Sidney stared at the file. It was sealed shut. She began tearing it open.

"Ah ah ah," Cyrus said, pinning the folder down with his hand. "You can look at this bullshit after I'm gone. I don't want any of this supernatural crap rubbing off on me. I've got big plans for tonight."

"Oh I see. You have a date then?"

He lifted his chin and said with a smirk, "As a matter of fact I do, and I'm pretty excited about it. She's so interesting." His eyes were fixed on hers. "Really interesting."

Fine, I'll entertain him. "And where did you meet her?"

"Work."

"Oh, well, I think that's a bad idea." *Not that I care.* "So, what's her name?"

"Rebecca Lang, and I believe you've met her."

"Yes," she nodded. "She seems nice. Good for you, Cyrus."

He reached into his pocket and grabbed his ringing phone. "Oh, that's her." He answered. "Hey Rebecca. Uh-huh. Uh-huh. Great. Eight it is." He disconnected and got out of his seat. "Sorry, but I've got to get back out on the street. I'm knocking off a little early today."

"Wait a minute," she said to him. "What about John Smoke? Isn't he going to be a part of this?"

"Don't know, don't care." He threw a buck on the table. "Read the file."

Back home inside her apartment early that evening, Sidney sat on her sofa staring at the unopened Black Slate file. Something was different. The hand-off from Cyrus for one thing. The lack of discussion about Smoke for another. She picked at the clasp that held the paperwork inside.

What are you waiting for, Sid?

Her phone buzzed. It was another text message from her sister. It read: I'm waiting.

Sidney texted her back:

90 min.

She'd agreed to watch Megan over the weekend, and that was part of her hesitation with the file. Once she opened it, she'd dive into it, and she just didn't want to do that right now. But what if the contents inside required immediate action? And wasn't Smoke supposed to be the bounty hunter, not her? She was just supposed to watch him. The phone buzzed again. It read: Pick up some dinner.

Sidney squeezed her phone. *That's just like her, not feeding Megan any dinner. It's 7:10 already. Geez! I suppose I might as well stock up on some groceries. Deadbeat!* She tapped the phone against her chin and stared at the file. The last two files had almost gotten her killed, not to mention all the mystery they had unfolded. What would the next file have in store for her? *A vampire? The New Jersey Devil or a Mothman?* The man from the cemetery who they called Boss had made light about one.

It's not like you to be a chicken, Sid. Go ahead. Tear Pandora's box wide open.

She ripped off the tape, peeled back the metal clasp, and dumped the contents on the table. The tab on the black folder read Mason Crow. After folding it open, she studied the portrait of a black man in sunglasses and mutton chops. "Oh Lord," she chuckled, "it's the Duke of New York." She pushed the picture aside and glanced at the next one and blanched. "On steroids."

The pictures were all labeled Mason Crow. The man was huge. Maybe seven feet tall and solid muscle. One picture was of him towering in the center of a group of men of several nationalities. They were in the bush and geared up like mercenaries. Mason Crow had an M-60 machine gun that looked like a toy resting on his brawny shoulder.

"I don't even want to know what kind of monster this guy turns into." She flipped through a few more pictures, and her stomach turned queasy. Mason Crow stood over a pile of butchered bodies with a blood-soaked machete in his hand. "He's a monster already."

CHAPTER 8

"Congressman Wilhelm? You're kidding, Allison. Tell me you're kidding?"

"No," Allison said, picking up her luggage and heading for the door. "This job's paying me seven thousand a month. I can't pass that up. I can't afford to pass up anything right now."

Sidney tossed her duffel bag onto the couch and glared at her sister. Allison wore a business pantsuit and she still looked sexy in it, like an airline attendant you'd see on some billionaire's private jet. "And David? Is he going to be there?"

"Nope," Allison said, checking her hair in her mirror. "I'm done with him." She smiled at herself in the mirror. "Wow, what a great view!"

"Seven-K a month seems a bit pricey for an internship," Sidney said, rubbing Megan's head. The little eyes were glued to the TV, watching cartoons. *I might need to look into her pay stub.* "And where are you going, exactly?"

"Oh, some sort of conference in Houston, Texas. I've never been there, but I hear it's pretty exciting. Do you think they still wear cowboy hats?"

"Sure, and the governor stables his horse at the capitol."

"Really?" Allison checked her make-up. "I bet that's fascinating." She loaded her luggage onto her shoulder. "Cab's waiting. Got to go. Kiss kiss, Megan."

Megan waved her pink-sleeved arm up in the air. "Bye, Mommy."

"Allison," Sidney started to say. Her sister disappeared into the hallway, and the door closed behind her. "Be careful."

"Are you worried about Mommy?" Megan said. She was leaning over the back of the sofa and looking up at Sid with her hands cupped under her chin. "Because you look worried."

Sidney took a seat on the couch and Megan curled up into her side. "Your mommy is my little sister, so I'll always worry some. Besides, that's what women do, too much and too often."

"Well, I'm not worried." Megan turned the TV off. "Can we play dress-up now?"

"How about we eat first? I brought your favorite takeout."

Megan clapped her hands. "Chinese?"

"Uh, no, I thought you liked Mexican."

"That was last year. I'm ten now, and I'm all about some Moo Goo Gai Pan."

"But you'll still eat Mexican, won't you?"

Megan shrugged her little shoulders and said, "I guess so."

"Good." Sidney got up from the couch and made her way into the apartment's kitchen. Grimy dishes were piled high in the sink. She stuck them in the dishwasher.

"That doesn't work anymore," said Megan, taking a seat on the kitchen barstool. She held a white teddy bear in her arms. "The landlord won't fix it because Mom's behind on her rent. You won't let them kick us out, will you Aunt Sid?"

"No, of course not." *Oh, great! Seven grand a month she says, and she can't pay rent.* "Well, you can still clean dishes with soap and water."

"I know. But I've been feeling kinda lazy lately." Megan stretched her arms out and yawned. "Plus, we're out of dish soap."

"I wasn't talking about you." Sid found a stack of paper plates in the cupboard, but there were water stains on them. "I was talking about your mother." She took the stryofoam containers of Mexican food out of the plastic bag and set them on the counter. "Looks like we're going to eat in a less formal setting." She fished some plastic utensils and napkins out of the bag. "Is that all right with you?"

Megan glanced at the trash can in the kitchen corner. It was stuffed with take-out containers. "What do you think?" she said.

The lukewarm food was good and the conversation light. Megan told her about school and her upcoming science project that she needed some help on. Sid noticed that Megan yawned a lot. She'd been with her niece plenty over the years, and usually, even later in the evening, she was bright eyed and bushy tailed. Normally, she'd be alert until she zonked out.

After they finished eating, Megan asked again if they could play dress-up, and they'd spent the last thirty minutes applying makeup.

Staring into the mirror, Megan said, "I look like a hooker."

"What?" Sidney gasped. "No, no, you don't." She started rubbing off some of the blush on her cheeks. *Morning Glory, I haven't overdone it that much, have I?* "What makes you think you look like a hooker?"

"Because I'm wearing a lot of makeup."

"Do you know what a hooker is?"

"Mommy says hookers are women who wear too much perfume and makeup."

"Well, not exactly. There are a lot of women who wear too much makeup, but they aren't hookers."

"Like old ladies that we see in department stores."

"Well that's one kind that aren't hookers."

"So what are hookers?"

Sidney grabbed a brush and began combing Megan's hair. "How about we braid it? You always look so cute when it's braided."

Megan said, "Sure. So, what's a hooker?"

"Well," said Sid as she braided Megan's soft and silky dirty-blond hair, "Hookers are women who sleep with men for money."

The little girl's jaw dropped, and her eyes filled with excitement. "Really? People will pay you to sleep with them? That sounds like a pretty easy way to make money. Sleeping's easy, but sleeping with boys seems kind of gross."

There's a lot of truth to that. "Well, there's a lot more to it than just sleeping with them."

"Like what?"

Be straight. "Kissing."

"Like sex kissing?"

Sidney eyed her reflection in the mirror. "Uh, something like that."

"Like I see on TV. I see lots of kissing on TV. Are all of those women hookers?"

"Only if they're paid for it." *Oh geez.* She stopped braiding. "What kind of shows do you watch?"

"Just what Mommy watches. I have a TV in my room, but the screen's all fuzzy. Mommy says she'll get me a new one now that she has a job."

"Okay, listen to your Aunt Sid, and I'll explain to you a little bit about hookers." *I shouldn't be having this conversation.* "Hookers sleep with men for money, but it's against the law. They can be arrested for it. So, talking about hookers, also known as prostitutes or call girls, is a bit of a no-no."

"Oh, I see." Megan smiled. "Thanks, Auntie Sid. That clears that up."

"Good." Sid resumed braiding the girl's hair.

"Aunt Sidney."

"Yes?"

"What happens if people sleep with each other for free? Is that illegal?"

Morning Glory!

CHAPTER 9

A
FTER A RESTLESS NIGHT OF sleep, Sidney rolled out of her sister's bed and rubbed her eyes. It was daybreak, and a soft light illuminated the edges of the bent mauve-colored window blinds. Megan slept at her side, curled up in a ball. A gentle rise and fall was in the little girl's chest and her face, despite some smeared makeup, was at peace.

Sidney kissed her forehead and brushed her cheek with her thumb. *Such a sweet thing.* She picked her way through Allison's bedroom. Drawers were half open, stuffed with clothes spilling out. Her closet was cramped with shoeboxes and fancy dresses. Sid rubbed the satin on a pearl-colored evening dress.

This would cost me a paycheck. How does she get these things? The conversation she'd had with Megan about hookers came to mind. Sid's neck tightened. *No. She wouldn't. Would she?* It would explain plenty of things. The clothes, the shoes… she opened a white jewelry box that sat on the dresser and gaped.

Look at this stuff!

She held up a tennis bracelet loaded in bright diamonds and shook her head. *And she can't buy any damn groceries!* There was more. More precious stones and fine metals of all sorts. A small hoard. Sidney slipped a ruby band flecked with diamonds over her finger. *Hmmm, I might keep this for myself.* A gold-leaf brooch studded with rubies caught her eye. She snatched it up. *That's Mom's!* She clutched it in her hand. *Is she stealing this stuff, or was it given to her?* She plucked another item out of the box. A pair of silver and onyx cufflinks she had seen their father wear. *Sonuva—?*

A rustle in the living room caught her ear. She scooted over to the bed and grabbed her Glock from under the pillow. On cat's feet, she crept down the short hallway. The back of a man's head could be seen sitting on the couch. He was leaning over the coffee table. She charged the slide of her weapon, readying a round in the chamber. "Get those hands up where I can see them."

Slowly, the man's big hands rose toward the ceiling.

"Clasp your fingers behind your head," she ordered, making her way to the kitchen.

The man let out a grunt but complied. He turned his face toward hers. "Smoke?"

The man looked amazing even in blue jeans, work boots, and a nondescript brown jacket. He swallowed. "Yeah. It's me."

She kept her gun on him. "What in the hell do you think you're doing?"

He grimaced. "Just keeping an eye on things, I guess." He eyed the barrel of her gun. "Do you mind?"

"Oh, I don't mind putting a bullet in your head. No, not at all."

"Maybe you should call the police." He started rubbing his neck.

Now that she looked closer, she noticed that his arm was skinned up. And the thigh of his jeans was torn, revealing a bloody gash.

He said, "You wouldn't happen to have a Band-Aid, would you?"

"No," she said, lowering her weapon. "But there's a hospital a few blocks up the road. Did you miss it on your way over here?"

"Guess so," he said, leaning his big frame over the coffee table. He clutched his side and eyed the Black Slate file that was opened on the table. "Interesting."

"There's nothing in here for you to see," she said. She stuffed everything into the file and tossed it onto the kitchen bar.

"I disagree," he said, running his eyes up her legs.

She was wearing only a long black shirt and panties and made no effort to hide it. Instead, she took a seat on the barstool and rested her gun hand on the bar. "Out with it. Why are you here—and why do you look beat all to hell?"

"Traffic problems."

"You didn't escape, did you?"

"Who, me? Nah, nothing like that. Just a simple misunderstanding on the way over, is all." He rubbed a lump on his head. "Got any ice?"

"No." She fidgeted on her stool, foot kicking. She was still mad at him for the cold shoulder in the detention center. She wanted an explanation for it. At the same time, Smoke was hurt. Bad enough to get stitches, maybe worse. *What is he up to?*

Smoke sat quietly eyeing the décor and pressing his jacket against the cut in his leg. "Look, I'm sorry for the brush-off, okay?"

"What are you talking about?"

"You know, back in the detention center. But I was in a hurry. You came at a bad time."

"Oh, were you missing out on some Bingo?"

"Something like that." He eased himself up off of the sofa and stretched his broad shoulders back. There was some popping of tendons and sinew. He lumbered toward the front door. "I guess I better get going." He glanced at the file. "I got all I need for now."

What is he up to? There was a strange thing about the file: no letter from the bureau and no mention of Smoke, either. *Is he still on my side?* "See you around, Mr. Smoke."

He stopped turning the doorknob. "You're one stiff lady."

"What did you expect, a welcome wagon?" She put the gun down and balled up her fists by her sides. "What kind of friend sneaks in while you're sleeping? It's creepy."

Smoke's face darkened a little. "I wouldn't do anything without good reason. Did you ever stop to think that maybe I was here protecting you and the kid?" He approached her, stretched his arm across the kitchen counter, and grabbed some paper towels off the roll. "We've been through enough together. You should trust me by now."

"That's not how it works."

"Guess not," he said, pressing the paper towels against a notch on his head and opening the door. "Later, Agent Shaw." Stooped over, he exited and closed the door behind him.

Sidney started out of her seat, then stopped. Something thumped into the door.

Wump.

She hopped out of her chair and opened the door. Smoke lay stone cold in the stairwell.

CHAPTER 10

S MOKE'S PULSE WAS STRONG BUT slow. Careful not to get any blood on the concrete stairs, Sidney dragged the man inside. "Geez, you're heavy." Closing the door, she left him on the floor, rushed into the bathroom, and grabbed alcohol and washcloths. In the kitchen she found a pair of scissors and cut the jeans off his leg. The sticky, matted blood was worse than it looked, and it had a rough stitch job on it. More blood still oozed out of the wound. "You need a hospital."

She grabbed her phone and had started to call 9-1-1 when a text popped up from an unknown caller.

Don't call the hospital. He'll be fine.

"What?"

The text continued.

I think.

She scanned the apartment, checked outside through the blinds, and checked the front door's spy hole. She had started to text back when another message popped up.

It's Mal Carlson.

"I'm getting a little sick of Mal Carlson." She kneeled alongside Smoke and applied pressure to the wound on his leg. His clammy face soured. "What kind of scrap did you get into this time?"

It wasn't the first time he'd shown up battered. It had happened when they were dealing with Night Bird. He had been slightly hobbled then, but this was worse. *What on earth was he doing?* She got up, fixed a damp washcloth, and put some ice in it. A knock sounded at the door.

Picking up her gun, she then checked the spyhole. Phat Sam and Guppy stood outside. She opened up. Guppy bustled through first and opened up a kit of some kind.

"Care to fill me in?" Sidney said to him.

Sam eased her way inside and said, "We have this covered. Just give him a moment." The gorgeous woman's tone was somber, and her forehead was creased with concern. "It's been a long night."

Sidney opened her mouth to speak but opted to close the door. "Fine."

Guppy pushed up his sleeves, revealing his thick and hairy forearms. He plucked a syringe from his kit and filled it with a clear liquid from a vaccine bottle. He injected it into Smoke's wounded leg.

"Care to tell me what that's for?"

"Smoke has a thing," Sam said, moving over to the sofa. She eyed it and sat down on the coffee table. "I think you're going to need a new blanket, but that leather upholstery should be good to go."

"Again, what is the shot for?" Sidney demanded. "And what kind of thing are you talking about? You make it sound like he's a diabetic."

Guppy tucked a penlight in his mouth and peeled Smoke's eyelids open with his thumbs. "He's gonna be out for a while. Better put him in the bedroom." In a slow but fluid move, he hefted Smoke up into a fireman's carry on his shoulder and headed down the hallway.

"Hold on a second," Sidney said, cutting into his path. "My niece is sleeping back there."

"She's not sleeping in both bedrooms, is she?"

"No."

"Then," Guppy said, "I'll use the one she's not using." He smiled. "And which one might that be?"

Sidney opened the door to Megan's bedroom and stepped aside. "Don't make a mess."

"Hmmm," he said, stepping inside. "Lots of pink and purple. I like it. It's not manly, but it's soothing. Good colors for healing."

Sidney shut him in and took a peek inside the master bedroom. Megan slept easy. Sid closed the door and headed back down the hall. Fat Sam had her nose buried in the Black Slate file.

"Do you mind?" Sidney said.

Sam waved her off. "Oh, we're all part of the same team. Get over it." Wearing only a dark-green hoodie and blue jeans, Sam was still an impressive sight. Her words somehow carried authority.

Sidney glared at her.

"All right," Sam said, closing the folder. "I guess we can sit here and stare at each other."

"Or you can fill me in on what happened to Smoke."

"Do you have any coffee in this rat hole?" Sam said toward the kitchen. "It goes great with conversation."

"No."

"Donuts?"

Sidney shook her head. "You don't look like someone who eats donuts."

"I have amazing genes."

"Yes," Sid said, taking a seat beside Sam, "you appear to have a lot of amazing qualities, but not pissing me off isn't one of them. Out with it, Sam."

Sam smiled. "Huh, I like that. A compliment with a dash of insult. Well done, Agent Shaw."

Sidney raised her brows at Sam.

"All right," the woman said, "Smoke got in a fight last night, but we've been keeping track of him and ended up here."

"With the help of Mal Carlson?"

"Yes."

"So you've met him?"

"Yes," Sam responded.

Sidney's tone tightened. "In person?"

Sam started to nod her head and then shook it. "No. But he sends us stuff."

The muscles knotted between Sidney's shoulders. Again, everyone seemed to know what was going on but her. "What kind of stuff?"

"Oh, a few software programs and some other gadgets, like that kit Guppy has." Sam checked her black-coated nails and mumbled. "A few weapons and articles of clothing." She huffed on her nails and rubbed them on her hoodie. "Hasn't he been sending you stuff too?"

"Not lately. Does the FBI know you're in on this?"

"Oh no. No no no no. Honestly, my skin crawls a little, hanging out with you, but it's fine since you're a shadow agent." She eyed Sid. "You *are* still a shadow agent?"

"Oh, I'm a shadow all right." Sid glanced down the hall. Inside, her feelings stirred. "He *is* going to be okay, right?"

"Sure. Believe it or not, he's even tougher than he looks." She nudged Sid. "And he has us looking after him."

"So, are you going to tell me what he got in a fight with and why he got in a fight with it? And how exactly did he get out of prison? I need some answers."

"Well, I don't know how he got out of prison. I was only notified after he got out, but I do know what he got in a fight with." She peered down the hall, and her beautiful face filled with excitement. She looked into Sid's eyes and squeezed her forearm. "It was a gargoyle."

CHAPTER 11

"A GARGOYLE, HUH?" SIDNEY SAID, STARING at Sam's fingernails digging into her arm. "And you saw it?"

"Well, no." Sam let go. "But I'm pretty sure that's what it was."

Sid recollected the gargoyle theory from back when they were in the cemetery during the last investigation. Smoke had claimed that was what he'd seen. "And where did this happen?"

"Smoke sent us word that he was investigating something at some old cemetery. And he told me what he saw that last time. He said it was a gargoyle." She pulled her chin up. "And I believe him. And," she poked Sid in the shoulder. "I believe in the werewolf and the harpy and I'm not alone."

You're a kook. Sidney squeezed her eyes shut and shook her head a little. *And I'm a hypocrite. I've seen these things—but I still don't believe anyone else sees them.* "I'll make some coffee." She headed into the kitchen and spied an espresso machine on the counter. "It's going to be pretty stiff."

"That's how I like it."

"Who are you?" said a little girl's voice with avid curiosity. Megan had made her way out of the bedroom and waltzed into the living room. She yawned and squeezed her teddy bear. "And why is my bedroom door locked?"

"Uh, hi," Sam said. "I'm Sam, and it's nice to meet you. You must be Megan." She looked at the bear and stretched out her hands. "And who do we have here?"

"This is Agent Fluff, and he doesn't like strangers." Megan sat down on the sofa, still staring at Sam. "But you're kinda pretty, so I guess it's all right." She handed over the bear.

"Nice to meet you, Agent Fluff," Sam said, shaking his paw.

"Aunt Sidney, I'm hungry."

"Okay," Sid said. She checked inside the fridge. No eggs. No milk. She closed the door and opened up one of her bags of groceries. "You still like cinnamon Pop-Tarts?"

"Yep!"

"Maybe the three of us should go out," Sam suggested. "I know a great place nearby that makes awesome pancakes."

"What? No." Sid rejected.

"Yeah! Let's go, Aunt Sidney. Pleeease!" Megan pleaded.

"What is *with* you people and pancakes?" Sidney said.

"Come on," Sam said. "I think it would be best." She eyed the hallway again. "If you know what I mean."

Sid shut off the coffeemaker and agreed, "Okay."

They spent the next couple of hours eating at the International House of Pancakes. Megan had a hundred questions for Sam. Sam had a thousand answers. All went well until they returned to the apartment and found out Smoke and Guppy were gone. Otherwise, everything was just as they left it, and even Megan's bedroom was cleaned up and organized.

"I guess that's my cue," Sam said, making a break for the door.

Sidney blocked it. "You aren't going anywhere until you tell me what's going on."

Megan took a seat on the couch and turned on the television. "Do you two mind taking it somewhere else? My show is coming on. Got to get me some Halley and Baby."

Sidney pointed down the hall and said to Sam, "March." Inside the master bedroom, they both took a seat on the bed. "So tell me something. Why did Smoke come here?"

Sam shrugged.

"All right then." Sid rubbed her hands on her thighs. "Since we're a team, and I'm pretty sure you pride yourself on being an honest woman, I'll rephrase the question. Why do you think Smoke came here?"

Sam's eyes brightened. She crossed her legs and said, "I think he was protecting you."

"All right, and what do you think he was protecting me from?"

"Gargoyles?" Sam lifted her shoulders a little. "Maybe that Mason Crow fella." She made a bitter face. "That's a scary-looking guy. And then, of course, as usual, you have the Drake to contend with, which I think we know is behind all this."

Sidney shrank back on the bed. Things began to click. "It's the file. They want the file!"

"You think?"

Sidney retrieved the file from the kitchen counter. She had taken it with her on the trip to eat but had left it in the car. From now on she'd be more careful. Back inside the bedroom, she dropped it on the comforter and opened it up.

"What are you doing?" Sam asked.

"Someone made sure the last file got burned up in a car accident. We still recovered pieces of it, and that was enough last time, but..." She studied the faces in the pics, looking for marks, tattoos, or distinct features. There were several notes and records too. "Everything is a clue, a puzzle piece, and each file ties them all together to complete the picture."

"In theory." Sam picked one of the pictures up. "Or Smoke missed you."

"Now that's a theory." Sid plucked a shipping manifest out of the file and noted a tiny logo on it. It matched some markings on people's arms, and one of the soldiers with Mason Crow had the image sewn on his camouflage shirt. "I think this is probably a good place to start."

"Assuming you survive until Monday. You and your niece both."

"We'll be fine." Wheels turning inside her mind, Sidney wanted to get out on the hunt, but that wasn't going to happen with Megan. She had been right about not looking at the file, but now that she had, she was hungry. Starving with curiosity.

"I can see this is eating at you. Tell you what," Sam suggested, reaching for the file. "How about I take the file, and you can pick it up on Monday, or Sunday night if you like. Out of sight, out of mind. Have some piece of mind with your little sunshine."

"I don't know about that." Sid stared at the file. She knew she couldn't control everything all the time. "You know, it wouldn't kill us to make a copy."

"Wouldn't that be breaking the rules?"

"I suppose, but I don't think you're going to tell," Sid said. "Come on. I know a place we can go."

Sam took her by the wrist with a firm grip. "Let go, Sid. Just let go of it."

Sidney started to pull away, but then she sighed. "All right. Let's do this. Take some pics with your phone."

"No, too many Cloud issues," Sam said. "Just let it go for a while, will you? Besides, I know you remember most of what you saw."

True. Sidney's sharp memory retained plenty, but she had only glanced through what she'd seen. She ground her teeth, eyed Sam, and released the file. "I want it back Sunday night."

Sam got up with a smile. "Oh, don't you worry. You'll have it back."

Sidney followed her to the front door and let her out. "I better."

Sam's shoes echoed off the concrete steps, and out of sight she went.

Sidney closed the door and rested her shoulder on it. Her hands clutched at her aching head. *Am I crazy?*

"Aunt Sidney," Megan said, popping up over the back of the couch. "Can I still have a Pop-Tart?"

"Sure, sweetie." Sid headed into the kitchen. Outside in the parking lot, a woman's voice cried out for help, and a blood-curdling screamed followed.

"AAAAIIIIEEEE!"

CHAPTER 12

"**S**TAY PUT," SIDNEY SAID, SNATCHING up her pistol, "and lock the door behind me. I'll be right back." Rushing outside and into the parking lot, she found Sam sitting on the blacktop clutching her leg. "What happened?"

"They got it! They got the file!" Sam pointed toward the parking lot exit. A dark blue sedan without any plates swerved and clipped the back end of a car that was backing out. Without slowing, it sped away and out of sight onto the highway. "I'm sorry, Sidney. I'm sorry."

Sid kneeled alongside Sam. The woman had a nasty gash through her jeans on the side of her thigh. "Are you okay?"

Grimacing, Sam nodded. Tears streaked down the corners of her eyes. "That's going to leave a scar, isn't it?"

"That's what you're worried about?"

"Well, that and the file," Sam said, stretching out her hand. "Help me up. I need to get out of here."

"Let's get you inside so I can take a look at that."

"No." Sam pointed at the car whose bumper had been clipped. A man with fuzzy hair was pointing and screaming. Sam started limping toward an all-white mustang convertible. "Cops will be coming. You'll have to cover for me."

"I need my file back!"

Sam closed herself in the car, fired up the engine, and drove away. Seconds later, Sidney closed her jaw, headed back for the apartment, and knocked on the door. "It's Aunt Sid, Megan. You can let me in now."

The door cracked open, and Megan peeked out. The chain held the door from completely opening. "Is everything okay?"

"It is now," Sid said, squatting down. "Are you okay?"

Megan nodded and closed the door.

Sid heard the chain come off, and then the door opened again. She eased her way inside and locked the door behind her. "You did good, Megan. You did just like I said. I think I'll let you eat the entire box of Pop-Tarts for that."

"Yippee!"

It took less than an hour to sort everything out when the police arrived. Sidney told the officers most of what she saw, but she didn't claim to know anything about who Sam was. Instead, she opted to not be forthcoming with all that she knew. It left her steaming inside. She wasn't big on half-truths and lies. Especially ones told to her. Telling them herself left her feeling dirty.

Somebody really needs to explain all this.

She was sitting on the sofa hiding her glum face with a smile when Megan asked, "Aunt Sid, can we watch a movie?"

"Sure, whatever you want. You pick."

For the latter half of the day, she played with Megan, feeling guilty because her heart wasn't in it. Her thoughts raced through every detail of her visit from Smoke, Sam, and Guppy. Perhaps the entire thing had been staged to get that file. A ruse. A deception. Was someone playing a game with her?

"Can we order pizza?" Megan asked at dinnertime.

"Sure. Whatever you want." Sidney scratched some images on a note pad. It was a picture of Mason Crow. His broad face and features gave him an inhuman quality. On a separate pad she made a list of people, places, and things she'd seen in the file. A tiny finger tapped her on the shoulder. "Huh?"

Megan looked up at her. "You need to call it in."

"Oh, I'm sorry." She set down her pad. "Where's the phone?"

Megan cocked her head. "You have it. In your pocket."

"I thought there was a phone in the apartment."

"There was, but it was discontexted."

Sidney laughed. "You mean disconnected."

"Yeah, that's what I said, discontexted." The little girl yawned. Her light eyes were weak and tired. "I like Hawaiian Style, with thin crust and extra ham."

Sidney readied her phone. "Your mommy likes that?"

"No. That's Grandpa's recipe."

"So it is." She knew that. They had practically grown up on it as kids. "And you want it from Husson's Pizza, I take it?"

"Either there or Grazianno's." Sidney curled up on the couch, sniffled, and closed her eyes. "Wake me up when it gets here. I think I need a little nap time."

The next twenty-four hours were more restless ones. On the outside, Sidney tried to entertain Megan the best she could, but the Black Slate was eating her alive on the inside. There was no word either. Not from Smoke, Mal, or anyone. She stewed over whether or not to report that the file had been lost, but it could wait until Monday. *Maybe later.*

Megan lay on the sofa napping again. Sid covered her with a blanket. The little girl's energy ran high in spurts before turning low. *She needs to see a doctor.*

Sid watched television on and off, but nothing eased her restless mind. It was 3:16 Sunday afternoon, and Allison wasn't expected back for hours. *I'm not going to make it.* She rubbed Megan's leg. *She must think I'm a horrible aunt.*

A jingle of keys sounded outside the door, and the knob rattled. Sidney unholstered her gun and slipped over to the door and peered through the spyhole. *Allison?* She removed the chain just before the door swung open.

Allison shuffled inside with her head down and tossed her luggage on the floor.

"You're home early," Sidney said, "Is everything all right?"

"I'm fine. Thanks." She made her way over to Megan and huddled at her side. She kissed her daughter's cheek. "I missed you."

"Are you all right?"

"I said I'm fine," Allison said again, not making eye contact. "And I appreciate it. I really do. But if you don't mind, I could use some time alone with my daughter."

"Well, if you don't mind, I'd like you to tell me that face to face."

Allison stood up with a sigh and faced Sid. She had a split lip, and her chin was bruised. "I partied too much and fell. And I don't need a lecture. I've embarrassed myself enough already."

Sidney reached for Allison's sleeve. "Let me see your arms."

"What? No!" Allison backed away. "I'm not using."

"I didn't think you were, but I can see a bruise on your wrist that wasn't there when you left. How'd that get there?" She reached out again. "And what's that on your neck?"

Allison smacked her hand away. "Get out of here!"

CHAPTER 13

T HERE WAS NO ARGUMENT. SIDNEY gathered her things, kissed Megan on the forehead, and left. She'd been driving around in the Hellcat ever since. Three hours of lonely road. She drove around Interstate 495 at least four times before pulling into a gas station.

The chill nipped at her ears as she pumped high-octane fuel into her car. Finished, she headed inside the store, fixed a large coffee, paid with a card, and hit the road. Inside her, a conflict stirred. Allison infuriated her. Whoever had hurt her sister made it worse. And the last thing Sid wanted was for Megan to have to see such things. It pained her heart. She said the serenity prayer.

"O God, give me the serenity to accept the things I cannot change,

The courage to change the things that I can,

And the wisdom to know the difference."

She took a swig of coffee and thundered down the road. *I can't do it all. At least not on my own.*

Cruising through the biting wind of the late-winter day, she headed toward Smoke's apartment. She wanted answers to her questions. *And somebody better be there to answer.* Off the interstate she went, onto the highway until she hit the back road that rolled right up to the remodeled service station that was now Smoke's home. The brakes squeaked as she came to a stop. No lights shone from within, and no cars were parked outside.

I thought Sam would be here.

She shut off the engine, made her way to the front door, and turned the knob. It was unlocked. She swung the door open and was greeted by a burst of warm air. Inside, the light was dim, but the gas furnace rattled above. She closed the door behind her. "Smoke?"

"You're early." Smoke sat in a chair that seemed too small for his frame, hunched over his computer desk, studying something.

"Am I? I didn't realize I was on your schedule. As a matter of fact, I'm not aware of any schedule."

He kept his back to her, igniting her blood.

She marched over and spun him around. "Tell me what in the hell is going on!"

Smoke tilted is head back and gazed up into her eyes. His color had returned, and his strong, handsome features were more pronounced in the dusky light. He offered a smile and shrugged his brawny shoulders. "I'd be happy to fill you in, Agent Shaw." He reached behind him and grabbed a sealed manila file and handed it over to her. "You might want to start here."

The file had some heft to it. She wanted to hit him with it. She ripped the top off and removed the black file that was inside. The tab on it read, Mason Crow. "What is this?"

"You might want to sit down."

"I'm fine where I'm standing."

"Suit yourself then, Agent Shaw." He got up and took a seat on the old black leather couch and sunk in. "It was all a setup. Sorry."

She opened the file. Most of the pages and pictures were identical, but there was more information. A notable amount. There was a smaller envelope inside with bureau letterhead in it. "What do you mean by 'setup?'"

Smoke rubbed his neck. "The other file was a ploy to draw the enemy out."

She stiffened. "And I wasn't consulted on this!"

"No. *They* agreed that it might interfere. That it was too risky. Keeping you in the dark was better. At least that's the version I got." He looked her in the eye. "I didn't agree. Things got dicey on Friday, and that's why I showed up."

She walked over, leaned down in front of him, and hit his knee with the folder. "Who are *they*?"

"Good question. I don't have the answer."

She let out a disturbing chuckle and flopped down on the sofa. "Am I even on the FBI's payroll anymore?"

"As long as the checks keep clearing, I'd say so. Besides, there are plenty of folks on the payroll that people never see or hear about."

"Yes, I know." From the file, she took out the letter and opened it up. "Everything's a conspiracy."

"And you still doubt that after everything you've seen?"

"No, I believe what I see, and I believe in things I don't see. I just don't share your disconcerted views."

He sat up. "Disconcerted?"

She read the letter to herself.

Agent Shaw,

Due to the unorthodox arrangement of this assignment, you will need to keep the following items under consideration.

John Smoke is a convicted criminal with special skills. Don't underestimate him. He's dangerous. Unpredictable. Possible escape risk.

You have eyes on him, and we have eyes on him. Allow him free range. We'll let you know if he needs reeling in.

If any alien objects or circumstances or individuals encountered, notify your superiors immediately.

Seek Mal Carlson for assistance when needed.

Shadow cover authorized on this Deep Black assignment.

Trust your instincts and good hunting,

The Bureau

"Care to share?" Smoke asked.

"You mean to tell me you don't know? Huh?" She handed him the letter. "Go ahead. Read. Have yourself a chuckle. After all, this is becoming a joke."

"It's anything but that," he said, staring at the letter and then chuckling. He did his Batman voice again. "*He's dangerous*. Hah. I just love that part. *Unpredictable*. I guess that's 'cause I'm Batman.*"

Sidney held her lips tight to keep from laughing and stuck her nose in the folder. There were a few more photos, and one of a woman stood out in particular. There was something about her, standing alongside Mason Crow with an M-16 assault rifle resting over her shoulder. A deep intensity shone in the tall and lanky woman's eyes. *She seems familiar.*

Absorbed in the photo, she hadn't even noticed that Smoke had gotten up until she heard a rustle behind her. "What are you doing?"

Smoke stood by the kitchen wearing only a pair of boxer-briefs. His long frame was layered in corded muscles. With a panther's ease, he slid the sweet heart suit up over his powerful legs. His arms were scarred and knotty. His smooth, strapping chest revealed something primal and powerful about him. A giant cat of a man ready to spring. "Getting ready," he said.

Sidney swallowed and caught her breath. Something stirred inside her. She ingested him with her eyes. It was just her. Just him. And nobody else for miles. He slid the rest of the suit over his brawny shoulders. "Where'd you get that suit?"

"Mal sent me a new one."

"Mal? Oh, your buddy Mal." Her urgings cooled. Her temper flared. "You sound like old buddies."

"I said he *sent* it to me." He put on his jeans and a burgundy hoodie that was similar to Sam's. "Do you happen to have yours?"

"Yes, why?"

"Because those people who stole the false file, well…" he strapped two guns to his hips, "I know exactly where they are."

CHAPTER 14

"**Y**OU KNOW EXACTLY WHERE THEY are, huh?" Sidney said. They stood outside her car in the rain twenty miles south of DC, looking at an open field. "Lead the way then."

Smoke stared at an app on his phone. According to him, *they* had planted a tracking device in the dummy file. That explained how Smoke had known Sidney was staying at Allison's apartment. He tapped the side of his phone with his palm.

"Really?" Sid said. "Is it named Ziggy, too?"

"Huh, good one." He stuffed his phone into his pocket and sauntered out into the field. "Something's here. I can feel it."

Huffing through the drizzling rain, Sidney followed his lead. On the ride over, she and Smoke had made amends and discussed the file—and a few other things. His apologetic words had given her some comfort, but there was still plenty of tension between her shoulders, even with the sweet heart suit on. Smoke had given her a hoodie too, like the ones he and Sam had, saying it was another of Mal Carlson's devices. Hers was dark blue.

"I see something," he said, pointing ahead.

Squinting her eyes, she made out a very high chain-link fence.

Smoke marched straight for it, stopped, and gawked at the crooked sign. "No trespassing."

"No surprise." She made her way a little farther down along the fence. "It says here, 'Property of Drake Real Estate.'" She cocked her head and stretched out her hands. "I wonder if it's electrified." She grasped it and started shaking uncontrollably. "Aaaaaiiiiiieeeeee!"

Smoke shook his head at her. "Really?"

She stopped shaking and let go. "You know, you're the first person that hasn't worked on."

"And you've done that how many times?"

Once. "I can't remember." *I'm really losing my humorous touch.* "It seems odd that the people who took the file would come this way. There isn't a road or anything."

"I'm not right on their trail. I'm staying a quarter mile off." He reached up, grabbed the lip of the fence, and pulled himself up and over. He eyed her through the fence. "I don't want them to see me. Are you coming?"

"I kind of like the view from right here," she said through the fence. "And I assume you're accustomed to it."

"You're cold."

She felt a little bad, but made no apologies. "Sam mentioned that you fought a gargoyle. Is there any truth to that?"

"Yep. Now are you coming over, or are you keeping the car warm for my return?"

"Just hold on a second. I think we need a little more planning before we do anything."

He put his hands on his hips. "Fine, let's hear it."

"First, the objective. Mason Crow. They want him alive."

"Yes, same as always." He shrugged and came closer, almost pressing his face to the fence. "Nothing new. Listen, I can go this alone. Retrieve. Report. Then we'll take step two. You can count on me."

They both clutched the fence, and her fingers touched his. She climbed over and hopped down. "We'll see."

Night had fallen. The pair cut through the darkness of the meadow. The rain slid right off their hoodies, and the second skin she wore left her feeling energized.

"I've got the signal back," Smoke said, staring at his phone. "Maybe a couple hundred meters that way." He pointed.

Wading through the tall grasses, she caught a whiff of manure. The landscape flattened and large bales of hay were scattered throughout the area. Peeking out of the night against the trees were a handful of silos. When they made a bead for the structures, several storehouses appeared.

Smoke stayed her with his hand and hunkered down. He produced a small pair of binoculars and put them to his eyes. He handed them to her.

Gazing through them, she got a better look at the ranch. A huge log cabin sat in the middle, with smoke billowing out of the chimney stack. The windows showed a warm glow within. The binoculars detected something else as well: heat signatures of men standing or strolling on the porch. With assault rifles in their arms. She surveyed more of the area. Guards were posted all around the complex. They stood among the silos, storehouses, and barns. There were vehicles too. Humvees. Vans. Farm trucks. Beyond the buildings was something else. A helicopter. *Morning Glory.*

"I counted fifteen, what about you?"

She handed him the binoculars. "Twenty."

"Hah," he said, pulling out his pistol. "I was testing you. Good eye. Besides, I like these odds better." He clicked out the magazine and slapped a different one in. "The more bad guys, the merrier." He tossed her a magazine. "Blue tips. Have fun."

"More presents from Mal?"

"Yep." Smoke stood up in the grass and grinned. "I don't know about you, but I'm ready to put some holes in things." He glanced at her. "So what's the plan?"

She switched magazines. "Tell me yours. If I don't like it, I'll tell you mine."

"Plan A, we disable the chopper first and recon. Plan B, we secure the chopper, find Crow, unleash a distraction, take him down, and whisk him away in the chopper."

"Are you flying the chopper? Just because I was in the Air Force doesn't mean I'm a pilot." Her fingertips tingled. "I'm a cop, remember?"

"I've got it covered."

Sidney didn't remember reading anything about him being a pilot. "Let's just find out if he's in there first. And stick together."

Staying low, the two of them circled around the ranch toward the chopper. Her nerves were on fire, and butterflies fluttered in her stomach. A step ahead of her, Smoke prowled with the finesse of a jungle cat. It eased her doubts. She split off to Smoke's right, stumbled over something, and pitched forward. *Crap.* She gathered her feet under her.

Smoke stopped and turned back.

"I'm fine."

He turned his back and marched forward again.

Sidney took her next step. Something seized her legs and jerked her down to the ground. A rock-hard fist clocked her in the side of the head, drawing bright spots. Cold and clammy hands clutched at her throat. Uncanny strength pinned her down. Dead yellow eyes found hers. It was a deader, stuffing her face down in the earth's soft grime. *Help!*

CHAPTER 15

FIGHTING AGAINST HER AGGRESSOR AS quietly as she could, she released her gun and fumbled for her knife. Her hand found the hilt and jerked it out. She stabbed wildly over her shoulder. The blade bit deep into flesh but the strong arms held her fast. Thrashing, she twisted onto her back and stabbed at its chest. The blade sunk into its belly.

Its expressionless leer didn't change. Its fists flailed at her head.

She covered up.

Wop! Wop! Wop! Urk!

The beating stopped. Her eyes snapped open. The deader that straddled her swayed with a knife tip sticking out of its chest. It teetered over into the grass.

Smoke stood there offering his hand. "How are you?"

Heart thundering inside her ears, she got back on her feet. "Fine." She kicked the monster. "Damn dirty deaders."

The monster still twitched.

Smoke kneeled down and wrenched his blade like a key, making a sickening crunch.

The deader's body went limp.

A beam of light shone from the compound.

She huddled down, hissing, "Great."

Smoke whispered back, "You didn't fire your weapon. I'm impressed." He offered over to her the gun she'd lost in the struggle. "Don't worry. I won't tell Cyrus you lost it."

She snatched it out of his hand, whispering harshly, "I didn't lose it."

As the light passed over their hiding spot, she took a glance. Three men were spread out and coming their way with assault rifles ready. Assuming these men knew what they were doing, it would be her last gunfight if they saw her first. A few quick blasts into her spot and it would be over. *This is bad. Really bad.*

Smoke crawled over to her side and whispered, "We could surrender."

"Are you nuts?"

He shrugged.

The light swept over their heads again, and she took another glance. The men were twenty yards away and closing in. *Do I shoot or not? Do I shoot or not?*

Smoke wiggled her knife in front of her eyes. "I'll handle this."

Suddenly, a buck rushed through the grasses and bounded over them. A cry of alarm went up. Shots were fired.

Blat-at-at! Blat-at-at!

"Stop shooting, you idiot!" said one of the guards. "It's a fricking deer!"

Still huddled beside Smoke, Sidney watched one guard in a pea coat march toward the one she thought had fired. He snatched the man's weapon away.

"Give me that!" He cocked the weapon back and stuffed it into the man's belly.

"Oof!" the man gasped, collapsing to the ground.

"Now I have to explain this mishap to the boss." The lead guard lowered the muzzle on the fallen one. "I should probably shoot you myself. It'd be better than seeing you turned into one of those deaders." He tossed the rifle at the man. "Let's get this over with. Better hope they're feeling merciful."

The guard pushed himself up with his weapon and trudged behind the other two. Near the log cabin, a small force had gathered. The lead guard held his arm up and waved. Before long there were some angry mutterings cutting through the steady rain.

Smoke nudged her. "We need to move while they're distracted. Come on."

Heart racing and keeping low, she pushed through the tall grasses with her gun barrel lowered. The thought of deaders prowling the grounds kept the alarm sounding in the back of her mind.

Smoke led her behind a barn that stood adjacent to the back porch of the cabin. The smell of hay and manure tickled her nose. She sneezed into her sleeve.

"This isn't the time for that," Smoke hissed.

"Then maybe we should vacate."

"Are you allergic?"

"No." She pressed her ear against the barn. Soft rustlings came from inside. She crept along the way, running her hands along the boards. Her fingers found an open knothole about knee high. She crouched down and peeked through. She stiffened. Children aged eight to twelve were busy packing, taping, and stacking boxes. A fire erupted inside her. *Not again!*

"What is it?" Smoke said, bending down.

She scooted away.

Smoke took a look through the hole, grunted, and eased back. "They'll have to wait."

"I'm sure they've waited long enough." She took out her phone and started to dial.

Smoke pushed her hand down. "One thing at a time. This is Drake space. Your comrades at the FBI aren't going to drop in without more evidence."

He was right. She didn't want to admit it, but he was. All she could think about was Megan. What if her niece were in that situation? The horror of it all. She took another look. There were five kids, wearing khaki jumpers. They all seemed so familiar. Their movements were purposed, fluid, and eerie.

"Hey," Smoke whispered. "I think I have an idea." He twisted a silencer onto the muzzle of his gun. "See that propane tank? How about I put a hole in it?"

"I think we need a more subtle course of action."

Smoke offered a smile. "I don't." He took aim and fired.

Ptew!

There was a metal *ting* sound, but no explosion.

"Idiot!" she whispered through her teeth. "Good thing it was empty."

He took aim again. "I see another one."

"No, it's too loud." She pushed his gun barrel down. "We just got here. Just wait a minute."

"Don't worry about it. We'll draw them out and then scatter. Easy peasy, Agent Shaw."

"Easy peasy?"

"You didn't have to come. And frankly, you're slowing me down."

"You arrogant sonuva—"

Smoke clamped his hand over her mouth.

The door on the back porch of the cabin opened. A towering man stepped out of the inner light and into the porch roof's shadows. His head was partly hidden by the rafters. Two guards sidled up to him, and he waved them away. There was a flicker of light, and a cigar was lit. Its fiery ashes burned bright and dulled again.

"That's him," Smoke whispered in her ear.

She peeled his hand away and said, "I know, you sonuvabitch. And you better not do that again."

The giant man took the wide-plank steps off the porch and into the rain. It was Mason Crow. Tall. Dark. Black bearded. Much bigger in life than in the pictures.

One of the men in pea coats came down the steps and said a few words to him.

Crow was every bit of seven feet tall. Maybe four hundred pounds, all muscle. He bent his ear toward the man and nodded.

Sidney whispered, "You really think you can carry him out of here?"

"Yeah, but I'm not sure the chopper can lift him." Smoke let out a strange chuckle. "I've never seen such big shoulders."

"Excuse me, but what are you doing?" A little girl in a khaki jumpsuit appeared beside Sidney, half-stopping her heart.

"Where did you come from?" Sid said, clutching her chest.

The little girl stood in the barn's shadows with them. She was a straight-haired towhead, pale-eyed, with a maturity about her. "Where did you come from?"

"We need to go," Smoke said with a sense of urgency.

"Can you tell me what your name is?" Sidney asked the girl.

"We need to go now," Smoke said

"Sure," the little girl said, "My name is—" Suddenly, she let out an ear-splitting scream.

CHAPTER 16

SIDNEY CLAMPED HER HAND OVER the little girl's mouth. "Sssssh!"

It was too late. The alarm sounded. Forces scrambled. Mason Crow, their target from the Black Slate file, ducked back inside the cabin.

"Way to go, Princess," Smoke said. He laid down a round of cover fire. Men screamed and fell. "Get inside!"

Gunshots rang out all over.

Budda-budda-budda... Budda-budda-budda...

Sidney lifted the girl onto her shoulder and scrambled for the barn entrance. The barn door opened, and a man in a pea coat stepped outside. Sidney cracked off a shot into his leg.

"Aargh!" he cried out, falling to the ground.

She leapt over him and dashed inside the barn. Children, four that she could see, stood inside handling the boxes the same as they'd been doing before, packing them into a black van's cargo doors. "Get in the van!" she said.

They all gave her a mute look.

She popped off a few rounds into the ceiling and yelled. "Now!"

The frightened children scrambled into the side door of the van. She jumped in the back with them and slammed the door shut behind her.

Smoke sat in the driver's seat and said, "Hang on!" The van lurched forward and powered through the barn wall and barreled through the ranch. Gunfire erupted all around. Bullets tore into the metal.

"Get down," Sidney said, covering the children as best as she could. "Stay down!" The van bounced up off of its wheels and landed hard. "What was that?"

"A person." Smoke cut the wheel hard and surged through the ranch. Bullets blasted the windshield. Smoke hunkered behind the wheel and stomped on the gas. "Here we go!"

The van's tires dug in, and the vehicle roared ahead, bouncing over the rough road. Sidney climbed into the front seat. The van was speeding down the driveway. Checking the side mirror, she saw other vehicles were in pursuit and closing in.

"Are you happy?" Smoke said.

"Happy?"

"Sure. Looks like this turned into a rescue after all." He flashed his teeth. "Happy?"

"Just drive."

The van now barreled down a country road toward where they had parked the Hellcat, slinging from side to side.

"You're going to crash!"

"No, I'm not," he said, slamming on the brakes and accelerating up a hairpin turn. "See? Besides, they can't get around us. The road's too narrow. Once we get around this crooked neck, it's practically a straight stretch to the city." He glanced at her. "What are you doing?"

"Calling backup."

"We don't need backup."

"Yes, we do—unless you plan on adopting these kids."

Smoke checked the rearview mirror. "Oh, them." He smiled. "Hi, guys." There was no response. "Pretty shy, I guess." He slung the wheel back and forth more times until they found themselves on a straight stretch of gravel.

Sidney could make out a faint line of cars traveling down the highway in the distance. Her breathing eased. "Everything's going to be fine," she said to the kids. "Just stay down."

"Yeah," Smoke said, looking up and out of the front window. "Everything should be just fine, assuming we can get past that."

A helicopter buzzed overhead, rattling the van. It landed on the road a half mile ahead.

"That's a problem." Smoke said.

"Go around it," Sidney said.

He shook his head. The straightaway had a steep valley on either side. "The only thing we can do is pull off and run for it. Maybe we can get to your car from here, but not with these kids—unless they're really, really fast kids."

One of the children popped his head up and said, "I'm fast."

"Yeah, me too," said one right after the other.

Ahead, the helicopter lifted off the road.

"Whoa!" Sidney said, squinting. A lone man stood in the middle of the road. His arms were spread wide, shaking toward the sky. Lightning flashed. Thunder boomed. "Is that Mason Crow?"

"It's something," Smoke said. He pressed on the gas. "And it's about to get rolled over!" The closer they got, the bigger the man became, filling the road. "Sweet mother of Pearl!" Smoke slammed on the brakes. "That's not a man..."

From less than fifty yards away, Sidney got a closer look. It was at least eight feet tall and padded in brawny muscle and coarse hair all over, and it had the head of a bull and the body of a man. It shook the horns on its head and let out a strange roar. Its hooved foot scraped over the ground, and it charged. *It can't be! It can't be!* She finished Smoke's sentence, "It's a minotaur."

Horns lowered, the man-bull made a bead straight for them.

Smoke put the van in gear and sped straight for it.

Frozen in her seat, Sidney said, "Why do I not like our chances?"

"Because this defies reasonable explanation." Smoke's knuckles were white on the wheel. "But can it defy the laws of momentum?"

Speeding toward each other, the van and the minotaur crashed. Twisted metal and shattered glass erupted from the impact. The van's wheels dug into the gravel road. The minotaur's horns pierced the hood. Its monstrous face growled and began shoving the van backward.

Sidney took out her pistol and started shooting. *Blam! Blam!*

The minotaur twisted its mighty neck and flipped the van over. The machine rolled over the hillside and slammed into the trees. Flames and smoke spilled out from underneath the hood. Smoke lay slumped on the wheel with his head bleeding. She shook him.

He groaned.

Dazed, Sidney clawed her way into the back that now lay sideways. The children were disheveled. Some had been knocked out. She found the latch to the cargo doors, twisted it, and shoved them open.

Wham!

The roof of the van buckled. Children screamed.

Wham!

Something had jumped on top of the van and started pounding on the roof. A horn ripped through the metal. A huge hand peeled it away. The minotaur leered inside, snorting.

Sidney went for her other gun and started shooting it in the face. *Blam! Blam! Blam!*

The minotaur let out a booming laugh, reached inside, and pulled her out of the van by the arm. It shook her like a doll and hopped down off the van. Her struggles were child-like against its raw power. Its animal eyes stared her down with hunger in them. Slinging her over its enormous shoulders, it said in a cavernous voice, "NICE. YOU'RE GONNA DO JUST FINE."

CHAPTER 17

T HE MINOTAUR HAD STARTED INTO a jog, jostling her entire body. It stopped at the sound of Smoke's voice. "Put her down."

"Move aside, mortal," said Mason Crow the minotaur, "your weapon is useless against me." He stomped his hooved foot. "Or watch as I run rough-shod over you. Oh, how I like the sound of splintering bones and cracking skulls."

Sidney twisted enough to get a look at Smoke. He stood tall, pointing the gun at the monster's skull. "Just shoot it!"

Crow jostled her. "Be silent, woman." He leered back at Smoke. "Go ahead. Let's see what your bullets can do. Be careful though. I don't want this woman damaged. That might make me angry. Crow likes his pretty playthings."

Ka-blam!

Crow let out an awful howl. "Mah-Rooooo!" He whipped Sidney around the front of his body. "Where did you get those bullets?"

"Where did you get those horns?" Smoke took aim. "Put her down."

The minotaur eyed the upper road. The forces from the ranch had gathered. He crushed Sidney against his powerful chest. "You have nowhere to go. And your bullets only sting. They cannot kill the likes of me."

"Is that why you're bleeding?" Smoke said, maintaining his aim. "Or is that blood a figment of my imagination?"

"It's only blood. I have plenty of it." Crow started to squeeze Sidney harder. "Let's see how much she has."

Sidney's eyes bulged. Her body felt like it had been stuffed inside a trash compactor. She let out a painful gasp.

Ka-Blam! Ka-Blam! Ka-Blam!

Crow dropped her in front of his hooved feet, lowered his horns, and charged.

Smoke skipped away and kept shooting.

The minotaur kept running up the hill, crashing over small trees, and bellowing, "Kill them! Kill them!"

The throng of men above opened fire. Smoke caught Sidney up in his arms and dashed behind the van. Bullets riddled the vehicle by the dozens. Smoke returned fire.

Sidney shook her numb arms and searched for a gun, finding nothing. *I'm useless.* She spied another gun tucked in the back of Smoke's pants and took it. It was an old single-action army, cowboy style. *Are you kidding me?* She pulled back the hammer and cracked a shot off up the hill. A man tumbled into the tall grasses. *Pretty accurate, but I've got a whole five shots left against their hundreds.*

"How do you like it?" Smoke said to her, talking about his gun.

"This iron would make a great paperweight." She took another shot. "But I bet it was quite the conversation piece a hundred years ago." She squeezed off another, and one more goon rolled down the hill. "Eh, it's a good shooter. But 'game over' once we're out of bullets."

"Never imagined it would end like this," he said, blasting away until he emptied his magazine. "A bad ending to a bad western. Nice knowing you, Agent Shaw." He snapped in another magazine. "I'll stay with the children, you run. Your car's just over that ridge."

"No."

"Yes!" he said. "Just go! Get help!"

"I'm not leaving you, and I'm not leaving these kids." She patted down his pockets. "Got any more bullets?"

"No."

She cracked off her last shots. "Then maybe we need to give ourselves up. Keep our lives a little longer."

He eased back behind the van and hunkered down beside her. He looked her in the eye and said, "If that's what you want to do, then so be it."

She grabbed his face and kissed him hard. Finishing, she said, "It's sexy when a man listens to me." She tossed her gun away and Smoke tossed his. They raised their hands up over their heads and waved them high. She said, "We give up."

The gunfire stopped.

She took a breath and eased away from the van. *This sucks!*

Wumpa! Wumpa! Wumpa! Wumpa!

A chopper soared overhead with searchlights burning bright. A voice came over its loudspeaker. "FBI! Drop your weapons!"

The mercenaries on the road tucked away their weapons and turned tail.

"FBI! Halt!"

Engines started up and headed back down the country road, disappearing into the night. A small convoy of cars with sirens gave chase, and the chopper landed.

Sidney let out a ragged sigh. "And you didn't want me to call them."

"I just said that because I knew you wouldn't listen to me." He touched the lips she had just kissed and added, "It was all worth it."

"I don't know about that." Stiff legged, she opened up the doors to the back of the van. Her jaw dropped. All of the children were gone. "That's impossible."

CHAPTER 18

"We survived," Smoke said, staring out of Sidney's car window. "I think that's a good thing. Soon enough we'll get another shot at that monster."

"Huh?" Sidney replied. She had barely heard what he said. Instead, she was in deep thought about those kids. What happened to them? They couldn't have snuck off so fast. "Oh, I suppose."

They spent less than an hour at the scene before the FBI let them go. Four men who had been wounded in the battle were taken into custody. Two more died from their wounds. Sidney and Smoke were lucky. The entire battle took place just outside of private property. Cyrus Tweel, her current supervisor, was there. The conversation was unpleasant. She wanted to go back into the compound and get the children. His response was a flat-out no.

"Are you going to take Smoke now?" she said to Cyrus.

His brow crinkled. "No, not this time. You don't have the mark yet. But it would be for the better. This is a mess." And with that, Cyrus departed.

"I wouldn't worry about them," Smoke said.

"About who?"

"Those kids. There's something strange about them."

"They're kids."

"Very odd ones." He shifted in the car seat. "You know what I'm talking about."

She did. The children's faces were almost identical to the ones they'd rescued months ago at Ray Cline's place. Their complexions and hair color were different. Otherwise, they were the same. "I know."

Cruising down the highway, she continued to gather her thoughts about all of the detail7s. Mason Crow was a minotaur. None of it seemed real. Not to mention the fact that there were dozens of men and women who had seen him. They had lives, family and friends, and they knew about this. *How can this madness be hidden?*

"Makes you think, doesn't it?" Smoke said.

She downshifted and let off the gas pedal, then accelerated into the turn. "About what?"

"About how these monsters are hiding in plain sight." He drummed his hands on the dash. "With all of the security videos and social media, you would think the entire world would know about it. Certainly someone has posted something, somewhere, and lived to tell about it."

Russ Davenport, the reporter for *Nightfall DC*, came to mind. She needed to check and see if he had survived or not. He was just the kind of person Smoke was talking about. "I guess the powers that be pick the stories that matter." She rubbed a knot on her head from the van's rollover. "Sometimes I feel like I'm in an episode of *The X-Files*."

"Yeah, where are the Lone Gunmen when you need them? So, where to now?"

She hadn't given her next move much thought. "I guess I'll drop you off at your place."

"Well, the cupboards are kinda bare. I wouldn't mind a round of pancakes. Fighting a minotaur can really work up your appetite."

Her tummy rumbled. "Fine. And I imagine you have a place in mind."

"Take the next exit and hang a left."

Her phone buzzed. There was a message on it. It read:

Time to meet. Carlson.

She showed it to Smoke.

His brows lifted. "Huh. An address and everything. But I'm getting my pancakes first."

Mal Carlson's home was a round structure full of glass windows, sitting on a massive stone, partially hidden in the trees that overlooked a place called Henson Creek. The unique circular architecture was odd to say the least, but beautiful the same. Sidney knocked on the red door. Smoke stood on the broad granite steps behind her, cleaning his teeth with a toothpick. She glared at him.

"What?" he said.

She plucked the piece of wood from his mouth and flicked it away. The door opened, and a pretty, oriental woman in an ivory silk gown bowed and said, "Please, come in."

They eased their way into the home. The woman led them down the landing into a room that appeared to be a combination of a living room, a bedroom and a kitchen. Like a massive studio apartment, it was wide open and decorated in tasteful décor from various cultures all over the world. There was only one little closed-off area, which Sid assumed was the privacy of a bathroom. The furniture was anything from colonial American to Italian Renaissance. There were small busts and statues on pedestals of figures she did not recognize. Nothing striking, but odd. She stared at one marble statue that had a bald head, an eye patch, and the grisly look of a pirate.

"That's Carl the Reaver," said an unfamiliar voice that spoke with what sounded like an early American accent, "eighteenth century hero, that is."

Sidney turned. Alongside the oriental woman, who stood just outside of the kitchen, was an elegant man with olive skin, in a simple white cotton outfit. His eyes were ancient and inquisitive, his demeanor purpose-filled, more charming than handsome.

"Finally, Agent Shaw, you can put a face to all of those troublesome texts." He walked over and offered his hand. "I'm Mal Carlson, and this is my wife, Asia. Welcome to our home. Ah, and this must be Mr. John Smoke." He looked up into Smoke's eyes. "I think you and Carl would have gotten along quite well. He was a Navy man."

"Who lived in the eighteenth century," Smoke said. "How would you know what he liked?"

"I'm a bit of a historian and very knowledgeable about peculiar things." He moved toward a dining room table that offered a wonderful view of the outdoors. "Come and sit. We have much to talk about. Asia is preparing some food for us. Something to drink first? Coffee, water, whiskey, wine—or Mountain Dew perhaps?"

"This is it?" Smoke said, taking a seat. "I was expecting something a little different."

"Like the Bat Cave?" Mal said, chuckling. "Be patient. This is only the first floor. I have a basement. So, drinks or no drinks?"

"Water's fine," Sid said, taking a closer look at Mal. He had strong features in his slender face, and high cheekbones. His nearly black hair covered his ears and rested on his neck. There was some gray in it.

"Asia!" he blurted out. "Bring out some water!" He leaned across the table. "Don't be alarmed. She's a little hard of hearing. Asia!"

"I'm coming!" She hurried into the room and rolled three bottled waters down the table. "There!" She smiled. "Anything else?"

"I'm sure our guests are hungry. A prepared meal would be nice."

Asia narrowed her eyes on her husband. "You did not tell me guests were coming. How about I order pizza?"

"I was thinking you could make one of your home dishes?" Mal said, pleading and whining a little.

"A Philly cheesesteak?"

"No! That thing with the rice."

"Rice-a-roni?"

"No!"

"Jambalaya?"

"Never mind," Mal said, shaking his head. "What do you two like on your pizza?"

"I'm not hungry," Sid said.

"I love everything on mine," added Smoke.

"Asia, one order of supreme will do," he said in a rich voice.

Asia slid a phone across the table. "You order. My show's coming on." She smiled at Sid and Smoke. "Nice meeting you." Then she planted herself on the sofa, turned on the television, and started laughing.

A little embarrassed, Mal said, "I didn't marry her because she could cook. I just married her because I love her." He picked up the phone and called in a pizza.

CHAPTER 19

A POLISHED METAL STAIRCASE SPIRALED BENEATH Mal's home. A security door waited at the bottom with a red light glowing on the pad. When he pressed his thumb to the scanner, the light turned green, and the door popped open. Inside was a large computer lab. A wall of oversized monitors was the first thing Sidney saw. The rest was cosmetic by comparison.

"Fifty screens and over a thousand camera feeds from all over DC," Mal said in admiration. "I know it's overkill, but it's quite effective."

There were plenty of places she recognized. Hotel lobbies. Monument buildings. High-rise apartments. Traffic lights. Bank buildings. *How does he have access to all of this?* "You're an employee of the government, Mr. Carlson?"

"No. I like to think of myself as a freelancer. 'Contractor' is such a rigid word, although I am under contract, so to speak." Mal glanced at Smoke. "Somewhat similar to your arrangement."

"I didn't sign any paperwork." Smoke took a seat in an ultra-modern scoop chair beside a long oval table. "I'm done signing my life away. This way, I can cash out whenever I want to." He rubbed the table's polished surface. "Is this pewter?"

"A hybrid metal." Mal motioned for Sidney to sit. "Please. I'm sure you have many questions about what exactly is going on."

She took a chair alongside Smoke and crossed one leg over the other. "So can you tell us why there's a minotaur on the loose in DC?"

Mal's jaw dropped as he gasped at the same time. He plopped in the seat beside Sidney with an excited look in his eye. "Mason Crow is the ancient beast?"

"Pretty sure," she said.

"Horns and everything," Smoke added, making little horns with his fingers.

Mal covered his mouth, uncovered it, and said, "I can't believe it. But I shouldn't be surprised. That's even worse than I suspected."

"You said ancient. What do you mean by that?" she asked.

"Of course." He made his way over to an alabaster bookshelf that was filled with many heavily bound tomes. He pulled a couple of books free, brought them over, and dropped them on the table. One was the Bible, and the other was a book filled with pages of Egyptian hieroglyphics. "Do you know the story in the Bible where Aaron confronts Pharaoh with his staff?"

"Exodus seven," Smoke said. "Aaron casts down the staff. It turns into a snake. Pharaoh's sorcerers cast down their staffs. They also turn into snakes, but the snake from the staff of Aaron devours them."

Mal pointed at him and said, "Right. That's the kind of evil powers we're dealing with. In theory anyway." He opened the Egyptian book of hieroglyphics and pointed at various pictures.

Sidney leaned forward. He pointed at people with bird heads and dog heads, the Sphinx, and more. A funny feeling overcame her.

"Seem familiar?" Mal said.

She made a reluctant nod. "I thought these were pagan images of gods?"

"Well, in most circles of history and archeology, they'd have you believe that. The truth of the matter doesn't fit the agenda of the powers that be." He flipped through the pages. "What they can't bury, they destroy. That's how *they*," he made air quotes, "control the information. It's the same today as it was thousands of years ago. *They* do their work in the dark. Behind the scenes. Pulling unseen strings."

"Who are *they*?" Sidney asked. *And do I work for a good* they *or a bad* they?

"That's much easier to ask than to answer. Even I don't know for sure, but I'll share my theories. Fallen angels, demons, evil spirits, nephilim, annunaki— those are a few of the more common names. They carry the supernatural seed that spoils humanity." He moved over to the computer and pulled up ancient images of Greek, Roman, Hindi, and other gods. "I believe these beings really did exist. Men and women of great renown and stature. Some records report them as being over twelve feet tall. The legends of Medusa, Prometheus, mermaids, sirens, unicorns—I think they are all various accounts of the truth."

Sidney started to say something.

Mal held up his hand to indicate he wasn't finished. "Over the centuries, or even the millennia, good men and women have been fighting these dark forces that continually try to take the world of men over. Empires rise and fall. Great cities are built up and buried. The truth gets distorted into lies or fables. The both of you have seen it for yourselves, and you've lived to tell about it. It's impressive."

Sidney's throat became dry. She glanced at Smoke. His eyes were fixed on Mal Carlson. A single thought ran laps through her mind. *This is crazy.* "Shouldn't there be a bigger team fighting against all this? A team of priests or archeologists, maybe?"

"There have been. There have even been knights and many kinds of crusaders," Mal said. "Not to mention our pirate friend you noted above, Carl the Reaver. They say his sabre dripped wet with giant men's blood."

Smoke let out a short gusty laugh. "I like this."

"So you wish to continue?"

"Without a doubt."

"And what about you, Agent Shaw?" Mal said, eyeing her with intent. "Are you still comfortable with your assignment?"

"I'm not sure what my assignment is anymore." *Or why they picked me.*

"Try not to overthink it. The mission is the same. You're going after what is believed to be a band of supernatural criminals that are listed on the Black Slate." He popped up a couple of pictures on the screen. It was Adam Vaughn the werewolf and Angi Harlow the harpy. "Ho ho. When you brought these two in, you opened some eyes. You certified this effort, and they had to acknowledge that sorcery was afoot. Still, they want discretion. And what you two are doing is working. Cutting out these two threw a big wrench into Drake's network."

"So Drake is *them*?" she said.

"So to speak. Yes. They are the ones behind this. AV and Night Bird were a pair of their top commanders. You sent ripples through that network when you took them down. Their cult-like henchmen scattered, and that made them angry. So now, the pressure is on in Washington."

"What do you mean?" she asked.

"They'll start digging around. Trying to figure out who's behind these efforts. Bribe and bully the congressmen and senators they have in their pockets."

On the monitors, pictures of Congressman Wilhelm and several others popped up.

Daggers of ice shot through Sidney's veins.

"They have their people in there," Mal said, "but don't fret. We have ours. So far as I know, the details of your missions are under wraps. There's still plenty of good people in the bureau protecting you both."

"But Wilhelm's already made us, and they've tried to kill us more than once. Not to mention they know we're in possession of the files. So whoever is protecting us is doing a lousy job."

"Well, I didn't say they were good at it." He tapped some more keys, and dozens of pictures of kids popped up. "If these faces seem familiar, it's because they are. We call them the Forever Children."

CHAPTER 20

S IDNEY GOT UP FROM HER seat for a closer look. Young boys and girls with different-colored hair and complexions were scattered all over the screens. The faces of all the girls and boys were almost identical. Some had freckles. Others red hair. Black. White. Asian. Many different styles of hair. "Who are they?"

Mal put on a pair of glasses and studied one of the faces on the screen. "Simply put, they're clones."

"That doesn't sound very supernatural."

Mal rubbed his chin. "Well, there is a supernatural element to it. That's what makes them breathe anyway. Genetic manipulation. Experimental. Combined with other things that defy scientific explanation." He pulled up another picture. A burly man with clammy skin was strapped to a table. "This is a deader we found wandering around the woods at AV's hospital site. Remember that. Blood runs through him like a reanimated corpse. It's fascinating. As long as his heart pumps, he won't die, at least not until the spell wears off. It happens sometimes."

Sidney took a closer look at the children on the screens.

"Why children?"

"Don't let these little minions fool you, Agent Shaw. They are faithful to their hive. Soulless slaves." He cleared his throat. "No one has any fear of a child. They throw your instincts off. They're the perfect workers. Remember the ones you found. Have no doubt they are back on the job again."

Sidney's stomach turned. Clones or not, they were children, just as real as any. Using adults was one thing, but using children was sickening. "It's not right."

"None of it is. Mother Nature is being turned inside out. Perverted. Most of these monsters volunteer for it. They want money. Power. The promise of immortality. They become roaring lions that prey on the weak humans who stand too close to the darkness." Mal faced her. "There are only good and evil. There is no in-between. Few know the difference, such as you and Mr. Smoke over there."

"What do you mean?"

"When it comes to battling these shape shifters, one has to come from a very solid foundation or else be lured in. That's one of the reasons why the pair of you were picked." He pecked on the keyboard and the screens went black.

"You'd be surprised at the number of good people who have fallen victim to their temptations."

Sidney swallowed, remembering how AV had ignited a passionate fire inside her that she'd never felt before. Dark, lurid, and sensual. Her eyes drifted to Smoke. He sat back, reading the Bible in one hand and switching the pictures with the remote in the other. *Pancakes and Butterflies.* If Smoke hadn't been with her, where would she be today? Was she that close to becoming one of them? An evil minion of Drake?

"Any thoughts, Agent Shaw? Doubts? Concerns?" Mal resumed his seat at the table. "After all, these are some extraordinary items that you've been presented with."

"It's an awfully big undertaking for a single agent and a bounty hunter."

"And me, naturally," Mal responded. "That's why I'm careful how we pick our battles. Much thought and consideration goes into it. The Black Slate is a unique list of people, or shifters. And I am convinced that one of those names is in charge of it all. Who knows, we might be lucky and capture the top dog by accident. Maybe Mason Crow is the one."

Sidney sat back down beside Smoke. His face was a mask of concentration. She could almost see the wheels turning inside his head. *What is he thinking?*

As for herself, after taking in all that Mal had shared, something began to stir. Her inner fire was stoked. An awakening charged in her blood. She had seen the face of pure evil. Her civilly tempered senses had denied it until now. She took out the postcard that Deanne Drukker had mailed years ago and set it on the table. It read, "Ted, monsters are real. Avoid the Slate."

Mal leaned over and read it. His eyes widened a little.

"You recognize it, don't you?"

"Yes," Mal said.

Smoke closed his books and picked up the postcard and studied it. "An interesting item."

"An even more interesting warning about the Black Slate," Sidney said.

"You aren't going to let a little postcard scare you off, are you?" Mal said. "Not after you've come this far. At least now you know what to expect."

"I'm more concerned about the message, not the monsters. The fact that it is seven words caught my attention, along with the sketch of the black sun. I think there's a greater message behind the warning.

"No doubt seven is special," Mal said. "There are seven days of the week, seven seas, seven continents, not to mention the seven deadly sins. I could go on for a long time. Some say seven is the number of completion and perfection."

She got the feeling there was something Mal wasn't telling her. "Maybe that's how many villains are on the Black Slate?"

"Er, no, not that few," he said, rubbing his finger under his lip. "That might just be a mystery between her and Chief Howard. Don't overthink it, hmm? We need to move on."

"Are we in a hurry?"

"Well, Mr. Smoke's free time is limited, and our objective, Mason Crow, is now on full alert to our presence, so we need a plan to take him." He made his way over to the desk and began typing away on the computer. The monitors came back to life with a myriad of city scenes. "Seems he's still holed up at his ranch, which is a good thing. Perhaps we should brew some coffee." He pulled up an image of his living room. His wife Asia lay on the couch snoring. He spoke into a microphone by the computer. "Asia." She didn't stir. "Asia," he said again. She shifted a little. "Asia!"

She jerked up into a sitting position, looking around in many directions and holding her head. "I hate it when you do that."

"Would you be a dear and bring us some coffee down?" Mal said in a charming voice.

Asia stood up, yawned, and rubbed her eyes. "Okay."

"Thank you, dear," he said, switching the screen to something else. "She actually loves to make coffee. Has a little thing that she does. Wait until you try it."

Sidney eased back into her chair and let Mal talk. He was doing his best to keep things simple. According to his own archives, the shifters had risen from the shadows over and over, aided by the forces of darkness. Good men and women would beat them back only to see them surface somewhere else and rise again. That somewhere was now DC, the most powerful city in the world. And the shifters could be anybody. She rubbed her temples with her index fingers. *I hope one is not the president.*

CHAPTER 21

"**W**AKE UP," SID SAID, WAKING from her sleep. She was resting on Smoke's shoulder. She pushed off of him and gave him a nudge. The ranging man slumbered over the table with drool dripping from his mouth.

Sidney made a face and shoved him again. Mal had gone off on a tirade that had taken until early in the morning. She felt like she'd been trapped in a dream, drifting between bizarre comic stories, movies, and reality. She stretched out her stiff limbs and groaned. She wasn't sure if all of this information was helpful to her cause or not. *Avoid the Black Slate.* Why would anyone want a part of this? But she did.

Smoke, who had been silent the entire time, helped himself out of his chair. He lumbered over toward a fresh pot of coffee that Sidney hadn't seen Asia bring in. "Want another cup?" he said, filling a mug. "It's good Joe. Nice kick to it."

"Sure." Looking for but not seeing Mal anywhere, she got up and cruised around the room. "Seems our host is gone." She rubbed her head. "I didn't think he was going to ever stop talking. Did you catch all of that?"

"I did, well, at least until I started sleeping. But I'm firm on the gist of it. These shifters are murderers, and murderers have to die." He rolled back his brawny shoulders and sent a heated glance her way. "Huh?"

"Huh, what?"

"You just have that morning air about you," he said, coming closer. "A swelteriness."

"I don't think that's a word. And it's creepy." She remained standing where she was and took the coffee that he offered. It was warm in her cupped hands, and for a moment she wondered if that was what she would feel like in his arms. "Care to try again?"

"Enticing."

"Really?"

"Enchanting."

She pushed her hair away from her face. "You're a strange man."

He made his way up to her, coming almost toe-to-toe. "I know, but you're all right with that, aren't you?"

His commanding presence drew her inches toward him. She could feel the warmth from his body. In the morning her juices started flowing. Apparently so did his. She set the coffee mug down on the metal table, bit down on her lip, and gazed up into his eyes. "What are you thinking?"

He gently rested his hands on her shoulders. "I'm thinking I don't want to go out of this world without kissing you again."

His hand glided down her back, sending shivers down her spine. Her heart raced. She eased her body into his. He leaned down and brought his lips to hers, delivering a soft kiss. It wasn't anything like the ones she'd give him. It was deep. Passionate. Real. Her fingernails dug into his lower back, and she returned his efforts in kind.

"Good morning, all!" Mal interrupted in a chipper voice.

Sidney broke off the kiss, gasping for breath a little. There was a thin stream of saliva still connecting them. She brushed it away and backed up with wide eyes. Smoke stood still with his eyes closed and lips still parted.

"Is he all right?" Mal said, sauntering over. He had a covered silver platter that he set down. "What's he doing?"

Sidney backhanded Smoke in the thigh. "Meditating, I think."

"Never seen that technique before." Mal took the lid off the platter. It was filled with steaming eggs, bacon, and pancakes. "I figured we could eat down here so I could continue."

Smoke plopped down into a seat and eyed Sidney. She lifted her brows. He said, "I think the food is the only course left that is needed. What do you think, Sid?"

"I agree."

"But there's so much to go over."

"We get it," Smoke said, grabbing a handful of bacon. "Just give us what we need to hunt the bad guys. I know you're dying to reveal something."

Mal's face lit up. "I'll be right back."

After Mal left the room, Smoke started to nuzzle back up to Sidney. She stopped him with her hand, only to find her palm pressed against his rock hard abs. *Morning Glory.* "Just what do you think you're doing?"

"I thought we'd—"

She cut him off. "Keep your thoughts to yourself. And to be clear, you took advantage of a moment of weakness, so get ahold of yourself."

He stepped back. "What do you mean by that exactly?"

"Funny," she said with a smirk. "Now just back away."

"But—"

"I'm not talking about this right now," she said, drinking her coffee. "And maybe never again, for that matter." She couldn't look him in the eye. "It happened. It's over. Move on."

"Okay," he said with a nonchalant shrug. "But just so you know, I thought that was a great kiss, and I think you thought so too." He walked out of sight.

He's right about that. She stared into the chocolate-colored coffee. *What is he thinking? What am I thinking?* She liked Smoke. What woman wouldn't? He had rugged good looks and a boyish charm about him, but he was odd too. Something about him unsettled her, leaving her uncertain whether or not she was truly attracted to him. *Probably just lust on both sides of the fence. But Lord can he kiss.* A fantasy of her and him started to unfold in her thoughts.

"Agent Shaw?" a voice said. "Agent Shaw?"

"Huh?" she said, twisting around and spilling her coffee.

"Oh, don't worry, I'll have Asia get that," Mal said, walking over and taking her by the arm. "It's time for the next stop." He eased her up out of her chair. "Come on now."

"Where's Smoke?" she said. The man was nowhere to be seen.

"He's a step ahead."

Sidney noticed one of the shelves in the back of the room was swung open. "A secret passage? Really?"

"Just a room actually," Mal said, leading the way inside. "Filled with many dangers."

CHAPTER 22

T HE ROOM WAS HALF AS big as the one they'd been in and laid out like a
weapons locker. Pistols and machine guns hung on black racks. Another
wall displayed a host of archaic weapons guarded by two burnished statues
of full plate armor. Smoke stood at a table, wearing only his second skin. He was
trying on a pair of western gun belts. He had a grin on his face.

Sidney didn't hesitate to share her thoughts. "That looks really stupid. Take
it off."

Smoke handled the chrome-plated, ivory-handled Colt .45 pistols with ease.
They blinked in and out of the holsters and spun on his fingers before he shoved
them back inside the black leather. To that effect, he added a mild, "Yeehaw!"

Sidney turned her back. *At least he didn't say Hi Ho Silver.* She ran her fingers
over several objects on the table. Bullets, magazines, hand grenades, and a silvery
pair of flex cuffs. *Hmmm.*

"I thought you might like those," Mal said from the other side of the table.
"Unlike your unfortunate experience with AV, those will hold just about anything."

"Even a minotaur?" she said.

"In theory."

"Are these stun grenades?" Smoke said, picking up a pair of flat black metal
disks.

Mal walked over, plucked them out of his hand, and set them back down
on the table. "Yes. They're on timers, and they can be activated by a radio signal
or app—which reminds me." He opened up a heavy-duty plastic toolbox and
withdrew a pair of boxes and tossed them over.

Inside, Sidney found a black watch with a flexible wristband. "No, thanks,"
she said, setting it down on the table. "Not my style."

"But it's sophisticated technology. Very helpful."

Smoke tossed his box to Mal. "No thanks for me either. These guns and
bullets will do." He eyed the wall filled with swords, axes, spears, and other
ancient weapons. "Some of those blades will, too."

"Those are antiques from my personal collection. Leave them alone."

Smoke's hand stopped short of a double-bladed battle-axe with a spike on it.

"Are you sure? I really would like to have this battle-axe. It'd fit perfectly between that minotaur's horns." He plucked it off the wall and swished it through the air.

Slice! Slice!

"Stop drooling over it, and put it away," Mal pleaded. "It's a priceless piece in my collection."

Smoke twirled it in the air one last time and then placed it back on the rack with a clank. "So be it." He started stuffing weapons and ammo into a duffel bag. Looking at Sid, he said, "I'm ready to go. Are you?"

She found an empty case on the floor and dropped guns, bullets, grenades, and a few other things inside it. She found a dark pair of sunglasses and slipped them on. They enhanced her sight. "Yeah, I'm ready."

Mal pushed his hair back. "You aren't taking all that."

"Why not?" Sidney said. "Who else is going to use it?"

"That's not the point."

"Come on, Smoke," she said. "You only have one more week, and we've got monsters to kill."

Mal cut off their path at the doorway. "A reminder. Bring Mason Crow in alive. And it's best to find him in the daytime. Most shifters prefer to change at night. That's when their power is at full zenith, especially when the moon is full." He poked Smoke in the chest. "And don't lose that *Zweite Haut* suit again. If you only knew what I had to go through to recover it."

Sidney landed some heavy slaps on Mal's shoulder. "Don't worry. I'll see to it that he wears it the whole time." She started to push by.

"No wait," Mal said, "Just hold on one more second." He rushed over to one of the walls that had a drawer in it, pulled it out, and produced a pill bottle. "Look. They're ready for you this time, and I'm not going to lie. You two are on your own. The truth is, no one thought you'd get this far on this project."

"You mean they thought we'd die," she said.

"Well, you in particular, yes, Agent Shaw, but you've proven to be a formidable survivor." His eyes brightened. "They're impressed."

"Well, they can kiss my ass," she said, "And I'm not taking any drugs." She squinted at the pill case.

"It's my own brand of sorcery," Mal said, dumping two bright-emerald pills into his hand.

"I thought magic was bad," Smoke said, leering down on him.

"No, it's not that kind. Sorcery comes from the Greek word *pharmakia*, hence it means drugs or pharmacy. Just a concoction of my own making." He tried to hand the bottle to Sidney.

"No, thanks. You know the FBI does random drug testing."

"You're going up against great evil. It might take more than bullets or brawn to stop them. These little pills," said Mal, shaking them in the bottle, "will certainly help level things out."

"How, by turning us into one of them?" Sidney said.

"No," Mal replied, "by enhancing your senses. Really. No side effects, but temporary. You'll thank me later."

"No," she said, pushing by him. "I'll put my faith in my wits and the guns on my hips." She'd heard enough. Seen enough. And now she was ready to get away from this place. Breathe some fresh air and find some normality. Without looking back, she made her way upstairs and passed by Asia, who was once again napping on the couch. Shaking her head, Sid exited the round glass mansion and walked to her waiting car. Shoulders slumped, she set the heavy case of munitions down. She rubbed her neck. *Damn, this is going to be a weird commute with Smoke.*

CHAPTER 23

Rest. Sleep. That's what Sidney needed. At 5:03 in the morning she sat up bleary eyed in her bed, contemplating her situation. She'd departed with Smoke the night before last, after leaving Mal's home. Little had been said about what was going on between them. Instead, they had talked about how they were going to find Mason Crow the minotaur. It was a little disturbing that conversations like this were beginning to seem normal. She flopped back onto the bed.

This is crazy.

She stuffed her face in her pillow and let out a scream. She followed it with an odd laugh she'd never let out before. The FBI had given her this nutsy assignment. It was loose. Dangerous. Mysterious. She had been a rigid by-the-book soldier, but now she was beginning to like the freedom of being a shadow agent. She could tell Smoke was into it too. A fire lit behind his dark eyes when he talked about it.

I wonder what he's doing now. She put her bare feet on the cool hardwood floor and shuffled into the kitchen. *Probably feeding hay to the minotaur by now.* She put on a pot of coffee, leaned on the granite kitchen counter, yawned, and rehashed their plans.

She and Smoke had decided to separate for the next few days. Supposedly, Mal was keeping tabs on any activity from the ranch and would let them know if anyone left. She didn't buy it. The ranch was pretty far out of sight and mind, and there had to be more than one exit. There was the helicopter too. There weren't video feeds in air space. Hm, but there was satellite tracking.

I hate counting on others.

She took a seat on the sofa, grabbed the remote, and turned on the twenty-four-hour local news. A reporter was on site at a fire scene. Fire trucks and flames were the landscape of the background. She turned up the volume and took her first drink of coffee and listened to what the reporter said.

"There are no confirmations of any casualties, but firemen are still clearing the building," he reported. "I can feel the intensity of the flames from where I'm standing, a good fifty feet away. Again, no casualties reported so far, and they are a long way off from clearing the building."

"Probably some bloody arsonist. What's wrong with the world?" She started to change the channel, but for some reason the reporter kept her attention. She leaned forward, hanging on the concerned tone in his voice.

The man on TV with a Geraldo mustache cleared his throat and continued with a worried look on his face. "I talked to one resident earlier, and she said it all happened so fast. Another witness said flames erupted in one lone apartment and then spread like wildfire." He glanced back at the burning building and shielded his face from the flames and added, "But it looks like DC's finest have the fire under control here at Rochester Apartments."

Sidney almost spit out her coffee. "*What?*" Her hand trembled. *That's Allison and Megan's place!* She rushed into the bedroom and snatched up her phone. She didn't have any texts. She punched one in to Allison. *Come on. Come on.* No response.

She practically jumped into her clothes, grabbed everything she typically needed, and in less than a minute she peeled out of the parking lot in her car. "Oh God, let them be all right. Please!" She dialed her contacts at the local police and fire department, but she couldn't get through. "Damn." She voice-texted Allison again. "Are you okay? Please answer!"

The Dodge thundered down the streets, but it was fifteen minutes later when she got there. The blaze was out, but half of the apartment complex lay in a smoky ruin against the day's first light.

Sidney parked and rushed to the scene, hollering out, "Megan! Allison!"

Two firemen approached and one female police officer. "Miss," the woman said, "can we help you? Do you live here?"

"Uh, my sister and niece do," Sidney said. Her heart was pounding. Her thoughts racing. "Did you get them out? Did you get them out?"

"Ma'am, it'll be fine."

"Is that where the fire started?" Sidney said, pointing. "Oh my, oh my!" Allison and Megan's second-floor apartment was nothing but charred remains. "Did it start there? Did it start there?" She rushed toward the remains.

The two firemen grabbed her and pulled her back. "Ma'am!" said the female officer. "You can't rush in there. Our people are on the scene. Let us handle this."

"Let me go! I'm FBI!"

"Then you understand standard protocols." The woman made sympathetic gestures. "Just trust us, and I'm sure everything will be okay."

Sidney's body slackened, and she eased out of the grip of the men. "Okay." It was torment. She couldn't stop visualizing her family being burned to death. In her gut, she knew something was wrong. She could feel it. *This can't be happening. Please don't be happening because of me.*

"Come on," said the female officer. She was a veteran lady with silver-black hair showing underneath her blue ball cap. "Guys, get her a blanket. She's shivering."

Sidney didn't even realize she was trembling. The firemen put a blanket over her shoulders, and she sat back on the hood of a black and white squad car. A stiff breeze kicked up, blowing the smoke into her face and stinging her eyes.

"Phew," the policewoman said, covering her nose. "I can't stand the smell of melted plastic." She squeezed Sidney's shoulder. "It's gonna be all right, uh—"

"Sidney."

"I'm Kate McFadden," the woman said, offering her hand. "I'll stick around, if you don't mind. Besides, I could use the overtime. When things like this happen, they need a little crowd control anyway." Her head swiveled around, and her eyes locked on a pair of reporters sliding through the police barrier. "Oh, no they don't. Excuse me." She darted away. "Hey! Hey! You two better get back behind that barrier. I'm not warning you again."

Sidney checked her messages again. Nothing from Allison. She sent another text out anyway and remained seated. She couldn't fight the fear swelling up inside of her. At this time of day she couldn't imagine Allison and Megan being anywhere else. All she could do was hope that maybe they escaped the fire, and Allison lost her phone in the process. Of course it wouldn't be beyond Allison to ignore her calls, especially after the fight they'd had earlier.

She said a prayer and started walking around the lot, searching the faces. Families and children were scattered all about. Tears streaked down a lot of faces. One woman was wailing. A man was arguing with the firemen and police officers. If Sidney had to guess, the apartment complex housed about fifty people, and judging by the looks of things, everything was gone. Her little thread of hope turned to despair as another section of the building collapsed in a whoosh of smoke. People started screaming.

A voice of authority caught her ear, and a handful of firemen gathered on a section of steps that hadn't burned in the fire. They vanished into the building with a pair of hand-carried gurneys. Teeth clenched and nails digging into her palms, Sid watched for them to emerge again. The female officer, Kate, stood by her side, humming. Sidney eyed her.

Kate stopped humming and said with a sympathetic look, "Sorry, but I get nervous sometimes."

"It's all right."

The second-floor fire exit door opened, and a group of firemen carrying two loaded gurneys made their way down the stairwell. Sidney started forward, but the officer grabbed her arm.

"Sidney, stay put, and let me take a look. It could be anybody." The woman ducked under the barrier tape and headed straight for the firemen.

Sidney felt her heart pounding inside her chest. *Please don't be them. Please don't be them.* Her keen hearing caught the brunt of the firemen's conversation. One said, "Pretty sure it's a woman and a little girl." Sidney leapt the barrier and charged over. Kate cut into her path, but Sidney slipped away. She jerked the blankets off the gurneys and choked out a sob at the sight of the lifeless charred remains.

CHAPTER 24

S IDNEY SWAYED OVER HER BUCKLING knees.

Kate caught her beneath the arms and steadied her. "Come on now. Come on. You don't know that's them for sure." The policewoman turned Sidney away as the firemen covered up the bodies again. "Just walk away. Walk away."

Sid shuffled through the parking lot and swallowed back the bile building in her throat. The strong stench of burning flesh hit her nose, and she began to gag. She covered her mouth with her clammy hand. *Get a grip, Sid. Get a grip.*

"You're in shock, honey. You're in shock," Kate said again, hugging her around the waist. "Just keep walking. Keep walking."

On spaghetti legs, Sidney managed to make her way back to the squad car. People were commenting and murmuring. Her rattled mind didn't comprehend anything they said. She squatted down and leaned on one of the hubcaps, huddled up with her head down. Tears streamed down her cheeks, and she shook uncontrollably. "Oh Lord. Oh Lord. Why?"

"It's probably a tragic accident," Kate said in a comforting tone. "But maybe it wasn't them. You never know. Hang in there."

No. Sidney had known something was wrong from the moment she saw the flames on TV. Her instincts had warned her of the danger. Emptiness filled her stomach. "Oh, Megan. Oh, Allison." She pounded the pavement with her fist. "No. No. No!"

"Easy now," Kate said, kneeling down beside her and trying to put a blanket over her shoulders. "You're gonna hurt yourself."

Sidney pushed the blanket aside and rose back to her feet. She wiped the tears from her eyes. "I need to walk."

"Sure. I'm right here if you need anything."

Hands on her hips, Sid took a shuddering breath and made her way through the crowd into the parking lot. *What do I tell Mom and Dad?* She could hear their hearts breaking. *What if this is all my fault?* The last thing she'd ever do was put her family in danger. A memory flashed in her mind. The text that had come with a picture of Allison and Megan and the message that read,

Watch your step.

Her blood turned to ice. *Wilhelm!*

Had Allison seen something? Maybe the congressman was covering up his tracks. Perhaps something worse had happened over the weekend while Allison was gone. *What kind of people play these games?* She found herself standing on the sidewalk across from the building. A flood of feelings rushed through her. Anger. Sadness. Despair. *Maybe the cop is right. Maybe it isn't them at all but someone else.* She closed her eyes and gathered her thoughts.

Be patient.

She'd find the cause in the fire marshal's report. An autopsy would have to be done on the bodies. There wasn't any sense in getting anyone upset until everything was confirmed. She checked her phone again. "Come on, Allison. Please. Be alive somewhere else," she muttered to herself.

"Excuse me," said a man who was passing by. He was much older, wearing a fedora hat and a brown trench coat. "Did you say something to me?"

"No, sorry," she said.

"Quite all right," he said, tipping his hat. "My hearing isn't what it once was." He gazed at the apartment's ruins and twisted the end of his grey moustache. "It's almost a tragedy to see such bad things happen."

"Almost?" she said.

"Oh, why yes," he said, without looking at her. His voice took on a sinister tone. "You know, Agent Shaw, bad things happen to those who dicker with the Black Slate."

Sidney slugged him in the jaw, knocking his hat from his head. He tumbled hard to the ground and lay out, on his back. She pinned him down with her knee and stuck the muzzle of her gun in his face. "Who did this? Who did this?"

The eerie man with a bleeding lip laughed and spat blood. "I don't know for certain. I'm just the messenger. Hahahaha."

She punched him in the face again. *Whack!* And again. *Whack!*

He continued to laugh. His watch started beeping. "Oh. It seems my time is up, Agent Shaw, but I'll give you a hint. The Drake send their condolences."

"You sonuva—"

The man convulsed and shuddered, and then his eyes froze upward to the sky. A foamy spittle oozed from the corner of his mouth.

She checked his pulse. He was dead. She checked his coat and grabbed his hat. They had a very musty smell, and the style looked to be at least seventy-five years old. She found a wallet and a paper driver's license belonging to Dwight Guilden. It had expired over sixty years ago.

"What's going on over here?" said Officer McFadden. She had a gun on Sid, and she wasn't alone either. "What did you do to that man?"

Another cop checked the pulse and said, "He's dead."

"Agent Shaw," Officer McFadden said, "put your hands down where I can see them."

"Why?" she said, holstering her weapon.

"Because you're going downtown until we get this all sorted out. Bart, cuff her."

"*What?* For what?"

"Assault and suspicion of murder."

"I'm a federal agent! I didn't kill this man."

"Then why's his face bleeding?" Kate took out her taser. "Now, Agent Shaw, don't make me use this."

"Have you gone mad? My family just got burned alive in there." Seething, Sidney took a pleading step forward.

Kate pulled the trigger on the stun gun.

Zzzzzzap!

Sid's body twitched, her teeth chattered, and she collapsed hard on the ground. She couldn't move her shocked and numbing limbs, but she could still see and hear.

Kate pulled out a card and read the Miranda rights to Sid. "You have the right to remain silent..."

CHAPTER 25

S IDNEY NIBBLED ON HER NAILS. For the past eight hours she'd been in the local PD's lockup while the FBI got everything sorted out. Cyrus Tweel had picked her up, and it had been a long trip back to headquarters.

"You can't cut loose like that, Sid," Cyrus said, pushing his spectacles up onto his nose. "It's bad for the agency, and you know we hate attention in the papers."

She sneered at him. One thing the weasel of a man lacked was compassion. He was all image. All agency from day one. If they made you walk around with your hat on fire, Cyrus would do it. "I don't need an academy lecture," she said, facing the passenger window. "And you don't know what the hell is going on either, so don't act like you do."

"Why don't you explain it to me then, *shadow agent?*"

She didn't miss the venom in his voice when he said it. "Ah, that's it, isn't it? You're jealous, aren't you Cyrus? They picked me over you, and it's just bugging the crap out of you."

"I could not care less about the Black Slate and your little ghost chases. Doesn't mean a thing to me at all. But as for you? Well, you're an excellent agent, but this assignment is a joke. Everyone thinks so."

"Everyone who, and how do they know about it?"

"Your special little assignment isn't a secret. Do you really think a bunch of special agents don't notice when someone like you," he glanced at her legs, "goes missing from time to time? The Slate is nothing but snickers at the water cooler."

"Oh, I see, so I'm making you look bad, huh Cyrus? I'm sorry." She reached over and patted his leg. "I really am sorry, little Cyrus."

"Geez, cut it out. Even you are above such mockery."

She dug her nails into his thigh. "Do you even give a shit about Allison and Megan? How can you sit here and act like you don't even know them?" She jerked her hand away. "That's your problem, Cyrus. If it doesn't help you and your career, it doesn't matter. You don't care if your fellow agent's family just perished in a fire. Jerk."

"You know I'm not like that, Sid. Look, I'm sorry." He steered the car to the exit ramp. "An autopsy revealed that those bodies were not your niece and sister."

She straightened up in her seat. "*What?* And you're just now telling me this?" She wanted to pound his face in. Instead, she punched him in the arm.

"Ow!"

"You're a rat, Cyrus. Just a little rodent who gets off toying with other people's feelings."

"No, I don't. I just have my orders. Chief Howard was going to brief you at his office." He rubbed his shoulder. "Geez, you hit like a dude."

She snorted. "You know Cyrus, this was one of the reasons why our relationship couldn't go any further."

"I beg your pardon."

"I never could put my finger on it. I mean, you do and say all the right stuff. But between us, I always knew the agency would come first." She sighed. "You would choose them over me. I could just feel it. And I think the agency, and the authority that comes with it, is how you get away with some bad things you like to do."

"Like what?"

"Like shooting people. Keeping secrets. Manipulating a situation. You thrive on it. I see that spark behind those icy eyes of yours. You delight in it. It disturbs me."

Cyrus turned on his blinker and turned into the headquarters garage. His face was stone cold. The brakes squeaked as he brought the SUV to a stop. He turned and looked at her. "I'll keep that perspective in mind."

❁ ❁ ❁

"Sid," Ted Howard said, sitting behind his desk, "we're trying to help. Honestly, you know that." He took a swig of bottled water. "It hasn't even been a day yet. You know how these things go."

She sat back in one of the chairs, arms folded, legs crossed, and foot kicking. "It's a little different when your own family is missing."

"It hasn't even been twenty-four hours yet," Cyrus added. He was sitting in the seat beside hers, facing Section Chief Howard. "Give our people, your people, a little more time. They'll turn up."

"Yes, they'll turn up dead if I don't get moving." She started up out of her seat.

"Sit!" Ted said, rising up from his chair. He lowered his voice again. "Please, Sid. Let's work on this together."

Reluctantly, she took a seat. "I know you don't have anyone on this. You don't have time for it. I'm only here because I got carried away and busted that freak Dwight Guilden in the face. What about his autopsy? Certainly you checked on him."

Ted and Cyrus looked at each other. Cyrus shrugged.

"You two are dropping the ball," she said. "How did you do an autopsy on the burn victims but not follow up on the man who got me arrested for attempted murder? Huh?"

"The man, Dwight you say," Ted said, checking out some papers. "He's at the county morgue. The burn victims went to the state where we have better connections. Look, I'm sorry. I'll get a man down to county as soon as I can find one."

"No hurry, Ted. He's dead, so I don't think he's going anywhere. At least not until the Drake make him disappear, just like they did with my niece and my sister!"

"Keep your voice down, Sid. Please. You aren't being yourself," Ted said. "It worries me."

No, she wasn't, and she knew it. Instead, she was coming unglued. It wasn't like her. But this was different. Her family had been taken. And by the sound of things, the two men she knew best in the agency didn't believe her.

"Look Sid," the chief said, "run this by me again. This Guilden fella. What exactly did he say?"

Cyrus took out his notepad and added, "Yes, walk us through it one more time. Word by word."

She got up again. "I've got a couple of words for the both of you." She pointed at each one. "Screw you, and screw you."

"You better button it up, Sid!" Ted said.

"I'm a shadow agent. I don't have to be here." She headed for the door. "You have no idea what I'm up against, because if you did, you'd be in the thick of this with me." She swung the door open and marched straight out.

Sitting behind her desk, Jane gave her a disapproving glance and opened her mouth to speak.

Sid cut her off and shot her a hard look. "Not a word if you know what's good for you." She made a bead for the elevator and noted the group of male agents mumbling and watching her go. "Worry about your own sorry cases, you bunch of jackasses." She punched the elevator button, tapped her foot on the tiles, shook her head, and blasted through the door to the stairs.

I'm beginning to hate this building.

She jogged down four flights, crossed through the lobby, and pushed her way outside through the main entrance doors. Taking the steps two at a time down onto the street, she realized something. *I don't have my car!*

CHAPTER 26

SIDNEY STUFFED HER HANDS INTO her jacket pockets and meandered down the sidewalk. *They're idiots. Then again, maybe I'm the idiot.* Throughout all of her career, everyone had preached teamwork—until the Black Slate. Now, it seemed no one wanted anything to do with her—or it. She felt like an outsider looking in. It hurt. It made her angry.

She took a breath and tried to flag down a taxi. It was getting dark now, and the busy streets had begun to thin. She didn't see a taxi anywhere and cursed. *Get ahold of yourself. What would you do if you were in their shoes?* She had never bent the rules before, but now things were different. Everything she knew about life was turned upside down.

"Hey! Hey! Taxi!" She dashed into the street as one went by. The driver waved. She smacked the back of his trunk with her hand. "Thanks for nothing!"

She headed back onto the sidewalk. A woman and her son were staring at her with widened eyes. *What are you gawking at?* She didn't say it. Instead, she tucked her chin down, picked up the pace, and marched down the street. She took out her phone. *I suppose I could call a cab.* She pressed the info button.

"How can I help you?" said a male computerized voice.

"I need a—"

A nearby car let out an awesome exhaust note.

Vrrrrooom! Vrrrrooom! Vrrrrooomm!

Sidney turned around. Her phantom-black Dodge Hellcat with orange highlights awaited in the street.

Smoke was in the driver's seat. He rolled down the window. "Need a lift?"

She walked over to his side, bent over to eye level, and said, "I'm driving."

He got out, walked in front of the hood, and entered the passenger side door.

Sidney took her place in the driver's seat. She adjusted her mirrors and seat. Cars honked as they passed by. She popped the sunglasses holder. The glasses from Mal's house fell into her hand. She slipped them on. The dark streets became brighter, distant images crystal clear. She squeezed the wheel. "Do you know what's going on?"

"Yeah," Smoke said, eyes forward, switching the magazine on his gun.

"You might want to get out. I'm going to see Mason Crow. Don't try to talk me out of it."

"I didn't swing by to give you a shoulder to cry on." He slapped the magazine into the gun.

"Good." She slapped the gear shifter into drive and punched the accelerator. The front end lifted off the ground and the rear tires dug in. "Now let's go get those bastards."

You can count on me. Smoke's words echoed in her mind. It was clear now. He meant what he said. It strengthened her. There weren't too many people she trusted in this world. Whenever she had trusted someone, they'd let her down. *Maybe my expectations are too high for most people. Not everyone can be a 'do the right thing or die' kind of person.*

The car engine purred as they traveled down the road back toward Mason Crow's estate. Or the Drake estate. It didn't matter to her whose it was.

"So, you plan on driving straight up to the front porch?" Smoke inspected the keen edge of the knife he had in his hand.

"I've got a feeling they're expecting me."

"You have a good sense of things. Guts too. I like it," he said. "Let's just hope they stay in you."

"I've got my sweet heart suit on. I figure my guts will be just fine. Getting my hair messed up is what worries me." She eyed his shaved head. "At least you don't have that problem."

He let out a low chuckle.

"You need to let that hair grow back out if we make it out. Just saying."

"All right, Delilah. If we live, I'll never cut it again."

"No, don't go all hippie on me, either." Her phone buzzed. She turned on the car's Bluetooth. "Hello, Mal."

"Good guess, Agent Shaw. Is Smoke with you?"

"Yes," she said.

"And I see that you're headed back. You need to turn around." Mal's voice was urgent. "Now."

"Can't do that," she said.

"It's a death wish. Turn around."

"It was nice meeting you, Mal. But we have to go now. If you recover our bodies, make sure it's a nice funeral."

"And if I'm gored to death," Smoke added, "be sure to hide the hole if it's in my head."

"Have you two gone mad? You're on a suicide mission. You need a plan."

"We have one," she said. "And it involves using all of your ammo."

"At least take the pills," Mal said. "Please, take the pills. Take them now. They're time release."

"I don't have any pills."

"I do," Smoke said, holding up two liquid green pills. "Sorry, but I couldn't resist. Reminded me of *The Matrix*."

"Well, you can take one for you and one for me then."

"Agent Shaw, listen to me. Your lives depend on it. So do your niece and your sister. Turn around."

"Good-bye, Mal." She disconnected the phone and powered it down. "I don't like being talked out of things."

"I know," Smoke said, "but if you don't care, stop for just a few seconds."

"Why?"

"Because I'd stop for you if you were asking."

She slowed the car down and put it into park.

Smoke shifted around in his seat and faced her. He held up the two green pills. "Who knows what sort of real monsters we'll find in there. I think we'll need an edge this time. These super vitamins might help."

"It doesn't seem like you," she said, eyeing the pills.

He shrugged his shoulders. "I won't take it if you won't."

Now the pressure was on her. She rubbed her palms on her jeans. "Don't you put this on me. If you want to take it, then take it. Don't blame me for dying if you don't."

His dark eyes bore into her. "If you won't do it for yourself, then do it for Allison. Do it for Megan."

"Fine." She snatched the pill from his hand and swallowed it down.

Smoke did the same. "See, that wasn't so bad."

She put the car into drive and hit the gas, pinning them both to their seats. "We'll see about that."

After they rounded the last bend, about a quarter mile in front of the ranch was a gate under heavy guard. Suddenly, a spotlight beamed on her car.

Sidney stopped the car about an eighth of a mile away. "Huh. I get the feeling they're expecting us." She squeezed the grip on her pistol.

Smoke held a gun in each hand. "They haven't started firing yet."

The sounds of small engines roared to life. Four ATVs zoomed in from the tall grasses, surrounding her car. A dozen gun barrels were lowered on them.

"Get those hands where we can see them!" yelled one of the men.

"Yep, they were expecting us." Smoke eased his hands up.

One of the men hopped out of an ATV, holding his fist up. He pecked on Sidney's window with the butt of his weapon.

She rolled it down.

"Are you Agent Shaw?" he said.

"No, I'm the tooth fairy."

The man lifted his bushy brows. "Nice car, tooth fairy. Now take a nice easy drive up the road, and come to a stop at the log cabin. Someone will meet you there." He spit tobacco juice on the ground. "I hope you're up for a long night. It's gonna be hell. It's gonna be death."

CHAPTER 27

Inside the oversized log home, a fire burned beneath a great hearth of cut stone that rose up through the ceiling. Sidney's face dripped sweat from the heat of the blaze. Her hands were bound behind her back, and she was on her knees. Smoke was in the same position beside her, with sweat dripping off his chin.

"Hot, yes?" said a man with a booming voice. It was Mason Crow, sitting in a grand chair carved from wood and animal bone. He was larger than life. Dark skin with large eyes underneath a head of shaggy brown hair. His shoulders were inhumanly brawny. A large machete rested on his lap. "Enjoy it. It's much warmer than the grave."

Sidney shifted against the bonds biting into her wrists and gave him a defiant look. "Where's my sister? Where's my niece?"

A tall well-built woman wearing a dark purple and gray suit with short salt and pepper colored hair strolled over and drove her booted foot into Sid's gut.

"Ooof!" Sid teetered over onto the floor, coughing and spitting.

"I doubt you are in a position to ask any questions," Mason said, rolling up his white cotton sleeves. "If I want you to speak, I'll ask."

Sid fought her way back onto her aching knees. She didn't care what he wanted. She hadn't come here to play games. She just wanted to know if Allison was alive or dead. "Just answer me, you fricking animal."

The woman launched a punch into her jaw. *Whap!*

Sid swayed, kept her balance, and leered up at the woman. "You hit like a girl."

Whap! "You bleed like one." The woman drew her fist back again. *Whap!*

Sidney's stinging eye began to swell. Her split lip tasted like blood. *I hate these people.* Like a fool, she had rushed into the lion's den, and now she would have to face the consequences.

"She is a spirited one, isn't she?" Mason said, cocking his head and giving her a study. Nostrils flaring, he took a deep draw through his nose. "I don't smell fear in her. Nor in him, for that matter. Much unlike her family."

Sid's head snapped up, and she stared him down.

"Yes, Agent Sidney Shaw," Mason said. "I have seen them, and you'll be glad to know that they live... for now."

"Show me!" she fired back.

The woman cocked her fist back to strike.

"Hold!" Mason said. "Let her save her energy, Double Dee. She'll need it. Humph." He picked up his machete, stood up, and made his way toward them. He brought the blade up under Smoke's chin. "You are the one who shot me. Humph. It takes a special bullet to penetrate my skin. My attendants marveled when they plucked it out of my hide. A breakthrough in ammunition. It will take more than that to kill me, but it's more than enough to kill mortals like you. I'm all about heavy blades and horns." He hefted the machete high over his head and brought it down hard with a tremendous yell. "Haaaaaaaaaaaaaaaaaaaaa!"

"Smoke!" Sidney yelled.

The blade quavered less than an inch from Smoke's skull. The man remained still as a stone.

Sidney gasped. "You're sick! What's wrong with you people! Are you nothing but bloodthirsty vampires?"

Mason withdrew the blade and stuck it into the hardwood floor. "Please, no need to insult us. We are nothing like those blood-sucking leeches. Leave those vermin to the European world." He backed up and resumed his chair. "Humph. Survivors. I like that. It's been quite some time since the attendants of the Drake have been tested. You took down the wolf man and the bird lady. Quite a feat." He stroked the coarse black hairs on his chin. "I'd say they underestimated you."

"That's an excuse," Sid fired back. "Your friend Night Bird didn't like lab rats who fought back. Well, we do fight back, and given the chance, we'll kick your hairy ass too."

Mason's chest heaved with great laughter. Some of the other guards in the room chuckled. The woman called Double Dee smirked. "Said like a true warrior. It's no surprise that *they* chose you, bold woman. You have guts." He stomped his foot, shaking the room. "And I aim to see them splattered underneath my hooves."

"Doesn't make for a very nice memory of the petting zoo," Smoke said. "Say, do any of you fiends turn into llamas? You know, half man, half llama. Now that would be formidable."

Sidney laughed.

"Fools," Mason said, "but cocky fools. Humph. That makes for great entertainment, but unlike the battles you had with my lesser colleagues, this one will be quite different." He snapped his fingers. "Let me see their weapons."

One of the soldiers carried Smoke's duffel bag over, bowed, and set it down at Mason's feet. Slowly he stepped off to the side.

Mason reached down and pulled the duffel bag up and into his lap. *Clank.*

"Let's see what our dear enemies have in store for us." He fished his hand into the bag and withdrew one of the daggers Mal had given them. He thumbed the edge. "Interesting." He ran the blade along his arm. A hairy clump of arm hair drifted toward the floor. "Now that's a sharp knife. I like it." He eyed the point, stuck it deep into his forearm, and sliced back until he drew blood.

Sidney grimaced. Blood dripped down Mason's arm and splashed onto the floor.

"'If it bleeds, then it can die,' the mortals like to say, eh, heroes?" Mason held his forearm out. The nasty gash closed itself together, and the shaved hairs grew back. "And that's true in most cases."

Sidney glanced at Smoke.

His eyes were on hers, and he said, "I've always wanted to be a matador."

"Yeah, me too," she added. "Do we get to wear those funny hats?"

"No," Mason said, "but you will be seeing a lot of red." In a lightning-swift move, he jammed the blade to the hilt into the soldier's chest. *Chuk!*

"Urk!" The man in the pea coat sagged to the floor, eyes wide and gasping for breath.

"Take this mess out of here," said Double Dee.

Two men rushed over, hooked the dying man under the arms, and bore him out of the room.

Sidney's nerves were on fire. She shifted on her knees. Eyed the exits of the room. *Maybe coming here wasn't such a good idea after all.*

CHAPTER 28

"THIS IS INTERESTING." MASON HAD fished a gun magazine out of the duffel bag and was eyeing it. He plucked a bullet with a red tip out and cocked his head. "Humph. Looks to be a little more than a tracer. What does it do?"

Sidney pulled her tongue off of the roof of her mouth and tried to speak. She was on a roller coaster of mixed emotions, fear and anger intermingled. Sweat dripped into her eyes. She wiped it with her shoulder. *Be brave. Be bold. Do it for your family.* "It kills people. And animals."

"Oh, I see." He slapped the magazine into the gun and handed it over to Double Dee. "Show me."

Double Dee charged the weapon's slide and took aim at Smoke. "It's gonna leave a mess," she said.

"Good, I like messes."

"Double Dee?" Sidney interrupted with a sneer, "What kind of stupid name is that?" She glanced at the woman's chest. She couldn't stop the words from coming. "Did you have a reduction and forget to change your stripper name?"

"You've got a pretty big mouth for a woman whose boyfriend is about to get shot in the head." Double Dee recharged the weapon's slide. "Anything else, *Agent Shaw*?"

"Nope."

"I'd like to state, for the record, that I'm not her boyfriend," Smoke said. "And I'd like lilies sent to my funeral. If I get one."

The woman huffed a laugh and said back to Mason, "Can you believe these two?"

"They'd make excellent jesters, Dee. Humph. I like it." He pointed at the guards posted at the windows. "Shoot one of those. Or both."

One man stiffened, and the other man moved.

Ka-Blam! Ka-Blam!

Sidney squeezed her eyes shut and hunkered down. Two explosions rocked the floor. *Boom! Boom!* Glass shattered.

"Holy shit!" Dee said.

Sidney opened her eyes. There was blood and guts splattered on Dee's face.

Dee wiped it off, held up the gun, and said to Mason, "Can I keep this?"
He nodded.

Sidney glanced over her shoulder. The pair of men lay dead, each with a massive cavity in his chest. Her tummy soured, and she turned away. "I told you they killed people. Pretty sure they'll work on livestock too."

Mason wiped the bits of scattered flesh from his arms and removed another item from the bag. It was the special flex cuffs that Mal said would hold anything. "They can have these. Humph. " He tossed the bag onto the floor. "The rest is now acquired by our arsenal."

Dee cozied up to Smoke and tugged at the sweet heart suit hidden underneath his collar. "What about this? I think this suit's made of fibro-gynnsynn."

"Leave it. It might save their skin, but it won't stop their bones from breaking or their innards from being crushed. If anything, it will only prolong their suffering." He cracked his knuckles. They each made a loud pop. "I love the sound of bone and sinew breaking."

"What about my family?" Sidney said. "I don't care what you have in store for me, but just let them go."

"Oh, but I'm going to leave their fate in your hands, Agent Shaw. Yes. All you have to do is find them. If you can find them, then you can save them. How does that sound?"

"It sounds like another one of your twisted games."

Mason shrugged. "When you've been around as long as I have, you find creative ways to entertain yourself. I'm so glad you volunteered your services." He stood up to his towering full height. "Dee, have them prepped and sent to the catacombs." He stood over Sidney. "I hope to see you both at the end." He turned his back and exited the room with loud and heavy footsteps.

"What does he mean by prepping us?" Sidney asked Dee. The woman had a vague familiarity about her.

Dee waved a few guards over, but she addressed her comments to Sidney. "It means search them again and take off their shoes. No one wears shoes down there. It's a thing. Now sit down on your ass."

Knees aching, Sidney was almost happy to comply. "How can you do this, Dee?"

"Please don't start trying to pick at my conscience. I don't have one." Dee started untying Sidney's boots. "Besides, you've only seen a glimpse of the power they have. Let me give you some advice. Let the devils in those holes take you quickly. They'll have more mercy than Mason will." She jerked Sid's boots off one at a time. "You'll understand once you get down there."

"I saw what you were thinking," Sidney said to Dee. "You have that gun, that power. You were tempted to shoot him, weren't you?"

"You're mistaken."

"No, I'm not. Women of your disposition often want to kill their lovers."

"Ha, well, I don't think you were paying attention." Dee tossed the boots aside. "He can't be killed."

"That's what AV and Night Bird thought. You know, Mason reminds me of my boss, Ted Howard."

Dee froze for a moment and then said, "Good for you."

"Huh, so the legendary Special Agent Deanne Drukker lives."

"I don't think so."

"What's the Double for then, Dee?"

"Just a stupid pet name for me," Dee said, looking Sid in the eye. "You should be able to figure it out, Special Agent." She then spoke with a hushed breath. "I warned Ted. Now you've come to die."

Something clicked deep inside Sid's thoughts. *Extraordinary Caution. Did Ted put me on this assignment hoping that I would find Deanne? Damn him!* "He misses you."

"He always was soft."

"Probably started after his mentor left."

"Uh-huh."

"Dee," Sidney said, pleading a little. "I don't care what happens to me. I just want to save my sister and niece. Free them."

"How noble." The rangy woman stood up. "But that's entirely up to you and him." She shook her head. "I really hate to see good troops go, but I'm excited to see how this ends." She pulled out her pistol and raised it behind the back of Sid's head. "Have a good death, Agent Shaw."

The gun came down. The butt of the weapon struck her skull. Sid's head filled with painful bright spots, stars, and then blackness.

CHAPTER 29

S IDNEY AWOKE WITH A SHIVER. Rubbing her bleary eyes and aching head, she managed to make it to her feet. *Where am I?*

She was in a round room about twenty feet across, with walls that were made of cut rock on a framework of iron beams. It was illuminated by dim yellow lights. The ceiling was maybe ten feet high, and a heavy metal door, no window, was closed behind her. *This must be where they dropped me off.*

She ran her fingers along the door's edge. There were no handles or latches, and the door was sealed up tight. "Great. Welcome to the catacombs, Sid."

The room she stood in was cold and lonely. She already missed Smoke, and despite the warmness her suit provided, a chill went through her. *Not a fan of caves. Or the dirt that's in them.* She'd gone spelunking once in her teens and sworn she'd never do it again. Getting trapped a few hundred feet underground had unnerved her then. It was worse now. She had a feeling she was so deep that no one would ever hear her scream.

"Well, Sid, let's go find your sister."

She shuffled forward. Something sharp bit into her foot. "Ow." She braced herself against the damp wall and hoisted her foot up. A sliver of something was stuck inside her foot and she plucked it out. *Is that bone?* She flicked it away. Something else caught her eye on the grimy floor. It was a few pairs of flex cuffs. "My, won't these come in handy." She looped them into her belt and shuffled—foot bleeding—down the corridor.

The walls and floor were slick and damp in some places but not all. Her feet found some cleared-off tiles cut from marble. Her nose found something else. She sniffed. Something somewhere was rotting. She balled up her fists and carried on, eyeing the ceiling from time to time. Every twenty steps or so she'd notice a small device mounted on the beams. *Are those cameras? What a bunch of sick people.*

The corridor winded left and right, making right angles and sharp bends and sometimes crossing over. Its grade went up and down, giving her the feeling she was inside some sort of military bunker. She'd been in them before, great man-made caverns and tunnels beneath the ground or built into the mountains. They were stockpiled with weapons and all kinds of other devices. She walked for minutes, twisting and turning, losing all sense of direction. *Morning Glory. I really am a lab rat.*

Her stomach groaned. A strong hunger gripped her. *Crap, how long was I out?* It could have been hours, and the suit tended to make her more hungry than normal. It gave her energy, but it made her want to eat more too. *Forget about it, and keep going.*

As her feet slapped over the wet floor, the foul odor became stronger. She covered her nose and forged ahead into an open room. A lone metal desk sat in the middle of the room with a body, seated in a chair, slumped over it. It was a man in uniform. The back of his blue shirt was stained in blood and showed a gaping wound. His flesh was rotting from his skin and it looked like rats, really big ones, had nibbled on it. He wasn't wearing any shoes.

Geez. Poor guy.

She gave his body a shove, and it collapsed onto the floor. She held back her shriek. The man's face was chewed up. His eyes were missing, and his mouth hung open in a silent terrified yell. There was a name badge on his shirt. She ripped it off. John Carter, DCPD. She remembered reading about how he'd gone missing. She glared up at the cameras.

"I guess I'm not alone fighting you minions! Screw you!"

She tucked the nameplate away in her back pocket. She ground her teeth thinking about his family and all they had been through since he went missing. It charged her blood. She patted down his body, searching for a weapon of any kind. Finding nothing, she searched the room. There were some empty shelves, boxes, and crates. A bunch of crap long abandoned. *Oh well.*

There was another corridor across, identical to the one that she came from. She started toward it and stopped. She heard footsteps coming her way. Steady. Purposed. She hid on the other side of the desk and waited. On her hands and knees, she peeked from underneath the desk. A pair of bare feet emerged from the corridor and slowly began to circle the room.

"Muh... muh," muttered an inhuman voice as something sniffed the room.

Sidney shifted her way around the desk, staying out of its line of sight. Her skin crawled at the sound of its voice.

"Muh... muh," it said, feet shuffling over the floor. Its movements stopped. Its voice fell silent. Only the hum of the yellow lights and the sound of dripping water remained—along with the foulness of the air.

Sidney swallowed and took a peek over the desk. Her eyes locked on a burly man with stringy hair and hollow eyes. A huge bloodstained club was in his hand. *A deader!*

Its eyes locked on hers. "Muh!" The weapon came down with all of its might, pounding at the desk. *Whack! Whack! Whack!*

Sidney sprang to her feet and backed away. A second deader emerged—bald and bearded— from the other corridor, dragging another crude club behind it. It raised the weapon up and came right at her, swinging left and right. The pair flanked her behind the desk, leaving only a straight path down the corridor where she had not been. *There might be another deader back there!*

The clubs came up and slammed down. Sid dashed between the pair of deaders and circled around the room. Their moves were mechanical but quick as a man of the same size and with unrelenting purpose. The clubs clanked off the walls, toppled the shelves, and ricocheted off the floor.

Chest heaving, Sidney ducked, twisted away, and spun through the pair of them. A bludgeoning blow ripped through the air, missing her and cracking the skull of the other deader. It teetered over and fell. Its club clattered to the ground. Sidney went for the weapon.

The shaggier one with the club charged. *Whack! Whack!*

It missed her curled-up legs. Her fingers stretched out, grabbing the club by the bottom and catching it up in time to block the next thunderous blows that rained down on her.

Clack! Clack! Clack!

The thunderous blows jarred her arms. She drew back her leg and kicked out its knee.

"Muh!" It said, teetering over and spilling to the ground.

Sid scrambled to her feet. A powerful hand snatched her leg and jerked her down. The first deader had her in its fierce grip. It balled up its fist and punched her hard in the thigh.

"Aargh!" Sidney yelled. "No more of that!" She hit it in the head with the club. *Whack! Whack!* "Die, monster, die!" *Whack! Whack! Whack!*

Its grip loosened.

She tore away, scrambling to her feet. Her lungs were burning, and her face was dripping with sweat. Sidney stumbled back against the wall. Two more deaders emerged from the corridors with clubs bigger than the last. "I hate you things."

CHAPTER 30

"Muh! Muh! Muh! Muh!"

"Oh, shut up!" Sidney swung with all of her force into the nearest one, dismantling its chin. *Clak!*

It fell backward, jostling the others.

Sid made her move. Fueled by another burst of adrenaline, she sprinted by the other deaders and darted into the corridor. *Catch me if you can!* She ran, leaving the distant 'muh muh' echoes of the deaders behind her. She slowed to a stop, legs cramping, and gasped for air. Her heartbeat was pounding inside her temples. The wound in her foot burned, but she ignored it.

Think of something, Sid. Think!

Feet splattering over the wet stone floor, she headed toward the sound of rushing water. Perhaps there was a drainage tunnel leading out. She picked up the pace, following the lights around a series of sharp bends in the tunnel. The path split off from time to time, but she followed the sound. It grew louder and louder. She turned down a narrow corridor until the sound of crashing water roared in her ears. The ceiling lowered and she stooped down, traveling toward the sound until the tunnel came to a stop.

No!

A wall of metal bars blocked the exit. Beyond them a series of tunnels roared with water rushing through them. She hit the bars with the club. The grid of iron rang out. She hit it again and again. *Clang! Clang! Clang!* She turned and slumped back against the bars. Took some deep draws through her nose and clutched the stitch in her side. It had been awhile since she'd run so hard.

"Muh..."

Her head snapped up. A deader bore down on her on stiff, fast-moving legs. Closing in, it swung its club. She sidestepped and walloped it in the side of the head. The creature's head tilted and snapped back. It swung again. She parried. She blocked. *Clack! Clack!* The unrelenting creature of the dead laid into her with heavy blow after heavy blow.

"Muh!"

"Muh you!" she yelled back. She clobbered it in the face, busting its nose. She was skilled. Quicker. She blasted it in the teeth. In the knee. The back of the head. She beat it down. Blasted it full in the neck. It lumbered aimlessly then cut loose a wild swing.

Crack!

"Aaaah!" Sidney cried out. It had busted her in the hand. The club slipped from her fingers. Tucking the wounded hand beneath her arm, she backed away. "Where's a flamethrower when you need one?" She shuffled back and ran into another deader. "Ugh!"

It locked its arms around her waist and held her fast. The other came at her and unleashed a furious swing.

She ducked her head. The club skimmed over her face and cracked the head of the deader holding her. It let out a ghastly groan, stumbled back, and slammed her hard on the tunnel floor. She grabbed its hands and tried to break free of its grip. She kicked, elbowed, and flailed. The other deader with the club attacked again. *Whap! Whap! Whap!*

It missed her and hit the other one. Sidney twisted in its loosened grip, pulled her feet under her, and shoved her way free. It fell back into the other, creating a pile of undead flesh. Gasping for breath, she found herself pinned between the deaders and the barred gate. *Morning Glory! How can I stop these things? I need my weapon!*

The deaders gathered themselves, blocking the path of any escape out of the tunnel, and closed in once more.

Sid's frantic hands found the handle on the club she'd lost. She got up on her feet. "Fine! Come and get me!"

"Muh!" one said with a dangling jaw.

"Muh!" said the other with a crushed eye socket.

She charged with her club high and brought it down with all of her might on the nearest one. The club clocked off of its skull and the handle busted. *No!* She tossed the broken weapon aside and launched a kick into one deader's gut, doubling it over. She locked her hands around the swinging club of the other and hung on for dear life.

Whop!

Something hard crashed into the side of her face.

She kicked back and kept kicking. Something hit back and kept hitting. She fought with everything she had, but she got tired. They didn't. She lost her grip on the club and sagged onto the tunnel floor. She looked up at her undead aggressor, spat out the words, "I can't go down like this," and launched a futile punch into its groin. "Not to some undead bastard."

CHAPTER 31

THE DEADER'S CLUB STARTED TO descend.

Glitch!

A blade erupted from the front of the deader's chest and ripped back out of it. The deader collapsed on top of Sidney. She shoved it off. *What just happened?*

The remaining deader whirled away from Sid and faced the new attacker. It was Smoke, standing tall with a gory spear in his hands. The deader charged. Smoke rammed the spear into its heart and clean through the back.

The deader let out its last cry. "Muh!" Its body slumped to the floor.

Smoke braced his boot on the deader's chest and pulled the spear out. He offered Sidney his hand.

She took it. "Where did you find a spear?"

Blood was dripping down from a gash in his forehead. He wiped it away. "Another deader. Come on. These tunnels are full of them."

"Hold on." She took the spear away from him, glared at one of the deaders, and stabbed it again. "Okay, now we can go."

Nodding, Smoke reached down for one of the clubs. "This all right with you?"

She shrugged. He led. Still catching her breath, she followed. Smoke moved with ease through the network, not moving too fast or too slow. They tread on bare cat's feet, stopping and listening. Deaders roamed. She could hear their heavy steps slapping the wet stones, but it was hard to tell where they were coming from.

Smoke stopped and held up his hand. Something was coming on heavy feet, but she couldn't see around the bend. "Go back," he said.

Turning, she crept back down the tunnel toward the last intersection that they passed. Just as she was pressing her back against the way, two more deaders, one very big, lumbered by carrying machetes. *Cripes!*

Smoke's hand gave her shoulder a gentle squeeze. His breath was on her ear. A tingling sensation raced through her. *Now's not the time for these kinds of feelings.* Something crawled over her feet. A rat the size of a cat was sitting on her bare toes. "Eek!" She kicked it off of her.

The two deaders turned around and ran right for her. Charged with adrenaline,

Sidney lowered the spear and ran the first one through. *Glitch!* She ripped it out, looking for the rat. "Where are you, little vermin?" She jabbed at a rat scurrying over the floor. "Not sure which I hate worse. Rats or deaders."

"Sid!" Smoke yelled. "Sid!"

She spun around.

Smoke—swinging two handed—was clubbing away for his life against a deader that towered over him swinging a machete like a butter knife.

She jammed the spear into its back. She missed the heart.

It twisted, breaking the spear shaft off in her hands and backhanding her in the face.

She landed hard on her ass. "Ooph!"

Smoke renewed his assault, hammering it in the face. "Can't hit what you can't see!" Whack! Whack! Whack!"

With a spear poking out of its chest, the deader chopped back. The blade slit Smoke's abdomen, doubling him over. The machete went up. Smoke's decapitation was soon to follow.

"No!" Sidney screamed. Her long legs churned. She slammed into the back of the deader's legs and knocked it from its feet. *Wump!* It tried to split her in half. She rolled away.

Smoke sprang like a panther and locked up its arms and neck. "Kill it!"

"With what?"

"The spear," he said. The veins in his neck bulged like purple roots. "Hurry. I can't hold it much longer!"

She crawled over, grabbed the gory spear in her hands, jerked it from the deader's chest, flipped it around, and plunged it into its heart.

Its long legs shivered and went still.

"That was gross," Sid said.

Smoke shoved the deader aside and said nothing, wincing and clutching his belly.

"Are you all right?" she said.

He fingered the clean slice in his clothes, revealing the black second skin underneath. "I can't believe my guts are still in me."

"Me either," she said, scooting closer. "You almost lost your head too, you know." She winced and glanced at her throbbing hand. Her pinky finger was out of joint. Her stomach turned sick.

"That looks nasty," Smoke said. "Let me take a look."

"No."

He made his way toward her and said it again. "Let me take a look."

Reluctantly, she showed her hand.

"Ever dislocated it before?" he said.

"No."

He rubbed his chin. "Hmm. I think you better let me fix it, Sid."

She shook her head.

"Come on. You can count on me. Just let me do it. You can't let yourself be distracted by that aching pain." He nudged her shoulder. "Come on. Time's pressing."

She stretched her hand toward him, looked him right in the eye and said, "Do it."

Smoke took her hand gently in his palm, looked right back at her and said, "Easy peasy."

Pop.

Pain lanced through her hand, back, legs, and shoulders. She winced and sucked through her teeth. Eyes watering, she said, "Thanks."

He stretched out his hand and took her other one in it. They pulled each other up together.

He looked deep into her eyes and said, "I'm glad I didn't lose my head."

"Oh," she replied.

"But it wouldn't be so bad if you were the last thing I ever saw."

"I can't believe you just fed me a line."

"I can't believe you're scared of rats."

She rose on her tiptoes, eyed the floor, and said, "If I see any more, you might have to carry me through here."

"It would be my pleasure."

CHAPTER 32

T HEY WANDERED: LONG TEDIOUS MINUTES avoiding the unnatural sounds that roamed the corridor.

"This looks different," Smoke said, scratching the dirt wall with his fingers. He eyed the ceiling. The beams were wooden instead of steel and iron, but the lights were still there.

"Do you think they used to mine something down here?" she said, bending over and picking up a small chunk of coal. "Or is it just another hideout?"

"It's a catacomb. Not sure what else you'd call it. The pattern's purpose is to confuse." He led her up a gentle slope that opened up into an oversized alcove. There were tables and chairs, and the shelves were stocked with dry rotten rations of some sort. Decayed corpses and piles of bones lay dormant in the corner.

Sidney ran her fingers over the table. Checked the grooves and markings. She had a knack for such things. Her parents had been avid antiquers. "This is early American," she said, looking at an emblazoned rising sun carved in the backs of the chairs. "Probably worth a small fortune."

"Maybe we can get Mark Wahlberg and *The Antiques Roadshow* down here," Smoke said, taking a knee alongside one of the corpses. "They might take a keen interest in these uniforms too. These are redcoats."

"You're kidding."

Smoke picked up the tattered uniform and what was left of the bones in it. He played with the skeleton's jaw and made funny talk with it. "The British are coming. The British are coming. Wait. I *am* the British. Say, how'd my legs get so bony?" The jaw broke off in his hand. "Whoops. The roadshow's not going to like that."

"I think we need to get moving, Smoke Revere."

Smoke picked up a redcoat hat and dusted it off.

"Don't put that on," Sidney said, easing her way around the alcove. It felt like she'd stepped back in time more than two hundred years. "You look silly enough already. Let's go."

"After you." Smoke gestured and shrugged. "I think we've survived the first wave of danger. They want us to be here. I can feel it in my bones."

Sidney resumed her trek, opting to take the tunnel on the right, rather than the option on the left or going back. For some reason the tension between her shoulders eased. Perhaps Smoke was right. It seemed that their pursuers had been called off. Trudging over the sloppy floors, she came to a stop at the top of a stone-cut staircase. Torches lit the stairway that spiraled downward. A lump formed in her throat. "Uh, Smoke?"

Like a big hawk, he leaned down over her shoulder. "Looks like a gateway to Hell, doesn't it?"

"I really wish you hadn't said that."

"Sorry," he said, brushing by. "I'll go first."

Heart racing, Sidney followed the stairs deeper into the bowels of the earth. *Allison and Megan better be down here.* One thing she remembered from spelunking was that you never could tell how deep you were on your own. It practically terrified her. When she was a girl, she'd found the Loraine Caverns fascinating. Now, she'd avoid those historic caves altogether.

This shadow agent stuff really should come with a hefty boost in hazard pay.

The tunnel got cooler and even damper. Her thoughts were on the rushing waters she'd seen earlier. Those had to be above her now.

Do heavy rains fill these tunnels? This is crazy.

Smoke stopped. "I think we finally hit bottom."

"I can't imagine being any lower." She stepped from behind his broad shoulders and gazed ahead. Her mouth formed a small 'O'. A monstrous black chasm loomed. The glimmer of two torches looked to be a hundred yards in the distance. A low howl of wind caught her ears, nipped at her toes, and finally chilled her straight to the marrow. "There has to be another way."

Smoke moved forward, fixing his hands on the wood beams that supported a rope bridge that looked to be in poor condition. It was the only thing between them and the other side. He looked back at her. "Can you do it?"

Her fingers twitched at her sides. "Uh…"

"I can piggyback you."

I would like that… Damn my pride. If he's not scared, I'm not either. She stepped onto the bridge, glanced back at Smoke, and said, "Don't get any crazy ideas, Dr. Jones."

"Huh, good one."

Squeezing the ropes with white knuckles, she ventured forward. The bridge swayed. She clutched the ropes with her arms.

"Just stay in the middle, Sid," Smoke said in a reassuring voice. "It'll be fine."

She sucked it up and moved on, one short step at a time. The wind licked at her toes and howled in her ears. *Where is that wind coming from?* There was nothing but darkness as black as pitch above her, below her, all around her. The void was the most terrifying thing she had ever seen.

"You're doing good, Sid. Keep going."

"Oh, shut up."

She lengthened her stride. The boards beneath her feet began to creak. *Morning Glory.* She took another step. *Morning Glory.* And another. *Morning Glory.* She thought of her mother's mother. 'Morning Glory' was the harshest thing Nanna Nancy ever said. Even though she'd been widowed at a young age, she had great patience with everything she did. *Her heart probably wouldn't skip a beat if she were on this bridge.* Sidney turned on her tiny engine and continued forward. *Morning Glory. Morning Glory. Morning Glory.*

Squawk!

Sid froze. "What in the hell was that?"

"A Night Bird," Smoke said.

She peered around. "That's not funny."

"Just keep going."

She did, but with ears honing in on the strange rustling that came from all around and on the scattered flaps of tiny wings. She summoned her inner strength. She'd closed at least half the distance to the other side, where an archway awaited, lit by torches. *Screw it.* She picked up the pace. The rope bridge jostled and twisted.

"Slow down," Smoke warned. "It's sensitive to our movements. Cat's feet, just like before."

Sidney felt exactly what he was talking about. The ripple effect moved up and came back stronger, pitching the bridge from side to side. Anything too rushed would twist the ropes right over. "Okay," she said in a hushed voice. "Okay. But we better find a shovel, 'cause I'm digging my ass back out of here."

She made it five more steps. Ten. Twenty.

Squawk!

The black sea surrounding them came to life.

Squawk! Squawk! Squawk!

Sid envisioned ancient winged predators darting down, plucking her off the bridge, and dropping her into the hungry black gorge, where gnashing teeth waited. *Keep going. Keep going!*

"Ignore it, Sid. Just go." Smoke said.

Something zipped overhead, clipping her skull. On instinct, she swung. The bridge buckled hard to the left. She lost her footing and started to fall. *Nooooo!*

CHAPTER 33

DANGLING OVER THE BRIDGE WITH just fingers locked on the ropes, she hung on for her life. *This is bad. Really bad.*

Squawk! Squawk!

Barely able to make out what she was holding onto, she climbed back on the swinging bridge and lay belly down. Huffing for breath, she said, "Smoke? Are you back there?"

No answer.

Oh no! Oh no!

"I'm here. Just be still, will you?" he said in a strained voice.

Slowly, she managed to look back over her shoulder. *Oh no!* Smoke held onto the lower rope of the bridge with one hand. "Hang on, Smoke. I'm coming."

"The thought had occurred to me," he said, "but don't you move. Stay flat and wide. It keeps the bridge stabilized."

"Okay."

Smoke began a gentle swing, swaying the entire bridge, and with a heave he latched his other hand onto the ropes. He pulled himself back up onto the bridge and said, "Let's get moving again."

"What about those bats?"

"Those aren't bats. Bats don't squawk."

"What are they?"

"Just go," he urged.

"Fine, but I'm crawling," she said.

"Suit yourself."

"Did you just drop a line on me from Moonraker?"

"Huh," he said, "I suppose I did. But really, you should get going."

Another stony screech erupted, followed by a burst of flapping wings.

Squawk!

She crawled onward and said, "You know what those things are, don't you."

Silence.

"Don't you."

"Yes."

"And?" she said, digging her hands between the planks.

"You don't need to worry unless you see the yellow glow in their eyes."

"Yellow glow?"

"Yes."

Something landed on the bridge, jostling the entire thing.

"Sid," Smoke said.

"What?"

"Run."

"I thought you said to go slow," she said, checking behind her. Smoke had his back to her. He was eyeing something else on the bridge. It was a small figure, little more than two feet tall, with burning yellow eyes, claws, and black wings. Her neck hairs stood on end. "Never mind."

"Run!" Smoke said again.

Up on her feet, Sid stretched her long legs out in full stride and raced to the other side. The bridge bounced, buckled, and swayed. She surged on, pulling at the ropes, closing on the glimmering torches. Something zipped overhead. Claws scraped over her ducking skull. She cried out. "Ow!"

"Go!" Smoke said. "Go!"

Almost there! Almost there! She wanted to get off the bridge more than anything. Her hands raced along the rope railing, steadying her balance.

Squawk!

A little gargoyle-like creature landed on the end of the bridge, barring her path. Another one landed on its shoulders. They grabbed the bridge ropes and started shaking them.

Sidney didn't know which was a worse fate: facing the grey-skinned fiends with burning-yellow eyes or being pitched into everlasting darkness. *Screw you, little monsters!* She lowered her shoulder that last ten steps, let out a cry, and charged. "Eee-Yaaaaaaaah!"

She plowed into the gargoyles, toppled them over, and spilled off the bridge onto the landing. She rose to her feet, shaking her head, and raised her fists up to fight. "Come on, whatever the hell you are!"

Smoke emerged off the bridge fighting two creatures that were latched onto his legs and arms. He ripped one off and stomped on its chest. He squeezed another by the neck and held it at arm's length. Its taloned fingers tore at his arms in an angry frenzy. He punched it in the face. "Ow!" He flicked his hand and flung it off him.

Sid searched for a weapon. They had left theirs on the other side to cross the bridge.

Squawk!

A creature landed on her back and dug its fingers into her neck. She grabbed its arm and slammed it hard into the rocky ground. She kicked it in the face, skipping it across the ground. "What are these things?"

"Gargoyles," Smoke said, ripping another monster from his leg. "Can't you tell?" He hurled it into the abyss, only to see it fly back and attack him again. "Argh!"

"How do you kill them?" she said, peeling another fiend from her waist. The gargoyles were strong for their size. Strong like animals and hard like stone.

"With a hammer. Preferably a big one."

"I don't have a hammer!" she said. She kicked and swatted at the two gargoyles that squawked and hissed at her. "Got any other ideas?"

Smoke held a gargoyle by the feet and started smashing it into the cave floor. The little monster started to chip and bust. *Wham! Wham! Wham!* It crumbled to dust.

"Good one," Sid said. She launched a kick at one, missing it. Another gargoyle latched onto her arm. She tried to shake it off. Punched it in the face. "Ow!" She shook her stinging hand. The other monster locked onto her free hand and let out a screech to the other. Their wings fluttered with new life and Sidney felt herself being lifted into the air. *Oh snap!* The gargoyles flew straight for the abyss. "Smoke!"

CHAPTER 34

FEET KICKING, SHE CRIED OUT again. "Smoke!"

The ranging man's head snapped up. He took two tremendous strides, jumped up, and locked his fingers on her ankles. The gargoyles shrieked. Their wings beat with fury, pulling them both toward the abyss.

Sidney's arms and legs groaned under the strain. Muscle and sinew popped. "You're ripping me apart!"

Smoke's toes dragged across the ground. He bunched up and heaved. The gargoyles faltered. Their efforts sagged. They let go.

Smoke landed on his feet and caught Sidney in his arms. "Are you all—"

She slipped out of his arms, let out a growl, and plucked the nearest gargoyle out of the air. She slammed it face-first into the ground and stomped her bloody foot on its back. Pinning it to the ground, she reached down, grabbed its wings, and tore them off its back.

It let out an ear-splitting shriek.

She tossed the wings aside and stuffed its face in the ground. "Shut up!" She grabbed it by the legs and slung it far into the abyss, listening to its fading horrified cry.

"Eeeeeeeeeeeeeeeeeeeeee!"

"Almost makes you think they have feelings," Smoke said. He pinned another gargoyle to the ground. "I like the way you think." He tore its wings off. *Riiiip!* Casually, he flung it away. "I think that's the last of them."

"For now," Sidney said, peering into the black chasm. She wiped away the blood that dripped into her eye. Ran her fingers over the gash in her head. *That feels nasty.*

"Let me take a look," Smoke said, easing up to her. He had deep scratches all over his hands and face. He examined it. "It'll clot."

"Gee, thanks."

"Did you want me to kiss it for you?"

She leered at him. *Yes.* "Shut up." She moved by him and stared at the door between the burning torches. It was a solid-steel door, modern by the looks of it, sitting just behind an archway cut from large stones. "That's a big door."

Smoke knocked on it with his knuckles. It made a hollow sound. *Bong. Bong. Bong.* "Makes you wonder if it's supposed to keep things in or out. Open sesame."

"Please don't." She placed her hands on her knees and caught her breath. Her lungs burned, and her body ached. She licked her dry lips. She'd worked out hard, but nothing had ever pushed her like this. "Are you sure this isn't Hell?"

"Hell isn't this much fun." Smoke rapped on the door again. "I want a peanut butter sandwich." He knocked again. "Kazam. Shazam." He spread his arms wide. "I am Batman!"

Sidney still struggled for her breath.

Smoke tilted his ear toward her. "Are you wheezing?"

"No," she wheezed. "Okay, yes?"

"You have asthma?"

"Yes, but I haven't-*wheeze*-had an attack in years." She practiced some deep breathing she'd been taught long ago. "I'll be all right, just give me a minute." *Damn. Not now of all times.* It had been so long, she'd almost forgotten the mild suffocation she suffered. It was demoralizing.

"Might be these moldy caves," he said.

"Or all of the life-threatening excitement." She gulped down some air and exhaled through her nose. Sometimes the attack would last for minutes, other times days, even weeks. *Well, at least we're not going anywhere.*

In an instant, the steel door slid upward.

Ssshluuuk!

"You ready, or do you want to wait?" he said.

Sid righted herself and headed for the door. In stride, the pair crossed the threshold at the same time.

Ssshluuuk!

"I guess we're staying," Smoke said.

The stone and mud-walled tunnels were gone, replaced by something far more modern. The dry floor had black-and-white checkered tiles. The walls were painted a medium gray, and fluorescent lighting dangled ten feet overhead. Sid ran her fingers over the wall and pecked her knuckle on it. It was limestone block. She wanted to hug it. "Not nearly as bad as I expected."

"Nope," Smoke said, moving forward. "Gray's still a depressing color though."

"I find its neutral base very soothing." Her breathing came a little easier.

"Well, spend a few weeks in prison, and then tell me what you think."

The corridor burrowed another hundred feet and came to a stop at a pair of double doors. They were yellow heavy safety doors, similar to the ones at her high school. She grabbed the handle and depressed the thumb lever. She eyed Smoke, he nodded, and she shoved it in.

"Welcome," boomed a voice within. "Please, come in."

Inside was an oval room with exits and doors similar to the one she'd just come through. The first thing Sid noticed was the floor. It was an archaic network of multicolor tiles with bloodstains splattered all over them. The musty smell of death lingered, and more corpses, some in dark aged armor, huddled dead along the walls.

There were large windows too. All the walls were cinderblock, and up above glowed gas lights in glass bulbs. There was a terrace, high above them, forming a platform around the room. Mason stood with his great hands on the rail in full minotaur form.

He snorted and shook his horns. "I am surprised you made it, humph!" It was strange how the words came from his bestial lips. "But I'm glad as well. Please, go ahead, take a look around."

"Where's Allison and Megan?" Sid demanded.

"As I said, take a look around."

In the center was a stone staircase that led up to a dais. An automatic pistol sat on the pedestal in the middle, locked in a case of glass. *That's my gun.*

Mason snorted above and paced over the catwalks. He was a monstrous figure, thick in muscles and hide hair. AV and Night Bird were rodents by comparison. His hooved feet made clopping sounds that echoed in the chamber. He held a great machete in his powerful paw.

Sid's breathing started to thin again. *Calm down, girl.*

"Sid," Smoke said, nodding her over. He was peering through one of the glass windows she'd noticed earlier.

"What is it?" she said, walking over. Smoke stepped aside. She gazed through the glass. "Megan!"

CHAPTER 35

S IDNEY POUNDED ON THE GLASS, but it made no sound. The sheet felt thicker than metal. Megan was inside, in a daycare-like facility decorated in fun colors and with tables, TVs, and shelves loaded with toys. She was playing with other children her age. Laughing and smiling along in a pair of pajamas adorned in pink and purple colors.

"Megan!" Sid hit the glass again. "Megan!"

"She can't hear or see you, Agent Shaw. It's a one-way mirror, similar to your interrogation rooms but made with impervious glass," Mason said from somewhere above. "But you can see that she is well cared for."

Sidney stormed to the nearest door. It was sealed tighter than a drum. She kicked it and moved on to the next one. It was the same result. She backed into the middle of the room and found Mason's bison-like eyes. "Where's your trough?" she said.

He cocked his horned head. "Pardon?"

"Your trough! I need to know so I can take a dump in it, you cud-chewing bastard!" She marched toward one of the fallen warriors and picked up a spear. She hurled it straight at Mason.

The minotaur plucked it out of the air and huffed a laugh. "I like your spirit, woman." He snapped the spear in half and tossed it aside. "But you'll need something far more deadly than that."

Smoke slid alongside her with a concerned look in his eyes. She was still wheezing. "Save your breath," he whispered in her ear.

"Please," Mason said, extending his hand. "Continue looking around. Make the most of it. After all, you'll need all the advantages you can get."

Sidney sauntered over to the next glass window. A group of men in a mishmash of uniforms lumbered aimlessly around an empty room. *Deaders!* Each had a bludgeoning weapon in its hand. Some carried two at a time. Bloody feet sticking to the tiles, she shuffled over to the next window. It was a supply room with an assortment of things: fire extinguishers, backpacks, rations, microscopes, other scientific equipment, and five-gallon jugs of water. "See anything useful?" she said to Smoke.

"No."

Her jaw dropped as she peered through the last window. Allison lay back in a salon-type room with cucumbers on her eyes. Two Forever Children in light-colored robes were in the room. One, a girl with frosty blonde hair, was giving Allison a manicure while the other one, a straw-headed boy, massaged her feet. Allison's creaseless expression was pure bliss. *She would be comfortable in this devil's pit.*

"These people really have a screwed-up way of doing things," Smoke said.

"Who are you calling people?" Sid marched out into the room, looked up at Mason, and said, "So, what's your game?"

"You kill me," Mason said, drumming his fingers on the rail, "or beat me into submission, humph, and you can all go free. Pretty simple."

She stepped onto the dais and eyed the gun encased in glass. There was a heavy padlock on it. "And this is the only thing we can kill you with?"

Mason lifted his monstrous shoulders up and down and said, "In theory." He stroked the coarse fibers of animal hair under his chin. "The key is in one of those rooms that you've seen. All you have to do is get the key and the gun before I get you. But be careful. In my labyrinth, not all is as it appears to be." He shifted over toward a great lever that jutted out from the wall behind him and laid his hand on it. "Ready?"

Smoke hustled over to the vanquished bodies lying along the walls. He plucked out a sabre and a bayonet. "Gear up," he said, tossing her the bayonet.

The bull-faced man brought the lever down a notch. There were sounds of metal moving against metal. *Clunk! Clunk! Clunk!* The chamber Sid stood in started to spin. She backed toward Smoke. "How come you gave me this and not that?" she said, eyeing Smoke's sword.

"Ever use a sword before?"

"No."

"A bayonet's much easier to learn."

Above, Mason ran his fingertips along his rack of black horns. "I'm going to enjoy this." He reached for the lever again and pulled it down. "Go."

All of the doors slid open, but because the room was spinning, all of them were blocked.

Mason laughed, "Humph! Humph! Humph!" In a single bound, he leapt over the rail and landed down inside the chamber, making a thunderous sound. Towering at eight feet tall, he spread out his muscular arms that were as thick as tree trunks. "If you only understood how much I enjoy this." He scraped his hooved foot over the tiles and lowered his head. "Goodbye now!" He charged.

Smoke took Sid by the arm and jerked her into one of the portals just as it opened. Eyes fixed on the minotaur, she watched it slide to a halt and rear up just as the portal closed. It was laughing. "Humph—Humph—Humph—Humph—" The sound was cut off.

"Are you finished standing around?" Smoke said, tugging her deeper into the limestone-block tunnel. It was wide and tall, an ideal fit for something as big as a minotaur. "Come on."

Sid hurried along on legs of jelly. The raw power of Mason rattled her. Suspended her thoughts and action in time. She shook her head. "I'm fine now, sorry."

They crisscrossed. Zigzagged. Doubled back. The minotaur man hadn't lied. It indeed was a labyrinth. A maddening one. As they ran along a curved wall, a door appeared on their right. Sid could only assume it was one of the rooms they'd already seen, but she was too disoriented to know which one.

Smoke pressed his ear to the door. "I can't hear a thing." He grabbed the door handle. "Are you ready?"

Brandishing her bayonet and wheezing, she said, "Yes."

He shoved the door inward. It was the colorful daycare room, but it was completely empty. A dark feeling sunk into Sid. *Lies! Nothing but lies!*

"Let's go," Smoke said.

Clop! Clop! Clop!

"I can smell you," Mason's grizzly voice said. "That means I can find you as easily as my fingers in front of my face. Humph."

"I've got a finger for you!" she yelled back.

Mason stepped into full view only twenty feet away from where they stood. "Do you now?" He lowered his horns and charged.

Sid was fast. Smoke was fast too, but the minotaur was faster. Sprinting, it closed the gap with great, powerful strides. They ducked into the next turn and weaved through the labyrinth. Mason thundered behind them. Sid's lungs burned. Her energy was fading. Smoke was pulling her along. She'd run marathons. Won ribbons in track. But all of her accolades and efforts were negated. "Go," she wheezed. She tried to peel Smoke's hand away. "Just go."

He came to a stop and said, "I don't think either one of us is going anywhere." He stared at the wall that closed off the corridor in front of them. "Dead end."

Clop! Clop! Clop! Clop! Clop!

CHAPTER 36

"I LIKE TO CALL IT 'DEAD MAN'S END,'" Mason said, blocking their only avenue of escape. He took a great snort. "I can still smell the blood. Can you see it?"

Crushed bones and tattered clothes were on the floor. Bloodstains graced the walls.

Slowly, the minotaur closed in, toying with the tips of his horns. "When I stick it to the good guys, I stick it to them good."

Smoke rushed in with his sabre high in the air and delivered a devastating chop.

Mason caught the blade in his hand and ripped it free from Smoke's grip. The monster clobbered Smoke in the chest with his fist, sending him staggering backward into the wall. Mason took the sword, bent its blade, and tossed it aside with a rattle of steel. "So young. So futile. So stupid." He cracked his knuckles and scraped his hoof over the floor.

Sid sagged, fighting for breath.

Slumped over, Smoke clutched at his chest.

She'd never seen the big man down like that before. Mason's punch was like a sledgehammer. She reached over and grabbed the cuff of Smoke's pants then glared up at Mason the Minotaur. "Do your worst," she said, shielding herself and Smoke with the bayonet.

"Humph. I plan to." He came forward, hooves thumping on the ground. A smirk formed on his bestial face. "Goodbye, Agent Shaw." He raised his hoof.

A spark ignited inside Sid's belly and spread. Her breathing eased. Time seemed to stop. Everything moved in slow motion. *What is happening?* A spring of limitless energy coursed through her body. Aches and pains disappeared. She felt like lightning in a bottle. And it was time to come out. She sprang like a gazelle. Jammed the bayonet in the monster's eye.

"Aaaaargh!" he said, clutching his face. He unleashed a wild swing.

Sid ducked under it. Smoke rushed into the minotaur, toppling it over and bounding along his side. Eyes as big as moons and smiling just as wide, Smoke said, "I feel awesome."

"The key!" Sid said. She sprinted off, feeling like the fleetest of deer. Her memory was crystal clear. Her focus razor sharp. She knew every twist and every turn of the labyrinth. Old memories and overlooked evidence from long-forgotten cases popped up inside her thoughts. *Oh my. I think I missed something back when. Poor bastard.* She weaved through the maze until she found another door. Breathing just fine, she said to Smoke, "Ready?"

"Oh, yeah!"

She swung the door open. It was the supply room. The pair of them rushed inside and rummaged through the goods. They opened boxes and crates. Tore through the shelves. Scoured through tables with beakers, microscopes, boxes of slides, and tuning forks. It looked more like a classroom than anything else. "Find anything?"

"No."

"Mah-rooooo!" The sound echoed down the halls.

Sidney stopped. "Sounds like beastie boy is angry."

"Yep, I don't think he liked the contact you gave him."

She laughed. She felt fearless. Invincible. *Whatever this is, I love it!* "Nothing in here. We need to move on."

"I think you're right." Smoke snapped his fingers. "I know where it is."

"You do?"

Smoke's lips curled as he said it. "The deader room."

A memory flashed inside Sid's mind. One of the deaders had on a necklace with a key on it. "Clever. Oh well, let's do it."

Clop! Clop! Clop!

Smoke slammed the door shut.

"What are you doing?"

"I have an idea." He gathered himself in front of the mirrored window.

Taking her place beside him, she said, "I think I know what you're thinking."

Horns first, Mason crashed in the door with one hand holding his eye. "See what you did? See what you did?"

"I thought you said it would heal," Sid said.

Smoke held his gut, pointed, and laughed like Bugs Bunny. "What a maroon!"

Mason perked up. "What!" He removed his hand. His eye was fine. "It did heal, you fools!" He charged, plowing straight through the tables.

At the last possible moment, Sid jumped left, and Smoke jumped right.

Mason's rack of horns shattered the thick glass into hundreds of crystals. His huge body became wedged between the walls and the spinning room.

Smoke huffed a laugh. "I can't believe that worked."

Mason's feet stomped at the floor. He roared on the other side.

Sidney and Smoke were on the move again. She followed the maze through the last paths she'd not yet taken. It took five minutes, and they were at their destination. The deader room.

"Do you think this is it?" Smoke said, taking the door handle in his hand. "Or somewhere else."

"Hey, it can't be any worse than that minotaur." She bounced on her toes. "Let's go for it."

"All right then, ladies first?"

"Said like a true gentleman."

Smoke shoved the door in. The dry stench of rotting flesh slapped them in the face. Sidney darted into the fray of decaying men. She ducked, dived, and disarmed. Every move the deaders made was in slow motion. She was on high speed. She stole a sword from one and impaled another. "And you thought I couldn't use a sword."

Smoke waded through the throng, letting loose skull-crushing blows with his club. "That one," he said. *Whack! Whop! Whack!*

Sid spied the one that he talked about, ducked under a chop, and skewered it through the chest. She jumped over the swinging blow of another and landed in front of the one with the key on its neck. With a lightning-quick swing, she severed its head. She grabbed the key from the body as the head tumbled to the floor, telling it, "Thank you." Back at Smoke, she yelled, "Let's go!"

Smoke pummeled through the broken bones and flesh for them, clearing a path to the door. Seven minutes and sixteen seconds later, they were standing back just outside the main chamber. The portal was only a quarter open. She and Smoke had to squeeze through.

Clap! Clap! Clap!

Still wedged inside the room and chamber, Mason continued to bring his oversized paws together. He stopped and said, "I have to admit. This has been one of the more entertaining challenges in my lifetime."

Sid ran up to the dais where the gun was displayed and took hold of the lock. She tried to jam the key in it, but it didn't fit. "Damn!" All of her strength and energy fled as quickly as it had come, and down on the floor she went.

Mason laughed. "Humph—Humph—Humph. Such a priceless expression. I wish I had my camera." Using his powerful back and hands, he pushed the entire chamber, freeing up his body, and stepped into the room. "Humph! Now it's time for you to play dead, forever."

CHAPTER 37

SIDNEY HUDDLED UNDERNEATH THE GUN pedestal. With all of the strength that she had left, she shoved the glass case off the stand. It bounced off the stone and landed at her feet, intact.

"It seems you found the wrong key," Mason said, marching straight for her. Smoke climbed onto his back.

The minotaur slung him off like a ragdoll. "Too bad for you. But I am curious what got into the both of you. I think a dissection will be in order. Maybe you'll be alive, just paralyzed while it's happening. Humph."

The super vitamin had worn off, leaving her completely exhausted, but Sid's spirits didn't dim. "I'll be just fine, but you'll always be an evil bastard."

He glowered at her. "Humph."

"Hey, pack mule," Smoke said, chiming in. He held a silver object up in his hand. A tuning fork. "Maybe this is the key you were talking about." He tossed the fork to Sid.

Mason's eyes became bigger than moons watching the object tumble through the air.

Sid snatched it and rapped it on the stone. The tuning fork wavered with life. She touched it to the glass case. It shattered.

"No!" Mason said, rearing up on his haunches.

In one fluid motion, Sid scooped up the gun, charged the slide, and took aim. "Yes."

Blam! Blam! Blam! Blam! Blam! Blam! Blam! Clik!

Mason stood tall as a statue with a grim smile on his face. He dusted the lead from his chest and watched it clatter to the floor. "Nice shooting."

"You cheated. Those weren't red-tipped bullets."

"And you believed me? Humph. Don't you know evil always lies?"

In a sudden move, Mason snatched Smoke up in his arms and bear hugged him. His mighty arms knotted up and Smoke's face turned purple. He started to gag. "Now listen, woman. Listen to the sound that makes your friend's spine snap."

"You mean you aren't going to gore him?" she said in a listless tone, trying to buy time.

"No, I'm going to gore you."

"I thought you were going to dissect me."

"Fool of a woman," Mason snorted. "You'll both be dead soon enough."

"Sid." Smoke somehow managed to croak out the word. "Catch!" He spat something from his mouth.

It was a bullet with a red tip on it. She snagged it from the air and loaded it into the weapon.

Mason cocked his horned head. "Eh, what trickery is this?"

Sid rose up and took aim between Mason's eyes. "Bye bye, Big Horns." *Blam!*

The minotaur's arms flung wide, dropping a gasping Smoke to the floor.

"Impossible!" Mason roared.

Boom!

Shards of bone, horn, and bull brain showered the room. There was nothing left of Mason above the shoulders.

Sid wiped the muck off her face and took a seat. Smoke crawled up alongside her. "Bye bye, Big Horns?"

She leaned against his shoulder. "What would you have said?"

"Actually, I think that's pretty good. Now we just have to figure out how to get our bounty out of here."

"Did you regurgitate a bullet?"

He showed a faint smile. "Sometimes I do strange things."

"Sometimes?"

The sound of metal grinding on metal brought the spinning room to a halt. Dee was standing by the lever, and another dozen men in pea coats had weapons pointed at them.

"For the first time in my life, I'm speechless." Her eyes locked on Sid's. "You're one helluva troop. The both of you."

"And now?" Sid fired back.

"And now, to my dismay, I'm going to let you go."

Leaning against the elevator wall, Sid allowed herself to breathe. She had never been fond of elevators, but this was the best ride she'd ever taken. It came to a stop, the doors split open, and prompted by Dee, who had a gun on her, Sid walked outside into a barn-like structure. She inhaled the air and rubbed her nose.

"Let's move along," Dee said. She poked the gun into Sid's back. "Quickly, before I change my mind."

"What about the body?" Smoke said to Dee. "There's a bounty I want to collect."

"If someone wants the body, they're more than welcome to come here and get it."

"Why, is the Drake going to blow another place up?" Smoke added.

"Well, maybe they'll just blow you up," Dee fired back. "I suggest you quit while you're ahead."

They made it outside of the barn and found the log cabin waiting under the moonlight. Allison and Megan were on the porch. Allison was kneeling down in front of her daughter, who was shaking her head and crying.

"What's going on?" Sid said, taking a step forward. A wall of guards shoved her back.

"Give it a moment, Sid," Dee said in her ear. "Not everyone wants to leave the Drake."

Allison hugged her daughter, took a quick glance Sidney's way, and hustled back inside the cabin.

"No! Allison!" Sid started to run for the porch.

Dee punched her in the ribs. "I said behave. Your little niece needs you now. Alive. Not dead. Stay away from the Black Slate, kid. Stay away for both your sakes."

EPILOGUE

T WO DAYS LATER, BACK AT FBI headquarters, Chief Howard's office.

"Sid." Ted stood up behind his desk and waved her over. "Please come in. Sit."

Cyrus remained seated in his chair and gave her a nod. "Uh, fascinating report." Sweat glistened on his balding head and upper lip. "Can I get you a drink? Some water perhaps?"

"No."

"Will you have a seat then?"

Eyes forward, she remained standing with her hands behind her back. "Where's Smoke?"

"Given the circumstances and in concern for his own safety, he's been relocated to an undisclosed location."

Her nails dug into her palms. The FBI had whisked him away within an hour after Sid contacted them.

"What's the matter?" Cyrus said, toying with his tie. "Didn't get a good-bye kiss?"

Ted stretched out his hand. "Cyrus, that's enough. She's your responsibility, you know."

The frosty man shrugged.

"Ted," she said, "when did you become such a putz?"

"Now, let's not get all insubordinate. I've warned you before. This time I'll write you up." He loosened his tie. "Will you sit down?" He eyed her. "Fine. Sid, the Black Slate, well, *they* want to move on. And they want me to talk to you about your next assignment. Given your situation with your niece, I think you'll like it. A forty-hour week supervising the range and armories and assisting the ballistics teams." He smacked the top of his desk. "It'll get your life back to normal."

She looked up, shook her head, and said, "You're such a putz."

Ted's cheeks reddened.

Cyrus jumped up from his chair. "That's it. I'm writing you up."

She glared into Cyrus's eyes and backed him down into his chair. "Go ahead." She tossed her badge and gun onto Ted's desk. "I resign."

CRAIG HALLORAN

THE SUPERNATURAL
BOUNTY
HUNTER
FILES

SMOKE ON THE WATER
BOOK 4

CHAPTER 1

A PPROACHING HER STAND AT A public outdoor firing range, Sidney donned her headset. There were signs everywhere: "Hearing Protection Required Beyond This Point." There were rules. She knew them all by heart. She took a deep breath through her nose. The smell of black powder and roasted brass awakened old military memories.

It was morning, warm and hazy. She wore sporty gym wear, black mixed with neon green. She set a soft leather duffle bag on her stand and unloaded her gear. Ten boxes of 40-caliber ammo, each box fifty rounds. *This will be fun.*

She pulled out her Glock 22. It wasn't the one the FBI had issued her. It was her own, a backup. She swung another bag up onto the table, beige and marked with a red Ruger stamp. From inside, she pulled out a small, short-barreled assault rifle with bipod legs built in. It was called a Charger. It had a built-in laser sight and a grey, camo-wood finish. She pulled out a box full of 22-caliber ammunition, a thousand bullets in all. *And this will be even more fun.*

Four magazines for the Glock 22 were already loaded. A typical Glock 22 held fifteen rounds. She had two that held thirty. The Ruger Charger held thirty as well. She slapped the magazine in and checked the sights. Down range, at forty yards, were barrels loaded with sand. At close range, fifteen yards, were metal silhouettes mounted in the ground.

"That's some fine weaponry you have there, young lady."

Sidney glanced back over her shoulder. It was an older man, big boned with a frosty mustache. He wore an NRA ball cap and a pair of six-shooters on his hips, nickel plated with pearl handles. Bowlegged in his jeans and wearing a Cabela's sweatshirt, he spoke louder than he needed to.

"Mind if I use this stand?"

Sidney glanced around. The range had more than fifty stands, and fewer than ten people were out there shooting. She shrugged. "Sure."

"I won't be crowding you, will I?" the older man said, lifting a brow. His voice was warm and friendly. "I'm just partial to this area on this side of the range. Eh, my name's Jake. They call me Big Jake."

"Hi, Big Jake," she said, extending her hand and shaking his. His calloused hand had an iron grip. "I'm Sidney."

"A pleasure, Sidney." He smiled, revealing a gold tooth toward the back. His bottom lip stuck out, and his breath had a minty scent of tobacco. "My, we sure don't see many gals out here. And you're a mite prettier than the last one I saw. She was coyote ugly and couldn't hit a barrel if she stood inside it. Woo! But, judging by her girth, she was a heckuva good cook. Wouldn't be surprised if she didn't have a stick of butter named after her."

He kept going.

Sidney kept laughing. Before she knew it, half an hour had passed, and she knew everything there was to know about who came and went at the range. For some odd reason, she enjoyed every bit of it. The last three months had been rough. Taking care of Megan was a delight, but still a chore. She needed some time to be around adults. Finally, she'd left Megan with her parents for a long weekend. Sally and Keith were about to leave on vacation, and it would do them all good to spend some time together first. It was the first time she'd been separated from her niece since they'd left Allison at the ranch.

"Sorry for talking your ear off, Sid," Jake said, plucking his six-shooter out of his holster. He opened up the cylinder and loaded in the bullets super quick and slapped the cylinder shut. "I don't get to talk to the ladies much since my wife died."

"Aw, I'm sure you get plenty of talking done when the opportunity presents itself."

He let out a Santa-like chuckle. "I sure hope you come around here more often." He loaded up his other pistol, holstered it, and squared up on his target. He turned his ball cap around and checked his earplugs. "Sid, this is where I like to show off a little. Watch this."

"Oh, you've got my attention." She leaned back against her stand and checked her headset. "Go for it."

Standing like a big ape, stooped over with his thick wrists hanging to his knees, Jake twitched his fingers and narrowed his eyes. His target was twenty yards away. It was a row of six small metal bull's eyes the size of fists. With uncanny speed, Jake eased one of his six-shot revolvers out of the holster. Two handed, he blasted away.

Blam! Blam! Blam! Blam! Blam! Blam!

Lead smacked into metal, making sharp plinking sounds. The bull's eyes spun around and around and steadied again.

"Woo hoo!" Jake twirled the gun on his finger before stuffing it into the holster. "Didn't miss a one!"

Smiling, Sidney clapped her hands. "That was awesome, Jake."

He pulled out the other loaded revolver and held it toward her butt first. "Care to give it a try?"

"Sure," she said with a shrug, "why not?" She took it from his grasp.

"It's heavy compared to that polymer thing you carry, so keep a firm grip on it. That forty-five will kick." He pressed his hands into her back and lined her up in front of the targets. A father helping a daughter. "Now listen. It's got a hair trigger. Put that in myself. It'll get away on you if you ain't careful." He gave her a little pat on the hip and eased away. "Show me what you got, girl."

Sidney pointed the heavy weapon toward the ground, closed her eyes, eased her breathing, and visualized herself shooting the targets. She loved the range. The smell. The muffled sounds of shots being fired. The wispy scent of gun barrel smoke. *Show this old fart what you got.*

Simultaneously, she opened her eyes, raised the gun, took aim, and squeezed the trigger.

Blam! Blam! Blam! Blam! Blam! Blam!

There was no triumphant sound of lead hitting metal, only six fresh holes in the dirt.

"Morning glory," she said, lowering the weapon with a frown.

Jake chuckled. "I told you. A big gun like that takes some getting used to." He took the gun. "Next time, take your time between your shots. You would have hit the other five if you'd taken enough time to think about it."

Shame on me!

CHAPTER 2

SIDNEY SPENT THE REST OF the day sharpening her aim. Hot and sweaty, she'd stripped down to a grey cotton T-shirt with a dragon logo on it. Taking command of the Ruger Charger, she emptied another magazine on the metal diadem 100 yards down the range.

"That's better," she muttered under her breath. Mopping the sweat from her brow, she reached over and upturned the box of .22 long rifle rounds. It was empty. She checked her duffle bag, fishing around inside. No ammo was left. With a sigh, she got out her cleaning kit and started breaking down her weapons. *At least I got my shot back. I hope.*

She ran a cleaning square into the barrel. Feeling disgraced by the lack of control she'd had with Big Jake's weapon, she hadn't stopped shooting until she'd gotten her edge back. It had taken a few magazines with her own weapon before she was back on the mark again. It ate her up. She'd been a crack shot since the first time she fired a weapon. She'd never before lost her touch once. She'd only lain off a few months, and she shouldn't have been off that much.

"Wrapping it up, I see," Big Jake said as he walked by. He'd been working the range all day, speaking with plenty of older hands. He seemed to make a point of knowing everyone. "I'm guessing you have things under control again?"

"I'm pretty sure." She ran the cleaning rod out of the barrel and checked the grimy square. "Thanks for the advice."

Drumming his fingers on the pommels of his guns he said, "Care to try it again?"

"No, I'm good, Jake. Certain of it."

"I know you are," he said. "Say, where'd you learn to shoot like that, anyway?"

"My father. The military. The fact that I love it."

Jake sauntered over and took a seat by her stand. He took his hat off and ran the back of his arm over his bushy brows. "Always feels hotter on the range than it is." He looked her dead in the eye. "You've seen some real shit, haven't you."

"What do you mean?" she said, wiping down the small rifle.

"I can see it in your eyes, Sid. They're pretty, but hard as iron." He huffed a little laugh. "When you missed those targets with my pistol, I thought your head was going to explode. That look. It was dismay. And then suddenly, a light went on behind those pretty eyes, bright as a furnace. You set that little jaw and started getting it on."

"These bullets don't shoot themselves."

"Heh!" He slapped his knee. "I suppose not!" His face reddened, and he started coughing. He tapped his chest with his fist. "Pardon me. Felt like I swallowed a butterfly. Anyway, what is it you do, if you don't mind me asking?"

"I used to be a cop."

"And what are you now?"

"Just between jobs."

Big Jake narrowed one of his eyes on her. "You aren't one of those mercenaries, are you?"

"What? No, why?"

"Eh, well—"

A very loud gunshot rang out. *Pow!*

Sid's head jerked up. "Geez! Was that a fifty cal?"

"Yep," Jake said, turning his head over his shoulder.

Two men on the far left end of the range were hunkered down over their .50 caliber rifles. They wore black ball caps and black T-shirts stretched over their muscles.

Pow! Two hundred yards down range, a canister of yellow paint exploded.

"Those two punks have been coming down here for weeks, blowing the crap out of everything. They're weird. Almost spooky." Jake spit juice on the ground. "They rub everyone the wrong way. Pushy types. You know. They talk, but it's like they see right through you."

Sid squinted her eyes. The pair of dusky-skinned men with slicked-back hair reloaded the monster bullets into their guns, speaking little. They were big men, like professional wrestlers. The one who wore mirrored sunglasses that looked small on his head glanced her way. He rolled a toothpick from one side of his mouth to the other and smiled. They had tattoos and triangle-shaped earrings in their ears. The other twisted his long neck around, revealing his cold, dead eyes. He sneered and turned away.

"Weird and ugly, ain't they," Jake said.

"Nothing surprises me these days," she said, wiping down her weapon and placing it in her satchel. She kept her eyes fixed on the men. They were different. The way they moved. Sat. Stretched. Talked. It raised the hair on her arms. "I think I might go say hello."

"What? Why?"

Sidney didn't say. She wanted a closer look. She needed to look for the mark. A black sun rising. The sign of the Drake. It ate at her. Every time she went out, she'd notice a little something she hadn't before the Black Slate. She had a new awareness. The way people spoke and dressed made all the difference. The weird signs on doors and even the slogans she read. Somehow, some way, there seemed to be subliminal messages that were tied to the Drake, or maybe to an even darker evil. "I'll be right back."

"Hold on now, Sidney. Uh," Jake looked over his shoulder. "I'm about as tough as they come, but those guys make even me a bit nervous. I did two tours in Vietnam, you know. Got a Purple Heart to show for it."

"I'll be fine." She glanced at the guns on his hips and gave him a wink. "Just keep those peacemakers ready in case things get a little hairy."

"Fine, just stay out of my line of sight."

Sid slung her jacket over her shoulder and headed down the range. Both men caught her coming their way. Both of them twisted around in their seats and faced her.

The one with the mirrored glasses spoke up. He had a heavy inner-city accent. "Something we can do for you, Miss?"

"I just wanted to get a closer look at those big cannons."

The stockier, bald one crossed his meaty arms over his chest. "Is that so? I think you need to move along, lady."

The other sniffed the air. "I smell cop. You a cop?"

"No," Sidney said. "Just a gun enthusiast." She eyed the weapons.

The first man, in the glasses, stood up, blocking her view. He was tall and rangy like Smoke.

"Awfully big for this range. You guys military?" she said, looking at the triangle earring in his ear.

"We're rabbit hunters," said the one sitting down. He slipped a buck knife out of the sheath on his waist and shaved a few hairs off his forearm. "I like to skin them. Cook them. Eat them."

"I don't imagine there's anything left once you shoot them with that," she said.

"Oh, I don't shoot them. I sneak up on them." He showed his calloused hands grasping in the air. "Catch 'em and squeeze them until they snap." He made a breaking motion. "I've killed lots of them like that."

Sidney's stomach soured. The man wasn't talking about rabbits. He was a killer. Both of them were. Hard-eyed, compassionless men. She ran her eyes up and down their arms and over their necks, feigning fear and fascination. No black suns. Mostly snakes, skulls, sharp blades, and guns. She started to back away.

"Where you going, little lady?" the first one said, tilting his head to the side and coming closer. "Don't you want to hear more about our rabbit hunts?"

The second man slid in behind her. "Yeah, why don't you come with?" he bumped up against her.

"Watch it!" she said. She tried to move around them, but the pair of them hemmed her in. Her cheeks flushed. "Move it."

"Or what, sweetie?" said the one with the long neck. He cornered her against the stand. His eyes were like a hungry predator's. Hypnotic like a snake's. Paralyzing her limbs.

Her knees weakened. "Go, go away," she said, trying to tear her eyes away from the long-necked man.

"You're coming with us, honey," he said.

Her shoulders sagged and her mouth dropped open. Heart pounding, she said, "Okay."

CHAPTER 3

"**B**OY!" JAKE SAID, STICKING HIS gun barrel against the long-necked man's ear. "You might want to step back, unless you want a ravine in your head."

The man who had cornered Sid froze and slowly lifted his arms. "That would be foolish, old man. And I'm unarmed."

"Don't give a damn." Jake pulled the gun's hammer back. "Get the hell away from the lady."

The man slipped to the side of the one in mirrored glasses and lowered his arms. "Just having a little fun with your daughter. She shouldn't be so nosey." He flicked his nose with his thumb and narrowed his eyes. "And you, foolish old one, shouldn't be so, heh, bold. You don't know who you're dealing with."

"I know your kind. Seen my share of men with venom in their eyes." He glared at them both. "My gut's telling me I outta shoot you both down where you stand." He stuffed his pistol back inside his holster. "Damn me for letting you live. Come on, Sid."

On instinct, she took his hand. Her eyes widened. She took a deep breath and followed him back down the range without looking back. Behind her, she heard the two huge men laughing. She swallowed. She'd lost herself to them somehow. Their hypnotic stares had sapped her will. Much like it had been with the wolf man, Adam Vaughan. "Thanks."

"You all right?" Jake said, helping her to a seat. "I hate to say this, but I saw your lights go out. You don't have a medical condition, do you?"

She rubbed her temples. "No, no." She couldn't shrug off the horrible feeling she had inside. She started stuffing her guns into her duffle bag. "Thanks, Jake, but I've got to go."

"Let me get you a beer. Settle your nerves." He looked beyond her shoulder. "Besides, those grease balls are moving out. Probably drug dealers." He hitched his thumbs in his belt. "I'm gonna have a few words with the owner about guys like that. Their kind seem to be coming around more often."

She slung her bag over her shoulder. "I'm fine. Don't do anything on my account. I'm a big girl. Nice meeting you, Jake."

Back inside the Dodge Hellcat and roaring down the road, her nerves began to settle. She wanted distance between her and the men at the range. The abnormal men. Long-faced and fluid. Smooth. Crass. Seductive. *This is exactly what Allison fell for.*

When it came to men with power, her sister was a moth to a flame. The Drake probably didn't have to promise her too much to get her to stay. A nice place to live and a line of credit. Allison would be all over it. Those were Sidney's first thoughts about her sister. She hated herself for it. *Shame on me.*

Allison wasn't without a heart. Not entirely. She loved her daughter, but she was weak. Still, Sid held out some hope that maybe, just maybe, Allison had done what she did to save her and Megan. Any loving mother would do that for her child. And a loving sister would do that for her sibling, too. It was that part that Sid struggled with. After all the years of bailing Allison out, had Allison made a sacrifice that bailed Sid out?

"Crap!" She banged on the steering wheel. "I don't know."

For the last three months, she'd put all her energy into Megan. She put the FBI behind her, even though they still called. She blew off Sam and Guppy whenever they reached out. Mal Gunderson had sent her a box, wanting his gear back. She'd been happy to oblige. And Smoke ... she did her best to forget about the man. His handsome façade and odd musings. It angered her that he'd come into her life only to be gone again.

She eased off the highway and pulled into the first gas station. She exited the vehicle and scanned her card. Pumping the gas, she leaned against her car and sighed. She noticed a couple police officers coming out of the convenience store. They were loaded up with sodas and hotdogs. They were smiling and laughing, too. She grimaced.

I miss Sadie.

She'd been blowing off her best friend. Her excuse was that Ted and Cyrus wouldn't want them communicating. The truth was, Sadie had called and texted numerous times. She'd even gotten pretty ugly about it when Sid fired back a bunch of canned excuses. Sid thumbed through her phone and read the last text Sadie had sent.

It read, "You see! This is why you're going to die single!"

Laughing, Sid took the nozzle out of her gas tank and placed it on the rack. Seconds later, she was driving down the road again, trying to sort everything out inside her head. Keeping Megan around kept her distracted from other things. The news. The job. The lies. With the girl gone to her grandparents' house, Sid's thoughts raced through everything that had gone on. It was driving her crazy. She didn't like not being able to carry a gun like she used to. She felt naked without it. Her concealed carry permit still hadn't been approved. *I should move to Texas.*

Her phone rang. Her mother's picture popped up.

"Hey, Mom. How are things going?"

"Hey Aunt Sidney," Megan said.

"Oh, hey, Megan. How are *you* doing?"

"Well, Grandma and Grandpa keep taking me to places that smell really old." Megan sighed. "And I'm getting tired of biscuits and gravy every morning. And smelling like bacon. They always eat bacon." She kept rambling on another ten minutes. Finally, she said, "When are you picking me up? I miss you."

The words crushed Sid's heart. It had only been a couple days, but Sid felt guilty. *How do parents do this?* She had decided to sacrifice everything for Megan, but not having a steady paycheck was starting to take its toll. At some point, she needed to find a job somewhere doing something. But she wasn't going to just take anything. "Can you hang in there until tomorrow?"

"Morning?"

"Come on, Grandma and Grandpa aren't that bad."

"They're boring. Nice, but you know, boring. And my bedtime is way too early."

"All right, no promises, but I'll try to be there by morning. Okay?"

"Okay. Bye."

The line went dead.

Sidney shook her head. *How long can I keep this up?*

CHAPTER 4

THE FOLLOWING MONDAY MORNING, SALLY and Keith had left on their vacation and Sidney was back inside her apartment getting Megan ready for school. The little girl sat at the kitchen table, eating cereal. She had a yellow bow in her hair and wore a khaki skirt and a white Oxford dress shirt. "I like cereal, so long as it doesn't taste like bacon," Megan said.

"You need to finish up and get the rest of your lunch packed," Sid said. She signed off on Megan's homework and stuffed the notebook in the girl's backpack. That was the thing she liked about the private school she'd enrolled Megan in: They ran a tight ship. And the school uniform made her life a lot easier than picking out different clothes. She could relate to the uniform. "And don't forget your milk."

"I won't," Megan said. She loaded a milk box, a juice box, chips, and a cheese sandwich into her lunchbox. "Can I take a chewy granola bar? I get hungry."

"Sure." Sid slung Megan's little backpack over her shoulder. "Let's go."

The drive to school took about ten minutes. There were two teachers, a man and a woman, standing outside at the student drop-off.

Sid waved at them.

They waved back.

"Aunt Sid," Megan said, "are you going to look for a job today?"

"Uh, I don't know, why?"

"Well, you need something to do. You can't just wait around on me all the time."

Sidney caressed Megan's face, looked her in the eye, and said, "I like doing this."

"I like it too, but…" Megan's voice trailed off.

"But what?"

"But you've got to be you." Megan popped the door open and hopped out. "See you later." She slammed the door shut and ran into the school.

After Megan made her way inside, Sidney pulled away. *What did she mean by that?*

Sid jogged around the Lincoln Memorial Reflecting Pool. It was one of her routines while Megan was in school. Jog. Work out. She was as fit as she'd ever been. And the time between that and when Megan got out of school was torture. She'd read the paper. Skim the news. She'd picked up reading books again. Fiction. Biographies. Maybe go home and watch some old shows on Netflix. She tried to avoid anything that made her think of the Drake or the Black Slate. Huffing for breath, clothes clinging to her body in sweat, she kneeled down and tightened her shoelaces. She walked over to a bench and sat down.

The DC campus was beautiful, but there was darkness hiding in the shadows of the magnificent architecture.

Washington, DC. Home of the greatest truths and the greatest lies.

That's what Smoke said. It had all been so very true. Sidney had learned the hard way that nothing in the world was as it seemed. More than she ever imagined was saturated with evil. Good men and women died for no reason because of it. People were careless in how they lived their lives. She couldn't be that way. She wanted to keep herself and Megan away from those shadows. They had taken her sister. They could take anything.

Never underestimate evil.

She rubbed out the tightness in her calf muscles, watching other joggers and walkers make their way around the great pool. It was midmorning, and the sun warmed her face. People loaded down with strollers and fanny packs took pictures. Some moved at a brisk pace, others with more leisure, noses stuck in their smartphones. Every one of them seemed lost to her.

Just a bunch of people wandering around waiting for someone to tell them what to do.

She got up, ran in place a bit, and took off around the reflecting pool. She picked up the pace, made one more lap, and then fast walked back to her car. There was a small newspaper pinned under her wiper blade. She didn't see any on the other cars parked nearby. She removed it. It was the size of a tabloid, only a few pages, similar to a college newspaper. She unfolded it, exposing the front. It was a copy of *Nightfall DC*. Her fingertips tingled as she scanned the area.

Grumbling, she spread the paper out on the hood of her car and started to read. There weren't any pictures, just bolded headlines.

Missing Girl. Strange Lights in the Park. Senator Howser, Man or Alien? Muggers in Fur Coats. Loch Ness Monster in Mallows Bay. Man Shot Ten Times and Walks Away.

She skimmed through them. The stories were bizarre. Odd. And clearly designed for the gullible. Her eyes froze on the next headline that she read.

Vietnam Vet Murdered. *"Jake Miller, known to his neighbors as Big Jake, was found dead inside his apartment, having been shot with his own revolver."*

She gasped.

CHAPTER 5

Russ Davenport's home was on wheels, with no engine. The old trailer was long and weather beaten, with a railed ramp leading up to the front door.

Sid shut off her engine, checked the surroundings at the trailer park ten miles west of DC, and exited the car. With that edition of *Nightfall DC* crushed in her hand, she stormed up the ramp and pounded on the door.

"Geez!" a rugged voice said inside. A glass bottle fell and rattled on the floor. "Aw, great!"

Sid pounded on the door again.

"Who is it?" said the man on the other side.

"It's Sidney Shaw."

Things got quiet for a moment. Then the familiar voice of Russ spoke up. "What do you want?"

"Answers."

"Ever hear of a game called Jeopardy? Give that a try," he said.

"Russ, are you going to open the door or not?"

"Eh." The door handle started to turn and the door swung open. Russ sat in a wheelchair on the other side of the threshold. He wore a Washington Senators jersey. A sawed-off shotgun rested back against his shoulder. "I don't like visitors."

Sid stepped inside and tossed the copy of *Nightfall DC* into his lap. "This isn't a social call."

Russ wiped a little bit of drool from his mouth and rubbed his eyes. The husky man backed his wheelchair toward a small table and picked up some glasses. He put them on, studied the paper, and grunted. "So, what do you want? It's my rag. So what?"

"Why'd you stick it on my car?" she said, noting all the newspaper clippings hanging on all his walls. The wood-paneled place was musty but organized. A computer was hooked up to three monitors, and a flat-screen television was on in the tiny living room. The trailer was plenty big for a single person. "Or did you have one of your reporters do it?"

"It's nice to see you too, Agent Shaw," he said. "You could at least ask how I'm doing, seeing how I'm back from the brink of death."

"Looks like you're doing fine. You even have new wheels. Good for you."

"You're cold."

She stepped closer and glared down at him. "I'm angry."

"I didn't put this on your car. And even if I did, why are you so bent out of shape about it? It's got nothing to do with you. Just more of my imaginary rubbish." He folded the paper up and set it aside. "What happened? One of the articles cut too close to some FBI informants?"

She eased back, shuffled some papers over on his couch, and sat down. "What happened?" she said more softly.

"With what?"

"The wheelchair. Why are you on wheels?"

"Oh, *now* you ask." He rolled his eyes. "Well, ever since I got shot, I have moments. I lose feeling in my extremities from time to time. It's scary. Sometimes it lasts a few hours. Other times, for days. Doctors can't figure it out." His eyes became sad. "I woke up this morning and couldn't move them at all. It's like I'm cursed or something."

"Sorry to hear that, but at least you're alive."

"Yeah, well, it's not much for living. If it keeps up, I'm going to have to give up on *Nightfall DC*." He wheeled toward the refrigerator. "Want a drink? I have cold beer and Gatorade."

She made a stop gesture and shook her head no.

"Suit yourself." He found a bottled beer and twisted the cap off. He flicked it with his thumb across the room into the trashcan. "I never miss." He grabbed a prescription bottle, took out a large white pill, flicked it into his mouth, and washed it down with beer.

"I didn't think you were supposed to take medicine with alcohol," she said. She'd noted the label already. It was a narcotic for pain. "And I thought you didn't feel anything."

"Sure, from the waist down. But this wound in my chest still hurts like hell." He took another drink. "You've seen action. You telling me you don't have aches and pains? Surely you've got monster scratches on you."

She did. Her scars and bruised bones would ache in the cold. Her knees would ache if she sat too long. Sometimes tiny, painful needles raced up and down her neck and arms. "So you still believe in monsters?"

"I know you've seen them. That's good enough for me. There've been others, too. That look in their eye when I asked them questions and heard their stories. I know the truth when I hear it." He wheeled closer and eyed her. "What brings you to me?"

"The Big Jake Miller story," she said.

"Oh." Russ nodded his round, scruffy face. "You knew him?"

"I met him, and I think I know who killed him."

Russ's eyes shone like moons. "You don't think I did it, do you? Are you investigating me?"

"No."

"Is this one of your cases?"

"No," she said. "I don't work for the FBI anymore."

He cocked his head. "You're serious."

"I resigned."

Russ smiled.

"What?" she said.

"I know you did. I just wanted to see if you'd admit it to me."

"I'm not very fond of games, Russ."

"Me neither. Since you're being up front with me, now I'm going to be up front with you." He reached back and found the local newspaper. "Your friend Big Jake. Huh. He wasn't the only one dead. The truth is, I was too scared to report all that I found, and anyway, the cops did a pretty good job covering up the rest."

"What do you mean?"

"Big Jake was shot with his own gun." He winced. "Poor guy was in the middle of a *Matlock* marathon, too. And that ain't all." He opened the paper up to the crime section and jabbed at it with his meaty finger. "In that same area, a woman was killed with a knife and another man was run clean over. Dead. Those were witnesses." He eyed her. "How come you think you know who did it?"

She told him the story about the two goons at the range.

Russ's face turned pale.

"What is it?" she said to him.

"I've heard about those guys before. They call them the Buffalo Brothers Assassins, and they say they can't be killed."

CHAPTER 6

"WHERE DO YOU COME UP with this stuff?" Sid said. "I've never come across any files dealing with any Buffalo Brothers. And why would they take out Jake?" She hit the arm of the plaid sofa. "Damn!"

"He probably shouldn't have stuck a gun in their face. Guys like that, they don't take threats lightly." He wheeled his chair back and eased his way in front of his computer. He started typing. "Sounds like they were making a point."

"If they can't be killed, why worry?" Her nostrils flared. Her face got flushed. Were the Buffalo Brothers the ones that had put the paper on her window? "Sickos!"

"My guess is they wanted you to know about it. Look, Agent, er, well, Sidney—that all right?"

"Yes."

"Seems to me they wanted you to know about it. Or somebody did for some reason." He eyed his screens. "Huh, this is interesting. Seems Big Jake had quite a unique history."

"What do you mean?"

"He was an ex-cop that worked a lot of strange cases. Looks like they made him retire early." He clicked through some more articles. "Yup. The top brass didn't like him. Hmmm, now that I think about it, his name's pretty familiar. When I started my rag ten years ago, he was one of the few that would talk. Not much, but better than nothing." He pulled up a picture of Jake, younger. Clean shaven and in uniform. "That's him. Now I remember what he said. I quoted it in one of my papers. He said, 'Monsters pull the strings, not men.' Huh." He rubbed his lip. "I burned my lip with my coffee when he said that one."

"That was the last time you saw him?"

"Yep. Of course, I was pretty self-absorbed back then. I moved on. He retired. He had an edge about him, though. I wouldn't be surprised if ol' Jake knew something. Or made some enemies. They decided to take him out."

"When you say *they*, who does that mean, to you?" Sid asked.

"Oh, well, you have the Black Slate. The Drake. The Hierarchy Enslaving

You. Probably several more they go by." He plunked away on the keyboard. "Who do you think *they* are?"

"The same, I guess." Sid's fingers drummed on the sofa arm. Were the Buffalo Brothers coming for her, or were they satisfied having gotten Jake? Who had put the paper on her car? It all seemed so convenient. It didn't help that she felt like someone was watching her all the time, either. The people she passed. The cameras in the streets and stores. They controlled all of them. "How do you know about the Buffalo Brothers?"

"Huh. It's another one of those dirty little DC secrets. That pair's been killing people around here for years. They're assassins. Hit men. It was the weird earrings, sunglasses, and the one's long neck that gave it away. When they show up, death follows." He guzzled down some of his beer. "Yep, real spooky. And they take out criminals mostly. Rats. People no one even cares about. The faces that don't make the papers. I think they're part of the Drake's cleanup crew, to be frank. Those monsters that leave tracks in the blood they spilled. They need looking after, too." He shook his head. "I sure hate to see someone go like that. Seems Big Jake was one of us."

"Us?"

"Yeah, us. People who aren't scared to shine the light on evil."

Sid nodded. "Tell me more."

"There was this one fella, worked the door in town at one of the strip clubs. Well, he said there was a scuffle in the alley. Said he saw a guy in sunglasses take a few gunshots at point-blank range and walk away." Russ finished off his beer. "The guy doing the shooting survived because the guy he shot vanished just as police arrived. The bouncer said it was lucky, because he saw murder in that assassin's eyes. The bouncer said that look scared the piss out of him. And he was a big dude."

"Maybe he wore a vest," Sid suggested.

"Well, that's one account. There was another club, the Night Ranger, where I met a pair of gals who'd stumbled on a murder victim. A guy was stabbed to death. No one saw anything." Russ turned toward Sid and leaned forward. "After the detectives left, I asked if they noticed anyone standing out in the crowd. They mentioned those guys. The weird earrings and glasses. Their eyes haunting them. One gal said she blacked out just from looking at him. 'Hypnotic,' she said. 'Evil.'"

Sid's throat tightened. *Those sound like the guys.* "Why do they call them the Buffalo Brothers?"

"Good question. Simply put, they started this stuff in Buffalo, New York. Oh man, I haven't talked about them in a long time. Uh, could you reach behind you? See those ratty books on the shelf?" He pointed. "Grab that one in the top right corner, third book over."

She turned, got up on her knees, reached over, and grabbed the book. "This it?"

"That's the one."

It was a small hardback book with a brown cloth cover. The title read *The Buffalo Murders*, by Jim Johann. She scanned the title page. "This was published in 1955."

Russ tossed his beer bottle in the trash can. "Yep."

Sid leafed through the pages. In the middle were some black-and-white photos of murder scenes. At the end of those pictures were mug shots. Her blood curdled. It was the faces of the two men from the range. "Impossible."

"You don't really believe anything is impossible, do you?" Russ said.

She'd already encountered more than a few corpses that came back to life. It was unsettling. "Says their names are Warren and Oliver Ratson. They were convicted. Went to prison for life and disappeared."

"There's a lot of people that have gone to prison and disappeared. You'd be surprised. Especially back in those days." He rubbed his thighs. "Legs're starting to tingle. That's a good sign. Anyway, the Buffalo Brothers are ghosts. Living and breathing ghosts. But you've seen them for yourself. Now what do you do?"

She thought about Jake Miller. He had been a good man. You took him seriously, but he was warm and friendly. He was the kind of fella that would help you move furniture on a rainy day. "So no one investigates these guys."

"Seems so. Not unless they trifle with someone that really matters."

Sidney got up, still holding the book. "Can I take this?"

"Sure. So what are you thinking about doing?"

"I'm thinking I'm going to find these bastards and take them down."

CHAPTER 7

Driving down the road, Sidney thought to herself, *Who am I kidding?* She had to take care of Megan. That didn't leave her any time to launch her own investigation. But what had happened to Big Jake ate at her. She had to do something. Protecting people. Serving people. It drove her. *Damn my pride!*

She missed being an agent, and it was beginning to catch up with her. She'd had access. Authority. The badge had given her an air of invincibility, and now that was gone. She'd given it up because she'd gotten mad. Because she felt guilty. She'd convinced herself that she couldn't trust her fellow agents anymore. Cruising down the highway, she pulled over into a Wendy's parking lot. She put the car in park, took out her phone, and sent a text.

The text read, "Looking for the Buffalo Brothers."

Her thumb hung over the phone. She was about to dig into something that she might not be able to finish. But those men! The arrogant sneers on their faces riled her. They had a dangerous air about them. Same as all the other monsters she'd encountered.

Morning glory, think about what you're doing, Sid.

Somewhere in her heart, she knew that she and Megan were safe so long as she didn't go nosing around. That was the deal she suspected Allison had made with the Drake. It was a cop-out, too, but a sacrifice nonetheless. But if Sid moved out of that lane, trouble might quickly find them. She held her breath.

I have to do the right thing. I have to be me.

She pressed send. The text went out to Phat Sam and Guppy. Sid let out her breath. She figured they'd probably changed their numbers anyway. She gave it a few moments. Nothing happened. Probably for the better. She put the car in drive, eased on the gas. The engine rumbled, and the muscle machine surged ahead to the thrill of a few gawkers that showed a thumbs up as she passed by. She smiled.

Maybe I should come here more often.

While she was merging onto the highway, her phone buzzed. There was an emoticon with an excited mouth wide open.

The message read. "Never heard of them. Doing research. Very interesting. We're in. Meet at Smoke's. Tonight."

At the stoplight she texted back. "No, tomorrow."

"No," Sam's text read. "Tonight. Bring Megan. We have plenty of ice cream."

Morning glory! I was afraid of that.

"Where are we going, Aunt Sid?" Megan asked.

They were heading down the highway after finishing up homework and dinner at Sid's apartment. She'd chewed one of her nails off contemplating what to do. She needed to get back in the action. But it killed her to think she might be putting Megan in danger.

"We're going to go see Sam and Guppy. Remember them?"

"Oh, that really pretty lady. Yay, I like her. She's funny." Megan checked her nails. "Do you think she'll give me another manicure?"

"I'm sure she'd love to."

"Good," Megan said. Her face had brightened. "I love getting my nails done. BTW, it looks like you need yours done, too." The little girl, now eleven years old, always carried some sadness within her.

Sid felt guilty. She couldn't keep Megan isolated all the time. They needed to get out. Be around people. It was finding people you could trust that was hard. Sam and Guppy could be trusted.

"I know."

"So, are you going to be doing cop stuff again? I hope so." Megan straightened the bow on a purple stuffed bear with burnt-orange plastic eyes. "I know you miss it. You can't just sit around on your butt and babysit me all the time."

"Megan!"

"Well, it's true. Listen, Aunt Sid, I know I'm only in the fifth grade, but I'm reading at a twelfth-grade level. And I've always been able to take care of myself. Not that I don't need you. I do. But you can't stop living your life because of me."

Sid's mouth dropped open. Recovering, she said, "You're starting to sound like your grandmother Sally."

Megan slapped her head.

Sidney laughed. Megan was a little adult. She had been since she was five. A lot of that came from taking care of her mother. Sid reached over and brushed her hand over Megan's soft hair. "You're something else."

"I know."

"Look, Megan. What I did before was dangerous, and I don't want to dive back into that. If something happens to me, who's going to look after you? It's not worth it."

"Nothing's going to happen to you, Aunt Sid. Besides, at some point you're going to have to go get my mother. That's what heroes do, right?"

Sidney sank behind the steering wheel. Her eyes started to water. Of course

Megan would expect her to go get her mother. Why shouldn't Megan expect her to save her own sister?

"Besides," Megan said, "most of the time, Mom doesn't know what's best for her."

"Well," said Sid, swallowing the lump in her throat. "I wish it could be easy."

"Haven't you been looking for her this whole time? Like when I'm in school?"

Lord, I'm a fool! How do I explain this? Megan was staring at her with her round pretty eyes. The young girl deserved an honest answer. "Megan, the people your mother is with are very dangerous. If I go after her and get too close, they'll come after us. I can't risk losing you again. Do you understand that?"

Sadly, Megan nodded her little chin and curled up into her seat. She hugged her bear tight to her chest.

"Megan, do you trust me?"

"Yes," the girl said, still looking away.

Sid took a deep breath. "Then I promise I'll find your mom, my sister. But you have to be patient."

Megan's face brightened. "Okay. Thanks, Aunt Sid."

It's going to be hard to find someone that doesn't want to be found. And they'll be waiting for it. "You're welcome."

CHAPTER 8

S MOKE'S GAS-STATION APARTMENT HADN'T CHANGED a bit since the last time she had been in there. The room was warm, and there was a lingering sent of oil in the air. Even after only being there a few times, Sid felt at home there.

"This place is cool," Megan said, gazing up at an old *King Kong* movie poster on the wall.

Sam shook Sid's hand. The gorgeous older woman was casually dressed in Buckle jeans and a snug designer T-shirt with a sequined design. She gave Megan a hug. "How about some ice cream while we get those nails of yours done?"

Megan clapped her hands and bounced up and down like the kid she was supposed to be. "Yay!"

It made Sid smile before she looked expectantly at Sam.

Sam winked. "Good to see you. Once we finish with this little angel, we're doing you next." She took Megan by the hand. "Come on."

Eyeing the studio apartment, Sid's eyes landed on Guppy. The short, burly man stood up from behind the computers as she approached. He gave her a warm embrace, locking his powerful forearms around her waist. "I was starting to think you weren't going to come around."

"It's not easy staying away. I'll admit that."

"It's in your blood," Guppy said. "It's who you are. It's probably who you've always been."

Nodding her agreement, Sid sat down in the chair beside Guppy. "So, what have the two of you been up to?" She eyed him. "Have you still been bounty hunting?"

"You know we keep our jobs confidential," he said, smoothing his hand over his bald head. "But we've been paying the bills, if that's what you're concerned about."

She wasn't. She wanted to know if they'd seen Smoke, but she wasn't going to ask. She set Russ Davenport's book, *The Buffalo Murders*, on the desk. "Have you dug up anything yet?"

"Maybe. Are you hiring us for a job?"

She leaned back. Her chest tightened. "Well, no. I just thought—"

"I'm teasing you, Sid. You're family to us. You know that. Any friend of Smoke's is a friend of ours." His chestnut eyes locked on hers. He patted her knee. "Till the end."

Relieved, she said, "I don't want to be any trouble. I just ... you know ... this guy, Jake Miller. He's dead. I feel like I'm a part of it somehow. She clenched her fists. "Oh, I don't need to drag you guys into this." She went for the book.

Guppy covered the book with his rugged hand. "Take it easy, Sid. Look, I'm not going to lie to you. We have things going on. That doesn't mean we can't squeeze you in."

Oh man, they're going to blow me off. "Are you shelving me?"

"No, no," he said, picking up the book. "Now you should know better than that. We trust each other, right?"

"A lot can change in a matter of months. For all I know, you have a really cushy gig." She tipped her head toward the window. "I noticed that Porsche Cayenne outside. That looks pretty new. Nice cream color." She started to get up.

"Sid, please sit down and let me finish my thoughts. Geez. I guess I do talk too slow. Either that or all women are impatient. At least to me. Sam really wears me out telling me to spit it out all the time."

"You're rambling now."

He sighed. "Okay, let me spit it out, then. Me and Sam have been talking. We want you in."

"In? What do you mean, in?"

"Become a bounty hunter. Like us. It's got great hours, and you'd be good at it."

Something ignited behind her chest. A spark. A flurry. She liked the idea. "I'm at a loss for words. Uh, how's your dental plan?"

Guppy rumbled a laugh. "And you'd fit right in."

"How do you do what you do and fly under the radar?"

"We have a legit operation that's our cover, and then we do other things as well." He shrugged his heavy shoulders. "We manage."

"I just thought that Smoke—"

"Did all the field work? No, no." He rolled up the sleeve of his plaid shirt. "Dog bite." He exposed his neck and ran his finger down a white scar. "Knife wound. I have many more, but I'm a gentleman. And nothing against Smoke, but he hasn't been around. We don't close shop without him. If I gotta bust heads to get my dough, so be it. "

"I didn't realize you did that. And so does Samantha?"

"Oh yeah. She's the hook and I'm the hammer. Her face works like a stun gun. Men are putty in her hands." Using his hands, Guppy made goggle eyes. "Thugs get that deer-in-the-headlights look." He glanced at Sam, smiling. "Never seen a mortal man that can resist her wiles."

Sid laughed. "You make her sound like one of Charlie's Angels."

"Lord, don't tell her that. The last person that said that to her got punched in the throat." He made a bitter face. "She just hates that show for some reason."

"Okay, I'll think about it. In the meantime, what have you dug up on the Buffalo Brothers?"

Guppy leafed through the pages of the book. He stopped on the mug shots. "Them's some ugly boys. Faces like that shouldn't be too hard to recall." He snapped a picture with his phone and uploaded it to the computer. He pulled the picture up on the monitor and cropped each face out. "I'm going to load this into the facial recognition database. See if we get any bites."

"What facial recognition database?" she asked.

"The taxpayer-funded one," he said, giving her a shifty glance, "that the FBI uses."

"You've hacked into the FBI?"

"Not exactly," he said. "Let's just say we have people on the inside. You know, like you used to be."

Sid's hands turned clammy. "They pick up on everything in there."

"No they don't. Trust me. I've been doing this awhile." He glanced at her. "Should I not have told you that?"

"Hey, Guppy!" Sam shouted across the room. "Stop incriminating yourself!" She started laughing and resumed painting Megan's nails. The little girl had headphones on, and her smile was as wide as the room.

"We'll be fine. He eased back in his chair and rested his hands on his stomach. Now tell me everything about these Buffalo Brothers."

Sid recounted the entire story all the way through her visit with Russ Davenport. "Say," she said, "you guys didn't put a copy of *Nightfall DC* on my windshield did you?"

"No," Guppy said.

"Not me," Sam said from across the room.

She believed them. "All right. So there you have it. Look, these men or whatever they are, they're bad. I want them."

"And if you find them," Guppy said, "what are you going to do with them? So you think they killed your friend, Jake Miller. You need evidence to convict them."

She got up and started to walk the room. "They'll have kept his gun, the one they shot him with. We find them, we find it. I'm sure of it."

"It's pretty thin," Guppy said. "Even if you root them out, you still have the powers that be to deal with. They might not even arrest them."

Sid made her way toward the door that opened into the garage. She put her hand on the knob.

"Sid, come back here. Let's sort through this conversation."

She pushed open the door. Her heart skipped inside her chest. The garage was empty. "Guppy, where's Smoke's Camaro?"

CHAPTER 9

"HOPEFULLY IN THE JUNKYARD," SAM said, averting her eyes.

"Guppy?" Sid said to him. "Any insights?"

The stout man's brow furrowed as he twiddled his thumbs. "We just got here ourselves. We don't know all about the comings and goings of Smoke."

"What do you mean, comings and goings?"

"He's got other people aside from us, you know. Perhaps one of them borrowed it."

Sid crossed her arms over her chest. "One of whom?"

"Uh, them?"

Agitated, Sidney brushed her hair out of her eyes. "Is he out?"

"Can't say if he is or isn't," Guppy replied. He turned back to the computer monitors. "All I can say is I haven't seen him."

Sidney didn't know whether to be mad or happy. She didn't like the thought of Smoke being in prison, but if he was out, he could have contacted her. *Why would he contact me? He doesn't owe me anything.* She sat down on the couch and eyed Guppy. He was hunched over the desk with his back to her. A quick glance over her shoulder, and she saw Sam had her back turned as well. *They know something.*

"He's out and working on the Black Slate, isn't he." She got up and poked Guppy in the meat between his shoulder blades. "Isn't he?"

"I can't say."

"Damn! He is out!" She squeezed Guppy's shoulders. "What's he working on? Tell me."

"I can't say. Look, Sid, we have to keep our mouths zipped. You know that."

"Then why did you bring me here?" she said.

"Well, er, that's more of a coincidence," he said, pulling out of her grip. He ˙ed up at her. "And, well, it wouldn't be our fault if you happened to run into

Seeing how you are a client and potential team member and all."

'l in favor of making Sidney Shaw a team member, say 'Aye'!" Sam blurted

raised an arm.

Guppy raised his hand. "See, you have two out of three. Of course, it has to be unanimous."

"Oh, stop it," Sid said. "I'm not in the mood for games." She huffed. "And I don't guess it's any of my business anyway."

"Yeah, but you miss him," Sam said. "Or else you wouldn't have come here. We miss him, too, you know. But we haven't seen him. That's word." She squeezed Megan's cheek. "So cute."

"Look," Guppy said. "He hits us up. We feed him. You know the routine. It's all pretty down-low unless he calls us." He cleared his throat. "He could be in prison somewhere for all I know. The truth is, we get odd requests from him all the time."

"What was his last request?"

"I can't tell you that," Guppy said. "Not unless you're a team member."

"Quit being silly; there is no team." She rubbed her forehead. She wanted to leave, but Megan was having such a good time. She looked happier than Sid had seen her in weeks. And there was always a lingering warmth about Smoke's place. It was like a cozy cabin in the woods. "There's just you two, covering for Smoke."

"Somebody's getting awfully frosty over there," Sam said. "I better put a sweater on if this keeps up."

"Oh, be quiet," Sid said. "Geez, can I make some coffee or something?"

"Oh, let me," Guppy said, jumping out of his chair. "I'll love making fresh brew."

Sam resumed her seat on the couch and sank in. Before long, the strong aroma of coffee drifted into her nostrils. Sam was quiet, but Guppy rumbled an old hymn of some sort under his breath. Considering her options, Sid decided to hang out for a while. She hadn't had much adult company in weeks. *Why not?*

"Here you go," Guppy said, handing her a ceramic mug with a handle on it. "You take it black, right?"

"The blacker the better." She took a sip. "Good. Very good."

Guppy eased in behind her. "This is one of the best parts of being a bounty hunter, enjoying some joe until all the action starts. The truth is, we've been pretty bored. I mean, we've been working the routine stuff with bail bondsmen, but not the, you know, supernatural stuff."

They all spent the next hour talking about black suns, the Drake, and the Black Slate. Even though Sidney wasn't really supposed to talk about the confidential information, she didn't care. She wasn't an agent anymore. She filled them in on what she and Smoke had seen. The Minotaur and the gargoyles. Sam especially hung on every word while Megan watched a kids' movie on the television with the headphones on.

"You really saw a minotaur?" Sam said, filing Sid's nails. "I mean, bull's head and everything?"

"Horns too," Sid smiled. All this talk got her juices flowing. That was one thing about Smoke. They had that bond. All the things they'd seen together. She loved talking about it with him. And for some strange reason, she enjoyed watching him eat, too. "But those gargoyles were some weird little things."

Sam grabbed her by the shoulder of her shirt and said, "I want to see those gargoyles! Man, Smoke didn't tell us anything!"

"Didn't tell you anything when?"

"Well, you know, whenever." Sam started filing Sid's nails really fast. "Don't be so paranoid. Smoke never tells us as much as he should. He's tight lipped about a lot of things."

"So are you," Sid said. "The both of you." She pulled her hand away. "Look, this is a bad idea."

"Ooh, you are testy," Sam said. She snatched Sid's hand back. "Now let me finish this."

"No. Megan!" Sid yelled. "Come on, let's go."

Megan took off her headphones. "What?"

"I said it's time to go."

"Aw, but I want to stay. Just a little longer," the girl pleaded. "Please?"

"Yeah, Please?" Sam said. "We haven't even had ice cream yet."

"No, we're going." Sid finished off her coffee, got up, and took the Buffalo book off the table. "Thanks for the coffee, Gilmore. And thanks for doing Megan's nails, Samantha."

"But," Samantha started to speak.

But Guppy held her off with his hand. The roughhewn man stood up. "We're here if you ever need us, Sid."

"Hey, what's that mean?" Megan said, pointing at one of the computer screens.

It was flashing red.

Guppy rushed over and squinted his eyes, then said, "I'll be. We got a hit on the Buffalo Brothers already."

CHAPTER 10

S IDNEY CRUISED DOWN THE ROAD. Guppy was buckled into the passenger, seat eyeing the dashboard of her Hellcat.

"You picked a fine machine," he said. "What's the fastest you've taken her up to?"

"One-fortyish," she said, cracking a smile. She felt good, being on the road, tracking some thugs down. It felt so good that she felt a little guilty leaving Megan behind with Sam. But the girl and woman hit if off great. She didn't want to ruin Megan's evening. Her niece deserved a little pampering and ice cream once in a while. Sid put her foot down on the gas. It pinned her and Guppy to their seats. They blasted by a pair of tractor trailers.

"Like that?"

"Love it," he said, eyeing the speedometer. "Man, one-twenty in a flash. I like it." He unzipped a leather pistol case on his lap. Inside was a pair of .45 caliber semiautomatic pistols. They were stainless steel 1911's. He charged the slides on both of them. "The boys haven't been out to play in a while."

"Interesting hardware," she said. "Are those Detonics Combat Masters?"

"Boy, you sure know your guns, girl."

"Yes, well, uh, those are pretty old school."

"Well, I'm pretty old. But I hated school." He laughed. "So, hotshot, what's your plan if we find these guys? You gonna take them down and haul them in to the judge? Or maybe we just gun them down, like Matt Dillon."

"I'd like that, but I'm not sure. I'll think of something when I get there."

He leaned back in his seat. "Really? I took you for a planner."

"We'll see what happens when we get there."

"Works for me."

They cruised back toward DC, got off the highway a couple miles outside the heart, and parked the Hellcat at a small shopping plaza. The mall's best days had been over decades ago, and the blacktop had cracks sprouting grass. Most of the yellow markers for parking spaces had faded away.

"Huh," Guppy said. "I haven't been down here since I was a teenager. Boy, half the places look closed."

"Well, it *is* after hours," she said, tucking her key inside the pocket of her jeans and opening the door. "But I smell danger."

"Huh-huh," Guppy said, closing his door. "I hate to say it, but I hope you're right."

There were cars spread out all over the parking lot. Small crowds gathered here and there in little tailgate parties. Many of the cars were souped up. Men and women sat in their cars' seats, doors open and engines revving. There was loud music pumping and beer bottles being sucked on, and the smell of weed was in the air.

A young woman approached. She had a dark complexion, ratty black hair, and smoky olive eyes. Her lip was pinned with rings. She smelled like she had just rinsed off in bong water. "Nice wheels, lady friend. Nice wheels. Hellcat. Woo. You got to enter. Got to enter." She held out her hand. "Take a look around. I'll keep an eye on it for you." She winked. "A real close eye."

"Sure," Sid said. "I'll set you up when I get back."

"No, I need something now."

Sid stepped on the girl's toe and got right in her face. "You be here when I come back later, and I'll take you for a spin, understand?"

The girl grimaced. "All right. All right. Tough lady friend. I like."

Sid eased off her foot. "See you soon." She and Guppy walked off.

"You sure have a way with people." He chuckled.

"Funny." Sid looked at all the loiterers. "Makes me wonder if any cops ever come around." She started to stroll through the parking lot with Guppy at her side. No one paid them any mind. It gave her a feeling that she was in a bad postapocalyptic movie. A scene from *Escape from New York*, perhaps. She glanced at the lampposts above. Most were out, and the lights flickered on some of them. Looking up at the cameras mounted on the posts, Sid said to Guppy, "Is that where you think you got your hit?"

"I'd say so," Guppy said, rubbing his short beard. "Eh, let's take a look around. All this funny smoke is making me feel a little lightheaded."

"You're worried about that? I didn't realize your bounty hunter department did drug testing. I might not be eligible."

"You! Really?"

"I'm not an agent anymore, you know."

Guppy stopped and looked at her. "Pah, you're just kidding. Right?"

"Come on." They walked the sidewalk, passing several stores. Most were still in business. Others had realtor signs in them. Sid stopped in front of a pair of glass doors with a realtor sign hung inside. "Drake Real Estate. No wonder this place stinks."

"You can say that again." Guppy scratched his back. "Just looking at those people makes me feel like something's crawling all over me."

"Let's keep walking," she said, rubbing her arms. As she walked, her keen eyes sorted through the crowd. If this was Drake property, then there was no telling what sort of fiends were running loose out there. The sound of revving engines caught her ears. Really loud exhaust notes were blasting across the lot. The people started heading toward the sound. "I guess it's time to see what this racing is all about."

Easing in with the throng of hoodlums, they made their way to the main strip of road that circled the mall. Sid checked her phone. It was ten past eleven, and she didn't have any messages. She didn't see any signs of the Buffalo Brothers, either. The closer they got to the action, the louder the exhaust notes became. She fought the urge to cover her ears. Beside her, Guppy said something that the engines cut off. "What?"

"I said, let's get a closer look!" He took the lead and pushed his stocky frame through the crowd until they made it onto the curb running along the main street. "This outta do."

Flames burst from the tailpipe of a lightning-black truck. It had four doors and giant off-road wheels and was lifted an extra foot off the ground. The plate said, "So Long."

"Ford F250," she and Guppy said at the same time. "Wish I could see who was driving," she said. She grabbed a frail young man in a dark-grey sweatshirt. "Give me the story here."

"One lap around the mall. The straight stretch here gets nasty. Those dudes in that black hulk got lots of nitrous. They usually win. But maybe not tonight."

The crowd started to cheer as another car with dim lights pulled alongside the black truck and revved up the engine. It was a primer-grey Camaro. Smoke's car.

CHAPTER 11

A JOLT OF ELECTRICITY WENT THROUGH Sid. "It can't be."

"It is. It is," the dude said. "That's Grey Racer. People been talking about this race all week long. No one's beat the Black Hulk, and no one's beat Grey Racer. They've never faced off before." He pulled out a wad of cash and squeezed it between his dirty fingernails. "Wanna make a bet? If not, I got to hustle."

Sid turned her back on the frail little creep. "Come on," she said to Guppy.

"Where?"

"To get a closer look." Keeping herself out of sight, she marched up through the crowd to the two revving vehicles just as the Black Hulk smoked all four tires. She covered her nose. Through the stinky mist, she noticed the passenger hanging his arm out the window. He stuck his head out and started screaming and waving his arm up and down. The crowd squalled with glee. "Idiots."

Suddenly, the hood of the Camaro floated up. The back wheels spun. The engine roared.

Sid coughed. *That's enough of this.*

The truck revved up again.

Sid turned and found herself looking at the man in the truck's cabin.

A pretty girl in high heels and little else was standing next to the truck, talking to him through the window.

Sid grabbed Guppy by the sleeve. "It's them."

"I'll be," he said, fanning the smoke from his eyes. "I don't suppose this is a coincidence."

It was them, the Buffalo Brothers. Both men had an air of superiority about them. They yucked it up with the girls that scurried around their windows. Now standing on Smoke's passenger side, Sid noted many other women fawning all over his car and blowing him kisses. His windows were closed, and the glass was tinted. She couldn't tell if it was him in there or not. "I'll be back."

"No, Sid!" Guppy yelled out after her.

She slipped away from his reaching hand and snuck up to the Camaro's side. Two girls blocked the passenger-side door. "Move."

"Yeah, right," one said, chewing a mouthful of gum. The other had her nose down inside her phone.

Sid shoved them both out of the way and popped the door open. Leaning inside, her eyes widened at the sight of the passenger. It was the little blonde, Agent Rebecca Lang, in a burgundy miniskirt. That rookie data analyst Cyrus Tweel had been dating. "What are you doing in here?"

"Me?!" the younger woman said. "I'm on a case. Now *you* need to go before you blow my cover!"

Crammed in the driver's seat and strapped in was a man wearing a navy-blue driver's suit. A gunmetal-grey helmet covered his head. He flipped up the mirrored visor. "Hey, Sid. How've you been?"

Blood charging, Sidney roared, "Get out, Rebecca!"

"I'm not getting out. Hey! Get off my seatbelt!"

Sid fumbled with the clasps on the harness that was like what you saw in racing cars. "Get out!"

"You are assaulting a federal officer, you retiree!" Rebecca squealed, swatting at Sid's hands. "Go away, or I'll press charges!"

"Sid," Smoke said. "Go. I'm on a gig." He motioned to the front.

A woman with a long white scarf and even longer white hair stepped out between the cars and raised her arms.

Smoke revved the engine. "It's racing time."

Sid glared deep into his dark eyes. "We're going to talk when this is over."

"No," Rebecca said defiantly, "you won't."

"We'll see, you little ferret." Sid backed out.

Rebecca slammed the door shut.

The crowd erupted in cheers just as the woman with the scarf dropped her arms. Powerful engines unleashed throaty roars. Wheels spun. Rubber burned. Everyone was left standing in the smoke as the two cars sped away.

Shoulders sagging and chest heaving, Sid watched the cars disappear around the first bend. *What is she doing here?!* Scanning the crowd, which was now on the move, she saw no sign of Guppy. Instead, her eyes met up with a pair of frosty eyes.

Her ex-fiancé was storming her way. "What in the hell are you doing here?" he asked her, his jowls jiggling and his glasses fogging up.

She looked him up and down. He wore some torn-up jeans over sandals, a dingy grey sweatshirt, a camo ball cap, and glasses that had clearly been designed for birth control. "I love racing. You know that."

"Get your ass out of here, Sid!" He was gritting his teeth and obviously fighting the urge to yell, knowing that a scene would blow his pathetic attempt at being under cover.

"Are you and Rebecca working the Black Slate?" Sid asked, sweetly feigning friendliness.

"You need to shut your hole," he said, glancing around. "That's an order."

"I don't work for you anymore, Cyrus. I'm free to be anywhere I want."

"Look, I don't know how you wound up here, but you are interfering with a federal investigation." Looking around, he was fighting even harder to keep his voice down. His arm shook when he pointed back toward the highway. "You need to get the hell out of here. Now!"

"I don't have to do anything." She tilted her head and smiled her sweetest smile. She would have batted her eyelashes if she thought he would have noticed.

"You are endangering us. Not to mention yourself." When Cyrus saw that line of reasoning wasn't getting him anywhere, he adjusted his ball cap and tried another tactic. "Of course, I'm not surprised that you and Mr. Smoke managed to hook up again. You know, he was under strict orders not to work with anyone on the outside. Especially you. And now you show up? Heh, he's not going to get out again anytime soon. He blew it."

"Wait a minute," she argued. "I didn't have any idea he was here, and I haven't seen or heard from him since before I left."

"Sure, Sid. Sure. I should have known he was sneaking in a little something on the side." He started away. "Look at you, giving booty calls to criminals."

She balled up her fist.

"Oh, seems I hit a little close to home," Cyrus said. He looked so sure of himself now that he could see he was getting to her. It made her even madder. "Go ahead," he said, "Take a shot if it makes you feel better. That way, I can take both of you out with one stone." He shook his head. "Man, Sid, you're such a disappointment."

"Are you friggin' kidding me? This is how you act?" She poked him in the chest. "I'm not a liar, and you know that. I'm here because those goons in that truck killed my friend."

Cyrus eyed her. "What friend?"

"Jake Miller."

Cyrus's brows lifted. Rubbing his chest, he said, "Huh, even Smoke didn't know about that. Look, I'll give you a pass, but you need to stay away from this case. Far away. I mean it, Sid."

"Well, I can't."

"Why?"

"Because I've been hired to bring those murderers in."

"Oh really, you're a bounty hunter now?" He laughed. "Who hired you?"

"Me."

A clamor rose up from the crowd. The grey Camaro screeched around the corner. The black truck was on its tail. One man was hanging outside the truck's window, aiming a gun. The sharp pop of gunfire rang out above the roaring engines.

"They're shooting!" Sid said, going for her gun.

A man running by said, "Anything goes! Anything goes! It's only lap one of the Death Race."

CHAPTER 12

WEAVING IN AND OUT OF the onlookers, Sid sprinted for her car. Clearing the massive gathering of crazed people clamoring to get closer to the gunshots, she made a bead for the Hellcat.

The young woman from earlier was standing on Sid's hood, whooping it up with her arm. She wasn't alone, either. A small horde of miscreants surrounded the car. They saw Sid coming and showed some tough looks on their faces.

"Get away from my car!" Sid yelled.

The woman on the hood waggled her finger. "You got to take us for a ride first. You promised. But we'll make it easy on you. Just give us the keys, and we'll do it for you." She opened up her palm. "Hand them over, and we won't hurt—"

Sid whipped out her Glock, took aim, and fired. *Pop!*

"Eek!" The woman screamed, clutching her ear. "I felt that. Shit! I felt that."

The horde scattered. The woman jumped off the hood, started to run, stumbled, and fell. She looked up at Sid. "You're crazy, lady thing. Crazy." Still clutching her ear, she scrambled up and fled.

Sid got inside her car and fired up the engine.

Cyrus hopped in the passenger side and shut himself inside with Sid. His chest was heaving.

"What are you doing?" Sid said, putting the car into gear. "The FBI doesn't have jurisdiction over my car."

Panting, he pulled out his badge and said, "I'm commandeering your car." *Puff-puff.* "Geez, I forgot how fast you were." He fanned his hand forward. "Go. Just go!" Cyrus mopped his forehead with a grimy and stained white handkerchief.

She stomped on the gas. The Hellcat surged forward, scattering miscreants like a flock of seagulls. She hit the main road, the pseudo-racetrack, and drove the opposite direction of where Smoke was headed. Between her teeth, Sid seethed at Cyrus, "Did you know this was a death race?"

Cyrus shook his head. "No." He buckled up and pulled out his phone. "I'm calling in backup."

"So you're going after the Buffalo Assassins? Why? Are they on the list?"

"You know I'm not saying." He checked his key pad and started dialing.

She smacked his phone out of his hand. "Don't call it in. You'll blow your own cover."

"Like you haven't? You're chasing them."

"I am," she said. "But not you. Just let me handle this." Doing eighty, the tires screeched around on the blacktop.

Ahead, Smoke the Grey Racer was side by side with the Black Hulk.

Sid saw a series of bright muzzle blasts. She locked up the brakes and formed a roadblock on the main drag. "Roll down your window!"

Cyrus was searching for his phone. "What? Why?" He glanced out the window. "Shit, you're going to get us pulverized, Sid! Move! Move!"

"They won't hit us." *I hope.* She pulled out her pistol. "Just shoot at the truck!"

She and Cyrus both started blasting away. The Camaro juked around the front end of the Hellcat. The truck swerved around behind her trunk.

"See?" Sid said, punching the gas and speeding after them.

Cyrus was on his phone again. "The steer is out of the stable! The steer is out of the stable!"

"Really?" she said, letting out a hearty laugh.

He sounded embarrassed when he said, "I didn't make it up."

Ahead, the F250 and the Camaro raced. Suddenly, the truck veered left and plowed over a handful of onlookers who were standing too close to the makeshift racetrack.

"No!" Cyrus cried. "Geez! That was intentional!"

Sid's heart sank. A pit in her stomach formed. "That's what monsters do. Haven't you met any before?"

"Damn, Sid. No. Not like these two freaks." He got back on his phone. "We have casualties. Send an ambulance." He glanced at the carnage and shock-filled wailing as they zoomed by. "Make it two."

The black truck veered off the track, off the road, bouncing over the berms toward the main highway.

"I think they're on to you," Sid said to Cyrus.

"Onto *me*? You're the one chasing them."

"You commandeered my car. Do you want me to stop and let you out?"

"No," he said. "Go. Just go!" He shook in his seat as if he could make the Hellcat speed up from there.

Sid followed the two racers to the highway, laughing the whole time and not being at all careful to avoid the bumps.

She just about lost it when she heard Cyrus gulp down some barf.

Smoke the Grey Racer's Camaro sped along, weaving through the traffic signs and lights after the Black Hulk, which picked up speed now that it was on the highway.

Sid swung her car left and right, fishtailing, spinning her tires before they bit into the road. Up the entrance ramp she went, right after Smoke.

"Rebecca," Cyrus said into his phone. "Are you okay?" There was a pause. "Good, good. Tell Smoke to follow. Don't engage. Let's just see where these bastards go. Be careful." He disconnected.

Sid eyed him. "'Be careful'?"

"What? It's a dangerous situation."

"I think being careful is implied in the FBI academy," she said. They were doing about ninety, weaving in and out of traffic and passing one car after the other. "So, she's my replacement on the Black Slate?"

"I can't answer that," he said, texting.

"I can only imagine you had a hand in picking her. Isn't she a little green? What kind of field experience does a data analyst have, anyway?"

He ran his forearm over his brow. "She's a good actress. Discreet and deceptive."

"Oh, a cute young female version of you. That's nice."

"Smoke seems to like her," he said. "They've gotten a lot done in the past six weeks."

She squeezed the wheel. *He better not have been out for six weeks.* "Well, I'm sure she finds him better company than you."

"Funny, I could say the same about you." He tipped his head up. "What did he say to me? She gives him a much longer leash. Something like that."

Sid ground her teeth. *It doesn't bother me. What do I care if he spends time with another woman? Dammit! It bothers me! Six weeks with Prissy Pants! Cyrus better be lying! Change the subject.* "So tell me. What do you want with the Buffalo Brothers?"

"No. Not going to say. But I'd be curious to know what you know about them."

Fine. I'll play.

"They're the Drake's cleanup crew. And the rumor around town is that they can't be killed."

"Interesting," Cyrus said. "I bet a pair of men like that have a lot of good stories to tell."

"Huh." *I'll be. They want to capture these guys. Interrogate them. Why am I surprised?* She glanced in the rearview mirror. Cop cars with flashing lights had filed in behind them. "We have company already."

"Yep," Cyrus said, sounding sure of himself and no longer about to puke. "And just a few miles up the road, a blockade will be set up. We have these jokers on manslaughter now." She could hear him smiling, imagine him showing his tiny little teeth. "Busted."

Cruising at high speed, Sid saw flashing cop lights up ahead.

The black truck screeched to a halt. In seconds, it was hemmed in by a fleet of cop cars, and so was Smoke and Rebecca's ride. The trapped truck did a circle of donuts, smoking up the area.

"What are those freaks doing?" Cyrus said, getting out of the car.

Eyeing the scene, Sid waved the drifting smoke from her face. The black truck's windows were rolled up. She couldn't make out the men inside. She tilted her head. Above and flying toward them was a black helicopter.

Whuppa! Whuppa! Whuppa! Whuppa! Whuppa!

A police officer was shouting through a bullhorn. He could barely be heard over the chopper that now hovered over the truck. Someone dropped a ladder out of the chopper. Suddenly the doors to the truck burst open. The big men hopped into the bed of the black truck and grabbed onto the ladder.

"No!" Cyrus screamed. "Halt! Halt!"

The helicopter soared away. The Buffalo Brothers gave them all a middle-finger salute and vanished into the night.

Pounding his fists against his thighs and stomping his foot, Cyrus screamed, "Dammit!"

An FBI cruiser pulled up. A small team emerged and approached Cyrus.

"I want a forensics team all over that truck. Now!"

A second later the truck exploded.

Boom!

CHAPTER 13

WATCHING THE FLAMING TRUCK BURN to the ground, Sid heard Cyrus say to her, "This is your fault!"

"My fault?" she argued. "You're the one watching a pair of mass murderers run around on the loose. I bet you could have apprehended them weeks ago, but you wanted to follow some ridiculous protocol."

"You know what, Sid?"

"What?"

"You're a joke. You can't even see your error in all this." He lifted up his phone like he was going to smash it into the ground. He held back. "Damn. Everything was fine until you showed up."

Two more people approached. Smoke was still in his racing suit. Beside him, Rebecca Lang lumbered along, holding her shoulder. Her face was wrought with pain.

Cyrus rushed over to her. "Are you all right? What happened?"

"I got shot," she said, sucking her teeth. "Sort of."

Cyrus rolled up her sleeve. She was wearing a dark mesh shirt Sid recognized. "Is that a Sweet Heart suit?"

"Part of one," Smoke said, taking off his helmet. His dark, wavy hair hung below his ears. His chiseled face was shaven, giving him a touch of a boyish look. "She wouldn't wear the whole thing. She said she wanted to sell it."

"I sold it, all right," Rebecca said, glancing at Sidney. "And I could have gotten more money if you hadn't ruined it. Ow!"

"Sorry," Cyrus said, inspecting her shoulder. "That's going to leave a beauty mark, but you aren't bleeding. Still, you better get that x-rayed. There might be a hairline fracture in there. Come on." He turned toward Smoke. "Don't either of you go anywhere. As a matter of fact..." His head swiveled around. "Lee! Lee! Keep an eye on these two."

A slender-faced man, tall and broad shouldered, sauntered over. He wore a dark navy suit, tinted glasses, and an earpiece. He clasped his hands in front of him and said, "Will do, sir."

Sid didn't know the man. She turned her back and faced Smoke. He had a funny look on his face. "What?" she said.

"I was wondering if you wanted to hug me."

Yes. "Not going to happen." Looking into his dark eyes, she found something she hadn't admitted to herself she'd been looking for. "Where have you been staying?"

"Can't say." He set the helmet down and started to unzip his racing suit. "Man, this thing's hot. It's nothing like the Sweet Heart suit."

"You don't have one, and she does?"

"Your ex-fiancé took it," he said.

"You didn't need to say that," she said, "but at least I know that still bothers you."

"That makes you happy?"

Yes! "Maybe."

"Huh. Well, it's good to see you, too. So, how did you stumble upon this?"

"Aw, crap. Guppy." She pulled out her phone and noticed a text.

It read, "Don't worry about me. On my way back. G."

"So," Smoke said, leaning back against her car, "I guess you've figured out I've been out of prison six weeks. And maybe you're mad that you haven't heard from me?"

Furious. "You could have let me know." Taking a place near him against her car, she shrugged. "Besides, Megan's asked about you."

"How is she?"

"Fine."

"You have to understand, Sid. I'm keeping things pretty close to the vest. If things go well, I can get out. Early." He glanced around. "Not that I trust them, but that's what they offered. And don't be bent at me because I haven't checked in. You're the one who left the Agency. Why'd you do that? I thought we had a good thing going."

She stiffened. There was a deeper meaning in his tone. He sounded hurt. "I had to. For Megan."

"When they came for me, it was like the first time we met. Remember? Except it was Rebecca, not you." His eyes found the little blonde, who was sitting in the back of a nearby ambulance. "She's a clever little bird. She asked an awful lot of questions about you in my interview. That said, for the record, I was disappointed."

"In what?"

"That it was her and not you. I knew something was wrong. I didn't want to take the job, but the offer, time plus money... I had to."

Sid leaned toward him. "You almost make it sound like they forced your hand. I don't take you for the kind of man who does things he doesn't want to do."

"She made it clear that if I didn't do what they wanted, things would get a little tougher on me. Besides, I thought I'd take the risk and hopefully bump into you. And here we are. Quite the coincidence, isn't it?" He eyed the star-filled sky. "Such a pretty nightfall."

She backhanded him in the shoulder. "You did that, didn't you."

Smoke feigned a look of surprise. "Did what?"

"You put that paper on my car, didn't you!"

"What sort of paper are you talking about? Notebook? Typing? News?"

"*Nightfall DC!*" She pushed him sideways along her car.

Chuckling a little, he let her. "Oh, never heard of it." Giving her an all-too-knowing smile, he said, "You look like you want to hug me now."

Heart pounding, she reached over and squeezed his hand tight.

His warmth raced through her.

Throat tightening, she quickly released his hand and his warmth. "No."

Cyrus approached with a handful of men. "I hope you two enjoyed your little reunion, but now it's over. I've got orders. Mr. Smoke, you're going back. This investigation's over." Several of the armed men closed in. "Don't try anything."

Smoke raised his arms over his head. "No problem, Cyrus."

"It's Agent Tweel to you."

"Cyrus, what is your problem?" Sid said, watching the men cuff Smoke's hands behind his back. "He's put his neck out for you, and you treat him this way?"

"You should have minded your own business, Sid." Cyrus had a familiar mean look in his eyes that scared Sid a tiny bit.

"What?" she cried. Numb from head to toe, she watched everything move in slow motion.

Smoke was led away in cuffs. His eyes caught hers one last time before he was shoved into a black SUV.

Cyrus got in Sid's face, pointing at her with anger. "And you interfered with an FBI investigation and have at least a dozen other charges, too. And I'm not even sorry to do this. Agent Lee, cuff her."

CHAPTER 14

S IDNEY SAT ON A COLD grey metal chair bolted to the wall of a small solitary holding cell. The walls were stark white. The fluorescent lights overhead flickered. The room was stuffy and warm. She stared at the heavy metal door. There was a square portal at the top. The last time a head had gone by had to have been an hour ago. Maybe longer. Using her T-shirt sleeve, she wiped the sweat from her lip.

Morning glory! What have I done?

Elbows on her knees, she sank her face into the palms of her hands. It was real. She was arrested. Spread out and searched and thrown into the slammer. Her nails dug deep into her hair. Her arms flexed. She had to have been in there a long time. Three hours, she guessed. She was good with time. But inside this little room, things had gotten weird. The isolation threw her off. Worry beset her. She stomped her foot.

"How stupid of me!"

Megan. That was her concern. Her niece should be safe with Sam and Guppy, but no doubt the little woman-to-be would worry. Sid's heart ached. She felt trapped. Helpless. More than a little scared now. She shifted in her chair. Got up and stretched her legs. Rose up on her tiptoes and peered through the portal. There was only the opposing wall of the corridor. She couldn't see much at all from left to right. She hit the door with her fist. The blow made almost no sound at all.

Keep it together. Don't act like a criminal.

Cyrus was right. She had interfered. If she'd kept her head down and lived the normal life, she'd be back home right now. Not waiting.

She sighed. The processing of paperwork took hours.

It might even run until tomorrow.

She'd been on the other side of that heavy metal door many times before. Taking her time. Getting the paperwork ready. Not giving the person in the cell a single thought. Guilty or not, no one ever rushed for them. No one heard their pleas. Their screams. No one asked about their responsibilities, their families. They just left them. Let them rot until the system sorted it out.

She sat back down on the bare-bones cot, pulled her legs up to her chest, and leaned back against the wall. All she heard was her own breathing. Her heart pumping in her chest. She swore her brain spun around in her head, running through every scenario and detail.

I'm a fool.

She had jumped into the action feet first, feeling justified. She had wanted to find Jake Miller's killers. She had opened up a can of worms. It had gotten her cop juices flowing. She had abandoned her responsibilities because of it. All because she wanted to go out and play.

Now Megan would pay for it.

What if they *stick it to me? What if* they *don't want me out?*

What if the Drake was calling the shots all along and this was what they wanted? What if they stuck her in an orange jumper, released her into the general prison population, and let a bunch of burly cons with shivs come to kill her?

Don't think like that, Sid.

Her stomach groaned. Above, the vent rattled as the air conditioner came on. It was icy cold. Chill bumps rose on her arms. Although she felt refreshed for a moment, it wasn't long before her sweat-slicked body chilled. She started to shiver. She rubbed her crossed arms up and down. She moved away from the vent, but it didn't do her any good. She couldn't go far.

Man, that's cold.

The temperature in the room must have dropped from ninety degrees to sixty in a minute. She stood up on the cot and stretched her fingers toward the ceiling vent, wanting to close it. She was at least a foot short.

"Come on," she said, teeth chattering. "This can't last forever." She rubbed her arms. Paced back and forth. She fought the urge to curl up under the cot like an animal.

Come on, Sid. You're tougher than them. Get mad. Don't give in. Fight them.

She'd trained in severe situations. Been through survival camps. Combat camps. Interrogation camps.

This should be a cakewalk.

Picking up her knees, she ran in place for fifteen minutes until the air shut off.

Yes.

Taking a seat and gathering her thoughts, she thought about Smoke. It stuck in her craw that he might not be getting out sooner because of her. Now he was gone again. Just when she had started to feel close to him.

Why do I hate to admit that I miss him?

The cold air kicked on again.

"Damn!" She stood up. "Fine. I can take anything you can dish out."

The cold air went on again, off again, minute after minute, hour after hour. Finally exhausted, Sid let out a tormented scream.

CHAPTER 15

EXHAUSTED, COLD, AND HUNGRY, SID huddled in the corner of her cell. A sound caught her ear. The cell door's lock tumbled over, and the door swung open. Muscles stiff as boards, she pushed up into a standing position.

A guard stepped into full view, an average guy in plain clothes, wearing an FBI jacket and ball cap. "Come with me," he said, stepping back out of view.

Sid headed out of the cell. The air in the hall was like a warm blanket. She followed the man down the hall and to the left, cutting across an office filled with a handful of empty cubicles. He cut into another hall, took a right, and opened a door. "Go on in. Have a seat," he said, running his eyes over her disheveled body. He gave her a funny look. "Someone will be with you in a minute."

"That's what they said last time."

"Sorry, I just came in. I've barely been briefed on it." He smiled. "I'll see if I can get you some coffee, but don't count on it."

"Oh, I won't." She entered the room. It was a typical interrogation room. A hard table and chairs. A big mirror and a camera in the corner. She turned as the door closed behind her and the lock was turned into place. "Great."

Rubbing her hands up and down over her cold bare arms, she yawned and sat down, glancing up at the camera in the corner. The little red light wasn't on, but that didn't mean anything. Often, they'd watch without recording.

Who's watching me now?

"Do you think I can get something to eat?" she said to the mirror. "Any chance I can make that phone call? I seem to have misplaced my phone."

Silence was the answer. She got out of the chair and walked around the table. At least the interrogation room was warm. That was intentional. The hotter the better. They liked to make the guilty sweat. She'd conducted plenty of interviews in places like this. The FBI had little offices all over. She didn't recognize this one, and she'd been inside many.

How many things does the FBI do that I don't have a clue about? Man, and they're only one agency.

The door popped open, and Cyrus Tweel entered. He was in a suit and looked refreshed.

Right on his heels came Agent Lang. The petite woman in a snug pantsuit wore a sling on her arm and a frown on her face.

"Sit down," Cyrus said to Sid.

"Good morning to you too, Cyrus," she said, resuming her seat.

He pulled out a chair for Rebecca then seated himself. "I'm sure you had a long night, but you know how paperwork goes."

"I know exactly how it goes! You can't hold me like this. You threw me in a cage like a hardened criminal. Like an animal!"

Cyrus held up his hand. "Don't raise your voice. You're in enough trouble already. Just so you know, I don't have to be here. Consider it a courtesy."

"I'm sorry," Sid scoffed. "Did I interrupt your morning? What's the matter, no time for you and your little bird to snuggle?"

"Sid, there's no need—"

Rebecca cut Cyrus off by whispering something in his ear.

He cleared his throat. "Tell us everything you know about the Buffalo Brothers." He pushed over a pad and pen. "Write it down."

She shook her head no. "Why?"

"Because I said so." He pushed his thick glasses up on the bridge of his nose. "You really need to do yourself a favor here, Sid. Things aren't looking good for you at all. Do you know how hard it is to get a job with felonies on your record? And what about your niece, Megan? Do you want her going into a foster home?"

"She has grandparents."

"That's for the state to decide. Everything doesn't always go your way, you know." He tapped the table with his fingers. "The charmed life you led is finally over."

In disgust, she said, "What are you talking about?"

His frosty eyes locked on hers. "Just start writing."

She slid the paper over and started to draw, humming as she did it. She lifted the top edge of the paper so that they couldn't see it. "No peeking." Like a schoolgirl, she bit on her tongue as she drew an obscene gesture on the paper.

Cyrus and Rebecca glared at her.

Finished, Sid tore the paper off the pad, folded it in half, and slid it over.

"A little quick," he said. He unfolded the paper in front of him and Rebecca and huffed. "Cute, Sid. Real cute."

"That's for the both of your eyes only," Sid said. "I'm sorry. You and your little bird look upset. Am I going to be additionally charged with insulting a federal officer now?" She leaned back in her chair. "I wonder if you can make that stick."

Cyrus wadded up the paper and tossed it aside.

Rebecca whispered something else in his ear.

He nodded. Rising from his seat, he said, "I gave you a chance. You blew it."

"What, you're leaving me?" Sid said, rolling her eyes. "How disappointing."

The door opened and the agent from earlier came in with a cup of coffee in his hand. Rebecca slid into his path, plucked the coffee cup from his hand, and said with a smile at Sid, "Why, thank you."

Cyrus followed her out, saying, "Have fun in the hole. I hear it can be rather chilly at times."

CHAPTER 16

SITTING IN THE CELL WITH her knees bouncing up and down, Sid pondered her situation. Cyrus was using coercion. Trying to pick her brain for some reason. She didn't really have anything, but she wasn't going to let him know that. She leaned her head back against the wall.

"Shoot."

She'd broken at least five laws in the last twenty-four hours. Sure, it was minor. Scuffing up against Rebecca while she sat in Smoke's car didn't seem like much, but it could be a problem. She'd seen things like this happen all the time. Agents getting out of control with their authority. It wasn't a problem agent on agent. But civilian on agent? Especially with an agent who had a grudge against you? That was different.

What cards do you have, Sid? Let them think you know something? Get them to drop the charges then exchange nothing? Maybe my unlawful imprisonment is a good example. No food. No visits to the bathroom. No calls. She slapped her head. *Megan. I need to be taking Megan to school right now!*

She hit the wall, winced, and shook her hand. The air conditioning fan kicked on. She balled up. Her eyes started to swell and her chest tightened.

I'm such a fool. Such a fool I am. Get it together, Sid. Don't let Cyrus and that little twit win.

She shuddered a breath and then recited the Serenity Prayer. "God, grant me the serenity to accept the things I cannot change, the courage to change the things I can, and the wisdom to know the difference." Her head sank between her knees. "Amen."

A moment later, the A/C fan kicked off. The cell door opened.

She lifted her head and saw Section Chief Ted Howard standing there.

"Sid," he said, stepping inside and clasping her hands. "I'm sorry about this. I just got word and made it over here as fast as I could. Come on. Let's get you sorted out and back on your feet."

She studied his face. Ted was a hard man at times. Tough. Old school. The hard lines on his face were softened by the sad look in his eyes. She took his hand. "No games, Ted."

"No, friend."

❀ ❀ ❀

Sid was inside a small office furnished only with a desk and half a dozen chairs. There weren't any decorations or evidence of personal effects. It was a typical satellite office, a place agents used when they went undercover. A place to meet. To plan. Off the radar from the main office. For the most part, the building was run by a skeleton crew that might consist of one field agent acting as a supervisor or guard.

Ted sat behind the metal desk in an old wooden swivel chair. His navy-blue suit jacket hung on an old coat rack in the corner. He rolled up his sleeves, exposing his husky forearms, and loosened his tie. He helped himself to something from a box of donuts and shoved them over.

Sid sipped coffee from a Styrofoam cup that read Donut Connection. Ted had given her some time to get cleaned up and make a call. Megan was fine, thanks to Sam, and had made it to school. Starving, she eyed the donuts, reached in, and plucked out an apple cinnamon. "So, did you pick these up as you rushed to come and see me?"

Taken aback, Ted said, "Well, I figured you'd be hungry. And it was on the way."

"Isn't there always one on the way?" She bit into the donut and chewed. *This is the best donut I've ever had in my life.* Washing it down with coffee, she grabbed another. "Bavarian. Interesting variety, Ted. Looks like it might have taken some time to pick out."

"Oh, don't start, Sid. I didn't have to bring anything at all, you know."

"You've known I was in there since last night, haven't you."

He looked her dead in the eye and said, "No."

She believed him.

"Okay. So what's happening now? Am I under arrest or not?"

"Yes and no."

"Yes and no? What does that mean, 'yes and no'?"

"I've gotten word that *they*," he said, making air quotes, "want you back on the Black Slate."

"Aren't Cyrus and *Agent Lang* handling that now?" she said, easing back into her chair. She made a face and tilted her head sideways when she said *Agent Lang*.

"Your sudden departure had consequences, Sid. Cyrus hounded me. Hell, he hounded everyone he could, trying to get into the Black Slate." Ted shook his head. "He'd kill to be a shadow agent. I really think he would. Well, somebody above gave him the pass. They even let him pick his team. He picked Rebecca."

Sid hitched her brow. "His girlfriend?"

"Actually, I think she has some connections that even I don't know about. I've never seen an agent so young promoted so fast. Anyway, as I understand it, the powers that be gave Cyrus what he wanted. Part of the reason was his familiarity with John Smoke and you. They even apprehended somebody on the Slate already."

Sid sat up and scooted her chair closer. "What? Really? Who?"

"I can't say."

Suddenly, the office door was flung open. Cyrus and Rebecca stormed in.

Cyrus slapped a document onto Ted's desk. "This is not happening!"

Rebecca, blue eyes smoldering like fires and arms crossed over her chest, huddled up to Cyrus's side and added, "You better not do this, Ted. You need to butt out!"

CHAPTER 17

"E XCUSE ME," SID SAID. "WHAT is going on here?"
"You shut up!" Rebecca shot back at Sid. "You washed-up has-been!"

Sid sprang out of her seat, pinned Rebecca down on the desk, and growled in the petite woman's ear, "Don't ever tell me to shut up."

"Get off her!" Cyrus said, taking Sid by the arm.

Sid twisted away and released Rebecca.

"I'm pressing charges! I'm pressing charges!" Rebecca cried out. Adjusting her glasses, the mousy little woman practically screamed, "Arrest her, Cyrus!"

Ted stood up with his fists on his desk and shouted over everyone in a thunderous voice. "No one is arresting anybody! Now sit down!"

Scowling, Rebecca pulled a chair over to the left of Cyrus, who took a seat to the left of Sid.

"I expect better from my agents," Ted said, slowly sitting back down.

Kicking her crossed leg, Rebecca said, "She's not an agent."

"Agent Lang," Ted said.

"What?"

He glared at her. "Call me Sir or Section Chief. Got it?"

Rebecca stuck her chest out and saluted. "Yes, Sir."

Ted took a breath and picked up the document Cyrus had slapped onto the desk. Examining it, he said to Cyrus, "I have no problem with this. You shouldn't either."

"Sir, I'm already working with one ex-con. Now I'm supposed to work with another? This is ridiculous."

"Sid's no convict," Ted replied. "You know better than that, Cyrus."

"What are we talking about?" Sid inquired.

"As I was about to say before I was interrupted, we, or rather the Agency, want to acquire your services, Sid."

"What do you mean?"

"We want to add you on as a consultant for the Black Slate," he said.

"We as in you, Ted?"

"We as in the same Agency folks who lined you up before. *They* want you on the Slate, Sid."

Beside her, Cyrus clenched his jaw.

Beside him, Rebecca lifted her chin and turned her head away while she sat there with her arms crossed tight over her chest, still kicking her leg.

"Tell me more," Sid said, sounding very interested. She swore she could hear both Cyrus's and Rachel's butts pucker. *Make 'em suffer.*

"The paperwork's ready. You'll be given consultant ID, and your former security clearances will be restored." He rubbed his chin. "Sorry, I'm making it sound simpler than it probably is. Anyway, you and Agents Tweel and Lang will work as a team on this."

"Just us?" she said.

"Mr. Smoke will be coming along, but he's not in a position of authority, hence not a team member, so to speak."

She heard Rachel shift in her seat. *Squirm, girl, squirm.* "What's the objective?"

Ted reached into the desk drawer, withdrew a black file, and slapped it down on the desk. He kept his hand over it and said, "Are you in or are you out?"

Eyes fixed on the file, Sid sorted through her thoughts. There was Megan to consider. Other than that, there was nothing else—aside from the satisfaction of pissing Cyrus and Rachel off. "I'm in."

"What!" Rebecca blurted out. "You have a nanny job to attend to. You don't have time for this! Sir, we don't need her. She'll just slow us down."

"Says the woman she just pinned to my desk," Ted said. "And you're borderline insubordinate. I'm getting tired of it. Don't make me warn you again."

"Or what?" Rachel said, getting out of her chair. "I'll have your job before you know what hit you, you frickin' dinosaur." Shooting Sid a look, she left the room.

Ted's face darkened. Normally, the veteran leader and agent would have taken immediate action. But something held him back. Sid wondered what that was.

"You need to get a better handle on that," Ted warned Cyrus. "That better never happen again."

Unfazed, Cyrus said, "I'll do what I can."

"I'm sure you will," Ted said, shoving the file toward Sid. "That's your copy. Now, we want to get the Buffalo Brothers, Warren and Oliver Ratson."

"We had them until she showed up," Cyrus said.

Ted clasped his fingers and rested them on the desk, staring at Cyrus until the flabby man backed down into his seat. "Continuing. We don't know much. They work for the Drake. And whenever they show up, someone important gets killed."

Thumbing through the file, Sid came across some familiar names and faces. Politicians and other high-ranking DC officials. Names that often made the papers. Important men and women. They were all dead. The papers reported natural causes. Maybe suicide. The photos showed something else. Grizzly photos. Blood and mutilation. Torment. "How is this possible? How is this covered up?"

"That's not the issue," Cyrus said.

"He's right," Ted said, giving Cyrus a warning glare, "not that it doesn't matter. The point is, these guys need to be brought down. Because they're here, we know someone's hired them to kill someone else. Mr. Jake Miller tipped us off to that."

"How's that?" she asked.

"The Buffalo Brothers have a calling card." He produced a transparent evidence bag and slid it over. "Those were in Jake's eyes."

Studying the contents, Sid observed two buffalo nickels. Her heart sank a little thinking about Big Jake. Like Ted, he was an old soul from a different era. "I imagine there is one for each of them."

"Of course, Jake's death didn't fit the profile. It looked more like vengeance. Sick thing is that they left fingerprints. And in the system, they are both registered to dead men. Got graves but no bodies."

Sid swallowed. If she'd stayed away from those men at the range, perhaps none of this ever would have happened. Jake's death was on her conscience. She gathered herself. "But Cyrus says he and Rebecca have been tracking these brothers for weeks. What tipped you off?"

"Check the dates in the files and you'll see where City Councilman Jeffery Ryson died in an automobile accident. Well, that's not what happened. As you can see."

She found a picture of a man pinned between a brick wall and his car. *I wonder what he knew. I wonder what he saw.* "They all have ties to the Drake, don't they."

Ted shrugged his husky shoulders.

Sid went on and told them about her encounter with the Buffalo Brothers at the gun range.

"Not good," Ted said, rolling his eyes. "It's bad enough what they're doing, but now they're using a sniper's weapon? Whoever they're after must be really high up. Damn. It could be anybody."

CHAPTER 18

"**L**ET HIM OUT," TED SAID into the intercom. "And bring him in."

Sid's heart raced.

A minute later, Smoke entered the room. His towering frame was back in his racing suit. He walked up to the desk, picked up the box of donuts, and sat in the vacant chair to Sid's right. He stuffed an entire donut in his mouth. Chewed. Swallowed. Stuffed in another. Repeated. And another, until the box was empty. He held it up and shook every last crumb into his mouth. And then he set the box back down on Ted's desk and dusted off his hands. "What's the plan?"

"Uh," Ted started, lifting his jaw up off the desk. "Well, Mr. Smoke, you've already been briefed. You might need to fill in Agent Shaw, excuse me, Liaison Shaw, on what you know. We have killers out there. An unknown target. We need to track them down before someone else dies." He rubbed the back of his head. "Cyrus, you're the lead, but the four of you have to work as a team on this. I mean it."

"You know I can't be accountable for these two," Cyrus said with a sneer. "They're reckless."

"They're proven. And if you want to continue to work on the Black Slate, you'll need to deal with it. That's the impression I get, anyway." Ted got up out of his chair and stared down at the empty donut box. "Looks like I'll have to make another stop on the way back to my office. Cyrus, report to me in the morning. You all can see yourselves out." He grabbed his jacket. "I'm out of here."

The room was very still and quiet after Ted left. Sid broke the silence. "So," she said to Cyrus, "what's the plan?"

Cyrus walked over to the window and pulled back the blinds.

Sid heard the sound of a car driving away.

Cyrus turned to her and said thoughtfully, "You two find something to do. I'll call you this afternoon." He took his phone from his pocket. "Sid, what's your new number?"

She gave it to him. "So that's it. Just wait."

"I have to wrap things up, seeing how you trashed the last assignment. We had them, Sid. We almost had them." He stuck his phone back inside his jacket pocket. "And you messed things up. Now we have to start all over again. Unless of course you have something to add?"

"Nope."

"See you around. Enjoy your conjugal." He walked out.

Smoke started to speak.

She held her hand up to his mouth. "Don't you dare say anything about me being engaged to him."

"I was just going to ask you if you wanted to get something to eat." Smoke smiled.

"You just ate half a box ... Oh never mind. Let's go."

They were back in one of the diners they'd been to before. An old rail car with blue booths miles from the heart of DC. Smoke had a stack of pancakes almost up to his chin and a Coke big enough to drown in.

"Aren't you eating?" he said, stabbing with his fork a pile of buttermilk pancakes slathered in syrup.

"Watching you eat fills me up somehow." She drank her coffee. "Just take your time. Sometimes you eat like an animal."

"Sorry." He wiped his mouth with a napkin. "Folks aren't really big on etiquette in prison. So, how have you been?"

She didn't want to get into it. For the moment, she was just happy to be with him. "Fine."

"You don't look fine," he said, adding a little grin.

"I'm sure I don't. But you've seen better days yourself. It's good to see your hair back, though. Even with the helmet hair."

He choked on his food and started laughing. "Helmet hair. If I'd shaven it, I wouldn't have that problem, now would I?"

"Don't shave it."

He made and air circle with his spoon. "Oh-kay."

"Let me ask you a question. Ted said that you and Cyrus brought in someone else from the Black Slate already. Who was that?"

"Maddy Ryan. A hunchback." He swallowed his food. "He wasn't anything like the ones me and you brought in. I mean, tougher than he looked, but not a big threat."

"So he was just a hunchback? Did he shift into anything?"

"No. He was just strong as a bull and exceptionally cruel." He stopped the waitress walking by. "Miss, could I get some whipped cream?"

"Sure, hun." The waitress in powder blue and white squeezed his cheek. "Anything for you." She looked at Sid. "He's a keeper. I think it's sexy when a man eats like that. And stays so fit. He's a keeper."

"Yeah, thanks," Sid said, watching the woman walk away. She eyed Smoke, who'd resumed his eating. "You were saying."

"Oh yeah. Uh, Maddy could hop like a rabbit. It was really weird. Scaled walls and ropes like a monkey."

"Was he wearing a Notre Dame jersey?"

"No, why?"

"Are you making this up?"

"Nope," he said.

"So, what was he doing?"

He pointed his fork at her. "Funny thing. I think he was running a day care. It was full of all those weird little kids. The Forever Children Mal told us about."

Sid felt a chill go up her spine. Something about those children disturbed her. She had no idea what to make of them. Were they dangerous, or were they in need of help? "What happened to them?"

"I don't know."

Of course not. "What about Maddy Ryan? What happened to him? Is he dead or alive?"

"Well, he should be dead. I beat the tar out of him." He huffed. "I'd knock him down, and he'd bounce right back up. I swear, that hump in his back, it's got a battery in it or something."

"Did Cyrus and Rebecca help?"

"Sure, they were a big help."

"Really?"

Smoke shook his head. "No. Not really. They're pretty useless without their guns, which of course Maddy deprived them of. It's a long story."

She leaned forward and rested her chin on her fist. "I'm not going anywhere, unless you are." Her phone buzzed on the table. She answered. "Hello?"

"It's Cyrus," he said in his snide voice. "Need you and Smoke to stake out 8505 Rummel Avenue. Be there now." *Click.*

CHAPTER 19

8505 Rummel Drive was a business park off Interstate 395 in Falls Church. Sidney parked her car in front of a UPS distribution warehouse. Drumming her fingers on the steering wheel, she glanced over at Smoke, who was looking out his window. His strong chin and muscular arms were appealing. Very appealing. She rolled down her window and fanned herself.

"So," he said without looking at her. "Do you think he'll be long?"

"I doubt it. He's pretty anal."

"Yep. But his little counterpart likes to play games. I bet they don't show for at least an hour. Maybe two." He rolled down his window. "At least it's a nice day."

"What do you mean about his counterpart?"

"Oh, Rebecca. Yeah, she's trouble. You better watch out for her. She'll get you killed."

"Get me killed?"

"Yeah, like she almost got me killed trying to take down Maddy. Music?" He reached for the radio.

She slapped his hand away.

"Uh, news?" he said, taken aback.

"How about you fill me in on this killing thing?"

"Either it was intentional or it was incompetent, but she had a clean shot on Maddy the Hunch and didn't take it. I took a beating because of it. Part of me thinks she let that happen. Plus, other things that don't add up."

"Like what?"

"Like the whisper thing. And she's always sneaking off. I don't think she's done anything helpful. All she's been is there." Looking out the window, he popped open the door and picked something up. He showed a copper coin to her. "Like a bad penny, she always turns up."

Sid flipped on the radio. Something cheesy from the eighties about balloons was playing. Smoke started to sing along, which was very awkward for a big guy, but he could carry a tune. Preoccupied, she remembered her early encounters with Rebecca. The younger woman had seemed fine. Just eager. She'd fooled Sidney entirely. It angered her.

"Well surprise, surprise, surprise," Smoke said, "look who's already showed up.

A black Cadillac Escalade pulled along their side. Cyrus got out of the passenger seat and walked over to Sidney's window. He had on dark sunglasses and gave her a file. "Sherman Investments. There's a man, Winslow Swift. Handles Drake Properties. Big community guy and donor. Well connected." He pointed to another building in the distance, a five-story building, all glass, with a big sign in front of it. "That's Law Park Offices. He'll be coming in and out of there. Keep an eye on him."

"I will until I have to get my niece," Sid said.

"Make arrangements," he said, glancing over at his SUV. "If you can't handle it, then you need to step away."

Sid stooped her head down and looked under Cyrus's arm at the black SUV he'd parked next to her.

Rachel, who was watching and listening intently, sneered at Sid from the passenger seat.

She's like a little blonde life-sucking rodent. Sid looked back up at Cyrus. "Sure thing."

Cyrus leaned down in her window. "Screw this up and you're gone, Sid."

"Got it." She fired up the engine and revved up while Cyrus was still speaking. *Vroom! Vroom!* "Sorry, what was that?"

Cyrus backed away and yelled something.

She pulled the car out and sped away, leaving Cyrus and Rachel out of sight but not out of mind. She tossed the file over to Smoke.

Without opening it, he said, "You know this is a decoy."

"Why do you say that?" She pulled the car into the parking lot of the Law Park Offices building and took a parking spot with a good view of the front entrance. A security guard at the desk could be seen inside the lobby. "Let me see that file."

Winslow Swift was a short, heavy man, very well dressed, dark headed, and with a devilish smile. "He looks like a Drake guy. A real shyster."

"That's right. Why would the Buffalo Brothers want to kill that guy?"

"Maybe he'll lead us to them," she said.

"But Cyrus says he's a potential target. No, this is a decoy. Keeping us on ice while they conduct their own investigation." He opened up the glove box. "What, no gun?"

"Sorry. I'm traveling a little light lately. Don't you have anything in your car?"

"No, little miss prissy picked me clean during our operation. Need to get back to home base to get them." He eyed the back seat. "Do you really not have anything else?"

"Why? It's just a stakeout. We aren't in any immediate danger, I don't think. Besides," she patted his leg. "You know I'll protect you."

He eased his seat back and closed his eyes. "Okay then. Wake me up if he shows."

Good idea. She yawned. Gazing at his body, she found herself thinking about taking him back to her place and curling up with him to ... sleep. *Bad idea. Get it together.* She poked his shoulder. "Did I really blow up your situation with the Buffalo Brothers last night?"

"No. You've seen those guys, right? We weren't going to catch them. There's something seriously different about them. Did you read the file?"

"No," she said, a little irritated. She reached into the back seat to grab it and accidentally braced her hand against Smoke's rock-hard belly. *Oh my.* "But what the heck. Why not take a look now."

"They're like deaders on steroids," he said. "At least that's what Mal said."

"And how's he doing?" she said.

"He's not happy," Smoke said. "He got ahold of me, briefly. Said his funding was cut off and they took all his stuff."

"So, no Sweet Heart suits? Blue-tipped bullets? Super vitamins?"

"Nada. He sounded pretty pissed off. Said to call if I needed help but that he couldn't offer much."

"Have you called him again?"

"I did, but he hasn't called back."

"Great." For all Sid knew, Cyrus and Rebecca might have a little bit of everything Mal had to offer. *Wouldn't that be something.*

Things fell quiet. The pair of them sat, listening to the local news radio. The minutes turned to an hour and cruised well past lunchtime.

Sid broke the silence. "I'm going to get Megan. Screw this stakeout." She drummed her fingers on the wheel, eyeing the Law Park building. "You can stay if you want."

"I don't want to stay. I want to go after the Buffalo Brothers. Besides, I already know where they stay."

"What?!"

CHAPTER 20

"E XCUSE ME?" SID SAID. "YOU'RE joking, right? How can that be?"

"No joke. It just is."

Sidney pulled out of the parking lot and headed for the highway. "And how long have you known where they were?"

"A few days. Well, more like eight days. Six hours and eight days."

"And you haven't shared this with anyone?"

"No."

"Why? If you brought them in, you could go ahead and get your time reduced."

"So they say, but that isn't always true. Besides, I'll need some help on this." He glanced at her. "And there aren't many people I trust to work with."

"Are you telling me you strung this hunt out so you could bring me in?"

He reached up and grabbed the handle over the car door. "Sort of."

Sid grinned. She'd been thinking about him every day, and now she knew that he'd been thinking about her.

"That makes you happy, doesn't it."

She clammed up. "No."

"Then why were you smiling?" he said, gazing at her.

"Because you screwed Cyrus."

"Huh, good answer. But I don't think that's really why."

Well it isn't, but there's still truth in it. "So where are they?"

"I don't know where they are right now. But I know where they hide out," he said.

"And how did you come across this information?"

He glanced at her. "You know me. Cyrus and Rebecca are pretty caught up with each other. That gave me a good bit of leash. I followed the brothers one night. They're cautious, but I pinned them down at Mallows Bay."

"The ship graveyard."

"None other." He pushed his hair out of his eyes. "Gave me the willies, too."

"What do you mean, the willies?"

"I watched them drive over the water and disappear," he said, shaking his head.

"They drove on the water?"

"Like a bad episode of *Knight Rider*. Pretty bizarre, huh?"

Mallows Bay rested on the Potomac River south of DC. It was filled with old steam ships and the ruins of other vessels that had been sunk in the 1920s. It had been a historic park up until recently. Now it was privately owned. Sid stared at the No Trespassing sign mounted on the chain-link fence. Beside it was another sign, a new one that read Drake Properties. She wanted to spit. "Boy, they own a little bit of everything, don't they."

"I'd say so." Smoke stepped over the metal gate that consisted of two steel bars crisscrossed over the road. "Ready to get a closer look?"

She grabbed a small gear bag, and then she and Smoke walked up the road. Before long, they found themselves in a parking lot that led to the boat ramp. The skies had darkened with grey clouds, and the wind was picking up.

They followed Wilson Landing Road to the edge of the dock. From there, Sid could see the ruins of ships scattered all over the bay. With the silt buildup caused by the tides, most of them had been clumped together into a small island, forming their own shoreline. A few of the boats still stood against time in the middle of the bay, fading ever so slowly into the murky waters.

"They drove over the water?" she said to Smoke. "From right here?"

"Yep." He took off his shirt, shoes, and pants.

"What are you doing?" she said, glancing at his legs.

Smoke handed her his pants. "Hold these." He waded into the water. It was murky.

Sid couldn't see his ankle-deep feet from where she stood.

Wearing only his boxer briefs, Smoke ventured out farther and farther, up to his knees but not sinking.

"Get back here!" Sid yelled, looking around. There weren't any people for miles, but she didn't like this place. It was too quiet. Odd. The water smelled a little rank. She rested her hand on her gun. "Smoke! Come back!"

"The water's a little chilly," he said, sloshing around from side to side. "But, yeah, there is definitely a road here." He resumed his walk farther out into the bay.

He must have been forty yards out before he came to a stop. He turned and waved. His lips were moving, but the wind ripping over the water drowned his voice out.

"What?" she yelled.

He waved at her. Then, suddenly, as he ventured farther out toward an old abandoned tanker-type ship, he disappeared.

"Smoke!" she cried. "Smoke!"

CHAPTER 21

ARMS CROSSED OVER HER CHEST, Sid paced back and forth over the boat ramp, holding Smoke's pants and seething. "I'm not going after him. I'm not going after him."

For all intents and purposes, Smoke had been missing for more than thirty minutes. The clouds had darkened in that span of time, and now rain began to sting Sid in the wind. Calm so short a time ago, the bay's waters now crashed against the shore.

She stowed Smoke's clothes in her gear bag and procured a pair of binoculars. Putting them to her eyes, she scanned the waters. The place Smoke had vanished had a shadowy look to it. She stepped out on an old floating dock that shifted beneath her feet and then spied the huge metal craft in the distance, maybe a hundred yards away. Sea birds rested on its edges. Nests jutted out from the anchor portals. Birds on the boat erupted in flight.

He's on there! I know it.

She noticed a figure drifting along topside on the boat. It looked like a man in an old trench coat. His shoulders were slumped, and he moved really slowly. She adjusted the focus on her binoculars. She watched the back of the man's head. He had a captain's hat on and was moving away. Slowly he turned. Sid's heart skipped a beat. The man's skin was taut and leathery, his chin whiskers grey and ragged. His spacy, dark eyes were sunken into the sockets.

A deader. Dammit!

The head of the man disappeared. Sid scoured the edges of the bay with the binoculars. It was just woodland beyond the bay that contained one sunken ship after the other. The rain began to come down a little harder.

I'm going to be soaked. I'm going to kill Smoke. I should just leave him.

She backed off the dock and onto the hard top. She found her gear bag and stuffed the binoculars back inside it. Grabbing her phone, she checked the time. Megan would be out of school in an hour. She started to text Sam. *Crap!* Sam wouldn't be able to pick Megan up. She didn't have permission and probably wouldn't ever be able to get it.

"I'm a horrible aunt."

Frustrated, she kicked off her shoes, rolled up her pants legs, and waded into

the water. The icy river sent tingles up her legs and through her neck. She felt
a hard surface like a road under her feet. She slipped on the grime, bashing her
knees and soaking her pants.

"Morning glory!"

She pushed herself up, teeth chattering, soaking most of her arms and shirt.

Lightning flashed in the distance. Thunder rolled across the river.

"Screw this." She turned around and stomped back toward the dock.

A deader popped up in front of her. It seized her leg in an iron grip and jerked
her down into the cold water.

In an instant, Sid was fighting for her life. Water filled her mouth, and she
was choking. Squirming against the force, she braced her legs against the wall of
the underwater bridge and shoved upward. Head clearing the water, she gasped
for breath, only to be submerged again.

Fighting for her life, she kicked at the undead person. She jammed her thumb
in its eye. Bit its finger.

Mindless, the deader held her down in the water, trying to wrap its paws
around her neck.

Somehow, Sid got her head up, took a breath, went under, and drove her feet
into its chest, pushing free of its grip.

Gasp!

She swam for the boat launch and made her way to where she could walk
up its slope. When she was shoulder deep in the bay, the deader pounced on her
again.

It tore at her, relentless. Fearless of a death that had already come for it. Now
it wanted hers.

Sid fought. Kicked. Screamed. Her water-soaked clothes felt like lead blankets.
Her chest heaved. She punched its face. Broke free of its grip and staggered up
the ramp.

God help me!

Arms heavy as anvils, chest heaving, she found her gun and pulled it out of
the holster. She turned. The deader crashed into her. Sid squeezed the trigger.
Blam! Blam! Blam! Blam! Blam!

Chest full of lead, the deader slumped. Waters washed over its decaying body.

Sidney half crawled up the ramp, soaking wet. Making it out of the bay, she
coughed and heaved. Blood dribbled onto the pavement. She raised her hand to
her head and felt a gash. A little woozy, she got up and stumbled to the dock and
held onto the post. The rain kept pouring.

I hate deaders.

More movement on the water caught her eye. Someone approached, walking
on the water. They were moving fast. She aimed her gun. Her wrist was shaking.
She started to squeeze the trigger.

"Don't shoot!" said a strong, reassuring voice. Smoke emerged in the rain, wearing nothing but muscle and shorts. He caught up to her and took her by the wrist. "Run!"

There was the whine of a motorboat engine. A fast craft appeared from around the other side of the tanker. Gun flashes sparked in the air. Bullets whizzed overhead and skipped off the ground. Smoke snatched up her gear bag and ran straight through the parking lot and into the woods.

Lungs burning, Sid fought to keep up. Her soaked clothes weighed a ton. Fighting for her life had taken a toll on her. She needed time to recover, bullets blasting away at them or not. She collapsed.

Smoke scooped her up in his arms. "I'm sorry. I've got you now, Sid."

She managed to drape her elbows over his neck. She was aware of Smoke laying her on the reclined passenger seat in her car. The roar of the engine. The screech of tires. Barreling through the rain, she took a long draw through her nose, put the seat back up, buckled herself in, and slapped Smoke in the arm. "As soon as I catch my breath, I'm going to kill you."

"You'll have to get in line," he said, checking the rearview mirror.

Sid looked back behind her. A car was giving chase. A Mustang, judging by the looks of it. Black as coal.

"I guess you found something," she said. Her eyes widened. A man hung out of the passenger side window with a large rifle in his hands. Even in the rain, she could make out the weapon. It was a sniper rifle. Its bullets were as big as her hand. "Those are the Buffalo Brothers!"

Smoke swerved the car just as the man fired.

The bullet rocketed into a passing semi-truck's cargo trailer. The entire back end exploded.

"That was nasty," Smoke said.

Chest pounding, Sid watched their pursuers take another shot. It hit some power lines ahead. They fell and barricaded the road.

Smoke slammed on the brakes, coming to a stop inches from the live power lines.

"Get out," Smoke said. He shoved her at the door. "Get out!"

CHAPTER 22

S ID JUMPED OUT OF THE car and scrambled onto the berm. The Buffalo Brothers' tires screeched as their car came to a sudden stop. The brother hanging outside the car window with the rifle took aim on her car. The Hellcat. She heard him speak before he fired. "Nice car. Too bad." He squeezed the trigger.

The Hellcat exploded, shaking the ground. *Boom!*

Face first on the ground, Sid rolled onto her back. One of her car's wheels was falling out of the sky. She rolled out of the way. The tire bounced off the berm and disappeared somewhere in the nearby pines. Gaping, she stared at what was left of her car. It was nothing but flames and black smoke. She clutched her head. "No. No!"

Nearby, the Buffalo Brothers were laughing. The one with the mirrored glasses lit up a cigarette. The shorter one, still tall and oddly long necked, held the rifle out so he could spit on the ground. He hefted the rifle back onto his shoulder and eyed her through the smoke. "Ah, there's the little bird." He started Sid's way.

She pulled out her gun and pointed at his chest. "You're going to pay for that."

He stopped in his tracks. "What do you mean, pay for that? Is that a revenge thing? Or do you mean I'm going to buy you a new car? That's so cliché."

She fired a round into his leg.

"Ow! You stupid bitch. You shouldn't have done that!" He started to lower the barrel of his gun.

Sid unloaded her magazine into his chest.

He staggered backward with his face aghast and toppled to the ground.

The other brother rushed over. "No! No!" he said, kneeling at his brother's side. "You killed him! You killed my brother."

Loading in another full magazine of ammo, Sid made her way over to the men. The one lay on his back, booted toes up, twitching. The other put his hands over his head. "I surrender. I surrender," he said, pleading. "Don't shoot. Don't shoot. I don't want to die like him."

Sid removed a pair of flex cuffs. She eyed her surroundings, looking for

Smoke. He lay face down on the ground, not moving, several yards from the burning car. She approached the first man on his knees. "You're Warren, right?"

"I am he," he said. "Look, lady, I'm really sorry about your car. Really. But your friend, well, he shouldn't be snooping where he doesn't belong."

She had started to cuff Warren when the brother on the ground, Oliver, caught her eye. He wasn't bleeding. Suddenly, he sat upright with a big smile on his face.

The closer brother, Warren, backhanded her in the face.

Sid staggered backward from the powerful blow and dropped down to one knee. Raising the barrel of her gun, she squeezed off a shot, but all it hit was the ground.

Warren clamped his hand over her wrist and wrenched the weapon free. "None of that now," he said. "It can't kill us, but it stings." He tugged her off the ground, twisted her arm behind her back, and held her fast.

"Uh!" she said, grimacing. The man who held her was strong, his grip a vise. She couldn't move.

Oliver chuckled a deep rumble. He inspected the bullet holes in his shirt. He dug in, squeezed a bullet out from under his skin, and flicked it away.

Sid's skin crawled.

He continued, saying, "I love it when they fall for the possum act. So stupid." He pinched Sid's cheek. "Huh, you're that gal from the shooting range. The nosey one. You know you got your friend killed, don't you?"

Sid kicked at him.

"Oh, ho, ho," Oliver said. "Now, now. You don't want to do that ... Sid, isn't it?"

Her eyes widened.

"Of course we know who you are, Agent—well, former Agent Shaw. We do our homework." He cocked his head and eyed her. "I thought you'd be a lot more tomboy, though. So, this is probably going to hurt worse than I first figured it would."

"What do you mean?" she asked.

He slugged her in the belly.

"Oof!" Sid sagged down to her knees.

"Quit playing around, Oliver," Warren said. "Just take care of the other one. We'll deal with her later."

Oliver shrugged. "Sure. Sure. I was just softening her up a bit. Besides, AV and Night Bird were my friends." He walked over and picked up the sniper rifle. He charged the chamber and stepped into the firing line of Smoke.

The rangy man was gone.

Oliver grunted.

"Well, go and get him," Warren said. "I can smell his scent. Get on it!"

"I am on it." Oliver marched forward.

Smoke stepped out from behind the front side of the burning car. His head was bleeding and he held his side. "Let her go," he said.

"Oh, he likes you," Warren said in her ear. "He wants to play hero. Dead men can't be heroes." He yelled over at Smoke, "I don't think you're in any position to negotiate, Mr. Smoke. You should have stayed in prison."

Smoke shuffled forward. "You don't want us. You have bigger things to deal with. Let her go. She's harmless."

"You're both harmless," Warren said. "At least that's what the others thought. No, I think it's time to finish you off, Mr. Smoke, but I think they have other plans for her."

"What do you mean," Sid said, "for me?"

"You'll find out soon enough. Oliver, just kill him."

The assassin slicked back his jet-black hair under his palm, hefted the weapon up to his shoulder, and aimed. "Bye-bye." He squeezed.

CHAPTER 23

S MOKE DOVE RIGHT.

The bullet exploded somewhere in the forest.

"How'd he do that?" Oliver said. "It's impossible."

Smoke charged through the pouring rain and slammed into Oliver. The two big men went down. Smoke clocked Oliver in the jaw. In the ribs. Oliver Ratson roared and countered with a flurry of his own. Then the two men were locked up. Warriors with fire-lit eyes slugging it out with everything they had.

"Oh, this will be fun. For a moment," Warren said in her ear. "Your friend will put up a good fight. Then, his lungs will burn like fire. Feel like they burst inside his chest. He'll be unable to move his limbs at some point, and then my brother will grind him into the dust. He should have just let Oliver shoot him."

"Don't be so sure about that," Sid said. "He's killed your ilk before. I'm sure he'll kill them again."

"You had help before. You don't have it now, foolish girl."

A glint of sharp metal appeared in Smoke's hand. He jabbed it into the back of Oliver's knee.

Oliver howled and staggered backward. He had a limp now. A bad one. If Sid were to guess, Smoke had torn out a tendon. "Looks like that hurt," Sid said. "Do you want to put a wager on it?"

Warren applied more pressure on her neck with his forearm. "Don't aggravate me, mortal."

Wary eyed, Oliver circled Smoke. "I'm gonna take that knife and gut you with it."

"Please," Smoke said, "by all means, try."

With a roar, Oliver charged. He sprang the last few feet like a wild beast pouncing on its prey.

Smoke leap-frogged the man, landed on his feet, turned, and pounced on Oliver's back. He drove the blade deep into Oliver's long neck. The huge man's muscular body went limp.

"No!" Warren yelled. He shoved Sid hard to the ground and glared at Smoke. "You will pay!"

"What's the matter?" Smoke said, rising back up to his feet. "Can't your brother handle a severed spinal cord?" Smoke waggled the knife. "You see, I'm quite the surgeon. Now, why don't you come over here and try to take the knife from me?"

Warren edged closer. "All you've had is a stroke of luck, but your luck has just run out." Warren coiled back like a predator ready to spring.

A helicopter buzzed overhead. *Wuppa-wuppa-wuppa-wuppa ...*

A voice came over the loudspeaker. "This is the FBI."

Warren looked up and sighed. "Yadda, yadda, yadda."

The chopper landed between the black Mustang and the road leading to the dock. FBI agents with assault rifles poured out of the chopper. A swarm of FBI vehicles blockaded the other side of the road. In seconds, Sid, Smoke, the burning Hellcat, and the Buffalo Brothers were surrounded.

Warren raised his arms over his head. "You got me, little G-men." He looked at his brother. "Get up, Oliver."

With a grunt, Oliver pushed himself up off the pavement. He cracked his neck from side to side and glared at Smoke. "That hurt," he said, spinning in a circle without a limp. "Next time—and there will be a next time—leave the knife in."

The Buffalo Brothers dropped to their knees and locked their fingers behind their heads. Warren glanced at Sid as they cuffed him. "See you around, girl."

She watched the agents bind up their hands and legs. They even put muzzles over their mouths and covered their faces. *That's really odd.* She breathed a little easier, but she wondered how many agents understood what they were dealing with. *Where are they taking them?*

Cyrus and Rachel appeared. He held an umbrella over her head. "You two are finished!"

Sid rolled her eyes.

Cyrus stared at her car and continued. "You're both too smart for your own good. I put a trace on your car when I gave you the assignment on Winslow Swift." He glared at Smoke. "I figured you knew more than you were telling. And as I suspected, you led us right to the Buffalo Brothers." He pointed at Smoke. "You're done, mister."

"It sounds to me like you got just what you wanted," Sid interjected. "So what's the problem?"

"The problem, Sid, is that he, like you, hindered our investigation and apprehension of two known murderers!"

"It's all a coincidence," Smoke said, putting away his knife. He rubbed the bruise on his jaw. "Dumb luck. We just came down here to go fishing."

"Have fun fishing another five years out of your prison toilet bowl, jerk!" Rachel's face went oddly calm then, and she turned and whispered something into Cyrus's ear.

He motioned a couple agents over. He pointed at Smoke. "Cuff him." He pointed at Sid. "Cuff her. Throw them in the van and get them the hell out of my sight."

"Will you get off it, Cyrus!" Sid said. "We still have to report everything that went down. You need to know the details. You can't just fill in the blanks yourself."

"You can do it later!"

"Boy, when did you become such a yeller?" she said, getting cuffed.

"Since I had to start putting up with you!" he pointed at her, "and you!" he pointed at Smoke. He rubbed his temple. "Just go. Get them out of my sight."

"Hey, I have to get my niece," Sid yelled, fighting against the agents. "Cyrus. You've got to get off this. Please."

Rachel whispered in his ear again.

Cyrus said, "Don't worry, I'll let Child Protective Services handle it."

CHAPTER 24

SITTING IN THE BACK OF the FBI van, Smoke said to Sidney, "Sorry."

She was turned away facing the window, which was being splattered by pouring rain. She didn't want to talk. She was mad. He'd pulled one of his stunts, and it had failed. Now she had no way of getting ahold of Megan—or anyone, for that matter. Her hands were literally tied. Not to mention, her car was gone.

I hate him.

"I know you hate me," he continued. "I figured we would nip this in the bud. Of course, when I went down into that tube, well, it was just kind of awesome. You see, it worked like a drainpipe, or one of those pools with an infinity edge. The water just gushed right over it, and into a tunnel I went. It reminded me of the Bat Cave."

"Just shut up," she said to Smoke, shivering. "Hey!" she said to the front seat. "Do you think you could turn the air conditioning down? I'm freezing."

The agents didn't respond. Their eyes were frozen on the road ahead.

"You have insurance, don't you?" Smoke said, trying to sound positive.

"Sure, I'll just tell them I lost my car to an exploding bullet."

"Well, it should qualify as a catastrophic accident." He cleared his throat. "You can use my Camaro while I'm back in prison. No problem. But I only have liability on it, so be careful."

She turned and gave him a deadly look. "Be careful? You turned my life upside down by being stupid. I don't know what I was thinking."

"At least the assassins are off the street, and we unveiled another one of their secret lairs." He pushed his hair back. "I think those ships are loaded with smuggled goods. It's going to cause them a problem with distribution."

"It's under water. Don't you think they'll just flood it?"

Smoke shrugged. "I guess that's what I would do."

"Hey, I need you guys to make a phone call for me. Just one," she said to the agents driving the van. "I'm begging you. Please."

"You need to keep silent," said the agent in the passenger side, a woman. She flashed a Taser that zapped with blue light. "I'm dying to use this."

Sid's chin dipped. She couldn't let Megan wind up with Child Protective

Services. It would take weeks, maybe months to get her back. Megan would be distraught. Hands cuffed in front of her, Sid balled up her fists and started hitting Smoke. "You idiot! You idiot! You idiot!"

"Hey, I told you to shut it!" said the female agent. She came back at Sid, Taser ready.

Smoke grabbed the Taser and zapped the woman. Smooth as a cat, he slid into the passenger seat and slugged the driver, knocking him out cold, unbuckling him, and flinging him back at Sid. He took command of the van. "Unlock yourself and let's roll."

Sid found the keys and uncuffed herself. She checked the agents. Both were breathing easy. "Have you gone mad?"

"You know this doesn't feel right," he said, looking at her in the rearview mirror. "Right?"

She couldn't ignore the pit in her gut. Cyrus, stiff necked as he could be, wasn't himself. "Wrong!" She jumped into the passenger seat. "Stop breaking the law!"

"Sure. Look, let's go get Megan, all right? It will be a great field trip."

"I'm sure the FBI will be expecting us, once these two fail to check in," she said.

"We'll find a way." He ran the van up the highway entrance ramp.

Sid settled back in her seat, picking at her lip. All her plans had turned to disaster. She was a better planner than this. *Who cares about the Buffalo Brothers? Who cares about any of this?* "So, you know what school Megan's in?"

"Uh, yep. Unless it's changed recently."

"Fine."

Flying down the road, it took twenty agonizing minutes to make it to the school. Sid, still wet from head to toe, rushed inside. Megan was waiting in the gym. Ignoring all the strange looks, she signed Megan out, saying to the lady, "I left my umbrella at home."

Outside in the parking lot, Smoke pulled up in the FBI van.

"Where's the Hellcat?" Megan asked.

"Somebody killed it," Sid said. Looking the confused little girl in the eyes, she added, "Megan, you trust me, right?"

"Of course."

"Well, get inside and don't ask any questions." She opened up the passenger door and pushed Megan inside. Smoke pulled out of the parking lot and shot out onto the main road.

"Hey, Smoke!" Megan said.

"Hey, Megan."

"So, what's up with the van?" the girl said, looking everywhere. And then she saw the bodies in the back and screamed.

CHAPTER 25

THEY DITCHED THE FBI VAN in a hotel parking lot and caught a ride on a city bus. Sidney had done her best to explain to Megan everything that was going on. The little girl, somewhat distraught, quietly nodded. It had taken some convincing to show her that the FBI agents in the back were alive and just knocked out.

"I'm hungry," Megan said. She sat with her backpack clutched on her lap. Sid sat beside her, and Smoke sat across from them, staring out the windows. "Can we eat soon?"

"Sure. Just a little longer," Sid said. *I'm a horrible aunt. Horrible.* She didn't have any of her gear. No gun. No phone. No connections. Nothing. She felt powerless. Across from her, Smoke looked at ease. He caught her staring at him. "The bus was a good idea," she said.

"Thanks. And don't worry about money. I borrowed from those agents." He looked at Megan. "So we'll get you whatever you want to eat."

Even Sid was relieved. And hungry. She put her arm over Megan's little shoulders and kissed her head. Taking the bus was a good idea. It took them off the grid. Away from the cameras and other prying eyes. It also gave them something they needed: time. She scanned the bus again. There were only a handful of other people on it. A young woman with two toddlers and a sack full of groceries. An older black fellow who mumbled a lot. A pair of old women wearing scarves on their heads and speaking Italian.

It didn't make for bad company. But the bus driver, a heavy fella with nervous eyes, stared back at them in his mirror from time to time. She and Smoke certainly weren't his typical fares. Soaked, cut, bruised, and swollen, they looked far from their best. She'd be suspicious, too.

"What are you thinking, Sid?" Smoke said.

"I think I should call Ted."

"It's your play. If I were in your shoes, I'd do the same, but ..."

His conditional word jolted her. She knew what was coming.

"... they'll probably expect that."

"They're going to find us. I need some kind of dialogue with somebody, and it has to be Ted. He's the only one I can trust. I think."

"You can trust me," Megan said, looking up into her eyes.

"I know I can." She stroked the little girl's hair. "I know I can."

They remained on the bus until the first wave of passengers got off and another one got on. That's when the bus driver said to them, "This isn't a tour. Are you going somewhere or not?"

"Are we committing a crime?" Smoke said to him.

"No," the driver answered.

"Then shut up and drive."

The bus driver stiffened in his seat.

"Aunt Sid, I'm really hungry. Really bad."

"Okay, Honey. Here's fine!" she said to the bus driver.

They all exited the bus into the rain and dashed up the sidewalk and into a café. It was humid inside, and plenty of people were in there avoiding the rain. The three of them crammed into a small booth made for two people. A waitress came by and said, "I'll be with you soon. Sorry, I'm the last one on duty."

"So, did you borrow any change?" Sid asked Smoke.

He slid some coins over.

"Get her something to eat." Sid got up and made her way toward the back, down the corridor to the bathrooms. A pay phone hung on the wall in between them. She dropped the coins in and dialed.

A young woman with pretty nails walked by and gave Sid an odd look.

She probably doesn't know what this thing does.

The phone rang. "Uh, hello?" said a woman on the other end of the line.

"Sadie, it's Sid."

The woman's voice was very excited. "What are you doing? I was wondering if you were ever going to call me. So, let me guess, no let me hope, you found a man and you want me to be the maid of honor in your wedding."

"No."

"Oh, well then I have to go."

"Wait, Sadie, this is important."

"It is? So you're calling to apologize, then?"

"Apologize," Sid said, "for what?"

"That's what I thought. Click."

"Did you just fake hang up on me?" Sid asked.

"Yes."

"Okay, I'm sorry. I should have called. Stopped by. Please forgive me."

"Hmmm, well, that's better. So, what do you want?"

"You don't know I'm back in the thick of this stuff?"

"What stuff?"

"My old stuff. I'm an FBI liaison now. Supposedly, but things are a bit upside down."

"Go on."

"Listen carefully. Being discreet, I need you to get a message to Ted. Avoid Jane, his secretary—and avoid Cyrus and Rachel if they happen to come in."

"Oh, that won't be a problem," Sadie said. "I'll tell you what, ever since you left, that Rachel acts like she's running the place. She has most of these three-legged hounds wrapped around her finger." She huffed. "They act like a bunch of horny puppy dogs."

"Sadie!"

"It's true. Now, I'll get the message to Ted. What is it?"

CHAPTER 26

TWO HOURS HAD PASSED SINCE Sidney had gotten off the phone with Sadie. Three empty plates sat on the café table flanked by four empty milkshake glasses. Sid picked at her lip. Megan was asleep against her side.

"I don't like this," Smoke said. His eyes were narrow and wary. "He should have been here by now."

"I'm sure he's being cautious," Sid said.

The waitress walked up to the table and refilled her coffee. "Aw, how sweet," the woman said, glancing at Megan. "Can I get you anything else?"

"No, we're fine," Smoke said. After the waitress left, he added, "I don't suppose we can consider this a date."

"After you destroyed my car? No, I don't think so."

"I didn't destroy it."

"Let's not get into it." She locked her eyes on his. "I need you to tell me something. The truth."

He leaned forward. "Okay. What?"

"How did you dodge that bullet?"

"Oh." He leaned back. "Well, that's just really good anticipation. I have a knack for it. And it wasn't point blank. I was fifteen yards away, at least."

His answer didn't satisfy her. She grabbed his forearm and squeezed. "Look, John. I don't have a lot of faith in people. Not lately, anyways. I need you to be straight with me. Are you like them?"

"Like who?"

"You know who. People with powers. Extra senses. I've seen you do some things that seem superhuman."

He made a smile. "I am pretty impressive, aren't I?"

"I'm not toying around with you, John."

"I'm not toying around with you, either. Sid, you can count on me. I swear I'm not one of those freaks." He sucked some residual milkshake out of a straw. "Sure, I'm gifted. I've always been. And sometimes I get carried away and venture a little too close to danger, but I can handle it. At least I think I can. And I'm sorry that I put you and Megan in danger. But I'm not one of those people. Let God strike me down if I am."

Her breathing eased. If anything, she felt a little sorry for Smoke. He was odd. Not one to fit in easily, even though he had his charms. He probably saw right through people. He probably knew exactly what they were before they even opened their mouths. Staring into his dark eyes, a thought occurred to her. *I feel like he knows what I'm thinking.* She let go of his arm.

He caught her hand in his. It was warm. Strong. Just what she needed. "Sid, I've come to a conclusion about something."

She tried to gently pull away, but he held her fast. His handsome eyes were caught up in hers. "About what?"

"Us. The truth is, every day I think about you. And when I saw you again yesterday, I realized that I didn't want to go another day without seeing your face."

She swallowed before she found something to say. "Now's not a good time for us. I mean, this. Don't do this to me, John." Her heart tapped like a hammer inside her chest. She wanted him, and he'd just confessed he wanted her. "We have to get out of this mess first."

"Life will always be a mess. And without this mess, I never would have met you."

She squeezed his hand. Her body became hot, her breath bated. "Not now. The timing's bad. And you'll be going back to prison. I'll probably be going to prison. Please, Smoke, don't make my life harder than it already is."

"You can count on me. Let me help make it better."

She wanted to curl up in his muscular arms and bury her face in his. Her body was a flame. It was clear now, in her heart, in her mind, that she wanted him as much as he wanted her. "I-I need time to think."

"Go with your heart."

"I—"

Smoke released her hand. The connection was broken. He leaned back in his seat and eyed the entrance to the café.

She turned.

Section Chief Ted Howard was coming. There were deep creases in his forehead, and he was sweating. He pulled a chair up to their table. "I don't know what in the hell is going on. I swear it." He touched Sid's shoulder. "Are you all right?"

She filled Ted in on everything, from the time he'd left that satellite office up to now. Glancing at Smoke from time to time, she noticed a lonely expression on the hardened soldier's face. He seemed lost. Almost alone.

"Sid, I'm going to make some calls and get this cleared up. In the meantime, go rest. Go home. Take care of the little one." He eyed Smoke. "As for you, well, I don't know. The Buffalo Brothers are in custody. I can only imagine interrogations will begin soon. At least they're secured, but we need their target. There's a lot of people still nervous about it. Rumor is the Buffalo Brothers might have been a decoy."

"What does that have to do with me?" Smoke asked.

"You'll probably be going back in the hole. Sorry for the expression."

"My time better be shortened."

"I'll find out. I'll find out." Ted took out a handkerchief and mopped the sweat off his head. "I swear, I'm having the worst time figuring out where the orders are coming from. I'm told to do one thing and Cyrus and that little witch do another."

"Get rid of her, Ted," Sid insisted. "You know what effect people like that have on the team. She's a cancer. It might be hard, but you have to get rid of her."

"I know. I know." He shook his head. His hands clutched in and out.

The waitress walked up and asked if he wanted something.

He said, "No thank you." He gazed at Sid. "I don't think there is anything I can do to her, Sid. I don't even know how she got hired. Her personnel file's nonexistent, but she's on the payroll somehow."

The little bell on the café door rang.

Smoke rose to his feet.

Sid looked around the booth.

A tall blonde woman in leather pants and a black jacket stood with her back to them. She locked the door and turned the Open sign around. Then she started closing the blinds. That's when Sid realized they were the only ones left inside the café except for the waitress and the man behind the grill.

"Hey," the waitress said to the woman. "What are you doing?"

The woman turned around and stuck a gun barrel in the woman's face. "I'm here for a reunion."

CHAPTER 27

"**D**EANNE!" TED SAID IN ASTONISHMENT.

Deanne Drukker. The imposing blonde was striking, her voice full of authority. "Have a seat, princess," she said to the waitress. The woman scurried into a booth, hands up. Deanne said to the man behind the kitchen counter, "Don't make me say it, dough boy."

The man scurried into the booth alongside the waitress. "The money's in the regist—"

Deanne stuck the gun barrel on his nose. "I'm not here to rob you, stupid. Didn't you hear? It's a reunion. And listen, boy, don't think I haven't killed people for being stupid." She kept the gun on him and turned her attention to Ted and Smoke. "And the rest of you sit tight. I talk. You listen."

"It's good to see you, Deanne," Ted said, gathering his composure. "What's on your mind?"

"You look older, Ted. Older and fatter. What did I tell you about all the snacks?"

"You said 'They'll make you old and fat.'"

"And I was right," she said. She rapped the butt of her gun on the table. "Wasn't I?"

"Yes! Yes!" said the waitress and grill cook, nodding their heads feverishly.

"Boy, it sure is a nasty day out there. I hate coming out on nasty days. Now I'm all wet and sticky." She took off her jacket, revealing nothing but a tank top. She was built, with well-defined muscles. "It pisses me off. I don't like coming out into the city. Especially to do shit like this."

"Maybe you should have brought an umbrella," Smoke said.

"Shut up, John. Pain in my ass number one. Well, actually, in today's case, it's number two." Deanne looked at Sidney. "You know, you had a good thing going, girl, but you had to stick your big nose back in it. You even got your sister's little girl all involved. Stupid. Plain old stupid. And I was beginning to think you were smarter than that." She waved the gun around. "But I have to hand it to Allison. She was right. You had a way out, and you jumped right back in it."

"So my sister's doing well?" Sid said.

"She's doing great." Deanne moved through the room and lined up on a view of Megan. The little girl was fast asleep. "She's longing for her baby, though. It's tough."

"You aren't taking her, Deanne."

"Oh, if I want to, I will, but be at ease. That's not why I'm here." She moved over to the counter and hopped up onto it. "You see, our boys, Warren and Oliver. Well, they won't talk. In less than twenty-four hours, they'll be out. And soon after that, someone is going to die. And you all need to let them do their job or else there will be more casualties. Take those two nitwits that work here."

The waitress let out a sob.

"Oh, don't cry. You aren't worth the bullet," Deanne said.

"What happened to you, Deanne?" Ted said. "You were one of us. One of the good guys. Now you're a megalomaniac."

"I enjoy megalomania. Living life without a conscience is so..." She cast her eyes up for a moment. "...liberating."

"So you're liberated," Ted said, "because you help people die."

"Oh, Ted, you wouldn't understand." She walked over and squeezed his shoulders. "Your heart's too big. Just too big. Like your belly."

Sid held Megan a little tighter. Deanne had an air about her. Like the Buffalo Brothers. Fierce. Fearless. She noticed a bead of sweat running down from Ted's hairline. *There's something else going on between them. He's scared.*

"So here's what's going to happen, boys and girls," Deanne continued. "Because I'm not a complete devil, I'm going to make you an offer. Forget about the Black Slate. Move on. Do something else and live. Keep at it and die."

"I didn't ask for the assignment," Ted said, pushing her hands away. "I don't think any of us did. And you know how it works. *They* choose you. And you don't have much of a choice in the matter."

"*They* are a problem, but I don't have any sympathy for your dilemma. Just think about it. Your family. Your friends. Their lives are on the line." Deanne shrugged. "Look, I'm here as a courtesy. You'd be wise to consider it a favor."

"I'd say you're here because we're getting too close to something," Smoke said. He pulled his shoulders back. "You're cocky. Why don't you just come out and tell us what that is?"

"Well, that's super-top-secret information, John." She gave him a little smile. "If you really want me to share it, I'll play your game, but I'll have to clear the room."

"Fine by me," Smoke said.

Sid's nerves fired. Deanne turned her gun on the waitress and fry cook. Sid tensed to spring. Ted plowed into Deanne and tackled her to the floor. The waitress and fry cook rushed for the door. Gunshots rang out. Bullets burst through glass.

"Get off me, Ted. I'm warning you," Deanne growled, fighting against the big man who had her pinned to the floor.

"Those are innocent people," he said, half spitting. "Are you mad?"

"Yeah," Deanne sneered, "I'm mad!" *Blam! Blam! Blam!*

Ted's large form sagged. His blood leaked onto the floor.

Megan screamed.

CHAPTER 28

D EANNE SPRANG BACK TO HER feet. Smoke crashed into her. He wrenched the gun from Deanne's hand and locked her up in an arm bar.

Lip bleeding, she started a nasty laugh. "You better save your friend Ted. Poor old guy. I used to like him."

Sid was on her knees. She rolled Ted over. His hands were clamped over his bleeding gut. Blood seeped through his fingers. His face was in torment. "Are they safe?" he said, spitting blood.

The waitress and fry cook were gone.

"Yes," Sid said, half choking.

Ted's eyes were glassing over.

"Hang on Ted, please, hang on."

"Fight the good fight, Sid," Ted said, spitting more blood. "Don't let those devils win."

Sid squeezed his hand.

"Such a sad thing to see. A decent man dying over a couple of nobodies," Deanne said. "Never understood it much myself. It's time you released me, Johnny Boy, if you know what's good for you."

"You aren't going anywhere," Smoke growled. "You're a murderer."

"Attempted murder on those sock puppets maybe. But I think in this case, it was self-defense. Oh well." She spoke something that sounded like German. The metal bands on her wrists lit up. A spark came out of her body.

Smoke jerked and spasmed. His grip on Deanne loosened.

The formidable woman slipped free of his grasp and drove the heel of her boot into his calf several times.

Smoke lay on the floor twitching.

As Sidney applied pressure to Ted's belly, Deanne retrieved her gun.

Walking casually over to Sidney, Deanne held the barrel on her head. "You need to let it soak in, what happened here this evening. Next time it could be you, your family, your friends." She cast a glance down at Ted's dying face. A glimmer of sadness was in Deanne's eyes. "I always liked him, but he was always kinda stupid."

"You're sick," Sid said. Her eyes swelled with water. "There's a special place for people like you."

"I know," Deanne said, backing away. "It's called the top." Police sirens squalled from outside in the streets. "Time to go. Sorry it ended this way, but maybe this was the plan all along." She backed toward the rear door of the building.

Sid felt Ted's hand find hers. Somehow, he stuffed his gun into her hand. His voice was barely a whisper. "Take her down. That's an order."

"Good-bye, Sid," Deanne said, still pointing her gun at Sid's chest. "Remember, stay away from this." Deanne turned and started to vanish into the back corridor.

Sid ripped out Ted's gun and unloaded several shots. *Blam! Blam! Blam! Blam!* She sprang to her feet and gave chase: down the hall, through the back door, and into the alley. Deanne was gone. Disappeared. Looking down, she noticed blood in the alley. *Damn! I shouldn't have missed. I shouldn't have missed.*

"You're lucky, Sid! Lucky!" Cyrus said, tapping his finger on the table. "But thanks to you, Ted is gone. How do you feel about that?"

Sitting inside an interrogation room painted with army-green walls, Sidney finished writing down the details of the incident at the café. She wiped a tear off the form and rubbed her eyes. She was hollow inside. Ted C. Howard, FBI section chief, friend, and mentor was gone. Another FBI agent was down, and to another ghost no less.

Cyrus had his sleeves rolled up over his flabby arms. He took his Coke-bottle glasses off his face. He continued his ranting. "Two witnesses saved your bacon. If it weren't for the both of them, I'd have you in jail again. You just can't play by the rules, Sid, can you? You're selfish. Dangerous."

"Shut up, Cyrus," she said in a stone-cold tone. "Everyone is hurting from all of this aside from you, it seems. I just lost one of the few men I trusted. It hurts. Hurts bad. And now you want to rub it in?" She shoved the paper across the desk and glowered at him. "I thought you'd be happy. You'll probably get a promotion."

"Huh," Cyrus said, picking up her statement. "You need to initial here." He set it back down. "Look, I'm mad that Ted is gone." He pulled out a chair and sat down. "I'm mad that you refuse to work with me on the Slate. I'm mad. I'm mad. I'm mad." He took out a handkerchief and cleaned his glasses. "We're supposed to be on the same side, you know? Deanna Drukker. Boy, a psychotic rogue agent." He leaned forward. "You see, Sid? That's what bothers me. What happened to her could happen to you. I'm looking out for you. You need to trust me."

She wanted to believe him. He was an agent, and she wanted to trust agents more than anything. But there were too many unanswered questions, and there was way too much weirdness with Rebecca's ear-whispering. *Let's wait and see how all of this is reported. What the papers say.* Deanne Drukker burned in Sid's mind. The older woman had half enjoyed Ted's death. *Why?* "Cyrus, I know you've always meant well." She paused. "So now what?"

"Well, we have two agents that were assaulted during your little incursion. Again, lucky for you, Mr. Smoke is going to take the fall for all of that. I'd say it's going to add a few more years to his sentence. But you are free to go. And so is Megan."

Her heart stung inside her chest. *This is my fault. All my fault.* She wanted to help. Be involved in the fight. But now Big Jake was dead. Ted was dead. Smoke was gone again. "So I'm not a liaison anymore?"

"It's early, Sid. Nothing is official yet. And you know there will be a ton of paperwork to follow." He leaned back. "I'd assume it's done, though."

"What about the Buffalo Brothers?" she said. "Deanne said they'd be out in a day. That they'd get their target one way or the other."

"Don't you worry about that."

"But I'm still official, aren't I?"

Cyrus's eyes narrowed on her. "You need to take Megan and back away from this thing."

"And if I don't?"

"Then I can have Child Protective Services over here right away."

CHAPTER 29

FBI AGENT SLAIN IN ATTEMPTED **Robbery**. That's what was all over the news the day after the incident. The story was nice and neat. It made Ted Howard out to be a hero. There were crystal-clear statements from the waitress and fry cook. It all added up. No one would suspect a thing.

Sidney set the remote down on the coffee table. It was about 6:30 a.m. Megan was still asleep in her bed. The little girl had cried until she soaked her pillow. Sidney had finally gotten her to sleep just before midnight by gently caressing her hair. Sid had been up ever since.

Why me?

All night long, she had rehashed everything. Doubted everything she'd done since high school. She was smart. She could have been anything. Why a cop? It was hard on families. Death and danger lurked at every traffic stop, routine building check, and simple apprehension. People were desperate. It made them deadly. Sidney was drawn to it.

I'm a foolish little girl.

She got up and poured another cup of coffee. She couldn't help but think of Ted's wife. His children. The funeral would be miserable. The tears would flow in streams. Her throat tightened. Her eyes swelled. She couldn't bear it. She made her way into the second bedroom. Megan lay on her back with her teddy bear tucked under her arm. Her chest gently rose and fell.

We should move south. To the beaches.

Back inside her living room, Sid turned on the television again. It was all bad news. Muggings. Murder. Scandal. Mayhem. "Fight the good fight." Those were some of Ted's last words. There had been power in them. An intense look in his fatherly eyes. He believed in what they did. What she did. She felt that in her gut. Ted used to say, "You know you're doing something right when you start pissing rotten people off."

But I don't want all this blood on my hands.

While she stared at the television, a familiar face came up. Her stomach soured. It was Congressman Wilhelm. Finely dressed and well manicured, he was a little pudgier than the last time she had seen him. His eyes had dark circles under them, and he sweated under the camera's light. He was accompanied by his son and two Secret Service agents.

"Agent Ted C. Howard," Wilhelm said, "was a dear friend of mine. A banner of law enforcement. Everything right with fine government agencies like the FBI. Let's pray that his colleagues and their associates bring the fugitive murderer to justice. My thoughts and prayers are with his family." He straightened his jacket. "Now, if you'll excuse me, I need to get to session. We've got an important bill to push through." He gave a thumbs up and walked away with his entourage in tow.

Snake.

Her sister Allison had come home battered from her last job with Congressmen Wilhelm. Defiant. Angry. It was people like Wilhelm that put people like her sister in bad places. They made promises to them then preyed on them. It was disgusting.

Now, for some odd reason, Sidney took comfort from knowing that her sister was safe with the Drake. Or perhaps it was more accurate to say Allison was just where she wanted to be: among the powerful. Standing alongside the ones calling the shots. Maybe they gave her the protection she needed. The attention that Allison always craved.

No. That's not what is best. But it's her choice. I have to help make a better life for Megan. Somehow.

She curled up on her couch and started to reassess things.

Put it together, Sid. You have to make sense of this. Did everyone die because of me? If I'm the problem, then why don't they just take me out? I'm just one person.

There was something Cyrus always said that irked her. Well, just about everything he said irked her, but there was one thing in particular. He said she led a charmed life. That she was lucky.

She never felt any more special than anyone else. Sure, she moved ahead of some people and excelled at many things, but she never thought of herself as special. It wasn't as if she used her looks to get away with things like Allison, although Sid knew being pretty did help her from time to time.

But when Cyrus said "charmed," it always felt like he meant Sid had an advantage that went beyond just being pretty.

Megan entered the room. She wore pink pajamas with cartoon characters on them. She yawned and stretched out her arms. "What's for breakfast?"

"Whatever you want."

"Pancakes and chocolate milk," Megan said. She shuffled over and snuggled up to Sidney on the couch. "I had a lot of bad dreams last night."

Sidney pulled her little niece closer. "I'm sorry. Is it anything you want to tell me?"

"Not until after I eat." Megan looked up into Sid's eyes. "I'm sorry your friend died."

"Me too." Sid kissed Megan's head. "Me too. I'm sorry you had to see that. Do you feel like going to school today?"

"You mean I have an option?"

"Of course. After all, yesterday was a bad day, and you probably didn't sleep well."

Megan yawned again. "No. School's fine. I have a math test, and there's a mobile petting zoo coming in for a visit. I want to see the llama. They make the funniest faces."

"Like this?" Sid contorted her lips and made a funny face.

Megan burst out in giggles.

Sid tickled the little girl and kept making the face.

"Stop it! Stop it, Aunt Sid!" Megan cried, laughing.

"All right," Sid said. She pulled Megan out of the couch pillows and dragged her to her feet. She gave her a big hug. "Now get ready. We'll swing by the Country Kitchen and eat there."

Megan's eyes widened. "Before school?"

"Yep."

"Yay!" Megan vanished into the bedroom.

Taking a breath, Sid turned off the television and drank down more coffee. *Now that's a much better way to start your day.* Heading for the kitchen with her empty mug, she heard a knock at her door. Slowly, she turned. On cat's feet, she made her way to the door and put her eye to the spy hole. Sadie stood on the other side. Sid opened the door.

Sadie burst in with tears in her eyes. She sounded a little hysterical. "What happened? You need to tell me what happened!"

CHAPTER 30

SADIE WAS DRESSED IN A tunic dress that hung just above the knees. She was an older black woman, always well dressed, and her decorated nails rivaled Sam's finest work. Right now Sadie's eyes were all puffy. She sat down on the sofa and blew her nose.

"Why, Sid? Why did you call me? I sent Ted to his death." Sadie sobbed. "I can't get over it. I read the paper and, and …" She blew her nose. "I knew it was my fault."

"Sadie, he was just in the wrong place at the wrong time."

The woman stiffened. Her eyes fastened on Sidney. "Don't you lie to me, Sid. Don't you dare lie to me. I'm not stupid."

"I know. But the news …"

"Don't you think I can put two and two together?" Sadie grabbed Sid by the arm. "You call. He dies. And with everything going on since you left, it makes perfect sense." Her eyes started to water again. "And now I'm part of this mess. I have to live with it." She fell forward into Sidney's arms and started sobbing. "I can't do this. I can't do this. They're going to come after me. I only have ten months, and I can retire."

Sidney felt like her chest was going to collapse. She'd gotten another friend into the crosshairs. "I don't think they're going to ask you anything."

"Why do you say that?"

"They'll move on," Sid said.

"How do you know?" Sadie leaned back and straightened up her dress. Using the tissue, she wiped her eyes. "I couldn't even get my makeup on. Now, out with it."

"Don't get mad at me for saying this—"

"Oh, I'm already mad."

"The less you know, the better."

"Huh, I figured." Sadie studied Sid's face. "You know who killed him, don't you. You were there, I bet. This whole thing is all a charade, isn't it?"

Sidney's eyes drifted away.

"Look at me," Sadie ordered.

"Not just this. A lot of things."

The room fell silent. Finally, Sadie said, "I knew it was all a bunch of horseshit. Heck, I've always known. I could feel it in my bones." She cupped Sid's cheek. "Aw, I'm sorry, Sid. I know you'll miss Ted. I'll miss him, too. He always brought me flowers on Secretaries' Day." She shuddered a sigh. "I think he knew too much. He was acting kinda nervous the last few weeks. Almost jittery. Man, I just wish it was Cyrus or that little vixen of his, Rebecca. There ain't nothing good in that one. It took me some time to figure that out, though. She's crafty like a bad Beastie Boys song."

Sid cracked a smile. "You know, I don't think Ted would want us to be whining around. Why don't you come with me and Megan to get something to eat?"

"Well, I'm not really hungry."

"Could you at least give us a lift? It's either that or a cab."

"What happened to your car?"

Sid headed for her bedroom. "I'll tell you on the way over."

Days later, Sid was lying in her bed staring at the ceiling. She wondered if she had told Sadie too much. She had held back as much as she could, but Sadie was pushy. Smart. She'd put it all together before she backed off. *I hope she's okay.*

Megan was in school. Sid had rented a car for the weekend and used it to go to Ted Howard's funeral. That had been a long, hot, miserable, rainy day. It had made her think of Jack Dydeck, her old supervisor who'd had his head ripped off by AV the wolf man. Jack's wife had been at the funeral alongside Ted's, with their kids in tow. Some young. Some old. All of their faces long, with not a single dry eye.

I live. They die. Charmed life.

She rolled onto her side and checked the clock. It was 9:40 a.m. She had no place to be. No word from Cyrus. There was just silence. A dead quiet that made her question whether she was even alive at the moment. She lay back down and rubbed her temples.

Maybe I should go for a run? Maybe I should go drink?

She ran through a mental checklist. Smoke was gone. The Hellcat was gone. Ted's murderer, Deanne Drukker, was gone. Someone needed to find that woman. Make her pay. Deanne had been so cold and calm after what she'd done. Soulless. *Is that what's in store for Allison? Can she be saved?*

"You can't save someone who doesn't want to be saved." Sid's dad, Keith, had told her that when she was a girl. He'd arrested so many people and had tried to help countless faces. He wanted to help get their lives back on track. But almost all of them didn't want to dig themselves out of the hole. No amount of convincing could change that. Her sister was like that. It was scary. Not even the love Allison must feel for Megan was enough to pull her out of the abyss. So it seemed. Perhaps Deanne Drukker was the same way.

Maybe I should move on.

A battle stirred inside Sid. One side wanted to quit. The other wanted to fight. Deanne needed to be brought to justice. Murderers and other monsters were running free. Someone had to stop them. She eyed her guns hanging inside the door of her closet.

Bounty hunter by day, babysitter by night?

Quickly she got up off the bed and made her way to the closet door. She checked her wallet. It still had her FBI liaison card. She had some access left. Some authority. Maybe Cyrus was wrong or lying. He just wanted her away from the case, but if anyone had answers, it would be him. *Him and that little snake, Rebecca.*

She strapped on her shoulder holster and gun. "That's better." She got a little bit of a charge from it. A feeling of wholeness. She picked up her phone from the nightstand and sent out a text to Sam:

"We need eyes and ears on Cyrus and Rebecca," Sid wrote.

A text came back. "We're on it like flies on stink. Glad you're back in the game."

CHAPTER 31

OVER THE NEXT TWO DAYS, Sidney lay low. She kept things routine. She took Megan to school in the silver Dodge Charger she'd rented. She texted with Sam a couple times a day. She paid close attention to the local news, both on TV and on the Internet. She even logged into *Nightfall DC*, but there weren't any new stories. Things were quiet. Oddly so, leaving her too much time to think. She couldn't help but think that the Buffalo Brothers were going to strike.

She pulled the car into the parking lot near the Washington Memorial. Wearing her bright-green-and-black jogging clothes, she donned her headphones and took off at a trot, thinking a few miles would do her some good. She made her way toward the Reflecting Pool and had finished two laps when the phone buzzed. She checked her screen.

The text from Sam read, "Cyrus is headed to Law Park Offices. Murder scene. Bad."

"Morning glory."

On long legs, Sid sprinted back to her car. The Law Park Offices were where Winslow Swift worked. She and Smoke had been assigned to stake it out that day, to keep an eye out for Winslow Swift. She'd pretty much forgotten about him. Now it seemed another mistake had come back to haunt her.

Back at the rental car, she hopped inside and fired up the engine. She noticed a case in the passenger seat. "You've got to be kidding me." The silvery metal case was just like the one she'd gotten before—from Mal Carlson. Glancing around the area, she shook her head and popped open the case.

There was a typewritten note on a small piece of white parchment paper. It said, "You'll probably need this. MC."

A Sweet Heart suit was inside. Special bullets in clips that fit her Glock. A matching pair of razor-sharp knives that would fit her hands. There was even a small bottle with a cork in it. She rattled around the glimmering emerald pill that was inside. It was a little different than the super vitamin she'd taken the last time.

"I'll be damned. Everyone knows what I'm doing but me." She got out her pistol and slapped the clip of green-tipped bullets into it and charged the handle.

Looking around, she ducked down in the front seat and started to slip out of her clothes to put on the Sweet Heart suit, saying with a smile, "Why not fight the good fight."

The parking lot at the Law Park Offices was almost empty. People in business attire were filing out of the building. It was more like a fire drill. No one hustled. There wasn't any panic in their voices. Calmly, they chatted among themselves, loaded into their cars, and headed home.

Sid got out of her car and approached a middle-aged woman in a dark-grey business suit. "What happened?"

"The power went out," the lady said, lighting up a cigarette. "They told us all to go home. Heh. I've been here twenty-three years, and I've never had a break like this. Hell, I never even get Christmas Eve off. I'm taking it." She looked Sid up and down. "Uh, you got business?"

"Yep."

"Well, you better reschedule." The woman blew smoke into the air and stared at the misty clouds. A power truck pulled up to the building's curb, and two men in white jumpsuits hopped out and rushed into the building with metal boxes. "I'd hate to be those guys. My bosses are a bunch of real a-holes, if you know what I mean. This'll cost somebody a buttload of money. It's always money." She sucked the cigarette down to the last ash and dropped it. She crushed it with her shoe. "Money, money, money, money. See you around."

Sid made a quick scan of the parking lot. There were only a couple unmarked FBI cars. She was pretty sure the black Navigator near the front was assigned to Cyrus. Some other men and women agents, in plain clothes, had positioned themselves at the corners of the building. The best that she could tell, no one coming out had any idea that somebody had been killed.

Feeling spry in the Sweet Heart suit, she navigated through the people and slipped unnoticed into the building. All of the lights were out, but the daylight illuminated most of the lobby with dim light. She found the directory near the elevators. Sherman Investments was on the top floor. Finding the emergency stairwell, she swung open the door. The emergency lights were on. She jogged up three flights of steps and peeked through the stairwell portal.

The office was dark but not without window light. The secretary's desk was abandoned. A flashlight beam flashed over cubicles deeper in the room.

Sid pushed through the door and quietly closed it behind her. The Sherman Investments lobby was top flight. Leather chairs and sofas. Chocolate marble walls. A waterfall dripped into the pond full of large goldfish. She passed the break room. There was an industrial-sized cappuccino machine. The scent of rich coffee grounds lingered in the air. On cat's feet, she pressed deeper into the facility. There were low voices and rustlings coming from a conference room that was enclosed in glass. Sid's heart skipped. There was blood splattered all over it. A flashlight glared in her eyes.

"Freeze!"

CHAPTER 32

IN A LIGHTNING-QUICK SWIPE, SID knocked the flashlight out of the man's hand. She wrenched his hand behind his back and drove him into the wall. Two more men burst out of the conference room with their guns lowered on her chest. One of them was Cyrus.

"Dammit, Sid!" he said. "What are you doing here?"

"Serving as a liaison," she said.

"I oughta shoot you." He shook his head and holstered his weapon. The other man did the same. "Since you're here, well," he stepped aside, out of the doorway, "be my guest."

She tilted her head to the side. "Really?"

"I don't think it's going to make a difference. Your life is finished anyway."

She walked into the conference room and surveyed the grisly scene. Five bodies sat around in office chairs with buffalo nickels inside their eyes. Four men. One woman. They'd been cut to ribbons. A knife still protruded from one man's chest. Another's neck was shoved backward. The woman had darkening bruises around her neck.

"I don't see Winslow Swift," she said. "So, where's your partner?"

Cyrus was texting someone when he looked up. "Huh? Oh, don't you worry about her. So what do you make of this?"

"Do we have anything other than the bodies? Any video?"

"Power's out."

"The power is out thanks to you."

"Heh. Look, you've seen. Now you can go."

"Just like that?"

"You stuck your nose into it, Sid. Get a sniff, offer some advice, and move on. I don't know what else to tell you."

She noticed a folded letter in the crook of his arm. She snatched it and opened it up to read it out loud. "This is what happens to thieves." There was a Drake stamp on it. "Interesting." She laughed. "He robbed the Drake, and we're worried about it? Excuse me, you're worried about it? So how much did this swindler steal?"

"Uh, Zed," he said to the other agent in the room, "give us a moment." Cyrus watched the man leave and then continued in a low voice, "Over a billion."

"Oh, now that must have hurt. So now the FBI is helping the Drake find their money?"

"No, we are following the money," he said. "And Winslow Swift has it. This is a message. A nasty one."

Her eyes searched the dead bodies. There were signs of torture on all of them. Broken fingers and missing ones as well. Sadistic carnage. "So the Buffalo Brothers came to deliver a message?"

"Er, and to find Winslow," he said with a twitch in his eye. "Naturally."

She knew he was holding back. The FBI, or someone over the FBI, was protecting Winslow for some reason. There was something bigger. Something deeper going on. Watching Cyrus text, she said, "You have Winslow, don't you."

Cyrus kept texting.

She stepped closer and covered his phone with her hand. "Look at me, Cyrus."

He glanced up. His eyes were all jittery. His forehead beaded in sweat. His Adam's apple rolled inside his neck. "I-I don't know what you're talking about."

Sid had never seen Cyrus nervous before. If anything, he had ice in his veins. Perhaps Ted's violent death *had* gotten to him. Perhaps he knew he could be in the crosshairs next. Something was on the man's conscience. Something bad. She decided to play nice. She put a little honey in her voice. "Come on, Cyrus. You've always known that I was trustworthy. And I've never lied to you. It's not like we haven't shared secrets before. Let's be a team again."

He stepped over to the door and closed it, leaving them in a stuffy room filled with the dead. "We have Winslow. We're using him as bait to capture the Buffalo Brothers. *They* want those guys off the Slate. They want them bad." He blotted the sweat from his brow with a handkerchief. He started shaking his head. "I shouldn't have agreed to this. I never should have let her do it." He kicked the chair. "How stupid of me!"

"Let who do what?" Sid said.

"Rebecca was guarding Winslow. Back in the same place we held you." His face filled with strain. His voice cracked. "They took her. They took Winslow." He handed her a cell phone. "Look."

There was a picture on it. Rebecca was bound up in a chair. Her face was bruised and swollen, her blonde hair matted. Two men with knives were in the picture as well, but their heads weren't showing. She moved to the other picture. Winslow was stripped down to his undershirt and lying on the floor. His nose was busted open.

There was a text message: "Return the money or they die."

CHAPTER 33

EVERY MAN HAD A WEAKNESS. Cyrus's was women. He fell too hard for them. He'd fallen hard for Sidney and overdone it. Now that same thing was happening with Rebecca. Sid could see it in his face. He was all torn up inside over it. The same tormented look was on his face like the day she had walked away from him. It tugged at her own heart a little.

"We'll get her back," Sid said to Cyrus. "I swear it."

Over the next few hours, they worked with a tactical team. During that time, Cyrus came clean with a few more things.

"Winslow embezzled one billion from the Drake," Cyrus explained. "Sort of. You see, according to Winslow, the money was supposed to be spread out among several political fund-raising organizations. As it turns out, that money never showed up. Instead, it wound up in the Cayman Islands and Switzerland. Maybe some of it's buried in Swaziland, for all I know. Well, May is coming up. Election time, and a whole bunch of incumbents are about to get burned." Standing outside the Law Park Offices, he strapped on his body armor and checked his gun. "So that's why we're involved. I hate to say it, but some congressmen and senators are all up in this, and they aren't happy at all. It's just a damned dirty business. Not what I signed up for." He holstered his gun. "I just want to get Rebecca out of this jam. But Winslow, he's screwed. He has names. They want to either control him or shut him up. I don't know. I just want to get Rebecca out."

The information was a lot for Sid to swallow, but she felt a chuckle inside. The Drake was out a billion in resources. It would cost them power and influence. The dirty politicians were screwed because many of them would be out of jobs. And it was all on account of one greedy little SOB.

The snakes devour each other. How poetic.

Sidney eyed the little case Cyrus had in his hand. Another agent had delivered it an hour earlier. It had a coded chip in it, and on that chip was an account for one billion in bitcoins. "So, if the money's hidden, how'd they scrape up a billion?"

"Huh. I don't even want to know, but clearly Winslow had insurance," Cyrus said. "He had names. I'm pretty sure if anything happens to him, then all of that dirt under the rug is going to be exposed. You'd think they'd kill Winslow, but it's like *Catch 22*. He's their lawyer. If he dies, then I think all their hard work is set back a decade." He almost laughed. "One way or the other, a lot of heads are going to roll because of this." He glanced at Sid. "So, are you sure you want to do this?"

A light rain began to speckle her rental car. The balmy day was unusually cool for this time of year. "I guess this is what liaisons do. Let's deliver the mail. My car or yours?"

The plan was simple. Per the request of the Drake, they were to deliver the chip to Mallows Bay. If everything was in order, Rebecca and Winslow would be released, and everyone could walk away. Sid pulled into the Mallows Bay parking lot. She was surprised Cyrus had let her drive, but he was preoccupied with his phone. He talked. He texted. She wasn't entirely sure who with. It seemed he had access to whoever was calling the shots, but the odd thing was—why was she included? Again, someone knew what she was doing before she did. It ate at her.

The brakes squeaked as she brought the vehicle to a halt at the edge of the Mallows Bay boat ramp. "Are you ready?" she asked Cyrus.

Cyrus rubbed his hands on this thighs. "Why do you think I let you bring your vehicle and not mine?" He coughed out an uncomfortable laugh. "I hope you got the damage waiver on this rental."

Sid studied the choppy waters of the bay full of sunken ships. Now that she knew what she was looking for, her keen eyes could make out the faint outline of a road underneath the water. She peered at the edges of it, envisioning the deaders crawling up onto them. *Come on out so I can run you over.* "All right, let's go."

The car eased into the water, tires almost a foot deep, following a straight line toward the half-sunken tanker. A dozen yards out they were surrounded by the murky waters on all sides. Sid sat up straight in her seat, peering over the edge of the car's hood. The hairs on her arms tingled. A gaping hole appeared in the middle of the bay. A rush of water poured around the tunnel's mouth, spilling into a great vat surrounding the submerged road. It was a marvel. A feat of engineering or something else. Something unnatural. The road moved deeper into the waters.

Cyrus looked at her and said, "I think I'm going to vomit."

"You can swim, right?" Sid asked.

"Yeah. Now why did you have to ask that?"

She made a little smirk and eased on the gas. The car's hood dipped down, and in seconds, they were below the waters and driving through a tunnel of glass or plastic. It was something similar to what Sid had seen at the massive National Aquarium in DC before it closed. There weren't any colorful fish, however, just glimpses of sunken ships in the muddied waters.

After they had driven along at five miles per hour for what seemed a long time, the great tanker's hull appeared. The tunnel led right into its belly. She kept driving, headlights on, into the darkness until some lights appeared ahead. After another thirty yards, they were inside the sunken ship's belly.

Cyrus's mouth dropped open. "You have got to be kidding me."

The inner hull of the ship gleamed with new metal. There were catwalks. Rows of metal shelving. A forklift. A Bobcat bulldozer. Several cars. Sid brought the car to a stop and turned the engine off. She and Cyrus got out. Behind them, a white cargo van with the Drake markings blocked their exit.

"Looks like we're staying for dinner," Sid said. Her thoughts drifted to Megan. *I'm a lousy aunt.*

The van groaned as the big man stepped out the door. It was Warren Ratson, mirrored glasses and all. Coming from the other side was his brother, Oliver. His chin jutted out from his long, crane-like neck. A nasty smirk was on his face. The two imposing men flanked them.

"Time for a patdown," Oliver said, closing in on Sid. "Don't get all excited, pretty girl. My sap doesn't rise like it did in the good ol' days among the living."

She turned her head. His breath was like the rot of the dead. He ran his hands down her shoulders and over her chest and stopped. He took her gun and tossed it aside. "Wouldn't do you any good against us anyway, but there's still a few other warm bodies around." His gruff hands rested on her hips. He swayed a little. "You know, I used to like to dance back in the day. I liked that Chuck Berry's Twist. Ew, what do we have here?" He slipped out the knives she'd pulled out of Mal Carlson's case. He thumbed their edges. "Very nice. I bet I could skin your eyeball with this."

"Or you could cut your tongue out with it," she said.

"Heh-heh," Oliver said. "You've got spirit." He ran the tip of the blade down her cheek, making a paper-thin cut. "It's going to be fun watching you bleed."

CHAPTER 34

S ID BALLED UP HER FIST.

Oliver glanced down at her side and said, "Don't get wise, little lady. You'll only bust a nail, and I'll bust you." He slapped her hard on the ass, half lifting her out of her shoes. "You liked that, didn't you."

Sidney lashed out. Turning into a back spin, she drove her elbow into his face. It crushed the cartilage that formed the bridge of his nose.

Oliver staggered back. "What the—"

Sid drove her booted foot into his gut, doubling him over. In a cat-quick move, she leg-swept his feet, knocking him flat onto his back. She heard laughing. Warren Ratson held Cyrus by the neck. His fingers were crushing his throat.

"I could snap it like a chicken's," Warren said. He shook Cyrus. "What a fleck of a man."

Sidney's ears caught a rustle on the metal deck. She turned.

Striking with speed that defied his size, Oliver pounced on top of her. He pinned her down, clamped his hand over her throat, and pulled his fist back to strike.

"That's enough!" A strong feminine voice echoed in the hollow metal chamber. "This is a business transaction. Not a bar fight."

Deanne Drukker stood on one of the catwalks overlooking the main floor. She was dressed in black cargo pants and a sleeveless camo shirt. Her hips sported a pair of Luger-like guns.

Oliver released Sid's throat and leaned back. He pushed his nose back into place with a sickening crunch. He took a big snort of air. He pointed his sausage-sized finger into Sid's face. "I'll get you." He stood up and moved away.

Sid gathered her feet beneath her and rose back up.

Warren Ratson dropped Cyrus to the new-metal floor.

The flabby man fell to his knees and started coughing.

Sid helped him back to his feet and said up to Deanne, "I was hoping I'd see you at Ted's funeral."

"I bet you were," Deanne replied. "Sorry I couldn't be there, but hey, I just didn't care." She put her fingers to her lips and made a sharp whistle. "Let's get this over with. I've got things to do."

A pair of upright gurneys with two bodies strapped to them were being pushed her way. On them were Rachel and Winslow. Both of them had bizarre masks over their faces, something similar to what Sid had seen in *The Silence of the Lambs*.

"Looks like you forgot the straitjackets," Sid said with disdain. "Is that really necessary?"

"The Ratson brothers have a twisted sense of humor," Deanne said from above. "Which is odd for deaders."

"We're not entirely dead," Oliver said with a grunt. "Just mostly dead." He rolled the sleeves up on his meaty arms. They were coated in mesmerizing tattoos filled with what seemed to be living arcane symbols. "Bet you ain't ever seen anything like that before, have you, Sweetheart?" He gave Sid a wink.

"They say anything you see on TV can become reality," Sid said, "so it doesn't surprise me. Who knows, if you survive long enough, maybe you'll get your own reality TV show."

"She's a funny one," Oliver said up toward Deanne. "I can see why you like her."

"Charming, aren't they?" Deanne said. She walked over the planks of the catwalk and made her way down a set of spiraling stairs. Upon hitting the main floor, she approached, stopping in between the undead Ratson brothers. "They are quite the marvel. Bloodless but still alive, thanks to the supernatural and some arcane medical advances. How can you kill something that cannot bleed?"

"Are you a deader too?" Sidney said to Deanne.

The woman stiffened at the remark. Regaining her composure, she said, "No. I can still bleed. For the time being," she said with a wink. "Now, I believe you have something for me. If all goes well, then we can part ways in peace. And Sid, you really need to get away from all this."

"I won't stop until I've taken you down. You can count on that."

Deanne huffed. "We'll see. You never know. You might just change your mind about that. I thought like you once." She laid her eyes on Cyrus. "All right, Specs. Get the payment." She patted the gun on her side. "And don't try to be clever."

Cyrus slid over to the car and retrieved the little silver case with the bitcoin codes in it. He tried to hand it to Deanne.

She sneered at him. "Open it."

Cyrus complied. The inside of the case revealed a small chip tethered to a smartphone cable. He plucked it up and dangled it in front of her face. "I don't think it's dangerous."

Deanne received it and plugged the device into her phone. "Bitcoin. Pretty hard to trace the source. What will the world of greedy men—and women— think of next? And the funny thing is, bitcoin is pretty volatile right now. But a few well-placed articles posted in the *Wall Street Journal*, and boom, one billion becomes ten. I just love how those one-percenters think."

"Of course you would," Sidney said. She was making a little small talk while scanning the insides of the ship. Her stomach filled with butterflies. Her hands turned clammy. Other than Deanne, the Ratson brothers, and the two deaders, there wasn't anyone else in there. It seemed odd. There had to be more. There was merchandise everywhere. "I hope you enjoy your cut," she added.

"It's uploading to our account," Deanne said, staring at her phone's screen. Keeping her eyes fixed on that, she said, "Oh, I don't do it for the money. I do it for the power. I do it for the thrill of it. It's so exhilarating." Her mouth fell open, and her brows buckled. "What's this?" She stormed over to Cyrus and stuck the phone in his face. "What's this?"

"Uh," Cyrus said, blanching, "it looks like only a hundred million dollars. Look, I didn't have anything to do with that. I'm just here to pick up and—"

Deanne punched him in the face. *Whack!* She smashed her phone on the floor. "Kill them! Kill them all!"

Quick as a snake, Oliver Ratson caught Sid up in his arms and picked her up off her feet.

Deanne then pulled out her guns and pointed one down at Cyrus and the other at Sid. "Aw, hell, I'll do it myself."

CHAPTER 35

C YRUS BALLED UP INTO THE fetal position and peed his pants.

Sydney could feel Deanne begin to squeeze the trigger. "No, wait!" she said.

"You had your chance," Deanne said.

Out of nowhere, the unexpected happened. The trunk of Sid's rental car, the silver Dodge Charger, popped open.

Deanne pulled her gun barrel up and cocked her head. "Check it out," she said to Warren Ratson, who stood to her right.

"Okay, Boss." The muscle-packed deader started toward the rear of the car. Just as he started to pass the hood, the car bounced a little. A tall, rangy man stepped into view.

Sid's heart leapt.

Smoke stood tall. Dressed in black attire from neck to toe, he seemed to leer down at all of them. In his large hands, he held a monster of a machine gun like a toy. It was an M-60, just like the one Rambo used in the movies. Smoke had two bandoliers of ammo crisscrossed over his shoulders. He lowered the barrel at Warren. "Don't move, dead man."

Warren froze but managed to cluck a chuckle. "You can't kill me. Go ahead. Take your best shot."

Smoke pulled the weapon tight to his chest and took aim. He squeezed the trigger.

Buppa-Buppa-Buppa!

Buppa-Buppa-Buppa! Buppa-Buppa-Buppa!

The first burst of ammo bored a hole through Warren's head so big that you could see clean through. The second burst tore out his heart. The third left the undead man disemboweled. Warren Ratson staggered around on clay feet before collapsing with a heavy *thunk* onto the ship's hull.

"Any more volunteers?" Smoke said. He pointed the smoking barrel at Deanne. "We're going to be leaving, and you'll be coming with."

"You! You! You killed my brother!" Oliver Ratson screamed.

He was still bear hugging Sid. His powerful arms were squeezing her ribs. She winced.

All puffed up and chest heaving, he rambled on. "You'll pay! You'll pay!"

"He might not be dead. He's still twitching," Smoke said. "Now, make yourself useful and get down on your hands and knees. Both of you."

"I don't think so, Mr. Smoke," Deanne said. She had both guns out, one pointed at Sid and the other at Cyrus. The woman was filled with eerie confidence. "You see, this ship, it's filled with deaders. And the only live person walking away from here will be me." She tipped her head toward Winslow. The man was wide eyed on the gurney. "And probably him. I guess we'll just have to skim our money off him. And of course, I'll have to put a nice hole in your girlfriend."

"She not my girlfriend," Smoke said. His eyes found Sid's. "Are you?"

Hands half up, she said, "No."

"You don't sound very certain," Smoke said. "Are you sure about that?"

No. "Yes." Sid glared at him. "This isn't the time for that."

"Oh, I think it is. I love to hear the famous last words of people who are half in the grave," Deanne said. "Believe me, I've heard the worst of them. So cliché almost every time. They tell me, 'You'll burn in hell' for this or that. Or, 'I'll see you in hell.' I'd be curious to hear what the both of you have to say. It's always so much more delicious watching people who care about each other go down."

"We aren't going down," Sid said. "You are."

"No, I don't think so." Deanne took a full step closer and pointed her Luger at Sid's nose. "Mr. Smoke. Set your weapon down or watch your, well, wannabe girlfriend die. I'll do it, you know."

"You're a murderer," Smoke said with a dark threat in his voice. "And murderers have to die."

"Oh, you won't kill me," Deanne said. "That's why they picked you out over many others. Sure, you'll kill the monsters, but you always spare the men—and women. It's such a weakness for those who hold onto such lofty standards. That's what separates the haves from the have-nots, you know. Conscience. People like me prey on fools like you. Now, set down the weapon, Smoke, and slide it over here."

"You're a murderer, and murderers have to die," Smoke said again.

"Stop saying that!" Deanne said. She jerked her head. "I'm only going to say this one more time. Give up your weapon."

Smoke set the machine gun down and slid it far away. He held his hands up. "You're a murderer, and murderers have to die."

"Ugh," Deanne sneered. "You really shouldn't have said that again." She took aim at Smoke with her left hand and fired. *Blam!*

CHAPTER 36

S ID'S LIMBS FROZE.

The shot rang out, echoing loudly inside the metal hull of the ship.

Smoke spun around and fell to the deck.

Sid fought against her captor, Oliver, but he held her fast. Finally, she pulled her tongue off the roof of her mouth and said, "You're evil!"

"And a good shot. Don't forget that," Deanne said.

"Not that good," the voice of Smoke said. He stood on his feet again. His countenance was fierce. Stark. "You missed."

Face contorted in rage, Deanne started to blast away with both barrels. *Blam! Blam! Blam! Blam!* The loud shots echoed all around. Bullet holes peppered Sid's rental car. Smoke, like a panther, slipped into cover and vanished.

From somewhere behind the car, Smoke said it again. "You're a murderer. Murderers have to die."

"Deaders," Deanne said to the two goons behind the gurneys. She motioned to Sid. "Seize her."

Just as Oliver released her, the two deaders latched onto her arms.

"Oliver, kill Smoke!" Deanne ordered. She started to circle the vehicle, firing shot after shot until her magazines emptied. "Dammit!" She bounced the guns off the floor. "Dammit!"

Sidney noticed Cyrus was still huddled on the new-metal hull with his eyes squeezed shut. He hadn't even cracked them open to see what was going on. Deanne walked over and kicked him hard in the back several times. Cyrus groaned. Deanne kicked him again.

Now, in front of a captive audience, Smoke and Oliver circled Sid's rented Dodge Charger.

"I'm going to tear you in half for what you did to my brother," Oliver said. He drove his fist into the car and put a dent into it. He crossed over the front of the car, shifting back and forth, trying to figure out which way Smoke would go. "What's the matter? You chicken?"

"No," Smoke said, mostly hidden by the popped-open trunk. "I'm just reloading." He slammed the trunk shut and stood with a synthetic shotgun in his hands. "Come and get some."

"Huh. Those little bits of grain won't stop me!" Like a great ape, Oliver leapt onto the hood of the car and scrambled over the roof.

Smoke opened fire. *Ka-blam! Ka-blam! Ka-blam!*

Chunks of flesh were ripped from Oliver's body, but he churned on and pounced on top of Smoke. The two vast men thrashed back and forth. They punched. Kneed. Kicked. A heavyweight bout of two relentless champions.

"This is good," Sid heard Deanne say. "Real good."

Smoke broke free and backpedaled away. His face was bleeding, and his shoulder dangled. Oliver circled him with hands clutching open and closed. Half of his face was shot off, revealing lots of teeth. A chunk of shoulder and another of leg were gone as well. "I'm going to make you feel every bit of what you did to my brother."

Sid recoiled in her captors' arms. Her heart sank. It was clear that Smoke's shoulder was dislocated. Oliver, with his supernaturally charged hulking frame, would make good on his words. He'd tear him apart. *I hope he has on his Sweet Heart suit.*

"I don't guess you'll be getting an engagement ring anytime soon," Deanne said to her. She put her fists on her hips. "This will be good. Just wish I had some popcorn."

Oliver charged.

There was a flash of silver like a strike of lightning. Oliver stopped in his tracks and glanced down. A blade was sunk hilt deep into his chest. "Aw, shit." He dropped onto his knees and toppled over on his side.

Smoke limped over to the car and leaned against it, panting. Bracing himself against the car, he shoved his shoulder back into place and yelled. He sagged to the hull floor, beaded in blood and sweat.

"Bravo," Deanne said, plucking up one of Sidney's knives. "And after all that, I'm still going to kill you all." She came at Sid. "You first."

CHAPTER 37

Held fast by the deaders, Sidney used their strength as an anchor. She leapt upward, launching a kick, disarming Deanne, and flipping over. Using her leverage, she pulled the deaders' heads together, loosening their grip. She twisted free.

"Seize her," Deanne ordered again. "Seize her!"

The deaders clutched after Sid.

Gunshots rang out. *Blam! Blam!*

The deaders recoiled. Each had a hole in the head. Adjacent to them, Cyrus had his Glock on them. The deaders resumed their attack on Sid. "Why aren't they falling?" he said with wide eyes.

"They aren't zombies," Sid cried out, trying to free herself from their clutches.

In a burst of movement, Deanne dashed away and wrenched the Glock from Cyrus's hands. She then said, "You have to shoot the heart." *Blam! Blam!*

The deaders fell flat.

Deanne cracked Cyrus between the eyes with the butt of the weapon and sent him bleeding to the shiny metal floor. She then turned the gun on Sid. "It's still over."

"Over?" Sid said, cracking her neck from side to side. She shifted into a fighting stance. "If you're such a badass, why don't you show me what you got?"

"Oh ho, I see the golden princess has some vengeance in her eyes." Deanne smiled. "I trained Ted. Ted trained you. This will be interesting. I tell you what. You win, I'm your prisoner. You lose? Well, you all die. And just to make sure that my efforts are secured," she put her fingers to her lips and let out a sharp whistle, "I'm bringing in some special referees."

The interior of the sweltering ship started to rattle. From the dark exterior of the ship's hull came a shuffling of feet. Deaders were coming. They moved slowly but determined. A mix of men and women, half-animated with blank faces. They held heavy working tools like clubs. On their heads were metal bands with faint blinking lights. They wore dark-navy pea coats with beige jumpsuits underneath. Twenty or so encircled all of them.

Sidney took a deep draw through her nose. She thought about Ted. His family. His friends. She set her jaw. "Let's do this."

"Let's do," Deanne said. "Ding. Ding." She came in high, feinted down, and executed a perfect leg sweep.

Sid landed flat on her back. "*Oof!*" On instinct, she pushed herself back to her feet. *That was fast. Really fast.* Sid had fought plenty of people in her days. Men. Women. She had a case filled with trophies from tournaments, but none of that compared to what it was like when your life was on the line.

"If you want, you can just give up, and I'll make it easy," Deanne said.

"No thanks."

"Suit yourself." Deanne lunged in. She kicked high. Punched low. Landed shot after shot after shot. *Wap! Wap! Wap!*

Sid counterpunched. Counterkicked.

Deanne slipped away, drove in again, and lit up her ribs. "Stings, doesn't it, little Sidney?" Deanne backed off and circled. "Yeah, those Sweet Heart suits are really good against puncture wounds, but that won't stop me from jangling up your innards." She mopped the sweat from her eyes. "This is where I'd normally say you'll be sore tomorrow, but you'll be long dead before sunrise."

"We'll see about that," Sid said. Nostrils flaring, she rushed in and unleashed her rage. Locking her hands over Deanne's head, she started driving her knee into the woman's ribs. She locked her fingers in the woman's hair, jerked her head back, and punched her in the jaw. Deanne's head rocked backward, and her knees buckled. Sid hit her again. And again. Bone smacked into bone. *Wap! Wap! Wap! Wap!*

Nose bleeding, Deanne spit out a mouthful of blood. In one swift move, she executed a judo throw and toppled Sidney over. She shoved her forearm into Sidney's throat and put her full weight on it. "You're tough. I'll have them put that on your tombstone."

Face reddening, Sidney pushed back against the woman's power. Deanne was strong. Solid. She had the leverage and the glazed look of a killer in her eye. Sidney drew her fist back and launched it hard into the woman's ear.

Deanne's teeth clacked together. Her taut body went limber.

Sid slugged her again, smiting her in the jaw.

Deanne's eyes flashed with anger. She still had Sidney pinned down, legs clamped over her waist. "I've had enough of this." She unleashed a flurry of hard punches.

Sid blocked some. She caught the full force of the others. Fighting against the unrelenting surge, her arms began to get heavy. Her arms juddered against every blow. *She's a maniac. She's a machine.* Fighting for her life, her limbs failed just as Deanne's fingers locked around her throat.

"Time to die," Deanne said, ramping up the pressure.

Sid took a halfhearted swing. The blow scraped off Deanne's brow, cutting a little slit above her eye. Blood dripped from the wound and onto Sid's face.

I can't die like this. I can't die.

CHAPTER 38

EGAN'S FACE FLASHED IN SID'S mind. Who would take care of her? New strength surged through her veins. She dug her fingers into one of Deanne's hands. *I won't die like this!* She locked onto Deanne's thumb and wrenched it backward.

Deanne let out a pained yelp. "Ouch!" The woman jumped up and away.

Sid held onto Deanne's arm and slung the rogue agent back down. Jaws clenched, she wrestled the older woman onto her stomach and rammed her elbow into her kidneys.

Deanne let out another yelp.

Sid shoved her onto her back and pinned her down the same way Deanne had her before. Like an MMA fighter, she started punching, one blow after the other. "You're going to pay for what you did to Ted!" *Whap!* A glint of steel caught her eye. It was one of her knives. Sid plucked it up off the metal floor and raised it over her head. You're going to pay!"

Deanne's body was limp. Her eyes were wide open, and she was panting. "Go ahead if you have the guts. Go ahead."

"Rrrrah!" Sid cried, bringing the knife down with all her might.

Deanne lurched. Eyes blinking, she stared at the blade stuck in the ship's hull by her side. She let out a ragged sigh.

On her knees, Sid rolled Deanne over.

Cyrus tossed her some flex cuffs, and with a knife, he cut loose Rebecca and Winslow.

Still, they were surrounded by deaders. The strange half-dead people clutched oversized wrenches, pry bars, and chains in their hands.

"Call them off," Sid said to Deanne. "Call them off."

"No. I can't do that. It would be disloyal." Deanne took in a sharp breath and started to whistle.

Buppa-Buppa-Buppa!

Buppa-Buppa-Buppa! Buppa-Buppa-Buppa!

Sid, Cyrus, Rebecca, and Winslow hit the deck.

Smoke stood like a giant unloading one blast of rounds after another into the deaders with the M-60 machine gun.

Bullets tore through their flesh. Heads were chopped up and severed. Body parts became tiny bits and pieces. It was carnage. Raw. Overwhelming. Smoke cut one deader clean in half. Its torso fell from its pelvis. One after another they fell under the heavy barrage of bullets. The gunfire stopped.

"Hold on," Smoke said, eyeing the heap of twitching bodies. He loaded up another belt of a hundred rounds of ammo. "Resume fire."

Buppa-Buppa-Buppa!

Buppa-Buppa-Buppa! Buppa-Buppa-Buppa!

Seconds later, all the deaders were nothing but a pile of rotten cat food. Smoke unslung the M-60 from his shoulder and tossed it back into the trunk. "Let's roll."

Everyone regained their feet. Cyrus's eyes were fixed on the leaf pile of exterminated bodies. He turned toward Smoke. "I'm not sure if that's sick or not." Taking out a handkerchief, he blotted the bloody spot on his forehead. "Ow."

"I'm glad I don't have to do all those reports like I used to," Sid said to Cyrus. "This case is all yours."

"Oh, you're still going to have to make a statement." Cyrus faced Deanne. "And you are going away for a very long time."

Deanne stood hunched over, listless eyes on the floor. Her spark was gone. It was as if a shroud of death had fallen over her.

"I bet she's chock full of useful information about the Black Slate," Sid said, still trying to catch a full breath. "Just don't let her get a reduced sentence."

"I won't."

An engine started up. Smoke was backing up the Drake van that was blocking the exit. "Hey, I've got shotgun!" he yelled out the window.

"Okay, let's load up, everyone," Cyrus said. He shoved Winslow into the back seat of the car. "Rebecca," he said, looking around. "Rebecca?"

Blam!

Sidney spun around. Rebecca had a gun pointed at Deanne. She intently watched the woman's figure collapse on the floor. Deanne had a bullet in the back of her head. Her eyes were glassy. She was dead.

"Rebecca!" Cyrus said, rushing over but showing some hesitation. "What have you done?"

Sidney found the woman's next statement eerie. With a bit of a deranged look in her eye, Rebecca said, "She's a murderer. All murderers must die."

CHAPTER 39

BACK INSIDE FBI HEADQUARTERS, SIDNEY sat in the lobby just outside Ted Howard's old office. Smoke sat on the opposite end of the contemporary orange sofa, leaning back with one leg crossed over the other, reading a law enforcement magazine. Across from him was Ted's secretary, Jane, pecking away at the keyboard. She looked stunning as usual, but her posture was stooped a little. Sid noticed a box of tissues on her desk where there had never been one before. Not ever.

I miss Ted.

Inside Ted's office, an occasional outburst caught Sid's ear. The offices were well insulated, but nothing did well to muffle raised voices. Sid had already been sitting there for more than thirty minutes, and Smoke had already been there when she came. He wore work boots, jeans, and a black T-shirt with a white dragon logo on it. All they did was say hi. She hadn't seen him since they left Mallows Bay, and that had been two days ago. She glanced at the nameplate on the office door for the twentieth time. She rubbed her swollen hands.

Cyrus Tweel. Interim Section Chief.

It gnawed at her gut. She could have been a section chief one day. She'd often thought about it. It was just part of the natural progression of the career path. But she wouldn't have wanted it under these circumstances. Still, that was how things happened sometimes. Usually people moved on. Sometimes they just died. In the case of Ted, he'd been murdered. She couldn't help but think there was a greater design to it. Deanne had made a strong hint about it. Now Cyrus was in place. Her eyes glided over to Smoke.

How can he always be so relaxed? He's going back to prison.

He looked over, and his face lit up in a pleasant expression. He turned back to his magazine. He'd made a confession to her. A deep one. She'd rejected it without any kind of good reason. "Love isn't a convenience. It's a commitment." That's what her mother Sally always said. Sid wanted Smoke, though. At least she thought she did, but she resisted. Every time he went back into the system, it tore her up a little more. She wasn't being selfish. She just couldn't commit to that. She scooted over toward him.

"Hi," she said.

He put the magazine down. "Hey, Sid, what's up?"

"Something's been eating at me."

His handsome, dark eyes widened a little.

She continued. "How'd you wind up in the trunk?"

His brightness dimmed. "I'm a hero. I had to be where I had to be."

"Huh," she said. "So, you're a hero. Sure, I guess I should have known that. Makes perfect sense. We're all about to die and you pop up out of the trunk like a jack-in-the-box."

"More like a Smoke-in-the-box," he corrected.

"Maybe more like a jack-ass-in-the-box."

Jane stopped typing.

Smoke bobbed his chin. "If you say so."

"Look, I'm sorry, that wasn't right. I just—"

Ted's office door popped open. Rebecca, dressed in a skinny business suit and high heels, exited. Her cheeks were flushed red. She glared at Smoke and Sid as she stormed by.

I hope that psycho got what she deserved. The electric chair, perhaps. Bzzt!

Cyrus stuck his head out. His entire forehead had a white bandage taped over it. "Come on in, you two."

Inside they went, and Cyrus closed the door behind them. "Have a seat."

One of the three chairs in front of the desk was already filled. A man sat in the chair on the right. He was older, wrinkle faced, with soft brown hair and wearing a light-grey suit. His eyes were saggy but with a deep intelligence behind them. He held out a pack of Big Red gum. "Help yourself," he said in an old, Southern voice.

"No thanks," Sid said, holding up her hand. She took the middle chair.

"Sure," Smoke said, taking a stick.

"I'm Leroy Sullivan. One of the *them* in *they*." He unwrapped a piece of gum and stuck it in his mouth. He placed the pack in his jacket pocket, revealing an early model 1911 pistol. An old Army issue. "We are impressed. With both of you."

He didn't say anything after that. He just stared at them, back and forth, with soft blue eyes.

Sidney felt like a schoolgirl on pins and needles. She rubbed her hands on her thighs. She jutted her chin out and said, "Thank you?"

"Heh," Leroy said. "Well, keep up the good work. I'll be in touch." He pushed himself out of his chair and extended his hand to Sid.

She shook it. His grip was gentle but with iron behind it.

Leroy shook Smoke's hand after hers, gave Cyrus a nod, and departed the room.

Sidney stiffened at Cyrus. "What was that?"

"One of the most powerful people in Washington, DC," Cyrus said. He gave a little shrug. "I think. Anyway," he pulled out a black file thicker than a Bible and dropped it on the desk, "he's one of the men behind the Black Slate." He nodded his chin. "Seems like there's an awful lot of people on the Black Slate."

"So ..." she said.

"They still want you on as a liaison." His eyes drifted up at Smoke. He rubbed his chin. "And you, too."

There was an awkward pause after that. Then Cyrus produced another document and slid it over the desk to Smoke. "And you can't be both a liaison and a prisoner."

Smoke picked up the paper and started to read. Sid leaned over to see it, but Smoke turned away. "I'm pardoned." He glanced up at Cyrus. "A free man?"

Cyrus nodded. "Just don't go on any big vacations. Either of you. We'll be in touch."

"But I haven't agreed to anything," Sidney said. She was still thinking about Megan.

"You'll agree. Now get out of here. We'll sort out all the details later. I've got another meeting at three." He glared at them. "Adios."

Smoke and Sid made it all the way out into the parking lot without saying a word. She swore there was a little bounce in his step. Maybe there was in hers, too, and her heart was racing. Smoke was free.

Inside the parking garage, they both stopped behind her rental car.

"I guess I'll see you around," Smoke said. He fingered one of the bullet holes in the quarter panel. "I hope you got the damage waiver."

Sid draped her long arms over his neck and said, "Shut up and kiss me."

He took her by the waist and pulled her lips up to his, and they both settled in for a long, passionate kiss.

EPILOGUE

I T WAS DINNERTIME A DAY later. Sid, Smoke, and Megan were at another one of Smoke's chosen diners. Megan was all smiles from ear to ear. The entire table was filled with food. Greasy hamburgers that half soaked the bun. Chocolate milkshakes in tall glasses with whipped cream and a cherry on top. Megan had whipped cream on her nose, and Sid was laughing. Smoke stuck his nose in his. Megan cracked up.

"You two need to stop it," Sid said, wiping off Megan's nose. "You're supposed to eat it, not wear it."

Megan giggled. Sidney's heart swelled. She hadn't had a moment like this for as long as she could remember. Still, she was a little stressed about how things with the Black Slate would work out. She thought of an older classic rock song she had heard earlier in the day. "Love Will Find a Way." She gave Megan a hug. She felt like she had everything she needed.

And then the tiny bell over the door to the restaurant rang.

A moment later, the conversation inside the diner fell silent.

Sid lifted her head.

Smoke turned and looked over his shoulder.

A woman stood in the aisle. She was stunning from head to toe. Her blonde hair was shoulder length and exquisite. A tight celery-green dress accentuated every curve. Jewels adorned her neck and fingers. Bright and tasteful. With a smoldering look, the confident woman approached, dropping every man's jaw.

Megan stood up on her seat and said, "Mommy! Mommy!" She jumped over Sid's lap and rushed into the woman's arms.

Sidney's heart dropped. She whispered in astonishment, "Allison?"

Allison hugged her daughter tight and kissed the little girl on the cheek. "Oh, I missed you, baby. I'm taking you home."

"Yay! I missed you too, Mommy!"

Sid's throat tightened. This wasn't the same Allison she'd grown up with. No, this woman was different. She had an air. A renewed confidence. A swagger very much like what she'd encountered with everyone from the Drake. Monsters and all.

CRAIG HALLORAN

THE SUPERNATURAL
BOUNTY
HUNTER
FILES

SMOKE & MIRRORS
BOOK 5

CHAPTER 1

S IDNEY COVERED HER NOSE WITH one hand and held her Glock in the other. A small beam of light shot out from a gadget mounted on top of the gun's barrel. Her feet sloshed through the muck inside the dark sewage tunnel. "There's got to be a better way to make a living."

"You wouldn't have it any other way," Smoke said. He walked step-for-step behind her, a shadowy protector with a pump-action shotgun in his hands. "Plus, it's good for the ole ticker. Keeps you from getting fat too."

"What's that supposed to mean?" she said, easing around the next bend in the tunnel.

"Just an expression."

"From where?"

"Somewhere."

Four months had passed since they took down Deanne Drukker at Mallows Bay. Allison and Megan had vanished. Sid hadn't slept well since. Now she was stuck in a sewer pipe hunting down another criminal on the Black Slate. She felt a tug on her arm and turned.

Smoke had a finger to his lips and was pointing at the light on her gun.

She turned the beam off, leaving only the two of them in the blackness. Reaching out her hand, she found his chest. His heart pounded slow and steady under her palm. Smoke was never in a rush. Never panicked. Her breathing eased.

With his soft breath on her ear, he whispered, "Listen."

The past few months with Smoke had been nothing short of odd. All business for the most part. A little pleasure in between. A strange platonic romance that neither one of them seemed to have figured out yet.

Footfalls splashed and echoed through the waters somewhere nearby.

Smoke took her hand and guided her deeper into the network of tunnels. She followed.

This wasn't their first rodeo. Just in the last few months there had been several others, but not from the Black Slate. Instead, they'd hauled in local criminals. Thugs. Bail jumpers.

Smoke called it 'easy money'.

She'd learned a few more things about Smoke that she'd never had time to notice before. He had instincts. He did things. Extraordinary things that she hadn't figured out yet, but she liked it.

Trying to ignore the stench, she followed along, one grime-soaked step after the other. She slipped and caught herself by grabbing one of Smoke's jean loops.

"This isn't the place for that."

"Hah, hah," she said, still keeping her voice low. "But I'd say our chances here are as likely as anywhere else."

Smoke didn't respond to her quip. Instead, his strong frame came to a stop.

Ahead, something soft scurried in the ankle-deep waters, sending chills down her spine. Swallowing hard, she aimed her gun barrel toward the sound.

"Easy," Smoke whispered.

The new mark on the Black Slate was just as trying as all the others. His name was Swift Venison. It was one of the stupidest names she'd ever heard. The man behind the name, a pale-faced rat of a man, was the definition of sinister. Six FBI agents had died at his hands over a month ago. That didn't count all of the innocents who had perished in his bloody wake, either.

It hadn't taken long for Sid and Smoke to catch up with the man in a frumpy diner. However, he had scurried away like a rat as soon as Smoke put a gun to his head. The man was fast, impossibly quick, and a street race on foot had led them down into these sewers.

Now Sid, twitching her nose, walked through the foul muck below the city. And there was more than stink all over it.

The scufflings ahead got a little louder then came to a sudden stop. The wretched tunnel had been deadly quiet, but now tiny voices made little squeaks. Stomach starting to knot, Sid said in a low voice, "I really need to shed a light on this."

"Go ahead."

She pressed the button on the small laser light mounted on her pistol. The bright beam cut through the darkness, illuminating the tunnel. There, at ground level, her eyes locked on dozens of others. She gasped.

Rats bigger than cats blocked the tunnel. Their eyes were small ruby beads. The sharp teeth in their mouths dripped with hunger.

Tugging on Smoke's pants, she started to back away.

Smoke remained.

"Let's go!" she urged.

"Not yet."

"Let me guess, you speak giant rat?"

"No, but he probably does." Smoke lifted her gun light higher.

A man stood just behind the horde of rats. His eyes were a deep red and his slender face was covered in grey fur. His supine figure bulged inside his clothes, in which several stitches were ripped. He removed the tie that hung from his neck and slung it aside. Showing a mouthful of rat-like teeth, he hissed more than spoke, but what he said was clear. "Eat, brothers and sisters. Feast on their bones!"

CHAPTER 2

S MOKE SAID SOMETHING. THE WORD was barely audible, but the meaning was clear. "Run!"

Sid took off at a full sprint.

Smoke was on her heels, with the sea of rabid rats nipping after him.

To make matters worse, the angry tide of rats squealed so much it hurt her ears. She hated rats. She hadn't even liked to feed squirrels when she was a girl. But rats, why? "Where am I going?" she yelled as she closed in on a junction of tunnels. She turned left and slipped to a complete stop.

More of the monster rats were coming right at her.

She unloaded a round of shots.

Blam! Blam! Blam!

"Ulp!"

Smoke jerked her up to her feet and took her by the hand. "This way." He crossed the junction in the other direction. The way was clear, nothing but smelly sock-soaking waters.

"We need to get aboveground now, John!"

"I'm working on it."

They'd already been inside the tunnels for more than an hour, and Sid didn't have any idea where they were. She wasn't so sure Smoke did either, but they didn't have any other choice but running at the moment. She glanced back. The rats couldn't be seen, but they were heard. A loud, continuous squeal from Hell itself. She cracked off a few more rounds that ricocheted off the walls and ping-ponged down the tunnel.

Blam! Ping! Pong! Pow! Blam! Ping! Pong! Pow!

"Save your ammo," Smoke said.

"I do what I want with my ammo, and you do what you want with yours."

They stopped in the middle of another intersection where the tunnels crisscrossed. The sound of more rats was coming from all directions. The path they were traveling was cut off. The turn to the right was another swell of rats.

"To the left it is," Smoke said, forging ahead.

"Brilliant choice," she said, running after him.

Hoofing it as fast as she could, Sid fought the urge to cover her ears. It sounded like the entire maze of tunnels was stuffed full of rats—hungry flesh-eating vermin.

Don't look back! Don't look back! Don't look back!

She did.

A lone rat—bigger than a cat—had surged ahead of the pack and started to nip at her heels.

She screamed. She fired.

Blam!

The little monster fell over dead and was instantly trampled and devoured by its brethren.

Sid's legs churned faster.

Lord, please don't let me die like this!

She turned and let the light on her gun find Smoke's back.

His broad shoulders blocked the view, leaving her chasing his back. He stopped on a dime.

She slammed right into him.

"What are you—*ack!*"

Smoke slung her around his back and formed a wall between her and the rats.

Ear-shattering shotgun blasts fired from his barrel.

Ka-blam! Ka-blam!

With her back to a sealed-off door and her ears ringing like bells, Sid took aim.

The entire horde of rats had come to a stop. They were all bunched up, one row on top of the other. A knee-deep wall of fur.

A squeaky sharp voice spoke.

The sea of rats parted from side to side.

There stood Swift Venison. Part human. Part rat. Another abomination of nature gone mad. "I see you both have finally found the end of the tunnel. Good. Now I just need to decide if I should let my friends devour you or not."

Sid started to squeeze the trigger.

Swift held up a finger. "I wouldn't do that if I were you. You see, if I die, then there is nothing to keep these rats from devouring you." He looked back behind him. "And notice, they stretch back as far as the eye can see. Besides, why waste a bullet? It can't hurt me." He made a command-like squeal.

The rats pressed closer. They were little more than a foot from Smoke's boots.

"Be wise now and set your weapons down."

Eyeing the rats, Sid set her gun down.

Smoke tossed his on top of the rats, drawing some squeaks.

"Very smart of you." Swift sniffed the air with his tiny nose. "Oh, how I love the smell of fear. It's in your eyes. In your sweat. All the way down to the hair on your toes." He flicked the shotgun up into his hands with his toe. "Now, turn around and open that door."

Sid and Smoke didn't move.

"Aw, I'm not going to shoot you in the back," he said in a calm and trustworthy voice. "It's just not my style. And I could easily tear the both of you to pieces. Oh, but how I hate to get my nails bloody. I just had them manicured."

"Really? Which veterinarian did you use?" Smoke asked. "I've been looking for a good one. You see, I have these little Pomeranians—"

"Shut up!" Swift pushed back the long rat fur on his head and took a breath. "Anyway, typically I let the rats eat you, which I probably still will. But a funny thing happened. I recognized you. John Smoke and Sidney Shaw, bounty hunters." He let out a shrieking laugh. "Heeeeeeee! The funny thing is, our kind has a bounty on your heads! It's the oddest thing. I only recently became aware of the facts. You see, so many of our special kind don't frequent my abode. I can only assume it's my gruesome exterior and preferred décor." He bounced the shotgun on his shoulder. "You took out the wolfman, Night Bird, the Minotaur, and those vile Ratson brothers. It seems you've really gotten the Drake's attention. Now there are bounties on your heads, big ones. More power. More territory, and it has all fallen right into my—eh?"

Sid and Smoke turned their backs to him and put their hands on top of their heads.

"Just shoot us in the back," she said. "Anything is better than letting you bore us to death."

"Wh-What?"

"Come on, just get it over with," Smoke added, shaking his head. "A talking rat. Say, are there any mutant turtles down here?"

Sid burst out in laughter. "Ha ha ha ha ha!"

Swift let out an angry howl. "Grrrrrrrrr! You dare! What are you fools babbling about?"

"Come to think of it, why are you pursuing us?" Sid asked. She wiped the tears from her eyes. "Shouldn't you be pursuing Shredder?"

The next warning from Swift froze the marrow in her bones.

"I'll shred you. I'll shred you both."

Out of the corner of her eye, she saw something come at her with blinding speed.

Smoke's head rocked forward.

A split second later so did hers. Pain filled her eyes, and everything in the world turned black.

CHAPTER 3

With painful effort, Sid lifted her chin from her chest and blinked her aching eyes. Skull throbbing, she found Smoke's eyes.

He sat adjacent to her with his hands behind his back. He was struggling. "Enjoy your nap?" he asked.

"I've had better." Grimacing, she fought against the bonds that had her arms pinned behind her back as well. She started digging into them with her nails. Her nostrils flared. The cell was a dingy spot with mold, mud, and who knew what else on the floor. Surrounded by concrete block, the only way out was through an iron grate with a solid but haphazard door. "Aw, great."

"Don't worry," Smoke said, "I'm sure the ninja turtles are around here somewhere."

"Ha ha." A desperate nagging started in Sid's stomach. "We really need to get out of here."

"I had a plan," he said, grunting with effort. "But you set ole Fuzzy-face off with that Shredder comment. He must have hated the show. But he was fast. I'm talking AV fast, and—"

"Hold up a second. Are you blaming me for us getting captured?"

"I was merely distracting him. Like I said, I had a plan." He winked at her. "Don't worry, I'll figure something else out."

She stretched out and kicked his boot. "You'll figure something out? How about I figure something out?"

Smoke sat still. "Okay, then you figure something out."

She leaned her head against the wall. "Sometimes I don't know if we make a good team or a bad team."

"Lighten up, Sid. I'm just stoking your fire."

"Why?"

"Because he's coming."

"I don't hear—"

"I hear voices!" It was Swift. The creepy shifter stood in front of the bars, holding a giant rat in the crook of his arm. It had a long tail and pink-painted toenails. "So it seems the little smart-alecky people are awake from a pain-filled and nightmarish slumber. Good." He stroked the rat's fur and added, "My friends are getting hungry, and I won't be keeping them at bay much longer."

"Just out of curiosity," Sid said, "why didn't you just kill us?"

"An excellent question, thought out. Most people just plead for their lives. But I have to say, the two of you are special." Swift stepped back, and another foreboding figure stepped in. It was a deader. An iron-thewed male with a long expressionless face. He wore bellbottom jeans and a black Styx concert T-shirt like a cursed body guard. "This is Jax. He's been with me a long time. You'll have to forgive the smell. I don't think he's had a shower since 1983." Swift rubbed the fiber on Jax's sleeve. "But look at the quality of these clothes. Not a hole in them. Sometimes I wonder if it's the bloodstains that keep them together."

Sid swallowed as Jax opened up the door.

The formidable figure lumbered in, bent over, and picked her up into its arms.

She coughed. "Morning Glory, he's foul! Put me down."

Jax walked out of the cell.

The door slammed shut behind them with a loud clang.

Sid flinched. Her heart raced. She craned her neck around, only to catch a glimpse of Swift blocking the cell door.

"What's the matter, dearie? Didn't I give you time to say a proper goodbye to your boyfriend?" Swift flashed his teeth and chomped them really quickly as he lowered his hand and snapped his fingers. "Oh rats."

The deader hauled Sid into another room, where oversized rats scurried over the floor.

Beady red rat-eyes bore into her.

This is bad. Really bad.

The room was nothing but slime-coated stone with some old tables and chairs. It looked like a guard shack from the fifties. There were chains and shackles hanging from metal loops in the walls. Skeletons hung all over the death chamber.

Gaping, she finally realized Jax had set her down, unbound her hands, and shackled her wrists to the chains.

He strung her up with her arms raised over her head and moved away.

Swift mounted a digital video camera on a tripod and pointed the lens toward her.

"What are you doing with that?" she said.

"Proof of life. Proof of death." Swift clasped his hands together. "My kind just loves this stuff. It's for our own version of YouTube. And just look at how happy my little brothers and sisters are." He waved his hand over the rat-covered floor. "Eating the homeless and those drug addicts isn't quite as filling for them as the likes of you." He squeaked to the rat in his arm, "Reeee!", and it licked him on the nose. He set the rat down on the table behind him, patted its head, and turned to Sid. "Now, try to look pretty as long as you can."

Sid started to tremble.

I can't believe this is happening! No! No! No!

"That's perfect!" Swift said. He stuck his eye to the camera. "Yes, they'll eat that up." He moved toward Sid and faced the camera with flare. "Let loose the rats of chaos and cry havoc! Oh wait, the record light isn't blinking. Damn!" He marched back to the camera and pressed a button until the red light stayed on. "Now let the show begin."

"Wait, wait, wait," Sid pleaded. She stomped her feet. "Wait! Don't I get a last request or something?"

"No. What you are supposed to do is beg and plead for your life. Promise me everything. Tell me you'll do anything." Swift grabbed her by the chin and looked her in the eye. "Anything."

Sid's shoulders drooped. "Okay."

"That's better." He leaned his ear towards her lips. "Tell me. Tell me what you'll do for me."

Her chin dropped. "I'll do anything you want."

Swift Venison the Were-Rat

CHAPTER 4

S WIFT PETTED HER FACE. "GOOD. Very good."

Sid rammed her knee into his groin.

"Ah!" he cried out, and then he slapped her across the face, drawing blood with his nails. "Fool of a woman. How miserable this is going to be for you! My brethren will eat you alive one chunk at a time."

"I don't think so!"

Swift whirled around. "You!"

Smoke stood beside the camera. He held Swift's pet rat by the neck and had Sid's pistol to its head. "Let her go, or the rat gets it."

Swift threw his arms up and pleaded. "No, no, not my baby!"

Jax the deader closed in on Smoke.

Smoke cocked the hammer back. "Your pet is going to be a pelt if you don't call off your goon."

"Stop, Jax!" Swift ordered. Hands up, palms out, he said to Smoke, "Now, let's be reasonable about this. There is no escape for you. You know that. And if anything happens to me, my rats will swarm you."

"True, but this critter will be dead, and so will you."

Swift the rat shifter eased closer. "Come now, be reasonable. You can't kill me."

Dangling the rat by the neck, Smoke turned the gun on Swift. "I have an exploding bullet in here, and trust me, you won't be doing anything after I blow a hole the size of your head through you."

"Impossible," Swift said with a grin, "we made a thorough check of both of you."

"You didn't check everywhere," Smoke said.

"That's gross." Swift looked back at Sid and added, "Do you date this man?"

"No, he just does strange things."

"And I thought I was weird."

"I regurgitated it," Smoke said, shaking his head.

"Oh, well, that's much more sanitary. I thought you—"

"Smoke, will you get me the hell out of these shackles!" Sid said.

"You heard the lady, Swift. Snap to it."

"Jax, free the woman," Swift said to the deader.

It took some effort, but the lumbering deader finally managed to unshackle Sid.

She rubbed her wrists and backed alongside Smoke. Keeping her eyes glued on Swift, she said, "Can I have my gun back?"

"Sure." Smoke handed it to her and said to Swift, "Get your hands behind your back and call off all your rats. I don't want to see a single one of them, except this one." He shook the pet rat. "Do you understand?"

Swift's eyes narrowed. He started to bend at the knees. His clawed fingers clutched in and out. "You're bluffing. There's no explosive round in there. I don't believe it."

Smoke held a red-tipped bullet in front of the rat man's face. "No, there isn't one. There's an entire clip of them. Now come quietly or come in pieces."

Swift cringed and followed it up with a quick shriek. "Eeeack!"

The rats scurried in all directions, stuffing their bodies into cracks and holes before vanishing, tail last, completely.

Swift put his hands behind his back. "Happy?"

Smoke put the flex cuffs on him and secured them tight. A knife appeared in his hand, and he held it under Swift's eye. "Now this blade, I think you know, will cut through anything. It's a real heart-stopper." He shoved Swift forward. "Take us out of here."

Head down, Swift said, "Jax, lead the way."

The undead man took them back into the next room. It was there that Sid gathered more of their things from a metal table. Everything seemed to be in order, but her heart still raced. She'd been certain she was a goner. How Smoke had appeared was nothing short of amazing. Still, she couldn't shake the dreadful feeling that something was wrong. Very wrong.

And from every crack and crevice, hungry rat eyes were all over her.

"Tell you what," Swift said. "I'll make it worth your while if you leave me be, hm? What do you say to that? I'm certain the FBI doesn't compensate you that well. Whatever it is, I'll double it."

"It's not about the money," Smoke said.

CHAPTER 5

S WIFT CHUCKLED. "OH, IT'S ALWAYS about the money. But I'm curious. If it's not about the money, what are you in this for?"

Smoke replied, "I just hate rats. I tell you what though. Maybe we can make a deal."

The rat man stopped and turned his ear. "A deal. What sort of deal?"

"We want to know who the heart of the Drake is."

Swift started laughing. "Ha ha ha! You'll never know that unless you become one of our kind. Heh-heh. But that can be arranged if you want to know bad enough."

Sidney's thoughts raced to her sister, Allison.

What kind of madness have they done to her? What about Megan?

"Let's get out and get paid, Smoke." She pointed the Glock's barrel at Swift's nose. "I'm running out of patience."

After a long and winding walk, the deader Jax led them through some metal double doors and up a stairwell. Soft light crept through the cracks in the doors above. Jax pushed them open, revealing the ground floor of a warehouse. It was empty, save for long rows of shelves and abandoned multipurpose appliances that were scattered all over.

Sid took a deep breath and dialed up the FBI on her phone. While she waited, she sent a text to Cyrus Tweel. She kept the gun on Swift. "You've been extremely cooperative."

He shrugged. "What can I say? You're a formidable pair that outwitted me. In truth, it's your bravery that I admire most. So many cringe. Cry. Some are so terrified that they have a heart attack and die. But not you two. It's no wonder you are wanted and hated so bad."

"Sounds like we're doing the right thing then," she said, checking her phone. There wasn't a text from Cyrus yet, which seemed odd. "It feels good keeping the vermin off the streets."

"Hah," Swift scoffed. "Who do you think really keeps the vermin off the streets, law enforcement? Hah. You see, that's part of what we do for your kind."

"Pardon me?" said Sidney.

"You know, long before I became what I am, I used to be a priest." Swift's form started to change. His bulging sinews and body hair thinned, leaving only a small man with a rat's head and thinning grey hair. "I took care of many. Drug addicts. The homeless. The wayward and desperate. There was no end to it. Then, a friend of mine introduced me to the Drake and showed me true power that let me embrace my inner nature." His eyes filled with lust. "There's nothing like it in the world."

Smoke tightened the flex cuffs on him. "And your point is?"

"That power can be yours, eh? And you won't have to answer to these fools that run your cities. Most of them work for us anyway. They are the ones who pay us to keep the unwanted off the streets. They become dinner for my rats." Swift glanced at his pet that Smoke still had in his hands. "Could you show some compassion and let my pet go before local law enforcement arrives? I fear they just might shoot her."

"Sure," Smoke said. He slung the rat up high in the air.

Sid took aim and fired.

Blam!

The rat exploded into bits and pieces.

Swift screamed, "Noooooo!"

"She's gone now," Smoke said. "You were saying something about dinner and compassion?"

Trembling with rage, the rat-man said, "You'll pay! You will pay!"

Sid caught a glimpse through one of the upper warehouse windows of a helicopter coming in for a landing. She kept the gun pointed at Swift's nose. "Looks like your ride is here, Mister Venison. Gee, I wonder who is going to feed all your rats when you're gone? Maybe DC's finest pest control will have to euthanize them."

"Don't you dare!" Swift said, puffing himself up.

Two squads of men stormed into the warehouse carrying automatic machine guns, dressed from head to toe in helmets and Kevlar body armor. One of them flashed an FBI badge.

Sid recognized him.

It was Agent Jonnie Wok, a stocky but short Asian with a Southern accent.

"We'll take it from here," said Agent Wok.

"I'm not releasing anyone until I hear from Cyrus Tweel." She checked her phone. There still wasn't any text from Cyrus.

The agents had them hemmed in, gun barrels on everyone's chests.

"Miss Shaw, we can't stand here and dilly dally," said Agent Wok. "I've got a job to do, and yours is finished. Now, step away and let us handle this."

Sid looked down at Agent Wok. "I need to hear from Cyrus."

Agent Wok stepped closer. "Well, maybe he's on vacation. Or maybe he's taking a sick day. Or maybe he's in the shitter? I don't have time to wait for him, and I don't have to either." He looked hard at her face. "Say, that's a pretty nasty scratch. You might want to get that looked at."

"Don't try to butter me up now, Wok." She texted Cyrus again, saying, "Wok here. Need your clearance." She hit 'send'.

"Agent Shaw—I mean Bounty Hunter Shaw or whatever the hell you call yourself—we need to move." He glanced over at Jax the deader. "Shit! Someone cuff that thing!" He focused on Swift Venison. "What's he do?"

"He's the Pied Piper," Smoke said.

"The what?"

Sid's phone buzzed. There was a text from Cyrus. It read, "On my way. Stay put."

Agent Wok took out his phone, checked the text, and rolled his eyes. "Aw, great. Looks like we're all staying. Damn, I was hoping to avoid Cyrus. Just seeing him gives me a brain freeze." He stuffed his phone inside his pocket. "Didn't you use to date that guy?"

"Yes."

"Man, what were you thinking?" Agent Wok twirled his finger beside his head. "Let's get these prisoners secured. Head to toe. We can't have these freaks getting loose. "

The agents put Swift and Jax into security straitjackets and muzzled their mouths. Their feet were shackled with short chains. After that, they sat them both down on the floor.

Agent Wok took off his cap and wiped the sweat from his brow. "Say, how much are you getting paid for this gig anyway?"

"More than you make in a year," Sid said, stuffing her weapon into her holster. "Why, you looking for a new job?"

"No." Wok fanned his face. "I'd rather not smell like a sewer. Besides, this gig pays well enough. I like it."

"Prisoner transport? Hah!"

"There's more to it than that," Agent Wok said. "I meet a lot of interesting people."

"Tell me more."

Smiling, Agent Wok said, "Maybe we should have dinner sometime and I'll tell you all you want to know."

Sid's eyes glided over to Smoke. He stood with his back to her, facing the prisoners.

She leaned in toward Agent Wok and asked, "Just tell me. Where do you take them?"

"Sorry, can't tell you that, even though I feel compelled to." He glanced over his shoulder and then said to her, "But I might give in over dinner and breakfast."

"Keep dreaming."

He shrugged, nodded, and stroked his chin. "I always have, and I probably always will."

Sid slipped away and found herself at Smoke's side.

He was staring at the prisoners.

Their hands and feet were covered in mitten-like gloves and booties. Their ears were covered with hearing protection, and blindfolds were on them. Both of the freaks seemed calm and at ease.

"What's on your mind?" Sid leaned close to Smoke.

"Maybe you should have dinner with him."

"What?" She leaned away again. "No! Why?"

"Well, the truth is, I want to know where they take them."

"So you want me to sleep with him?"

"Well no. Just get him drunk and make him think you'll sleep with him. He'll fall for it."

Sid's neck muscles tightened. "You'd better not be serious."

Stone-faced, Smoke turned and looked her in the eye. "No. I don't think I'd like that."

"Well, now that I think about it, maybe it's not such a bad idea. After all, Jonnie is pretty funny, and he loves to party."

Smoke's stone-faced expression turned dark.

Good. "So do you have any more stupid ideas?"

"No, but I do want to know where they take them."

Sid's breathing eased. She brushed her hand against his. "So do I, but why are you so worried about it?"

"Sometimes I have a hard time believing they're actually incarcerating them."

"Me too."

"Look sharp, everyone," Agent Wok said, "Section Chief Tweel just landed."

Here came Cyrus, marching through the warehouse doors wearing a beige trench coat and looking as thin as ever. He wasn't alone either. Rebecca Lang was with him.

"Damn," Sid said, "she's back."

CHAPTER 6

S WIFT VENISON WAS GONE. JAX the deader, gone. Agent Wok the Chinese redneck and company, gone. Only Sid, Smoke, Cyrus, and Rebecca Lang remained. Sidney hadn't seen the mousy blonde since the day she killed Deanne Drukker in cold blood. 'She's a murderer, and murderers must die.' That's what Rebecca had said, and it still gave Sid chills to this day. And now, the woman who should be as far away from law enforcement as possible was back.

How in the hell did this happen?

"My bitcoin account is awfully low," Smoke said, holding up his phone. "About twenty-five grand by my count."

Sid checked her account as well and shook her head. "What's the deal, Cyrus? The bounty was one hundred grand split between me and him. This is only half. Where's the rest?"

Cyrus opened his mouth to speak, but Rebecca—wearing a blouse and a knee-length skirt—cut him off. "I can answer that. We aren't paying you that much. Budget cuts."

"I don't care about your budget cuts. We are going to be paid what we're owed."

Rebecca faced off with Sid, made a sour face, and stepped back. "Ew, what have you been into?"

"It's not what I've been into that should worry you, but what I'm about to get into." Sid balled up her fist. "Now release my money!"

"The way I figure it," Rebecca said, "you stand to make a lot of money if bitcoin soars again. So be patient and make do."

"You aren't my financial advisor, and we didn't just risk our necks for a measly fifty K. We just about died down there!" Sid wanted to knock the woman's head off her shoulders. It wasn't about the money either, even though she could use it—she was way behind on all her bills. No, it was principle. A bargain struck. A deal. But worst of all, she hated Rebecca's involvement. That tramp was an arrogant, prissy, conniving little witch. "I'll just get ahold of Leroy then."

"Leroy's dead," Cyrus said. He was cleaning his glasses with his tie and put them back on. "Heart attack, I believe. Hey, he was old."

"Very old," Rebecca added, "and very dead."

"When did this happen?" Sid asked.

"A couple weeks ago," said Cyrus. There was something different about Section Chief Cyrus. He was more reserved, less arrogant. He rubbed his hands together, caught Sid looking at them, and stopped. "I didn't find out about it until after he was buried."

"And you couldn't have told me this?"

"It wouldn't have made any difference," Rebecca said with a sneer. "It's not like you'd quit. After all, you need the money."

Sid shifted her hips and prepared to let loose a roundhouse kick.

Smoke stepped in her path of attack. "Are you going to pay us the rest or not?" He addressed Cyrus, but Rebecca answered.

"No, I'm not. And seeing how this is all off the record, consider yourselves lucky you got what you got."

Towering over Rebecca, powerful arms crossed over his chest, Smoke looked down at her. "Do you want to know what happened to the last person who didn't pay me what they owed me?"

Rebecca swallowed. "I could not care less." She spun around on her heel. "Let's go, Cyrus."

"Hold on!" Sid said. "What about the Black Slate?"

Rebecca kept walking.

Cyrus turned to look at Sid as he walked backward. "We'll let you know."

A week later, Sidney lay in bed inside her apartment. It was early morning after what had been another long and restless night. She rubbed her temples. A nagging headache hadn't left since she'd seen Rebecca and Cyrus.

I can't stand that woman.

Sid had blown Smoke off too. She needed time to think. Sort things out. She was supposed to be getting some steady pay as a liaison for the FBI, but the deposits weren't coming through. Now, Rebecca had stiffed them on their last bounty. Even worse, Bitcoin had taken a twenty-five percent hit the day after that last deposit. She tugged at her hair.

Am I an idiot?

Then there was the other odd thing. Leroy Sullivan. He was a big shot with the FBI who was supposed to be overseeing her dealings with the Black Slate. Now he'd died. Supposedly. Allegedly. Had he really? Sid had exhausted herself searching the obituaries and found nothing. It was more than odd. More than strange. The ice-blue-eyed old man had vanished.

Her financial stability had vanished with him.

What am I going to do?

She picked up her phone and pulled up the photo album. She found some pictures of Megan in there. She stopped on one of her favorite pics. Megan was on a swing with her teddy bear, looking as happy as she could be. Sid's eyes started to water. Working on the Black Slate gave her hope of finding Megan and saving her sister. If she could find that monster at the top of the Drake, then she could put an end to it. But now, she wasn't any closer than she'd ever been. She wiped her eyes and sniffed.

"I'm so sorry, Megan."

She swung her legs off the bed, got up, and shuffled into the bathroom. Looking in the mirror, she said to herself, "Good Lord, I'm a mess." She ran her fingers over the gash that Swift Venison had given her. She huffed a laugh.

What a stupid name, even for a rat.

The claw marks were still red and itchy. From the vanity drawer she pulled out a tube of Neosporin. She squeezed some on her finger and rubbed it in. "At least I don't have anywhere to go."

In the kitchen she scraped out just enough coffee grounds to make a cup of coffee. Her machine was out of coffee pods. It was one of the first expenses she'd shaved, by whittling down her coffee budget to a plastic can of Folgers. As she took a seat at the kitchen bar, the smell of fresh brew got her going a little bit again.

Routine. That was what she needed to get out of this funk she was in. She closed her eyes and made a mental list.

Coffee.

News.

Stretching.

A long run.

Workout.

Hit the heavy bag.

Kick the heavy bag.

Smoke popped into her mind.

Sex.

She squeezed her eyes tight.

No. No sex. No Smoke. Morning Glory, Sid. The man eats bullets!

Oh, but those eyes.

CHAPTER 7

S ID COMPLETED THE GAUNTLET OF activity she'd planned for herself and returned to the apartment. Sweat soaked, she removed her neon-blue-and-jet-black jogging suit and tossed it onto the overstuffed hamper.

Oh boy, I can sit at home and do laundry today. Whoopee!

She took a hot shower, dried off, and slipped into the only clean clothes she could find: the gunmetal-gray Darkslayer T-shirt Guppy had given her and a pair of khaki shorts. She threw in the first load of laundry, headed into her small living room, and sat down. She turned the TV on to the local news.

A hard rain started outside.

Glad I got my run in.

The outside weathercaster was getting drenched. The sewer drain behind him was overflowing.

Sid thought of the massive rats inside those tunnels and cringed. She'd almost died ... again. Devoured by rats like in an Indiana Jones movie. Her father, Keith, loved those movies. It got her thinking again about Swift Venison. The things he'd said about power. Money. The temptation.

He said he'd been a priest. He made it clear that the Drake worked for or with the politicians. They cleaned up the streets in grisly ways. And he'd said there was a bounty on her head. On Smoke's head. But she didn't feel any less safe than she had before. And Swift Venison hadn't seemed that worried when they took him in. He'd almost seemed relieved.

It had all been too easy.

"Something stinks." She rubbed her cheek. "Stinks bad."

Knock! Knock! Knock!

The sound jostled Sid from head to toe. Images of fiendish bounty hunters ran through her head. She found her Glock and took a quick peek through the blinds. Her breathing eased, and she opened the door.

"Hi," Smoke said with a sparkle in his dark eyes. He was clean shaven, and his lustrous hair was combed back in waves. He wore a burgundy polo shirt in a nice cotton blend and dark-blue jeans that stopped at the toes of his leather boots. "Nice shirt."

"You should call first," Sid said, stepping aside and closing the door behind him.

"But that would ruin the surprise," he said, taking a seat on the couch.

She crossed her arms over her chest. "Well, I'd rather you ruin a surprise than ruin my day."

"That's kinda harsh." He patted the sofa cushion beside him. "Why don't you just sit down?"

"Look, I'm sorry, John. I really am. But that's not a good idea." *He smells good. Really good. And the semi-preppy thing really works for him.* "And what's with the clothes? Did you swing by the mall on your way over here or something?"

"I thought we could go and have lunch? Somewhere nice."

"Like a waffle house?"

"Maybe a little nicer than that. I know a great 24-hour breakfast buffet at Truck Stop Ninety-nine."

"Shut up," she said, letting loose a little smile.

There was something innocent and boyish in Smoke's expression. He seemed a little nervous, maybe.

"So, is this visit business or pleasure?"

Smoke's eyes brightened. "Pleasure?"

"Just an expression. Bad choice of words. I should have said, 'social.'"

"But you said 'pleasure'. You've been thinking about me, haven't you."

She cozied a little closer to him, just a hair out of his reach. "You're all my dreams and nightmares wrapped up in one."

"You just can't give in to the plus side of me, can you."

"I guess that's just the woman in me."

"Well, I like the woman in you." He reached out and tried to grab her hand.

Sid drifted back. "So, I take it this is a social visit? Or is it business? Do we have a case where you get to go undercover as a mall dad?"

Smoke started laughing. "You really are cold, aren't you. Come here."

"No. I'm not in the mood. I've got a lot on my mind."

Striking fast, Smoke seized her wrists and eased her onto his lap. "Now this isn't so bad, is it?"

"Yes." *No.*

He coiled his arm around her waist and squeezed her thigh with his hand. He leaned in and kissed her.

Lips to lips, heart to heart, she gave in. It wasn't the first time either. She and Smoke had moments here and there, but nothing serious. She was holding back because there was something mysterious about Smoke that she didn't understand.

Something also seemed to hold Smoke back, an innocence or lack of experience.

She was drawn to it. She tangled her fingers into his thick locks, straddled him, and kissed him harder.

He returned in kind.

It went on for minutes until she broke it off, gasping for breath.

"Is something wrong?" he said.

"No. Do you think something's wrong?"

Smoke shook his head no.

Sid could see something was still on his mind, eating at him. Panting, she swiped her hair back over her shoulders.

Here we go again.

"Okay, do it."

"Do what?"

"*You* know what. Do what you always do that screws the moment up so that we can get on with it." She grabbed him by the collar of his shirt and kissed his handsome face, broke it off and then said, "Make it fast."

Smoke rubbed her thighs with his big hands. "Let's just keep doing what we're doing?"

"What, keep making out like we're in an episode of Happy Days? I'm a woman, Smoke. I want you, you want me. Take me!"

Smoke's face paled. His expression grew uncertain, almost embarrassed. This was the man who faced down death with nothing short of ice-water in his veins. Nothing rattled him. Now, he seemed confused.

Sid's engine cooled. She pushed herself up off his lap.

Smoke reached for her.

But she glided away. "Do you want me or not, John?"

"Of course I do. It's not you though, it's me."

"'It's not you, it's me'? What the hell is this, a bad Matthew McConaughey movie?" She drew back her fist and kicked him in the knee instead.

"Ow!" he said. "And who's Matthew McConaughey?"

"Ow!" She hopped over to the kitchen counter, shaking her hand and wincing. "Just get out of here!"

"Sid, it's not that. It's not that at all. I just want to do things right."

Without looking at him, she said, "Are you sure? Because you really seem to enjoy doing things wrong."

"Look, I'm good at a lot of things. Shooting people. Beating up people. Killing people. And eating pancakes. But relationships? Well, they aren't my strong suit. Of course, you seem to have figured that out on your own."

She could see him fidgeting with something, but she kept her gaze fixed on the kitchen.

"That's the reason," Smoke continued in his strong but gentle voice, "why I don't want to mess this up."

The stiffness in her back started to melt a little. She almost turned her head. "Sid, look at me."

She turned on her stool and lost her breath.

Smoke was on one knee holding a diamond engagement ring in his hand. "Will you marry me?"

CHAPTER 8

S ID'S EYES FASTENED ON THE jaw-dropping diamond ring.
The cut, clarity, and color were astounding. And it was big. It winked at her from the gold ring in which it rested. It spoke to her, saying, 'Take me.'

She glanced at Smoke then back at the ring. She leaned closer. Her keen eye didn't pick up a single inclusion. She found Smoke's eyes again. Sweet and innocent. "What did you just say?"

"Will you marry me?"

She couldn't feel her fingers or toes. She held her head as the room began to spin a little.

"Sid, are you all right?"

"I–I ... did you just ask me to marry you?"

"That's what the ring is for ... a wedding." Smoke rubbed his sweaty palms on his jeans. "Like I said, I want to do things right."

In a hushed breath, she replied, "You're crazy." She shook her head a little and felt her senses start to return. She checked out the diamond again. Her heart was pounding. "That really is beautiful, John, but this ... this is crazy. Uh, I'm sorry to ask this, but why?"

Smoke rose up, looked deep into her eyes, and touched her chin. "Because I love you."

"Me?"

"Yes, you."

It wasn't sinking in.

"John, you can't just walk in here and ask me to marry you." She moved away and curled up in the chair. "It's crazy. What are you trying to do to me anyway?"

"I'm trying to marry you. Take care of you. Be your husband if you'll have me." He sounded nice about it, but there was a hint of irritation in his voice.

"You couldn't have possibly believed that you could come in here and ask me to marry you and that I'd just say yes."

"I wanted to do it over lunch."

She made a frustrated growling sound. "Most people talk about these things. They don't just do them." She stuck her face in her hands. "Nobody does that."

"Well, don't get mad at me. I didn't realize there was a rulebook."

"Well, there is!"

Smoke took a seat on the couch, set the ring box down, and didn't say a word. The silence was uncomfortable.

Sid's thoughts were a tangled mess. She wasn't much different than most women. She too dreamed of a diamond engagement and a nice wedding. She and her mom and Allison had even talked about those things from time to time. Of course, Allison had done most of the talking. She'd always had big plans, and Sid knew that her sister would be full of envy if she saw a ring like this. "It's beautiful," she whispered.

Smoke eased forward. "Would you like to try it on?"

Yes! "No. I can't."

"Why not?"

It was a fair question. Smoke deserved a fair answer. She gave him the best one she had. "I don't know why." She qualified it. "Yet."

Smoke rubbed his clean-shaven chin. "Look, I realize this might not have been in your plans, but you really shouldn't have expected anything different from me. It's supposed to be a happy moment, you know."

She let out a little laugh. "Heh! No, you're right. But I honestly think I would have been less surprised if you'd asked me in the sewers. But like this? Something's not right."

"Maybe you don't feel the same way about me that I do about you. I can live with that. Well, maybe I can't. But since the first moment I saw you, I knew I wanted to marry you." He closed the case on the diamond. "I don't know how long 'yet' takes, but I can wait."

His closing of the box felt like her own coffin being sealed as she watched Smoke get up to leave. Her wide eyes were on his back as he started walking for the door. His long, dark hair. His powerful, rangy frame.

Tall, dark, and handsome—and I'm going to let him get away. He's saved my life and almost died for me. Am I crazy, or is it all him?

Smoke put his hand on the doorknob and started to turn it. "Just call me."

Sid's heart started to break.

What do I do?

But then it was too late. Her heart had broken the moment the door closed behind him.

Clutching her chest, she took a seat on the couch.

What just happened?

She reached over, picked up the ring box, and popped it open.

The ring was as bright as a shining star.

Morning Glory!

She hopped out of her seat, ran to the front door, and opened it up.

Smoke was gone. There was only the rumble of his primer-gray Camaro pulling out of her parking lot and vanishing into the traffic on the streets.

"Dammit."

She closed the door and sagged down with her back against it, holding her head. With the ring box still in her hand, she started laughing—a bit derangedly— as the torrent of mixed emotions toyed with her brain. Smoke loved her! He had said so. She knew she loved him too, but marriage? Was it really that kind of love? Deep. Long lasting. Meaningful?

As she ran her finger over the diamond's edges, a smile crossed her lips. "I guess I could be a big girl and talk to him like a woman about this. Boy, I sure didn't handle that very well." On her hands and knees, she crawled over to the couch to lie down on it. She tucked the ring box under her arm.

I need to call him. What do I say? Yes? No? Maybe? Not now? Good Lord, why did that man have to propose to me?

She yawned, and her chest shuddered. She reached over to the coffee table, grabbed her phone, and pulled up Smoke's number.

Should I text, or should I call him?

The phone buzzed in her hand.

"Eek!" Expecting Smoke, she got another surprise, a text from Cyrus Tweel. It read, "Turn on the local news and don't go anywhere! On my way over."

"What in the world is going on now?" She found the remote and turned on the television to the local news.

Ambulances, police cars, and fire truck lights were flashing like the Fourth of July fireworks. Behind them was the site of a new construction project, a new mega-shelter for the homeless that Congressman Wilhelm and some other prominent business leaders had been working on. If Sid's memory served her well, today was the grand opening. She turned up the volume.

A black female reporter stood just inside the building's overhang, out of the pouring rain. She was soaked, but unaffected. "This is Angie Gentry, TV1Y News, and we have confirmation from local law enforcement officials that Congressman Augustus Wilhelm has been shot and presumably killed. The congressman has been rushed to Mercy Angels hospital." She read more details from a rain-soaked piece of paper. "Witnesses at the ceremony reported that a tall white male in a ball cap and raincoat stepped out of the crowd and opened fire. Security has already released this video footage." She held up the paper, revealing a crystal-clear picture of John Smoke.

Sidney dropped the ring box and gasped.

CHAPTER 9

S ID'S UPSIDE-DOWN WORLD HAD JUST been turned inside out. Two FBI agents were posted outside her front door. Inside with her were Cyrus Tweel and Rebecca Lang. Neither were happy. Both showed frowns as long as football fields.

"I could have come down to the station," Sid said as soon as they arrived. It was all business though. Pressure. A congressman had been shot. DC's entire world was rocked. And her want-to-be-fiancé was the prime suspect. "This isn't an ideal place for an interrogation."

"Do you have any idea where he is?" Cyrus said, staring at her with his hard, beady eyes. "And don't play any games, Sid. We're not in the mood for them."

"We're?" Sid replied, looking at Rebecca.

The petite agent was every bit as frosty as she'd ever been. Her eyes gave Sid's apartment the once-over more than once.

"What did I say about the games?" Cyrus said.

"I'm not playing games, and no, I don't know where Smoke is. He just left twenty minutes before you got here. Cyrus, there is no way he did this. He was here, not there."

Rebecca stepped over. "The shooting was an hour and a half ago. That's plenty of time to come over here and have a booty call before he goes back to prison."

Sid's eyes flashed. She was up on her feet, shoving Rebecca into the bar stool.

"You bitch!" Rebecca hauled back, ready to unload a punch.

Cyrus caught her arm.

"You dare!" Rebecca said to him. She smacked him hard in the face.

Cyrus's eyes filled with astonishment. A blue vein popped out on his forehead. "This is no way for agents or former agents to act. Rebecca, Sid, sit down!"

"Don't you dare tell me what to do!" Rebecca straightened her business coat and sat back down on the stool. "I'll legally castrate you."

"Sid, I know you like this guy, but we warned you, me and Ted. He's a loose cannon. A bit of a nut job." He rubbed the back of his head and sighed. "And I also know about your history with Congressman Wilhelm. You and him, his son, and your sister, well, let's just say you have a colorful history."

"Wait a second. You think I said something that triggered this?"

Cyrus and Rebecca glanced at each other, then Cyrus said, "So you think he did it?"

"No. Absolutely not. He'd never do such a thing. John might be a lot of things, but he's not a murderer."

"He's psychotic," Rebecca said in a cold voice.

"You're the one who's psychotic."

"I spent some time with him too, if you remember," Rebecca said. "He's crazy. Certainly capable of doing a lot more harm than good."

"I think you have him mixed up with yourself. You're the only one I ever saw gun anyone down in cold blood. Yet here you are!"

The door popped open. A black agent filled the doorway. His head was shaved clean, and he had a dangerous look about him. "Everything okay?"

Cyrus gave him a nod. "We're fine, Calhoun."

The man closed the door behind him, but not without giving Sid the eyeball first.

Her skin prickled. "Calhoun? I thought he was fired. I thought he was in prison!"

"That's not your concern, Agent—I mean Sid." Cyrus took out his iPad and pulled something up on the screen. He set it down in front of Sid. "Now, I need you to watch this closely."

She did.

It was video surveillance footage from the new homeless center. It started out on the open streets where a man in a raincoat, on foot, weaved through the traffic in the pouring rain. He made his way up the steps and tilted his chin up just high enough for the camera to get a perfect shot of his face.

It was Smoke. No question about it. Even the height and build were right.

Heart empty, Sid glanced up at Cyrus.

"Keep watching if you're not convinced," he said.

New footage continued inside the shelter. Dripping-wet people from all walks of life were standing inside the lobby. Smoke stood among them, half a head taller than all the rest at least, wearing a Washington Redskins ball cap.

In front of the crowd was a podium where Congressman Wilhelm was making a speech. There wasn't any audio, though. Just a camera shot right over Wilhelm's shoulder and into the crowd.

Not too far into the speech, Smoke pushed his way through the throng, aimed his semi-automatic pistol, and cracked off several shots.

Wilhelm fell.

Everyone scattered, and Smoke disappeared with the masses.

Sid's stomach seeped down into her toes. "It can't be him."

Cyrus put the iPad in his coat pocket. "Sorry, Sid, but it's him. And you need to do whatever you can to help us bring him to justice. Anything you can think of that will make this easier will make a difference."

Sid's throat was dry and she didn't have any words to say. She'd seen him on the video. But it wasn't him. It couldn't be. There was no reason for him to do something like that. Not unless there was something else. Something bigger that no one else knew about. Maybe the Drake had blackmailed him. Feebly, she managed to say, "I assume you checked his place?"

"It's clear. No sign of him anywhere. We're keeping an eye on it though." Cyrus took a seat on the barstool and sat with his hands clasped together. "Have you and him talked about your relationship with Wilhelm?"

"He knows enough. I don't like Wilhelm. Neither of them. And they don't like me."

"Be careful what you say, Sid."

"Well shit, Cyrus. You make it sound like I pulled the trigger. I didn't!" She caught Rebecca rummaging through one of her end-table drawers. "Excuse me, do you have a warrant?"

"This is interesting." Rebecca held the ring box in her hand, opened it up. "Wow. That's one fine rock. Where did you get this?"

"Let me see," Cyrus said.

Rebecca tossed it over.

He snatched it from the air. "Whoa. That is impressive. An engagement ring, Sid?" His expression was twisted. "Who gave this to you?"

"That's none of your business." She averted her eyes for some reason. "Long story, just hand it over."

"No," Cyrus said, "I think I'd like to hear that story. Hmmm." He tapped the ring box on his chin. "There's only one man in your life that I know of. Is this ring from John Smoke?"

"I don't want to talk about it." She held out her hand. "Hand it over, please."

Cyrus removed his spectacles and huffed on the lenses. He cleaned them with his tie and placed them back on his head. He brought the ring in for a closer look. "My, I can't see a single inclusion, and it's so ... white. Mister Smoke gave you this, didn't he?"

Sid didn't reply.

"Well, it's certainly a superior product compared to the one I presented you with. It kinda makes me feel like a turd."

"Excuse me?" Rebecca said, tapping her foot on the floor.

"Nothing, dear," he said, still gazing at the stone. "So when did he give this to you?"

Sid didn't want to say it, but she did anyway. "Today."

"Hmmm, interesting timing. You know, until today, we were working on another case. A jewel heist of sorts. I hate to break it to you, Sid, but I believe this ring was stolen."

CHAPTER 10

S ID SAT WITH HER FACE in her hands.

It can't be true. It just can't be true.

Her heart told her one thing, the presented evidence said another. The pragmatic side clashed with the gut. Doubt swelled inside her. If there was one thing she was sure of, Smoke was a good man. But he might just be crazy.

"We could take you in for possession of stolen goods," Rebecca said. She'd found one of Sid's emery boards and started to file her nails. "Not to mention the fact that you might be an accomplice to murder. Aiding and abetting a known fugitive. Tsk tsk. Looks like the deck is quickly stacking against you."

"You're really starting to get on my nerves," Sid said to Rebecca. She faced Cyrus. "You know I don't have anything do to with this, right?"

"That's not for me to decide, Sid. Love can do funny things to a person. For all I know, you and Smoke might be today's Bonnie and Clyde. And you know how the FBI is. They don't like to take any chances." He picked up a picture frame that stood on the end table. It was an image of Megan. "And people not only do unordinary things, but sometimes extraordinary things for family." He glanced at Rebecca.

She gave him a little shrug.

He got up and straightened his tie. "Sid, if you know or find out anything, I'd better know first. Don't leave town."

Really? Wow.

She found Rebecca's face.

The mousy woman seemed satisfied.

"I won't."

Cyrus closed the ring box and stuffed it in his pocket. "I need to check this out. I'll let you know."

As soon as Cyrus and Rebecca departed, Sid took a long, shuddering breath. Her head pounded. Life was upside down again.

Smoke, what have you done to me!

She took a peek through the blinds.

The parking lot was in full view. A little farther down the lot was a black

Chevy SUV. She wasn't certain, but it looked like Agent Calhoun was in the driver's seat.

Great!

She wanted to go see Sam and Guppy, but that would be a bad move. That left her with nobody to talk to. The only other ally she thought she had was Smoke, and maybe Mal Gunderson, but she hadn't heard from Mal in what seemed to be forever. Wringing her hands, she sat down and watched the TV again.

It was all over the news. Every major network. It seemed like every channel.

It isn't every day that a high-ranking Washington official is shot. Even though Augustus Wilhelm is a good start.

She squeezed her temples.

Don't even think it, Sid. Geez!

Her phone buzzed. An image of her friend Sadie from the FBI office popped up.

"Hey," Sid said.

"Hey, are you all right?" Sadie said. She sounded really worried.

Pacing throughout the apartment, Sid said, "You have no idea. Cyrus and Rebecca just left. Look, Sadie, don't get involved in this—"

Her phone vibrated. Her mother Sally was calling.

"Crap. My mom's on the other line. Look, I'll check back in with you. I'm fine."

"Just let me know if you need anything, Sid," Sadie said. "You know you can count on me."

"I will." Sid switched lines. "Hi, Mom."

Her mother was all over the place. The woman couldn't even get a complete sentence out.

"Mom, slow down. I'm all right. ... No, I don't think it's him, it just looks like him. ... Yes, I know he seemed like a nice guy. ... No, I'm not in any danger. ... I don't need money. ... No, don't come down here."

Sally rambled on and on.

Sid paced. She found a notebook of paper and slapped it on the table. She put the phone on speaker, set it on the counter, and began scribbling down notes, half listening to her mother as she wrote. "Uh-huh. Uh-huh. Uh-huh."

Watching the television, she jotted down the dates and times the reporters gave. She noted the hospital. Paid attention to the details on the police cars, ambulances, and fire trucks. She watched the replays of the brutal shooting, looking for things that she should and shouldn't see. She wrote down the times that Smoke, Cyrus, and Rebecca had come and gone. She included the things they'd said and not said, too.

"Sidney, are you there? Are you listening to me?" Sally asked on the other line. "And you know your father can't handle all this excitement. He doesn't know that I'm calling. Don't you dare call him."

"I won't, Mom. Look, I need to run some errands while all of this mess gets sorted out. My love to you and Dad. Got to go."

"But—"

Sid disconnected and sagged onto the counter. "Morning Glory, who's going to call next?"

In case her line was being tapped, it was good that she'd maintained a normal conversation. That was real. Genuine. It would be odd if no one called at all. That would have aroused more suspicion.

All of a sudden, Sid sat up straight.

Damn, they probably planted a bug.

Gently she inspected every place Cyrus and Rebecca had been. Thankfully, they'd been confined to the kitchen/living room the entire time. Sid ran her fingers under the counters and tables, and then she rummaged through her two plants and vases.

Nothing, but it doesn't feel like nothing.

Eyeing the room and spinning around slowly, she saw one place she'd almost overlooked: the picture of her and Megan. Without touching the frame, she bent over and took a look behind it. There was a tiny black chip mounted on the velvet back of the frame.

Ah-hah.

Her phone buzzed again. She walked over and picked it up. The screen was blank. It buzzed again, but not in her hand. It came from somewhere else.

Buzz. Buzz. Buzz.

Standing inside her kitchen, Sid slowly spun around.

There.

The sound came from inside a set of jars for baking ingredients. They'd been a house-warming gift from her mother, and not a single grain of salt, flour, or sugar had ever been placed in any of them.

Sid took the lid off of the one in the middle and found a burner phone.

Oh my. It's got to be Smoke.

She answered and put the phone to her ear.

"Ah, Sid. Don't say a word. We need to meet. The Reflecting Pool. Forty minutes. I'll find you." The line went dead. It had not been Smoke.

CHAPTER 11

S IDNEY THREW ON A HALF-DRY pair of blue jeans, gathered some gear into a backpack, and headed out the door. The hard rains had subsided, and she made her way across the water puddles and opened the door of her car. The automobile, a dark-blue 1995 mustang GT, wasn't the Hellcat, but it was cheap. Lousy on fuel but good on speed. The door groaned as she closed it and fired the engine up. Three seconds later she was on the wet main roadway. At the first stoplight she checked the rearview mirror.

"Ah, there you are."

Agent Calhoun was four cars behind her. She could see him hunched over the steering wheel. There was a story about him. Several that she recalled. He abused power. Abused criminals. He'd even abused his supervisor. A couple of witnesses had died in his protection. Fleeing criminals had been blown away—and one of his partners, an agent named Muriel Davis, had vanished without a trace. There were question marks all over the man. He was supposed to be gone. He was a troublemaker, but he was back—and with eyes on Sid.

"So, how do I lose him?" She tapped her fingernails on the steering wheel. The light turned green. She didn't move. It couldn't have been a split second later when the honking started. Horns blared. Car windows filled with angry faces. Sid got out of her car and threw her arms up. "Sorry."

That was when the obscenities started. Everything foul from A to Z with many F's in between. Not one person offered to help.

So much for chivalry.

Sid popped the hood and checked the engine.

I can't believe I'm doing this.

Out of the corner of her eye, she watched the other lanes of traffic blast by until the light turned yellow. She slammed the hood shut and jumped back into her car. She stomped the gas as the light turned red and cruised through the intersection unmolested. Agent Calhoun sat stuck in his lane. His hands slapped the steering wheel.

Sid smiled. "Thanks, Dad. If you hadn't made me watch 'Beverly Hills Cop' with you twenty times, I might never have thought of that." She chuckled. "Every cloud really does have a silver lining."

It didn't take long for her to get to the Reflecting Pool. She even parked in her usual spot. After getting out of the car, she slung the backpack over her shoulder and headed for the pool.

There weren't many people out. The rain was between a mist and drizzle. The Reflecting Pool was usually a pretty popular place during lunchtime. Plenty of joggers, walkers, and tourists. But not today. It was quiet.

Sid tied her hair back and started walking.

Great.

As she headed toward the Lincoln Memorial, a flash of light caught her eye. She figured someone was taking a picture with a huge flash until the light hit her in the face again. Picking up the pace, she marched up the stairs and inside the monument where Abe Lincoln sat. He wasn't alone.

A wrinkle-faced man with soft blue eyes and brown hair wore a black trench coat and was chewing gum. It was Leroy Sullivan.

"I thought you were dead," Sid said, walking up to him.

"Oh, you should know better by now. You can't believe everything you hear." Leroy stuck out his hand. "Gum?"

"No thanks."

"It's everlasting cinnamon."

"Don't you know by now that nothing lasts forever?" she said.

Leroy half cackled and half laughed. "Shit, that was kinda funny. Good for you, Sid." He tucked the gum away. "So, my little buddies Cyrus and Rebecca paid you a visit. Told you I was dead. Boy, they're something, aren't they?"

"So they know you're alive?"

"Oh yeah. They're just trying to cut me out of the Black Slate. You see, they want control of it, and they don't have that. Some people just can't stand to not have control of everything. That's the problem with this country. Well, the world for that matter. Anyway." He came closer and put his arm over her shoulders. "We got a helluva problem. The manhunt for John Smoke has begun."

"So you don't think he did it?"

"If he did it, he wasn't in his right mind when he did. There's always things, dangerous things, lingering out there. Mind control. Hypnosis. It would be mighty hard to get him to go against his nature, but they want him off the streets. You two are causing problems. They don't like it."

"How can we clear him? I mean, there's video. Eyewitnesses."

"Yes," he said with some admiration. "Clever, aren't they. The only thing I can tell you is that you need to find out who really did it. But Sid, it could be him. And if Congressman Wilhelm doesn't survive, then this will never be over with. Even if he does survive, I'm not sure Smoke won't be buried out of sight for a long, long time."

"How am I supposed to do anything with the FBI all over my ass?"

"I'll take care of that." He squeezed her shoulder. "It's time to suit up, soldier."

"So I'm supposed to trust you now?"

"You don't really have anyone else." He handed her a set of keys and pointed back to the parking lot with his other thumb. "Everything you need is in the car."

"What about my Mustang?"

He offered his palm. "I'll see that it's properly retired. Goodbye, Sid. And happy hunting."

CHAPTER 12

H ANDS STUFFED IN HER POCKETS, Sid made the long walk back to the parking lot. She hadn't even looked at the keys Leroy had given her. Instead, she squeezed them tight.

Where am I even supposed to start?

Deep in thought, she kept walking, eyes forward, not really paying attention to what was ahead of her until she stood in the space where her car should have been.

Where's my car?

She spun around. The old Mustang was gone without a trace. She checked the keys in her hand. Dodge. With a curious look on her face, she pressed the auto-start button. A throaty engine note followed.

Vrrrooooom!

About ten car spaces away and partially concealed by a silver Volvo crossover rumbled a Dodge Challenger. Sid closed the gap between her and it and came face to face with a new phantom-black Hellcat. Her fingers tingled. "I'll be."

She ran her fingers over the triple coat of black on the hood. Traced the edges of the orange racing stripes. It was just like the one she had lost, but better. She opened the door and sat inside. The leather welcomed her like an old friend. She checked the console and glove box. All of her belongings were there. The registration and insurance were even in her name. She revved it up. "Purr, Hellcat, purr."

Vrrrooooom! Vrrrooooom! Vrrrooooom!

A charge went through her. New life. Exhilaration. She rubbed the dash, leaned back, and with one leg still hanging out the door she took in a deep breath and closed her eyes. "Man, I love fast cars."

Ring! Ring! Ring!

It sounded like the ringer from the old Adam West Batmobile. Sitting up, she fidgeted with the dash and answered the console.

The small digital screen in the middle came to life.

Mal Gunderson's face was on it. "Hi, Sid, how have you been?"

"It hasn't been the best day, but it's getting better."

"Do you like the car?" he said, smiling. The older, olive-skinned man looked as refined and studious as ever.

"Love it."

"Good."

Someone shoved into him, and another face crammed into the screen. It was Sam, stunning and happy. "Hey, Sid. Check out the trunk."

Guppy pressed his face into the picture. "Hey, Sid, did you check out the trunk yet? Check out the trunk!"

"Why, is Smoke in it?"

Sam and Guppy froze, and a frowning Sam said, "That's not funny."

"Oh, sorry."

Sam's face brightened. "Just kidding. No, he's not in it. Only God knows where he is. Now check out the trunk."

"Will you two get back!" Mal said to the both of them. Regaining his composure, he politely said, "Sid, go ahead and check out the trunk."

"All right." She headed outside, checked over her shoulder, and popped the trunk open. "Oh my."

Guns. Big and small. Ammo. Loads of it. A pair of L.A.W. rockets.

Is that a flamethrower?

There were two small metal cases too, like the ones Mal had equipped her and Smoke with before. She unfastened one and opened it up. A sweetheart suit. A vial full of pills. A Glock 22 with a pair of 30-round clips of ammunition. There were bullets too: red, blue, and green tipped. She picked her way through some other supplies. More knives. An ammo belt. A lighter. Watch. Glasses. "Are you trying to turn me into Jane Bond or something?"

Chuckling erupted inside the car.

She closed the trunk, got back in the car, and closed the door. All three faces were crammed onto the screen. "Am I being deployed? That arsenal was full of everything but a parachute."

"Oh, there's one in there," Guppy said with a wink.

"You know, all of that extra weight is going to infringe on my quarter mile time," she said.

"I think you'll be fine," Mal said. "Now Sid, do you think you're ready?"

"Ready for what?"

Sam said, "To kick some bad-guy ass."

"I think you all know I was born ready." Sid adjusted her seat and locked in her radio channels. "What's the plan?"

"We need you to come in," Mal said.

"To the Bat Cave?"

"No."

"The Hall of Justice?"

"No."

"The Avengers—"

"We are staying at the Hyatt Regency Downtown, suite 1111," Mal said, shaking his head. "See you soon."

Just before the image faded, Mal's Asian wife, Asia, popped her head in the screen. "Pick up some good food. Hotel food is shi—"

Sid cut her off, dropped the car into drive, and laid her foot down on the gas. Shoulders pinned to the seat and smiling from ear to ear, she made it to their hotel in no time flat.

CHAPTER 13

ROOM IIII. A BUSINESS SUITE. Suitable for all occasions.

"What do you mean Cyrus took the ring?" Sam said. Her face was red, and her perfect brows were creased. "It wasn't stolen. I'm the one who picked it out. Geez!"

As soon as Sid entered the room, a new interrogation had begun. Half embarrassed, Sid had told them everything, and Smoke's proposal was the worst part of all. "You knew about it?"

"Of course we did," Sam said, shaking her head yes.

"All of you knew?"

"It was a pretty ring." Asia was lying on one of the beds in a hotel robe, watching a soap opera on TV. "I prefer princess cut."

Sid grabbed a pillow and screamed into it. "Eeeeaaaaahhhh!"

Why does everyone but me always know what's going on!

Red-faced, she said, "So did everyone go out shopping for my ring? Guppy, were you there too?"

"There was a lot of shopping going on. Somebody had to hold the bags."

"If it's any consolation," Mal said, "I was the last one to know. Well, obviously you were the last one, but I certainly would have picked a better day to pop the question."

"You can say that again," Asia said. "Fool of a man proposed to me behind a liquor store. Can you believe that?"

"It was a nice view of the river. The liquor store just happened to be there," Mal said. "And I was, well, nervous. It's not like I'd ever asked anyone to marry me before."

"Aw, it's all right, honey," the little woman said. "I've forgiven you, but I'm still waiting on that second honeymoon to Vegas."

Sid sat down on the edge of the bed, exhausted and embarrassed. Smoke sure had awfully weird ways of doing things. She recalled the first time she'd read his profile. No hint of a schoolboy romantic anywhere in there. If anything, it had said he was a dangerous, lawless terror.

How can I marry an enigma?

Sam threw her arms up. "We can't have a wedding without a groom, so I suppose it's time we got to work."

"Indeed." Sitting behind his laptop, Mal pecked at some keys.

Guppy fed some paper into a portable printer. "And pardon everyone, Sid. This certainly is serious business, having to clear Smoke."

"Clear the Smoke. Funny," Asia said.

"You'll have to pardon my wife, Sid. She suffers from a mild but still annoying form of Tourette's."

"What is Tourette's?" Asia asked.

"Continuing," Mal said, "I don't think anyone here believes Smoke did what we think we saw him do. We're going to have to find out who did do what we saw." He turned on a projector, and his computer's image appeared on the wall. "Lights."

Guppy lumbered over to the door and turned off the lights.

The projector's light kept the room lit up.

Mal ran the video that the television stations had played during the assassination attempt. "We should be able to find some clues right here. Let me know if any of you sees anything out of the ordinary."

Sid had a very strong memory, borderline photographic. Several things jumped out at her. When the video stopped, she spoke first. "The shooter wore gloves. I don't recall seeing Smoke in a ball cap before, either. Back up to when Wilhelm is behind the podium."

The video image cruised backward.

"Stop it there. See this," she said, pointing with her finger. "This is a full view of the entire stage. One of the first things I said to myself was, 'Where's the Secret Service?' Wilhelm always has two of them nearby. There weren't any today."

"Very good," Mal said.

"Also," Sid continued, "Smoke doesn't move like that. This guy's stiff. Smoke is graceful. And look at Wilhelm. His eyes land on the audience and freeze on Smoke. If he felt he was in danger, then he would have moved out of harm's way, but he doesn't. He keeps talking." She put her finger on Wilhelm's image. "Run it right up to the point when the gun is fired."

Mal did, and then he froze the camera angle on Wilhelm's face.

"Look," said Sid. "He's tightening up. You can almost see that paunchy face of his pucker up, and the shot doesn't come until a couple of seconds later. If I were to guess, I'd say he was expecting it."

"Pretty good, Sid," Mal said with admiration. "I didn't even pick up on all that. Of course, it's not my forte."

"Good work, Sid," Guppy said while he rolled up the sleeves of his flannel shirt. He dabbed his sweaty forehead with a handkerchief. "I'd be lying if I said

I wasn't worried. Still, how are we going to prove that it wasn't him? We weren't there, and whoever did that looks just like him—and he has disappeared."

Sid sat down at the table.

Sam and Guppy joined her.

Every eye was fixed on her, looking for leadership. Looking for answers.

She took out the notepad where she'd jotted her notes in her apartment. "Let's start with what we do know. Time. Place. Hmmm. Witnesses. Did anyone see any interviews with the witnesses?"

"A couple," Guppy mumbled.

Sam was checking her nails until she found Sid's eyes on her. "Uh, nope."

"Tell you what, Sam. Maybe you and Guppy can contact Russ Davenport. If anyone else is on this who we can trust, it's him."

"Listen, Sid," Mal said, "all of this that you are suggesting is fine and well, but I don't see how any of it will help Smoke. We need a body and a gun. We aren't a bunch of attorneys who can clear his name. No, this is deep, and it's got the Drake's stink all over it. And as we all know, they have deeper pockets than we do."

"Aw, quit being such a sissy," Asia said.

"Will you shut up?" Mal fired back. "Now, I do think you should follow your instincts. That's fine. But I need to dig into some deeper things." He pecked at the computer and pulled up a new screen. "Look at this."

Images of faces from the Black Slate showed up. AV, Nightbird, Mason Crow, the Ratson Brothers, the forever children, the hunchback, Swift the rat-wolf, gargoyles and a handful of deaders.

"Creepy," Sam said with awe, "but kinda cool."

"What are you getting at, Mal?" Sid asked.

He gazed at all of them. "These are shifters. Men and women that change forms. What if there's one out there who has shifted to look just like John Smoke?"

CHAPTER 14

SID RUBBED THE CHILL BUMPS racing up her neck and shoulders. "Are you telling me that might not have even been him in my apartment at all?"

"No, that's not what I'm saying," Mal said. "Did you get a creepy feeling? Was there something odd about him?"

"Yeah, was he creepy?" Sam said.

"No, not exactly. Just the fact that he proposed to me."

"Aw, did he get down on one knee?" Sam said. "I love it when they do that."

"I take it you've been proposed to before," said Sid.

"Oh yeah, lots of times." Sam studied her nails. "But I only said yes once." She winked at Guppy.

"Let's not get ahead of ourselves," Mal said, closing the laptop.

Guppy powered down the projector. "It's only a theory."

Sam and Guppy got up and headed toward the door.

"Where are you two going?" asked Sid.

"After Russ Davenport, like you said." Sam was giving her a look.

"Forget it, I'll go."

"What? Wait a minute, why?" Sam said. "I think we can handle it."

"It's not that," Sid said, "it's just that I don't know where to start, so it might as well be there."

"I don't see any reason why we can't come with," Guppy said.

"Because three's a crowd." She felt someone tapping her on the shoulder.

It was Asia. The little woman said, "And four's even worse. No, let's go get something to eat. I'm tired of sitting in this stuffy room. Feels like a hospital." She made a sour face. "Uck!"

Asia sat in the front seat of the Hellcat, staring straight ahead and stuffing her face with French fries. Sam and Guppy were in the back, and neither one of them stayed quiet longer than one second at a time.

"You know, this car's fairly roomy back here. Needs more leg room, but heck, it's a sports car," Sam said. She had a copy of Nightfall DC folded in front of her. "Hey, it says here there are giant rats living in the sewers." She shoved Sid's shoulder. "Duh."

"Why don't you lay into this thing, Sid? I want to feel that power. Say, I know a great track that we can take it for a spin on," Guppy said. He pushed himself up toward the dash. "Maybe time the quarter mile. See? You have a timer in your console here, and you can figure out your G-forces as well. Look, see the race light?" He poked it with his pudgy finger. "Sweet, huh."

Sid smacked his hand. "Do you mind?"

"Can't say that I do."

Sam shoved him back in his seat. "Behave yourself."

Asia stuck her hand in Sid's face. "French fry?"

"No thanks," Sid said.

Geez, what is wrong with these people?

That was one of the things that bothered Sid about these people most. They didn't seem to worry. It was both weird and refreshing. Since she graduated high school and went into the service, most of the training had been intense. The job was serious. She pushed herself to the highest levels and gave herself the biggest challenges. Heck, there were plenty of days when she probably didn't crack a smile. And come to think of it, the FBI was notorious for its frowns.

Sheesh.

But this crew, they seemed to delight in danger.

"How much farther, Sid?" Guppy asked.

"A few more miles of highway and a few miles of old roadway after that," she said. "Why?"

"Oh, I think I'm starting to get a little carsick is all."

"Oh honey," Sam said, petting his head, "do you want us to pick you up some Dramamine?"

Sid tuned them out. Or at least tried to until they got to the camp where Russ Davenport kept his trailer. She shut off the engine and popped open her door. "We're here."

Guppy hustled out, a little green. "I call shotgun on the ride back."

"Tell you what," Sam said, stretching her long frame out of the car and putting on her sunglasses, "this is pretty much how I imagined it."

Russ's two trailers stuck together looked just as shabby as they had before. The wooden deck needed paint, and the wood was aged grey. Rust was apparent on the corner edges of the trailers, and the screen door banged a little in the wind.

"Why didn't you just call?" Asia said, crinkling her nose. "This place is shitty."

"He doesn't like phones," Sid said.

The steps creaked beneath her feet on her way up to the front door. She pounded on the frame. "Russ! It's Sid. Sidney Shaw."

No answer. She scanned the camp area. A white convertible Chrysler LeBaron was parked nearby. Its best days had been at least two decades ago.

Guppy walked over to it, put his hand on the hood, and showed Sid a shrug.

She banged on the trailer again. "Russ!" She opened the screen door. The main door was cracked open behind it. She looked back over her shoulder and pulled out her gun.

Asia's eyes popped open.

Sid went inside.

Russ's trailer was a mess. The books were all over the floor. Computer equipment was busted. Anything that opened had been pulled out or torn off. Glass crunched under her feet. "Russ?"

Thump. Thump. Thump.

Swallowing hard, Sid ventured deeper into the trailer toward the bedroom. There was nothing but ruffled sheets, torn up pillows, and loose papers. "Russ?"

Thump. Thump. Thump.

She whirled and faced the tiny door that led to the bathroom. Gun ready, she grabbed the handle and jerked the door open. Russ's heavy frame rolled out. His mouth, hands, and legs were bound. He was barely breathing—and bleeding from the head.

CHAPTER 15

"**A**W MAN," RUSS SAID, HOLDING a wet towel to his head. He was propped up on his sofa, surrounded by Sid and everyone else. "I gotta tell you, I'm sure glad you guys stopped by. I thought I was a goner."

"What happened?" Sid asked.

"I'm sitting at my computer, you know, doing my thing and working on my paper." He sucked his teeth and winced. "When I hear a sound. I turn, and *pop,* I get hammered right between the eyes. The next thing I know I'm bound up and lying on the floor. Some dude's tearing up all my stuff, and I yell at him. He turns, and then things get spooky. His eyes are pitch black, and his face is weird and pasty. His hands are huge. He snatches me up off the floor with one hand and tosses me back onto the bed. Man, I thought I was dead."

"Did he say anything?" she asked.

"He—or it—asked me where Smoke was. I said, 'I don't know, ask the fuzz.'" Russ's breath shuddered. "That's when everything went black. Well, after his fist exploded into my head." His eyes found Sam's face and brightened. "But it looks like my day is getting better."

"Looks like you're going to make it," Sid said. "You might want to check and see if he—or it—took anything."

Russ leaned forward with a groan and let Sid help him to his feet. Scanning everything, he shuffled into the other trailer. It was a little more suitable for company and had a bigger desk with more intact computer screens. He took a seat behind the desk. "Well, doesn't look like anything is broken in here. So, uh, can one of you grab me a beer out of the fridge? It'll do me better than this rag."

Asia—petite, expressionless, and pretty—brought over two bottles and set them on his desk. She twisted the caps off both of them. "The only thing decent in here is your beer. Everything else sucks." She gulped some down, took a seat, and turned on Russ's TV.

"Uh," Russ said, grabbing his beer, "so what brought you guys over here?"

"You know about the Wilhelm shooting?" Sid said.

"Of course. That's what I was working on when that goon showed up."

"What were you working on?" Sid asked.

"Ah, well, like everything else I write about in the city, I was working on the conspiracy." Russ took a long sip of beer. "And that shooting is another doozy."

Arms crossed over her chest, Sid said, "What do you mean?"

"You know, one thing that I do all the time is interview. I've done hundreds of them, heck, maybe thousands, I don't know, but I'll tell you this. I know when someone's not being honest. And, I'm pretty good with faces." He turned his screen around so that everyone nearby could see. He typed on the keys, and a pair of images showed up. "For instance, this guy who I like to call jackass number one."

Sid, Sam, and Guppy leaned closer. The man on the screen had kinky hair and was going bald. His cheeks were saggy, and so was his jaw. Russ played the eyewitness interview, and the man sounded like a real know-it-all. He recalled a lot of interesting details: how many shots were fired and what the shooter was wearing.

"Okay, where are you going with this?" Sid asked.

"Well, watch this other interview. Same guy, right, but different shooting. This was from a taping just outside of Atlanta. Remember that shooting at the university? Guess who was there." He played the video.

"Hah!" Sam said. "That SOB recited the same MO. I'll be damned. You know I read an article that said the Atlanta shooting never happened."

"That was my article," Russ said, giving her a smile.

"Well, it was a good one. But reading that, and seeing this all for myself, now that is something." Sam walked away. "I need a beer."

"I'll take one," Guppy added.

"Sure, help yourselves," Russ said. "And I can only assume you guys are going to stick around long enough to help me clean up this mess."

"*Phllyyt!*" Asia said. "This place is hopeless."

"It ain't that bad." He shook his head. "Tough crowd. Anyway, I've got this guy on two other videos and two more separate incidents. And he's not the only one. There are others too. He's just the one I hate the most."

"Why do you hate him? Have you met him?" Sam said, coming back with two beers.

"The man's a liar. I just can't stand liars."

"Maybe you should consider moving out of this city," Sam said, taking a seat on the edge of his desk. "Ever consider that?"

"Nope." Russ guzzled down the rest of his beer and tossed the bottle into a little trash can that toppled over. "Because that's just what they want."

"So you think Congressman Wilhelm wasn't even shot?" Sid said.

"Have you seen his body, dead or alive? Has anyone? No, this stinks, and it's got the Drake written all over it. Crap. Uh, can someone beer me?"

Asia got up and returned with a beer. She tossed it to him. "Hope you can take the cap off by yourself, sloppy man." She returned to her seat.

Looking around his screen at Asia, Russ said, "I can't tell if I like her or not. Pretty and mean. Huh. What's her story?"

"Mean," Guppy said.

"Russ, what's your theory then? Why the setup?" Sid asked.

He twisted the cap off his bottle and replied, "It's pretty clear to me. They have a DC-wide manhunt going on because they want your pal John Smoke dead."

CHAPTER 16

S MOKE DEAD. SIDNEY FELT HOLLOW inside on the drive back to the hotel. It didn't help that everyone else was a little quiet as well.

"Oh, he'll be alright," Sam said, reaching up and rubbing Sid's shoulder. "He hasn't been caught."

"It hasn't even been a day," Sid said, cruising the streets of DC. A tingle went up and down her spine as she passed by a police car with flashing lights on. A man was handcuffed and being stuffed into the back of the patrol car. Everyone in Sid's car was looking. "Has anyone heard anything at all from him?"

"No," Guppy said. "And I don't suppose we will either, too risky. You know what I mean."

"Your weird boyfriend likes to hide," Asia said. She was checking her makeup in the visor mirror. "He be fine. Say, how about we stop and get something to eat before we go back to the hotel? I'm in the mood for some Indian cuisine, eh? Spicy food makes your worries go away."

"I'm not hungry," Sid said, irritated, "but I'd love to drop you off so you can gorge your little self."

"Don't be so frosty," Asia said.

Sam chuckled. "Forgive her, Sid. It's taken us some time to get used to her too."

Sid had gotten used to Sam and Guppy over the last few months, since they'd all been working together as bounty hunters. The pair had been nothing short of reliable, sharp witted, and effective. They would make great FBI agents, but they were pretty heavy on the big government conspiracy side. On the one hand, they seemed pretty kooky with their theories, but on the other hand, there was the Black Slate. It made it kind of hard to rule out anything they said. "I think we need to see if we can figure out where Congressman Wilhelm is. If this was staged, he's probably alive somewhere."

"He's at Angels of Mercy Hospital, right?" Sam said. "Me and Guppy can handle it. I'm a pretty persuasive woman when I put my mind to it."

"You're always persuasive," Guppy said.

"Aw!" Sam kissed Guppy on the forehead. "You're so sweet, honey."

"Honey?" Sid and Asia both said together. Sid continued. "Are you two dating or something?"

"Dating?" Sam took out a compact mirror and started putting some lipstick on. "Certainly not dating."

Guppy chuckled. "We're married."

"What?" Sid and Asia both said with alarm. "You're serious?"

"Of course. Geez, didn't you know that?" Sam said. She held her hand out and flashed the many rings on it. "See that rock. Or those rocks?"

Sid had noticed Sam's bejeweled fingers before. The woman had plenty of rings, and she changed them out all the time too. Sid had never paid any mind to the small engagement ring that was always there. "Interesting. So where's your ring, Guppy?" she said into the rearview mirror. "I don't see any rings on your fingers."

Guppy pulled out a heavy chain around his neck. There was a gold band attached to it along with a pair of dog tags. "I've gotten a little heftier since we got married, so it don't fit no more."

"Then go on diet," Asia said, "chubby dwarf."

"Great," Sid said. She took pride in figuring things out for herself, but she'd totally missed on Sam and Guppy. The pair worked so well together, and neither ever fawned or argued. Of course, she wasn't with them most of the time, but still …

How did I miss that?

She'd even done background checks on them and didn't recollect anything about them being married.

Guppy, sitting in the back, eased up between the front seats. "I know what you're thinking, Sid. How'd you miss that? You see, not everything's on public record. That's just what they want, and they can use it against you. But don't worry." He pointed up and gave her a wink. "He saw the entire ceremony."

Sid showed a little smile. "So, are there any other secrets I need to know about that my thorough research missed?"

Sam and Guppy sank back into their seats.

Asia started humming.

Sid smacked the wheel with her hands. "Seriously? There's a bigger secret than you two being married?"

"No one said it was a secret," Sam said, tucking her lipstick away. "You just missed it."

"What else did I miss, then?"

"Uh, well, there's only one other oversight I can think of," Sam said. "I'm Smoke's sister."

Sid pulled the car over into a grocery parking lot, slammed it into park, and turned her shoulder toward Sam. "What?"

"Well, half-sister, sort of."

"Which is it?"

"It's complicated?"

"Do you have the same father or the same mother?"

"More complicated than that," Sam said. "Look, I don't really want to discuss it. But at least now you know." She flipped her hands up. "There. No more secrets."

"You can't just leave me hanging," Sid said, taking a demanding tone.

"You know enough. That's it." Sam made the zipped-lips motion and looked out the window.

"She won't talk now," Guppy said. "Trust me."

"True, but I'm sure you know as much as she does," Sid said.

"That is true, Sid, but I know better than to open my mouth and tick off my wife. You'll have to get it from her someday. Or him."

"Yeah, right." Sid put the car in gear and headed toward Angel of Mercy Hospital. A long twelve minutes later, she dropped off Sam and Guppy at the hospital's ER entrance. Getting out and letting Sam out of her side, she took the woman by the arm, a little torn between mad and happy when she said, "The more I know, the more likely I am to say yes. I don't like secrets."

Sam gave her a tough little nod. "I'll be in touch."

Sid sat back down in the car and looked at Asia. "Do you have any secrets that you want to share?"

Asia patted her belly. "No secrets here. Hungry."

Sid started pulling out of the emergency room entrance.

A man walked right in front of her car toward the hospital.

She hit the brake and laid on the horn. "Idiot."

The man kept moving. Head down and clutching his side, he vanished through the sliding glass doors.

"I can't stand hospitals," Sid grumbled.

"Me either," Asia agreed.

While she was driving down the parking lot, a crash of glass exploded from somewhere outside. A man toppled out of a third-floor window. The bushes broke his fall. Another man sailed out of the window and hit the pavement hard.

"Holy crap!" Asia said. "Men don't fly so well."

Standing inside the third-floor window was a tall and ranging man with his back to them. He moved fast, fading in and out of sight. He wore green scrubs and had a surgeon's cap and mask on his head. The sharp pop of gunfire sounded from somewhere inside the building. The man dressed as a doctor jumped out of the window and landed in the bushes.

"Looks like another person going to need emergency room," Asia commented.

The man sprang up out of the bushes and took off at a full sprint.

Men in dark suits and glasses hung out of the window and started firing.

"What kind of hospital is this?" Asia said, folding her arms over her chest. "They shooting at the doctors!"

"Asia, that's not a doctor," Sid said, "that's Smoke."

CHAPTER 17

"REALLY?" ASIA SAID. "HE'S A doctor and a bounty hunter? Looks like he's probably a better bounty hunter."

"Shut up, Asia." Sid stomped on the gas, peeling rubber.

Smoke's head popped up between the cars in the parking lot briefly, and then she lost sight of him. "Damn!" She cruised up the parking lot, looking left and right. "Where did he go?"

"I think we better get out of here," Asia said, peeking in the side-view mirror. "Angry patients everywhere."

Men in suits poured out of the emergency room exits and spread out all over the parking lot.

Sid counted eight of them with guns ready.

What have you done now, John?

"Look, Sid, you need to get us out of here." Asia tapped on her shoulder. "Look!"

Police cars with flashing lights were coming. In seconds the entire parking lot would be sealed off.

Sid couldn't get pulled over and have the trunk searched either. She eased on the gas and squeezed off the lot and onto the main road just as two cop cars blew by. She pulled off on the berm and looked back for Smoke. "Whew!" she said, heart racing and looking forward.

The whine of a motorcycle engine caught her ear.

She looked back.

Smoke was on a street bike, hemmed in by Secret Service and cops. The only way off the lot was through the police barricade. Officers from all over were swarming in from all directions now. Smoke revved up the bike and took off straight toward the shooters.

"No!"

Like a bullet, the bike screamed down the parking lot straight into the path of the shooters. Smoke and the ultra-fast bike covered the distance to the barricade in two seconds.

The shooters jumped aside just as Smoke squeezed between the bumpers of two cars and jettisoned out onto the main road. A hail of gunfire and screams of shock and alarm followed.

The wide-eyed Asia turned to Sid. "If you marry him, you better get a lot of life insurance."

"I will," Sid said, gunning the engine, "if I don't kill him first."

The Hellcat's engine revved. Rubber burned.

Pinned to their seats, Sid and Asia chased after the diminishing speck of John Smoke.

"Slow down, slow down!" Asia screamed.

Sid did no such thing. She blew by three cars merging onto the highway and was up to a hundred miles per hour before Asia screamed again.

"Aiyeee!"

The Hellcat closed in on Smoke.

With Smoke's hair flying in the wind behind it, the big green ghost had slowed, but it still weaved in and out of the cars on the highway.

"Where are you going, John?" Sidney checked her rearview mirror.

Police lights sparkled, but they were still far behind. It wouldn't be long before every police car in town packed the interstate. She pressed on the gas. A hundred and twenty. A hundred and thirty.

"You're crazy!" Asia yelled.

It was crazy. Illegal. Dangerous. Stupid even, but she had to catch up to Smoke. Ahead, she saw the helmetless man glance over his shoulder. "But he's crazier than me. He doesn't even have a seatbelt."

Asia balled up in the seat, clutching the seatbelt with her eyes squeezed shut, chanting, "Please don't wreck. Please don't wreck. Please don't wreck. I don't want to die yet!"

Smoke's motorcycle slowed and moved over to the right lane. Sid caught up and pulled alongside him. They both backed off to about seventy miles per hour. She rolled down her window.

"Hi, Sid!" Smoke yelled.

"Don't you 'Hi' me, you idiot. What do you think you're doing?"

"Evading law enforcement." His eyes scanned the Hellcat. "Nice ride. Where'd you get it?"

"Never mind that, John! What's going on? What's your plan?" she asked.

"I need to clear my name and probably blow up a few things. Look, Sid, stay away from this. I can handle it." Still cruising down the highway at seventy miles per hour, he put his hand on the car door and peeked in. "Hey, Asia."

"Shut up, crazy man!" said the little woman.

"John, you can't do this alone. It's too big." She could hear the sirens now. "They're going to kill you."

"Aw, Sid, don't worry. You can count on me." He glanced back. "Tell you what, follow me off the next exit ramp. I've got a plan." He sped the bike up, but then he slowed down and approached her window again. "Oh, wait. Do you happen to have an extra gun in there?"

Asia popped open the glove box and tossed over a 1911 semi-auto with an extra-long clip.

Sid handed it to him.

Smoke stuffed it down the front of his pants. "Thanks. Now follow me." He led them off the next exit ramp, where traffic was bumper-to-bumper at the red light.

"Morning Glory. What is he doing? Is he stupid?"

Smoke turned around and saluted. Revving up the bike, he squirted through the traffic, raced through the intersection, popped a wheelie, and roared back up the other side of the entrance ramp.

"No you didn't!" Sid screamed, banging her hands on the wheel.

"Yes he did," Asia said, dabbing the sweat off her brow. "And I'm happy for it. He's crazy, but in a sexy way."

Sid ground her teeth.

I can't believe he did that.

Police sirens roared by on the interstate over their heads. Looking up through the window, Sid saw two choppers zoom overhead. Men were manning the machine guns on both of them. Helpless and gaping, Sid felt doom creep between her shoulder blades.

CHAPTER 18

"THE MANHUNT IS STILL ON for this suspect the authorities have not identified," said the female reporter on the television screen. She was standing outside the Angels of Mercy hospital. A picture of John Smoke, a little blurry, appeared in the right-hand corner. "Authorities say this man is armed and dangerous. If you see him, do not approach him, but send any information you have to the contacts listed on your screen."

Sid turned the television off and lay back on her couch, rubbing her temples. "What are you doing to me, John Smoke?"

"Did you say something?" Sam said, popping her head out of the kitchen. She wore an apron, and her hair was up in a bun. "Say, why don't we make some cookies? It will make you feel better." She rummaged through the cupboards, opening and closing the doors. "Or maybe not. You don't cook very much, do you."

"I don't eat a lot."

"That's a good thing. Too much gluten in everything."

Sid leaned over on her side, facing Sam. "And you're wanting to make cookies?"

"I didn't say we had to eat them. I usually just give them to Guppy. Maybe that little Chinese lady. She eats like she has a tapeworm or something."

Sid put her feet on the floor and rubbed her eyes. It had been two days since Smoke lost her on the highway, and she'd barely slept a wink because of it. And things had been quiet. Too quiet. It didn't seem possible that Smoke could have escaped just about every law enforcement official in DC. And those helicopters really put the fright in Sid. What if Smoke was already dead?

"Don't do that," Sam said.

"Do what?"

"You're biting your nails."

"Oh. Thanks."

"Why don't we go out and get some fresh air?" Sam suggested. She took off her apron. She was wearing a sequined shirt with a dragon on it, jeans, and high heels. "Maybe some good news will find its way to us."

Sid headed for the bedroom. "I need to change."

"Why don't you put that sweetheart suit on? It'll make you feel better. Besides, you never know when we might run into danger."

"Then why don't you wear one too?" Sid said. She took off her shirt and opened the case to the sweetheart suit.

"Not my thing," Sam replied. "But if I were you, I'd be wearing it. Especially after what you told me about those rats. Ew!"

Sidney removed her jeans, took up the suit, and started slipping it on. It was snug but energizing, a warm second skin that made her body feel alive.

Her stomach groaned.

Sam stuck her head into the bedroom. "Was that you?"

"The suit does that."

Sam eyed her up and down. "It does look good on you. Hmmm ... Maybe I *will* try one of those things."

Moving to her closet, Sid slipped on some new jeans and a shirt over the suit. She grabbed her boots—light but durable hiking ones—and laced them up. After she cracked her neck from side to side, she strapped on a pair of shoulder holsters and adjusted them in front of the mirror.

"Not bad," Sam said. "You look like the Punisher."

"Ha ha." Sid gathered her gear, and out the door they both went.

Agent Calhoun was leaning on the trunk of the Hellcat. He was a little bigger and thicker than Smoke, heavy shouldered with a dangerous and lazy look in his eyes. His hair was really short, bald in places, and his voice was a warning thunder when he spoke. "I see you upgraded to a better set of wheels. Nice."

"What do you want, Calhoun?"

"Oh, just the same thing every officer of the law in DC does: John Smoke." He pushed off the car and rose to his full height. Looking down on Sidney like a drill sergeant, he added, "Dead or alive."

Leroy Sullivan had told Sid that the FBI dogs wouldn't be a problem. Yet, here Calhoun was. It put a crimp on things. "I don't like your chances," Sid said. "You can't even keep up with me. What makes you think you can keep up with him?"

"A quarter of a million dollars," he said. "That's the bounty on his head."

"You can't collect that. You're an agent."

"Was. You see, I'm on an extended leave of absence." He flashed a broad smile. "Family problems." He opened up his long coat, revealing a pair of guns and a long knife hitched in his belt. He took out a handkerchief and mopped the sweat from his brow. "It's gonna be a hot few days, Sid." His eyes gave her and Sam the once-over as he walked away. "Real hot."

"That's one shady bastard, isn't it," Sam said, getting into the Dodge.

"To put it mildly." She pulled the car out and stopped in front of Calhoun. He was hunched over the wheel inside his black Suburban. She loaded some blue-tipped bullets into her Glock's clip, charged the weapon, took aim on Calhoun's engine block, and squeezed off a few rounds.

Blam! Blam! Blam!

The armor-piercing bullets ripped through the SUV's metal, and the engine started to smoke. Agent Calhoun's face darkened, and his eyes narrowed on Sid.

"Let's go eat," Sid said as she drove away with Sam's laughter filling her ears.

The long lunch that went into evening was good. The return back to Sid's apartment was bad. The front door was busted open, and two police officers were inside. Her entire apartment had been ransacked.

CHAPTER 19

"Is this your place?" the one officer said. He wasn't very tall and had a friendless demeanor. A real sourpuss. The other cop, much younger and taller, had a cocky smile.

"It's mine," Sid said, forcing her way inside. The cabinets were empty. Glass was broken. Her bed was overturned, along with many other things. The padding on the sofa and chairs was cut open and the stuffing pulled out. "What happened?"

"Anything missing?" the older cop said, writing on a small notepad.

She held up a picture of Megan that sat on the end table. The glass and frame were broken. Sighing, she said, "Let me look around and see."

"Do you have a boyfriend or husband, miss? Maybe a fallout?" asked the younger cop.

"No."

"Er, what's your name, Miss?" asked the older cop.

"Who called this in?" Sidney fired back.

"Beg your pardon?"

"Who called this in?"

"Er, it was a 911, I guess. Look, I'm asking the questions here. Name?"

She pulled out her badge and held it in his face. "Sidney Shaw."

He leaned in and tilted the cap back on his head. "FBI Liaison. What's that mean? You some kind of consultant or something?"

"Maybe you should call them and find out," she said.

"Hey, we're just doing our jobs," the older cop said. "You just need to cooperate, Miss FBI Liaison. I can still haul you in for obstruction, you know."

There were plenty of obstinate cops she'd crossed before, but there was something different about this one. His uniform was a bad fit. The buttons were tight, the cuffs on his pants too low. The other cop's pants were too high, and the grin on his face was a bit abnormal. He leered at both Sid and Sam with a hungry look in his eyes. "What is your badge number?" Sid asked.

"My what?" the older cop asked.

Sid enunciated. "Badge number."

"It's, uh—" He looked down at the badge on his chest. "Five. Four. One. Two."

Sid eased away and took Sam by the wrist and led her toward the front door. "You know, I didn't notice a police car outside. Did you two walk over from the station?"

Both officers' nostrils flared. Their eyes narrowed and dimmed. Hands clutching in and out, the taller one said in a throaty voice, "Where's Smoke, woman!"

Sid went for her guns.

They were halfway out when the old officer collided into her. He clamped his hands over her wrists and wrenched the guns out.

"Run, Sam! Run!"

The gorgeous woman made it down two steps. The tall cop snatched her by the hair and yanked her back. "Hey!" She started to scream, only to have the man's hand clamped over her mouth.

He dragged her inside and slammed the door shut.

Sid launched a kick into the cop that had her.

He laughed it off.

She twisted away, only to have him pounce on her back.

He pinned her down with inhuman strength.

"Damn. You're a deader, aren't you."

"In the undead flesh," he said. "It's the price we pay for being superhuman."

She drove her head into his chin.

His grip loosened, but he held firm. "Aw, you're only going to hurt yourself more fooling around like that. Now tell me, where's Smoke?"

"That seems to be the question everyone is asking, but I don't know."

The deader cop forced her onto her back and slapped her in the face. "I don't like your tone."

Grimacing, Sid managed to snake a knife out of the back of her pants. She sliced his throat. "I don't like yours either."

The man staggered back, holding his throat but not bleeding.

Sid scrambled for her gun and got the drop on the first deader cop. "One hole through the chest will end you!"

The first cop froze. The second cop had his arm wrapped around Sam's throat. "Yeah, but one hard squeeze and her trachea will cave in. Who's going to save her then? Now tell us where Smoke is!"

Blam!

A bullet ripped through the tall deader's forehead. He staggered back with a face full of alarm.

Blam!

Sid's second shot tore clear through the dead man's heart. He dropped to the floor.

The other deader cop rushed out the door.

Sid couldn't get a clean shot at him.

"That was crazy!" Sam said, catching her breath and rubbing her neck. She kicked the deader cop lying on the floor. "He's not even bleeding, but he was so real." She glanced up at Sid. "I thought deaders were slow and stupid."

Tucking her weapons back inside her holsters, Sid said, "They were, but they're getting better. More real." She kneeled down by the dead man on the floor and pulled down his collar. There was a Drake tattoo of a black rising sun on his neck.

"Spooky, huh," Sam said, trembling.

"You okay?"

"I'm just getting the chills." Sam pulled out her phone and started texting. "Let me get the word out to Guppy. He gets worried if I don't check in."

"Tell him we need some cleanup. Cops, real ones, will be all over this place. Not sure we have a good explanation for this man down here." She gave her apartment a long, sad look. "I think I'm going to need a new place to live."

Looking at her phone, Sam said, "We need to get out of here. Guppy and Mal will handle the cleanup."

Sidney got a sinking feeling she might not ever see her apartment again. All she had left that hadn't been destroyed fit in her two suitcases. And then she picked up the picture frame, removed Megan's picture, and tucked it inside her shirt. Taking one more quick glance around, she said, "Let's go."

Driving her new car, she made her way out of the apartment complex. It being midday, there weren't too many people standing around. A couple of old ladies stood on the sidewalk, wearing colorful robes. A maintenance crew in a golf cart passed them by.

Eyes forward, she pulled out onto the main highway and let out a breath. "You know, I don't really understand why they want John so bad. Why him and not me?" she said to Sam.

"You're easier to control, I guess."

"What's that supposed to mean?"

"Think about it. You have more family than he does. Or at least you don't think yours are expendable."

"Does he really think that way?" Sid asked. "That you're expendable?"

Checking her makeup in the vanity mirror, Sam replied, "Eh, we're covered. Besides, Smoke's a 'kill them all, let God sort them out' kinda guy."

"I think he's more compassionate than that."

Sam shifted toward Sid. "Let me tell you something, sister. Where we come from, we don't compromise with evil."

CHAPTER 20

S ID LAY LOW THE NEXT couple of days. She slept at Sam and Guppy's place, a tiny apartment on the other side of town, much like the one Sid had to abandon. It was morning, and coffee was brewing. Sam had some eggs and bacon on a griddle. Sitting on the sofa with the television on, Sid rubbed her bleary eyes.

Every day, on every channel, they talked about the manhunt. They never mentioned John's name or anything about his past. They just called him the unknown man and showed a slightly blurred picture. The experts were popping up on every outlet too. They had all kinds of theories about who Smoke was. Prior military. An ex-con. A deranged madman. A jilted employee.

Sid smiled.

They don't know how close they are.

Sam set a steaming mug of coffee on the table.

"Thanks," Sid said. The hot brew stung her lip. "Say, Sam, you didn't see Wilhelm in the hospital, did you?"

"No, everything was chaos when we went in there. I only got a glimpse into the room, but it was cleared out."

"Nothing odd?"

"No, nothing's come to mind since the last time you asked. Or the time before that." Sam fixed up a couple of plates of food and sat down beside Sid. "You aren't doing all right, are you."

Sid nibbled on her bacon and shook her head. "I am. I just have a feeling someone got to him before we did."

"It's not hard to hide in a city like this. It's pretty big, and Smoke knows it pretty well. I'm sure he's blending in with a stack of hot cakes somewhere right now." Sam stabbed the scrambled eggs with her fork and ate. Swallowing it down with some coffee, she said, "Don't worry, something will surface."

Digging into her meal, Sid fished through the news channels. She needed to find something, anything that would be a good starting point. Everything had happened so fast two days ago that she was just now getting a chance to sort things out. She flipped from channel to channel, and then there it was. An eyewitness. And not just any eyewitness, but the same slob that Russ Davenport from Nightfall DC had pointed out. Elbows on her knees, Sid leaned forward.

"What is it?" Sam said, squinting her eyes at the screen.

Sid paused the TV. "If this guy is indeed an actor like Russ says, then maybe he can provide a few answers."

"Yeah," Sam agreed, "he really has been making his rounds, hasn't he? I'll get right on it."

Sid finished up her breakfast, slipped some clothes on over the sweetheart suit, and loaded up her gear.

"Where are you going?" Sam asked.

"Out to catch the bad guys."

"What? I thought we were gonna hang out and watch the Bewitched marathon." Sam leaned over the back of the sofa. "Say, which Darren did you like better?"

"Dick York, of course." Sid slung her pack over her shoulder and nodded at the TV. "Let me know what you find out about that witness, I mean that camera-hogging bearded tub of lard. I'm on my way."

"I'm on it like Larry Tate on ad money."

Sid departed with a chuckle. The Hellcat's engine roared, and before long she was cruising down the highway. With the radio off, she had some time to think, but she liked Sam's company.

Sometimes you need time to yourself.

Thirty minutes into the drive, she got her first text from Sam. It was the location of a small television station just outside the northwest rim of DC.

Man, she's good.

She pulled into the parking lot of the station ten minutes later. She backed the car in with a good view of the front door. It was a one-story white building made from long channels of concrete. The groundskeeping had seen better days. Two people were smoking inside a nearby gazebo. There was one parked news van. Everything was quiet.

She texted Sam. "Are you certain he's here?"

"He wouldn't miss it for the world. Dude has a Twitter account. Blowing up all of his appearances. Loser."

"Gotcha. Tks."

Social media might be one of the greatest windfalls to law enforcement of all time. People just can't keep quiet about their business.

The phone buzzed. A picture of the man she was looking for popped up. Bald and bearded, the heavyset man's name was Clarence Williams.

Tap. Tap. Tap.

Sid's heart jumped. A man was standing by her window.

She trained her gun on him.

"Whoa," the man said with his fingers spread wide. "Don't shoot."

It was Russ Davenport. She lowered her window but kept the gun aimed on his chest. "What are you doing here?"

"Same as you," he said, scratching his nose, "just following the clues. Heh, I'm impressed. Widened my eyes when I saw you pull up in this big black machine." He eyed her gun. "Do you mind? I've been shot before, if you don't remember."

She put the pistol away. "So you're after Clarence too?"

"Yep." He rubbed the back of his neck. "I've been here since he went in. He ought to be out any minute. Say, you think I could have a seat? Kinda hot today."

"Why don't you take that jacket off?"

He peeled back his coat, revealing an old wheel gun. A stainless steel 357 Magnum by the look of it. "I'm a lot more cautious these days."

"You know that's illegal."

"Every Constitutional right seems illegal in DC these days. I say screw 'em."

Sid nodded. "Get in."

"Thanks." Inside the car, Russ adjusted the seat back and dabbed the sweat off his face with a handkerchief.

"So, do you have anything else?" Sid asked.

"Like what?"

"Anything on Smoke or anyone else?"

"Nah, it's been quiet. No one's talking. And it's a pretty big city. Lots of ground to cover—and lousy parking."

Sid shook her head. It didn't help that Russ smelled like sweat and a submarine sandwich. She sat there for quite a while, hands on the wheel and eyes on the television station door.

A pair of people came out.

"That's him," Russ said with a scowl. "Man, I can't stand the look of that guy. He reminds me of a walking gourd or one of those killer space clowns."

"What? Never mind." Sid noticed the other person with Clarence. She was a bulldog of a woman. Black jeans and a grey T-shirt, short dark hair and husky arms. "Who's that?"

"I'll be damned," Russ said in awe from the edge of his seat. "It's Jean."

CHAPTER 21

W HO'S JEAN?' WAS THE OBVIOUS question, but Sid didn't have to ask. Russ became a burbling fountain of excitement. Sid put the car in gear and followed Clarence and Jean, who pulled out of the parking lot in a beat-up white painter's van and then drove through town, light to light, street to street.

"Man, I can't believe it. I can't believe it," Clarence said, sweating again.

"Believe what exactly?"

Russ caught his breath. "That's Jean Moffat, a legend."

"What do you mean by a *legend*?"

He took out an asthma inhaler and took a puff.

Sid cocked a brow. "Asthmatic, huh?"

"Only when I get really excited." He gasped for breath. "I just didn't expect this."

She could relate to the asthma, but not the excitement. "Settle down and spit it out."

"Well, me and a bunch of my cronies, well, not a bunch really—most of them are dead—but anyway"—he sucked in some more breath—"we studied a bunch of old films. I mean archived stuff from any old tragedies that we could find. The stuff's not sealed up or anything, but still hard to come by. Finally, on YouTube, a bunch of good stuff showed up." He wheezed and pounded his chest. "Oh man, this attack's bad. So as I was saying, like our boy Clarence, who shows up at all of these disaster interviews, so comes out Jean Moffat." He went into a fit of coughing.

Sid leaned over, still eyeing the road and the van, and thumped his back.

"I'll be fine. Thanks." He tucked the inhaler away in his pocket. "Remember the Hindenburg?"

"Of course."

"Well, she was there, being interviewed. I swear it's her. And the Kennedy assassination, Dealy Plaza, the Grassy Knoll. She was an eyewitness. Same woman, same pug face, and same mole on her chin. You would really think she'd get that thing removed."

"Maybe she has family, a daughter."

"I can't imagine anyone procreating with that. Not because she's ugly, but flat out mean looking. I'm talking scary." He wheezed in another breath. "I'm telling you, that face has been at all kinds of disasters. Some of the guys say they saw pics of her at the Holocaust."

A chill raced up and down Sid's spine. Goosebumps rose on her arms.

"See?" Russ said, looking at her arms. "You know it's true. Put your friends on it."

The van pulled off to the side of the road in front of an old apartment building. It was small—just five stories—and crammed between two business-office juggernauts. Clarence and Jean got out and headed up the steps of a red brick building and vanished.

Sid parked half a block away. "Wait here."

Russ grabbed her arm. "No wait, are you nuts? Be patient. Wait."

She bent his thumb backward.

"Ow! Cripes, lady!"

"Don't do that again," Sid said. She hopped out, closed the door, and took some strides up the sidewalk.

The streets weren't too busy in this part of town. Some folks hung out on the staircases she passed. One of them asked her for money.

She moved on. She spied the building from the bottom of the front steps. It was old, maybe a hundred years or more, a testament to a time long forgotten. She took the steps one by one to the top. The entrance door was painted with decades of chipping black enamel. The door groaned open at the hinges as she pulled and slipped inside. A narrow stairwell going up. The hanging lights were dim, and there was a heavy musty smell.

Smells even older than it looks.

Up she went, steps creaking beneath her shoes. She pulled her gun and crept up to the first landing. Two apartment doors were at the top, and everything was quiet. She made her way up the next flight of steps, unable to shake the feeling she might be the only person in the building. Up on the second floor landing, she listened at the doors. Stark silence. It fed her, pumped more adrenaline that mixed with the sweetheart suit and charged her blood. She peered around the corner on the next level of steps. Her nostrils flared.

Tobacco?

She hadn't noticed either Clarence or Jean smoking. It was probably a tenant passing through with the smell lingering. Up she went to the next level. Two more doors. No more sounds. No scuffles. No breathing came from the other side. There was only her heart pounding inside her ears. Up she went toward the next floor.

Halfway up, the stair underneath her foot made a mechanical sound. *Click.*

Sid froze. Her instincts fired.

Morning Glory! It's a trap!

Above, the stairs groaned under heavy footsteps.

Clarence appeared on the landing with a shotgun in his hand and a cigar in his mouth. "Looks like we caught ourselves a little squirrel. Heh." He came down a couple of steps, his big body filling the stairway. An over/under shotgun was pointed at Sid's head. "I'd toss that piece you got if I were you."

She kept the gun barrel pointed at his head. "You're the one who needs to disarm, not me."

"Is that so?" He shrugged his shoulders. "Well, I'm not the one standing on a mine now, am I? I suggest you give yourself up unless you want your legs blown to pieces."

Maybe's he's bluffing, and I have the suit on.

Sid fixed her eyes on his.

Clarence's expression was stone cold. His eyes said, "I dare you."

Sid hunkered down and set the Glock down behind her. "Now what?"

Clarence let out a short whistle. The doors on the landing behind her opened up, and two well-knit men emerged in black T-shirts. One had a black sun rising on his neck. They seized her arms and bound them up behind her. Clarence popped open a concealed panel on the wall and pressed something downward.

Click.

The pressure plate beneath Sid's feet seemed to deactivate.

"Smart girl," Clarence said, hefting the shotgun over his shoulder. "Bring her up. Jean would like a word with her. But not now. Later. Time to take a nap, Miss Shaw."

Sid lunged forward. She twisted and kicked, but the men held her fast.

One covered her mouth with a rag.

Chloroform!

Life turned blurry and black.

CHAPTER 22

S ID LIFTED HER CHIN AND opened her heavy eyes. She was tied to a chair. Ropes dug into her wrists. Her struggles were in vain. Sitting still, she scanned her surroundings. It was an old apartment room, sparsely furnished, with paint peeling from the walls and ceiling. The glass on the window was painted over. It smelled of smoke and grime.

"Ugh," a voice said. Russ Davenport was bound to a chair on her left. His face was swollen. Lip bleeding. "Did you get the name of that anvil that hit me?"

"Keep it down," she said.

A television set was on somewhere. Footsteps approached. A man came in the room and eyed them both. It was the goon in the black shirt who had clocked her in the head. He had an assault rifle strapped over his chest and a hunting knife tucked in his belt. "Say, Clarence, they're up."

The floorboards creaked, and Clarence stepped into the room with a smirk on his face. The man seemed even bigger than the last time. He had an unnatural swagger about him. He bent down and held Sidney's head up by the chin. "We've caught quite a fish in you, it seems. Heh. Sidney Shaw. Fallen FBI agent and now a bona fide bounty hunter." His dark eyes gleamed. He toyed with her hair. "I can see why the Drake wants you, but I'm not so sure about him."

Sid recoiled. Clarence's breath was worse than stagnant pond water. She launched a kick into his groin.

He didn't flinch. His expression darkened. "None of that now!" He backhanded her across the cheek.

Sid teetered onto the floor.

"Clarence," a female voice squalled. Jean stormed into the room. She looked about half as tall as Clarence, but far meaner. "We'll have none of that. If you want to slap somebody, slap him. I don't like the looks of him."

Clarence backhanded Russ so hard he toppled the heavyset man to the floor.

"Feel better?" Jean said.

Clarence shrugged.

"Well, pick him up!"

Clarence rolled his eyes and pointed to the goon. "Do it." He walked over to

Sid, scooped her up, and set all four legs of the chair back down. "Keep your feet to yourself this time."

Fast as a cobra, Jean drilled Clarence in the groin with her fist.

The man doubled over. "Oof!"

"That's for swatting my prize, Clarence—you oversized idiot."

"I told you he was an idiot," Russ said. "Anyone that looks like that has to be an idiot."

"Quiet, reporter man," Jean said. She rolled up her sleeves, revealing a hard pack of muscle. "Don't make me sock you too. Now—" She reached over and grabbed a chair, dragged it to her, and sat down. "Let's have a little discussion, shall we? Tell me, pretty face, why are you following us?"

"As if you don't know," Sid said.

"Oh, good answer. Of course I know. You want to know who is behind this assassination attempt on Wilhelm. Sticking up for your friend, aren't you." The brute of a woman took a can of Copenhagen from her back jean pocket and put a rub in. "Want some?"

Sid gave her head a gentle shake no.

"It'll give you the giggles. Hah. I'm a country girl. Old, old country. Picked up the habit from my grandma. Grew our own tobacco back then. Makes you tough." She flexed her arm. A rising sun was branded on it. "Real tough."

"You gotta be tough to be as old as you," Russ said. "You're at least a hundred and twenty by my account. Maybe a hundred and fifty."

Jean turned toward the reporter and showed a creepy smile. "Good for you, Nightfall DC. Ha. I read your little pissant paper. Too bad only a handful of weirdos have enough good sense to believe you." She turned back, pinched Sid's face in her hands, and eyed her with cold, dead eyes. "Yes, I've seen lots of things. Things that'll make your worst nightmares seem like an amusement park."

Sid swallowed.

"And if you don't cooperate," Jean said, whisking out a knife hanging from her jeans, "I'll see to it you experience it all for yourself." She pressed the blade against Sid's throat. "Now, tell me, what do you want?"

Not averting her eyes, Sid said, "I want to clear John Smoke."

"He's a murderer." Jean laughed. "Killed a congressman."

"Allegedly," Sid said.

"Ha! The entire country saw it with their own eyes. The only freedom for him is death, and that's coming soon enough, thanks to you."

"What do you mean?"

"Aw, come on, Sidney. As soon as I made some calls and found out who you were, I got a plan. You see, there is a bounty on your head, but there's a bigger one on Smoke's. They want him really bad. A rare breed, that one is. A real hawker."

"Why?"

"I'm not going to tell you that, but I'll tell you this. You're the bait that's going to bring him in."

Sid clenched her teeth. Not so long ago, she'd thought she was getting a handle on things, but now she was in over her head. She wriggled at her bonds.

Jean just laughed.

Just play along, Sid. Play along.

"Of course, it might take a few days to flush your friend out. He'll be careful, but I'm sure he'll make it here to try and save you. They say he has a real shine for you." Jean spat on the floor and got up. "I love that kind of leverage. It lets me twist those tender hearts in circles."

"Where are you going?"

Jean looked over her shoulder. "Aw, miss my company already, do you? No surprise. I do have a special charm. But I'll be back. In a day or so. Just hope you and big boy don't starve to death."

CHAPTER 23

"**W**AIT!" SID SAID.

Jean stopped.

"Look," Sid continued. "Let's quit beating around the bush and playing these games. Just tell me, who's behind all this?"

"Oh, I see. You want to take the boss down," Jean said. She kneaded her dimpled chin. "Well, we don't talk about the boss. Heck fire, not many even know who he is, but I do."

At least I know he's a he now.

"Seeing how the odds are stacked against me," Sid said, showing a struggle in her bonds, "what does it hurt to tell me? Think of it as a last request."

"Giving up so soon, are you?" Jean cackled. "Oh, I doubt that. Look, little miss. You don't meet the boss unless the boss wants to meet you. Hmmm." She rubbed the back of her neck. "Seeing how it's going to be a long wait, maybe we should play a little game."

"What kind of game?"

"I'll give you a clue if you earn it," Jean said.

She'll probably lie about that, but at least it will give me some time.

"What game did you have in mind?"

Jean walked up to Sid and slipped her hunting knife out. It was bloodstained and old crafted. She waggled it in front of Sid's eyes. "This blade was a gift. A gift from an Indian warrior I killed. Heh heh. A handsome savage too. He wanted to make me his little squaw. I told him he'd have to fight me for it. He laughed. We fought. He died."

Sid's fingertips tingled. "That's a very touching story," Sid said with a smirk. "Do you share that at Tupperware parties?"

"You've got a smart mouth." Jean toyed with Sid's hair. "And such a pretty brunette. I'd hate to shave off all that lovely hair." She leaned in close and whispered in Sid's ear, "But I have, and I will."

Damn, she means it.

"You said something about earning a clue?"

"Yes, I did," Jean said, thumbing the knife's edge. She eyed Clarence, who was leaning against the wall, biting his nails and spitting them out. "Think you can take him down? If you can, I'll give you a name. But if you lose, you get shaved."

Clarence pushed himself off the wall and crossed his hairy forearms over his chest. He was at least six foot six and three hundred pounds.

"Kind of a sadistic game, isn't it?"

"Pfft! This is nothing. Boy, you have a lot to learn, and besides, you're the one that wanted a clue. But I'm fair. You don't have to play if you don't want to."

Sid weighed her options. Even if she won, she wasn't going anywhere. Jean would have guns on her and Russ. She could jeopardize his life. And getting her head shaved by that ... woman?

That would be grisly.

"Why don't you let her shave him if she wins?" Russ said, glaring at Clarence. "Of course, there ain't much to shave."

"Heh. So what's it going to be?" Jean said. "You want to take a shot at some answers or not?"

"Sure, why not?"

Jean's brows lifted. "I like it." With the knife, she started severing Sid's cords. "Don't try anything stupid. I've been around a long time. Know most every trick in the book."

Sid nodded. Her wrists were free. She rubbed the blood into them. With the sweetheart suit on, she felt like she could do anything. In a few seconds the numbness in her wrists was gone. She faced Clarence.

He had a look on his face that was easy to hate. Arrogant. Crass.

"Kick his ass, Sid," Russ said.

Cackling, Jean slid her knife back into her sheath and backed away. "Go for it, girlie."

Leering down at her, Clarence spread his arms wide. "Come on. Give me a kiss."

Like a cat, Sid sprang. She drove her boot heel into Clarence's heavy gut.

Unmoved, he laughed. He pounded on his belly. "Go ahead, try that again."

Sid went in, kicked hard, pulled it back, jumped up high, and socked him right between the eyes.

"Ow!" Clarence said, staggering back into the wall. "That hurt!"

Wincing, Sid shook her hand. Clarence was solid.

"All right," he said, beckoning with his long arms. "You want to fight, let's fight then."

Rushing in, Sid unloaded some punching and kicking combos.

Clarence's beefy forearms countered with a grace that belied his girth.

Morning Glory, he can fight!

She pressed the attack, jabbing and kicking at his ribs. Her hard blows were muted. His body was like a heavy bag of sand.

What's this guy made of?

Clarence, no longer playing around, starting throwing heavy punches.

Pinned back in the corner, Sid ducked a thunderous punch that went clean through the wall. Skipping away, Clarence tripped her with his long leg, sending her sprawling to the hardwood floor. His fingers seized her by the ankle. "I gotcha now!"

Sid kicked at him.

He kicked back.

"Oof!" The foot to her gut left Sid breathless.

Jean's cackling and Clarence's laughter followed.

"I can't wait to shave that pretty hair!" Jean taunted.

Sid was jarred from the impact and half stunned.

Clarence dragged her limp frame into the center of the floor.

Her nails dug into the hard wood.

"Get up, Sid! Fight!" Russ yelled.

I'm trying. Damn, I can't feel anything.

The big man grabbed her in a vice-like grip and kept her pinned to the floor on her stomach. "Too easy," he said. "How about that kiss now?"

Sid flung an elbow back into his side.

Clarence chuckled. "She's still got plenty of fight in her. This ought to take care of that." He shoved her head into the hardwood planks over and over.

Stars exploded in her eyes. Warm blood dripped down her face. Her body went limp.

"First I kiss her, then you shave her," Clarence said. "I'm not smooching no bald-headed chick."

CHAPTER 24

ARMS DANGLING BY HER SIDES, Sid felt herself being lifted up off the floor. Clarence's iron grip squeezed her neck as he brought her face to face with him. Her nostrils flared.

The stench of his breath was putrid. He squeezed her neck harder. "Now, how about that kiss, baby, though I do prefer a little more fight in them." He leaned in.

"Aw no, Sid," Russ said, head down, "aw no."

Using one free hand, Sid clutched him by the beard. "Kiss this." With her other free hand, she drove her knuckles into his temple with all of her force.

Clarence's eyes popped wide, fluttered and closed. His body flopped over onto the floor and lay still.

"Dammit, Clarence!" Jean squalled.

"That was badass," Russ said, head up and smiling. "Badass."

Gasping for breath, Sid wiped the blood from her eyes and rose to her feet. "You have a clue for me?"

"Boys!" Jean declared. "Tie her up." She eyed Sid. "Sure, I'll tell you. I'm a woman of my word. The man you want is called Kane. But I'm not going to tell you one bit more."

"Fair enough," Sid said, taking a seat in her chair just as the first guard approached. One stood in the front, and the other entered the room from the hall. He had a piece of rope. "You think maybe you can stop this blood from running into my eye?" she said about the oozing gash in her forehead.

Jean walked over and eyed the wound. "Gonna need a couple of stitches. Too bad for you my needle-and-thread days are long behind me. Looks like a duct-tape bandage will have to do. Heh. Tie her up good. I'll be back."

The first guard, in front of her, watched Jean go.

The second, behind her back, started to bind up her hands.

"Not so tight, please," she said, sounding nice.

"Huh, you're the one that's looking tight," the second guard said. "Sad to see a fine woman like you go to waste."

Flirting, Sid said, "Let me go and I'll make it worth your while. Both of you."

The man behind her paused, and the breathing of the leering one in front of her became heavy. Behind her, the man tightened up one wrist. "No chance. Jean would eat us alive. Literally."

"That's too bad," Sid said. She winked at the one in front of her and rapped the side of her boot heel on the floor. A toe blade licked out. *Flick!* Exploding into action, she kicked the thug in front of her just behind the knee with the toe blade.

He went down with a howl. "Yeow!"

Sid drove her head backward into the chin of the man behind her. She sprang on the man in front and ripped the assault rifle free. She kicked him in the chin with her heel, knocking him out cold.

The last guard whirled his gun around toward her.

Sid shot two quick rounds into his legs.

Blat! Blat!

The man howled and fell to the ground.

"Throw the gun away!" Sid ordered.

The man did.

"What the hell is going on in there?" Jean yelled.

Sid was on the move. She took out one of the guards' knives and cut Russ free.

"Thanks," he said, rubbing his wrists. He lumbered over to a nearby table and picked up his wheel gun.

Jean walked in. She had duct tape in one hand and her knife in the other. "Stupid, stupid, stupid men!" She tipped her head toward the chair. "Sit down."

"Excuse me, but I think you're the one who needs to sit down," Sid said, keeping the barrel pointed at Jean. "We're getting out of here."

"Honey, you aren't going anywhere. There's more of us in here than you think. They'll be waiting."

"I'll take my chances."

"You'll die," Jean warned.

"Just drop the knife and toss over the tape."

"No. What are you going to do, shoot me?"

Sid pointed the gun at Jean's head. "You're armed with a deadly weapon. It would be self-defense."

Jean's face darkened. Her throat growled. Her eyes turned pitch black.

"Oh man," Russ said, backing toward the window.

"Screw this!" Sid unloaded a hail of gunfire. Bullets ripped into the changing woman.

Jean slammed into Sid and drove her hard into the wall.

Sid dropped the rifle and fought for her life.

Jean whaled on her. Her face was more hog than woman. Tusks popped up from her lower jaw. Her arms were coarse, powerful, and hairy. Taking Sid by the collar, Jean beat her into the floor. "Foolish woman! You're no match for a shifter!" She champed her teeth. "Dead or alive, they want you! That means I can eat part of you. Now stop squirming before I do."

Blam! Blam! Blam!

Jean recoiled and glared at Russ.

The man's smoking gun barrel shook in his hands.

The pig-faced Jean kicked Sid in the gut and marched toward Russ.

He fired again.

Blam! Blam!

Swat!

Jean hit Russ so hard he spun around like a top and collapsed on the floor. She picked Russ up over her head and hurled him out the window.

Eyes wide, Sid darted for the next room.

"Get back here!" Jean yelled with a snort.

Sid caught a glimpse of her Glock on the kitchen counter and went for it. Snatching it up, she wheeled around.

Jean rammed her head into Sidney's chest and kept charging. Wrapping Sid up in her arms, the boar-faced woman drove her clear through the wall.

Plaster dust exploded everywhere.

Sid found herself on her back and pinned down at the top of the staircase.

Jean wrenched the Glock from Sid's hand.

"Ah!" Sid cried out.

"Shut up!" Jean grabbed Sid's hair and slammed her head on the planks. "See what a mess you made." The woman snorted. Still holding Sid in a grip of iron, she said, "You're too much trouble. I'm gonna have to cripple you." She grabbed Sid's arm and yanked.

Sid's shoulder popped out of the socket. "Aaaaaggghhhhhhhhh!"

CHAPTER 25

THE PAIN WAS BLINDING. SID could barely comprehend the words coming from Jean's sweaty lips.

"Do you still want to play games with me, woman?" Jean said, holding Sid down by the chest.

Gasping, Sid sputtered out the word "No." Tears filled her eyes. Blood still ran in her face. She went limp. "No."

"That's a good girl." Jean eased up. "The better you cooperate, the sooner we get this over with."

"I couldn't agree more," Sid said. "The sooner the better." In an instant, she pulled her knees up into her chest, drove them into Jean's gut, and launched the swine-faced woman down the steps.

Jean bounced down the steps to the bottom and scrambled back to her feet. Pointing, Jean said, "You die for that." She started up the steps.

Sid's eyes searched for her gun and found nothing.

Where are you?

She turned back.

Jean's face was a mask of rage, the self-control gone. She stomped up the steps with murder in her eyes.

A faint familiar sound caught Sid's ear.

Click.

Jean took another step.

Sid turned away and flattened herself on the landing.

Boom!

The stairwell burst into splinters. The hall filled with plaster dust.

Sid started coughing and fanning at the smoky mist. Feeling around the floor with her hand, her fingers found her Glock. The pistol was an old friend in hand. She pointed it down the stairwell. Heart racing and arm dangling, she forced herself up to her feet.

I have to get out of here. But Russ!

She lumbered back into the living room, cozied up to the broken window, and peeked out.

A hand seized her wrist.

She jerked away and stuck her gun in a man's disheveled face. "Russ!"

"Oh man," he said, rubbing his head. "I thought I was a goner. That freak picked me up and tossed me like a hay bale! I'm a two-hundred-and-seventy-five-pound man." He sniffed the air. "Do I smell bacon?"

Sid glanced down.

Russ was on the emergency fire escape.

"Let's get out of here." She climbed out the window. Both of them raced down the stairs and dropped into the alley.

"Ow!" Russ said. He was sitting down and holding his ankle. "Feels like I broke it."

Shoulder dipped, Sid said, "I can't carry you." She pulled him up to his feet with her good hand.

Heads emerged from high above, and gunfire erupted.

"Hop to it, Russ!"

They took cover behind a dumpster. Sid returned fire.

Bullets skipped and ricocheted everywhere.

"We're toast!" Russ said.

A roar sounded from behind them. A black car thundered down the alley and screeched to a halt. It was the Hellcat.

Smoke popped out of the driver's window with a LAW rocket hefted on his shoulder. He pointed it upward at the apartment Sid and Russ had escaped from.

The gunfire stopped, and the guards vanished.

Still aiming at the apartment, Smoke barked an order. "Get in!"

Sid got in the front seat, and Russ stuffed himself in the back. "Get us out of here, man!"

Smoke got back in the car, slammed it in reverse, and stomped on the gas. The car screamed back out of the alley and skidded into the street. He put it into drive, gunned the gas, and zoomed into the nearest highway tunnel.

Groaning a little, Sid said, "How have you been?"

Eyes forward, Smoke said, "I've had better days."

The car emerged from the tunnel and flowed into the traffic.

Grimacing, Sid shifted in her seat. "Thanks for picking us up."

Smoke nodded.

Odd.

"So, where are you taking us, to the bat cave?"

"No," he said. "Parking garage. We'll lie low there until things cool off." He glanced at her body, but not her eyes. "Shoulder dislocated?"

"Very astute of you," she said. "Thanks for noticing."

"So, what happened up there?" Smoke said, eyeing the road.

Russ jumped in. "I'll tell you what happened. This city is full of crazies! I'm moving to Arizona."

"Well, fill me in," Smoke said, eyeing Russ through the rearview mirror.

Russ offered up the entire ordeal.

Sid filled in some other details.

Smoke seemed unaffected.

"John," she said, "we were trying to find out who framed you. We didn't have much luck with that though. All I got was the name Kane."

Smoke nodded.

Geez, he won't even look at me. He must be having a really bad day. I hope this isn't over the engagement thing. And I'm not going to bring up the ring being stolen.

"You know," Russ said, "that name Kane rings a bell."

"I'd hope. It's Cain from the Bible," Sid said.

"No, not like that. One with a 'K'. K-A-N-E. Like the wrestler."

"Why's that matter?" Sid asked. She was grimacing, her shoulder throbbing.

"I did a story a long time ago—geez, at least two decades, maybe longer—about the Lancasters."

"The crime family?"

"Yep. They really hated the cops. Back in the seventies they blamed the cops for the death of their son Kane. Things got brutal for about ten years but quieted after that. The Lancasters kind of faded away in the nineties, but there's been some murmurings of late. A Lancaster here, a Lancaster there. Arrests. Mugshots. Kinda weird."

Sid had read some of those files on the Lancasters. They'd taken two FBI agents down in the late seventies. It was an extremely rare thing back then. But it was one of those things that Ted Howard, her now-deceased boss, had told her about. Fallen agents. The FBI was family, disjointed sometimes, but still family. They took things like that personally, but more so then than now. Things had changed. Ofttimes now, the agency seemed divided.

Smoke took the next exit in south DC. It was a rougher neighborhood than downtown. More poverty. More homeless. He cruised the car into a parking garage that drove down underneath an old office building. The tires squealed on the hairpin turns. The motor sounded like thunder down below. There weren't many cars parked either. The ones that were pulled in looked abandoned and dusty, a graveyard of bad car models from the eighties and nineties.

"Hey look, a K-Car. I used to have one of those," Russ said. "Love that Cream-of-Wheat yellow."

Smoke backed the car into a slot near the elevators, shut down the engine, and got out.

Struggling with the door, Sid finally got it open.

Russ squeezed out.

"So, what's the plan?" Sid asked Smoke. "I could use a sling, you know."

Smoke sat back on the hood and crossed his arms. "We're waiting on somebody."

Aggravated, she asked, "Care to fill me in?"

Smoke turned toward her. His dark eyes fastened on hers and started to change.

The blood drained from Sid's face.

Smoke's eyes turned black as eight balls, and then he scowled. "No."

CHAPTER 26

S ID PUT A GUN ON Smoke.
He showed a wicked sneer.
"Who are you?"

"Oh, put that away," said the man who looked just like Smoke. "You don't want to get hurt."

"Me hurt?" said Sid, trying not to wince. "You're the one looking down the barrel."

"True," said the black-eyed man, calmly, "but you can't know for sure. After all, maybe I really am John Smoke and you've been fooled all along."

"I say shoot him," Russ suggested. "We'll figure out the truth later."

"Oh, I doubt that," the man said. He reached into his jeans and pulled out a soft pack of cigarettes. A black Zippo lighter appeared in his other hand. He flicked the Zippo open, started the flame, and lit his cigarette. He snapped the top shut and tucked it all away. It was just him, smoking, with a smile on his face. "I've probably smoked more of these things than anybody, and it never gets old. Always wondered why."

"Nicotine, dumbass," Russ said.

"No, not with my chemistry," the man said. "I can't be harmed by the usual mortal means."

"I doubt that," Sid said, easing herself into a better position. She pointed the gun toward his back. "You're the one who shot Wilhelm, aren't you."

The man shrugged. "It doesn't take a genius to figure that out at this point. Of course, I've shot a lot of people. You know," he chuckled a low laugh, "I've been around since Lincoln. Makes you think, doesn't it."

"You're coming with me," Sid said.

The man turned. His eyes were dark blue like Smoke's. Every detail was just right on the outside. Only the voice was off a little. "Oh, I'm not going anywhere, and neither are you, Miss Shaw. You see, we're all trapped. Well, not me so much, but you certainly don't have a way out."

A dreadful feeling dropped into her stomach like a cup of castor oil. She summoned her courage. "I'll make a way out. Now get back in the vehicle."

The man held his hands up. "Shoot me, Sid. Shoot me, the man you love."

He winked. "I'm a murderer, so shoot me. It will do me some good. But shoot me, and you'll never see me again."

"Screw this." She squeezed the trigger. *Click!*

The man chuckled. "Such a fool. You know, Sid, we switched your bullets out. Yes, those fancy ones with the blue tips. Very nice. Very gone. You're lucky Jean didn't kill you back in the apartment building. But it seemed your resourcefulness prevailed. We anticipated it."

"What are you talking about?" she said.

"Why, your audition. You know, the Drake could use someone like you: a loner, but loyal. We can make all those bills go away. Reunite you with your sister and niece. You'd never have to worry about your parents, their safety."

"I don't want any part of what you're offering. I just want to take you in."

"Really? Which one of me to you want to take in?" The man changed. He had Cyrus's face. "This me?" He turned again. Rebecca Lang appeared. "Or this one? Hah. No one has ever captured me. No one ever will. I'm the greatest shifter of them all. Why, I could even be the President if I wanted. Maybe I have been before. So many strange goings-on these days." He changed back to Smoke. "So do you still want to kill me—or kiss me?"

"Kill you. Definitely kill you."

"You know, I was like you once."

She rolled her eyes. "Oh please, I don't want to hear it. I've heard it twice now: once from Double Dee and a second time from the rat guy."

"Miss Shaw, take it from me, there is no better life than what we have. Power. Money. You, like your sister, should consider it." He blew a smoke ring. "It would be best for you and your family."

"They can take care of themselves just fine."

"Don't be so sure of that." Rubber tires rubbing on cement echoed above. An old black Cadillac limousine with a very high roof pulled up in front of them. "Well, if I can't convince you, perhaps they can."

A deader in a limousine driver's cap lumbered out of the car and opened the back doors.

Someone swung a leg out. The foot attached to it was impossibly big. The limo groaned as the most towering figure she'd ever seen stepped out. A huge man, eight feet of solid muscle packed into a grey gym suit. His head almost touched the ceiling.

Sid tilted her neck just to look at him.

The towering figure would make Shaq look like a child. His face was fierce and hard. Dark wild hair hung over his eyes.

"Holy shit," Russ muttered. "That just ain't possible."

The deader limo driver walked over to the other side of the limo and opened the doors. Sid expected some man or woman, maybe her sister Allison, to step out. The limo groaned and bounced again. Another giant stepped out, bigger and taller than the first.

The man posing as Smoke let out a sinister chuckle. "Let there be giants."

CHAPTER 27

SID FELT ALL OF HER blood seep down into her toes. AV the minotaur hadn't been as big as these men.

She heard the door of the Hellcat shut. The door locks popped closed. Russ tapped the window, said to her softly, "I'm not here. I'm not here," and crawled into the back seat.

The monstrous men stood still. Shaggy. Hairy. Beastly. They each must have been six hundred pounds easily.

That's really not normal! I need to get out of here.

"Big fellas, aren't they?" The man who looked like Smoke puffed on his cigarette. "You can't find them that big at the carnivals. Well, that was a long time ago, anyway. Care for a cigarette? It'll settle your nerves."

Sid gently shook her head no, still gaping at the giant-sized men. They made NBA players look like dwarves.

Just when I thought I'd seen everything.

"Do you have a name?"

"Me?" said Smoke's double. "I've had many. My given name is Reginald, but you can call me Reggie. No need to be formal."

"Are there any more like you?"

"Ah, now that's a good question. Well, the truth is, so far as I'm concerned, I'm the only one that matters. The doppelganger. One of a kind. That's all you need to know." He fixed his eyes on the limousine. Another person was getting out. "And now it's time to meet our next guest."

Sid's jaw dropped.

Older, heavy and swarthy, a slick politician eased his way between the giants and buttoned his dress coat. It was Congressman Augustus Wilhelm. "Hello, Sidney," he said with brightened eyes, "surprised to see me?"

"More like disappointed."

"Hah. Well, you're not the only person to say that. Oh, and by the way, before I forget, Allison and Megan send their regards. Megan, so sweet and growing up so fast. She's going to be such a pretty thing."

Sid stormed forward.

The giant men blocked her path to the congressman. One of their hands could fully engulf her head.

She could hear Wilhelm laughing behind them.

"Oh Sidney, you're such an overprotective hothead. I can't stand people like you. You get in the way of progress." He stepped out from behind the giants and faced her. His face was smug. "Lay a finger on me, and these two will rip you apart. And you wouldn't want them to do anything to your precious little Megan, now would you?"

Casting a glance up at the giants then back to him, her chin dipped and she said, "No."

"Good girl." He lightly smacked her cheek. "It's good to see that as you grow older, you can grow wiser as well."

"What's this all about, Wilhelm?" she asked. "Why the big show?"

"It's all about me, of course. You see, I live." He spread his arms wide. "Miraculously! Now, my path to the Senate will be far easier than it was. In case you haven't noticed, I'm not exactly the most likeable guy with the people, so I made a deal and got a little boost. Oh, won't it be wonderful to come out of that coma a changed man."

"That's it?" she said. "All this, just to remain in the Senate?"

"Oh, well, I'm being modest. It's certainly not my ambitions alone. The Drake supporters have their interests—and they pay well."

"Of course. Just what we need. Another leader who cares nothing for the people but is all in for himself."

"At least you realize I'm not the first," he said.

"Why Smoke?" she asked, turning as Wilhelm paced around her.

"He wasn't my choice, but your friend, well, he gets under their skin. After all, since he came on the scene, you've rounded up several members of the Black Slate. They're a rare and useful breed, so that's a problem." He stopped pacing and faced her. "Now, I know what you're thinking. You helped too. And to your credit, I'm shocked that you live. But your friend Smoke, he's unique." His eyes scanned her from head to toe. "But you're quite impressive yourself. Some might say, special." He glanced over at Reggie. "Did you mention the offer?"

"I did. She wasn't interested."

"Your sister is thriving in the Drake's organization," Wilhelm said to her. "Really rising up the ranks. You know, you and her are more alike than you think. When she wants something, she'll do whatever it takes to get it. And, Sid, with Deanne Drukker gone, there's an opening for a gal with your talents."

"No thanks."

"Double Dee said no the first few times too, but everyone has their price."

"So what tipped her over, blackmail or murder?"

Wilhelm checked his nails and dusted them on his tie. "She lost someone significant, so I'd say it was a little bit of both."

"You know," Sid said, tilting up her chin, "all of you bastards really need to die."

"Good luck with that," Wilhelm said. He clapped his hands together. "Now, back to business. The offer still stands for you to join the Drake. But just so you're clear, John Smoke will die. Either right in front of our eyes or in some prison, but he will die. But, if you want him cleared, and we can clear just about anything, you can just join us. Maybe he'll join as well."

"I'm not buying it."

Wilhelm's prideful grimace soured. "You're a fool!"

The Hellcat's engine roared to life. Russ Davenport was behind the wheel. The car squirted out of its spot toward the doppelganger. Reginald dove out of the way. Window rolled down, Russ yelled at Sid, "Get in!"

She made a mad dash for the passenger door and dove through the open window.

The car surged forward.

One of the giant men caught the front end of the car with his chest. Car fenders clutched in his humongous hands, the massive man heaved and brought the car to a standstill.

"Holy Schnikies!" Russ said. He laid on the gas.

The 707 horsepower throttled with hungry life. Still on the pavement, the back tires spun. The rubber smoked in great white rolling plumes.

The giant's feet slid over the garage floor.

"Come on baby! Come on!"

The giant's eyes were wide, its face straining against the car's force. It was losing.

The car was winning.

"You've got this, Russ!"

Suddenly, the rear tires lost their grip.

Sid looked behind them.

The other giant had grabbed the car by the back bumper and lifted it up ever so slightly. The engine screamed for traction, but caught only air.

"Oh man!" Russ banged his hands on the steering wheel. "Blasted rear-wheel drive."

With a snarl and a groan, the giant in front lifted the front wheels off the pavement as well.

"Oh, this is bad," Sid said, reaching into the back seat and trying to find anything she could.

"Oh no! Oh no!" Russ said.

"What?"

With a heave, the giant men flipped the car over.

It landed on its hood.

Crash!

Sid hit her head hard. The impact had flopped Russ on top of her. Gathering her senses, she shook her head.

But the car started to spin. Gusty laughter like that of a coming storm could be heard. The giants, like children, were spinning the car round and round, faster and faster like a giant top.

CHAPTER 28

T HAT SID WAS QUEASY WAS an understatement. As soon as the car stopped spinning, one giant reached in and pulled her out by the hair. All she did was hold her stomach.

Please stop spinning. Please stop spinning.

"Mrah mrah mrah mrah!" the huge man laughed. He set her down on her feet.

She staggered around and fell down again.

Nearby, someone was retching.

Forcing herself up to her hands and knees, she caught a glimpse of Russ doubled over.

The second giant put his big paws on Russ's shoulders and lifted him up to his feet.

Russ fell back down.

"Mrah mrah mrah mrah!"

"We don't need that one," Wilhelm said of Russ. "Feel free to tear him apart if you want. No one will miss him."

The giant grabbed Russ by the arms. The second one grabbed him by the legs and picked him up off the ground.

"Hey! What are you doing?"

They started to pull him apart.

"Ah! No! No! Ah! Stop it!"

Wilhelm chuckled. "This would make such a great story for Nightfall DC. Too bad you can't write it, Russ. Or your own obituary."

Sid rose to her feet, holding her shoulder, and managed to mutter, "Stop this. Stop it."

A shadow crept up behind Wilhelm and stuck a gun in his ear. "Yes," the man said, "stop it. Now!"

Something in Russ's body cracked. He let out a horrifying scream. "Eiyaah!"

"Now!" said the man holding Wilhelm hostage. It was the big black man, Agent Calhoun.

"Don't be foolish," Wilhelm said. Sweat beaded on his forehead. "There's been too much of that going around."

"Call off those big shaggy hounds," Calhoun said, cocking back the hammer on his gun. "Or whatever they are."

"Rexor! Thorgrim! Release him!"

Russ hit the ground with a thud.

"Are you happy?" Wilhelm said, trying to turn his head.

"Don't know about that," Calhoun said. "I'll just wait for my colleagues to arrive, and we'll let them sort this freak show out." He eyed Reggie. "That ain't normal." He turned back and surveyed the whole scene. "None of this is. Here I have the congressman that was supposedly shot and killed. I had a lot of money coming for that. Not so sure how I'm going to collect it now, seeing how none of what I've seen's been real."

"Oh ho," Wilhelm puffed. "Is money all that you want? There's plenty of that to go around. How much? A hundred grand?"

"Two-fifty buys my silence."

"A negotiator, how quaint," Wilhelm replied. "Two hundred?"

Calhoun's stature eased. "I don't think you have that kind of cash on you."

With a finger, Wilhelm eased the gun barrel from his neck. "Just stay silent. I'll take care of all your needs and more."

"Boss," Reggie said, cocking his head. "I hear sirens."

"Thorgrim! Rexor! Get in the limo! You too, Reginald!" Wilhelm turned and looked up at Calhoun. "I'll be in touch, eh ..."

"Calhoun. Cort Calhoun. You better not stiff me, Congressman."

"You have my word, Cort. Play along, and you'll have even more than that."

Thorgrim and Rexor stuffed themselves into the limo.

With a wink at Sidney, Reggie followed suit.

Wilhelm was the last one in and said to Sid, "You can't say no forever." The door closed, and the limo screeched away.

"Fine job," Sid said to Calhoun. Arm hanging, she made her way over to Russ. His right leg was at an unnatural angle. "Oh Lord!"

Russ was sitting upright, eyes like moons, hands shaking over his contorted legs, repeating, "I'm okay. I'm okay. I'm okay."

Calhoun stepped over both of them, shaking his head. "No, you ain't okay. None of this is."

CHAPTER 29

"**Y**OU TELLING ME WILHELM'S ALIVE and well?" Cyrus Tweel talked as he typed at his desk at FBI headquarters. "Living and breathing. Made alive again?"

"It's in the report. Didn't you read it?" said Sidney. Her dislocated shoulder had been reset, but she still wore it in a sling. She was sitting in a chair in front of his desk.

Rebecca Lang sat to Sid's left, reading a copy of the report she'd prepared. Rebecca had the same condescending look on her face that she always did.

Sid tried another tack. "What don't you understand about this? You've seen some of these monsters for yourself."

Cyrus huffed and pushed his glasses up on his nose.

Sidney had spent the entire night writing up the incident—in a tiny guest room at FBI headquarters, since they knew her apartment was in shambles and she didn't want to drag Sam into all this. The hollow feeling in her stomach seemed to tell her the FBI wanted the entire incident to go away.

"Eight and nine feet tall?" Cyrus laughed, finally reading her report. "If that were the case, those guys would be playing in the NBA. What a laugh. Huh." He peered at Rebecca. "What do you think?"

"I'm like you, Cyrus. Seeing is believing." Rebecca glanced once more at her copy of the report and then tossed it on his desk. "And I haven't seen anything that I believe." She turned to Sid. "In case you didn't know, we have agents on site at Mercy of Angels hospital right now. Wilhelm is comatose. What do you think about that, Miss Shaw?"

"Seeing is believing." Sid glared at Rebecca. "What about your boy Calhoun, you know, the one you stuck on me? What did his report have to say?"

"I don't have his report yet," Cyrus said. He seemed a little withdrawn.

"He's gone, isn't he," Sid said. "You lost him."

"He's a liaison like you, and if I were to guess, I'd say he was still trying to find your boyfriend Smoke, whom you are clearly trying to protect."

Sid jumped up out of her seat. "Are you serious? Who do you think flipped my car over on the hood? Giants, that's who!"

"Keep your voice down and stay seated!" Cyrus ordered, getting up. "I know what I've seen, and I don't need you to tell me."

Sid stood there and crossed her arms in a way that said, "I don't have to obey orders anymore, remember?"

Rebecca whispered something in Cyrus's ear.

He sighed and sat down.

Frustrated, Sid slapped both of her hands on Cyrus's desk.

He jumped. Just a little, but it gave her a thrill.

"What about Russ Davenport?" she said. "Who do you think bent his leg back over his head, huh? No normal man or woman could do that!"

Rebecca put her hand on Cyrus's back and started to say something.

That woman has to go!

Sid balled up her fist and looked at Rebecca. She had no doubt that everything Leroy had told her about Rebecca and Cyrus was true. They were hiding everything. Keeping it all to themselves. It was infuriating. One day they were helping Sid, and the next they were against her. "I ought to slap that smug look off your face."

"It wouldn't do you or your murdering boyfriend any good."

"It's not Smoke! Geez! Talk to Davenport."

"He's not credible, Sid. Just another kook. You know, your kinda people. Now listen, Sid. I think you saw your boyfriend. Actually, according to Calhoun, he was there. He saw him. And you need to quit covering for the guy."

"Covering for what, an assassination that didn't happen? Look, you two idiots! Wilhelm is alive and well! Before long he's going to rise from the dead and talk about his run for Senate."

Cyrus and Rebecca burst out into mocking laughter.

Cyrus said, "Nobody even knew he was a Congressman until he got shot. Boy, why didn't you put that in your report?"

Shaking her head, Rebecca said, "I can't believe even you are that stupid. I think it's time we had you reevaluated." She whispered some more to Cyrus.

Sid's jaws clenched.

Please really be shifters so that I can kill you both. Maybe someone will turn you into deaders. Oh, that would be nice. I can't believe you! Either you are complete idiots, or else you are paid extremely well. Morning Glory, I don't understand it.

"Are we finished?" was all Sidney said.

"Sid, I have to tell you, the entire Reginald-the-doppelganger theory almost had me. After all, that would explain this entire mess. It's believable. Actually, it's so believable I think they made a movie about it." Cyrus pecked on his keyboard and turned his screen around. "Yes, they did make a movie about it. It's called *Doppelganger*, and it starred Drew Barrymore. See, there she is."

Rebecca slapped her knee, held her gut and laughed.

Sid struck. She grabbed Cyrus's hand that held the mouse and twisted his thumb back. "I'm not in the mood for this. You know these things exist. We all do. Now quit treating me like some kind of fool!"

Rebecca hopped out of her chair and closed in on Sid.

A quick kick to Rebecca's gut sent the mousy woman toppling over her chair. Still holding Cyrus by the thumb, Sid said, "I'm going to clear Smoke. You"—she cranked the pressure up on his thumb—"better stay the hell out of my way." She released him.

Cyrus gasped. His face was a mask of pain. He started rubbing his hand.

Looking at Sid full in the face with hatred, Rebecca started to rise.

On her way to the door, Sid stopped and said to her, "Get up and I'm going to Ronda Rousey you."

Rebecca stayed down.

Sid opened the door and found herself face to face with Ted's old secretary, Jane. "Step aside."

Without a word, Jane shirked away.

Sid headed for the stairwell and flung open the door. On her way down she got a text from Sam. It read, "Meet at the Hyatt."

"Great." Sidney didn't even have a car. The FBI had impounded it, or so she'd been told. She was low on money, too, and the Hyatt was a long walk. Not that she minded long walks, but storm clouds loomed above. She'd made it one block and was crossing a four-way intersection to another when a hard rain started coming down. Her shout startled other passersby. "Great!"

Seething, she stepped out onto the curb to hail a cab.

A dull-orange minivan pulled alongside the curb.

Sid flung open the door, hopped in, and slammed it closed.

The cab driver locked the doors, pulled out into the street and barreled down the road.

"Hey, I didn't even tell you where I was going."

"I already know where you're going," the driver said, eyeing his rearview mirror.

"Smoke!" she exclaimed. She eased forward and then eased right back, withdrew her gun, and pointed it at his head. "Or is it Reggie?"

CHAPTER 30

THE MAN DRIVING THE CAB, the one she hoped was Smoke, wore an Irish tweed cap and glasses. The usually clean-shaven hair on his face was overgrown. He didn't turn or stop driving. Instead, he kept his eyes between the road and Sidney's.

"You got a text from Sam, right?" the man said. "Meet at the hotel?"

"Maybe the text wasn't from her," said Sid, still holding the gun on him. "After all, you can't believe everything you read. Now pull over."

"Aw, you won't shoot me, Sid. Look, I'm not the doppelganger. You know that. Besides, I saw him. His eyes aren't as dazzling as mine."

She warmed up inside a little. "So maybe you aren't the doppelganger. That still doesn't mean I won't shoot you."

"Why would you shoot me?"

"Because you're you."

"Or I'm Reggie? Or," he posed, "I'm—"

"Don't say it."

"Batman!"

She lowered the Glock. "Only an idiot would say that, so it must be you."

"That's my girl. I knew you'd come around. So, how have you been?"

"How have I been?" She couldn't believe how calm he was about everything. There was only an enormous manhunt out for him. She sank back into her seat. "You're nuts."

"I thought you'd be happy to see me."

I am. "Well, I'm not. I mean, what have you been doing the past few days, playing cab driver?"

"Actually"—his voice brightened—"yeah, I have been. I've met some of the most interesting people. There sure is a lot of foreign interest in DC. But the most interesting fare I had was this family from West Virginia. Super nice bunch. Good tippers. I got a big kick out of them because they were here for, get this, a Supernatural convention. They said I looked like one of the dudes that stars on the show."

"Never heard of it."

"Oh, it's about these brothers—"

"Will you shut up!"

"Sorry," he said. "Did you have something you wanted to share?"

Stress. It didn't exist to Smoke. It infuriated her.

"So," he continued, "have you given any more thought to my question?"

"You aren't serious?"

"No, I'm Smoke."

Sid leaned forward and knocked the cap off him. It revealed a nasty wound stitched in a bare spot on the back of his head.

Oh my!

"Hey, that's my disguise." He put the cap back on.

"What happened to your head?"

"I got cornered by some deaders. Those things seem to be getting a lot deadlier."

"You can say that again. There were a couple of cops I had to deal with that I think were deaders. They were looking for you." She eased closer. Something about his presence, aggravating though it might be, drew her to him. "Look, John, we have to get you cleared. I don't know how to do that yet, but this isn't going to stop until we clear you. We need to think. We need to plan. You might need to leave the country."

Smoke pulled the taxi over, and the brakes squeaked as it came to a halt.

They were parked in front of an old church. It was quaint and laid out with heavy stones. He turned and faced her. "Seriously, have you given my question any more thought?"

"About marriage?" *Yes.* "No. John, now's not the time to talk about weddings."

"I didn't say wedding," he said, smiling. "I was only talking about the engagement." He bobbed his chin. "So you have been thinking about it. You know, you're going to have to be more honest with me if we're going to pursue a long-term relationship."

"People are trying to kill you, and some of them are trying to kill me, and you're worried about our courtship?"

"A good man has to have his priorities straight. And I like the sound of that."

"The sound of what?"

"Courtship."

She sank back into her seat, hand over her head. "Morning Glory."

"You know I'm not getting any younger, and you aren't either." Smoke was staring at the church as he spoke. Rain splattered on the window. "And we might not have that much time left on this earth, you know. I mean, seeing how a bunch of people want us dead and all. At least me. I just never thought I'd die single."

"Really? With all of the stupid risks you take, it never occurred to you that you might die single? That's the dumbest thing I ever heard." A sliver of uncertainty slipped through her.

Geez, maybe he thinks he won't survive this.

"Smoke, are you okay?"

"Of course. But I have pissed off a lot of people." He caught her eyes. "Bad people."

"I can't even begin to imagine what you do when I'm not around. Aside from eating pancakes and taxiing people around. And being annoying."

And charming.

She fixed her eyes on the church doors. She eyed him. "You don't have anything set up in there, do you?"

"Only one way to find out."

"I'm not going in there."

"If you knew this was your last day, what would you do?"

Sid's heart beat a little faster.

I suppose I'd marry you. But I'd prefer more sun, rice, and some church bells. Huh, Sidney Smoke. Not too bad of a ring to it.

"I'd take down the Drake."

"I see," he said, a little dejected. "Oh, and by the way… Sam, Guppy, and Mal are in there."

"I thought they said meet them at the hotel."

"No. I found some eyes there." He got out of the cab, fished an umbrella out of the back, and slid Sidney's door open. He stood like a gentleman, holding the umbrella for her. "Coming?"

"Fine, but this better not be a surprise wedding."

Without a word, Smoke led her up the steps under the alcove and put the umbrella aside. He opened the door, saying, "After you."

CHAPTER 31

A SIDE FROM THE WOODEN PEWS and stained glass, the church was empty. Sid's heart sank a little.

Smoke's soft-strong voice echoed when he spoke. "You look disappointed."

I guess.

Just above a whisper, Sid replied, "I thought you said we were meeting Sam and Guppy here?"

Smoke took her hand. "Come on." Down the aisle they went together.

She glanced up at the marble arches in the ceiling. The angels carved from the stone. The podium and flowers that waited ahead. Her throat tightened.

What is he doing?

A door squealed somewhere in the church. A tall figure emerged from behind the choir chairs on the stage.

"Hey, Sid!" It was Sam, and she was waving. Her loud voice echoed everywhere. "Come on down. We've been waiting for you." Her eyes widened. "Aw look, they're holding hands. How sweet." She stepped out of sight.

Taking the steps up onto the altar, Smoke brought her to a stop. He took both of her hands in his and faced her. It was just them and rows of empty pews. He looked deep into her eyes. "You know, we might not make it until tomorrow."

She swallowed the lump in her throat. "Well, then if you want to marry me, we better."

With the side of his mouth turned up in a smile, he bent down and kissed her.

She felt her body melt in his strong arms. It was a great kiss. Soft. Sweet. Everlasting. One to live for. One worth dying for.

"Ahem," a voice interrupted.

They broke it off. It was Sam. "Sorry, but they're pretty eager downstairs."

Gathering her breath, Sid rubbed the palms of her hands on her jeans, glanced at Smoke, then to Sam. "Okay."

Behind the curtains they went, and down an old set of well-built stairs crafted from a fine dark oak. The area beneath the church was a lot of stone archways and alcoves, a little damp and musty.

Sam ducked into one of them, and they followed.

Inside was a large chamber filled with wine racks and whiskey barrels—hiding a modern lab that had been set up inside. Large computer monitors, a network server, conference table, and chairs. A coffee pot was brewing.

"Hey, Sid," Guppy said. He sat reading a magazine at the conference table, which was piled with papers. "Nice place, huh?"

Mal Carlson was behind the monitors, pecking away. "Actually, it used to be an old speakeasy. Can you believe that? Right below a church, of all things. But it's been a safe house for well over a century. Almost two."

"And it stinks," Asia said. She was propped up on an old loveseat that looked like it came out of a fraternity house. She faced a television and held a steaming mug of joe in her lap. "TV reception is crap."

"So what's the hurry?" Sidney said, making her way to the table and pulling up a chair behind Mal. A familiar scene was on the screens. It was live images of the battle with the giants in the garage. "Hey, how did you get that?"

"I've got cameras in the Hellcat," Mal said, taking a sip of coffee. "Among other things."

"So when I was down there fighting for my life, you sat watching?" she asked.

"We were close," he said. His eyes drifted to Smoke. "At least he was. You're all right, aren't you?"

She moved her sling and elbow. She'd dislocated it before, but it still felt like hell to move. "My wing's busted, but I can still shoot if I have to."

"Asia!" Mal called out.

"What!" the Chinese woman yelled, still glued to her TV.

"Fix up Sid's shoulder, will you?"

The little woman huffed, got up, and shuffled over. She eased around the table. "Which shoulder?"

"Uh, the one with the sling on it."

Asia yanked it off.

"Ow!"

"Shut up and be still. Take your shirt off."

"What? No!"

"Don't be so modest. You have nice body. You can leave your brassiere on."

Sam and Guppy started chuckling.

"Look, I think I'll be fine."

A pair of scissors appeared in Asia's hands and she began cutting Sid's top off. "Hey!"

Asia tossed the shirt aside. No one was looking at Sid except Sam, who walked over and handed Asia a tube filled with long needles. "You'll love this, Sid." She cleared the papers off the table and rolled out a sleeping bag on it. "Here, lie down and just relax. But don't look. That makes it kinda weird." She produced a small dowel rod. "Oh, and bite down on this. You might not need it, but every little bit helps."

Sidney lay down on the sleeping bag. The smell of something calming filled her nostrils.

Asia's warm hands began massaging her shoulders.

She's got strong hands for such a little woman.

"Relax," Asia said, but her voice was far from soothing. "You are too tight. Stiff like old woman." She continued to rub. Her fingers dug deep into Sidney's skin and bore into the muscle.

Sid's forehead burst out in sweat. Something in her shoulder popped and cracked. She bit into the dowel rod hard. "Ugh!"

"Be still," Asia ordered.

Sid saw a long sliver of silver from the corner of her eye. Something sharp pinched her skin. It pierced deeper and deeper. It burned like fire.

"This is the cool part," Sam said, "but maybe you should close your eyes."

"Why?" Sid mumbled with the dowel in her mouth.

Sam's eyes were glued to Sidney's bad shoulder.

Sid glanced at it. The skin began to poke out. Her head broke out in a cold sweat just as the long needle poked clean through the skin. Sid's first instinct was to jump away. Her courage held. It was rewarded. The throbbing pain in her shoulder was replaced with pure euphoria. The dowel rod dropped from her mouth. "Morning Glory! How did you do that?"

"Ancient Chinese secret," Asia said. "Just stay still. I'm not finished yet." She poked more needles into Sid's back.

Sid didn't feel a one of them. She said, "Again, what's the rush?"

"Well," Mal stated, "We've come to a conclusion about this fine mess we're in."

"And that is?"

Mal rubbed his temples, shook his head. "We need to close in on them before they close in on us. If we don't pull this off now, Sid, I'm afraid it's all over."

CHAPTER 32

"**O**VER?" Sɪᴅ ɢʟᴀɴᴄᴇᴅ ᴀᴛ Sᴍᴏᴋᴇ, whose dark eyes were fixed on Mal. "I don't follow."

"We've got a pretty big mess on our hands. They want Smoke gone. They want the Black Slate team defunded, and they're getting pretty close to pulling it off. The main concern is Smoke's safety, and they've gone to an awful lot of trouble to get him out of the picture." Mal sighed. "An awful lot."

"What did you do to piss them off so bad?" Sid said to Smoke.

Smoke shrugged.

"It's not what he did; it's what he didn't do," Mal said. "Well, that's not entirely true. Smoke's been throwing wrenches into their missions right and left. It really gets them bent out of shape. Of course you know that. But in this case, they made him an offer and he refused. Actually, they've made him several offers."

"Like they did me?" Sid said. She turned to face Smoke. "And why are they so interested in you anyway? You aren't a shifter, are you?"

Taken aback, Smoke said, "Me? No."

Sid's eyes narrowed on him. There were plenty of things Smoke did that were hard to understand. Being a shifter would explain a lot of them.

"You say they made you an offer?" Mal asked Sid.

"Wilhelm did. He said they needed a replacement for Deanne Drukker." She squirmed a little. Asia was still over her, doing some insane method of acupuncture. There was a little biting here and there, but the sensation still felt good. "Basically he says they'll keep asking until I say yes."

Mal pulled more video up on the screen. It wasn't the best picture, and the angle was bad. "I can't read lips as well as I used to, but it seems what you said was truth. I need to get that microphone on the Hellcat fixed. It should have been working. Then we would have had Wilhelm talking."

It was a little bit surreal watching herself having a conversation with Wilhelm and Reggie. She was transfixed. She felt violated. "Wait? Microphone? You can record me inside the car?"

Sam leaned over Sidney's shoulder and said into her ear, "Just because we can doesn't mean we are."

"I only activate the surveillance systems when needed," Mal said, "so you have your privacy most of the time."

"Where is the Hellcat?" she asked.

"We got it back," Guppy said. "It was a heck of a thing getting it flipped back over."

"Yeah, play that giant thing again," Sam said, twirling her finger, "the part when they flip Sid over and spin her around like a carnival top."

Mal pulled it up. The two giants' strength was freakish. Everything about them was. The one that Sid could see didn't even strain when he helped flip the car over.

Hanging by Sid's shoulder, Sam said, "Those guys are awesome. And really gruesome."

Sid eyed her.

"But evil, of course."

"I'm sure an exploding bullet will take care of them," Sid replied.

"Maybe. Maybe not," Mal said. He zoomed the screen in on another image of the giants. "Based off our analysis, the bigger these shifters are, the tougher their bones and skin. It might take more than an exploding bullet to upend them. But those giants aren't the mission; Reggie the Doppelganger is. We need him to turn himself in, for Smoke's benefit." He removed a jump drive. "So the goal is to blackmail them. After all, we have Wilhelm on video, alive and well. With giants. It might be enough to call this manhunt off Smoke. Call it an ace in the hole."

"And if we deliver it to them and they don't bite?"

"Then you and Smoke will have to bring Reggie in yourselves." He handed Smoke the jump drive. "Like I said, the walls are closing in. This needs to be done, now."

Sidney winced. Asia was taking the needles out of her shoulder one by one. "So, who are we supposed to take this to?"

"We were able to track that limousine. There's an estate several miles out of town. It parked there. It's all loaded in the Hellcat's GPS now." Mal turned and faced her. "Since they're recruiting you, I think you should deliver the package. We'll stay close by in case things get too scary."

"Can't we just call them out and meet them on neutral ground?" Smoke said.

"I don't think they'll hurt Sid." Mal looked up at her. "Do you?"

"No, I don't guess."

"Look, we can't talk all day. At first I wanted to hit them hard and heavy. Rattle things. But I think this tactic is better. It will at least get them off our backs for a while. Give us some time to figure out who Kane Lancaster is."

"Don't they have a bounty on me and Smoke?" Sid said. "Do you think this is enough to settle them down?"

"I think you can convince them of that," Mal said, "but just in case there's going to be a fight on your hands, you might want to take a super vitamin and suit up before you go." He handed them each a sweetheart suit.

Sid made her way into the next alcove and put hers on.

"Shoulder feel better now?" Asia asked her, suddenly right there.

Sid rolled her shoulder. "I can't remember the last time it felt this good."

"Good, then don't screw it up again."

Sam was there too, holding out a long-sleeved T-shirt.

Sid put it on and smiled gratefully at Sam.

"Um, you guys?" Guppy interjected. "You might want to take a look at the breaking news on the television channels."

"What? Why?" Sam said, making her way to Guppy's side. "Oh crap. It's a conference at the hospital. It's Wilhelm."

Sid ran over to the television.

Guppy turned up the volume.

Wilhelm was speaking to a host of reporters from a hospital bed. "I pulled through. Thank the Almighty, I pulled through." He shifted in his bed and grimaced. "But I think it was the good news that woke me up. A little bird whispered in my ear telling me that they caught my so-called assassin. Well, looks like I fooled him, didn't I?"

The captivated reporters chuckled.

Wilhelm started coughing. "Anyway, I want to thank the fine men and women of so many law enforcement agencies that came together to bring this man to justice, though I am sad that he won't see a day in court. Death seems like an easy way out to a menace like him."

Sid stood staring at the screen with her mouth half open. She wasn't the only one either. "They're covering the entire hoax up. I can't believe it."

CHAPTER 33

WILHELM DROPPED A NAME: REGINALD Baker. There were pictures too. A dead man on the streets who looked a little like Smoke, but his face was bloated.

"I don't suppose that video is going to do us a lot of good now," Sid said to Mal, "but does this mean Smoke's off the hook?"

Mal rubbed his chin. "I've still got a bad feeling that the walls are closing in." He started pulling up images from the cameras on the streets around the church they were in. It was pouring rain so hard you couldn't make out anything. "You know, it wasn't supposed to rain today."

Sid hadn't been paying attention, but of course strange weather patterns often happened when you lived near the coast. She pointed at one of the smaller camera views on the screen. A tight knot of men were rushing up the church steps through the pouring rain.

"We've been breached." Mal pecked away on the keyboard. "We need to get out of here."

"Too late," Smoke said. He started loading clips of ammo into guns. "Did you say you had some more of those vitamins?"

"Yeah, why?" Mal said.

Smoke pointed at the screen. Two monstrous men strode up the outside stairs, great arms swinging five steps at a time. "That's why."

Mal took an Rx bottle out of his pocket, filled with bright green pills. "Take these. There's still some issues with the time release." He tossed one to Sid. "Better something than nothing."

Heart racing, she said, "Bottoms up," and swallowed down the pill.

Mal, Sam, Guppy, and Asia scurried to gather whatever equipment they could get their hands on.

"We'll hold them off," Smoke said, slapping a clip into his gun. "You guys just get out and get out now."

The four of them fled out of the alcove and down the corridor. Smoke and Sid faced the opposite way out to the upstairs. "Maybe this church is sacred ground to them. You know, like in Highlander." He eased forward. "What do you think?"

"I don't think anything is sacred to them," she replied. She loaded a clip of blue-tipped armor-piercing bullets. "I just want to shoot them."

Things were quiet, dead quiet, for just a few seconds. And then a rush of fleet feet clamored down the steps. Half a dozen men, maybe deaders, appeared—decked out from head to toe in tactical gear.

Sid and Smoke fired.

One of the deaders tossed a grenade. It seemed to float in the air.

Sid heard Smoke yell, "Stun grenade!" He shoved her into the alcove. The grenade hit the floor.

Boooomph!

Sid's entire body shook with ram-like force. The tight confines of the basement made the stun grenade's impact ten times worse. She saw bright spots. Felt the floor moving. Every nerve in her body was a jangled mess. As she fought her way to her knees, the floor spun. She started to puke.

Smoke was on his feet. He staggered between Sid and the oncoming deaders, holding only a knife in his hand.

That's when it happened.

A deader emerged from the shadows behind Smoke, slack-jawed and ugly. It swung a crude piece of steel like a club and landed a blow in the meat of Smoke's shoulder.

The knife fell from Smoke's fingers.

The deader cocked back to swing again.

No!

Sid lifted her hand and squeezed the trigger.

The gun didn't fire. The Glock wasn't there.

She spread her fingers wide and stretched them out for the gun that lay inches from her grasp. It might as well have been ten yards. She couldn't get it in time.

There was a heavy thud as Smoke got whacked again.

Another deader emerged in full tactical gear. Wielding its club like a cleaver, it closed in on Sid and chopped at her.

Summoning all she had, Sid rolled. Her fingers wrapped around her gun and she opened fire.

Blam! Blam!

The bullets ripped through the deader's face. Its club still came down on her hip.

Whack!

Shrugging off the blow, Sid kicked out its leg, climbed on top of it, and blasted into its chest with a scream.

"Aaaaeeeeeeh!"

Blam!

The deader died.

Game over.

"Smoke," she said, looking around. "Smoke?"

The rangy man was gone. Only a trail of blood remained that disappeared around the bend of the alcove. Forcing herself to her feet, Sid stumbled headlong into the corridor. It was packed with deaders.

They swarmed her.

She unloaded her clip.

Blam! Blam! Blam!

Some stumbled, others fell. The rest covered her like bears on honey.

She fought and kicked with all her might.

But they dragged her battered body across the floor like a soaked mop, bouncing her head off the tiles.

She couldn't see anything. All she could do was smell the wretched stench of the decaying bodies.

They propped her up against a wall and backed away.

Smoke was there, holding his head. Blood seeped through his fingers. He said something to her about a helmet, or forgetting it.

She still could barely hear. The sweetheart suit had absorbed a good bit of the stun grenade's impact, but she thought it might be a long time before her senses returned to normal. Panting, she surveyed her surroundings.

"Oh no."

Mal, Sam, Asia, and Guppy were bound up and held at gunpoint.

There were at least twenty deaders in the basement room. It was some old auditorium of some sort, maybe a municipal room. The deaders weren't the only ones in there either. There was a man, the mirror image of Smoke. And behind him, heads just inches below some colorful banners, were the giants, Thorgrim and Rexor. One held a huge hammer, the other an axe with four blades.

Reginald the doppelganger applauded. "The bounty on your heads is still good. I think it's time I cashed in on it. Oh, and I don't need the money. I just like drama."

CHAPTER 34

E VERYONE HAD A GUN ON them. Sid. Smoke. Their friends' hands were bound up behind their backs. Their mouths were gagged. Sam's eyes were wide with fear. Mal's face was a mask of concentration. Guppy's eyes were hard and cold. Asia looked agitated. But the group's intent was clear. They wanted Smoke and Sid to get them out of there.

"So are you taking us dead or alive?" asked Sidney, eyeing the barrel of an assault rifle.

It was a man holding it. She could see the whites of his eyes. He wore dark-gray tactical gear and had a black rising-sun tattoo on the back of his hand.

"Oh, well, the price is the same," Reggie said. "But the Drake like to keep things entertaining." He scanned the large room they were in. High ceilings. Old stone architecture blended with new painted drywall. The tiled floor was marked off for volleyball and basketball. A rim stood at either end. "This place should make for an interesting arena."

"Beg pardon?" Sid replied. Her voice echoed a little.

More men funneled in, some of them holding video cameras. The deaders huddled up in tight formation in front of the only exits. There must have been twenty of them. Two other men rolled out some bleachers. The odd auditorium had enough room for a few hundred people. Extra incandescent lighting hung from the ceiling.

Arms folded over his chest, Reggie's form started to change. The visage of Smoke was gone and replaced by a face far more vicious and sinister. With high cheekbones, a hawkish nose, and shoulder-length white hair, what Sid assumed was the real Reginald stood in front of them. He slipped a cigarette pack from his jacket and popped open the lid to a black-logoed Zippo. With a flick, he charged the lighter.

"There's no smoking in here," Smoke said to Reggie.

"Funny," the doppelganger replied. Some of his men-at-arms took to the top of the bleachers and aimed their cameras down on the center court.

Sid felt the hollow feeling expand on her stomach. A memory flash occurred. She remembered what the rat-shifter, Swift Venison, had been going to do to her.

The Drake wanted her death recorded. They wanted to see the whole thing. It was their sick brand of entertainment.

"For the record," Smoke said, folding his feet under him and sitting cross-legged, "any unauthorized use of my image will be subject to the full prosecution of the law."

Reggie laughed.

So did Sid.

"I'm sure you both have excellent lawyers," said the doppelganger.

"He's a fine notary too," Smoke said, laughing.

"Oh, that's good," Reggie said, blowing out a puff. "The audience loves a sense of humor. You know, we have our own dark network at the Drake and lots of video of both of you in the most unlikely places. We call it Deathflix. As a matter of fact, part of your bounty is based on the viewers wanting to see the two of you in action. Some of it is just for study. That whole thing with the minotaur, Mason Crow, do you know we have most of that on film?"

"Film?" Sid laughed. "You didn't use digital media? Doesn't sound very efficient."

Narrowing his eyes, Reginald glided over to the bleachers and climbed halfway up. He placed a hearing device in his ear and spoke into a device on his wrist. "How's the view?" He nodded. "Excellent. I'll send in the deaders first. Let the wagers begin."

"So people are out there betting on us?" Sid said, shaking her head. "You're a sick bunch."

"No, not at all. We just like to have fun, at your expense. And it's not just us, but your own representatives as well. You know, those helpful elitists who give gobs of money to charity." Reggie rubbed his hands together. "They love a bloody fight as much as anybody." He held his finger to his earpiece and spoke into his wrist. "Roger that." He gave a quick nod to the men holding guns on Smoke and Sid.

The henchmen backed away.

Glancing over at Sid, Smoke said, "Time for round one, I guess. You ready?"

"No," she said, putting her fist on the ground. "I'm angry."

"Just so you don't try anything too clever," Reggie piped in, "remember we have guns on your friends over here. However, I feel generous. If even one of you survives this, I'll let them all go. But if you don't … well, what difference does it make anyway?"

"Why don't *you* fight us?" Sid said. "After all, you were boasting about how you were the greatest shifter."

"Oh, I'll be hanging around, don't you worry. But you'll have to at least beat Rexor and Thorgrim before you ever get a crack at me." He checked his wrist. "And right now, those odds are about one thousand to one."

"I like those odds," Smoke said. He shrugged at Sid. "It's much better than flying through an asteroid field."

"The audience is getting antsy," Reggie said. He pointed to a row of undead men sitting on the first row of bleachers. "Deaders! Kill!"

Smoke and Sidney

CHAPTER 35

S LACK JAWED, SLOW AND STEADY they came, one heavy metal pipe in each deader's hands.

Sid and Smoke rose to meet the deaders head on.

She swayed a little.

Smoke stepped between her and the threat. The back of his head was still caked with wet blood. "I'll handle this."

Moving at a stiff fast walk, the first deader came in hard and fast. It brought the long rod of steel down with a fierce two-handed chop.

Smoke sidestepped the blow and kicked the deader hard in its side, knocking it off its feet. Still moving, Smoke closed in on the second deader and in one smooth move, he twisted the pipe free from its swinging arms. A split second later, the pipe Smoke had stolen collided with hard bone, making a sickening smack.

The deader teetered over, holding a hand on its temple.

Smoke didn't slow.

The first deader started to rise from the marked-up tile floor.

Smoke busted its knee. *Whack!* Its chin. *Whack!* He hit it in the head so hard its skull cracked. *Whack!*

The pipe fell from its fingers when the final blow collided with its temple. *Whack!*

Both of the deaders lay on the floor, not dead but twitching oddly. They fought to get up, only to fall back down.

Smoke hit the second one, which had almost managed to make it to its feet, in the temple again.

It flopped to the floor.

He tossed the pipe he had to Sidney. "Aim for the temple. It won't kill them, but it screws them up really good." He picked up the other pipe. "Got it?"

Sid clutched the cold steel in a tight grip. "I've got it alright."

"Well, the odds were only two to one, in your favor," Reginald said. He sucked on his cigarette. "The next round is three-to-one odds. Against you." He turned and spoke to his men. "Send in four deaders. The fast ones. Edged weapons."

Four more men in tactical gear popped up. Their faces were taut, eyes dark. They reminded Sid of the cops who'd invaded her apartment. Two of them had axes like firemen carry, and the other pair wielded big machetes. The tallest was bigger than Smoke, and the smallest was shorter than her. They all had stringy, dry hair, sneers, and crooked smiles. A flash of evil marked all of them.

"It's a good thing you have those German-engineered suits on," Reginald said. "They'll slow down the process of them carving you to pieces."

Sid swallowed. Wary eyed, she watched the deaders close in.

Their blades whisked from side to side, cutting the tension in the air.

Aim for the temple. Aim for the temple.

The smallest deader waggled his machete, eyeing her with fierce intent. He flicked his tongue in and out as he said, "I'm going to cut that hair. I'm gonna cut that pretty, pretty hair." The little man snaked in.

Smoke busted that deader's teeth out.

That was the last thing Sid caught out of the corner of her eye. Right in front of her, she saw a hefty man with a deadly axe swinging her way. She ducked beneath the blow and cracked him in the knee.

He rumbled with slobbering laughter and brought the axe down with a hard chop.

Sid skipped away.

The axe chipped the tiles on the floor.

She had a clean shot on his temple and put all of her weight behind the swing. The steel pipe hit hard.

The deader dropped even harder.

Instincts on fire, Sid whirled around.

Smoke delivered a lethal blow to another deader's head.

Two others were already on the floor. All four were down now.

Chest heaving, Sidney gasped for her breath. "You could have saved at least one more for me."

Smoke gave her a funny look and said under his breath, "You're wheezing."

"I ain't got time to wheeze."

"Two. Four. Hmmm." Reginald lit up another cigarette. "I guess eight will be next. Oh, and now, the odds are heavy against you. But one man from China is still betting on you. Odds of your survival are twenty to one."

"That's better than I thought," Smoke said. He picked up the axes. "Come on," he said to Sid.

They backed toward one of the corners of the room, on the opposite side from the giants. The huge men stood quietly with their arms folded over their weapons. A dangerous look was glimmering in their eyes.

"Send in the next eight!"

Smoke lifted two axes high over his head. "Eight would be great! Why not ten!"

"Are you crazy?" Sid said, wheezing. There was a wild look in Smoke's eyes. A savage fury that had come to the surface. It stirred her blood.

The deaders came at them in a dangerous and shambling mob. Crossing the small expanse, they hemmed Smoke and Sid in without hesitation and attacked.

Smoke's axes sang a riddle of hard steel.

Two deaders' faces collapsed under their unrelenting weight.

Sid went for the temple on the nearest. Her steel club glanced off the fiendish man's arm and skipped off its head.

Something sliced into her arm.

"Ugh!" She held onto her pipe, unleashed a hard swing, and connected with bone. She swung again.

The enemy cut and stabbed.

So far, the sweetheart suit had kept her from being cut to pieces, but the blows of the deaders were heavy—not accurate, but heavy. Her lungs burned. Blood dripped into her eyes from a small cut on her forehead. She kept swinging and swinging and swinging until she felt she couldn't swing anymore. "Smoke," she wheezed.

Deaders were piled up at his feet. His axe strokes were like lightning from the sky.

One deader somehow still fought him without a head.

And then Sid heard Reginald scream, "Send in the rest!"

There were more deaders and men than she could count, and she didn't have anything left.

Smoke dropped to a knee. Covered in gore and sweat, he said to her, "Got any plans for Saturday?"

CHAPTER 36

IT WAS A SEA OF monsters. A rising tide.

Sid stumbled to Smoke's side, fighting for her breath, and they faced the oncoming horde together. She lifted the rod in her hands and shifted her feet. "We gonna make it?" she said.

"Not sure," Smoke replied. "We just have to keep hitting and hope the bodies keep falling. Stay close." He stepped over and drove the axe's back spike into the nearest monster's head.

Sid summoned all of her reserves.

Ignore it. They're just lungs. Who needs them?

The deaders didn't. They were tireless automatons. Dangerous. Unrelenting.

Sid caught a devastating chop with her pole. It jarred her arm. Clacked her teeth. It ignited the survival instinct in her. She felt no pain. Avoided some stinging blows, fought through the others. She was a little faster than her assailants. Smarter. She unleashed wild and clumsy blows. Some connected. Others did little to slow the deaders.

"Just keep swinging," Smoke roared.

She couldn't see him. She could feel him. Her shadow. Protector. It inspired her.

Clack!

Something hard glanced off the back of her head. She fell into a pile of bodies.

Hands from disabled deaders clutched at her wrists and hair, pinning her down, where more deaders closed in for the kill.

Chest burning, barely breathing, she glared at them. "Screw you dirty deaders!"

One with a busted eye socket let out an ugly laugh. It raised the axe over its head with two hands. "Good-bye."

Sid's heart quickened. Her eyes popped wide. Her lungs filled with air. Lightning raced through her veins.

Yes!

Mal's super vitamin had finally kicked in.

She sat up. "Hell yes!"

The deader's axe came down.

Swish!

Sid laughed. Popping up right in front of it, she smashed in the temple of its head.

Now I'm cookin'.

She unleashed all of her outrage. Her hatred. She waded into the deaders. Piece by piece, skull by skull, she felled one right after the other. She was Neo. She was Electra. She was worse. She was a pissed-off Sidney Shaw.

Crack! Crack! Pop! Pop! Whack! Bang! Smack! Smack! Smack!

Limbs were broken. Skulls were smashed. The floor was slick with greasy blood.

Sid danced to her own deadly song. She weaved between attacks. Executed flawless counters. It was fun. Exhilarating.

"Feeling better, I see," Smoke said, sliding alongside her.

She dropped another deader. "Yep. And how about you?"

"Never deader. Er, I mean better."

Only four deaders remained. Standing firm, they crowded in.

Sid and Smoke turned them into dog food and strode out in the center of the room. Not even winded, she looked over at Reginald.

His ageless face was creased.

She yelled over to him, "What are the odds now, jackass?"

Reginald opened up his clenched jaws. "Rexor. Thorgrim. Kill them both!"

Something about the way the giants moved tempered Sid's electrified nerves. They were fluid. Carnal. Savage. Primordial. It was all bundled up in their soft brown jumpsuits ready to be unleashed.

Smoke cracked his neck from side to side. "Which one of you wants to die first?"

Sid looked over at him. "Did you just quote a line from Conan the Barbarian?"

"It seemed fitting." Chin up, Smoke took center stage.

Rexor stepped forward with his oversized four-bladed axe. The massive man, standing over eight feet tall, was built like a train station. With his oversized paw of a hand, he beckoned for both Smoke and Sid. "Come," he said in a cavernous voice, "taste the steel in my hands."

Smoke and Sid charged.

The giant's devastating axe was swift, but not swift enough. It cut over their ducking heads.

Smoke chopped the axe into its thigh.

Sid cracked it in the nose with her pipe.

"Fleas!" the giant said. "You cannot hurt me." Rexor pressed the attack. His axe blades fell with speed and precision.

Morning Glory, he's fast!

She busted him behind the knee. Cracked a kneecap. Smacked his jaw.

Smoke attacked him like a lumberjack hewing down a tree, heavy chop after heavy chop.

Rexor swatted. Jabbed. Chopped. His strikes were getting closer and closer. "See, you cannot hurt me. My bones are iron. My skin is steel. Haaruagh!" With a flick of his wrist, he made an incredible back swing.

The flat of the blade smacked hard into Sid and sent her flying from her feet. Bones aching, she struggled to rise.

"Sid, watch out!" Smoke yelled.

She glanced over her shoulder.

The other giant, Thorgrim, brought his hammer down.

She sprang back like a cat.

The great hammer busted up the tiles between her legs.

"How are we supposed to kill these things?"

"Try kindness," said Smoke.

"What!"

Thorgrim's hammer came down again and again.

She ducked and dived. Evading his blows wasn't the problem, not being able to hurt him was. And the clock was ticking inside her brain. The super vitamin wouldn't last forever.

"Aaargh!" the giant man Rexor bellowed. He staggered back, covering his eye.

"Aim for the softest spot you can find," Smoke said, pressing his attack.

Sid drifted back toward the heap of fallen deaders. She needed a better weapon. She needed an edge.

Thorgrim, hammer high over his head, closed in on her.

She slung her pipe at his face.

He deflected it with his elbow and laughed.

Sid snatched a machete off the floor. She was fast, but the giant's strength and size negated some of that. It didn't help her much if she couldn't hurt him.

Got to find a weakness. Everything has a weakness.

She leaped away from a powerful downward attack.

Thorgrim's hammer made a sickening smack into a deader. Bone crunched. Guts squished out.

That was nasty!

As the giant brought the hammer back up, Sid poked the machete at the giant's eye, clipping the skin just below it.

Thorgrim jerked back and kicked her feet from beneath her.

She flipped head over heels and cracked her head hard on the tiles, pulling up onto her elbows just in time to see the massive hammer closing in on her eyes.

CHAPTER 37

S ID SQUIRTED AWAY. THE HAMMER fell again and again. Closer and closer.
She rolled away.

Crap! Is he getting faster, or am I getting slower?

In a sudden move, she leapt down between Thorgrim's legs and slid through.
Using both hands, she swung the axe into the back of the giant's heel with all her
might.

"Rargh!" Thorgrim hopped up on one foot, spun around in a half circle, and
took an off-balance swing.

Sid jumped back up to her feet and skipped away.

The giant hunkered down, hammer ready, eyes wary. Blood seeped from his
ankle.

Yes! I found his weakness!

"Smoke! Go for the Achilles."

Smoke fought Rexor with the grace and power of a striking panther. He
chopped into the monster man with precise blows.

Rexor's chops were devastating and angry. The massive four-headed blade was
an arc of death, striking just an inch from the evading Smoke.

The elusive man hammered away on Rexor's blind side. He started cutting at
the enormous man's ankles.

Rexor parried with his arms, his axe. "Fat chance, little man! You may have
clipped my brother, but you'll not clip me! Rargh!"

The axe came down hard and fast. The blow would have split a horse in half.

Smoke slipped away and unleashed a fierce backswing into Rexor's good eye.

The giant lost his grip on the axe and teetered back, holding his eye. "Aargh!"

Thorgrim averted his attention from Sid.

She charged in and cut out his other Achilles tendon.

Flailing and roaring, he tumbled hard onto the tiles with visible blood oozing
from his wounds. "You still can't kill me."

Rexor dashed the blood from his ruined eyes and said to Smoke, "I can't see
you, but I can smell you."

Smoke picked up the humongous battle axe that was almost as tall as him. He hefted it over his shoulder and faced off with the giant. "Smell this!" He rushed in hard and fast, swinging. He sank the blade right between the giant's eyes. *Split!*

On his hands and knees, Thorgrim abandoned his hammer and began crawling toward his brother. He bellowed. "No, Rexor! No!"

Sid tossed away the machete and grabbed Thorgrim's hammer. She teetered off balance.

Holy bat crap, this thing is heavy!

She hefted it up on her shoulder and marched right up behind Thorgrim.

The giant man clutched his brother's arms with tears in his eyes.

"Put him down, Sid!" urged Smoke. He was covered in sweat and down on one knee. "Hurry."

She raised the great hammer and dropped it down hard on the back of Thorgrim's shaggy skull. *Crack!*

The giant went limp.

Her legs turned to noodles. She fell, almost face-planting on the floor. The super vitamin was done for. Her stomach started to growl.

"How are you feeling?" Smoke said, resting his hands on his knees.

"I need a plateful of pancakes."

Holding his stomach, he huffed, "Make that two plates." Smoke's head twisted around.

Reginald was coming down the bleacher steps. He was softly clapping his hands, but there was a look of disappointment in his eyes.

Smoke said to him, "So what were the odds on that one?"

"Fifteen hundred to one." Reginald removed his jacket and flicked his cigarette away. He started rolling up the sleeves of his dress shirt. "Needless to say, some heavy hitters lost a lot of coleslaw. Heh. Even though I expected better, I should have known. After all, giants are stupid. That said, I'm still not so sure how you pulled off what you just did. That ... adrenaline surge was quite unique." He glanced backward at Sid's friends. "I suppose one of them will supply the answer to that."

Can't let that happen.

Sid groaned on her way up to her feet. Even with the suit on, her arms felt like lead.

Smoke rose up on two legs and swayed in place a little.

She'd only taken the super vitamin once before, and she'd forgotten the tremendous toll it took, not to mention what the sweetheart suit demanded of her.

At least I'm not wheezing anymore. I'm just so hungry I could eat a goat.

Reginald checked his watch. "Looks like the bets are in." He turned and said to his men, "Keep the cameras rolling, boys."

Even though all of the deaders were down, more men with assault rifles still remained. Half of them were operating the cameras. Two others had guns on Mal and company, and the remaining men's eyes were locked on Sid and Smoke with barrels pointed right at them.

She wiped the blood from her mouth. "So now what? We fight you and it's over? You let us go?" Sid asked. She nodded at Smoke. "What are the odds on that one? Two to one in favor of us?"

"Oh, no no no. Let me assure you, it's more like five thousand to one. In my favor."

"Why's that?" Smoke said, lifting a brow. "Are you going to turn into a snake or something?"

"Funny, but no. It's simply because I'm awesome. But I could turn into a snake if I wanted." His muscular arms were covered in tattoos that seemed to slither like snakes. "Oh, and pick up a weapon of your choosing." He picked up one of the metal pipes that the deaders had used and bent it end to end. "Make it two of them if you like. I'm ready when you are."

CHAPTER 38

"I THINK HE'S A TERMINATOR," SMOKE said, and he followed up with, "I'll be back." He stepped around the giants and picked up a pole and axe, shook his head, and tossed them away. "I think I'll try something different this time."

Sid balled up her fist and closed in on Reginald.

The doppelganger was a statue. Not the slightest hint of worry in his eye.

She lunged in and threw a roundhouse kick.

He ducked away from it and hid his arms behind his back.

She kicked.

He evaded. His head bobbed and weaved.

She let loose a side kick.

Reginald countered this time, unleashing one quicker and more powerful of his own.

She left her feet and landed hard on her back. "Oof!"

"Wah-tah!" Reginald unleashed a roundhouse kick on Smoke. The doppelganger had changed into some weird combination of Bruce Lee and Chuck Norris. "Wah-tah!"

Wap! Wap! Wap!

Smoke countered with a flurry of his own. Hard, heavy punches landed all over Reginald's body.

The doppelganger shrugged them off and hit back even harder. A nasty front kick sent Smoke sprawling all over the floor. "Wah-tah!"

Sid regained her feet and renewed her attack.

Reginald had changed again. He was a woman now. Not any woman either. He—or it—was Samantha.

Sid cast a quick glance over to the prisoners. Sam was bound up. One of her eyebrows was perched. "Screw it!" Sid unloaded a combination of kicks and elbows.

Sam the doppelganger swatted them aside and danced away laughing.

"Come now, Sidney. Don't hold back." Reginald started to shift again. He turned into Rebecca Lang. "I know you hate me."

A new fire burned in Sid's belly. She attacked.

The doppelganger squared up and took punch after punch after punch.

Sid hit and kicked until she couldn't anymore.

Rebecca's Lang's body didn't have a scratch on it.

Hands on her knees and gasping for breath, Sid said, "I hate you."

"Me, or Rebecca?" said Reginald's Rebecca-like voice.

Sid unloaded a kicked in its gut. "Both!"

The doppelganger shoved her down. "Be wise and stay down."

Sid wasn't sure she could get up again. She felt her face swelling. She was wheezing again.

I hate shifters!

Smoke crept up on the doppelganger with another axe in his hand and turned loose a decapitating blow.

Elation raced through Sid. *Yes!*

Reginald ducked with a split second to spare. The axe swished over his head.

"No!" Sid cried out.

Smoke had missed. Still chopping away, the rangy ex-SEAL fought to connect on a new mark.

Reginald skipped away. Baiting. Laughing. He shifted again. Into Sid. "I hate that thing."

Smoke backed off. He labored for breath, and his brawny shoulders sagged. Sid could see in his eyes that he didn't have much left.

"As I said," Reginald added in Sid's own voice, "I'm the greatest shifter in all the world. There's a reason for that. I don't have a weakness."

Smoke spat on his hands, rubbed them together, and lifted the axe up by the handle. "Everything has a weakness."

"Well, certainly, at least in your cases. You're both human." He blew Smoke a kiss with Sid's lips. "I'm your weakness." He pointed at Sid. "Or at least she is, and you're hers. You'll see soon enough what I mean." He strolled over the gore-slickened floor and picked up an axe like Smoke's. He flipped it around a few times and transformed into Smoke. Glancing at Sid, he said, "See if you can keep track of who's who." And then, axe high, he charged.

Axe heads collided together. The brawling men were identical, but their clothes were different. Sid wanted to help, but she barely had the strength to move.

Find a weakness, Sid. Find a weakness!

She made a pleading glance at her friends. They weren't going anywhere. All eyes were fixed on the battle.

"Oh please, this is too easy," Reginald said. He blocked or dodged everything Smoke threw at him. "Really, I don't know what kind of speed you were on earlier, that was thrilling, but this will be a disaster."

The pair of men locked axe heads.

Reginald ripped Smoke's free from his hands, sending it skipping away.

Shoulder dipping, Smoke limped forward.

Reginald brought down a brain-splitting swing.

"Noooooooo!" Sid wheezed.

Smoke's hands locked on Reginald's wrist, and the pair of formidable men stood eye to eye. "Drop it," Smoke said in his face.

"Done."

The axe clattered to the floor.

Both versions of Smoke circled one another.

Reginald removed his shirt and tossed it aside. He had a black sleeveless T-shirt underneath it. He lifted up his fists and transformed into a hulking black boxer. "It's time for a knockout."

Smoke rushed in with a flurry of punches. Hard and fast, he pounded on Reginald's face with swift, hard smacks.

The doppelganger's bullish neck didn't yield. His big meaty hands unloaded a pair of heavy uppercuts into Smoke's gut and ribs. "Oh! That's got to hurt!" Reginald said. He tore into Smoke with a rapid fighter's frenzy.

The punches were so hard Sid swore she felt them.

Smoke was down, and the punches were still coming. Hard and fast. *Wap! Wap! Wap! Wap! Wap!* Smoke's legs twitched.

Reginald reared up and shifted again, this time back into Sid. "You're killing him, Sid," Reginald said. *Wap! Wap! Wap!* "You're killing him, Sid!" *Wap!* "You're killing him!" *Wap! Wap! Wap!*

Sid's heart exploded inside her chest, and she screamed, "Stop! Please! Stop!"

Reginald held back his punch. Blood dripped from his knuckles. "You have something to say?"

"Spare him. Spare them," she said, wheezing. "I'll come to the Drake. That's what you wanted all along anyway, right?"

Reginald flung the blood from his fingers. "Well, not me. And I do like punching him. He's tough. But I think he's dead." He rubbed his knuckles. "It's been a few weeks since I beat my last man to death."

CHAPTER 39

Sid crawled over to Smoke and huddled over him. His face was a battered and bloody mess. Eyes swollen. Nose broken. Lips split. She almost didn't recognize him. "John," she said, pushing his matted hair from his eyes. She held his head in her lap. "John?"

Smoke's eye popped open. He rolled over on one elbow and spat blood, saying, "I didn't find a weakness." He coughed. "I will next time." He eyed Reginald, who had shifted back into his normal self. Smoke leaned back onto Sid's lap. "Don't deal with them, Sid. It's not worth it."

"I already gave him my word." She held his face in her hands. "I couldn't let any of you die. Not on account of me."

Grimacing in pain, Smoke forced himself to a knee and gasped. He held his ribs. His face was wracked with pain. "Don't go."

"She has given her word, Mister Smoke. You know how that goes. Reneging would result in the painful deaths of every last one of you." Reginald put his jacket back on, found a pack of cigarettes, and lit one with his black Zippo lighter. He eyed Sid. "Are you having second thoughts, Miss Shaw?"

She glanced at her friends—Sam, Guppy, Mal, and Asia. All eyes were glued to her.

Smoke rubbed a knot on his head. "Don't give them what they want."

"I can't watch all of you die," she said, still wheezing. "I can't. What else am I supposed to do?"

Gritting his teeth, Smoke rose to his feet. "I know I'd rather die first."

"Don't worry, Mister Smoke. I'm sure that can still be arranged." Reginald beckoned to Sid. "We need to leave now. As in right now. Precious seconds could wipe this deal away. And remember, I still have men with two barrels on each and every one of you."

Empty hearted, Sid got up and draped her arms over Smoke's shoulders. There was tension in his iron limbs, like a great cat ready to spring. She expected a surprise. A last-ditch effort. A miraculous rescue. His iron jaw gave a gentle shake. His eyes said there was nothing left. He'd lost this fight. They both had. "You look like you could use some pancakes."

"Don't say that. I'm one of those stress eaters. They used to call me big boy when I was a kid."

She choked out a sob.

"Oh please, don't be so tiresome," Reginald said. He puffed out some smoke rings. "Give him one final kiss, and let's be gone. The things I do for humanity. Death is such a greater mercy than this sickening forlorn suffering. Rexor! Thorgrim! Get up, you two lazy bastards!"

What? Really?

Smoke's best eye popped wide.

Sid looked over Smoke's shoulder at the giants.

Thorgrim sat up and started rubbing the back of his head. He eyeballed Sid and grabbed his hammer.

Rexor's great arms came to life, and with the help of Thorgrim, he wrenched the four-bladed axe from his face. The mutilated giant gave Smoke a nasty leer. Rising up to his towering height, he pointed at Smoke and then turned and walked away with his brother.

"Stupid and lazy. It's their biggest flaw. They aren't used to fighting so long, so they took a little nap. Pathetic," Reginald said. "Guards, take Miss Shaw into custody and see that she's well secured. I don't want to come looking for her or her friends again. Not for a while anyway."

"I guess this is goodbye," Smoke said with a bit too much finality.

She searched his pummeled face for a place to kiss and ended up kissing his chin.

"That was awkward," he said.

The guards started pulling her away. "Well, you shouldn't have gotten your face all messed up."

"If you think my face looks bad, you should see my heart."

Sid's own heart dropped into her stomach. Being hauled away, she yelled toward Smoke with tears running down her cheeks. "Smoke ..."

"Don't say it," he said back. "I already know you love me."

EPILOGUE

D AYS LATER, SID WAS BROUGHT into a magnificent dining room, the largest she'd ever been in. Aged wood was everywhere. Exquisite china like one might see in the Smithsonian Museum. All around was nothing short of old family wealth. It was the kind of stuff you'd see in the Biltmore or the Vanderbilt. There was a grand fireplace, but no flame, no warmth. The room was cold.

Rubbing her elbows, Sid ventured in. She'd been cleaned up and adorned in the finest evening gown and jewels her eyes had ever beheld. She'd been treated like nothing short of a queen the last few days. She tried not to gape at the sparkling crystals on the mammoth chandeliers.

"Enjoying your stay?"

The strong and rich voice startled her. A man appeared in the room. He was refined, powerfully built, and wearing a dark suit. His salt-and-pepper hair was slicked back. His skin was dark, and his moustache was waxed.

Sid kept her silence.

"Please, Sidney, sit down." He beckoned toward her seat. "And allow me to introduce myself. My name is Kane, Kane Lancaster, and we have much to talk about."

Stay tuned for Book 6, Up in Smoke, available February 2016

FROM THE AUTHOR

Hello! First off I just want to thank you for reading. I've gotten a lot of feedback on this new series of mine, and it's really keeping me going. Seeing how this is the end of the fifth book, I wanted to fill you in on a few things. This one ends on a bit of a cliffhanger. That's not my custom, but I always have at least one in every series I write. This series is scheduled for at least 10 books, so we are halfway there. When I write a series, I think of it as one big story written in 10 parts. It's written so that when it's completed, someone can read the story from end to end without waiting. I really hate waiting and I don't want readers to wait so much either, but heck, everything worthwhile is worth waiting for, right? And if you are a fan of my other book series, at least you have other books coming out. I try to do at least 10 per year, but I'd rather do 12. It's a tough pace, but it works best so I can keep as many readers as I can happy. Hopefully the next book will be out January 2016. No later, I'm pretty sure. I always take a break during Christmas, and I'm still writing the other two series, plus I like to squeeze in new things when I can.

All of that said, it's always great to get feedback from you. Follow me on Twitter, Facebook, or email anytime.

The first of the final 5 books (6 thru 10) in this series will be coming out February 2016. Up in Smoke is the title of book #6 and available for order. In the meantime, check out my other book series listed below. Thanks.

Best,
Craig

ABOUT THE AUTHOR

Craig Halloran resides with his family outside his hometown of Charleston, West Virginia. When he isn't entertaining mankind, he is seeking adventure, working out, or watching sports. To learn more about him, go to: www.thedarkslayer.com.

CHECK OUT ALL OF MY GREAT STORIES

CLASH OF HEROES: Nath Dragon meets The Darkslayer

THE CHRONICLES OF DRAGON SERIES

The Hero, the Sword and the Dragons (Book 1)
Dragon Bones and Tombstones (Book 2)
Terror at the Temple (Book 3)
Clutch of the Cleric (Book 4)
Hunt for the Hero (Book 5)
Siege at the Settlements (Book 6)
Strife in the Sky (Book 7)
Fight and the Fury (Book 8)
War in the Winds (Book 9)
Finale (Book 10)

THE CHRONICLES OF DRAGON: SERIES 2, TAIL OF THE DRAGON

Tail of the Dragon
Claws of the Dragon
Eye of the Dragon
Scales of the Dragon
Trial of the Dragon
Teeth of the Dragon

THE DARKSLAYER SERIES 1

Wrath of the Royals (Book 1) Free eBook
Blades in the Night (Book 2)
Underling Revenge (Book 3)
Danger and the Druid (Book 4)
Outrage in the Outlands (Book 5)
Chaos at the Castle (Book 6)

THE DARKSLAYER: BISH AND BONE, SERIES 2

Bish and Bone (Book 1) Free eBook
Black Blood (Book 2)
Red Death (Book 3)
Lethal Liaisons (Book 4)
Torment and Terror (Book 5)

THE SUPERNATURAL BOUNTY HUNTER FILES

Smoke Rising (2015) Free ebook
I Smell Smoke (2015)
Where There's Smoke (2015)
Smoke on the Water (2015)
Smoke and Mirrors (2015)
Up in Smoke (2016)
Smoke Signals (2016)
Smoke Em' (2016)
Holy Smoke
Smoke Out

ZOMBIE IMPACT SERIES

Zombie Day Care: Book 1
Zombie Rehab: Book 2
Zombie Warfare: Book 3

You can learn more about the Darkslayer and my
other books deals and specials at:

Facebook – The Darkslayer Report by Craig
Twitter – Craig Halloran
www.craighalloran.com